William Minto

# Characteristics of English Poets

From Chaucer to Shirley

William Minto

**Characteristics of English Poets**
*From Chaucer to Shirley*

ISBN/EAN: 9783743389878

Manufactured in Europe, USA, Canada, Australia, Japa

Cover: Foto ©Raphael Reischuk / pixelio.de

Manufactured and distributed by brebook publishing software (www.brebook.com)

William Minto

# Characteristics of English Poets

# CHARACTERISTICS

OF

# ENGLISH POETS

# CHARACTERISTICS

OF

# ENGLISH POETS

## FROM CHAUCER TO SHIRLEY

BY

## WILLIAM MINTO, M.A.

PROFESSOR OF LOGIC AND ENGLISH LITERATURE IN THE
UNIVERSITY OF ABERDEEN

SECOND EDITION

WILLIAM BLACKWOOD AND SONS
EDINBURGH AND LONDON
MDCCCLXXXV

# PREFACE TO THE FIRST EDITION.

Two things are attempted in the following work, which the author believes have not hitherto been systematically accomplished.  My chief object has been to bring into as clear light as possible the characteristics of the several poets within the period chosen.  And as a secondary object to this, I have endeavoured to trace how far each poet was influenced by his literary predecessors and his contemporaries. This is what I have attempted to do.  The reader must not in this volume expect to find the works of our poets treated with reference to their race or their social surroundings. "What sort of man was he?" not "How was he formed?" is the leading question to which I have endeavoured to supply an answer.

In thus deliberately adopting a method that is in one vital respect the opposite of M. Taine's, I should be sorry if it were supposed that I am insensible to the value of what M. Taine has done for English literature.  It may be, as one of his critics has said, that M. Taine has added little to the popular conception of the Englishman, as expressed in the nickname "John Bull"; but none the less on that account is it a great and valuable work to have shown that the characteristics thus vaguely summed up really pervade the whole of our literature.  Justly viewed, indeed, the method pursued in this volume is not so much the opposite as the complement of M. Taine's.  His endeavour was to point out what our writers had in common; mine has been to point out what each has by distinction.  I might advance, as a justification of my attempt, that a thorough study of

the individual is indispensable to that higher study which
has for its object the determination of the characteristics of
the race.   And besides, the most interesting study for mankind will always be the individual man.

It may be objected to my method that it does not systematically follow successive periods in the career of the individual, the opening of new veins, the development of new
powers, the subjection to new influences.   That is a method
by itself, with its own value and its own dangers.   It is
the method suitable to monographs, or to history on a larger
scale than is here attempted.   I must say that it seems to
me to have been of late somewhat overdone.   It has been
pursued without due respect to the individuality of the
individual.   Men's lives have been divided into clear-cut
periods, and those periods characterised as if it were a law
of nature that the individual became at sudden and definite
epochs a wholly new creature.   All division into periods,
unless cautiously carried out, tends to obscure the fact that
every animated being retains its individual characteristics
from birth to maturity, from maturity to decay.   The child
is father to the man : a young cabbage does not become an
old fig-tree.   To trace the gradual growth of powers and
qualities, extended range of effort, increased mastery of
materials, is a most interesting task.   This I have inciden-
tally endeavoured to do.   But I conceive that it is of prior
interest to know what characteristics are of the essence
of a man's being, and are manifested in all his outcomes ;
and therefore my chief aim in each case has been to seize
those characteristics, and to make my interpretation of
them as plain and unmistakable as lay in my power.

A smaller point in which I am especially open to hostile
criticism, is the modernised spelling of the texts of Chaucer
and his contemporaries and immediate successors.   I have
done this after much consideration, resolving to attempt it
more by way of experiment and for the purpose of eliciting
opinion, than from any settled conviction that it is the only

proper course. I am not insensible to the charm of the archaic spelling; and I know that to some minds modernisation of spelling is as obnoxious as the performance of Othello in a dress-coat. My object is to help my readers to forget such small points as orthographical differences between them and those poets of an elder time, and to get nearer to the living spirit of them. The tendency of all archaisms, as I shall point out more fully in the case of Chaucer, is to impart into the text a sentiment of old age and childishness, very delightful in itself, but not so favourable to truth of criticism.

W. MINTO.

*August* 1, 1874.

## PREFACE TO SECOND EDITION.

THERE are three points in particular on which I have made any considerable alteration from the text of the first edition —the relation of Chaucer to the English Court and to French poetry (chap. i.); the connection, or rather the non-connection, of the Wars of the Roses with the decadence of English poetry in the fifteenth century (chap. ii. sect. iii.); and the "causes" of the development of the Elizabethan drama (chap. vi.) On these points I have tried to express more fully and clearly the views originally put forward. In revising this edition I have gained less than I had expected from the enormous mass of interesting commentary on Chaucer and Shakespeare published within the last ten years, the reason doubtless being that my book is concerned with one main purpose—the exposition of the characters, personal and artistic, of the poets dealt with. Every student of English literature must rejoice to find so many able and ingenious scholars at work in this field, and everybody must be sensible of the great value of their results; but as regards my own special purpose, I have not found occasion for material change. How far this is due to prejudice and preoccupation, others must judge.

Some of the writer's incidental essays in the hazardous work of verifying anonymous allusions in Elizabethan literature, have been more favourably received than he had ventured to hope. Two of them have been almost universally accepted, the identification of the rival poet of Shakespeare's Sonnets with Chapman, and the identification of Spenser's "Aetion" with Drayton, under his poetical name "Rowland." The identification of "Our pleasant Willy" with Sidney, and of "That same gentle Spirit" with Spenser himself (Appendix A), I regard as equally certain, but such does not seem to be the general opinion of those who have taken any notice of my arguments.

The discussion of the age and character of Hamlet is much more argumentative than I should make it now when Goethe's view of the character is less generally accepted. The views I contended for were novel at the time. The arguments for Hamlet's age contained in the body of the play (see p. 309) had strangely escaped the notice of Shakespearian critics.

I have added in an Appendix a commendatory sonnet, of date 1591, and have put forward some considerations, originally printed in the 'Examiner' some ten years ago, for believing it to be Shakespeare's. I cannot expect many to take the trouble of following arguments of such minuteness. Most readers will judge, as I did myself at first, from a general impression. But I must beg those who do interest themselves in such a dilettante inquiry, to observe the nature of my argument, that it is not founded on single coincidences of expression, such as might be made out from any Elizabethan author, but on coincidence with a whole circle of associated ideas, images, and words.

W. M.

*August* 1885.

# CONTENTS.

### CHAPTER I.—GEOFFREY CHAUCER.



### CHAPTER II.—CHAUCER'S CONTEMPORARIES AND SUCCESSORS.



### CHAPTER III.—RENAISSANCE AND TRANSITION.

## CHAPTER IV.—EDMUND SPENSER.



## CHAPTER V.—ELIZABETHAN SONNETEERS.



## CHAPTER VI.—DRAMATISTS BEFORE SHAKESPEARE.



## CHAPTER VII.—WILLIAM SHAKESPEARE.

## CHAPTER VIII.—SHAKESPEARE'S CONTEMPORARIES AND SUCCESSORS.

# CHARACTERISTICS

OF

# ENGLISH POETS.

———•———

## CHAPTER I.

### GEOFFREY CHAUCER.

### (1340-1400.)

#### I.—His Life, Character, and Works.

To regard Chaucer as the first genial day in the spring of English poetry, is to take, perhaps, a somewhat insular view of his position. On a more comprehensive view, it would appear more apposite to call him a fine day, if not the last fine day, in the autumn of mediæval European poetry. He may be described as the father of English poetry—the first great poet that used the English language; but it is more instructive to look upon him as the English son and heir of a great family of French and Italian poets. He was the great English master in a poetic movement that originated in the south of Europe, among the provinces of the Langue d'Oc, which had been going on with brilliant energy for more than two centuries before his birth, and had produced among its masterpieces the 'Romance of the Rose,' and the poetry of Dante and Petrarch.

How the Troubadours came by their poetry is not, and perhaps cannot be, sufficiently ascertained. Probably great significance

ought to be attached to the fact that the south of France and
the east coast of·Spain received a large infusion of Greek blood
from the Phocæan colonists of Massilia (now Marseilles) and their
offshoots.    These Greek colonists were something more than
a handful of adventurous settlers, such as might be absorbed in
a community without appreciably affecting its character.    Their
chief city, Massilia, soon after its foundation, became one of the
most prosperous and powerful communities on the coasts of the
Mediterranean, the successful rival of Carthage, the independent
ally of Rome, and, under the early emperors, the chief dispenser
of liberal education to the young rulers of the world.    It may well
have been that, in these representatives of her race, taken from the
home of lyric poetry—the region of Alcæus and Sappho—ancient
Greece left to Western Europe a more precious bequest, a bequest
that gave a more vital impulse to modern literature than all the
fragments of her art.    In the eleventh and twelfth centuries, the
various provinces speaking the Langue d'Oc, and especially Pro-
vence, were in a high state of commercial prosperity and political
freedom.    We may therefore, in the absence of certain knowledge,
venture to speculate that, when the Provençals, having achieved
the material basis for a great literary outburst, came in contact
with Arabian poetry through the Moors, the artistic tendency of
the Greek quickened with irrepressible life, and throwing itself
into the metrical forms that had given it the awakening stimulus,
blossomed and bore fruit with voluptuous luxuriance.    But whatever may have been the origin of Provençal poetry—however the
Troubadours caught their happy art, found it, or came by it—they
certainly are the poetic fathers of the Trouvères and the early
Italian poets ; and through them the grandfathers of our own
Chaucer.

Although the Trouvères of the north of France received their
impulse from the Troubadours of the south, they were not simply
imitators and translators, rendering the productions of the Langue
d'Oc into the Langue d'Oil.    The bent of their genius was no less
decidedly epic than the bent of the Troubadours was lyric.    They
poured out of fertile imaginations hundreds of chivalrous, amorous,
and humorous tales.    The history of this great creative movement,
within its limits of two centuries, is a subject in itself.    Englishmen took part in it, as a result of the close political connection
between England and the north of France, but no writer of mark
used any dialect of English.    Geoffrey of Monmouth wrote in
Latin ; Walter Map in French.    These are great names in the
literature of England and of the Middle Ages, but they do not
belong to English literature.

Chaucer was the first writer for all time that used the English
language.    But viewed as a figure in European literature, he must

be regarded as the last of the Trouvères. His works float on the surface of the same literary wave; a deep gulf lies between them and the next, on the crest of which are the works of our great Elizabethans. Some patriotic Englishmen have strongly resented the endeavour of M. Sandras[1] to consider Chaucer as an imitator of the Trouvères. They are justified in taking offence at the word "imitator." It is too much to say that Chaucer produced nothing but imitations of G. de Lorris or other Trouvères, till he conceived the plan of the 'Canterbury Tales'; and that the 'Canterbury Tales,' though so far original in form, are animated throughout by the spirit of Jean de Meun. To say this is to produce a totally false impression as regards the decided individuality and pronounced English characteristics of Chaucer. He undoubtedly belongs to the line of the Trouvères. He was a disciple of theirs; he studied in the school of Guillaume de Lorris and Jean de Meun, by the side of Guillaume de Machault and Eustache Deschamps. He adopted the same poetical machinery of vision and allegory. He made the same elaborate studies of colour and form. From French predecessors he received the stimulus to his minute observation of character. It was emulation of them that kindled his happy genius for story-telling. The relation between Chaucer and the Trouvères is much closer than the relation between Shakespeare and the foreign originals that supplied him with plots, or than the relation between Mr Tennyson and the Arthurian legends. Making allowance for differences of national character, Chaucer owed as much to Guillaume de Lorris as Shakespeare to Marlowe, or. Tennyson to Wordsworth; and in spite of national character, there was probably more affinity between pupil and master in the one case than in the others. At the same time, we should keep clear of such a word as imitation, which would imply that Chaucer had no character of his own. He received his impulse from the French: he made liberal use of their forms and their materials; yet his works bear the impress and breathe the spirit of a strong individuality; and this individuality, though most obvious in the 'Canterbury Tales,' is throughout all his works distinctively English. Finally, to add one word on the comparative extent of Chaucer's obligations to Italian sources: while he translated largely from Boccaccio, and while it may be possible to trace an expansion of his poetic ideals coincident with the time when he may be supposed to have made his first acquaintance with Italian poetry, it is not to be questioned that he was most deeply indebted for general form, imagery, and characterisation to the Trouvères, whose language and works he must have been familiar with from boyhood.

[1] Étude sur G. Chaucer considéré comme imitateur des Trouvères, 1859. See, in particular, Mr Furnivall's 'Trial-Forewords,' *Chaucer Society*.

Various circumstances helped to bring the son of a London vintner under the influence of French poetry. Many details of Chaucer's life have been gradually recovered by successive generations of antiquaries, from Thynne and Speght to Nicolas and Furnivall,[1] but none of them is more significant as regards the influences that shaped the growing poet than the recently discovered fact that in 1357 he was a page in the household of Prince Lionel. His age was then probably fifteen, or at the utmost seventeen, and whether or not he had been at Cambridge before—the University age being then much younger than it is now—this position ensured him the best education of the time. And while the youth was in this much-coveted service, a great public event happened. The French king, captured at Poictiers by the Black Prince, was brought to London in triumph. In accordance with the chivalrous usage then dominant at the English Court, the royal prisoner, so far from being treated with indignity, was received with as much show of respect and georgeous ceremony as if he had been a distinguished potentate on a friendly visit. He brought a large retinue with him, and he was lodged in what was then considered the finest house in England, John of Gaunt's Savoy Palace. During his four years' captivity, tournaments were frequently held in his honour, hunting and hawking parties were arranged for his diversion, and everything possible was done to make life pleasant for him. Chaucer, as a member of Prince Lionel's household, must have made the acquaintance of some of King John's numerous retinue. He would naturally be thrown into company with youths in a similar position to himself, and as one of a page's duties was to amuse his master or mistress with reading, and the French king was a lover of poetry, Chaucer must thus have had his attention vividly turned, if it had not been turned before, to the French poetry then fashionable. Soon afterwards he had another opportunity. The page was advanced to the dignity of "squire" in 1359, and in Edward III.'s unfortunate expedition of that year into France, was taken prisoner and detained till the following year. Of his treatment during this captivity we know nothing specific, but we may assume from the custom of the time that it was not harsh, and that the young squire, if he had a passion for poetry, would have access to congenial company. The king paid £16 for his ransom after the Peace of Bretigny.

It may almost be said to have been an accident that Chaucer did not write in French, as his contemporary Gower began by doing. But he had the sense to discern a capable literary instrument in the nascent English, which the king at this time was

[1] Of late years Mr Furnivall and the *Chaucer Society* have left hardly a paper unturned in extant official records.

doing his utmost to encourage. A poet is not begotten by circumstances, but circumstances may do much to make or mar him, and a man of genius, able to make the new language move in verse, was sure of a warm welcome at the Court of Edward III. The atmosphere was most favourable to the development of a poet of genial pleasure-loving disposition. Edward's reign was the flowering period of chivalry in England. It was the midsummer, the July, of chivalry; the institution was then in full blossom. All that it is customary to say about the gladness of life in the England of Chaucer's time was true of the Court; if a whole nation could be gladdened by the beautiful life of a favoured few, then all England must have been happy and merry. Pageantry was never more gorgeous or more frequent, courtesy of manner never more refined. The Court was like the Garden of Mirth in the ' Romance of the Rose'; there were hideous figures on the outside of the walls, but inside all was sunshine and merry-making, and now and then the doors were thrown open and gaily attired parties issued forth to hunt or tournament. These amusements were arranged on a scale of unparalleled splendour.

It was a most gladsome and picturesque life at the Court of Edward III., and in that life Chaucer's poetry was an incident. This is the key to its joyous character. Animated playing on the surface of passion without breaking the crust, humorous pretence of incapacity when dull or difficult subjects come in the way, an eye for the picturesque, abundant supply of incident, never-failing fertility of witty suggestion—these are some of the qualities that made Chaucer's poetry acceptable to the audience for which he wrote. He never ventured on dangerous ground. He kept as far as possible from disagreeable realities. We search in vain for the most covert allusion to the painful events of the time. Devastating pestilences, disaster abroad, discontent and insurrection at home—he took for granted that his audience did not care to hear about such things, and he passed such things by. They wished to be entertained, and he entertained them charmingly, with lively adventures in high and humble life, pictures of the life chivalric with its hunts and tournaments, pictures of the life vulgar with its intervals of riotous mirth, sweet love-tales, comical intrigues, graphic and humorous sketches of character.

It would seem that Chaucer, like Shakespeare after him, was brought professionally face to face with the people whose sympathies he wished to command, and thus, like Mr Gladstone's orator, drew from his audience in a vapour what he gave back to them in a shower. Seven years after his return from imprisonment in France, he received a life pension of twenty marks for good service done the king as a "valettus," and in the year following he appears in the Exchequer Rolls as an Esquire of the

Household. Unfortunately the Household Book of Edward III. has not been recovered, so that we cannot know directly what Chaucer's official duties were. But Mr Furnivall has examined the book in which Edward IV.'s domestic system is set forth, with a word of compliment to Edward III. as "the first setter of certainties among his domestical meyne,". and it appears there that the Esquires of Household "were accustomed, winter and summer, in afternoons and evenings, to draw to Lords' chambers within Court, there to keep honest company after their cunning, in talking of chronicles of kings and of others policies, or harping, singing, or other acts martials, to help to occupy the Court and accompany strangers till the time of their departing." This, then, was probably the practice when Chaucer served the king, and it was one of his official duties to make the time pass pleasantly for the king's visitors. He could, if he liked, instead of harping or singing, or talking history or politics, try the effect of his own verses on an audience not likely to submit to boredom. At the time when Chaucer passed into manhood, in the seventh decade of his century, there was a remarkable concurrence of circumstances favourable to the development of an English poet. Given a man of poetic genius within the circle of the Court, the time had come if the man was there : he could hardly escape such a conspiracy of influences to stimulate and foster his gift. Poetry was recognised as one of the graces of a courtly life ; the queen was interested in the art, and had French metricians about her, Froissart among the number ; the king also was an emulous patron, and besides was anxious, along with all his Court, for a poet who should do honour to the language which had at last established itself as the language of the whole nation. The opportunity was there ; the call was urgent. Chaucer was able to respond. The hour had come, and the man as well.

Chaucer continued to rise steadily in royal favour, and in the prime of his life was frequently employed in important diplomatic missions—a sufficient testimony to his powers of making himself agreeable. Up to 1386, fortune would seem to have been uniformly kind to him. Among other places, he had an opportunity of visiting Italy while Petrarch was still alive and Boccaccio was in the height of his fame. In 1372 he was appointed one of the commissioners for arranging a commercial treaty with the Genoese, and visited Florence and Genoa in the following year. Unless royal favourites were then intrusted with very unsuitable posts, our poet must have had a decidedly commercial turn. In 1374 he was appointed Comptroller of the Customs and Subsidy of Wools, Skins, and Tanned Hides in the Port of London ; and he had to perform his duties in person, without the option of a deputy. In his "House of Fame," perhaps with a reference to these duties, he speaks of going home when his reckonings were made up and poring over books till his eyes were dazed; and doubtless, between business and poetry, he must have been closely occupied. For several generations before Chaucer's time, the successful poets of France had been in the habit of receiving munificent presents, which enabled them to give their whole time to poetry. Chaucer was not so fortunate, or unfortunate; his patron, instead of handing over to him jewels, horses, houses, or lands, obtained a moderate pension for him from the Crown, and the privilege of discharging the dry duties of a moderately lucrative office—an arrangement which may, perhaps, be considered peculiarly English, and which probably combined a certain amount of leisure with a solid feeling of independence. Besides his pension and his salary, he seems to have had an allowance for robes as one of the king's esquires; and he received the custody of a wealthy minor, which brought him something equivalent to about £1000 of our money. The accession of Richard II. (1377) did not injure his position: his pension was confirmed, and he received, besides, another annuity of twenty marks, in lieu of a daily pitcher of wine. The Issue Rolls contain further entries of money paid to him for his expenses abroad on the king's service. In 1382 he was appointed Comptroller of the Petty Customs of the Port of London, with the privilege of appointing a deputy. In 1385 he was allowed to name a deputy for his other comptrollership. In 1386 he sat in Parliament as a Knight of the Shire of Kent. This was the zenith of his fortunes. In that year John of Gaunt lost his authority at Court. A commission was issued for inquiring, among other alleged abuses, into the state of the subsidies and customs, and Chaucer was superseded in his two comptrollerships. The new brooms had probably little difficulty in finding an excuse for sweeping away the *protégé* of the fallen Minister. As is often the manner of poets, he had saved little of his pensions and salaries as a royal favourite and a public officer; if, at least, we may draw the natural inference from his two years afterwards getting both his annuities transferred to another man. The revival of John of Gaunt's influence in 1389 again brightened his prospects. He was appointed Clerk of the King's Works. In 1394 he obtained an annuity of £20; but the decay of his fortunes is too plainly indicated by the fact that he was several times under the necessity of applying for small portions of this pension in advance. It is pleasing, however, to know that the last·year of his life was made happy by the accession of his patron's son, Henry Bolingbroke, who immediately more than doubled his annuity by the additional grant of forty marks. He would seem to have retired to a tenement in the garden of the chapel of the Blessed Mary, of Westminster. According to the

inscription on his tomb in Westminster Abbey, confirmed by the
cessation of the minutes of his pension, he died on the 25th October
1400.

These main facts in Chaucer's life are drawn from official records.
While they leave the imagination room enough to picture the
poet's life at Court, they mark the outlines of that life with
sufficient distinctness.   We must be careful about filling in details
of his inner history from supposed autobiographical references in
his poems.   Chaucer's biographers too often take the poet literally,
ignoring his ironic humour and his conventional artistic pretences.
They argue from one or two jests at his wife's expense, of a kind
that might be made by the most affectionate of husbands, provided
there was no real ground for them, that his wife was a shrew and
his married life far from happy.   They accept as matter of fact
to be gravely discussed the poet's statement in the opening of the
'Book of the Duchess,' which serves happily as part of the artistic
setting of that poem, that he has been unable to sleep night or
day for eight years.   This confession of a long and hopeless love-
passion is taken with such unhesitating faith, that it is set against
and allowed to overbear otherwise plain documentary evidence of
the date of Chaucer's marriage to one of the "damoiselles" of the
Queen's Chamber.   But why take such conventional artistic pretences literally ?   In the beautiful Prologue to the 'Legend of
Good Women' the poet tells us that on the first of May he hied
him to the fields before sunrise to see the daisy unclose, and that
he spent the whole day leaning on his elbow and his side,

> "For nothing ellës, and I shall not lie,
> But for to look upon the daïsy."

The scent and colour of the flowery meadow were so sweet that the
poet thought he could live in it the whole month of May,

> "Withouten sleep, withouten meat or drink."

Are we to take this pretty fancy literally, as a modern imitator
of the mediæval poets is said to have done ?   Extravagant love-
sorrows, fantastically transcending poor human nature's powers of
endurance, were equally a commonplace of the school in which
Chaucer wrote.

What was the personal appearance of this soldier, scholar,
courtier, poet, man of business, and successful wooer of a queen's
maid of honour ?   The portrait procured by Occleve[1] represents
him probably after his retirement to St Mary's, and with the
monastic dress and gesture of a grave teacher in dark gown
and hood, pointing with the forefinger of the right hand, holding

[1 See a photograph of it in Mr Furnivall's 'Trial-Forewords,' *Chaucer Society*.]

a string of beads in his left, and having an inkhorn dangling at his breast. The eyes are large and grave, and the features regular, and small in proportion to the size of the head. In the description of himself in the ‘Canterbury Tales,’ put into the mouth of the imperious host (*Prol.* to “Sir Thopas”), he probably was indulging his favourite habit of ironical bantering. The small size of the waist is certainly jocular, seeing that the host is described as a large burgess. The mysterious elfish reserve, and attitude of quiet listening, are in keeping with his position as the observer and recorder of his companions; and the thing is no more trustworthy as a veritable portrait of Chaucer than the reserved “Spectator” as a sober description of Addison.

Knowing that Chaucer was a successful courtier, we look in his works for the necessary qualifications. In the contrast between Placebo and Justinus in the Merchant's Tale, we see that he had theorised on the conditions of success at Court. Justinus, as his name partially implies, was outspoken and honest, churlish and cynical towards human frailties: the sort of man that succeeds only when his services are indispensable, or his eccentricities amusing. But Placebo was a true courtier, who understood the courtier's golden rule of never obtruding advice: he was wise enough to agree with his superior's plans, and so evade dangerous responsibilities—

> “For, brother mine, of me take this motif :
> I have now been a court-man all my life,
> And, God it wot, though I unworthy be,
> I havë standen in full great degree
> Abouten lordës of full high estate ;
> Yet had I never with none of them debate.
> I never them contraried truëly
> I wot well that my lord can more than I,
> What that he saith I hold it firm and stable ;
> I say the same or elles thing semblable.
> A full great fool is any counsellor
> That serveth any lord of high honour
> That dare presume or onës thinken it
> That his counsel should pass his lordës wit.”

Admirers of sturdy English independence—independence that is more candid in the exposure of faults than in the acknowledgment of merits, will desire always to think of Chaucer as having been more of the Justinus than the Placebo. Perhaps he was a judicious mean between the two—neither a churl nor a sycophant. At any rate, it is worth noticing that he understood the arts of the courtier if he cared to avail himself of his knowledge. One thing could hardly have failed to be of service to him in his diplomatic negotiations, and that was equability of temper. There is every indication in his works that he was not an eager, excitable man ;

moody and uncertain. On the contrary, he would seem to have been tranquil and leisurely, with his wits in easy command; patient, not self-assertive, yet with sufficient backbone to defy Fortune when the worst came to the worst. Such, at least, he appears in his works, and such, from his diplomatic success, we may presume him to have been in actual business; though we should err greatly if in every case we concluded that the diplomatist with the pen has equanimity enough to be diplomatic with the tongue. In his works, at least, he displays the most artful and even-tempered courtesy. We see him with easy smile deferentially protesting ignorance of the flowers of rhetoric; throwing the blame of disagreeable things in his story on some author that he professes to follow; dismissing knotty inquisitions as too difficult for his humble wit; evading tedious or irrelevant narrations by referring the reader to Homer, or " Dares," or " Dyte." He conducts us through his narratives with facile eloquence, smoothing over what is unpalatable, waving aside digressions, interspersing easy reflections; never staying too long upon one topic. If he had equally ready command of his resources for the purpose of keeping people in good-humour face to face with himself, no wonder though the king found him useful in embassies. Perhaps the best evidence of his equable unhurried ways is his patient following of the windings and turnings of the protracted subtlety of Pandarus in mediating between Troilus and Cresside. This is the unique gift of the epic poet and of the novelist: it is their special function, with due precautions against tediousness, to exhibit operations that are too subtle or too extended for the stage. Contrast this engineering of Pandarus with the wooing of Anne by Richard III.; the deception of Othello by Iago; the fooling of Ajax by Ulysses. These are all triumphs of active audacity as distinguished from patient intrigue: they are examples of working upon the feelings no less perfectly adapted for stage effect than the calculations of Pandarus are for subtle epic. And as these cases illustrate the distinction between what is suited for the different species of composition, so I believe they illustrate a distinction in the characters of the authors. Coleridge, generalising as usual from himself, has said that all great men are calm and self-possessed, and that "Shakespeare's evenness and sweetness of temper were proverbial even among his contemporaries." There is, perhaps, more truth in the generalisation than there is in the professed statement of fact, though both are open to considerable limitations and explanations. There is no record of *evenness* of temper as a characteristic of Shakespeare; and although there were, one would be inclined to think, from the evidence of his life and works, that while he may have been even-tempered as compared with Marlowe and Ben Jonson, he was a much more excitable man than Chaucer. I doubt very much whether Shakespeare had the easy equable self-possession of Chaucer: with all his fundamental tranquillity and clear grasp, there was more fire in him—more of a tendency to take daring liberties, and to mock danger with cool assurance. I do not suppose that Shakespeare could have practised the cruelty of Richard III. any more than Chaucer could have undertaken the service that Pandarus rendered to Troilus; but I believe that Shakespeare was capable of the cool daring requisite in the one case, while Chaucer had the easy equanimity requisite in the other.

How about Chaucer's qualifications for winning the heart of a queen's maid of honour? His works show that he was not likely to fail in the respectfulness that women are said to love. He is on all occasions the champion of "gentle women, gentle crëatures;" and, however much sly fun he makes of their foibles, he makes ample compensation in praises of their beauty, their constancy, their self-sacrifice. M. Sandras could not have made a greater mistake than when he said that Chaucer imitated the chivalrous Guillaume de Lorris out of deference to the taste of the Court, and had naturally more affinity of spirit with the satirical Jean de Meun. There was nothing monkish in Chaucer's spirit. Gower bears a message from Venus to Chaucer, in which she greets him as her own disciple and poet, with whose glad songs the land is fulfilled over all, and to whom she is especially beholden. And Chaucer himself more than once expresses his devotedness to the Queen of Love, and claims credit for meritorious service. In middle life he seems to have sobered down into becoming gravity, translating Boethius on the Consolations of Philosophy, and writing a Treatise on the Astrolabe for his little son Lewis— no less fitting as an employment for grave years than significant as an indication of his substantial strength of intellect. But all his best work as a poet was done at the instigation of love and humour, and his humour was not monastic. It is remarkable that, while both his serious and his comic productions are founded in most cases on pre-existing works of art, in the serious pieces he follows his original much more closely than in the comic. In his comic tales, as Tyrwhitt says, "he is generally satisfied with borrowing a slight hint of his subject, which he varies, enlarges, and embellishes at pleasure, and gives the whole the air and colour of an original." His imagination dwelt by preference in the regions of brightness, sweetness, softness, and laughter, in its broadest as well as its subtlest varieties. He passed lightly over his opportunities of sublime description; he picked small personal threads out of the mighty web of public transactions. Such grandeur as appears in his pages is the grandeur of magnifi- cent buildings, splendid pageants, assemblies, and processions of knights and ladies in gorgeous array. Affairs of the heart in high and humble life are his themes; he is the sympathetic poet of the aspirations, sorrows, and manifold ludicrous complications of the tender passion. And though there is a strong serious strand in the thread of Chaucer's life, coming more into prominence as the soft outer nap is worn off by the rubs of time, his youthful poetry contains an immense preponderance of the gay over the grave. He was not a mere butterfly; but, on the whole, he preferred the sun to the shade.

Therein he showed his natural affinity for the Court. In the 'Canterbury Tales' it is the Monk that bores the merry pilgrims with his humdrum tragedies; and it is the Knight that interposes to put a stop to him. The Knight does not like to hear of sudden falls from great wealth and ease; tales of prosperous elevation are more to his liking. It is the grave professional men that tell the piteous tales: the Man of Law recites the sufferings of faithful Constance, the Clerk the trials of patient Griselda, the Doctor of Physic the heartrending fate of Virginia. These things do not occur by accident; there is a studied epic propriety in them. Chaucer evidently had his theory concerning what pertained to the Court, and what went naturally with the hard mental work of the learned professions. Looking back upon his own life, we see that his mixed career had given him experience of both, and that in his youth he inclined more to the one, while in his old age, as was natural, he felt drawn more towards the other.

When we look closely at the construction of his poems, trying to realise how they were built up in the poet's mind, we are confirmed in our first impressions of the equability of his proceedings. We are not to suppose that he sang as the birds sing, without effort—out of "the inborn kindly joyousness of his nature," as Coleridge says. His work is too solid for that. Those perfect touches of character in the Prologue to the 'Canterbury Tales' were not put together with unpremeditated flow: we should as soon believe that a picture of Hogarth's was dashed off at a sitting. And, indeed, Chaucer tells us himself, in his "House of Fame," that he wrote love-songs till his head ached, and pored over books till his eyes had a dazed look. Still, he worked equably, with patient elaboration. He is not carried away into incontinent fine frenzies of creation; his words and images do not flash together with lightning energy like the words and images of Shakespeare. His imagination is not overpowered by excited fecundity. Perhaps none of our poets combine such wealth of imagination with such perfect command over its resources: such power of expressing the incident or feeling in hand, with such ease in passing from it when it has received its just proportion; perhaps none of them can put so much into the mouth of a personage, and at the same time observe such orderly clearness, and such propriety of character. If you wish to understand his processes of construction, you cannot do better than study such passages as the elaborate self-disclosure of Januarius, when he consults with his friends about the expediency of marrying, or the imprudent candour of the Pardoner, or the talk between Chanticleer and Pertelot in the tale of the "Nun's Priest." We are there struck by another consideration, and that is, how much he must have owed to his predecessors the garrulous inventive Fableors of northern France; and with what clearness of eye, and freedom and firmness of hand, he gathered, sifted, and recombined their opulent details of action and character. The 'Canterbury Tales' could no more have grown out of the imagination and observation of one man than the 'Iliad,' although one man had scope for the highest genius in adding to, taking from, kneading, and wholly recasting the materials furnished by many less distinguished labourers.

It were a nice question to raise, whether Chaucer or Shakespeare had the best knowledge of men. They exhibit character under conditions so very different that it is hard to make a satisfactory comparison. The epic poet has a choice between describing his personages directly, accumulating characteristic traits in a full portrait, and making his personages reveal themselves, as it were, unconsciously in what they say and do; and usually he supplements the one method by the other. He can put before us at his leisure their whole outward personality, voice, colour, general build, tricks of gesture, peculiarities of dress. We are left in no doubt as to his ideal; and are in a position to say at once whether the details are consistent or inconsistent; complete or meagre. Now, the dramatic poet is much more limited. He may introduce a striking feature now and then, such as Falstaff's fatness, Bardolph's red nose, Aguecheek's flaxen hair; but for the most part, he must leave the outward personality, with all its suggestiveness, to the "make up" of the actor. Hence, so far are we from seeing easily the consistency or inconsistency of a dramatist's creations, that his intention not unfrequently becomes a subject of dispute—the situation within the compass of a play rarely being sufficiently varied to make the exhibition of character unequivocal. Unless, indeed, the personages either describe themselves, or are described by one another, or (as in Greek tragedy) are known to the audience beforehand, their characters must always be more or less enigmatical, seeing that every action is open to several interpretations. It can never, therefore, be quite satisfactory to compare a dramatist, as regards knowledge of character, with an epic poet, and that, too, an epic

poet whose peculiar province is the epic of manners and character.
Although Shakespeare's personages are not all so definitely, fully,
and consistently characterised as Chaucer's, we must not conclude
that his knowledge was inferior. In the case of such masters,
one might do worse than follow the commonplace advice to study,
enjoy, and admire both, without troubling one's head about their
respective merits. It is enough for us to know that Chaucer
observed with clear eye the characteristic features and habits of
the different classes in the England of his time, and has set them
down for us with the most patient elaboration and the most
genial spirit.

In trying to make out Chaucer's character from his poetry, we
can never be quite certain that we do not carry our notions of
his equability, not to mention his inborn kindly joyousness, a
great deal too far. The gay predominates in his works over the
grave. They seldom turn to the gloomy side of things. Yet
the more intimately we know him, the more we begin to form
suspicions that, after all, his equanimity is only comparative, and
that perfection in this is as difficult to be attained as in any other
virtue. We see him chiefly in his flower-garden and summer-
house; but beneath his gay manner as he receives visitors there,
we discover, after longer acquaintance, symptoms of sensitive
tenderness as well as sternness and strength where the smiling
serenity at first appeared to be imperturbable.

Chaucer's works are assigned by Professor Ten Brink to three
periods: the first ending with his departure for Italy in 1372,
comprising his "A B C," his translation of the *Roman de la Rose*,
and his "Book of the Duchess," and representing his subordination to French influence; the second, ending in 1384, the supposed
date of the "House of Fame," comprising, as well as that work,
his "Life of St Cecile" (Second Nun's Tale), his "Parliament of
Fowls," his "Troilus and Cresside," and his first version of the
Knight's Tale, and representing his subordination to Italian influence; and the third, comprising "Annelida and Arcite," the
"Legend of Good Women," the 'Canterbury Tales,' and the
"Complaint of Mars and Venus," and representing Chaucer's
maturity and independence. I should be inclined to reject this
division as throwing a factitious, and, upon the whole, misleading
light on the natural development of Chaucer's genius. There is
a certain advance from the "Book of the Duchess" to the "House
of Fame"; but I do not think that that advance is explained by
supposing French influence to have operated on the one, and
Italian influence on the other. The difference mainly represents
an increasing width of knowledge and mastery of expression, fully
accounted for by the interval between the works. It seems to me

that Chaucer had from first to last more affinity with the French than with the Italians. I can distinguish no change either in his methods or in his spirit that is fairly attributable to Italian influence. He was master of his own development from the time that he received his first impulse from the French. The Italians merely supplied him as they supplied Shakespeare with material. English obligations to Italian impulse belong to the sixteenth century. The greater part of "Troilus and Cresside" is Chaucer's own.[1] He exalts the character of Cresside in the chivalrous spirit common to him and Guillaume de Lorris; and recasts Pandarus with a power of characterisation inferior to nothing in the 'Canterbury Tales.'

Mr Furnivall's refinement of a fourth period, a period of decay, into which he puts all the minor poems that he does not like, seems purely arbitrary, so far as I can judge; but Mr Furnivall's devotion to the subject gives him a very great authority. I should have been disposed to refer Chaucer's "Flee fro the Press" to his final retirement from the world, to the same date as his "Parson's Tale."

The "Testament of Love," the "Assembly of Ladies," and the "Lamentation of Mary Magdalene," are now universally allowed not to be genuine works of Chaucer; and of late, the genuineness of the "Court of Love," the "Flower and the Leaf," and "Chaucer's Dream," has been disputed by Professor Ten Brink and Mr Bradshaw, and their arguments have been accepted by Mr Furnivall. In a previous edition of this book I showed that the arguments then adduced against the genuineness of the "Court of Love" were inconclusive. The case has since then been strengthened by Mr Skeat and Mr Furnivall, who also contend that the extant translation of the *Roman de la Rose* is not Chaucer's. Textual criticism on such a point is entitled to every respect, and they have also in their favour the fact that in the unique MSS. of these works no author's name is given. The grammar differs in important and obvious particulars from Chaucer's, and the works have been ascribed to him on conjecture. The case against genuineness is so strong, that Mr Skeat is pardonably impatient with those who do not at once own themselves convinced. Now I am not particularly concerned to stand up for the "Court of Love" as Chaucer's, for the simple reason that my business is with his character as a poet; and it seems to me so thoroughly Chaucerian in spirit, that my impressions of the man

---

[1] See Mr W. M. Rossetti's admirable prefatory remarks to his comparison of the work with Boccaccio's Filostrato, *Chaucer Society*. I do not quite agree with Mr Rossetti, upon his own showing, that the chivalric passion and gallantry came in great measure out of Boccaccio's poem into Chaucer's. Troilus's courtship is modelled more, it seems to me, on the pursuit of the Rose.

would be the same whether it was written by him or not. In its curious mediæval doctrine on the subject of love, it is in complete harmony with the Prologue to the 'Legend of Good Women,' —Cupid's martyrology, the Lives of the Saints of Love. If not written by Chaucer, it must have been written by a very clever and observant imitator—one might even say, looking to small coincidences,[1] a deliberate and dexterous forger. The great difficulty in the way of not assigning the "Court of Love" or the "Flower and the Leaf" to Chaucer is this, that between him and Surrey there is no English poem half so good, and that it is next to incredible that the name of any poet capable of such work should have perished. If Chaucer did not write it, who did? This, I take it, is the feeling of everybody who still thinks it possible that Chaucer may have been the author. That the grammatical differences, which are doubtless very striking, should have been introduced by a transcriber, seems to them more likely on the whole than that a nameless poet, in an age whose known poets never rise anywhere near such a level, should have produced works that have received enthusiastic admiration from such judges as Dryden and Mr Swinburne. Mr Skeat, although he has committed himself to the opinion that the "Court of Love" is "utterly unlike Chaucer"—an opinion which is to me simply unintelligible —made the suggestion at one time that the author might be Sackville. But the age of the MS. makes this impossible by a generation at least, and there is no other likely claimant among the poets that are known to us. When a possible claimant is discovered, nobody will have a word to say for Chaucer's authorship of the doubtful poems, and in the meantime Mr Skeat and Mr Furnivall deserve thanks for their thorough examination of the text.

It is an interesting fact that Chaucer did not complete the scheme of the 'Canterbury Tales' or of the 'Legend of Good Women,' and that he left half finished "The story of Cambuscan bold." This looks as if his manifold other occupations indisposed him to long-sustained efforts. The incompleteness of the Squire's Tale is particularly interesting. One is inclined to conjecture that he may have thought of it as the beginning of a larger enter-

---

[1] Philogenet, the name of the writer of the "Court of Love," comes curiously near Philo Ghent, which Chaucer might well subscribe himself; and Philobone would pass for a pretty transmutation of Philippa, the name of Chaucer's wife. True, Philobone is not Philogenet's mistress—she only introduces him ; but this is in accordance with the Troubadour rule (which may explain, also, the apparent inconsistency of "Chaucer's Dream"), that, when the poet's mistress was attached to a court, he addressed his songs to the presiding princess (see Mr Rutherford's Troubadours, p. 150). Rosial, though intended for Philippa, may thus have been formally Lady Blanche, on whom Philippa attended. Once more, compare the name Rosial with ll. 41-48 of the Romance, where the translator tells his patroness that she "ought of price and right be cleped *Rose* of every wight."

prise, a cycle of stories like the Carlovingian or the Arthurian, with Cambuscan as the central figure. It would have been a worthy enterprise for the last of the Trouvères. The old cycles of romance were hackneyed, worn out; otherwise one might wonder that the great poet of English chivalry never dealt with the legend of Arthur. His predecessors had exhausted every great name known to their histories. But Genghis Khan, whose fame filled Europe in the fourteenth century, was a new and tempting hero; and the far East was an untrodden field for the romancer. Cambuscan might well have been the centre of a new romantic cycle. Hence it strikes one as possible that Chaucer stopped short with the Squire's Tale because he had. larger views, and put off completing it as he put off completing the full scheme of the 'Legend' and the 'Canterbury Tales,' because he shrank from long continuance of high-strung labour.

## II.—His Language, Metres, and Imagery.

Our philological authorities do not seem to be quite at one about Chaucer's English. Mr Earle ('English Philology,' pp. 75-97) says that Chaucer and Gower wrote King's English, the language that had grown up at Court about the person of the monarch; and that this was distinguished from all the contemporary dialects by its being formed more under the influence of French. This position is not refuted by counting the number of words derived from the French, as Mr Ellis does for the Prologue to the 'Canterbury Tales,' and finding that the proportion of words so derived is "not quite one word in a line on an average." It is not so much the number of words borrowed that Mr Earle insists upon, as the general strain or rhythm of the language. Not that he means to say that the King's English adopted the French rhythm, but that, growing up as it did among persons familiar with French, it acquired a rhythm of its own, different both from the French rhythm and from the rhythm of the provincial dialects. To understand this, compare the English of Chaucer or Gower with the English of Robert de Brunne, or of Langland's 'Piers Plowman.' Difference in the inflections and in the proportion of French words do not account for the immense indescribable difference in the general movement of the language. This movement, this rhythm, Mr Earle considers the distinctive feature of the King's English.

Whether Dr Morris would accept Mr Earle's position or not, I do not know. Dr Morris lays down that Chaucer wrote in the East Midland dialect, and so far is at variance with Mr Earle's statement, that the language of the Court differed from all other

dialects.  But perhaps Dr Morris means only that Chaucer uses
the inflectional system of the East Midland as distinguished from
the Northern and the Southern.  These dialects have been defined
by Dr Morris with new precision.[1]  The Midland was the most
widely spread, and of its many varieties the East Midland was the
most important.  It was first cultivated as a literary dialect as
early as the beginning of the thirteenth century; and it had then
thrown off most of the older inflections, so as to become in respect
of inflectional forms and syntactical structure as simple as our
own.  It was the dialect of Orm and of Robert of Brunne.
Wycliffe and Gower added considerably to its importance, and
Chaucer's influence raised it to the position of the standard
language.  In Chaucer's time it was the language of the metropolis, and had probably found its way south of the Thames into
Kent and Surrey.  Such is Dr Morris's account of the East Midland.  So far as appears, he has not been struck with differences
of rhythm, and it has not occurred to him whether the language
of the Court was different in other respects than inflections from
the language of the metropolis.  The probabilities seem to be overwhelming in support of Mr Earle's hypothesis, and justify him in
saying that the facts admit of no other explanation.  The frequent-
ers of the Court, when they were ultimately forced to adopt the
language of the people, could not but have found it poorly equipped
for the varied needs of polite conversation; and even when they
were not under the necessity of importing words from the more
cultivated French, must have been compelled to introduce turns
of expression to the extent of altering the complexion of the
language.

Whatever may be our conclusion as to the sources of Chaucer's
language, there can be little doubt that his genius made it the
standard language.  A poet cannot, of course, invent a language:
what he writes must be intelligible to his readers, and his admirers
are constrained by the same necessity of being intelligible to their
readers.  But if a great poet had arisen before Chaucer in the
Northern dialect, or if Chaucer himself had written in that dialect,
the course of the English language might have been substantially
altered.  In corroboration of this, Mr Earle remarks that "the
Tuscan form of modern Italian was decided by the poetry of
Dante, at a time when Florence and Tuscany lay in comparative
obscurity, and when more apparent influence was exercised by
Venice, or Naples, or Sicily."  I suspect, however, that in all
such cases the poet must be backed by a cultivated society; and
that the only possibility likely to have affected the course of
standard English would have been the existence of a high culture

---

[1] Garnett and Guest, however, are still worth reading.

in the Court of Scotland, and the ascendancy of a great poet there before the date of Chaucer.

One of the many directions of thorough antiquarian study in this century has been towards the remains of old English; and one of the most valuable triumphs of this patient scholarship has been to restore the versification of Chaucer. Chaucer's metre had been a vexed question ever since he had been reduced to print. The change of pronunciation had seriously affected the number of syllables in his verses; and his editors, Thynne and Speght, while they valiantly abused detractors, could not, or at least did not, show how to supply the missing syllables. Ascham, Sidney, Spenser, and others of that age, recorded their admiration of the old poet; but they omitted to say on what principles they scanned his lines. A century later, Dryden, with his vigorous habit of saying what he could not as well as what he could admit, expressed the greatest veneration for Chaucer, but considered that the rough diamond needed smoothing for modern senses. He laid down in the most positive manner that Chaucer's lines often have a syllable too many, and often a syllable too few. His peremptory opinion received a considerable shake from the publication of Tyrwhitt's edition in 1778, with its "Essay on the Language and Versification of Chaucer;" but even then a certain amount of scepticism might have been pardonable. One might have been forgiven for entertaining some doubts about Tyrwhitt's liberal restoration of final *es*, to make up for the deficiency of feet when the text is pronounced with the modern allowance of syllables. Tyrwhitt did not apply sufficiently convincing scholarship to show that these *es* were "survivals" of French and old English (or Anglo-Saxon) terminations, and, still more largely, of old English inflections. This was first thoroughly done by Guest, who pointed out that the dropping of the final *e* is the exception, and expressed a hope that we should one day have a list of all the words in which Chaucer has taken that liberty. I am not aware that the more recent labours of Mr Ellis, Mr Skeat, and Mr Furnivall, have realised this hope, but they have gone a considerable way towards its fulfilment. The general reader should see the sections added to Tyrwhitt's Essay by Mr Skeat, in the Aldine edition of Chaucer, vol. i.

But not only have the missing syllables been recovered by modern scholarship: an attempt has been made by Mr Ellis, in his elaborate and ingenious work on Early English Pronunciation, to recover the sounds of the vowels, so that Chaucer may be declaimed as he was by his contemporaries. Mr Ellis proceeds on the supposition that no two words were set down as rhymes unless their sounds agreed perfectly; and he starts from known vowel-sounds of Latin, French, and English of the sixteenth century.  The investigation is interesting, and the results are as trustworthy as the undertaking is courageous; but nothing can restore for us the old music of Chaucer's verse.  It is musical to us—exquisitely so—but the music is not the music that delighted the Court of Richard II.  We may learn to repeat the articulations of his contemporaries, but we cannot hear with their ears.

Chaucer has three principal metres: four-accent couplets (the metre of Milton's "Comus"), in the "Romance of the Rose," "Chaucer's Dream," the "Book of the Duchess," and the "House of Fame"; rhyme-royal [1]—the metre of Shakespeare's "Lucrece" —(a stanza of seven decasyllables, with rhymes of 1, 3 + 2, 4, 5 + 6, 7), in the "Court of Love," the "Parliament of Birds," the "Flower and the Leaf," four of the 'Canterbury Tales,' and "Troilus and Cresside"; and heroic, or five-accent couplets, in the "Legend of Good Women," and most of the 'Canterbury Tales.'

The four-accent couplet is the original metre of the *Roman de la Rose* and nearly all the French *fabliaux*, and was the most common metre in English poetry during the thirteenth and the fourteenth centuries.  It is the prevailing form in Dr Morris's 'Specimens of Early English,' being used for all kinds of narrative matter, fables, romances, tales, 'Sunday Sermons,' and political songs.  Its facility is rather a temptation than a check to a loquacious narrator; and Chaucer dances along in his jingling fetters with the greatest vivacity, as if his fertile invention wanted some severer restraint.  He dashes off every now and then into digressive reflections, and recalls himself with an effort, as if he could hardly refrain from throwing in a few more of the facile couplets before he had done.

"Troilus verse" was the favourite form of the fifteenth century, and was frequently used in the sixteenth.  It was, indeed, the great stanza of English poetry, till Spenser superseded it with the fuller music of his more elaborate structure, and is a simpler

---

[1] "The epithet *royal* seems to be derived from the *chant-royal* of the French, a short poem in ballet-stave, written in honour of God and the Virgin Mary; and by which, according to French critics, the abilities of the king were tested in the poetical contests at Rouen."—Guest's English Rhythms, ii. 359.  According to Warton, the title "Balad-Royal" was first used in English by Caxton, being applied to Herbert de Burgh's stanza in his Translation of Cato's Morals. Gascoigne calls the same stave "rythm-royal."  It is sometimes said that the epithet "royal" was derived from the circumstance that the stave was used by James I. of Scotland in the 'King's Quhair'; but this is probably a later supposition based only upon the coincidence.  If it had been the tradition, James VI. of Scotland would hardly have applied the term "ballet-royal" to the stave of eight, designating the seven-line stave—after its first memorable appearance in English—*Troilus* verse.

and homelier dress corresponding with the youth of the English muse. It may be disputed in which of the two stanzas the greatest quantity of English poetry has been written; for while Troilus verse was used by many poets of the fourteenth century whose names even are seldom repeated now, the Spenserian was the favourite stanza of the great revival at the close of the eighteenth century, numbering among its patrons Shenstone, Thomson, and Beattie, Campbell, Scott, Byron, Shelley, and Keats. Chaucer used the seven-line stanza to embody graceful allegories, and tales of sweet pathos. His choice of this medium for the touching stories of Constance and Griselda, and the woful legends of Cecilia and little Nicholas, is approved by the later employment of it in Spenser's "Ruins of Time," Daniel's "Complaint of Rosamond," and Shakespeare's "Lucrece" and "Lover's Complaint." It is worth noting that though Lydgate adopted the same stanza for his tragical "Falls of Princes," Chaucer employs a heavier eight-line stanza for his Monk's "Tragedies," or brief commiserations of potentates that had fallen out of great prosperity. The seven-line stave with its single repeat and appended couplet, a form that lends itself naturally to the expression of graceful after-thought or irrepressible sob, is too quick a measure for the embodiment of statelier feeling. This was felt by Michael Drayton, when, after composing his poem on the wars of the Barons of Richard II. in Troilus verse, he recast the whole into heavier *ottava rima*. But *ottava rima* (the stanza of 'Don Juan'), though strong enough for the vigorous march of Drayton's narrative, would not have been sufficiently inwoven for the grave reflective sentiments of the Monk's Laments, which are written in eight banded lines (1, 3 + 2, 4, 5, 7 + 6, 8)—the Spenserian stanza without the concluding Alexandrine.

Five-accent couplets are more suited for comedy and the comic epic, than for tragedy and the grand epic. This can be called "heroic verse" only when heroism is taken to imply a minimum of dignified feeling. There is, doubtless, a certain strenuousness in its movement when the matter is heavy; it may be used to convey the impression of bold splendid energy: but dignity and stateliness are out of the question. If the ear attends to the rhyme at all, the expectation of it must be more or less of a distraction from the feeling of massive grandeur. With the lighter material of comedy, the regular beat of the rhyme is cheerful and animating, if the couplet is occasionally divided and other means are used to prevent the regularity from becoming tedious. If one were disposed to venture on fine distinctions, one might say that the *ottava rima* of 'Anster Fair' and 'Don Juan' is the peculiarly appropriate metre of the light epic, while the couplet is the predestined vehicle of dramatic comedy. In the theatre the ear cannot wait for the close of a stanza through several verses without fatigue, and the quick recurrence of the rhyme is imperative. In a light narrative intended to be read, longer suspense is permissible, while at the same time the nature of the subject forbids intricacy ; and *ottava rima*, with its simple even structure, seems to answer the purpose about as exactly as could be desired.

Chaucer's similitudes are taken from such familiar sources, that M. Sandras charges him with giving a vulgar tone to his renderings of the chivalrous romances of Boccaccio. Whether it was that his English humour now and then broke out through his chivalrous sentiment, or whatever may be the explanation, there certainly is some ground for the charge. The comparison of Cressida to the "chief letter A," is so like our modern vulgar "A 1," that we are not perhaps unbiassed judges in that particular case. But there are a few similitudes in the Knight's Tale expressed with a primitive simplicity that must have drawn a smile from the poet himself. Such is the comparison of Palamon and Arcite quarrelling about Emily to two dogs fighting for a bone, while a kite comes in and carries off the object of contention. And still more amusing and unworthy of the subject is the comparison of poor humanity struggling on through the dark world with uncertain footing, to a drunk man, drunk as a mouse, who knows that he has a house, but does not know how to reach it, and finds the way very slippery. These similitudes are undeniably vivid : but unless our judgment is biassed by modern feelings, they belonged even in Chaucer's age more to the quaint monk than the chivalrous knight.

Most of Chaucer's similitudes, however—and he uses comparatively few, either as extended similes or as metaphors—are simple without being quaint or humorously inadequate to the subject. In this respect he contented himself with commonplaces, and made no effort to embellish his style with far-fetched flowers. He gives his warriors the look of griffins and lions, and makes them fight like cruel tigers and wild boars. Occasionally he expands the comparison, and gives it a certain local colour after the Italian manner, as when he introduces the Thracian hunter, or the tiger of the Galgopley, or the lion of Belmarie, or the pale face of the criminal on his way to execution. In extolling the charms of his heroines, he describes for the most part directly ; and when he wants a brief illumination, makes use of the immemorial comparisons from the simple beauties of inanimate nature, the rose and the lily, sunlight and moonlight, spring-time and morning.

We are accustomed to think that Chaucer was able to dispense with a richly loaded diction, because he wrote for a primitive audience, thankful for small poetical mercies. But they were not so unsophisticated that a poet could make a reputation for colour, or as they might have called it, flowers of rhetoric, "the blossoms fresh of Tullius' garden sweet," upon the strength of comparing lovely women to roses and lilies, sunshine and spring, perennial as is the charm in thinking of such a likeness. Chaucer might have had to bestir himself for less familiar "tropes" and figures, had it not been that the structure of his poems gave him the opportunity of flooding his pages with colour in direct description. Beautiful women, heroic men, gorgeous buildings, gay processions, splendid armour, gardens and fountains, woods and rivers, birds and beasts, come in his way as the poet of fables and allegories, love, character, and romantic adventure; and he describes them enthusiastically with the utmost opulence of detail. His pictorial imagination was not called upon for many fragmentary contributions, but every now and then it received steady employment. What need had his readers for isolated touches of colour when their poet gave them such accumulations to revel in as the Gardens of Venus, the Temple of Venus, the House of Fame, the Court of Love, the Tournament before Theseus, the rival troops of the knights and ladies of the Flower and the Leaf?

The "Parliament of Birds" is perhaps the richest of Chaucer's smaller poems—"imitations," as M. Sandras calls them,—but the "Book of the Duchess" is as good an example as need be of the poetical machinery that he inherited. The central aim of the poem is to commiserate the death of Blanche, Duchess of Lancaster, and to express the sorrow of her husband; but this object has grown into fold after fold of richly coloured and animated conception. The poet begins by telling how, for eight years, he has suffered from restlessness and sleeplessness, and how one night, as he lay awake, he called for an old romance (apparently Ovid's 'Metamorphoses,' in the original or in a French translation), and read the tale of Ceyx and Alcyone. A less skilful artist might have explained to us that his tale of devotedness was a proper parallel to the mournful separation of united love, of which he was preparing a memorial. But though this was doubtless the real motive, the poet skilfully invents another, which makes it appear as if the correspondence were an accident, and varies the commonplace of falling asleep over the introductory tale. The ostensible motive is that the story of Ceyx and Alcyone involves the agency of the god Morpheus, of whom the poet had never heard before. Partly in game, he vows to make Morpheus a present of a bed of down, if only he may obtain an evidence of his divinity. Scarcely had he breathed this vow when he fell asleep.

Next comes the dream, the opening of which is exceedingly beautiful.

" Me thought thus that it was May,
And in the dawning I lay—
Me mette[1] thus in my bed all naked—
And looked forth, for I was waked
With smallë fowlës a great heap,
That had affrayed me out of my sleep,
Through noise and sweetness of their song.
And, as me mette, they sat along
Upon my chamber roof without,
Upon the tiles over all about,
And songen everych in his wise
The mostë solemnë servise
By note that ever man, I trow,
Had heard.   For some of them song low,
Some high, and all of one accord.
To tellen shortly at oo word,
Was never heard so sweet a steven[2]
But it had be a thing of heaven ;
So merry a song, so sweet entunës,
That, certes, for the town of Tunis
I nold[3] but I had heard them sing :
For all my chamber gan to ring
Through singing of their harmony ;
For instrument nor melody
Was nowhere heard yet half so sweet,
Nor of accord yet half so meet.
For there was none of them that feigned
To sing, for each of them him pained
To find out merry crafty notes.
They ne spared not their throats. "

Then the decorations of his chamber are described, and how, as he
lay admiring the bird concert and the bright beams streaming
through the painted window, he heard a hunter try his horn, and
footsteps of men, horses, and hounds, and confused talk of hunting.
He got up, and rode to the forest, finding out by the way that the
hunter was the Emperor Octavian.   By-and-by the hounds are at
fault, and as the poet is loitering about, an incident happens that
conducts to the main subject of the poem.

" I was go walked fro my tree,
And as I went, there came by me
A whelp that fawned me as I stood,
That had y-followed and could no good :
It came and crept to me as low
Right as it haddë me y-know ;
Held down his head and joined his ears
And laid all smoothë down his hairs.
I would have caught it, and anon
It fleddë, and was fro me gone.
And I him followed, and it forth went

---

[1] Dreamed.          [2] Sound.          [3] Ne would.

> Down by a flowery greenë went [1]
> Full thick of grass, full soft and sweet,
> With flowerës fel [2] fair under feet,
> And little used, it seemed thus ;
> For both Flora and Zephyrus,
> They two that maken flowrës grow
> Had made their dwelling there I trow.
> For it was on to behold
> As though the earth envyë wold
> To be gayer than the heaven,
> To have more flowrës suchë seven [3]
> As in the welkin starrës be.
> It had forgot the poverty
> That winter through his coldë morrows
> Had made it suffer; and his sorrows—
> All was forgotten, and that was seen,
> For all the wood was waxen green :
> Sweetness of dew had made it wax.''

While looking at the beasts that were roaming through the wood, more in number than Argus could have counted, he became aware of a knight in black, sitting with his back against a huge oak-tree. This knight is supposed to represent the mourning Duke of Lancaster; and thus, through the story of Ceyx and Alcyone, and the various scenes and incidents of the May morning, we reach the main subject of the poem.


### III.—THE CHIEF QUALITIES OF HIS POETRY.

It is not unlikely that our impressions of the chief qualities of Chaucer's poetry are different in some respects from those felt by his contemporaries. In all probability we pass lightly over many things that fascinated them, and admire many things that they received with comparative indifference. Their captivating novelties have become our commonplaces, their impressive reflections have become trite; and, on the other hand, many passages that would doubtless have seemed tame and commonplace to them, strike us with all the freshness of reawakened nature, or with the strange interest of things exhumed after long ages of burial.

We cannot recover, with any assurance of certainty, the feelings of Richard II.'s courtiers when first they were charmed by the English language in the compositions of a great poet. We cannot imagine how his descriptions of fair women, fine buildings, flowers, trees, and bird-singing, were heard or read by those familiar with the " Romance of the Rose "; nor how his ' Canterbury Tales ' affected minds that knew such plots and incidents by the hundred. We know what a master of language can do with the most familiar

---

[1] Path.    [2] Many.    [3] Seven such, seven times as many.

materials; we know how fervently Chaucer's power was acknowledged, not only among his countrymen, but also on the other side of the Channel: but how they felt his power, which of its elements appealed to them most irresistibly, must ever remain matter for speculation.

Archaisms of word and inflection cannot but be inseparable elements in the sum total of the effects of Chaucer's poetry on us. Single words have changed their associations very materially since the days of Chaucer; and there are many that signify nothing to the present generation, many that are empty sounds, whose meaning may be attained only by dim approximation through glossarial synonyms. Words faintly picked up from a glossary have not the same power as the words of our mother-tongue. Even if we have a literary familiarity with them, the matter is not altogether mended. In all cases we may be sure that a passage with obsolete words in it does not move us as it moved contemporary readers. What may have been the effect of the passage when its words were hung about with the associations of the time, we cannot realise either by patient study or impatient flash of imagination: it is a dead thing, that no intellectual alchemy can resuscitate. We only know that it must have been different from what we experience. A phrase in a modern poem, even, does not go with equal power to the heart of every reader. Chance associations are fruitful sources of colouring peculiar to the individual. But to none of us can an obsolete word of Chaucer's have the same associations that it bore to men in whose mouths and ears it was a familiar visitor.

The natural effect of archaisms on pathetic passages is to make them sweeter and simpler by making them more childlike. Such lines as—

> "The newë green, of jolif ver the prime
> And sweetë smelling flowerës white and red;"

or—

> "And as I could this freshë flower I grette,
> Kneeling alway, till it unclosed was
> Upon the smallë, softë, sweetë grass,
> That was with flowerës sweet embroided all"—

come to us like the prattle of childhood, and fill us with the freshness of spring as no modern words could do. Even lines that are not so appropriate in the infantile mouth, are made prettier by their archaic garb. Take the following:—

> "She was not brown ne dun of hue,
> But white as snow y-fallen new.
> Her nose was wrought at point devise,
> For it was gentle and tretis,

> With eyen glad and browës bent ;
> Her hair down to her heelës went,
> And she was simple as dove of tree ;
> Full debonaire of heart was she."

These lines, particularly the two about the lady's nose, are such as a modern reader would apply to a beautiful pet ; they probably carried a more elevated sentiment when first written.

Look now at a passage that, apart from the quaintness of the language, should carry the sense of splendour—the march of Theseus upon Thebes.

> "The red statue of Mars with spear and targe
> So shineth in his whitë banner large,
> That all the fieldës glitteren up and doun :
> And by his banner borne was his pennoun
> Of gold full rich, in which there was y-beat
> The Minotaur which that he wan in Crete.
> Thus rid this duke, thus rid this conquerour,
> And in his host of chivalry the flower,
> Till that he came to Thebës and alight
> Fair in a field there as he thought to fight."

The archaic inflections and turn of language give this a quaint unction, as if it were the imperfect utterance of an astonished child.  The influence of the diction co-operates largely in reminding us that the splendour is a thing of bygone times, strange and wonderful in our imaginations.  In the following astrological passage, matter and manner go together in the same way.  It is the reflection of the " Man of Law " on the infatuated passion of the Soldan for Constance.

> " Paraventure, in thilkë largë book
> Which that men clepe the Heaven, y-written was
> With starrës, when that he his birthë took,
> That he for love should have his death, alas !
> For in the starrës, clearer than is glass,
> Is written, God wot, whoso could it read
> The death of every man withouten dread.
>
> In starrës many a winter there beforn
> Was written the death of Hector, Achilles,
> Of Pompey, Julius, ere they were born ;
> The strife of Thebës, and of Hercules,
> Of Sampson, Turnus, and of Socrates
> The death ; but mennës wittës been so dull
> That no wight can well read it at the full."

Later on in the same tale, there is another astrological passage —an impassioned appeal to the starry destinies—when Constance is setting sail for the East to the marriage that proves so fatal.

> "O firstë moving cruel firmament !
> With thy diurnal swough that crowdest aye
> And hurlest all fro East to Occident
> That naturally would hold another way !
> Thy crowding set the heaven in such array
> At the beginning of this fierce voyage,
> That cruel Mars hath slain this marriage."

In this passage the archaic trappings, and particularly the bit of dogma about the natural course of the firmament, are rather in the way—interfering with our perception of the dignity and passion of the apostrophe.

The archaic diction makes itself felt with peculiar harmony in the narrative of supernatural manifestations, such as were ascribed to devils and magicians. Sir Walter Scott might have envied the following account of the ritual of Arcite in the temple of Mars, and the answer to his prayer :—

> "The prayer stint of Arcita the strong :
> The ringës on the temple door that hong,
> And eke the doorës clattereden full fast,
> Of which Arcita somewhat him aghast.
> The firës brende up on the altar bright
> That it gan all the temple for to light ;
> A sweetë smell anon the ground up gave
> And Arcita anon his hand up have,
> And more incense into the fire he cast,
> With other ritës mo, and at the last
> The statue of Mars began his hauberk ring,
> And with that sound he heard a murmuring
> Full low and dim, and said thus, 'Victory !'"

This is a more active and instantaneously impressive sorcery than the calm power of the stars, and the archaisms seem to go with it in readier harmony.

Take now another point. Chaucer sympathises deeply with the victims of deceitful love, and assails false lovers with cordial anger. If he were a dreamy poet like Spenser—a poet whose indignation assumed a wailful and regretful tone—the antique words and turns would be in perfect unison ; they would help to translate the objects of our pity and anger farther and farther away from the living world—farther and farther back into a dim distance from indignant tears and frowns. But Chaucer is the opposite of a dreamy poet ; his feelings are fresh and quick, his expression direct and demonstrative ; he pities Dido, Ariadne, Phyllis, Medea, and flames out with fierce passion against Æneas, Theseus, Demophon, and Jason, as heartily as if they had all been his personal acquaintances. He cannot think of the treachery of the false lovers without getting into a passion.

> " But welaway! the harm, the ruth,
> That hath betide for such untruth!
> As men may oft in bookës read,
> And all day see it yet in deed,
> That for to thinken it a teen is."

He utterly repudiates the pretence of Æneas that he was urged to leave Carthage by a destiny that he could not disobey; he treats this with scorn as a shallow and commonplace excuse for leaving a love that had become stale. He travels beyond his authorities to imagine the complainings of the forsaken queen; refers his readers for the whole of the touching story to Ovid; and cries with sudden energy—

> " And were it not too long to endite,
> By God, I would it herë write!"

He is no less furious at Theseus—

> " How false eke was Duke Theseus,
> That as the story telleth us,
> How he betrayed Adriane;
> The Devil be his soulës bane!"

Demophon, the son of Theseus, wicked son of a wicked sire, prone to deceit as the young of the fox, is treated with contemptuous scorn for his treachery to Phyllis—

> " Me list not vouchësafe on him to swink,
> Dispenden on him a penful of ink,
> For false he was in love right as his sire;
> The Devil set their soulës both on fire!"

Jason is held up to especial contempt; the poet proceeds to impeach him with especial zest—

> " Thou root of falsö lovers, Duke Jason!
> Thou sly devourer and confusion
> Of gentle women, gentle crëatures!"

Now there is no mistaking the genuineness of all this passion. But can we echo all these imprecations with true fervour? Do they not sound strange in our ears? Can we feel them as the poet's contemporaries did?

It was the opinion of De Quincey that, in the quality of animation, Chaucer is superior to Homer. The comparison is not, perhaps, altogether fair, because Chaucer's themes, as a rule, admit of lighter treatment than Homer's: but certainly no poet could well be 'more animated than Chaucer. All his works are full of bright colour, fresh feeling, and rapid ease and gaiety of

movement. There is no tedious dulness in his descriptions; no
lingering in the march of his narrative. With all his loquacity
and vivacity, he knows when his readers have had enough of one
thing, and passes easily on to something else. The ease of his
transitions is very remarkable. Some writers drive so hard at the
expression of what lies before them for the moment, that they
cannot recover themselves quickly enough to make a graceful turn
to what succeeds : they throw themselves off the track, and become
confused and uncertain in their apprehension of the main subject.
This Chaucer never seems to do; he always keeps his main subject
clearly and firmly in view; and his well-marked digressions add
to the general animation, by dispersing the feeling of rigid restraint without tending in the slightest to produce confusion.

It is in the Knight's Tale and the Squire's Tale, which deal to
some extent with martial subjects, that Chaucer may most fairly
be compared with Homer. The comparison is not unfavourable
to our native poet. Even in conveying a vivid impression of the
stir of an excited crowd, in which Homer is so excelling, we
cannot allow that Chaucer is inferior. What could be more animated than Chaucer's account in the Squire's Tale of the bustling
and buzzing multitude that assembled to stare at the magic horse,
broad mirror of glass, and ring of gold, and to exchange specula-
tions concerning the nature of these wonderful presents? Take,
again, the gathering to the tournament before Theseus, in the
Knight's Tale. What could be more inspiring, more alive with
bright movement, splendid evolution, and fresh air than this?
The herald has just proclaimed that the more deadly weapons are
excluded from the lists; whereupon—

> " The voïce of the people toucheth heaven,
> So loudë criedë they with merry steven :
> ' God savë such a lord that is so good :
> He willeth no destruction of blood ! '
> Up goth the trumpës and the melody.
> And to the listës ride the company
> By ordinancë through the city large,
> Hanging with cloth of gold and not with serge.
> Full like a lord this noble Duke can ride ;
> These two Thebanës upon either side :
> And after rode the Queen, and Emily,
> And of ladies another company,
> And of communës after their degree.
> And thus they passeden through that city,
> And to the listës comen they by time.
> It was not of the day yet fully prime,
> When settë was Thesöus rich and high,
> Hippolyta the Queen, and Emily,
> And other ladies in their degrees about.
> Unto the scatës presseth all the rout ;

> And westöward, thorough the gates of Mart,
> Arcite, and eke the hundred of his part,
> With banners red is entered right anon;
> And in that selvë moment Palamon
> Is under Venus, eastward in that place,
> With banner white, and hardy cheer and face."

We should expect the courtier of Richard II., even when writing in his old age, to be more animated in his treatment of love than the blind old man of the rocky isle. And such he is. We shall see that Chaucer specially excels in depicting the tender aspects of the passion, but he was a master also of its cheering inspirations. Everybody has by heart his cheerful description of the youthful squire. That gay gentleman, however, was basking in the unbroken sunshine of love; you must take one who has known its dark eclipse, if you wish to see an example of its full power. Take Arcita of the Knight's Tale, who has been changed by his passion out of all recognition: he has become lean, hollow-eyed, and sallow, and his spirits have been so low that the sound of music brought tears into his eyes. Consider the change wrought on this woful lover when he has made some progress towards success, and his youthful energies return to their natural tone. Take him when he walks out of a May morning with his rising hopes, and drinks in the sympathy of nature, which also is rejoicing in its recovery from darkness and winter.

> " The busy larkë, messenger of day,
>   Salueth in her song the morrow gray;
>   And fiery Phœbus riseth up so bright
>   That all the orient laugheth of the light,
>   And with his streamës dryeth in the greves
>   The silver droppës, hanging on the leaves.
>   And Arcita, that is in the court royal
>   With Theseüs, his squiër principal,
>   Is risen, and looketh on the merry day.
>   And for to doon his observance to May,
>   Remembering of the point of his desire,
>   He on his courser, starting as the fire,
>   Is ridden into the fieldës him to play,
>   Out of the court, were it a mile or tway.
>   And to the grove, of which that I you told,
>   By aventure his way he gan to hold,
>   To maken him a garland of the greves,
>   Were it of woodëbind or hawthorn leaves,
>   And loud he sung against the sunnë sheen:—
> ' May, with all thy flowrës and thy green,
>   Welcome be thou, fairë freshë May!
>   I hope that I some greenë getten may.'
>   And fro his courser, with a lusty heart,
>   Into the grove full lustily he start,
>   And in a path he roamed up and down."

When we go for a feast of tender feeling to a poet possessing in large measure the quality of animation, we should not go in a languid mood. We need not, of course, follow his lead; we may choose our own pace. Instead of going with the surface of the lively brook, and seeing no more of its pebbles and the beauties of its banks and winding nooks than the rapid glance that its speed allows, we may fix on delicious spots, and feed there to our heart's content. It is this quality of animation that makes Chaucer so peculiarly the poet of outdoor summer weather, the most delightful of companions on the hillside, or by the running streams.

Chaucer's heart fitted him well to be the poet of tender sentiment. He seems to have dwelt with fond observation on everything that was bright and pretty, from "the smallë fowlës that sleepen all the night with open eye," to the little herd-grooms playing on their pipes of green corn. He watched the little conies at their play, the little squirrels at their sylvan feasts; he looked into the "coldë wellë streamës, nothing dead," to admire

> " The smallë fishes bright
> With finnës red, and scalës silver white."

He knew, too, the colour of every feather in Chanticleer, and had minutely studied his majesty's habits towards his subjects. But of all things of beauty in nature, the singing-birds were his most especial favourites. He often dwells on the ravishing sweetness of their melodies. His finest picture of their exuberance of joy in the spring—their tuneful defiance of the fowler, their billing and chirruping, their vows of eternal fidelity—occurs in the opening of the "Legend of Good Women."

A man of the world himself, Chaucer still could enter into simple love-making among unsophisticated gentle creatures of a larger growth than the amorous little birds. Perhaps no passage shows the poet's exquisite tenderness better than the wooing of Thisbe by Pyramus, so well known in its ludicrous aspects from the caricature in "Midsummer Night's Dream"; and it is but an act of justice to these two faithful lovers to let them be seen as they were conceived by a sympathetic poet.

> " This wall, which that betwix them bothë stood
> Was cloven atwo, right fro the top adoun,
> Of oldë time, of his foundatioun.
> But yet this clift was so narrow and lite
>
> .      .      .      .      .      .
>
> But what is that that love cannot espy?
> Ye lovers two, if that I shall not lie,
> Ye founden first this little narrow clift!
> And with a sound as soft as any shrift,

> They let their wordës through the cliftë pace,
> And tolden while they stooden in the place,
> All their complaint of love and all their woe.
> At every timë when they durstë so,
> Upon the one side of the wall stood he,
> And on that other sidë stood Thisbe,
> The sweetë sound of other to receive.
> And thus their wardens wouldë they deceive,
> And every day this wall they wouldë threat,
> And wish to God that it were down y-beat.
>   Thus would they sayn :—'Alas, thou wicked wall !
> Through thine envyë thou us lettest all !
> Why nilt thou cleave, or fallen all atwo !
> Or at the leastë, but thou wouldest so,
> Yet wouldest thou but onës let us meet,
> Or onës that we mightë kissen sweet,
> Then were we covered of our carës cold.
> But nathëless, yet be we to thee hold
> In as much as thou sufferest for to gone
> Our wordës through thy lime and eke thy stone,
> Yet oughtë we with thee been well apaid.'
>   And when these idle wordës weren said,
> The coldë wall they wouldë kissen of stone,
> And take their leave, and forth they wouldë gone."

Thoroughly as his heart seems to go with this simple, earnest passion, almost infantile in its fondness, he can strike many another key in the infinitely varied art of love. Especially is he skilled in the chivalrous profession of entire submission to his lady's will, and humble adoration of her pre-eminent excellence. Take, for example, the opening stave of his humble prayer to Pity, which, without doubt, the cruel fair was at liberty to apply to herself.

> " Humblest of heart, highest of reverence,
> Benignë flower, corown of virtues allë !
> Sheweth unto your royal excellence,
> Your servant, if I durstë me so callë,
> His mortal harm, in which he is y-fallë,
> And not all only for his evil fare,
> But for your renown, as I shall declare.
>
> .      .      .      .      .      .
>
> What needeth to show parcel of my pain,
> Sith every wo that heartë may bethink,
> I suffer; and yet I dare not to you plain,
> For well I wot, although I wake or wink,
> Ye reckö not whether I float or sink.
> Yet nathëless my truth I shall susteen,
> Unto my death, and that shall well be seen."

All forlorn lovers have his best services at their command. We may apply to him his own favourite line, many times repeated—

> "For pity runneth soon in gentle heart."

How feelingly he depicts the situation of Palamon—imprisoned and love-sick Palamon !

> " In darkness and horrible and strong prison
> This seven year hath sitten Palamon,
> Forpined, what for wo and for distress.
> Who feeleth double sorrow and heaviness
> But Palamon ? that love distraineth so,
> That wood out of his wit he goth for wo."

The woful pangs of sweet Aurelius too, his languor and furious torments, are followed with deep sympathy ; and the heart-broken agony of forsaken Troilus is most intimately realised.   In the expression of " deep heart's-sorrowing," Chaucer's words always flow with peculiar richness and intimate aptness of choice.

Naturally, however, it is womanhood in distress that enters his heart with the keenest stroke.   He might well plead before the god and goddess of love that, if he had laughed at some of the foibles of the sex, he had not been indifferent to their virtues and their sufferings.   His gallery of distressed heroines was as wide as the range of legend and history that was known to him : Constance, Griselda, Virginia, Cecilia, Alcyone, Alcestis, Cleopatra, Thisbe, Dido, Hypsipyle, Medea, Lucrece, Ariadne, Philomela, Phyllis, Hypermnestra.   The thought of their suffering agitates him, destroys his composure ; he cannot proceed without stopping to express his compassion, or to appeal to heaven against the caprice of Fortune or the wickedness of men.   But he never dwells long on such scenes.   It was not for him to harrow the feelings of his audience ; when he has said enough to move them, he at once proceeds to effect a diversion.   Lingering agonies were not to his taste.   His representative the Host is almost choked with emotion 'at the Doctor's tale of Appius and Virginia ; he relieves himself with furious denunciation of Appius, and tries to laugh the painful theme out of his memory.   The legends of Constance (Man of Law's Tale) and Griselda (Clerk's Tale), have the happy termination of comedy ; and the story of their prolonged sufferings is relieved by many a passing word of indignant blame against the guilty causes of their misery.   Mediæval readers liked long-drawn martyrdoms, but in the hands of such an artist as Chaucer, whether he dealt with the martyrs of religion or the martyrs of love, the pathos is never hard and overbearing ; our pity is kept quick and fresh, and not allowed to stagnate in oppressive anguish.   Such a poem as Wordsworth's ' Margaret ' was impossible for him.

One of the most delightful of the ' Canterbury Tales ' is the Franklin's Tale.   The incorruptible fidelity of the beautiful Dorigen, the equanimity and magnanimity of her brave husband

Arviragus, the resolution of the Squire Aurelius not to be outdone in generosity by the Knight, capped by the resolution of the Knight not to be outdone by the Squire, make this tale a unique embodiment of the highest ideals of chivalry : scrupulous adherence to a rash promise on the one hand being met by renunciation of unfair advantage on the other. The chivalry of the tale is fantastic, but the poet's art makes it credible and beautiful.

Chaucer's humour is the most universally patent and easily recognised of his gifts. The smile or laugh that he raises, by refined irony or by broad rough jest and incident, is conspicuously genial. Mephistophelian mockery and Satanic grimness are not in his way. This had nothing to do with his being the bright morning star of English poetry—writing with the buoyancy of youth at a time when the struggle for existence was less fierce, when there was no bitter feeling between high and low, no envenomed warfare of civil or religious party. There never has been age nor country in which the fierce spirit has wanted fuel for its fierceness. It was simply the nature of the man to be genial, —"attempered and soft" as the climate of his gardens of Venus. He would have been so in whatever age he had lived.

The great criterion of good-nature, the indispensable basis of humour, is the power of making or sustaining a jest at one's own expense; and none of our humorists bear this test so well as Chaucer. He often harps on his own supposed imperfections, his ignorance of love, his want of rhetorical skill, his poverty. His poverty, real or pretended—and, unfortunately, it would seem to have been real—is the subject of several jokes in his poems, as it must have been in his private talk. In the "House of Fame," when describing how the walls, roofs, and floors of the temple were plated with gold half a foot thick "as fine as ducat of Venice," he cannot resist the temptation to add—

> "Of which too little in my pouch is."

His "Complaint to his Purse" is conceived in a very gay spirit :—

> "Now voucheth safe this day, ere it be night,
> That I of you the blissful sound may hear,
> Or see your colour like the sunnë bright,
> That of yellowness haddë never peer.
> Ye be my life ! ye be mine heartës steer !
> Queen of comfort and goodë company !
> Beth heavy again or ellës mote I die."

We must know this hobby of his to understand the full comic force of his comparing Alison to a newly forged noble, bright from the mint.

The freedom of his humour, as one would expect, was progressive. There are unequivocal touches of humour both in "Chaucer's Dream" and in the "Court of Love"; witness the sly treatment of Morpheus, and the poet's timid entry into the sacred court; but the humour, as became the subjects, is lurking and subordinate. It is worth noting, that in the "Court of Love," though he could not profess entire ignorance of the passion as he did so often afterwards, he professes to have kept out of the service of Venus for a most unconscionable length of time; he was actually eighteen before he went to her court, and then he had to be summoned. But the humour is much less overt in the "Court of Love," than in the more mature "House of Fame." In that poem, as in the 'Canterbury Tales,' he treats his own personality with reckless contempt. When the poet is caught up, at first he loses consciousness; but by-and-by the eagle wakes him up with comical remonstrances at his timidity. Half reassured, he begins to wonder vaguely what all this can mean :—

> "O God, thought I, that madest kind,
>  Shall I none other wayes die?
>  Whe'r Jovës will me stellify,
>  Or what thing may this signify?
>  I neither am Enoch, ne Eli,
>  Ne Romulus, ne Ganymede,
>  That was y-bore up, as men read,
>  To heaven with Dan Jupiter,
>  And made the goddës botteler!
>  Lo, this was then my fantasy!
>  But he that bare me gan espy,
>  That I so thought, and saidë this—
>  'Thou deemest of thyself amiss;
>  For Jovës is not thereabout,
>  I dare will put thee out of doubt,
>  To make of thee as yet a star.'"

The comparison between his own stout person and Ganymede, and the implied conception of himself as the butler [1] of the gods, are delicious. But, indeed, the passage throughout is so rich, that it is difficult to say which is its most comical touch.

The outcome of his broad humour is seen in the general plan of the 'Canterbury Tales' as much as in some of the pronounced particulars. With the rougher sort of the pilgrims, and as we shall presently see, only with them, the pilgrimage is a tipsy revel, a hilarious holiday "outing." They are the merriest company that mine "Host of the Tabard" has had under his roof for many a day; and they are such jolly noisy good fellows that, at supper overnight, the host is tempted to propose that he should

---

[1] This, however, is one of those cases where Time has lent an additional touch to the humour. The butler was a higher functionary than we should understand now by the name.

go with them and direct their merriment on the way. In the energy of his good-fellowship and confident sudden prospect of a hilarious journey, he cries for immediate decision on his plan—

> " Now by my father's soulë that is dead,
> But ye be merry, smiteth off mine head.
> Hold up your hands withouten morë speech."

They agree ; and the idea thus conceived is carried out with no less spirit. The pilgrims must have made a sensation as they rode out of town. The more respectable members of the company doubtless bore themselves with becoming gravity, but the wilder spirits put no restraint upon their mirth. The Miller brought them out of town to the music of his bagpipes—and a bagpipe in the hands of a drunk man is an instrument likely to attract some attention. The harum-scarum pimple-faced bacchanalian Summoner had put on his head a garland large enough for an alehouse sign, and flourished a cake as a buckler. His friend and compeer the Pardoner had, " for jollity," trussed up his hood in his wallet, and let his yellow flaxen hair hang in disorder on his shoulders, saying that it was the new fashion.

> " Full loud he sang 'Come hither, love, to me.'
> This Summoner bare to him a stiff burdoun,
> Was never trump of half so great a soun."

A company with spirits so uproarious in it tasked all the Host's powers of maintaining order, authoritative though he was. Of course they broke through. The Knight, who drew the lot for telling the first tale, was allowed to finish it ; but as soon as he had done, the drunk Miller struck in and insisted on telling a noble tale that he knew. Though hardly able to keep his seat, he was not so drunk as not to know that he was drunk ; he knew that, he said, " by his soun," and he besought them, if he said anything out of place, to lay the blame on the ale of Southwark. His tale does ample justice to his inspiration. The Host having once let the reins out of his hands was not able to resume them : the president of such a company must keep his authority by giving his subjects liberty to take their own way. The butt of the Miller's Tale was a carpenter ; and the Reeve being a carpenter thought himself aggrieved, and wanted to return the compliment by telling an equally coarse tale about the cuckolding of a miller. The Host, with the true instinct of a ruler, at once humoured him, and asserted his own dignity by cutting short his prologue, and commanding him to tell his tale. Then the gross Cook, chuckling over the discomfiture of the Miller, wanted to tell " a little jape that fell in our city," and the judicious Host granted permission. There was more intoxicated personality, wrangling, and peace-

making, as they went on.    The Friar enraged the Summoner by
relating an awkward adventure that happened to one of his profession ; and the Summoner gave a merciless Roland for his Oliver.
After a long draught of ale, the Pardoner recklessly exposed all the
tricks of his trade, and had the audacious assurance, after this full
confession of his roguery, to try to work upon the feelings of his
brother pilgrims, and extract money from them.    It is to be feared,
too, that the Host required a little too much of the " corny ale " to
drown his pity for poor Virginia : one cannot otherwise account
for his getting into a hot quarrel with the Pardoner, which required
the intervention of the Knight to smooth it over.    Towards the
close of the pilgrimage the Cook showed symptoms of being overcome with sleep and ale, and seemed to be in danger of falling
from his horse.    The Host rebuked him, and the Manciple fell out
upon him with such a torrent of abuse, that poor Robin over-
balanced himself and tumbled to the ground in a furious futile
effort to articulate a reply, and there was much shoving to and fro
before they could set him in the saddle again.    A pretty pilgrimage
to the shrine of a saint !    There is endless food for deep animal
laughter in the humours of these riotous pilgrims—particularly that
madcap pair of ecclesiastics—the Summoner and the Pardoner.
One is constantly finding fresh points of comical view in that
precious couple.    It is a mistake, I may remark, to look in the
'Canterbury Tales' for satire.    If there is any, it is there by failure
and imperfection ; it is a flaw in the poet's design, which was to
provide material for disinterested laughter, zealous and profound.
To suppose that there is any satire in the candid revelation of the
Pardoner's gross deceptions of the credulous vulgar, is to fail to
rise to the height of the humour of that great character.    There is
no more ill-nature in the elaboration of his reckless freaks, than in
the often-quoted and justly-praised delicate irony of the opening of
the Wife of Bath's Tale.[1]

As regards any lurking satirical purpose in the 'Canterbury
Tales,' if we suppose that we discern any such purpose, we may
take for granted that we are still on the outside of their riotous
humour.    It is true that a good many of the pilgrims are men of
somewhat damaged reputation, or, at least, doubtful virtue.    The
Merchant is not beyond suspicion ; the Miller steals corn ; the
Reeve has secured a comfortable feathering for his own nest ; the
Cook is a profligate sot ; all the ecclesiastics, Monk, Friar, and
Pardoner, exhibit a wide difference between their practice and

---

[1] If M. Sandras had understood English humour, which seems to baffle French-
men as Scotch " wut " baffles Englishmen, he would hardly have said that in the
' Canterbury Tales ' Chaucer's natural affinity with the spirit of Jean de Meun is
made conspicuous.    In the following section I shall show how Chaucer maintains
his agreement with the spirit of chivalry.

their doctrine; and even the respectable professional men, the Lawyer and the Doctor, have a questionable liking for large fees. But these failings are not dwelt upon from the point of view of the satirist. With all their sinful taints, the pilgrims are represented as being on the whole jovial companions, satisfied with themselves and with each other; the taints, indeed, are not shown in the aspect of sins, but rather in the aspect of ludicrous peccadilloes or foibles. The sinners are elevated by the hilarity of the occasion above the sense of sin; and the poet does not hold them up to scorn or contempt, but enters genially into the spirit of their holiday revel. He does not join them to backbite and draw out their weaknesses for the bitter amusement or sharp dislike of his readers: he joins them to enjoy their company. Chaucer's humour in the 'Canterbury Tales' is not in the spirit of Jean de Meun; it comes much nearer the spirit of Burns in the "Jolly Beggars."

## IV.—His Delineation of Character.

It is somewhat startling to put together, as I have done in the preceding section, the buffoonery that went on throughout the Canterbury pilgrimage. We remember the tales of high chivalrous sentiment and exquisite pathos, and we ask how these were compatible with such noisy ribaldry. The explanation is, that the tales are suited to the characters and manners of the different pilgrims; and that while one set of them indulge largely in ale and inebriated freaks and loud animal mirth, the more respectable sort preserve a becoming dignity.

To a certain extent Professor Lowell is right in saying that there is no caste feeling among Chaucer's pilgrims. Knight and yeoman, monk and cook, lodge all night in the same inn, set out in a company on the same errand, and contribute to a common entertainment subject to the direction of one man, and that an innkeeper. But we should greatly misunderstand the delicacy of Chaucer's sense of manners as well as of character, if we went away with the impression that in the 'Canterbury Tales' there is no trace of the distinctions of rank, and that in the pilgrimage there is no respect paid to persons.

In the Prologue, the poet begs pardon for not setting the pilgrims in their degree—

> "Also I pray you to forgive it me
> All have I not set folk in their degree
> Here in this tale, as that they shouldë stand:
> My wit is short, ye may well understand."

He had a livelier plan in view than to make them tell off their tales in the order of their rank. But though he did not adopt this palpable and unmistakable way of indicating caste, he does really show respect of persons in several less gross and obvious ways. A line is drawn, though unobtrusively and with delicate suggested art, between "the gentles" and the other pilgrims. If this had not been done, we should have been compelled to say that our poet had inaccurately portrayed the life of the time. But he has done it, and done it not by harsh angular forced assertion, but easily and naturally in his clear-sighted shaping and working out of his materials. The careful reader gets the clue from such passages as that at the end of the Knight's Tale, where we are told that the whole company, young and old, praised it as a noble and memorable story, "and namely," that is, particularly, "the *gentles* every one." That was the sort of tale that the gentles felt themselves at liberty to approve of. When the Pardoner took up with animation the Host's request that he should tell a merry tale, forthwith "the gentles" began to cry that they must have no ribaldry: "Tell us," they said, "some moral thing that we may learn." It is very misleading to apologise, as some writers on Chaucer do, for the gross obscenity of certain of the tales, on the ground that this was the outspoken fashion of the time—that decorum then permitted greater freedom of language. The savour of particular words may have changed since the time of Chaucer; but then, as now, people with any pretensions to refinement were bound to abstain strictly in the presence of ladies from all ribaldry of speech and manner, on pain of being classed with "churls" and "villains." In the "Court of Love," the gentle lover is warned emphatically that he must not be

> "Ribald in speech, or out of measure pass,
> Thy bound exceeding; think on this alway:
> For women been of tender heartës aye."

And in the 'Canterbury Tales,' Chaucer carefully guards himself against being supposed to be ignorant of this law. The ribald tales are introduced as the humours of the lower orders, persons ignorant or defiant of the rules of refined society, and moreover, as we have seen, excited, intoxicated, out for a pilgrimage as riotous and wild as our pilgrimage to the Derby.[1] Such riotous

---

[1] That the behaviour of the more uproarious of Chaucer's pilgrims was based on real life we may see from one Thorpe's indignant account of the actual pilgrimages to the shrine of St Thomas (quoted in Morley's English Writers, ii. 291): "They will ordain with them before to have with them both men and women that can sing wanton songs, and some other pilgrims will have with them bagpipes; so that every town they come through, what with the noise of their singing, and with the sound of their piping, and with the jangling of their Canterbury bells, and with the barking out of dogs after them, that they make more noise than if the king came there away with all his clarions and many other minstrels. And if these men and women be a month in their pilgrimage, many of them shall be a half-year after great janglers, tale-tellers, and liars." In saying that in

mirth was very far indeed from being the fashion of the time among fashionable people. Mark how careful Chaucer is to shield himself from the responsibility of it. In the Prologue (l. 725), he prays his readers of their courtesy not to set down his plainness of speech as his "villany": he is bound to record faithfully every word that was said, though it had been said by his own brother. He does, indeed, whether seriously or jocularly, allege the example of Christ and Plato as authorities for plainness of speech; but he does not repeat this when he returns to the matter before the first of his freespoken tales. In the prologue to the Miller's Tale, he is most explicit. He says that the obstinate Miller would not forbear for any man, "but told his churlish tale in his manner." And then he makes this clear and elaborate apology for rehearsing it,—

> "And, therefore, every *gentle* wight I pray,
> For, Goddës love, deemeth not that I say
> Of evil intent; but for I must rehearse
> Their talës all, be they better or worse,
> *Or ellës falsen some of my matter.*
> And, therefore, whoso list it not to hear,
> Turn over the leaf and chose another tale;
> For he shall find enowë great and small,
> Of *storial thing that toucheth gentilesse,*
> And eke morality and holiness.
> Blameth not me, if that ye chose amiss.
> *The Miller is a churl, ye know well this;*
> *So was the Reeve and other many mo,*
> And harlotry they tolden bothë two.
> Aviseth you, and put me out of blame;
> And eke men shall not maken earnest of game."

Observe, accordingly, how the tales are distributed. Nothing ribald is put into the mouth of the gentles, and nothing ribald is told concerning their order. The "very perfect gentle knight," who never said any villany to any manner of man, recites the tale of Palamon and Arcite, with its chivalrous love and rivalry, its sense of high womanly beauty, its gorgeous descriptions of temple, ritual, procession, and tournament. His son, the gallant, well-mannered, well-dressed squire, embroidered like a mead, with his head full of love, romance, song, and music, gives a fragment of a romance about King Cambuscan and his daughter Canace, and the wonderful exploits of a magic horse, a magic mirror, and a magic ring. The professional men—the busy lawyer, the studious clerk, the irreligious but good-hearted doctor—give the pathetic

Chaucer's company "each fellow-traveller carried his wit for bagpipe," Professor Morley seems to have overlooked the Miller's instrument, and generally he seems inclined to make the pilgrimage a much tamer affair than it would appear to have been. I have endeavoured to show how the poet's decorous self-respect is reconciled with fidelity to the manners of the time.

stories of Constance, Griselda, and Virginia: the two first of
which may be justly described as tales of morality.  The Franklin
tells the old Breton lay of Dorigen and Arviragus, models of
chivalrous virtue.  The Prioress and the Second Nun relate holy
legends of martyrdom.  These are "the gentles," and such are
their tales.  The tales of vulgar merriment are told by the Miller,
the Reeve, the Wife of Bath, the Friar, the Summoner, the Merchant, the Shipman.  And as regard is had to the condition of the
narrator in the character of the tale ascribed to him, so the persons engaged in degrading adventure are below the rank of the
gentles.  Januarius, indeed, in the Merchant's Tale, is called a
worthy knight; but he is a blind dotard, long past knightly
exercise and knightly feeling: and his May, who is so easily won
to play him false, is represented as a maiden of small degree.  The
rank of all the other befooled heroes is plain : they are a carpenter,
a miller, a summoner, a friar, and a merchant.[1]  The gentle order
is respected.  They join the company, and enjoy the ribald speech
and behaviour of their riotous, inebriated, vulgar companions; but
they do not forfeit their self-respect, by contributing a share to the
noisy merriment.  When they have had enough of it, or when
the tales threaten to become too boisterous, they use their influence
to give a more sober tone to the proceedings.  They do not break
rough jests on each other as the vulgar do.  And mine host knows
his place sufficiently well to be less familiar and imperious with
them than with the Miller and the Cook; he is courteous to the
Knight, and ludicrously over-polite to the Prioress.

I may seem to have insisted too much on this distinction between the "gentles" and the "roughs" in the Canterbury pilgrimage; but the truth is, that we cannot have too vivid a hold
of this distinction if we wish to understand either the 'Canterbury Tales,' or Chaucer's poetry generally.  Unless we realise
this, we cannot feel how thoroughly and intimately his poems are
transfused with chivalrous sentiment.  What is more, we cannot
appreciate the perfect skill with which he has maintained this
sentiment in the 'Canterbury Tales,' and at the same time
transferred to his pages a faithful representation of vulgar manners
in their wildest luxuriance.

Waiving all questions as to whether Chaucer was most of Norman or of Saxon, of Celt or of Teuton, we cannot escape from

---

[1] Observe, in passing, another evidence of Chaucer's sense of courtly propriety
in his Troilus and Cressida.  The knights and ladies that heard his poems read
would not have tolerated Shakespeare's representation of Pandarus, one of the
knights of Troy, as a gross procurer, or of Cressida, a lady of rank, as an incontinent wanton.  Chaucer's Pandarus is an accomplished knight, moved to his
questionable service by pity for the despair of his friend; Cressida the loveliest,
most refined, and most discreet of widows, overcome by passionate love, dexterous
intrigue, and favouring accidents.

admitting that he was deeply impressed with the wide difference between chivalrous sentiments and the sentiments and manners prevalent among the dependants of chivalry. The difference may not have in reality been so profound as it was in ideal: but Chaucer felt it deeply. How deeply, we see most clearly in the "Cuckoo and Nightingale," and the "Parliament of Birds," where the antagonistic sentiments are placed in express contrast. The Cuckoo is a vulgar bird, and takes gross ridiculous views of love: the Nightingale is a gentle bird, and regards love with delicate seriousness. Similar types are represented, with greater epic variety, in the "Parliament of Birds." There is no mistaking the contrast in these allegorical fables; the vulgar birds, the Water Fowls, the Seed Fowls, and the Worm Fowls, are sharply snubbed for their chuckling vulgarity by the haughty and refined Birds of Prey. But in the 'Canterbury Tales' the poet has achieved the triumph of making the antagonistic sentiments work smoothly side by side, and that is really their main triumph as a broad picture of manners and character. There, with dignified carriage, are seen the type of men and women whose sensibilities were trained to appreciate the tender refinement of Chaucer, and who allowed themselves more boisterous entertainment only under decorous pretexts, listening without participating. Side by side, following their own humours with noisy independence, are their vulgar associates, stopping at every ale-stake to eat and drink, half choked with ribald laughter, finding in the contrast between themselves and the reserved gentles an additional incentive to their gross open mirth. The 'Canterbury Tales' embody two veins of feeling that powerfully influenced the literature of the fifteenth century—the sentiment that fed on chivalrous romances, and the appetite for animal laughter that received among other gratifications the grotesque literature of miracle-plays.

If we fail to perceive this contrast between the serious and the ludicrous side of the Canterbury pilgrimage, if we miss the poet's reconciliation of the two without repression of either, Chaucer's genius, in so far as regards manners and character, has laboured for us in vain. A dead weight flattens his figures into the page. The exquisite delicacy of his delineation is confused. We drag down the Knight and the Prioress by involving them in the responsibility of the Miller's Tale: we crush the life out of the Miller and the Summoner, and reduce them to wretched tameness by supposing them to fraternise with the Knight in a certain amount of decorous restraint. The pilgrimage becomes a muddled, jumbled, incoherent, unintelligible thing.

We must not, however, allow our attention to two large divisions, however much that may be the key to a right understanding of the 'Canterbury Tales,' to make us overlook the varied

types that lie within these divisions. Every character, indeed, is
-typical—Knight, Squire, Yeoman, Prioress, Monk, Friar, Merchant, Clerk, Sergeant of Law, Franklin, Cheapside Burgess,
Cook, Shipman, Doctor of Physic, Wife of Bath, Parson, Ploughman, Miller, Manciple, Reeve, Summoner, Pardoner: and the
characteristics of their various lines of life are drawn as no other
generation has been in equal space. I shall not attempt to pick
out supreme examples of Chaucer's skill. The compression of
masterly touches in that Prologue can hardly be spoken of in sane
language: there is not one of the seven or eight hundred lines
but contains something to admire.

Apart from the skill of the delineation, one typical individual
is specially interesting from his relations to the time, and that is
the poor Parson. He cannot be said to belong, in rank at least,
to the gentle class: he is of poor extraction, the brother of the
Ploughman. He represents the serious element among the lower
classes. During the riot of the pilgrimage, he is put down and
silenced. He ventures to rebuke the Host for his profane language,
and is jeered at and extinguished by that worthy as a Lollard.
But when the ribald intoxication of the road has exhausted itself,
his grave voice is heard and respected: and he brings the pilgrims
into Canterbury with a tale more in harmony with the ostensible
object of their journey.

# CHAPTER II.

## CHAUCER'S CONTEMPORARIES AND SUCCESSORS.

### I.—English Contemporaries.

### (1332-1400?)

#### 1. William Langland—*Piers the Plowman.*

This chapter deals with second-rate, third-rate, and fourth-rate poets or versifiers who flourished from the time of Chaucer down to the early part of the sixteenth century. Chaucer had no worthy rival among his contemporaries, and no English poet worthy to be placed by his side appeared before the time of Spenser. Still, it is well to characterise the poets of this sober interval, however humble. The task may be dreary, but we cannot always live with the great minds, and we are rewarded by the study of mediocrities with a more vivid sense of the beauty and strength of their betters.

The most noteworthy of Chaucer's contemporaries was William Langland, author of the 'Vision of William concerning Piers the Plowman,' commonly known as the 'Vision of Piers Plowman.' Not much is ascertained about his life. Mr Skeat[1] considers it probable that he was born about 1332, at Cleobury Mortimer; that he wrote the first version of his poem (the A-text) in 1362, the second version (the B-text) in 1377, and the last version (the C-text) between 1380 and 1390; that he wrote a poem on the Deposition of Richard II.; and that he did not long survive the accession of Henry IV. He is generally supposed to have been a secular priest. It is obvious that he was familiar with London; and it

[1] See his elaborate Introduction to the Clarendon Press selection, and his editions of the various texts for the Early English Text Society. Mr Skeat accepts the argument of Professor C. H. Pearson ('North British Review,' April 1870) that the poet's name was Langley.

may be inferred, from his mention of the Malvern Hills, that he lived at one time in their neighbourhood.

Langland wrote in the old English alliterative metre; but he went to the fashionable modern poetry for the machinery of dream and allegory. He walks abroad on a May morning, like any poet of the period, lays himself down by a stream under a broad bank, and as he looks into the water, is lulled to sleep by the merry sound. He then dreams, and sees an allegorical field, full of folk; an allegorical tower, and an allegorical dale, with a dungeon. He is visited by a supernaturally lovely allegorical lady, who explains the meaning of what he sees. He is next witness of an allegorical drama; an allegorical marriage is proposed, the banns are forbidden, the whole party is carried before the king; and, after several symbolical incidents, judgment is pronounced. Wishing now to change the scene, the poet awakes his dreamer, and presently sends him asleep again, and opens up to him the vision of the Seven Deadly Sins, and of Piers the Plowman. The same artifice for changing the scene is used nine other times in the course of the poem.

But though the machinery of the poem reminds us that Langland had read in the same school of poetry as Chaucer, he writes in a very different spirit. The author of Piers the Plowman was the Carlyle of his generation. He may be said to be the complementary opposite of Chaucer. His criticism of life is stern. He refuses to enter the Garden of Mirth, which Chaucer was unwilling to quit; he holds the mirror up to the ugliness, the misery, the discontent to be found outside this pleasant habitation. Chaucer and Langland furnish our first examples of the conflict between sensuous art and Puritanism. Langland is not a rabid Puritan— he is not a rabid man; but he regards the votaries of the lust of the flesh and the lust of the eyes mournfully as deluded victims, and he denounces all minstrels and mirth-makers as heartless insulters of the miseries of the world. With what scorn he must have read, if he did read, the Legends of the Saints of Cupid! Langland would have used even stronger language towards such a work, than Milton used towards Sir Philip Sidney's "Arcadia," when he called it "a vain amatorious poem." He makes no distinction between wandering minstrels and other purveyors for idle luxury; he scorns them collectively with no less vehemence than the Puritans of the seventeenth century scorned the strolling player. Langland was far from having Milton's genius to tempt him into violations of his own doctrine; but he had some difficulty in reconciling even the modest flights of his muse with his paramount and imperious moral earnestness. He had qualms about "meddling with makings," when he might have been saying his psalter or praying for his benefactors; and had to reassure himself by quoting the example of Cato and other holy men, who played a little that they might bo more perfect in many places.

The contrast between Piers and the 'Canterbury Tales' is most instructive. Chaucer's pilgrims are not perfect, very far from it, but their shortcomings are exposed in a genial light. The poet shows us a company of people on the whole happy and self-satisfied, and alleges no reason why they should be otherwise. He is, in short, an artist of manners and character, who chooses a moment when his personages are seen to advantage, and when their imperfections are amusing without being painfully offensive. Langland writes with a very different purpose. His aim is, not to seize the happy moment in things as they are, but to make a stern comparison of things as they are with things as they ought to be—to place the existing state of society side by side with a lofty ideal, and elevate the depraved by energetic reproof and exhortation. What renders the difference in spirit between the two poets all the more remarkable is, that they treat of the same period; and that, when we reflect independently on the substance of what they convey to us, we draw from both the same conclusions regarding the prevalent state of society. There is, indeed, one exception. Langland gives us no idea of the refinement of sentiment among the gentle folks: he includes them in the general censure of ribald amusements; and, on the other hand, Chaucer, in his portrait of the "very perfect gentle knight," drew an ideal rarely realised, and suppressed the fact that knights very often treated their vassals with scant justice, and tyrannised over them like a cat among mice. Concerning the lower classes, we gather from them substantially the same facts. We learn from Chaucer, as well as from Langland, that merchants, millers, and cooks cheated their customers; that reeves (or stewards) cheated their masters; that doctors and lawyers were bent upon making money; that monks were more conversant with field-sports than religious duties; that friars were unconscionable beggars; that pardoners told atrocious lies, and made audacious extortions from the credulous vulgar; and that, amidst considerable drunkenness, waste, and ribaldry, there lived also men of honest industry and sincere piety. And if we look beneath the surface of Langland's invective, we see that poor people were not reduced to a state of uninterrupted wretchedness by the oppression of the rich, and their own intemperance. We reflect that, though their recreations were not to the poet's taste, their life must have been occasionally brightened by these japers and jugglers and janglers of jests. But so different are Chaucer and Langland in the spirit of their pictures, that it needs an effort of reflection to discover the shadows of the one and the lights of the other.

Take a few details of Langland's picture of the life of England. In the "fair field of folk," described in his prologues, he sees all manner of men moving about, the mean and the rich, "working and wandering as the world asketh." As Chaucer puts the knight in the foreground, so Langland gives the first place to his ideal of humble virtue—the hard-working honest ploughman—

> " Some putten them to the plough, played full seld,
> In setting and in sowing swonken[1] full hard,
> *And wonnen that wasters with gluttony destroyeth.*"

The sight of conscientious labour at once arouses the moralist's anger at unprofitable indolence. He places in immediate contrast a form of immorality most ·despicable in his eyes, and most pardonable in the eyes of the artist—

> " And some putten them to pride, apparelled them thereafter
> In countenance of clothing comen disguised."

In this category he would probably have placed Chaucer's youthful squire, embroidered as a mead. After his ideal of active life, with the unproductive display that consumes its fruits, comes an ideal of contemplative life—

> " In prayers and in penance putten them many;
> All for love of our lord liveden full strait,
> In hope for to have heavenric bliss ;
> As anchorites and hermits, that holden them in their cells,
> And coveten not in county to kairen[2] about,
> For no lickerish livelihood their likam[3] to please. "

Then follow various contrasts : Thriving merchants—"as it seemeth to our sight that such men thriveth"—minstrels, beggars, palmers, hermits, friars, pardoners, absentee parish priests ; idle and dishonest men—

> " Bidders[4] and beggars fast about gede,[5]
> With their belly and their bags of bread full y-crammed ;
> Faiteden[6] for their food, foughten at ale ;
> In gluttony, God it wot, gone they to bed,
> And risen with ribaldry the Roberdes knaves ;
> Sleep and sorry sloth pursueth them ever.
>      Pilgrims and palmers plighted them together,
> To seek Saint James and saintës in Rome ;
> They went forth in their way with many wise tales,
> And hadden leave to lie all their life after.

---

[1] Toiled.     [2] Carry themselves, gad.     [3] Body.
[4] Synonym for beggars.     [5] Gced—went.
[6] Made up tales—used false pretences.

> I saw some that saiden they had y-sought saintes ;
> To each a tale that they told their tongue was tempered to lie,
> More than to say sooth ; it seemed by their speech.
>     Hermits on an heap, with hooked staves,
> Wenten to Walsingham, and their wenches after ;
> Great lubbers and long, that loath were to swink,
> Clothed them in copes to be knowen from other ;
> And shapen them hermits their ease to have."

How different is this righteous animosity from the spirit of such artists as Burns and Chaucer, whose eyes are all for picturesqueness and humour ! The difference is still more marked in his picture of the interior of an inn. Glutton is tempted to enter on his way to confession ; goes in swearing, and finds a collection of habitual topers,—Cis the shoemaker's wife, Wat the warrener and his wife, Tim the tinker and two of his apprentices, Hick the hackneyman, Hugh the needle-seller, Clarice of Cock Lane, the clerk of the Church, Daw the dyker, Sir Piers of Pridie, Pernel of Flanders, a ribibe-player, a rat-catcher, Robin the roper, Clement the cobbler, Rose the dish-seller, Godfrey of Garlickhithe, Griffin the Welshman. All the ugly details of the debauchery are brought into prominence. They barter clothes, with noisy squabbling over their value ; they pass the cup greedily, snatching it from one another's hands with laughs and frowns, and continue their noisy carouse till evensong. Glutton drinks a gallon and a gill of ale, and manifests the most repulsive symptoms of intoxication. The picture, as a whole, is graphic, but intentionally coarse and disgusting ; throughout, the author's purpose is to make debauchery odious by showing its ugliest side. The glutton is not the hero of the evening, the triumphant leader of coarse delights ; he is a moral spectacle, a warning to drunkards and ne'er - do - wells. Contrast Langland's treatment of him with Chaucer's treatment of the Cook, at the close of the pilgrimage, before the Manciple's Tale. The Cook is roundly reproved by the Manciple for making a beast of himself ; but his drunken eccentricities are presented in such a way as to make them laughable rather than disgusting.

Langland is not without genuine humour,[1] though his moral purpose forbids him to allow it anything like full scope. He shows unmistakable enjoyment of fun in his account of the career of "Lady Meed," the allegorical embodiment of wealth ; he narrates with much gusto the respectful treatment she received from judges, clerks of the court, and confessors, and even from the king himself. In his account of the Seven Deadly Sins, also, whose characteristic appearances he describes with consider-

---

[1] Mr Lowell finds in Langland an equal sense of fun with Chaucer's ; but Mr Lowell would find a sense of fun in the demonstrations of Euclid.

able pictorial force, he sometimes relaxes into a smile or a laugh. Perhaps the most unequivocal flash of humour in the whole poem is his making Avarice mistake the meaning of "restitution "—

" 'Repentedest thou ever,' quoth Repentance, 'ne restitution madest?'
'Yes, once I was harboured,' quoth he, 'with an heap of chapmen ;
I rose when they were a-rest, and y-rifled their mails !'
'That was no restitution,' quoth Repentance, 'but a robber's theft ;
Thou hadst be better worthy be hanged therefore
Than for all that that thou hast here showed.'
'I weened rifling were restitution,' quoth he ; 'for I learned never read on book,
And I can no French in faith, but of the farthest end of Norfolk.'"

But humour is, on the whole, rare in Langland's work, and certainly it was no part of his purpose. He was a moralist, not a humorist. If his ridicule had produced laughter for laughter's sake, and raised no moral disapprobation, he would probably have taken himself to task for having missed his mark. He laughed at things that he wished to see abolished, and used ridicule as a means to make them hateful and loathsome, and to secure their abolition. He wished to make the glutton odious as a waster of the fruits of honest labour, and so discourage intemperance. He caricatured Lady Meed to make people ashamed of paying respect to riches. He represented the palmer as ignorant of the way to truth, and made the friars pretend that Do-well dwelt only with them, in order to expose and thereby reform their hypocrisy and exaggerated pretensions. He satirised the unscrupulous impositions of the pardoners, because he hated their unprofitable idleness and luxury, and was indignant at their robbing the poor man of his hard-earned bread. Langland is, in short, a Puritan of the fourteenth century. When we look from the 'Canterbury Tales' to his stern series of visions, we see that the antagonism between Cavalier and Roundhead began long before it culminated in civil war. Only, in Langland's time, the champion of the poor was still hopeful of redress. Langland was an apostle of purification, not of reconstruction. He believed devoutly in Holy Church, and desired only to see churchmen acting up to their professions. He raised not a word in dispute of the privileges of the nobility ; he desired only that they should remember and discharge their duties to those beneath them.

The cardinal virtue in Langland's eyes is industry. Like Carlyle, he proclaims a gospel of work. He expresses the teaching of Kind Wit—that is, natural wit or common-sense, in a form that reminds us of Carlyle's—'Two men I honour and no third.'

> " Kind wit would that each a wight wrought,
>   Or in dyking or in delving or in travailing in prayers ;
>   Contemplative life or active life, Christ would men wrought."

The paramount obligation of this duty is preached at every turn of the poem. The mere choice of Piers as the man that he delights to honour, still more his final transfiguration of the honest ploughman into a type of Christ, is a bold assertion of the dignity of the humblest labourer, and the contemptibility of idleness. And there are many minor inculcations of the same doctrine. When the Seven Deadly Sins are converted and cry out for a guide to Truth, Piers steps forward and offers to conduct them when they have helped him to ear his field of corn ; and he sets them all sturdily to work, with the exception of the Knight, who undertakes to secure him protection for the fruits of his toil. The substance of the teaching of Holy Church is, that faith without works is "dead as a door-post" ; and this is in part another aspect of the same doctrine. Two of the five sons of Inwit (Conscience), the constable of the castle that Nature has built to hold Anima (the Soul), are Work-well-with-thy-hands and Sir Godfrey Go-well.[1] Again, industry is the most prominent of the qualifications for obtaining the company of Do-well. And as Langland resembles Carlyle in his earnest upholding of the duty of work, so the resemblance extends to the provision of strenuous punishment for idlers. We have seen how our poet denounces sturdy beggars and lazy lubbers of hermits. When these gentry come to honest Piers, pretending that they cannot work for him, but offering to give him the benefit of their prayers, he allows hunger to restore them the use of their limbs. In like manner, Conscience is a strong advocate of the rod for the lazy back.

Another doctrine, less obtrusively expressed, is the right of individual judgment in matters of religion. This is not exactly a protest in favour of reason as against authority. It really is part of Langland's championship of the illiterate but honest poor. He pits their Kind-wit or common-sense against the learning of the clergy. He does this indirectly through the medium of his allegorical personages. Piers obtains from Truth a pardon containing only two lines—

> " They that have done good, shall go into eternal life ;
>   They that have done evil, into eternal fire."

A priest laughs at this pardon, and at first Piers is in despair, and thinks of leaving his plough and taking to prayer and pen-

---

[1] Mr Skeat commits a slight and natural inadvertence in describing these five sons as The Five Senses. They are See-well, Hear-well, Say-well, Work-well, and Go-well.

ance; but after a little he is emboldened to dispute the priest's authority. At another time, William the poet in his own person opposes Clergy, one of his characters, and stoutly maintains that learning is more of a hindrance than a help towards the kingdom of heaven—

> " Aren none rather y-ravished from the right belief
> Than are the cunning clerks that con many books ;
> Ne none sooner saved ne sadder[1] of belief
> Than plowmen and pastors and poor common labourers.
>
> Souters[2] and shepherds, such lewed[3] jots
> Piercen with a pater-noster the palace of heaven,
> And passen purgatory penanceless at their hence parting
> Into the bliss of paradise, for their pure belief."

Further, he makes Nature Wit laugh at the voluble talk of Dame Study. It is remarkable, however, that in his enlargement of the original poem he qualifies this extreme disparagement of learning. In *Passus* XII., Imaginative reminds him of the good done by men of learning, bids him never despise them, and tells him that Learning and Nature Wit are of the same kindred, and, indeed, near cousins.

The poem, as a whole, is not a connected historical allegory like the 'Pilgrim's Progress' or the 'Holy War.' The poet evades the difficulty of weaving the action of his allegorical personages into a simple connected story. He presents us with a series of eleven more or less disjointed visions or dreams, and leaves us to divine for ourselves whether or not these visions are allegories of consecutive stages in the religious life. On examination, we find that the visions are not consecutive. The first vision is a view of life by itself, designed to symbolise the corrupting influence of wealth ("Lady Meed"), its frequent union with falsehood, its doubtful compatibility with truth and conscience, its possession of the services of wisdom and wit. The next vision is a complete change of scene with a new set of allegorical personages ; it represents the conversion of the Seven Deadly Sins by Repentance, and their reformation by Piers Plowman, a poor husbandman, who is afterwards seen to typify the condescension of Christ to human nature. Then follow the Vision of Wit, Study, Clergy, and Scripture ; The Vision of Fortune, Nature, and Reason ; The Vision of Imaginative ; the Vision of Conscience, Patience, and Haukyn, the Active Man— a series of visions all bearing on the life of Do-well, the good life, the life of honest industry. Next we have the Vision of the Soul and of the Tree of Charity ; the Vision of Faith, Hope, and Charity ; the Vision of the Triumph of Piers the Plowman—

---

[1] More sober and sure.   [2] Shoemakers.   [3] Illiterate.

a series of visions bearing on the life of Do-bet, the better life, the life of faith, hope, and charity. Finally, we have two visions —the Vision of Grace and the Vision of Antichrist—bearing on the life of Do-best, the best life. Taken as a whole, these groups of visions do not allegorise any religious progress, any growth of religion in the soul; the one is not deduced from the other. In the last three divisions of the poem certain virtues and heavenly endowments are set forth in order from good to best; but this is an order of regular exposition, a climax, and not an order of development in the progressive Christian. Piers Plowman is the hero of the poem, and the chief connecting link of the dreams, inasmuch as the author, once having seen him, is very desirous, in more than one of the subsequent dreams, to see him again.

In describing the various personages of his allegory, Langland, as we have already said, has another object than to produce an artistic picture. Yet in his description of the Seven Deadly Sins—a subject that often engaged mediæval artists—the word-painting, simply as such, is exceedingly powerful. The effect cannot be said to be pleasing; the poet or preacher was himself full of strong abhorrence of the subject, desired to disgust and repel his reader no less strongly, and has emphatically succeeded —at least for modern readers. But the energy of the character-isation is tremendous—

> " And then came Covetice—can I him not descrive,
> So hungrily and hollow Sir Hervy him looked.
> He was beetle-browed, and babber-lipped also,
> With two bleared.eyen as a blind hag;
> And as a leathern purse lolled his cheeks,
> Well sidder [1] than his chin : they chivelled for eld;
> And as a bondman of his bacon his beard was bedravelled.
> With a hood on his head, a lousy hat above,
> And in a tawny tabard of twelve winter age,
> All to-torn and bawdy, and full of lice creeping;
> But if that a louse could have leapen the better,
>     She should not have walked on that walsh [2] so was it threadbare."

Such hideous and loathsome ideals, though *caviare* to the general run of moderns, may have been enjoyed by our Middle Age ancestors. They were realised in the moral-plays, doubtless with the best intentions; but they probably rather amused than instructed the rude audience. Spenser also applied his genius to similar subjects; but whether from moral enthusiasm or from a disinterested taste for horrors, it is difficult to say.

As regards the use of the alliterative metre in 'Piers Plow-

[1] Longer.

[2] Filthy garment. (?)

man,' although Langland was contemporary with Chaucer, we must not look upon this as an archaic affectation or a proof of uncultivated rusticity. Langland acted wisely in choosing the alliterative metre. Of the forms then in use, it was decidedly the best for a didactic poem. Some critics have shown an unreasonable prejudice against alliteration; it has even been stigmatised as "a vulgar trick." Old Thomas Fuller, and the unknown framers of our popular proverbial wisdom, knew its value for aphorisms and epigrams—at least they used it, consciously or unconsciously, with good effect. And in like manner, Langland, whether by chance or by good judgment, adopted the form best suited to his materials. Not to mention its value as a help to the memory, how much better than jingling octosyllabics, sing-song ballad metre, or even than heroic couplets, is its incisive emphasis suited to the vigour of Langland's thought and sentiment.

The poem on the deposition of Richard II., ascribed by Mr Wright to Langland, has every appearance of being his composition. There are constant minute coincidences of expression; and the general strain of the sentiment, the fierce scorn for wasteful idleness, and the burning indignation against oppression and neglect of the weak, as well as the general energy of .the verse, are in eminent correspondence with 'Piers Plowman.'


### 2. JOHN GOWER (d. 1408).

Gower is intrinsically a much less significant figure than Langland, but his name is more closely associated with Chaucer's, and occurs most readily next to his in any enumeration of the poets of the time. The basis of this reputation is very clearly stated by Mr Earle (English Philology, p. 76): "One is apt to imagine, previous to a study of their works, that they" (Chaucer and Gower) " were a *par nobile fratrum* — brothers and equals in poetry and genius; and that they had contributed equally, or nearly so, towards the making of English literature. But this is very far from being the case. That which united them at first, and which continues to be the sole ground of coupling their names together, is just this, that they wrote in the same general strain and in the same language. By this is meant, first, that they were both versed in the learning then most prized, and both delivered what they had to say in the terms then most admired; and, secondly, that both wrote the English of the Court. If affinity[1] of genius had been the basis of classification, the author of 'Piers Plowman'

---

[1] I should consider the word "affinity" rather loose in this connection. I have enlarged upon the disparity, or even antagonism, of genius between the two. But Mr Earle's general meaning is obvious.

had more right to rank with Chaucer than the prosaic Gower. But in this Chaucer and Gower are united, in that they both wrote the particular form of English which was henceforward to be established as the standard form of the national language; and their books were the leading English classics of the best society down to the opening of a new era under Elizabeth."

Even this modified title to rank with Chaucer needs some qualification. Gower was of about the same age as Chaucer, probably several years older, but he did not write in English till his old age. Up to 1393 he was known to the reading public only as a writer of French and Latin; and after that date he continued to use Latin as the medium for his political poetry.

It requires some courage to begin a course of reading in Gower after Professor Lowell's energetic summing up and appalling illustration of his demerits. "Gower, he says, "has positively raised tediousness to the precision of science; he has made dulness an heirloom for the students of our literary history. As you slip to and fro on the frozen levels of his verse, which give no foothold to the mind; as your nervous ear awaits the inevitable recurrence of his rhyme, regularly pertinacious as the tick of an eight-day clock, and reminding you of Wordsworth's

> ' Once more the ass did lengthen out
> The hard, dry see-saw of his horrible bray,'—

you learn to dread, almost to respect, the powers of this indefatigable man. He is the undertaker of the fair mediæval legend, and his style has the hateful gloss, the seemingly unnatural length, of a coffin. Love, beauty, passion, nature, art, life, the natural and the theological virtues—there is nothing beyond his power to disenchant, nothing out of which the tremendous hydraulic press of his allegory (or whatever it is, for I am not sure if it be not something even worse) will not squeeze all feeling and freshness, and leave it a juiceless pulp. It matters not where you try him, whether his story be Christian or pagan, borrowed from history or fable, you cannot escape him. Dip in at the middle or the end, dodge back to the beginning, the patient old man is there to take you by the button and go on with his imperturbable narrative. You may have left off with Clytemnestra, and you may begin again with Samson; it makes no odds, for you cannot tell one from t'other. . . . Our literature had to lie by and recruit for more than four centuries ere it could give us an equal vacuity in Tupper, so persistent a uniformity of commonplace in the 'Recreations of a Country Parson.'" Warton's verdict is more solemn than this, but hardly more favourable; and it is a melancholy thought that the old man tedious has of late found no sympathisers.

John Gower was an esquire of Kent.[1]  He was not in priest's orders, but he was so far connected with the Church that he held the living of Great Braxted, in Essex.  He was the most widely read scholar of his age; saw but little of the Court; had a recluse's peevishness and unfavourable views of life; and a recluse's pleasure in rank-flavoured tales.  One cannot but have a certain compunction in transcribing Mr Lowell's wicked rending to pieces of the industrious old rhymer's reputation: all the more when one sees from his description of the effects produced upon him by his lady's voice and the metres of the old romances, that, prosy and feeble though his writings are, he was not altogether dead to the higher emotions.  If it could be of any service in making his dulness more acceptable, one would be glad to apply to him Chaucer's account of the dejected Arcite—

> " And if he heardë song or instrument
> Then would he weep, he mightë not be stent;
> So feeble were his spirits and so low."

In this susceptibility of ear, "moral Gower," as Chaucer called him, bore a resemblance to the judicious Hooker, whom he resembled farther in scholarship and in feebleness of constitution.

Gower's principal French work, entitled *Speculum Meditantis* ('Mirror of a Meditating Mind')—which seems to have been a didactic poem on Vices and Virtues, and the principal support of his "moral" character—is now lost: but some French *Balades* of his have been preserved.  His Latin poems were political in their scope.  The first of them—*Vox Clamantis*, 'The Voice of one crying aloud,' or 'An Earnest Appeal'—was evoked by the rebellion of Jack Straw in 1381.  In this poem, while satirising the corruptions of society, which he considers the distempering causes of such insurrections, he shows a warm attachment to the young king, from whom he had received tokens of favour; but in subsequent productions, in the same tone of complaint against the times, he seems to have changed sides, and includes the king among other social corruptions.[2]

His principal English work—almost his only preserved composition in English—is *Confessio Amantis*, 'The Confession of a Lover.'  The word "confession" is here used in its ecclesiastical sense: *Confessio Amantis* is not an autobiographical work like Augustine's Confessions, or the Confessions of an Opium-eater, but a dialogue between a penitent and his confessor.  Strangely enough for the "moral" Gower, the religion of the parties is not

<hr>

[1] Sir Harris Nicolas.  See Morley's English Writers, ii. 69; and Thynne's Animadversions on Speght's Chaucer, *Early English Text Society*, p. 14.

[2] Wright's Political Poems and Songs, in the Master of the Rolls series.

Christianity, but love; the confessor is a priest of Venus. Substantially, the work is a miscellany of tales, fantastic love-philosophy, pseudo-Aristotelian mysticism (embracing alchemy, astrology, magic, palmistry, geomancy). The confessional form is merely a device for stringing this heterogeneous lore together. The love portion of it is described by Warton:[1] "The ritual of religion is applied to the tender passion, and Ovid's ' Art of Love ' is blended with the breviary. In the course of the confession, every evil affection of the human heart, which may tend to impede the progress or counteract the success of love, is scientifically subdivided, and its fatal effects exemplified by a variety of apposite stories, extracted from classics and chronicles." Some of these stories, particularly two cases of incest, were pronounced by Chaucer very "immoral"—

> "Of whichë cursed stories I say fy !"

For himself, Chaucer said that—

> "He of full avisëment
> Would never write in none of his sermons
> Of such unkind[2] abominations."

In spite, however, of these "incidental divertisements," readers of Mrs Stowe literature would find Gower very dry material : these oases occur in a very wide Sahara.

The inaccuracy of his statements regarding personages mentioned in Scripture and in Latin and Greek classical literature, becomes credible only when we remember that he lived before the revival of learning. Before the invention of movable types, the multiplication and diffusion of books in manuscript was not calculated to preserve accurate historical knowledge. The student was not likely to have access to many books, and the few accessible to him probably bore no indication of the relative dates and general position of their authors. He was to be pardoned under the circumstances, if he believed that Ovid was the founder of the Latin language, or that Noah and Abraham were old writers on astrology and magic. Gower had to trust voluminous compilations of theory, fact, and fiction, made by men whose scholarly advantages were little superior to his own: *Secretum Secretorum Aristotelis* ('The Secret of the Secrets of Aristotle'); *Memoriæ Seculorum* ('Memorials of the Ages'); *Speculum Regum* ('Mirror of Kings'): *Gesta Romanorum* ('Acts of the Romans'). His notions of chronology are sufficiently well illustrated by his sum-

---

[1] History of English Poetry—Section xix. (on Gower).      [2] Unnatural.

mary of the wonderful knowledge and the renowned teachers of
Ulysses :—

> " He was a worthy knight and king
> And clerk renowned in everything.
> He was a great rhetorian ;
> He was a great magician :
> Of Tullius the rhetoric ;
> Of King Zoroastes the magic ;
> Of Ptolemy the Astronomy ;
> Of Plato the Philosophy ;
> Of Daniel the sleepy dreams ;
> Of Neptunë the water streams ;
> Of Solomon and the Proverbs ;
> Of Macer all the strength of herbs ;
> And the physic of Hypocras ;
> And like unto Pythagoras
> Of surgery he knew the cures."

### 3. MIRACLE-PLAYS AND MYSTERIES.

Though there is no pre-eminent chief in this species of composition, they formed so large a part of the entertainment of the
vulgar during the fourteenth and fifteenth centuries, that we must
try to make out their characteristics.   There are at least three
allusions to them in the 'Canterbury Tales,' all in the Prologue
and Tale of the Miller.   The Miller cries in *Pilate's* voice (*Prol.*
16) ; Absolon is said to " play Herod on a scaffold high " (*Tale,*
198) ; and Nicholas makes reference to Noah's difficulty in getting
his wife into the ark (353)—a stock incident in the Mysteries.
We may therefore suppose that, when Chaucer wrote the Miller's
Tale, he was fresh from an exhibition of these Scriptural dramas.
It will be seen in what here follows, that though they were pro-
fessedly designed for the encouragement of morality and holiness,
they harmonise in spirit more with the Miller's Tale than the
Parson's.

Miracle-plays, in the strict sense of the term, were dramatic
representations of miracles performed by saints ; Mysteries, of incidents from the New Testament and elsewhere, bearing upon the
fundamental principles of Roman Catholicism.   This distinction,
however, is hardly kept up in the practical application of the
terms.   They were performed in the churches, or on stages erected
in the churchyard or in the fields, or, as at Coventry, on movable
stages wheeled from street to street.   The actors were in some
cases the brethren of a monastery, in some cases the members of
a trade guild.   The authors were monks.   As regards other particulars of the representation, "it appears," says Mr Wright in
his Introduction to the 'Chester Plays,' "that the spectators paid
for the sight : either seats were purchased, or a collection was

made. At a later period we find that . . . there were different floors or partitions to represent heaven, earth, and hell, and that very intricate and ingenious machinery must have been used to produce different effects. Masks were also used, at least in the thirteenth and fourteenth centuries, so that the whole performance must have borne considerable analogy to the rude Greek comedy in the days of Thespis."

Besides a few isolated plays, as old as the fifteenth or even the fourteenth century, there have been preserved three complete sets . of Mysteries dramatising Biblical and apocryphal incidents from the Creation to the death and resurrection of Christ, and His ascension and return in glory on doomsday: the 'Townley Mysteries,' published by the Surtees Society in 1836; the 'Coventry Mysteries,' edited for the Shakespeare Society by Mr Halliwell, 1841; the 'Chester Plays,' edited for the same Society by Mr T. Wright, 1847.[1]

Though the ostensible object of these plays was to instruct the illiterate in a knowledge of Scripture, and edify them in love of God and fear of the devil, the effect of them as a whole must, to use Chaucer's classification, have partaken more of coarse comedy than of either morality or holiness. It was natural that they should occur to Chaucer when he began to write the first of his series of ribald tales, and that he should strike the key-note of boisterous humour by making the Miller break through the decorous reception of the Knight's Tale with a voice like Pilate's in the Mysteries. Various liberties were taken with Scriptural personages for the sake of comic effect. Both in the Chester and in the Townley series, Noah's wife is represented as somewhat of a shrew, who gives the patriarch a great deal of trouble before he can get her into the ark. In the 'Coventry Mysteries,' Joseph is represented as a contemptible and impotent old man, who marries Mary under compulsion, alleges that he is neither able nor willing to act as a husband, is certain that he has been dishonoured when Mary proves to be with child, and expresses his conviction in very plain language. Mary's account of her condition is treated with coarse incredulity by everybody, till her veracity is vindicated by a miracle. The shepherds to whom the angel declared the birth of Christ give another opportunity for ludicrous invention. Herod is a favourite character—a ludicrously inflated tyrant, blasphemously rampant and boastful, carried off in the end by a demon. Even the Massacre of the Innocents becomes a rude burlesque: the mothers assail the soldiers with gross language, and beat them with extravagant fury. In this way is the Scripture brought

---

[1] There is an elaborate account of Miracle-Plays, Moral Plays, &c., in Collier's 'History of Dramatic Poetry.' Hone's 'Ancient Mysteries Described' is an entertaining book.

down to the level of the multitude; and one does not wonder that
these Mysteries were often denounced by earnest preachers. There
doubtless is religious feeling in them, earnest praise and adoration
of God; but it is difficult to suppose that the serious element pre-
dominated over the comic. The coarse comic incidents must have
flavoured the whole; in judging of the probable effect of the
serious portions, we must take into account the ludicrous surroundings, and we must not suppose that the rude audience were
so very differently constituted from ourselves that they viewed
with gravity things that appear supremely ludicrous to us. The
cooks and millers, cobblers and carpenters, of the fourteenth
century, were by no means blind to comic effect; and if they had
their chuckle over some of the grotesque figures in church architecture, they were not as solemn as Methodists at the exhibition
of a Mystery. It is apparent on all hands that the sense of the
ridiculous was very powerful in the fourteenth century; religion
no more than love was sacred from its rude sport. Remember
that these Mysteries were exhibited at festivals, and consider the
following picture of how the common people enjoyed themselves
at Christmas [1]—

> " The lewed people then algates agree,
> And carols singen every Christmas tide,
> Not with shamefastëness but jocundly,
> And holly boughs about; and all aside
> The brenning fire them eaten and them drink,
> And laughen merrily, and maken rout,
> And pipe and dancen and them rage : ne swink
> Ne nothing else twelve day they wouldë not. "

The Mysteries exhibited on holidays, either general Church holidays or days sacred to the memory of some patron saint, were part
and parcel of this hearty enjoyment. At York, previous to the
year 1426, the revelling and drunkenness at the representation of
the Mysteries was such that they had to be discontinued. We
have a curious evidence of the amusing character of Mysteries
generally in a portion of a Latin story quoted by Mr Wright.
Certain persons walking in a meadow "saw before them a vast
crowd of people assembled, and heard them now hushed and silent,
now bursting into loud laughter. Wondering, therefore, why
there was so great a congregation in such a place, they concluded
that a performance was going on of those plays that we call
*miracles.*" What could be more significant ? One class of personages seem to have been special objects of merriment—the devil
and his attendant demons got up with horns, tails, claws, and
hideous mask. Professor Morley, who holds that the chief interest

---

[1] Quoted in Hone's Ancient Mysteries, p. 90.

of the Mysteries was tragic, affirms that the whole endeavour in the make-up of the demons was to render them terrible. I am very far from agreeing with this. The women and children among the spectators might be horrified, as they still are at ugly masks; but a sturdy Englishman out for a holiday and well lined with beer would probably laugh the louder the more shrilly his weaker friends were excited to scream. When we study the demons closely, it becomes obvious that terror was not the sole aim of their existence. Take, for example, the devil of the 'Coventry Mysteries,' the most serious of our three sets. How does he express himself when cast by God out of heaven?—

> " At thy bidding thy will I werk,
> And pass fro joy to painë smert,
> Now I am a devil full derk
> That was an angel bright.
> Now to hell the way I take,
> In endless pain there to be pight,
> For fear of fire a —— . . . . . . .
> In hell dungeon my den is dight."

A single utterance like this, accompanied doubtless by the sound of a horn, as the blowing of the nose is still rendered in pantomimes, would effectually destroy the devil's influence for terror, at least in that representation, not to say that it would unsettle any serious impression from what preceded. I have noticed two other places in the 'Coventry Mysteries' where the great enemy of mankind expresses his emotion in the same way. So far from helping to make demons more terrible, the Mysteries embodied the hideous ideals of the popular imagination, and raised temporary laughter by making them ridiculous—treated them for the time being, as so much ludicrous capital. If superstitious fears had been absolutely bodiless before then—if the Mysteries had been the means of clothing the devil in popular imagination with claws, hoofs, horns, and tail—it might have been argued that they did add to the dreadful attributes of his fallen majesty. And even as it is, it may reasonably be maintained that the laughter was temporary, and that the actual representation of the hideous being had a permanent effect of terror. I am inclined, however, to believe that the Mysteries left the fear of the devil where they found it, and simply provided the vulgar with a good day's sport.

#### 4. METRICAL ROMANCES.

The mythopœic faculty or unstudied imagination of the Middle Ages was occupied in the main with two kinds of matter: the heroism of religion, and the heroism of chivalry, miraculous saints and no less miraculous knights.   The legends of the saints and the romances of the knights grew out of the same unchastened desire of the natural man after superhuman ideals ; the desire to escape from the chilling limitations to perfection of character and nobility of achievement in actual life.   Such, in the broadest view, was the origin of Middle Age romances, religious as well as secular ; they were produced by the generating force that created Romulus, Numa, and Egeria, Achilles, Ulysses, and Circe,—a passion for the marvellous that still survives and operates, and promises to bid defiance for many coming generations to all appliances for the discovery and diffusion of verified knowledge.   Doubtless in all ages many less generous motives have conspired to the invention and spread of fictions ; patron saints have been made wonderful in the eyes of devotees, and ancestors have been magnified to move the bounty of descendants.   In most cases, too, the passion has taken a patriotic turn.   It was inevitable that men should, in creating heroes, show a preference for their own country and kindred.   Still, vanity much less than disinterested love of the marvellous has ever presided over all such creations.

In the voluminous discussions regarding the origin of mediæval romance — whether it was Scaldic, or Arabic, or Classic — too little respect has been shown to the permanent sources of romance in the human mind.   It has never required any great impulse to excite those sources to productive activity.   The magnificent enthusiasm of religion and chivalry that sent the crusaders to Palestine could not have failed to evoke a frenzy of romantic invention.   When the English began to be conscious of a national unity, they made for themselves a fabulous connection with such ancient history as was known to them : derived their government from the Trojans, and their Christianity from Joseph of Arimathea.   They provided themselves with a national hero, surrounded him with knights, and engaged him and them in honourable adventures.   It is vain to look for a historical basis to the operations of the romantic imagination ; this faculty owns no allegiance to fact.   Our business, however, is not with romance in general, but with the very humble romances extant in English in the time of Chaucer.

Chaucer has burlesqued the metrical romances of the wandering minstrels in his tale of Sir Thopas.   He enumerates some of the productions that will bear comparison with his parody—

> " Men speaken of romans of price
> Of Horn Child and of Ypotis,
>     Of Bevis and Sir Guy,
> Of Sir Libeaux and Pleindamour ;
> But Sir Thopas beareth the flower
>     Of real chivalry."

All these romances, or at least romances on all these heroes,
except Pleindamour, are still in existence; and if they are the
same, the parody cannot be said to depart far from the original.
They deal with the usual subjects of romance—giants, enchantments, obstructive knights, and invincible champions—and their
diction may fairly be described as unmitigated doggerel. The
following two stanzas are from 'Lybeaus Disconus,' *Le Beau
Desconnu*, The Fair Unknown (Ritson's Metrical Romances):—

> "Anon that maid Helen
> Was set with knightes ten,
>     Before Sir Lambard;
> She and the dwarf I mean,
> Told seven deedës keen,
>     That he did thitherward:
> And how that Sir Lybeaus,
> Fought with felë shrews,
>     And for no death ne spared:
> Lambard was glad and blithe
> And thankedën felö sith[1]
>     God and St Edward.
>
> Anon with mildë cheer
> They set to the supper
>     With muchë glee and game;
> Lambard and Lybeaus, in fere,[2]
> Of aventures that there were
>     Talked both in same.
> Then said Lybeaus, Sir Constable,
> Telleth me withouten fable,
>     What is the knightës name,
> That holdeth so in prison
> The lady of Synadon
>     That is so gentle a dame."

All, or nearly all, English romances were translated from the
French. In the case of a few unimportant ones, no French
originals have been discovered, and they may therefore be presumed to have been written in English to begin with; but all the
romances belonging to the great Arthurian cycle were originally
composed in French, though some, if not most of them, by
Englishmen for Anglo-Norman readers.

The Romance of Ywain and Gawain, sons respectively of Urien,
King of Gore, and Lot of Orkney, and nephews of Arthur, is
ascribed by Ritson to the reign of Richard II. This romance is
considerably superior to Horn Child or Lybeaus. The two
cousins, and firm friends, are really noble mirrors of knighthood.
Their prowess is supreme at Arthur's Court, and they are the
very flowers of courtesy and generosity. Ywain (Ewen, or Owen)

---

[1] Many times.  [2] In company.

is the hero of the piece in so far that its object is to relate his adventures. He kills a fair lady's husband, marries her, rides away on promise of returning within a twelvemonth, is tempted by his love of tourneying to stay beyond his time, incurs his lady's fierce displeasure, goes mad, is restored to his wits, and, after many perils and successes, is reunited to the object of his faithful affections. The romance abounds in the marvels of its class. A knight-errant comes to a well of cold water, with a basin of gold hanging near; he takes the basin and sprinkles some water on an emerald stone; immediately there arises a furious tempest of hail, rain, snow, sleet, thunder, and scorching lightning. When the storm subsides, a flock of birds alight near him, and by-and-by comes a knight, with the sound of many horsemen, spurring on eagerly to do battle to the stranger, who has dared so to trouble the realm. Ywain's lady gives him an enchanted ring with various wonderful properties—

> " I shall tell to you anon
> The virtue that is in the stone :
> It is no prison shall you hold,
> All if your foes be many fold ;
> With sickness shall ye not be ta'en,
> Ne of your blood shall ye lose nane."

One of the most striking wonders in the romance is the attachment of a lion to the person of Ywain. The knight had saved his life in an encounter with a dragon, and from that moment the royal beast becomes his faithful attendant and body-guard, and renders him very valuable service in his encounters.

Though Ywain is the hero of the romance, his cousin Gawain is a still nobler and more illustrious figure. Ywain, indeed, when they are unawares matched against each other, fights with him through a whole long day till darkness sets in, without losing ground; but Gawain is represented as the most famous of Arthur's knights, to whom the distressed naturally apply for succour. Gawain's fortune has been very hard in the growth and variation of Arthurian romance. Other heroes of later invention have been exalted at his expense. In the romance of Merlin,[1] which is the chief authority for the early history of Arthur, Gawain is the noblest ideal of knighthood. Again and again the romance dwells upon his irresistible strength and generous disposition. King Bors says, that if he live he will be the most illustrious knight that ever was. He is "a wise knight, and without pride, and the most courteous that was in the Bloy Breteyne, and the best taught in all things, and ever true to God and to his lord." And, again,

---

[1] An English fifteenth-century version of this romance is published by the Early English Text Society.

he is said to be "one of the best knights and wisest of the world, and thereto the least mis-speaker and none avaunter, and the best taught of all things that longeth to worship or curtesy." But this reputation was too bright in the eyes of other romancers with heroes of their own to celebrate; and so Gawain was depreciated, that more unrivalled lustre might accrue to Lancelot, Pelleas, Lamorak, or Tristan. All these knights were brought into conflict with him, and came off victorious. Worse than that, the glory of his courtesy was tarnished by a base explanation. It was fabled that he was sworn to courteous behaviour as a punishment for a most unknightly action done in his youth. And last of all came Lord Tennyson, and pursued the unfortunate knight with bitter hatred and spiteful detraction, because he was the half-brother (Lord Tennyson would say the full brother) of Mordred; and it suited the laureate's purpose to argue that treachery, masked by smiling manners, ran in the blood.[1]

## II.—Scottish Contemporaries.

### 1. John Barbour (d. 1396).

The impulse of mediæval poetry had no very considerable effect on Scotland till the end of the fifteenth century. Not till then was there anything that could be called a flowering period of Scottish song. In the fourteenth century, however, there was a certain emulous response to the Continental singers: a response, too, that was inspired by no small ambition. The Scottish poets of the fourteenth century were not content to echo with or without variations the favourite romances of the west of Europe: they struck a bolder, a more original, a more closely patriotic note. Events had recently happened that fascinated them more than the most dazzling achievements of the European models of ·knighthood, and filled them with pride as well as reverence. Alexander, Arthur, Charlemagne, were faint personages to them in comparison with their own national heroes. Their country was fresh from a successful struggle to maintain her independence against English aggression; and in the exultation of their triumphant resistance, they had no interest in weaving romantic webs of splendid colours round ideal champions of other causes. Even the great cause of Christian against Saracen, in which the religious imagination of the Middle Ages had exhibited Alexander, as well as Arthur. and Charlemagne, stirred them with a vaguer and

---

[1] National jealousy of the Scots may have had something to do with the degeneration of Gawain in the romances. The romance of Ywain and Gawain is in the Northern dialect.

feebler enthusiasm than memories of their own recent deliverance from impending slavery. And in the leaders of their war of independence, they were proud to be able to show to the world fresh mirrors of chivalry. They were not ashamed to place Douglas side by side with Hector of Troy, and to claim for Wallace and Bruce endless honour among the foremost heroes of romance.

John Barbour, Archdeacon of Aberdeen, who undertook to relate the exploits of the Bruce in four-accent couplets, was a scholar, an ardent patriot, and a warm admirer of chivalry. Zeal for study, both of books and of men, the enthusiasm of knowledge, may be said to be characteristic of the Scotch; and Barbour was in this respect a Scot of the Scots. In 1357, when he had already attained the dignity of archdeacon, he applied to his king, David II., to procure him a passport from Edward III., and went south with three scholars under his charge to study at Oxford. Again, in 1364, he obtained permission to "study at Oxford or elsewhere as he might think proper." In 1365, and again in 1368, he passed through England towards France to prosecute his studies in Paris. The terms of the safe-conducts granted to him show that he travelled not merely as the superintendent of the studies of youthful wards, but for the increase of his own knowledge.[1]

While thus devoted to the life contemplative, the life active had a strong hold of his imagination. "The heart of the soldier beat under the frock of the churchman." The spirit of chivalry found a fit dwelling-place in the grave Scotch student: nowhere did its attributes of courage, gentleness, generosity, fidelity, and high honour meet with a warmer reception, and nowhere was everything antagonistic to it excommunicated with heartier indignation. Believers in race will not fail to observe that Barbour was born in the north-east of Scotland, and that in the population of this district there was a large admixture of settlers from the opposite coasts of Norway and Denmark—men of the same race as the Norman founders of chivalry—so that the patriotic, warlike-minded churchman may have inherited from roving and reaving ancestors his passion for celebrating heroic achievements. At all events, race or no race, the passion was strong within him. He enters the battle with his hero, and lays about him with sturdy enthusiasm. The shock of Bruce's spear is irresistible; and when his spear is shivered and his good sword drawn, there is death in every sweep of his arm: heads are smitten off, helmets cleft, shoulder-plated arms shorn away like corn before the scythe. He does not hesitate to oppose the Bruce single-handed to two hundred men, and bring him off victorious after much slaughter;

---

[1] See Mr Innes's preface to the Spalding Club edition.

comparing this incomparable achievement with the defeat of fifty
men by the hardy son of Tydeus. With what energy he recounts
the discomfiture of the three gigantic Macindrossans, who attempted to take Robert alive! How thoroughly he enjoys the
feat of the king in bringing the giant who has leapt on his horse
behind him round from the crupper within reach of· his deadly
sword! Our archdeacon had a most admiring eye for a strong
arm. When the patriots, in the beginning of the enterprise, are
rowing towards Cantyre as a safe winter retreat, he imagines
crowds of spectators on the shore looking at them as they rise
on the rowing-benches, and admiring the stalwart hands that
were more familiar with the spear than with the oar. Sir Walter
Scott must have envied his description of the doughty Douglas—

> " But he was not so fair that we,
> Should speak greatly of his beauty.
> In visage was he somedeal grey,
> And had black hair as I heard say ;
> But of limbës he was well made,
> With bonës great and shoulders braid ; [1]
>
> .      .      .      .
> When he was blithe he was lovely,
> And meek and sweet in company;
> But who in battle might him see,
> All other countenance had he."

This trim carpet-knight and grim champion had the noblest
attribute of strength—generosity. When Bruce sent him to help
outnumbered Randolph at Bannockburn, he halted when he saw
the enemy begin to give way, that he might not rob his friend of
any part of the honour of success.

But courage was not the only chivalrous virtue that the Scottish poet of chivalry held in admiration. There are other elements
in his portrait of Douglas—

> " He was in all his deedës leal,[2]
> For him dedeigned not to deal,
> With treachery ne with falset.
> His heart on high honour was set,
> And him contained in such manner
> That all him loved that were him near."

This disdain of falsehood Barbour was prepared to practise as well
as to admire. He held it to be his duty to give impartial praise
to brave achievements—

> " But whether so he be friend or foe
> That winnës prize of chivalry,
> Men should speak thereof lealëly."

---

[1] Broad.                                                     [2] Faithful—*loyal*.

And he scrupulously fulfilled the obligation in his own case. We may be certain that he added only the attractions of rhyme to the traditional glory of his hero; and he does not fail to recognise and honour a valiant enemy. He duly records and extols the magnanimity of Sir Giles de Argentine in raising his battle-cry and rushing to certain death rather than leave the field of Bannockburn alive. Nor is Barbour deficient in apprehending the chivalrous respect for women. He particularly commends the sturdy Douglas for his assiduity in hunting and fishing for the ladies of the party when their fortunes were at the lowest. And Bruce himself is almost Quixotic in his devotion to the tender sex. On a critical occasion he delays the march of his army rather than imperil the safety of a poor laundress in his train. No act on record of any knight of romance can exceed that: it is as incomparable a proof of his tenderness as the combat with two hundred is of his courage and strength.

The enthusiastic Pinkerton preferred Barbour, "taking the total merits of the work together, . . . to the melancholy sublimity of Dante, and the amorous quaintness of Petrarca;" and every Scotchman whose patriotism would be above suspicion must wish that he could agree with Pinkerton. There is, indeed, a certain epic swing and momentum about the romance of the Bruce; its vigorous opening picture of the prostration of Scotland under the English, and its passionate aspiration after freedom, place a powerful arrest on the wandering attention, and summon us with no small cogency to hear the story of enfranchisement through its ups and downs of hope and danger to the triumphant end. If he had stopped with the battle of Bannockburn, Barbour's Bruce might have been called a historical epic, bearing to the epic proper the same relation that the chronicle history bears to the regular drama. But by carrying his story on to the death of Bruce, he conforms it to the laws of the metrical romance, which, doubtless, were the laws that he set himself to observe, and very likely the only laws known to him. The manners and sentiments, as we have seen, are those of chivalry. Barbour was a distinct observer, and he had the consistent, pure, defined sentiments of a clear-headed man, careful always to establish a harmony between the sentiment and the object. There is not much embellishment in his style. He presents us with but few studies of natural scenery, and those bare and meagre; and he draws no extended portraits of the beautiful women that moved among and commanded the homage of his brave men. His diction rises considerably above the rude doggerel of rhyming chronicles; he is superior to the necessities of make-rhymes. Undoubtedly, however, the main charm of Barbour's Bruce lies in the cordial energy of its battles and rencounters.

### 2. Henry the Minstrel, "Blind Harry."

The champion of the fame of William Wallace, was born at least
half a century later than Barbour. One does not like to say
severe things about a poor old wandering minstrel. Like many
other bygones that were interesting to bygones, he and his heroic
verse, once an acceptable arrival at many a lively feast and proud
residence, would be considered a terrible visitation in modern
society. Blind Harry has not the elements of perennial interest.
Only strong patriotism could have composed, and only strong
patriotism could have listened to, his strains. Till very recently,
however, he was popular among the Scottish peasantry, circulating
no longer in oral recitation,[1] but in printed copies, often boardless
and well-thumbed. Of late he has been superseded by Miss
Porter's 'Scottish Chiefs.'

### III.—English Successors.

It does no great violence to fact to treat all the English poets of
the fifteenth century as the disciples of Chaucer. Almost everything of value in the poetry of that century—and not much has
been preserved, if there was much to preserve—was due to the
impulse given by Chaucer. A great deal of versification went on
out of the reach of that impulse, in the shape of chronicles, lives
of saints, translations from the French, and other miscellaneous
lines. Prose romances also were translated. But the two or three
poets that rise above the herd had, or professed to have, an acquaintance with Chaucer, and acknowledged allegiance to him,
though all of them were far from catching any tincture of the
charm of his verse. It is, indeed, significant of the general dulness
of ear, as well as poverty of execution, that Skelton places Gower
and Lydgate on the same level with the master from whose greatness to their littleness is such a fathomless sheer descent.

The extraordinary collapse of English poetry after the death of
Chaucer is one of the most curious phenomena in literary history.
When he died he carried his mantle with him ; or at least it fell
upon no worthy successor in England. We have to look to the
Scottish Court for any memorable traces of his influence. A
Chaucerian school was established in Scotland, and flourished
there for nearly two centuries, decaying only with the transference
of the Stuart dynasty to London. But in England itself his example fell dead, and there was no stirring of poetical vitality till

---

[1] I remember, however, a sturdy beggar of the name of Wallace, who was
much revered by schoolboys as a lineal descendant from the national hero, and
who used to recite from "Blind Harry" violent incidents, such as the breaking
of the churl's back, with appropriate gesticulation.

poetry came under new influences. The wide literary desert corresponds with an inglorious political interval, and it is usual to connect the two as effect and cause. The Wars of the Roses, more particularly, are commonly held responsible for the decadence of English poetry in the fifteenth century. But this current explanation will not bear looking at, even if we give a wide meaning to the Wars of the Roses, so as to include all the long-protracted struggle of the House of Lancaster to keep itself in power. The state of affairs was disturbed, but not more so than it had been in Chaucer's time. A poet's audience, before the invention of printing, was necessarily limited, but a poet of genius would have found an audience even in the reign of Henry VI. Abundant patronage was given to inferior artificers; the poet was in no danger of having his genius chilled by indifference. Men's minds are never wholly engrossed even by such national calamities as unsettled succession and civil war. Some of the sweetest and lightest love-poetry in our language was published during the heat of the Great Rebellion. Tottel's ' Miscellany,' with its songs and sonnets fragrant of sweet marjoram, as the publisher put it, found eager purchasers in the reign of Bloody Mary. The reign of Richard II. was one of the darkest periods in English history, yet it was in this reign that Chaucer wrote his ' Canterbury Tales.' The immense expansion of England in the eighteenth century has no counterpart in its literature. Instances might be multiplied to show that the connection between poetry and public affairs is by no means so close as it is the fashion to assert. The influence of social conditions and political events is accidental rather than essential. It may convey germs of poetic life to virgin soil, but it cannot originate new forms ; it may fertilise and foster, but it can neither generate nor prevent decay. The main causes of literary developments and literary degenerations must be sought for in literature itself, and in the individual characters of men of letters.

### 1. Thomas Occleve (1370-1430 ?).

Of the immediate successors of Chaucer, the most celebrated is Lydgate ; but Occleve, or Hoccleve, comes first in order of time. It is to Occleve that we owe our standard portrait of Chaucer. He was a most ardent and admiring disciple of the great poet, and more than once lamented him in such strains as these, extolling his knowledge in rhetoric, philosophy, and poetry, and inveighing against the indiscriminate ravages of death—

> " O master dear and father reverent,
> My master Chaucer, flower of eloquence,
> Mirror of fructuous intendement !

> O universal father in science,
> Alas, that thou thine excellent prudence
>   In thy bed mortal mightest not bequeathö !
>   What ailed Death, alas ! why would he slay thee ?
>
> O Death, thou didest not harm singular
> In slaughter of him, but all this land it smarteth !
> But, nathëless, yet hast thou no power
> His name to slay : his high virtue astarteth
> Unslain from thee, which aye us lifely hearteth
>   With bookës of his ornate inditing,
>   That is to all this land enlumining."

And again—

> " She might have tarried her vengeance a while
> Till that some man had equal to thee be.
> Nay, let be that ! she knew well that this isle
> May never man bring forthë like to thee.
> And her officë needës do mote she ;
>   God bade her do so, I trust for the best.
>   O master, master, God thy soulë rest ! "

In Thynne's edition of Chaucer, in 1532, there was printed, among other miscellaneous pieces, a "Letter of Cupid," written in 1402. No other production ascribed to Occleve appeared in print for more than two hundred years ; and after Warton characterised him as a feeble poet of cold genius, the very titles of whose poems were chilling to the searchers after invention and fancy, the unfortunate poet ran a considerable risk of extinction. In 1796, however, George Mason printed various poems from an MS. that Warton had not seen, and pleaded for a more favourable verdict.

Occleve is certainly an interesting character, if not an interesting poet. "Cold" was a singularly inappropriate word to apply to him. He seems to have been a fellow of infinite warmth and geniality. He is supposed to have been born in 1370, and he emerges at the Court of Richard II. in 1387. The luxurious extravagance of that Court found in him a congenial spirit. He could never pass the sign of Bacchus, with its invitation to thirsty passengers to moisten their clay, so long, at least, as he had anything in his purse ; and he spent much money in the temples of a goddess of still more questionable character. He was a favourite among cooks and taverners, from the circumstance that he always paid them what they asked. Only two men of his acquaintance could equal him in drinking at night and lying in bed in the morning. The only thing that preserved his life from the brawls incident to such habits was an invincible cowardice : he never traduced men except in a whisper. All this we know from his own humorous confessions. He tells us also that his excesses exhausted his money, although he held a valuable office—and impaired his health, though nature had given him a strong constitution. He would seem to have received a pension of twenty marks a-year from Henry IV., and various begging poetical addresses are extant to show that he suffered from a chronic scarcity of coin. In the introduction to his poem *De Regimine Principum* ("On the Government of Princes," written in 1411 or 1412), he relates his distressed circumstances, and how an old man had advised him to write a work and dedicate it to Prince Henry, who might perhaps be induced thereby at least to see that his annuity was regularly paid. There would seem to have been not a little of Falstaff in his character. He addressed a poem to Sir John Oldcastle, full of grave disputation, which receives a somewhat mock-serious air from his advice to the good knight to leave off studying Holy Writ, and read 'Launcelot of the Lake,' or 'Vegetius,' or 'The Siege of Troy,' confining his Bible reading, if he must read the Bible, to Judges, Kings, Joshua, Judith, the Chronicles, and the Maccabees, all of which are most authentic and pertinent to chivalry. Although he had been appointed a writer to the Privy Seal, probably in 1387,[1] his hopes were long set on obtaining a benefice in the Church, but at last he married in despair. In the beginning of the reign of Henry VI., he wrote an appeal for pecuniary help to Carpenter, afterwards Bishop of Worcester; and unless his conduct was more respectable in his later years, when seventy winters had passed over his head, this petition must be taken as being very much of a piece with Falstaff's application for a loan to the Lord Chief-Justice. His last patron seems to have been the Duke of York; and he lived to the good old age of eighty, having contrived probably to pass through life very easily, from his success in conciliating patronage, and in borrowing without repaying.

The "Letter of Cupid" is full of sly humour and tender feeling. It is addressed by Cupid to all his subjects, to warn them of the grievous complaints that have been made to him by ladies of honour and reverence concerning the deceitful outrages and offences done them by men. They complain particularly of the little island of Albion,—

---

[1] This is the most probable date, and the date also of Occleve's coming to Court. In his "Address to Health," Occleve speaks of twenty years of misspent life; in his *De Regimine Principum*, he speaks of having been a writer to the Privy Seal for "twenty year and four come Easter." The date of the one poem is supposed to be 1406, and of the other 1412; but the circumstances make 1407 and 1411 equally probable; and if we accept these dates with an interval of four years between the two compositions, it becomes likely that Occleve's memory went back to the same date as the beginning of his dissipation and his official appointment. The date of the appointment is usually given as 1392, from a curious mistake of "twenty years *and four*" for twenty.

" Passing all landës on the little isle
That cleped is Albion they must complain.
They say that there is crop and root of guile
So can the men dissimulen and feign,
With standing droppës in their eyen twain
  When that their heartës feeleth no distress
  To blinden women with their doubleness.

Their wordës spoken be so sighingly
With so piteous a cheer and countenance,
That every wight that meaneth truëly
Deemeth they in heart haven such grievance.
They say so importable is their penance
  That but their lady lust to show them grace
  They right anon must sterven in the place.

Ah, lady mine, they say, I you ensure,
As doth me grace, and I shall ever be,
While that my life may lasten and endure,
To you as humble and low in each degree
As possible is, and keep all things in secre,
  Right as yourselven listeth that I do,
  And else mine heartö motö brast in two."

This is what the wicked men do; and Cupid deeply compassion-
ates the injured women—

" O faithful woman, full of innocence,
  Thou art deceived by false apparence."

He proceeds to show how men overcome silly, simple, innocent
women, and then go and boast of their success; he asks them, Is
this an honourable vaunt?  To be sure, men say that women are
unfaithful—but what is this but envy and pique at failure to
achieve their infamous designs?  Granted that here and there may
be found a woman unfaithful: did not some of the angels fall, and
was not one of the apostles a traitor?  Cupid then administers a
severe rebuke to men that slander women, bidding them think of
their own mothers—

" Oh, every man ought have an heartë tender
To a woman and deem her honourable,
Whether his shape be thick or ellës slender,
Or he be good or bad.  It is no fable,
Every wight wote that wit hath reasonable,
  That of a woman he descended is;
  Then is it shame of her to speak amiss.

A wicked tree good fruit may none forth bring,
For such the fruit is aye as is the tree;
Take heed of whom thou took thy beginning,
Let thy mother be mirror unto thee,
Honour her, if thou wolte honoured be.
  Despiseth her then not in no manner,
  Lest that thereby thy wickedness appear."

It is a fashion with poets whenever they mention women to rail at them, and rake up the stories of Adam, David, Samson, and Solomon; this, says Cupid, is a tyranny that he will not permit, and is exercised chiefly by worn-out old scoundrels who try to discredit what they can no longer enjoy. He threatens to punish them by making them maugre their will fall in love with "the foulest slut in all the town," and extol her as a duchess or a queen. He refers to the 'Romance of the Rose' as a manual of the arts of love, and says it is no wonder though women prove unfaithful when men assail them with such craft. He draws unfavourable contrasts between Jason and Medea, Æneas and Dido. He even defends Eve: it was her trusting confiding nature that induced her to believe the serpent; no thought of guile entered her mind; only a man, himself accustomed to deceit, would have suspected any harm. Finally, he bids men honour women for the sake of the Virgin Mary, who next to God is man's best friend, at whose girdle hangs the key of mercy; and commends the fidelity of women to Christ when men forsook Him, and the heroism of female martyrs.

The *De Regimine Principum*, translated from Ægidius, with an original introduction in the form of a dialogue between the author and an old man, is a didactic poem on the duties of the king, involving the discussion of domestic and foreign relations. There are some faint traces of Occleve's jocularity in the opening dialogue. He is very rich in one thing, and that is indigence. Some people complain of Fortune as my Lady Changeable: she is too much my Lady Steadfast and Stable with him, for she keeps him constantly in poverty. These, however, are rare touches of light in the sombre didactic, which is simply rhymed politics, of interest only to the political historian. Occleve belongs to the numerous class of abuse-mongers: an easy trade, and nothing but a mechanical trade to a man of his temperament. He asks where pity is gone, that so many gentlemen who spent their substance in the wars with France now go about in poverty; inveighs against the degeneracy of knights, who fight not for honour as in the old time, but for gain; attacks the clergy for their desire of pluralities, and their stingy neglect of church roof and altar; laments the necessity of propitiating men of power in the courts of law; condemns infantine betrothals, the abundance of paramours, and the lack of conjugal fidelity. His advice to the king, Henry V., Falstaff's Hal, is all very sound, and all very commonplace. Perhaps the most striking of his precepts is his deprecation of the wars between France and England. Christian princes should not make war on each other; they should combine against the infidel. Henry should make peace by marriage. All this might be very creditable to honest Thomas's humanity, were it not to be suspected that he had got wind of this basis of peace-making as a thing in contemplation. At least, however, let him have the credit of concurring; and let us hope that Henry took in good part another hint of a more personal nature—that he should never grant pensions unless he meant to pay them.

### 2. John Lydgate (1370-1450?).

One expects to find in Lydgate, who belonged to the Church, a supreme exponent of saintly ideals. But though the Monk of Bury wrote several lives of saints, he was not so much a religious enthusiast as a professional poet, with facile pen at the command of many patrons for many different purposes.

Lydgate is the most celebrated of the successors of Chaucer, and for more than a century after his death almost divided the honours of poetry with his great master. Later posterity, however, has not confirmed this reputation; and it is but justice to him to say that he himself made no pretension to the high rank accorded him by his own and several following generations. If the "Flower of Courtesy" is his, the ending is a modest and fair estimate of his powers; and if it should turn out not to be his, other passages no less modest may be produced from his undoubted compositions. It runs thus—

> "Ever as I can surprisen in mine heart,
> Alway with fear, betwixen dread and shame,
> Lest out of lose [1] any word should astart
> In this metre, to make it seemen lame.
> Chaucer is dead, which that had such a name
>   Of fair making, that was withouten ween [2]
> Fairest in our tongue as the laurer green.
>
> We may assayen for to counterfeit
> His gayë style, but it nill not ybe ;
> The well is dry, with the liquor so sweet
> Both of Clio and of Calliope ;
> And first of all I will excusen me
>   To her that is the ground of goodlihed,
>   And thus I say unto her womanhead."

It would be ungenerous to take the poet at his own modest estimate, framed in accordance with the poetical etiquette of his time, were it not that still more unfavourable estimates have been given by some modern critics. Percy, Ritson, and Pinkerton treat him with contempt: Ritson, in particular, scoffing at " these stupid and fatiguing productions, and their still more stupid and disgusting author." Even after he had been vindicated by Warton, the editor of ' A Chronicle of London' quoted some of his poems with the

---

[1] Order.　　　　　　　　　　　　[2] Doubt.

remark, "It seems no subject escaped that eternal scribbler's attention." Now, although his verses, as they have come down to us, are often intolerably lame, let us, out of respect for the judgment of our ancestors, see what good can be said of the sum total of his literary exertions. Seeing that Warton is his most indulgent critic,[1] it may be well to let Warton speak for him as much as possible, leaving severe and exacting criticism to make what deductions it thinks proper.

If Lydgate is deficient in quality, he makes up in quantity. He was a most indefatigable and versatile poet. In 1598, Speght enumerated 114 different pieces, original and translated, ascribed to Lydgate; and Ritson, in 1782, was able to bring the number up to 251. Speght's catalogue embraces Lydgate's three principal works — The "Siege of Thebes;" "Bochas upon the Fall of Princes: at the Commandment of Humphrey, Duke of Gloucester;" "The History, Siege, and Destruction of Troy: at Commandment of K. Henry the Fifth, 1412," — followed by a strangely heterogeneous assortment of psalms, hymns, calendars, pedigrees, lives of saints, moral allegories, prayers, astrological and philosophical memoranda, popular ballads, disguisings, mummings, and direct moral exhortations. The best known of his minor poems are "The Dance of Death" and the "London Lackpenny." "No poet seems to have possessed a greater versatility of talents. He moves with equal ease in every mode of composition. His hymns and his ballads have the same degree of merit; and whether his subject be the life of a hermit or a hero, of Saint Austin or Guy Earl of Warwick, ludicrous or legendary, religious or romantic, a history or an allegory, he writes with facility. His transitions were rapid, from works of the most serious and laborious kind, to sallies of levity and pieces of popular entertainment. His muse was of universal access; and he was not only the poet of his monastery, but of the world in general. If a disguising was intended by the company of goldsmiths, a mask before his majesty at Eltham, a May-game for the sheriff and aldermen of London, a mumming before the lord mayor, a procession of pageants from the creation for the festival of Corpus Christi, or a carol for the coronation, Lydgate was consulted, and gave the poetry."

We may, then, consider Lydgate as a facile and accomplished versifier, with a flexible wealth of second-hand poetical beauties: if his own imagination was superseded by wide knowledge and fluency, he at least was able to put the imaginations of others under judicious exactions. He cultivated poetry as the Greek rhetoricians are said to have cultivated rhetoric. He came after a long line of Middle Age poets who had discovered and refined all

---

[1] See also an eloquent tribute to the old poet in Professor Morley's English Writers, ii. 424.

the nuggets of their peculiar mine.  The Italian and the French poets had exhausted the commonplaces, and Chaucer had carried away all the best of the new vein of English life and manners.  A very original genius might have been powerful enough to open a new mine, though it may be doubted whether the time was then ripe for it: but Lydgate's genius was pliant and obsequious, and he contented himself with selecting and fusing into new combinations the refined gold of his predecessors.  "After a short education at Oxford, he travelled into France and Italy, and returned a complete master of the language and the literature of both countries.  He chiefly studied the Italian and French poets, particularly Dante, Boccaccio, and Alain Chartier; and became so distinguished a proficient in polite learning, that he opened a school in his monastery for teaching the sons of the nobility the arts of versification and the elegancies of composition."

The "Flower of Courtesy," from which we have already quoted, whether Lydgate's or not, is a fair illustration of his manner as a hack versifier.  It is written in Troilus verse—Lydgate's favourite metre, which he used with wooden indifference for all sorts of subjects—and is a eulogy of the wondrous beauty and many virtues of a lady, an expert recombination of the chief commonplaces of enamoured praise.  She is as the sun among the stars, the sovereign ruby among rich stones, the sweet rose among fresh flowers; she is in all truth and soberness (soothfastness) the fairest and the best of her sex, a pattern of steadfastness, a mirror of seemliness; she is "of port benign and wonder glad of cheer," discreet and wise, with all her desires governed by wit and high prudence; her busy charge is virtue; she is the consolation of the sick and the enemy of slander; there is no changing nor doubleness in her.  Her poet is rude; he has not the skill to describe her praises; he knows no rhetoric.  She is good as Polyxena, fair as Helen, steadfast as Dorigen, constant and faithful as Cleopatra; citron (bright of hue) as the white Antigone of Troy; meek as Hester, prudent as Judith, kind as Alcestis, patient as Griselda, discreet as Ariadne, honest as Lucrece, faithful as Penelope, fair as Phyllis, innocent as Hypsipyle, seemly as Canace, &c., &c.

One of his mechanical arts is rather curious.  In his narratives he seems to intersperse descriptive and moralising passages at short intervals for the deliberate purpose of agreeably breaking the march of events.  It is not probable that the intervals are studiously regular; but it does seem as if, after a considerable reach of narrative, he took counsel with himself and said—"It is time now that we had a break; I must seize the first opportunity."  What begets this suspicion is the fact that he occasionally seems to make such opportunities, when they do not occur naturally.

His abundant command of poetical language and imagery betrays him into diffuseness and pleonastic accumulation. This is the vice of his position as the heir of many generations of creative poets. Inheriting vast poetical wealth, he spends it prodigally; he does not refine his rich inheritance with tasteful activity, but enjoys the easy luxurious pleasure of telling out and heaping up his glittering hoards. We spoke of his fusing into new combinations, but very often he simply accumulates. This appears particularly in official pieces rapidly made to order. Take for example his description of the seven attendants in the pageant of Nature, Grace, and Fortune, set forth in a poem upon the reception of Henry VI. in London after his coronation as King of France, 1429[1]—

> " On the right hand of these Emperesses,
> Stood seven maidenës very celestial;
> Like Phœbus' beamës shone their golden tresses,
> Upon their heads each having a crownal,
> Of port and cheerë seeming immortal:
> In sight transcending all earthly crëatures,
> So angelic they weren of their figures.
>
> All clad in white, in token of cleanness,
> Like pure virginës as in their ententës,
> Showing outward an heavenly fresh brightness;
> Streamed with sunnës weren all their garmentës:
> Afore provided for pure innocentës:
> Most columbine of cheer and of looking,
> Meekly rose up at the coming of the king."

This is doggerel five-piled, though the elements thus mechanically piled up were originally exquisite. It is, however, an extreme example, and perhaps when Lydgate falls to be edited, it may be shown that this rude stuff is unworthy of him. Mr Wright ascribes to him an address to the boy-king on the same occasion, very little superior, it must be confessed, in workmanship.

What chiefly recommended him to his contemporaries was, we may conjecture, his narrative vigour; or, generally, his qualifications for writing a serious epic. Chaucer being so much the servant of the comic muse, with an eye for the humorous, the pathetic, and the picturesque, in familiar life and manners, the moment was singularly opportune for a poet prepared to deal with the darker side of life and the weightier incidents of national or civic history. Lydgate himself might not have seen the opening: the versatile monk was probably fully occupied with miscellaneous orders for hymns, prayers, lives of saints, and disguisings—too busy or too contented to look beyond his orders, except in an occasional popular ballad for relaxation. But a

---

[1] Attributed to him in Mr Halliwell's edition of his Minor Poems for the Percy Society. Quoted also as his in 'A Chronicle of London.'

tragic epic was suggested to him by a noble patron: it was at the gracious command of Humphrey, Duke of Gloucester—a royal minister sensible of the insecurity of his own position—that Lydgate undertook to translate "Boccaccio's Fall of Princes," a collection of short poems like the Monk's tragedies in the 'Canterbury Tales.' The work was undertaken to satisfy a thirst for tragical recital; and it fulfilled that mission till superseded by the fruits of the next great poetical season. It was sufficiently comprehensive in its catalogue of unfortunate celebrities; it travelled downwards through all history, sacred and profane, known to the author, from Adam and Eve to John, King of France, and his misfortune at Poictiers in 1356.

Lydgate had no special call to tragic poetry. He had neither depth nor refinement of poetical feeling. But he had abundance of poetical language, and he was able to express the conceptions of his original in a style not so very unworthy. His "gigantic and monstrous image of Fortune" is quoted by Warton as an example of "Gothic greatness":—

> "While Bochas pensive stood in his library,
> With cheer oppressed, pale in his visage,
> Some deal abashed, alone and solitary; ·
> To him appeared a monstruous image,
> Parted in twain of colour and courage,
> Her rightë sidë full of summer flowers,
> The tother oppressed with winter stormy showers.
>
> Bochas astonied, full fearful to abraid,[1]
> When he beheld the wonderful figure
> Of Fortunë, thus to himself he said :
> 'What may this mean ? Is this a crëature,
> Or a monster transformed again nature,
> Whose burning eyen sparkle of their light
> As do the stars the frosty winter night ? '
>
> And of her cheerë full good heed he took ;
> Her facë seeming cruel and terrible,
> And by disdainë menacing of look ;
> Her hair untrussed, hard, sharp, and horrible,
> Froward of shapë, loathsome and odible :[2]
> An hundred hands she had of each a part,[3]
> In sundry wise her giftës to depart.[4]
>
> Some of her handës lift up men aloft,
> To high estate of worldly dignity ;
> Another handë griped full unsoft,
> Which cast another in great adversity,
> Gave one richesse, another poverty."

According to Warton, our poet's chief excellence is in florid description. He is very gorgeous in his architecture; giving to

---

[1] Rise.    [2] Hateful.    [3] On each side.    [4] Distribute.

Greeks and Trojans all the magnificence of Gothic masonry. The following passage from Warton illustrates this peculiarity, and, at the same time, the absurdity of his anachronisms : "The poet (following Colonna) supposes that Hector was buried in the principal church of Troy, near the high altar, within a magnificent oratory, erected for that purpose, exactly resembling the Gothic shrines of our cathedrals, yet charged with many romantic decorations.

> " ' With crafty arches raised wonder clean,
> Embowered over all the work to cure,
> So marvellous was the celature,
> That all the roof and closure environ,
> Was of fine gold y-plated up and down,
> With knottës graven wonder curious
> Fret full of stonës rich and precious.'

"The structure is supported by angels of gold. The steps are of crystal. Within, is not only an image of Hector in solid gold ; but his body embalmed, and exhibited to view with the resemblance of real life, by means of a precious liquor circulating through every part in golden tubes artificially disposed, and operating on the principles of vegetation. This is from the chemistry of the times. Before the body were four inextinguishable lamps in golden sockets. To complete the work, Priam founds a regular chantry of priests, whom he accommodates with mansions near the church, and endows with revenues, to sing in this oratory for the soul of his son Hector." Lydgate's contemporaries doubtless enjoyed these descriptions, at a time when their senses were being opened to similar splendours in the churches, monasteries, and public buildings of their own towns and villages. Even to modern readers, in spite of their "capricious incredibilities and absurd inconsistencies," they are not without a certain charm of barbaric magnificence.

The particulars of Lydgate's "florid landscapes" are picked and chosen from hundreds of preceding artists. We have the newe green, and the younge green, the soft blowing of Zephyrus, the sweet dew, the soft showers, the wholesome balm, the lustie licour, the tapestry of divers flowers in the meadows, the singing of birds, the glancing of leaves in the sunshine. "The colouring of our poet's mornings is often remarkably rich and splendid," says Warton ; and quotes the following :—

> " When that the rowës and the rayës red
> Eastward to us full early ginnen spread,
> Even at the twilight in the dawning,
> When that the lark of custom ginneth sing,
> For to salutën in her heavenly lay
> The lusty goddess of the morrow gray,

> I mean Aurora, which afore the sun
> Is wont t' enchase the blackë skyës dnn,
> And all the darkness of the dimmy night,
> And fresh Phœbus, with comfort of his light,
> And with the brightness of his beamës sheen,
> Hath overgilt the hugë hillës green,
> And flowerës eke, again the morrow tide,
> Upon their stalks gan plain their leavës wide."

### 3. SIR THOMAS MALORY.

The date of Caxton's print of Malory's 'Morte d'Arthur' is 1485, the year of the deposition of Richard IIL, and the final settlement of the strife between the Houses of York and Lancaster. From the prime of Lydgate's life (1420-30) to this date, is a long interval, during which the English muse contented herself with very humble efforts at poetry. Rhyme and metre were used rather plentifully for chronicles, moral treatises (translated from Latin), chivalrous romances, lives of saints, by such versifiers as John Harding, William of Nassington, Benedict Burgh, Hugh Campden, Thomas Chester; but none of their performances rise to the humblest grade of mediocrity.

Sir Thomas Malory's 'Morte d'Arthur' is a condensation of an extensive literature—the prose romances on the subject of Arthur and the Knights of the Round Table. Its humble prose is all that we have to show as a national epic. It is compiled and abridged from French prose romances written during the thirteenth, fourteenth, and fiftcenth centuries, and contains the most famous exploits fabled of our national heroes. Its chief pretence to unity is that it begins with the birth of Arthur and ends with his death. It is, further, consistent in recognising throughout the invincible superiority of Lancelot of the Lake. Otherwise, its variety is somewhat bewildering, in spite of the obliging printer's division into twenty-one books. It is a book to choose when restricted to one book, and only one, as the companion of solitude ; there might then be some hope of gaining a clear mastery over its intricacies, a vivid conception of each several adventure of Gawain and his brothers, of Pelinore, Lancelot, Pelleas, Tristram, Palamides, Lamorak, Percival, Galahad, and their interminable friends, foes, and fair ladies.

Lord Tennyson's "Idylls of the King" have drawn especial attention to Malory in this generation. The old knight is very pleasant reading. He describes warlike encounters with great spirit and graphic homely language ; and his simple old English is very telling in the record of such pathetic incidents as the unhappy love of the maid of Astolat. His work being more or less of an abridgment, he is obliged to sacrifice much of the picturesque detail of his originals, and the story sometimes becomes a catalogue of encounters, with but little variation of the familiar incidents of knights hurled over their horses' tail, swords flashed out, shields lifted high, and helmets struck with stunning blow. Yet the 'Morte d'Arthur' is, as it was designed to be, a most entertaining book.

Lord Tennyson has taken considerable liberties in his adaptation of the legends or fictions collected by Malory. This he was fully entitled to do : there is nothing sacred in them, and an artist may do with them as he pleases, bearing always the responsibility of treating the subject in such a way as to justify himself. So far from being offended at any modification of the story of the 'Morte d'Arthur,' we should owe no gratitude to a modern poet who should simply versify Malory's prose, whether in substance or in detail. We can have no quarrel with a modern poet for using the 'Morte d'Arthur' as so much raw material to be worked at discretion. It is vain to look for any profound and consistent unity in such a compilation of the unconcerted labours of different authors —authors working not only without concert, but even with conflicting aims. And therefore I think that Mr Hutton, in his eloquent defence of the "Idylls of the King"[1] from the strictures of Mr Swinburne, commits a mistake when he tries to make out that Lord Tennyson's conception of the story is more consonant with the original designs than Mr Swinburne's. Lord Tennyson is fully entitled to bend the story to his own purposes ; and Mr Hutton is much more happy in his interpretation and justification of the Idylls upon their independent merits.

What the laureate has really done, has been to take up one motive to the creation of Arthur, and to regenerate his whole life in rigorous conformity thereto. This generating or regenerating motive is considerably different from any of the several motives that produced the heterogeneous character of the 'Morte d'Arthur,' but it may be said to be the modern and idyllic equivalent of one of them. So far, the character and achievements of Arthur may be described with Mr Hutton as a "mystic mediæval vision." There is a certain "halo of spiritual glory" round Arthur's head. He ministered to other sentiments than religious enthusiasm : he was a mirror of perfect knighthood, an object of national pride, and the adventures of himself and his knights furnished a luxurious feast to the passion for the marvellous. But religious enthusiasm was undoubtedly one motive, and a great motive, for his creation. He was the champion of Christianity against the heathen, and his return was looked for to aid in the recovery of the Holy Cross. And it is this side of Arthur's character that Lord Tennyson has set himself to treat in his own way. His Arthur

---

[1] Macmillan's Magazine, December 1872.

is still a perfect knight, a national hero, and a centre of marvellous adventure; but he is, above everything, a defender of the faith according to Lord Tennyson's ideal, and according to the moral sense of the present generation—a hero of divine origin, of immaculate purity, of unwavering and unintermitting singleness of purpose. Now, in these particulars, the modern poet departs from the Arthur of the old story. There was something supernatural in the origin of the old Arthur, but he was not literally heaven-sent: he was a child of shamefulness—not begotten in lawful wedlock. His father, Uther Pendragon, was transformed by the art of the magician, Merlin, into the likeness of Ygerne's husband, and Arthur was the issue of this illicit love and supernatural delusion of a faithful wife. Again, the Arthur of the old story was not stainless in the sense of loving one woman and cleaving to her. When he was a young squire, and before his origin was known either to himself or to the public, he lay with Morgause (or Bellicent), the wife of Lot, his half-sister; and in that unwittingly incestuous connection begat Mordred, who became afterwards his fatal enemy. After the battle with the eleven kings at Bredigan, he gratified, by the help of Merlin (who would not seem to have been scrupulous about playing the pander), a passing fancy for Lionors. And even after his marriage with Guinevere, not to mention his unwitting adultery with the false Guinevere, he was not the high, cold, self-contained Arthur of the Idylls. On one occasion, at least, he showed the wantonness of gallant curiosity, when he persisted, against Lancelot's dissuasion, in riding up to the fair Isoud, and staring at her until he was smitten off his horse by Sir Palamides for his discourtesy. Finally, as regards his singleness of purpose in driving out the heathen, therein also the modern Arthur is a refinement upon the Arthur of the old story, who made great war for the common selfish purpose of "getting all England into his hand;" and did not scruple to try to secure his power by committing to the mercy of the waves all children born on May-day, because Merlin told him "that he that should destroy him should be born on May-day."

Arthur is not the only personage in the old story whose character Lord Tennyson has chosen to modify. In the romance of Merlin, the magician falls hopelessly in love with Nimian, a maiden of great beauty and wisdom, teaches her all his enchantments, and is ultimately enclosed by her in a magic house without walls, that she may enjoy his love without interruption. In the 'Morte d'Arthur' this lady is Nimue, one of the damsels of the lake; Merlin persecutes her with his love, letting her have no rest; she "is ever passing weary of him, and fain would be delivered of him, for she is afeard of him, because he is a devil's son;" and at last she gets an opportunity to enclose him under a stone

for ever.  Nimue was afterwards one of the good angels of the
Round Table, gained the love of Pelleas, brought up Lancelot,
and more than once saved the life of Arthur, ever doing "great
goodness unto King Arthur, and to all his knights, by her sorcery and enchantments."  This exquisite creation of romance, to
whose father Diana had promised that her beauty would subdue the wisest man of all the world, the laureate has replaced
by Vivien, a wanton lady of the court, wholly without precedent
in romance, who, out of vulgar ambition to outwit the great
wizard, wrings his secret from him by wearing him out with
voluble flattery and such arts as the female Yahoo applied to
the naked Gulliver.[1]  The sons of Bellicent, again, are seriously
transfigured in the Idylls.  In the old story, Arthur's death,
through the treason and by the hand of Mordred, his own son
by unconscious incest, appears as the inexorable vengeance of an
iron law that accepts no plea of ignorance.  The king is punished
by the fruit of his own involuntary crime.  Lord Tennyson wipes
off this blot of incest from the life of his spotless hero, and attributes the treason of Mordred, whom he represents as the lawful son of Lot, to simple depravity of nature.  And to deepen
the colours of this natural taint, he extends it to Gawain, the
son of Bellicent and Lot, incriminating the whole of them as a
crafty deceitful race, with traitor hearts hid under a courteous
exterior.

These modifications of the old story and the old characters must
be left to justify themselves, very much as if the modern version
were a wholly new creation.  It is best on all grounds to regard
it as such : we should spoil the 'Morte d'Arthur' were we to
read it by the light of Lord Tennyson's conceptions ; and we should
be unfair to Lord Tennyson were we to condemn him for departing from the somewhat uncertain outlines of the ' Morte d'Arthur.'
We must take the "Idylls of the King" on their own merits.
If the poet had been writing a tragedy on a theme that appears on the surface, at least, so admirably suited for tragedy,
one cannot see that he would have gained anything by reject-
ing the incestuous birth of Mordred and its fatal consequences.
But the "Idylls of the King" are idylls ; it is obvious that their
greater simplicity is in accordance with the idyllic nature of the
poetry.  We are not distracted by bewildering mixtures of good
and evil in the "Idylls of the King": the king is blameless ;
Mordred is wholly vile, with no justification as an instrument
of Nemesis, or a revenger of the inhuman attempts upon his own

---

[1] I am not sure that Mr Swinburne is right in speaking of Vivien as a vilifica-
tion of the Lady of the Lake.  Lord Tennyson has kept up the Lady of the Lake
as a benignant enchantress, only he has disconnected her from the disappear-
ance of Merlin, and ascribed that to an independent and wholly new personage.

infant life; Lancelot and Guinevere are noble natures stained by one great sin. As the simple clearly outlined figures pass before us, we are not agitated by changing admiration and abhorrence; their first impression is ever deepened as they come and go by repeated strokes on the same spot of our moral vision. When the catastrophe comes, and death passes over them, we look back upon their lives without the conflict of emotion that appertains to tragedy. They affect us as visionary types, not as men and women of mixed passions.

### 4. JOHN SKELTON (1460-1529).

This is a fresh, audacious, boisterous, wayward pupil of Chaucer's, very different from the tame decorous Lydgate. He plays wanton freaks with the time-honoured copy-books of the school: writes a few lines in sober imitation, and then dashes off into all sorts of madly capricious irregularities. He is, indeed, so independent of models that he should have a chapter to himself, were it not that this would exaggerate him out of all proportion to his poetic importance. It wants some leniency in the definition of poetry to allow him the title of poet at all; he was not much more of a poet than Swift.

A genius thus " wild, madding, jocund, and irregular," is naturally a puzzle to his critics, and he has been very variously estimated. He had no doubt of his own position himself: in his genial impudent way he wrote a poem of sixteen hundred lines (the "Garland of Laurel") in which Fame and Pallas hold a complimentary dialogue over him; Gower, Chaucer, and Lydgate overcome his modest scruples to enter the Temple of Fame; and a bevy of fair and noble ladies embroider a rich crown for him with silk threads of green, red, tawny, white, black, purple, and blue. Other critics have been less favourable. Webbe, in his ' Discourse of English Poetry ' (1586), was tolerably gracious: " I with good right yield him the title of a poet; he was doubtless a pleasant conceited fellow, and of a very sharp wit, exceeding bold, and would nip to the very quick where he once set hold." But the courtly Puttenham, in his ' Art of English Poesy ' (1589), found Skelton's coarseness more offensive: he is " a sharp satirist, but with more railing and scoffery than became a poet-laureate; such among the Greeks were called *Pantomimi;* with us, Buffoons, altogether applying their wits to scurrilities and other ridiculous matters." However, he found a champion in D'Israeli, who pronounced him " too original for some of his critics; they looked on the surface, and did not always suspect the depths they glided over."

There is one depth that we may very easily glide over, if we are not on our guard. If we are not accustomed to distinguish between occasional moods and predominant character, we may fail to notice that the most furious occasional riots of ridicule and laughter are compatible with prevailing seriousness and good sense. Reading "Philip Sparrow," or the "Tunning of Elinour Rumming," we may refuse to believe in the possibility of the solid qualities that procured for Skelton the charge of educating the young prince (afterwards Henry VIII.), and the honour of being hailed by Erasmus as *unum lumen ac decus*—the only light and ornament—of British letters. But a little knowledge of the versatility of human nature will prevent us from falling into Miss Strickland's mistake of describing Skelton as a "ribald and ill-living wretch," who probably "laid the foundation for his royal pupil's grossest crimes." This is not merely judging without allowance from Skelton's writings, but taking for granted as gospel truth all the mythical tales that have accumulated round Skelton's name; it is like describing George Buchanan from the chap-books as the "king's fool." Skelton belongs to a type by no means uncommon; a man habitually serious and laborious, but endowed with the ungovernable energy that under excitement displays itself in rude bursts of extravagant mirth, and effusions of demonstrative affection.

When we look through the two volumes of Skelton's works collected by Mr Dyce,[1] we find underlying the mantling humour abundant evidence of a clear and capacious mind. The "Bowge of Court"—"*Ship* of Court," a satirical allegory—and the moral interlude, "Magnificence," are written with consistency and force of character, and abound in terse maxims of worldly wisdom: these productions show that the "ribald and ill-living wretch" was a penetrating observer, and might have been a sage counsellor. In Skelton's writings, however, it is not to be denied that the extravagantly ludicrous intrudes itself on every other quality; before he can go far in a serious vein, the humour collects again, and explodes at the slightest touch, irresistibly forcing his personages into violent movements and extreme manifestations. For instance, in his "Bowge of Court," he goes on for a little with his delineation of personified Disdain in tolerable soberness, though with occasional strong touches verging on the ludicrous; but this serious proceeding has not endured long when we come to a livelier stanza—

---

[1] 1843. Mr Dyce says that, "of almost all Skelton's writings which have descended to our times, the first editions have perished; and it is impossible to determine either at what period he commenced his career as a poet, or at what date his various pieces were originally written." Many of the works enumerated n the "Garland of Laurel" are no longer in known existence.

> " Forthwith he made on me a proud assault,
>     With scornful look moved all in mood ;
> He went about to take me in a fault ;
>     He frowned, he stared, he stamped where he stood.
>     I looked on him, I weened he had been wood.
> He set the arm proudly under the side,
> And in this wise he gan with me to chide."

All his personages are thrown more or less into these laughable exaggerated attitudes : the poet's irrepressible humour transforms them all into caricatures.   Prince Magnificence is the Herod of the Mysteries out-Heroded, blown up with absurd pride, declaring himself peerless and incomparable, threatening to drive down everybody like dastards with a dint of his fist, or flap them like fools to fall at his feet.   In extreme contrast to this heavy tyrant is the airy skipping and strutting sprightliness of Courtly Abusion—

> " What now, let see,
> Who looketh on me
> Well round about
> How gay and how stout
> That I can wear
> Courtly my gear :
> My hair busheth
> So pleasantly,
> My robe rusheth
> So ruttingly :
> Me seem I fly,
> I am so light
> To dance delight."

Not less extravagant is the wild hilarity of Liberty, singing as he dwells on sweet recollections—

> " With, ' Yea, marry, sirs,' thus should it be :
> I kissed her sweet and she kissed me ;
> I danced the darling on my knee ;
> I garred her gasp, I garred her glee,
> With, ' Dance on the lea, the lea ! '
> I bassed that baby with heart so free :
> She is the boot of all my bale."

This last passage reminds us of the demonstrative fondness of Swift's "Journal to Stella," and the suggestion of resemblance is still stronger in the lament for "Philip Sparrow," written in name of a young lady to commemorate her loss of a pet.   The tender bits in "Philip Sparrow" and in the "Journal to Stella" are written in exactly the same strain of fondling affection.   We should not have been surprised to find the following passage in the "Journal," as Swift's interpretation of Stella's feelings on a similar occasion :—

" It was so pretty a fool :
It would sit on a stool,
And learned after my school
For to keep his cut,
With, ' Philip, keep your cut !'
    It had a velvet cap,
And would sit on my lap,
And seek after small worms,
And sometimes white bread crumbs :
And many times and oft
Between my breasts soft
It would lie and rest ;
It was proper and prest.
    Sometimes he would gasp
When he saw a wasp ;
A fly or a gnat
He would fly at that ;
And prettily he would pant
When he saw an ant ;
Lord, how he would pry
After the butterfly !
Lord, how he would hop
After the grassop !
And when I said, Phip, Phip !  .
Then he would leap and skip,
And take me by the lip.
Alas, it will me slo
That Philip is gone me fro !

    .       .       .       .

Alas, mine heart it slayeth,
My Philip's doleful death !
When I remember it,
How prettily it would sit,
Many times and oft,
Upon my finger aloft !
I played with him tittle tattle,
And fed him with my spattle,
With his bill between my lips ;
It was my pretty Phips !
Many a pretty kuss
Had I of his sweet muss ;
And now the cause is thus,
That he is slain me fro
To my great pain and woe."

With all his buffooning and humour, Skelton was capable of sharp
satire and fierce invective.   He was not so wrapt up in grotesque
fancies and ebullient self-complacency as to be satisfied with the
whole world as well as with himself.   He was a good and an
extensive hater.   More than one of his contemporaries felt his
power to nip to the quick.   He had personal quarrels with one
Garnesche, a gentleman usher at court ; Barclay, the Scotch
author of the 'Ship of Fools'; Gaguin, a French ambassador ;

and Lily, the grammarian.  His poems against Garnesche are preserved, and are rare studies in foul language.  A more illustrious object of his aversion and rude railing rhymes was Cardinal Wolsey.  At one time Skelton enjoyed the patronage of the Cardinal, and rendered homage in his dedications; but afterwards he took or received offence, and assailed his former patron with remarkable boldness and scurrilous rancour.  The following is a specimen of his voluble abuse :—.

  " Our barons be so bold
   Into a mouse-hole they wold
   Run away and creep,
   Like a mayny of sheep ;
   Dare not look out at dur
   For dread of the mastiff cur,
   For dread of the butcher's dog,
   Would worry them like a hog.
    For and this cur do gnarr,
   They must stand all afar,
   To hold up their hand at the bar.
   For all their noble blood,
   He plucks them by the hood,
   And shakes them by the ear,
   And brings them in such fear ;
   He baiteth them like a bear,
   Like an ox or a bull :
   Their wits, he saith, are dull ;
   He saith they have no brain
   Their estate to maintain ;
   And maketh them to bow the knee
   Before his majesty ;
   Judges of the King's laws
   He counts them fools and daws.

   In the Chancery where he sits
   But such as he admits
   None so hardy to speak ;
   He saith—" Thou huddy peak,
   Thy learning is too lewd,
   Thy tongue is not well thewed
   To seek before our grace ;
   And openly in that place
   He rages and he raves
   And calls them cankered knaves.
   Thus royally he doth deal
   Under the King's broad seal ;
   And in the Chequer he them checks ;
   In the Star Chamber he nods and becks,
   And beareth him there so stout,
   That no man dare rout,
   Duke, Earl, Baron, nor Lord,
   But to his sentence must accord
   Whether he be knight or squire
   All men must follow his desire."

Although himself in orders and not averse to preferment in the Church, Skelton did not refrain from exercising his satire on the state of religion. "Colin Clout" is one of the most celebrated attacks on the clergy prior to the Reformation, and must have helped materially to increase, or at least to support, the popular dissatisfaction with the Church. His position may be said to be characteristic of English Church reformers. He attacks the officials, but spares the institutions. He is most scornful towards certain presumptuous young scholars who had shown some desire for reform of doctrine. He tries hard to make them ashamed of their little rags of rhetoric, their little lumps of logic, their pieces and patches of philosophy. In "Colin Clout," with a certain assumption of irony, he disclaims the character of a reformer, because people do not like the inquisitive, prying, meddlesome ways of such a character. For himself, the time seems so utterly out of joint, that he doubts the use of trying to set it right. He proposes merely to repeat what he, Colin Clout, hears as he wanders in and out among the people. He merely retails what they say hugger-mugger, or the "logic that they chop"—

> " And in their fury hop
> When the good ale sop
> Doth dance in their fore top."

The common people, he says ironically, are doubtless liars, slanderers, and railing rebels; but they have much to say about the pride, venality, luxury, and debauchery of the clergy, both great and small. The higher clergy, forgetting their humble origin, keep great state; treat the lords temporal with open insolence; hunt, hawk, neglect their duties, rob and spoil their charge, admit to holy orders worthless untaught drunkards—men of small intelligence and great sloth; have their houses adorned with lascivious pictures. The begging friars intrigue with the servants, encourage them in discontent, flatter them with filed tongue and pleasant style, and wheedle from them the good things of the larder. It is really too bad of the common people to make such accusations—

> " What hath laymen to do
> The gray goose for to shoe?
> Like hounds of hell
> They cry and they yell
> How that ye sell
> The grace of the Holy Ghost:
> Thus they make their boast
> Throughout every coast
> How some of you do eat
> In Lenten season flesh meat,

> Pheasants, partridge, and cranes !
> Men call you therefore profanes.
> Ye pick no shrimps nor pranes ;
> Salt-fish, stock-fish, nor herring,
> It is not for your wearing :
> Nor in holy Lenten season
> Ye will neither beans nor peasen,
> But ye will look to be let loose
> To a pig or goose ;
> Your gorge not endued
> Without a capon stewed
> Or a stewed cockle."

The chief production of Skelton's that has laughter for its ultimate end, is the "Tunning of Elinour Rumming," a picture of a low alewife and her customers. It is too coarse to quote. It deals with the same materials as Burns's "Jolly Beggars"; but the treatment is as widely different as the character of the writers. Burns, with catholic sympathy, enters into the spirit of the "splore" held by his "gangrel bodies," his vagrant waifs. In the excitement of the festivity their sorrows are forgotten, their rags unheeded ; they are raised to the rank of gods. Skelton, on the other hand, writes in a strain that would please a teetotal lecturer. Elinour and her friends are reduced by their craving for drink to the level of beasts. They are painted with harsh, coarse, cynical feeling, as by one utterly revolted and enraged at their squalid, uncared-for persons, their unclean habits, and miserable shifts to get their fill of the old hag's filthy ale. We laugh at their preposterous mishaps, but it is a bestial orgie.

### 5. STEPHEN HAWES.

This well-intentioned versifier was contemporary with Skelton ; but two men could not well be more dissimilar. Hawes is said to have been a travelled Oxonian, and to have obtained a place in the household of Henry VII. by his knowledge of French and facility in repeating the English poets. Of this last accomplishment there are many traces in his "Pastime of Pleasure," a didactic poem in a thin disguise of romantic allegory ; and it is pretty nearly the only accomplishment or claim to interest that the poem exhibits. If Skelton is fresh as a relief from Lydgate, Hawes is doubly dull and spiritless after Skelton. When we come to Hawes, we regret that Professor Lowell threw away his eloquent illustrations of tediousness upon Gower. He should have kept them for the so-called "Pastime of Pleasure." Gower cannot boast of such a perseverance in drivel ; and it beats either of the two living exemplars, whom cis-Atlantic politeness forbids us to name.

In the prefatory address " To the Reader," we are informed that the title of the work is a pious fraud : that the design of the writer is to entice young men, by the promise of pastime and pleasure, into a course of valuable instruction in the seven sciences and in moral habits. He holds out the unsophisticated bait that "herein thou mayest easily find (as it were in pastime), without offence of nature, that thing, and in short space, which many great clerks without great pains and travail, and long continuance of time heretofore could never obtain nor get." The various precepts are made attractive to youth by being represented as the course that a young man must follow before he can hope to win a lady's favour. The hero of the poem, Graunde Amoure, relates how he met Fame : how she fired his fancy by a description of the incomparable La Belle Pucelle : how she directed him to the tower of Doctrine, where he was instructed in succession by seven mistresses, Grammar, Logic, Rhetoric, Arithmetic, Music, Geometry, and Astronomy : how in the chamber of Music he met his fair lady, wooed and won her love, but was parted from her and warned that he must conquer certain giants before she became his : how he conquered those giants with the help of certain personifications whom he met on the way, and married La Belle Pucelle. When he had lived many years with his wife, Age walked into his house, bringing Policy and Avarice. Fame celebrates him after his death.

Warton has said that Hawes "has added new graces to Lydgate's manner ;" and we may admit this if we are allowed to give our own interpretation to the words. But what are we to make of Southey's saying that the "Pastime of Pleasure," composed as he himself states in 1506, is "the best English poem of its century"? That such a judgment should have been given by any one that had read any of Hawes's predecessors, is a standing puzzle and bewilderment. As we plod conscientiously through the dreary pastime, we cannot help wondering whether Southey, who could not "afford either time or eyesight for correcting the proof-sheets of such a volume" as his British Poets, but who afforded the floating power of his name to the most execrably inaccurate reprint ever offered to the public, had ever been foolish enough to waste either time or eyesight on Hawes in any form whatever. Nothing short of a few pages of the poem can give the reader an adequate idea of its lustreless retailing of borrowed beauties, its mechanical piecing together of lines and rhymes with unmeaning and tautologous fag-ends and bits. Take his description of his matchless heroine, La Belle Pucelle, which he has laboured with especial care—

"In which dwelleth by great authority
La Belle Pucelle, which is so fair and bright ;
To whom in beauty no peer I can see :

> For like as Phœbus, above all stars in light,
> When that he is in his sphere aright,
> Doth exceed with his beamës clear,
> So doth her beauty above other appear.
>
> She is both good, aye wise, and virtuous,
> And also descended of a noble line ;
> Rich, comely, right meek, and bounteous ;
> All manner virtues in her clearly shine ;
> No vice of her may right long domine :
> And I, dame Fame, in every nation
> Of her do make the same relation."

Take another specimen, in the old spelling, and see whether that flavour of antiquity makes the style more enjoyable. I give also the original uniform pointing as it appears in Southey's text, not venturing to make a new distribution of the adjuncts—

> "The roufe was painted, with golden beames
> The windowes crystall, clearely clarified
> The golden raies, and depured streames
> Of radiant Phœbus, that was purified
> Right in the Bull, that time so domified
> Throughe windowes, was resplendishant
> About the chamber, fair and radiaunt."

There is a grammatical connection among these scattered members, and to discover it will be a fair exercise in punctuation.

The "Pastime of Pleasure" is said to have been composed in 1506. It was first printed in 1517, and it was reprinted in 1554 and in 1555. It was included in Southey's selection from Early British Poets in 1831. Antony Wood lamented that, in his time, it was "thought but worthy of a ballad-monger's stall." We are less astonished at this than at the fact that Southey considered it worth reprinting in full in a selection that had no room for a single passage from Lydgate or Dunbar. Some of the critics of Southey's generation, in their laudable zeal to make Art the handmaid of Morality, seem to have been betrayed into criticising upon the principle that everything moral is poetical, no matter how tame, stupid, and lifeless.


## IV.—Scottish Successors.

The Scottish disciples of Chaucer are, on the whole, a more brilliant line of descendants than their English brethren. The seeds of mediæval poetry found a virgin soil in Scotland ; and though the stems and flowers had something of the Scotch hardness, the crop was luxuriant enough.

### I. James I. (1394-1437).

This accomplished and unfortunate king—born in 1394, held as a captive in England from 1405 to 1424, and assassinated, after a firm and popular reign, in 1437—was by far the most successful imitator of Chaucer. Though he has no title to the rank of original poet, which some of his admirers claim for him, his "King's Quhair" (*Quire* or *Book*) is justly the most celebrated English poem of the fifteenth century. It is written in *Troilus* verse, and is commonly said, though the notion is probably erroneous,[1] to have given that stanza its designation of rhyme-royal. In general structure, the poem belongs to the same family as Chaucer's graceful fantasies. The main incident is imitated from the Knight's Tale; and many turns of expression have been caught from the master.[2] The poet supposes himself, after his restoration to his kingdom, to waken at midnight, when—

> "High in the heavenës figure circulere
> The ruddy starrës twinkled as the fire,
> And in Aquary Cinthia the clear
> Rinsed her tresses like the golden wire."

He falls a-thinking, and, finding that he cannot sleep, reads 'Boece's Consolations.' But Boece is no sleep-compeller, and keeps his majesty awake with thoughts on the variableness of Fortune. He tosses about, and travels restlessly over his past life—

> "Among these thoughtës rolling to and fro,
> Fell me to mind of my fortune and ure,[3]
> In tender youth how she was first my foe,
> And eft[4] my friend, and how I gat recure
> Of my distress, and all my adventure
>   I gan o'er-hale, that longer sleep no rest
>   Ne might I not, so were my wittës wrest."

Suddenly the matins bell begins to sound, and seems to say to him—"Tell on, man, what thee befel." He resolves at once to do so; gets up, takes a pen, makes the sign of the cross, invokes Calliope and her sisters in the name of Mary, and forthwith proceeds to tell the story of his captivity and courtship. He relates how his father prepared to send him to France, and how he was captured by an English ship and imprisoned in the tower. There he lay bewailing his sad fortune through the long days and nights. But suddenly joy came out of torment. From his prison window he could see into a fair garden, with flower-beds, hawthorn hedges, and leafy trees, filled with singing birds; and there one fresh May morning came to gather flowers a vision of beauty

---

[1] See before, p. 20.

[2] See Mr T. H. Ward's essay in 'English Poets,' and Mr Skeat's edition, 'Scottish Text Society.'

[3] Use—hap.          [4] Again.

that sent the blood of all his body to his heart—a lady with
"beauty enough to make a world to dote," so fair that she might
be taken for "god Cupido's own princess," or "even very Nature
the goddess," the painter of all the heavenly colours of the garden,
come in person to survey her handiwork.  For a moment he was
astounded ; but soon he began to feel that he had become for ever
thrall to the fair apparition.[1]  He drank in all the particulars of
her beauty ; noted her attire, which was loose and simple, and
feasted his eyes on a heart-shaped ruby hanging from a gold
necklace, and burning like a wanton flame on her white throat ;
chided the nightingale for not singing to her ; and after her
departure, sat at his window in despair till night came on, leaning
his head on the cold stone and bemoaning his destiny.

The conception of all this is well calculated to give scope for
luxurious execution.  It is a spacious and effective framework for
studies of melancholy reflection, pangs of thwarted love, scenical
richness, and womanly beauty.  The execution, however, is not
equal to the conception : it comes very far short of the softness,
delicacy, and voluptuous richness of Chaucer.  In what follows of
the poem—for the above is comprised in two out of the six cantos
—one is no less struck by the largeness and clearness of the plan,
the vigorous judgment in bringing good situations naturally and
fitly within the course of the poem.  In Canto iii. he is transported to the Court of Venus, to plead for mercy from the Queen
of Love, whose power he has long set at nought.  In Canto iv. he
is conducted to the Palace of Minerva, and receives much wise
counsel.  In Canto v. he goes in quest of Fortune, along the
banks of a river, and through woods filled with all manner of wild
beasts ; finds her "howffing" on the ground, with her wheel
before her, and obtains assurance of her favour.  In the last Canto
a turtle-dove presents him with a formal notification that his
prayers have been heard, and that his desires will be speedily
fulfilled.  Readers familiar with Chaucer will see that the royal
imitator has contrived to run the stream of his story past the
very best opportunities for description, through the very heart of
the country pictured in the "Court of Love," the "Parliament of
Birds," and the "House of Fame."  And it must be owned that,
while the "King's Quhair" seems deficient in richness and delicacy of colouring when placed side by side with the work of the
master, it reads remarkably well when removed from damaging
comparison, and is infinitely the best composition produced in
the school of Chaucer.  There is real passion in it, and a real

---

[1] This is commonly supposed to be a true narrative of King James's first
vision of Lady Jane Beaufort.  There is not the slightest reason to believe that
it is anything but a romantic fancy, imitated from the appearance of Emily to
Palamon and Arcite.  As a real incident, it is as probable as that a turtle-dove
brought him the blissful news of relief from his pain (Canto vi. 5-7).

sense of beauty, though the expression fails to strike through and rise above the embarrassing self-criticism that cramps so many Scotch attempts at eloquence and poetry. The proportions are good, but the surface is dry and hard.

In confirmation of this, the lover's approach and address to Venus (Canto iii. 25-28) may be compared with similar passages in the " Court of Love." The third of these stanzas is modelled on the invocation to the Virgin in the 'Canterbury Tales' of the Second Nun.

> " With quaking heart astonate of that sight
> Unnethës[1] wist I what that I should sain,
> But at the lastë feebly as I might
> With my handës on both my kneës twain,
> There I begouth[2] my carës to complain ;
>    With ane humble and lamentable cheer
>    Thus salute I that goddess bright and clear.

> ' High Queen of Love ! star of benevolence !
> Piteous princess, and planet merciable !
> Appeaser of malice and violence !
> By virtue pure of your aspectës hable
> Unto your grace let now been acceptable
>    My pure request, that can no further gone
>    To seeken help, but unto you alone.

> As ye that been the succour and sweet well
> Of remedy, of careful heartës cure
> And in the hugë weltering wavës fell,
> Of lovës ragë, blissful haven and sure :
> O anchor and true of our good aventure,
>    Ye have your man with his good will conquest,
>    Mercy, therefore, and bring his heart to rest.' "

The beginning of Canto v., describing his journey in quest of Fortune, also comes into direct comparison with Chaucer (" Parliament of Birds," 180, 360, &c.)

> " Where in a lusty plain took I my way,
> Along a river, pleasant to behold,
> Embroiden all with freshë flowrës gay,
> Where through the gravel, bright as any gold,
> The crystal water ran so clear and cold,
>    That in mine carë made continually
>    A manner soun melled with harmony.

> That full of little fishës by the brim,
> Now here now there, with backes blue as lead,
> Leapt and played, and in a rout gan swim
> So prettily, and dressed them to spread
> Their coral finnës as the ruby red,
>    That in the sunnëshine their scalës bright
>    As gesserant aye glittered in my sight."

---

[1] Hardly.　　　　　　　　　　　[2] Began.

Two humorous poems—"Peebles to the Play" and "Christ's Kirk on the Green"—dealing with the riotous merry-making of the lower orders, and written with very heavy spirit, are ascribed to James I. by some authorities. Since, however, their authorship is disputed, and we shall have abundant illustration of Scotch humorous poetry in Dunbar, I shall pass them over.

### 2. ROBERT HENRYSON (1425-1495 ?).

The schoolmaster of Dunfermline had much less power than King James, but his poetry was more self-determined and less imitative. The only ascertained date in his life is his admission to the newly founded University of Glasgow in 1462 : he may thence be conjectured to have flourished midway between King James and Dunbar. He seems to have been a grave, religious, gentle scholar, observant, full of prudent precepts, melancholy reflections, and quiet humour. He wrote little, and elaborated that little with Virgilian care. He generally imposed upon himself the double restraint of rhyme and alliteration, and fitted most of his ballads with a refrain : he used considerable variety of metre. King James's style was opposed to the English in point of diffuseness, but Henryson studied compression even more than his royal predecessor : he would seem to have struggled to express himself in few words and circumstances, and to make the few as pregnant as possible. His scenes are masterpieces of delicate and faithful word-painting.

Henryson's most celebrated composition is a continuation of Troilus, called the "Testament of Cresside," written with a view to providing a suitable retribution for the fair lady's breach of faith : in an important council of the Gods of the Seven Planets, she is doomed to leprosy, and bequeaths a lamentation and a warning to all false lovers. He is also the author of the first pastoral poem in the language—"Robin and Malkin"; and of one of the earliest Scotch ballads—"The Bluidy Serk," a religious allegory. He wrote also a poem on Orpheus and Eurydice, and versified certain 'Fables of Æsop.'

The opening stanza of his "Praise of Age" is a fair specimen of his most spirited manner, though containing perhaps less alliteration than usual :—

> " Intill a garth,[1] under a red rosere,[2]
> An old man and decrepid hard I sing ;
> Gay was the note, sweet was the voice and clear,
> It was great joy to hear of such a thing :
> And to my doom, he said, in his diting,

---

[1] Into a garden.　　　　　　　　[2] Rose-bush.

> For to be young I would not, for my wiss
>   Of all this world to make me lord and king :
> The more of age the nearer heavenës bliss."

The following seven-line staves display considerable power :—

> " Syne[1] Winter wan, with austere Æolus,
>   God of the wind, with blastës boreal
>   The green garment of Summer glorious
>   Has all to rent and riven in pieces small :
>   Then flowrës fair, faded with frost, mon fall,
>     And birdës blithe changes their notës sweet
>     Intil mourning, near slain with snow and sleet.[2]
>
> Syne comës Ver, when Winter is away,
>   The secretar of Summer with his seal ;
>   When columbine up keekës[3] through the clay,
>   Whilk fleyed[4] was before with frostës fell ;
>   The mavis and the merle begins to mell ;[5]
>     The lark on loft, with other birdës small
>     Then drawës forth from dern,[6] o'er down and dale."

### 3. WILLIAM DUNBAR (1460-15 ?).

The pride of early Scottish poetry is William Dunbar.  He is usually spoken of as being, next to Burns, the greatest poet that Scotland has produced.  Looking upon him simply as a Scottish poet, we may regard King James and Henryson as his precursors, and as isolated fine days before the confirmed summer.  But this altogether exaggerates his importance in a more cosmopolitan view.  Employing the machinery of allegorical dream, and sweet spring proemiums, he must be considered as being through Chaucer one of the numerous poetical progeny of the *Roman de la Rose :* he is the best Scottish representative of the movement initiated and transmitted by that poem.  Other influences went to the making of his poetry, but his main impulse came from Chaucer. He was formed in the school of Chaucer, as Chaucer was in the school of Guillaume de Lorris and Jean de Meun.

The first record of Dunbar's name is on the register of the University of St Andrews, where he appears in 1477 as a "Determinant," or Bachelor of Arts, and again in 1479 as Master of Arts. The next record is in the register of the Privy Seal : in the year 1500 he obtained a yearly pension of ten pounds for life, or until he should be promoted to an ecclesiastical benefice.  But· the gaping spaces between these meagre and insignificant records are filled up from hints in the works of the poet and his poetical

---

[1] Then—next.
[2] The readings " austern," " changit," and " in still murning," are obviously erroneous.
[3] Peeps.    [4] Frightened.    [5] Mingle.    [6] Secret—hiding-place.

antagonist, Walter Kennedy.   In early life he joined the Franciscan friars, and begged in the habit of that order.   Addressing the
pretended St Francis, he says :—

> " Gif ever my fortune was to be a friar,
>     The date thereof is past full many a year ;
>         For in to every lusty town and place
>         Of all England, from Berwick to Calais,
>     I have in to thy habit made good cheer.
>
>     In friarës weed full fairly have I fleeched ;[1]
>     In it have I in pulpit gone and preached
>         In Derntoun kirk and eek in Canterbury ;
>         In it I passed at Dover o'er the ferry
>     Through Picardy, and there the people teached."

By James IV., who came to the throne in 1488, he would seem to
have been employed as a clerk to foreign embassies, visiting Paris
more than once in that capacity.   Later in life he proved the
value of his early practice as a beggar by the ingenuity and variety
of his supplications to the king.   He received occasional gratuities,
and an increase of his pension ; but he never attained the fat
Church benefice that he coveted and prayed for so earnestly.

This jolly quick-witted friar and courtier is sometimes called the
Scottish Chaucer.   The two have, indeed, a good many points of
resemblance.   Both were men of the world and favourites at
Court ; companionable men, witty and good - humoured : both
showed sufficient address and business dexterity to be employed
on embassies of state.   But if we wish to give the title of
"Scottish Chaucer" its full significance, we must place considerable emphasis on the adjective.   Dunbar and Chaucer belong to
the same class of easy self-contained men, whose balance is seldom
deranged by restless straining and soaring ; but within that happy
pleasure-loving circle they occupy distinct habitations : and one
way of bringing out their difference of spirit is to lay stress upon
their nationality.   Dunbar is unmistakably Scotch.   He is altogether of stronger and harder—perhaps of harsher—nerve than
Chaucer ; more forcible and less diffuse of speech ; his laugh is
rougher ; he is boldly sarcastic and derisive to persons ; his ludicrous conceptions rise to more daring heights of extravagance ;
and, finally, he has a more decided turn for preaching—for offering
good advice.   Not that he is always strong-headed, extravagantly
humorous, or gravely moral ; there are green places in his heart,
and his fancies are sometimes sweet and graceful ; but the strength
of head, the extravagance of humour, and the gravity of good
counsel are, upon the whole, predominant in his composition.

, It is significant of Dunbar's intellectual activity that his versifi-

---

[1] Begged.

cation is more varied than we find in any of his English predecessors.   He studies variety of stanza by interweaving lines of
different length, with rhymes and refrains at different intervals.
Besides the familiar Troilus verse of seven lines, he uses stanzas of
four lines, of five lines, of six lines, of eight lines, of nine lines,
and of twelve lines.   In some of his stanzas the lines have five
accents, in some four.   In his "Dance of the Seven Deadly Sins,"
he uses the arrangement adopted in the opening of Burns's "Jolly
Beggars"—couplets of four-accent lines separated by single lines
of three accents : his stanza, however, is of twelve lines.

His most finished poem is an allegory called the "Golden
Targe," printed in 1508, and evidently intended to show the world
at large what he could do.   The "Golden Targe" is the armour of
Reason against importunate Desire ; but the weapon itself is but
a small figure in the poem.   He opens with a description of a
mirthful morning in May ; in which he shows that the habit of
St Francis did not prevent him from enjoying the favourite season
of the lover.   He has fairly succeeded in his ambition to strike
out new fancies.   The picture is most carefully studied, and the
colours are really gorgeous.

> " Full angelic the birdës sang their hours,[1]
> Within their curtains green, into their bowers,
>     Apparelled white and red, with bloomës sweet :
> Enamelled was the field with all colours ;
> The pearly droppës shook in silver showers,
>     While all in balm did branch and leavës fleet : [2]
>     To part fro Phœbus did Aurora greet ; [3]
> Her crystal tears I saw hang on the flowers
>     Whilk he for love all drank up with his heat.
>
> For mirth of May, with skippës and with hops,
> The birdës sang upon the tender crops,
>     With curious notes as Venus chapel clerks ;
> The roses young, new spreading of their knops,[4]
> Were powdered bright with heavenly beryl drops,
>     Through beamës red, burning as ruby sparks ;
>     The skyës rang for shouting of the larks ;
> The purple heaven o'erscailed[5] in silver sops ;
>     Oergilt the treës, branches, leaves, and barks."

After five stanzas of such elaborate delineation, he proceeds to say
that he fell asleep, and begins to relate his dream :—

[1] Orisons.                 [2] Float.                 [3] Weep.                 [4] Buds.
[5] Overflowed.   Cf. Douglas's Virgil, Prol. Book xiii. l. 26,
          "The recent dew begynnis doun to *skale*."
From the same passage I have conjectured that " sops" and not "slops" is the
true reading here.   See l. 41—
     "Out ouer the swyre " [hill-top] " swymmys the *soppis* of myst."

" What through the merry fowlës harmony,
And through the river's sound that ran me by,
  On Flora's mantle I sleeped as I lay ;
Where soon into my dreamës fantasy
I saw approach, against the orient sky,
  A sail, as white as blossom upon spray,
  With merse [1] of gold, bright as the star of day,
Whilk tended to the land full lustily,
  As falcon swift desirous of her prey.

And hard on board unto the bloomed meads,
Among the greenë rispës [2] and the reeds,
  Arrived she ; wherefro anon there lands
An hundred ladies, lusty into weeds,
As fresh as flowrës that in May upspreads,
  In kirtles green, withouten carol or bands :
  Their brightë hairs hang glittering on the strands,
In tresses clear, whippëd with golden threads
  With pappës white, and middles small as wands."

He then portrays some of the personages in this ravishing vision
of beauties : among others—

" There saw I May, of mirthful monthës queen,
Betwixt April, and June, her sister sheen,
  Within the garden walking up and down,
Whom of the fowlës gladdeth all bedeen : [3]
She was full tender in her yearës green.
  There saw I Nature present her a gown
  Rich to behold, and noble of renown,
Of every hue under the heaven that been
  Depaint, and broad by good proportion."

His own situation is very luxuriously painted :—

" Full lustily these ladies all in fere [4]
Entered within this park of most pleasere,
  Where that I lay o'erhielt [5] with leavës rank ;
The merry fowlës blissfullest of cheer,
Salute Nature, methought, on their manner,
  And every bloom on branch, and eke on bank,
  Opened and spread their balmy leavës dank,
Full low inclining to their Queen so clear,
  Whom of their noble nourishing they thank."

Thereafter follow more of these studies of luxurious spectacle
and situation, which must be owned to be no mean emulation of
Chaucer ; and at last, just in the middle of the poem, he introduces
what the title indicates as its main purpose : narrating how he
was espied by the Queen of Love ; how she sent her fair minions
in pursuit of him—Beauty, Fair Having, Fine Portraiture, Pleas-

[1] Mast.        [2] Coarse grass.        [3] Immediately.
[4] Company.        [5] O'ershielded.

ance, and Lusty Cheer; how Reason defended him with her golden targe; how his assailants were reinforced; how Reason was for a time overborne and the poet taken prisoner; how Æolus dispersed the brilliant gathering, and sent them all to sea again; and how he awoke and found himself in his pleasant valley, amidst soft air and tender sunshine, with the birds singing merrily around him. He ends off with a panegyric of Chaucer, Gower, and Lydgate, and a modest address to his own "little Quhair," his humble book. With all its transparent artificiality, the ingenious author had no small reason to be proud of it. He was an imitator of forms that had lost the freshness of youth, and he belonged to a nation never conspicuous for softness and delicacy; yet he could send forth his book with a feeling that he had made a very creditable contribution to the mediæval play of fancy and study of form and colour.

The "Golden Targe" was obviously, as we have said, one of his most ambitious and laboured compositions. Another allegory, which was reprinted in 'Brydges's Restituta' with a very high encomium, is called the "Thistle and the Rose." This was written in 1503, to celebrate the marriage of King James IV. with the Princess Margaret of England; and a very ingenious and flattering epithalamium it is. After an elaborate description of the usual May morning, the poet makes Dame Nature summon before her the birds and the beasts, the flowers and the herbs. In delicate flattery of his patron, the red lion rampant is described as a most terrible beast; and receives Nature's injunctions to extend his protection to the inferior kinds—

> "Exerce justice with mercy and conscience,
>    And let no small beast suffer scathe ne scorns,
> Of greatë beasts that been of more puissance;
>    Do law alike to apes and unicorns,
>    And let no bowgle [1] with his boisterous horns
> The meek plough-ox oppress, for all his pride,
> But in the yoke go peaceable him beside."

When Queen Nature comes to the flowers, she looks with profound respect upon "the awful Thistle," and his environing "bush of spears," and bids him maintain order among the herbs and flowers like a discreet king as he is. In particular is the Thistle told to honour the fresh Rose; and under the symbol of that flower, the poet celebrates in most flattering stanzas the "blissful angelic beauty" of the Princess Margaret.

In the moral apologue of the Merle (or Blackbird) and the Nightingale, we have an example of the same species of composition as Chaucer's Cuckoo and Nightingale. The Nightingale, however, is no longer the representative of chivalrous love as

_______
[1] Buffalo.

opposed to the vulgar love of the Cuckoo.  She represents the
love of God in antagonism to the love of earthly creatures,
symbolised by the Blackbird.  The following are the opening
stanzas :—

> "In May, as that Aurora did upspring
>     With crystal eyen chasing the cloudës sable,
> I heard a Merle with merry notës sing
>     A song of love with voice right comfortable,
> Against the orient beamës amiable,
> Upon a blissful branch of laurel green ;
>     This was her sentence sweet and delectable,
> A lusty life in Lovë's service been.
> Under this branch ran down a river bright,
>     Of balmy liquor, crystalline of hue,
> Against the heavenly azure skyës light ;
>     Where did upon the tother side pursue
>     A Nightingale with sugared notës new,
> Whose angel feathers as the peacock shone :
>     This was her song and of a sentence true,
> All love is lost but upon God alone."

It would appear that the Scotchman had never seen a nightingale
in the course of his wanderings.  His opposition of religious love
to love in general, and his alienation of the nightingale from
chivalrous love, shows the spirit of the friar predominating over
the spirit of knighthood.  Dunbar has none of the chivalrous
feeling of Barbour or of King James.

In the above extracts we have specimens of the sweet moods of
Dunbar's rugged good-humoured Scotch nature.  He shows little
inclination for the loftier flights of poetry : he had not the soaring
genius of Burns.  Partly, this is owing to his natural easy temperament; partly, no doubt, to his circumstances.  There was
little encouragement to soar in writing for the Court of James
IV., among jealous rivals ready to pounce with keen sarcasm and
hearty madcap derision upon any attempt at fine composition.
All Dunbar's attempts in the way of serious sublime writing are
upon religious themes.  He has a hymn on the Nativity, another
on the Resurrection, and a curiously rhymed "Ballet of our Lady."
His hymn on the Nativity is commonplace and uninspired in
comparison with Milton's.  The following is one of the best
stanzas :—

> "Celestial fowlës in the air
>     Sing with your notës upon height !
> In firthës and in forests fair
>     Be mirthful now at all your might
> For passed is your doleful night ;
>     Aurora has the cloudës pierct
> The sun is risen with gladsome light,
>     *Et nobis Puer natus est.*"[1]

---

[1] And to us a son is born.

Undoubtedly the most striking quality in Dunbar's poems and ballads is his wild Scotch humour—the humour of robust nerves, delighting in extravagantly ludicrous conceptions of exalted things, and dealing hard knocks to persons without malice, and with the redeeming consciousness of being prepared to receive the same in return. It is only under the afflatus of this spirit that his imagination is rapt up and hurried on beyond its usual sober pace. His other productions are comparatively cold-blooded and mechanical—mere exercises of skill.

The bedlamite philosophy of his wilder moods is expressed in the following stanza, which concludes a poem designed to express the folly of having money without enjoyment—

> " Now all this time let us be merry,
> And set not by this world a cherry:
>  Now while there is good wine to sell,
> He that does on dry bread worry
> I give him to the Devil of Hell."

The last expression is an instance of his habit of making humorously free with dread ideas and personages. He does so very frequently. He is especially familiar with the enemy of mankind and his myrmidons, and credits them with many a ludicrous prank. His "Dance of the Seven Deadly Sins," set agoing in hell by "Auld Mahoun,"[1] is a phantasmagoric extravagance as wild and grim as could well be conceived: mirth could not well be more demoniacally riotous. It is totally different in purpose from Langland's "Vision of the Seven Deadly Sins;" there is not the faintest suspicion of a moral in it. Even the fast and furious "splore" of the "Jolly Beggars" is less fantastic. Pride, Ire, Envy, Covetousness, Idleness, Lechery, Gluttony, each with a train of representative followers, dance in characteristic fashion on the floor of their house of torment; while fiends stand by enjoying the sport, and encouraging the dance with various hot applications. The Covetous vomit hot gold at each other, and the fiends stand ready as they discharge one shot, to fill them " new up to the throat" with another. The followers of Idleness ("Sweirness") require special stimulus to dance. Belial lashes them with a bridle-rein, and that failing, the fiends lose patience, and try a stronger measure—

> " In dance they were so slow of feet,
> They gave them in the fire a heat,
>  And made them quicker of cunnyie."

The concluding stanza of the poem is a ludicrous derision of the

---

[1] Mahomet, a synonym for the arch-enemy.

Highlandmen, to whom the Lowlanders always had a strong aversion. Mahoun sends for one of them, and has a coronach sung over him, whereupon the Erse men assemble and so deafen Satan with their outlandish clatter, that in a fury he sinks them to "the deepest pit of hell," and smothers them with smoke. It needs a strong nerve to laugh over such horrors; but to one with the requisite vigour there is considerable humorous body and power in the stanza—

> "Then cried Mahound for a Highland pagean :
> Syne ran a fiend to fetch Macfadzean
>   Far northward in a nook;
> By he the coronach had done shout,
> Erse men so gathered him about,
>   In hell great room they took :
> These termagants, with tag and tatter,
> Full loud in Erse begowth to clatter,
>   And roup [1] like raven and rook.
> The Devil so deaved [2] was with their yell,
> That in the deepest pit of hell
>   He smothered them with smoke."

Dunbar is no less free in his ridicule of persons. He and another poet, Walter Kennedy, in the enjoyment of their gift of rhyme and metre, amused themselves and the Court generally with a pitched battle of "flyting" or vituperation. They are said to have been very good friends, and to have abused each other purely in sport, as was done by the Italian poets Luigi Pulci and Matteo Franco; but friendship put no restraint upon their tongues; they could hardly have been more abusive, if they had been in virulent earnest. They threw into the struggle their whole wealth of gross epithets, and neither of them was poor in the commodity. It is hardly worth while to quote any of this curious amusement. Dunbar found better subjects for his humorous derision in Andro Kennedy and the Abbot of Tungland. Mr Andro seems to have been a graceless and inveterate winebibber, and Dunbar writes a testament for him in lines of four accents, alternated with the formularies of a will and shreds of the breviary in Latin. The old sinner is made to leave his soul to his lord's wine-cellar, and his body to a brewer's dunghill. He will have no decorous funeral, but a rout of his own boon companions, drinking and weeping, as he had been wont to do, and preceded by two rustics with a barrel slung on a pole. No anthem is to be chanted over his grave, no bell to be rung, but he must be buried to a "spring" on the bagpipes: and instead of a

---

[1] Croak.　　　　　[2] Deafened.

cross by his side, he must have four flagons of sack to frighten away the fiends.[1]

On the poor Abbot of Tungland, Dunbar is still more severe. The Abbot was one Damian, a naturalised French physician, a bold, boastful, ingenious fellow, who undertook to transmute metals into gold, and to fly in the air, and who succeeded in keeping the king's favour and getting Church preferment before Dunbar in spite of all his failures. The poet's device is to make him figure in wonderfully ludicrous dreams. In one vision he appears hand in hand with a person in the habit of St Francis, who turns out to be the Devil, and vanishes "with stink and fiery smoke." In another, in ridicule of his attempt to fly, he is represented as soaring into the air "as ane horrible griffoun," meeting with a she-dragon in the clouds, and begetting the Antichrist. But he is assailed most openly and licentiously of all in the "Feigned Friar of Tungland": he there mounts into the air, much to the astonishment and speculation of the regular winged denizens, and as a strange new bird becomes a mark for most ludicrous and coarse indignities.

When we read Dunbar's "Twa Married Women and the Widow," and his burlesque "Jousts between the Tailor and the Shoemaker," we become less and less surprised that the poet never rose to the dignity of the mitre. Humour nowhere runs riot in madder intoxication than in his pages. His appetite for mirth is unbounded— Brobdingnagian. He turns the world topsy-turvy: seizes on the most venerable and dreadful things, and dances them about on the top of their head. He subjects his rivals to imaginary indignities with all the freedom and zest of Aristophanes : he burlesques the services of the Church ; and as a crowning variation of the sober march of ordinary life, visits hell, that he may revel with Satan and his imps in their glee over the tortures of the damned.

### 4. GAWAIN DOUGLAS[2] (1475-1522).

The Court of James IV. was, in many respects, a Scottish repetition of the Court of Edward III. James lived in more splendid

---

[1] " I will no Priestës for me sing
 *Dies illa, dies iræ ;*
Nor yet no bellës for me ring
 *Sicut semper solet fieri :*
But a bagpipe to play a spring,
 *Et unum* ale wisp *ante me :*
Instead of banners for to bring
 *Quatuor lagenas cervisæ :*
Within the grave to set such thing
 *In modum crucis juxta me,*
To fley the fiends, then huirdly sing
 *De terra palmasti me.*"

[2] The works of Douglas have recently been edited, and new light thrown upon his life by Mr John Small. See also Dr Ross's ' Early Scottish Literature.'

state than any of his predecessors: with more of chivalrous pageantry and sport, and with a definite ambition to imbue his Court with the highest ideals of chivalry. James I. would have done the same, but the materials were too stubborn for him : three generations of civilising influences had made them more tractable, and his great-grandson had more success. There were many poets besides Dunbar at James IV.'s Court, but none of them men of any mark, except Gawain Douglas, third son of the great Earl of Angus, Archibald "Bell-the-Cat." This third son was educated for the Church, and family influence soon procured for him more than one of the benefices for one of which Dunbar pleaded with such humorous importunity. The learned leisure of the young "pluralist" was spent in writing poetry. He produced an elaborate scholarly allegory, "The Palace of Honour," in 1501, and another, much less stiff, much more full of life, some time later, "King Hart." But his most memorable work was a translation of Virgil's Æneid into heroic couplets, begun in January 1512, and finished two months before the battle of Flodden. In the troubles that followed this calamity, Douglas lost both his livings and his character. The house of Douglas seemed at first likely to gain the highest honours, nearest to which it had long stood. The Earl of Angus married the widowed Queen Margaret eleven months after her husband's death. But the prosperity was short-lived. Gawain's share in it, the bishopric of Dunkeld, was not entered upon without a struggle, and was held but for a short time. He died in England in 1522, a dishonoured exile, a political intriguer burdened with the unpardonable sin of failure. The most charitable construction of his conduct is that he was dragged by family connections into a stormy strife for which he was utterly unfitted by his scholarly habits.

Each of the Books of the Æneid, as well as the Thirteenth Book added by Maffeus, is furnished by the translator with a prologue: and it is generally agreed that these prologues are the most favourable specimens of his ability. Most of them are disquisitions of a religious and moral nature, as became his reverend character; but those prefixed to the Seventh, the Twelfth, and the Thirteenth Books, describe the season of the year in which they were begun—a winter day, a May morning, and a June sunset. These scenical studies are remarkable for magnificent opulence of detail, and strength of colour. In the prologue to the Twelfth Book in particular, he seems to have braced himself for a final effort, and resolved to gather together every personification of the phenomena of morning, every appearance of sky, cloud, earth, and water, every attitude of every herb, flower, bird, beast, and insect. Nothing is left in a state of suggestion for the reader to fill up : the particulars of the richly coloured landscape are tumbled out before us with unreserved profusion. It is difficult to convey an idea of the tedious diffuseness of this description without quoting the whole : but the following few of the two hundred and seventy lines are as much as we have room for :—

> " And blissful blossoms in the bloomed yard[1]
> Submits their heads in the young son's safeguard:
> Ive leavëes rank o'erspread the barmkin[2] wall ;
> The bloomed hawthorn clad his pikës all ;
> Forth of fresh burgeons[3] the wine grapës ying
> Along the trellis did on twistës hing ;
> The locked buttons on the gemmed trees,
> O'erspreading leaves of nature's tapestries ;
> Soft grassy verdure after balmy showers
> On curling stalkës smiling to their flowers ;
> Beholding them so many diverse hue,
> Some pers,[4] some pale, some burnet,[5] and some blue,
> Some grey, some gules, some purple, some sanguare,
> Blanched, or brown, sauch[6] yellow many are,
> Some heavenly coloured in celestial gre,[7]
> Some watery-hued as the haw[8] wally[9] sea,
> And some depart in freckles red and white,
> Some bright as gold with aureate leavës lite.
> The daisy did unbroad her crownal small,
> And every flower unlapped[10] in the dale
> In battled grass burgeons, the banewort wild,
> The clover, catchook, and the camomile ;
> The flour de lys "—

But we need not proceed with the catalogue, nor transcribe the ten or twelve lines that labour to express the fragrance of the scene. The reader must imagine the effect of two hundred and seventy lines on the same scale of minute description. The voluble poet had no notion of artistic restraint : he poured out his stores of synonym and circumstance with immoderate prodigality. When we open his Virgil, the first dozen lines of the Preface astound us with a torrent of eulogistic epithets addressed to the great master: and this first impression of overpowering volubility is often repeated in the course of perusal. He apologises for not being able to render the sententious Virgil word for word—

> " Some time the text mun have an exposition,
> Some time the colour will cause a little addition,
> And some time of one word I mun make three "—

And remarkable though the undertaking was, and meritorious the execution, one cannot help smiling at the translator's notions of unfolding the effect of his compressed original. He felt uneasy

[1] Garden.     [2] Rampart.     [3] Sprigs.
[4] A grey colour.     [5] Dark brown.     [6] Willow.
[7] Degree.     [8] Adjective of colour.     [9] Wavy.
[10] Unfolded.

at the thought of leaving a condensed expression to make itself understood.

These diffuse descriptions give a good opportunity for comparing the diction of the poet with contemporary English. It is peculiarly instructive to compare his description of Winter with the opening of Sackville's "Induction" in the 'Mirror for Magistrates.'[1] Three points of difference are disclosed: he is fond of taking, direct from French, words never received into English; he makes considerable coinages from Latin; and his names for familiar things are in many cases peculiar to Scotch and northern English. These differences are more marked in Douglas than in Dunbar, not so much, I believe, because Douglas was an extensive innovator as because he was so immoderately copious. They would probably have used the same names for the same things or ideas; but Douglas ranged over a much greater variety of particulars, and thus exposed his vocabulary to view at a much greater number of points. There was, however, undoubtedly a tendency among Scotch writers of that and the following generation to introduce new vocables from French and Latin.

### 5. SIR DAVID LINDSAY (1490-1557).

Though Lindsay's poetry takes us down to the middle of the sixteenth century, his most fitting place is among the poets of the present chapter. He was formed almost exclusively by their influences. While his English contemporaries, Wyat and Surrey, received their main impulse from Italy, his acknowledged masters were Chaucer, Gower, Lydgate, Henryson, Dunbar, and Douglas. We should, however, be misleading were we to call him an imitator of Chaucer. He used poetical forms chiefly for political and social purposes; and this being the chief motive of his productions, he did not go far afield for models, but accommodated to his own spirit such shapes as were fashionable around him in the Scottish Court. He had not enough disinterested enthusiasm for poetry to read the Italians, or the revived Greek and Roman classics. There is no allusion to Dante or Petrarch in his works, and only a second-hand allusion to Boccaccio; while of Greek and Latin classics, he selects for special mention "the ornate Ennius," and Hesiod—"of Greece the perfect poet sovereign." I should doubt whether he was very familiar even with Chaucer: Lydgate and his own Scotch predecessors would seem to have been his principal reading. But it is difficult to trace obligations in works

[1] Both these descriptions of winter are intended to harmonise with visits to the infernal regions: Douglas has been there, and Sackville is going. They proceed upon Henryson's maxim—

> " Ane doleful season to ane careful dyte
> Should correspond and be equivalent."

that sacrifice poetical graces to practical aims. Lindsay did not cultivate poetry for its own reward. His poems were very famous among his countrymen; but they were admired not so much for their poetical charms as for their powerful help to the good cause of the Reformation.

Sir David Lindsay of the Mount (his family seat in Fifeshire) was a great power in the Court of James V. He had been appointed gentleman-usher to that prince in 1512, after a course of study at St Andrews and a visit to Italy, and he never lost the favour that he established with his youthful charge. He was knighted and made Lion King of Arms in 1530, was employed as an ambassador, and represented the burgh of Cupar in four successive Parliaments from 1543 to 1546. But, above all, he was allowed the utmost freedom of pen; and was tolerated in trenchant abuse and biting satire of the Church, as well as in very frank advice to the King himself. Most of his poems,—the "Dream" (1528); the "Testament of the Papingo" (1530); "A Satire of the Three Estates" (1535); the "Complaint of the King's Auld Hound Bagsche" (1536); "Kitty's Confession" (1549),—make a free distribution of blows, cuts, and stings among ecclesiastics and courtiers.

The parts of royal favourite and Church reformer have not much natural affinity: it must be rare to find the two combined in one person. Lindsay had a good many humanities in him that one does not expect to find in the active antagonist of an established faith. He was an eminently genial man. When we read how he nursed and amused his young master, we do not wonder that he was beloved and favoured in return. In the epistle to his "Dream," he reminds the King as follows :—

> " When thou was young I bore ye in mine arm
> Full tenderly, till thou begouth to gang ; [1]
> And in thy bed oft happit [2] thee full warm,
> With lute in hand, syne sweetly to thee sang :
> Sometime, in dancing, feiraly [3] I flang ;
> And, sometime, playand farces on the floor ;
> And, sometime, on mine office takand cure :
>
> And, sometime, like a fiend transfigurate ;
> And, sometime, like the grisly ghost of Guy ; [4]
> In divers forms, oft times, disfigurate ;
> And, sometime, disguised full pleasantly."

Most undignified relaxation for a Church reformer. The reminiscences of the "Complaint" bring up other particulars of this romping and affectionate relationship ; disclosing the young prince astride the gentleman-usher's neck, or borne on his back like a chapman's pack, or urging with imperfect articulation—"pa, da

---

[1] Began to walk.　　[2] Covered.　　[3] Wonderfully.　　[4] Guy of Warwick.

lyn," Play, David Lindsay, upon the lute. There were also many tales told of Hector, Arthur, Alexander, Cæsar, Jason, Troilus, sieges of Tyre, Thebes, and Troy, prophecies of Merlin, Bede, and Thomas the Rhymer. Lindsay was evidently no narrow Puritan in his notions of training young royalty. He has left also among his works one unmistakable evidence of the breadth of his sympathies—his "History of a noble and valiant squire, William Meldrum," written, not in his green youth, when feats of arms and amorous adventures are most likely to captivate, but in 1550, when he had reached the mature age of sixty. It certainly is remarkable that the historian of Squire Meldrum should have been with Knox at St Andrews in 1547, acting as one of the Reformer's most urgent supporters; and should have written the grave morality of the "Monarchy" in 1553. The great body of his verses, however, bore on practical life. While the kindly exuberance of spirits that made him so delightful a playmate for the infant prince gave vivacity and verve to all his compositions, and spread their popularity far and wide, the substance of them was moral and political; amusement was not their end and aim, but a means to secure goodwill for the underlying doctrines. The siege of the Papingo's (parrot's) deathbed by her kind friends the Magpie, the Raven, and the Kite, was amusing enough; but the fact that the Magpie represented a "canon regular," the Raven a black monk, and the Kite a holy friar, excited a much keener interest than if the fable had symbolised nothing but the greed of legacy-hunters in general. The "Satire of the Three Estates," though inclined to be tedious from its inordinate length, was very entertaining as a morality-play; but it must have owed its main attractions to its bearings on what was in immediate agitation throughout the kingdom. And, to take his attempt at a "tragedy"—in Lydgate's sense and not in Marlowe's—the fall of Cardinal Beaton was impressive merely as an illustration of the caprice of Fortune; but Lindsay would not have undertaken to make a poem on the subject, had he not been desirous to impress his countrymen with the crimes that led to the Cardinal's overthrow.

One might select from the ornamental fringes to Lindsay's satirical verse occasional passages of genuine poetical enthusiasm, in which he has suspended and forgotten his didactic, and done his best to express the situation. His "Dream" is the earliest and most poetical of his works; in it his satirical aims were considerably abashed and qualified by emulation of his models, and it contains passages that will bear comparison with anything in his Scotch predecessors. Take, for instance, part of his description of Winter in the prologue. It is fit and proper that the strength of both Douglas and Lindsay, these last survivors of the Chaucerian school, should lie in the description of winter. Douglas wrote

nothing superior to his prologue to the Seventh Book of his translation, and Lindsay wrote nothing superior to the following.   He has
walked out well wrapt up in cloak and hood, with "double shoen"
on his feet, and "mittens" on his hands :—

> " I met Dame Flora, in dule [1] weed disguised,
> Whilk into May was dulce and delectable ;
> With stalwart storms her sweetness was surprised ;
> Her heavenly hues were turned into sable,
> Whilk umwhile were to lovers amiable.
> Fled from the frost the tender flowers I saw,
> Under Dame Nature's mantle lurking law. [2]
>
> The small fowlës in flockës saw I flee,
> To Nature, making (great) lamentation :
> They lighted down beside me, on a tree ;
> Of their complaint I had compassion ;
> And with a piteous exclamation,
> They said—Blessed be Summer with his flowers,
> And waryed [3] be thou, Winter, with thy showers.
>
> Alas, Aurora ! the silly lark gan cry,
> Where hast thou left thy balmy liquor sweet,
> That us rejoiced, we mounting in the sky ?
> Thy silver drops are turned into sleet.
> O fair Phoebus, where is thy wholesome heat ?
> Why tholës [4] thou thy heavenly pleasant face
> With misty vapours to be obscured, alace !
>
> Where art thou, May, with June, thy sister sheen,
> Well bordered with daisies of delight ?
> And gentle July, with thy mantle green,
> Enamelled with roses red and white ?
> Now old and cold Januar, in despite,
> Reavës from us all pastime and pleasure.
> Alas ! what gentle heart may this endure ?
>
> O'ersoilëd are with cloudës odious
> The golden skyës of the orient,
> Changing in sorrow our song melodious,
> Whilk we had wont to sing with good intent,
> Resounding to the heavenës firmament ;
> But now our day is changed into night.
> With that they rose and flew out of my sight."

In the course of his dream, Lindsay is conducted by Remembrance
—not so very appropriate a personification in this case—to hell,
but his description of it is entirely subordinate to satirical purposes, and contains about as little grandeur as could possibly be
thrown into any verses on the situation.   He proceeds at once
to the popes, emperors, cardinals, prelates, priors, abbots, friars,

---

[1] Doleful.          [2] Low.          [3] Cursed.          [4] Endurest.

monks, clerks, priests, and "bings" or heaps of all sorts of church-men, and specifies the causes of their perdition with an eye to personages still in the land of the living. Lindsay probably took the idea of this visit to the nether regions from Douglas's translation of the Æneid.

### 6. NORTH-COUNTRY BALLAD-MAKERS.

The border-land between England and Scotland was the scene of many tragedies—of daring exploits, violent outrages, fierce acts of vengeance; and the feuds, loves, and humours of the robust Borderers, if they found no great poet to commemorate them, found many sympathetic minstrels whose simple and often powerful verses were committed by oral recitation to the memories of the common folk. It was not till the middle of last century that any attempt was made to collect and print these popular treasures, and consequently we cannot be sure that we have any pieces as old as the fourteenth or even the fifteenth century in their original form. They must have been more or less modernised, if not otherwise altered, as they passed from minstrel to minstrel, and from one generation of reciters to another. Still, there is reason to believe that there were current in the North Country during those centuries, ballads upon most of the themes in our extant ballad-literature: Border battles such as Chevy Chase and Otterburne; freebooting raids by such heroes as Kinmont Willie and William of Cloudesly; outrages such as that committed by Edom of Gordon; tragical jealousy, love between the children of enemies, love between high and low, stepmother cruelty, deadly mistakes, such as we find in the ballads of Young Waters, Helen of Kirkconnell, Clerk Saunders, the Child of Elle, Annie of Lochroyan, Gil Morice, and many others; the mysterious dealings of fairies with such heroes as Tamlane and True Thomas. In short, there circulated in that wild border-land in the ballad form, and steeped in a superstitious atmosphere of thrilling omens and apparitions, such tales as afterwards formed the material of English tragedy and the romantic drama. And yet two curious things are to be remarked: that the North Country never produced a great dramatist; and that no great English drama, with the exception, perhaps, of Macbeth, was based upon the incidents commemorated in these ballads.

# CHAPTER III.

## RENAISSANCE AND TRANSITION.

MOST of the poets discussed in this chapter received their main impulse from Italy.  We have seen how the impulse given by Chaucer directly and through his immediate disciples gradually died away, sinking into the inane repetitions of Hawes, or awakening the more individual energies of Skelton or Lindsay, who paid only a formal allegiance to the ruling powers, and substantially followed their own personal will: and we have now to deal with a more varied literature, which was largely influenced by the study of Italian.  Not that Italian influences only were operative on the writers embraced in this chapter, but these were the main influences.  Nor did our poets follow at the heels of Italian masters with slavish imitation: still, they received from Italian masters their most potent stimulus.  Wyat, Surrey, Sackville, Gascoigne, and even Spenser, while preserving their individual and national characteristics, formed themselves upon Italian models much more than upon any previous productions of the English imagination.

Tottel's Miscellany, published in 1557, but containing the poetical efforts of the preceding quarter of a century, marks an epoch in English poetry.  A collection of songs and sonnets by the courtiers of Henry VIII., it is a fit spring prelude to the great Elizabethan season: of somewhat uncertain glory like April itself, struggling out with its sunshine and bird-singing through clouds and rain, yet on the whole victorious in hiding the rotten wrecks of winter with fresh vegetation.  It was a hopeful thing for those days that the enthusiasm of poetry had seized upon the Court: before this time, though several noblemen had extended their patronage to poets, no person of rank in England had endeavoured to sing for himself. The new "courtly makers," as Puttenham calls them, of whom the two chiefs were Sir Thomas Wyat and Henry Earl of Surrey, had "travelled into Italy, and there tasted the sweet and stately measures and style of the Italian poesy," and came home filled with the zeal of "novices newly crept out of the schools of Dante, Ariosto, and Petrarch." Love was the natural theme of these ardent disciples of the gay science; and Petrarch was their model. Tottel's Miscellany is our first collection of love-lyrics : and after the droning narratives and worn-out rhymes of Lydgate and Hawes, the "depured streams," "golden beams," and "fiery leams," these eloquent and freshly worded complaints of the malice and treachery of Cupid are a blessed relief.

It is not hard to discern general causes that must have favoured this brilliant efflorescence of English genius. The case of James I. of Scotland shows that a century before the time of Henry VIII., the royal families at least received some sort of literary education. But if we may trust the statement of Erasmus, it was not till the end of the fifteenth century and the beginning of the sixteenth that the English nobility began to be solicitous about the education of their children, and to engage as tutors the most eminent scholars that were to be procured. We may therefore suppose that about the middle of the reign of Henry VIII., our "young barbarians" began to revel in the spirit of newly-acquired freedom from ignorance, and like the French after the Revolution, thirsted for an outlet to their energy. Their king had been educated under Skelton, a poet, however eccentric, and had imbibed among his many accomplishments a love for the generous arts. The cultivation of poetry at the Court of Scotland might have shamed them into exertion; but abroad they had in the brilliant Court of Lorenzo de Medici the traditions of a nobler example to excite their emulation. The interest of literary Europe had for some time centred in Italy. The tutors of the young English nobility had gone there to study the ancient classics under masters whose patient enthusiasm had gained the key to those treasures; and coming home brimful of the Italian scenery and the Italian manners, as well as the wonderful old learning, had created among their pupils a universal desire to travel into this Land of Promise, and see its marvels with their own eyes. And there the youthful travellers found and brought to England with them a treasure more valuable even than had been imported by their sage instructors : they found a new literature, palpitating with fresh life, and they were fired with ambition to emulate its beauties in their own tongue. This secondary and accidental result of the revival of learning was of more value to our literature than the primary movement itself : the most profound and wide-reaching impulses come from living sources.

Why poetry at the Court of Henry took the form of songs and sonnets is a more perplexing question. Petrarch was probably known to Chaucer and to Lydgate; but they were not moved by his example. I can venture on no deeper explanation than that

Petrarch suited the taste of Wyat and Surrey as Boccaccio suited the taste of Chaucer and Lydgate. One might speculate at length and plausibly on the why and the wherefore, but with little satisfaction to one's self and probably less to one's readers. Among the poets included in this chapter most of the great Italians found congenial disciples : Sackville studied Dante ; Gascoigne translated from the plays of Ariosto and the prose tales of Bandello ; and Spenser owed considerable obligations to the romantic epics of Ariosto and Tasso. I do not see that you can account for the choice of master except by supposing a natural affinity in the individual pupil.

## I.—SIR THOMAS WYAT (1503-1541).

The names of Surrey and Wyat are usually placed together as two great reformers of English verse, and often in such a way as to convey the impression that Wyat was the humble friend and imitator of Surrey. A close attention to dates and other circumstances leads us to reverse this position of the "chieftains." Whoever was the first of Henry's "courtly makers," it seems tolerably clear that Wyat was the poetical father and not the pupil of Surrey. Wyat was born in 1503. He was admitted to St John's College, Cambridge, in 1515, the year before the supposed date of Surrey's birth. In 1525, when Surrey was nine years old, and was living at Kenninghall under the care of a tutor, Wyat took a leading part in a great feat of arms at Greenwich, and was a favourite of Henry on account of his wit. There is a tradition that shortly afterwards he went to travel in Italy ; but this fact does not rest on contemporary authority. In 1537 he was sent as ambassador to the Court of Charles V. in Spain— Surrey's age at this time being twenty-one. Seeing that from 1537 till his premature death in 1541, Wyat was with short intervals closely occupied in public business, we may reasonably presume that most of his poetry was written before 1537 ; we may at least be certain that he had studied French, Italian, and Spanish, and had begun the practice of poetry, before that date. If we suppose Surrey to have been the prime mover of Wyat's literary activity, we must suppose that accomplished young nobleman's influence on his senior to have begun at a very early age, and to have worked its perfect work before he was one-and-twenty. The thing is not perhaps impossible ; but it is much more likely that the influence proceeded the other way. In proof thereof, we may notice that Surrey addresses Wyat with the reverence of a pupil, thus—

> " But I that knew what harboured in that head,
> What virtues rare were tempered in that breast,

> Honour tho place that such a jewel bred,
> And kiss the ground whereas thy corse doth rest.
>
> .    .    .    .    .    .
>
> A head where wisdom mysterics did frame;
> Whose hammers beat still in that lively brain,
> As on a stithe : where that some work of fame
> Was daily wrought, to turn to Britain's gain.
>
> .    .    .    .    .    .
>
> A hand that taught what might be said in rhyme :
> That reft Chaucer the glory of his wit."

In another of Surrey's sonnets, entitled "A Praise of Sir Thomas Wyat the elder, for his excellent learning," Wyat is compared to the deified heroes who introduced arts "in the rude age when knowledge was not rife;" and putting together the praises bestowed on him by Surrey and others, the dates of his life, and the known character of the man, we need have little doubt that Wyat was the first of Henry's courtly makers, and the initiator of the new movement in English poetry. Surrey's brilliant character, romantic life, and untimely fate, must not be allowed to rob his humbler friend of due honour.[1] Wyatt had more natural affinity with certain parts of the Southern character. His outward features, his "visage stern but mild,"—dark complexion, long grave face, and retreating forehead,—do not belong to a common English type. He was probably selected as ambassador to the Spanish Court because his manners were suited to the position. His poems abound in non-English characteristics; grave dignity and sweetness, delicate irony, temperate gaiety, absence of incontinent excitement under the influence of strong feeling. This greater natural affinity with his models, is the cause both of his being and of his appearing less original than Surrey, at the same time that it fitted him to lead the way in appropriating a vein of love-poetry new to English verse.

There is perhaps no better way of bringing out the self-

---

[1] Dr Nott's account of the relations between Wyat and Surrey is exceedingly hazy and inconsistent. He supposes Wyat to have adopted the iambic (that is, the fall of the accent regularly on every second syllable) from Surrey; yet he also supposes certain poems in this metre to have been addressed to Anne Boleyn, and to have been writtten before 1530, when Surrey was only thirteen years old. He contends that Wyat's versification became smoother after he was in contact with Surrey, and that they translated certain sonnets together as it were for practice : yet one of those sonnets (which we shall presently quote) is perhaps the most irregular of all that Wyat wrote. Mr Guest also, usually an indisputable authority, is here found inadvertent. He makes Surrey the great leader in introducing new forms, ascribing to him the first use of the banded three-line stave, of *ottava rima*, and of the sonnet. Yet Surrey never used *ottava rima* at all : and in another place, Mr Guest assigns a stave of one of Wyat's odes to the year 1520, at which time Surrey was only four years old. The prime cause of all these mistakes about the relations of the two poets is the fact of Surrey's name appearing first on the title-page of Tottel's collection, which was probably out of compliment to his rank.

controlled gravity of Wyat's spirit than comparing him with the
more excitable and demonstrative Surrey in their translations of
the same sonnet.   They will illustrate at the same time another
thing, and that is how thoroughly translators colour originals with
their own feelings.   The run of the thoughts being the same, we
might easily overlook this; but after a minute study and patient
realisation of the effect of every epithet, the lines, which remain
dead to the casual reader, come to life and assert their individuality
and difference of origin.   Take the two in succession :—

### WYAT.

" The long love that in my thought I harbour,
 And in my heart doth keep his residence,
 Into my face presseth with bold pretence,
And there campeth, displaying his banner.
She that me learns to love and to suffer,
 And wills that my trust, and lust's negligence
 Be reined by reason, shame, and reverence,
With his hardiness takes displeasure.
Wherewith Love to the heart's forest he fleeth,
 Leaving his enterprise with pain and cry,
And there him hideth and not appeareth.
What may I do when my master feareth,
 But in the field with him to live and die ?
 For good is the life ending faithfully."

### SURREY.

" Love that liveth and reigneth in my thought,
 That built his seat within my captive breast,
Clad in the arms wherein with me he fought,
 Oft in my face he doth his banner rest.
She that me taught to love and suffer pain,
 My doubtful hope and eke my hot desire
With shamefast cloak to shadow and refrain,
 Her smiling face converteth straight to ire.
And coward Love then to the heart apace
 Taketh his flight, whereas he lurks and plains
His purpose lost, and dare not show his face.
 For my lord's guilt thus faultless bide I pains.
Yet from my lord shall not my foot remove ;
Sweet is his death that takes his end by love."

Now compare the two versions as regards their predominant spirit.
The master of Wyat's heart has long held dominion there, but
fears to encounter the all-conquering lady : at last he musters
confidence, presses boldly forward into the face "and there campeth,
displaying his banner."   A long period of quiescence is suddenly
broken by a grand imposing movement.   Surrey's tyrant is more
energetic ; he strikes us as a more stirring blustering fellow ; he
reigns actively, he has built a seat, he has the insignia of power
about him ; and as soon as he has conquered the heart, he *often*

sallies out and makes a show against the dreaded enemy. Whereas
Wyat's master is normally reserved and self-contained, and rouses
himself to one grand effort, Surrey's master is restlessly active.
When Wyat's master does resolve to move, he fortifies himself
in a camp, and unfolds his colours firmly; Surrey's master seems
to be always fiddling in and out with his banner. When we
study their behaviour after the lady's angry look has put them to
flight, we find the same contrast. Compare the three following
lines in Surrey's sonnet with the corresponding three in Wyat's—

> "And coward Love then to the heart apace
> Taketh his flight, whereas he lurks and plains
> His purpose lost, and dare not show his face."

Wyat's Love, when resolution fails him, retreats with inarticulate
cry, and hides himself as it were in a forest: Surrey's Love, with
the epithet "coward" on his back, lurks about bemoaning his
failure. It is a small but important element in the effect that in
the one sonnet Love's brief challenge in the face is an "enterprise,"
undertaken after long misgiving, and abandoned with inarticulate
despair: while in the other it is simply a "purpose," often entered
upon, and often departed from with demonstrative timidity.

Wyat's poems are full of melancholy, dispersed sometimes by a
firmer and more confident mood, but frequently deepening into
bitterness. The poet has suffered much at the hands of Cupid—
"his old dear enemy, his froward master." His youth has been
shamefully abused by falsehood. He has been made a filing
instrument to sharpen the advances of another. His mistress has
been taken from him by a wealthier rival. If this, however, was
his only passion,[1] he must have suffered a great deal before it
came to this end. Sometimes armed sighs stopped his way when
he had resolved to pray to her for comfort; sometimes his
traitorous tongue betrayed him at a critical moment, and refused
to proceed with his suit. He was constrained to cry for death or
mercy. His bed was wet with his tears; the snows could not
redress his heat, and the sun could not abate his cold. He com
pares his love to the Alps—

> "Like unto these immeasurable mountains
> So is my painful life the burden of ire:
> For high be they and high is my desire:
> And I of tears and they be full of fountains."

----

[1] He complains that May was a peculiarly unhappy month to him: and seeing
that Anne Boleyn was executed in May, and was certainly taken possession of
by a more powerful man than Wyat, Dr Nott conjectures that she was the
mistress of our poet's heart. We English take things so seriously that we cannot suppose Wyat's mistress to have been imaginary, or to have given him no
just ground for his many complaints of her cruelty.

He calls on woods, hills, and vales, to resound his plaints: he finds a voice for his anguish in the huge oaks that roar in the wind. His very life threatens to give way, if he receive no comfort—

> "So feeble is the thread, that doth the burden stay,
>  Of my poor life, in heavy plight that falleth in decay:
>  That but it have elsewhere some aid or some succours,
>  The running spindle of my fate anon shall end his course."

By-and-by, in the depth of his agonies, he shows some resentment against his unkind mistress—

> "What rage is this? what furor? of what kind?
>  What power, what plague, doth weary thus my mind?
>  Within my bones to rankle is assigned
>  What poison pleasant sweet?
>
>  Lo, see, mine eyes flow with continual tears:
>  The body still away sleepless it wears:
>  My food nothing my fainting strength repairs,
>  Nor doth my limbs sustain.
>
>  In deep wide wound, the deadly stroke doth turn,
>  To cureless scar that never shall return.
>  Go to: triumph: rejoice thy goodly turn:
>  Thy friend thou dost oppress.
>
>  Oppress thou dost, and hast of him no cure:
>  Nor yet my plaint no pity can procure:
>  Fierce tiger, fell, hard rock without recure,
>  Cruel rebel to Love,
>
>  Once may thou love, never be loved again:
>  So love thou still and not thy love obtain:
>  So wrathful love with spites of just disdain,
>  May fret thy cruel heart."

This resentful mood gains strength; he begins to curse the time when he first fell in love—

> "When first mine eyes did view and mark,
>  Thy fair beauty for to behold;
>  And when mine ears listened to hark
>  The pleasant words that thou me told:
>    I would as then I had been free
>    From ears to hear and eyes to see."

He complains sadly that he has been deceived and forsaken: "they flee from me that sometime did me seek." He reminds himself bitterly of better days; tortures himself with rapturous memories of her visits to him in his chamber. Then he makes an effort, and addresses her with resolution to know the worst—

> " Madame, withouten many words,
> Once am I sure you will or no ?
> And if you will, then leave your bords,
> And use your wit and show it so ;
> For with a beck you shall me call.
> And if of one that burns alway,
> Ye have pity or ruth at all,
> Answer him fair with yea or nay.
> If it be yea, I shall be fain :
> If it be nay, friends as before.
> You shall another man obtain
> And I mine own and yours no more."

And finally he summons up courage to take leave of her for ever : but his courageous resolution to part friends breaks down, proves to have been a self-delusion ; he cannot part from her with equanimity—

> " My lute, awake ! perform the last
> Labour that thou and I shall waste,
>   And end that I have now beguu.
> And when this song is sung and past
>   My lute, be still, for I have done.
>
>   .    .    .    .    .    .
>
> Proud of the spoil that thou hast got,
> Of simple hearts through Lovës shot,
>   By whom unkind thou hast them won ;
> Think not he hath his bow forgot
>   Although my lute and I have done.
>
> Vengeance shall fall on thy disdain,
> That makest but game on earnest pain.
>   Think not alone under the sun
> Unquit to cause thy lovers plain,
>   Although my lute and I have done.
>
> May chance thee lie wither'd and old,
> In winter nights that are so cold,
>   Plaining in vain unto the moon :
> Thy wishes then dare not be told.
>   Care then who list, for I have done." [1]

The gravity and dignity, the tones of mournful and bitter sweetness in Wyat's verse, are not a mere cultivated imitation of Italian models : they flow from a deep - seated constitutional sadness. Henry's favourite wit would not seem to have been a happy man. One of his sonnets is a defence of himself from a charge of variability or moodiness. He is familiar with the concealment of the mind by colour contrary of feigned visage.

---

[1] This may have suggested Tennyson's " Lady Clara Vere de Vere," which differs considerably in tone, from its accusing the lady of presuming on her rank, and its recommendation of charitable works as nobler employment than flirtation.

Despondency is often his companion : he turns to his dumb
dependants and fondles them with bitter reflection on the faith-
lessness of his human friends.

> " Lux, my fair falcon, and thy fellows all,
>     How well pleasant it were your liberty !
> Ye not forsake me, that fair mote you fall.
>     But they that sometime liked my company,
> Like lice away from dead bodies they crawl.
>     Lo ! what a proof in light adversity !
> But ye, my birds, I swear by all your bells,
> Ye be my friends, and so be but few else."

Active cynicism—cynicism no longer mournful, but kindled into
delight by its own exercise—is seen in Wyat's satires, written
in imitation of Horace.    There are three of them, all in the *terza
rima* or banded three-line stave : their titles are, " Of the mean
and sure Estate, written to John Poins," "Of the Courtier's Life,
written to John Poins," and " How to use the Court and himself
therein, written to Sir Francis Bryan."    These are our first
English imitations of Horace ; and if Horace is taken as the
standard of satire, Wyat has the best claim to the position of
first English satirist, which is sometimes assigned to later satirists,
Lodge, Donne, or Hall.

Although Wyat preceded Surrey, and should not be robbed of
the honour of that position, it is not to be pretended that he had
Surrey's ease and accuracy of expression.    He has indeed occasional felicities of higher and more delicate charm than anything
to be found in Surrey ; single lines and parts of lines whose words
have fallen together with the perfection of instinct.    But he is in
general awkward and embarrassed in his management of the complicated staves which he had the courage to attempt.    His rhymes
are exceedingly faulty, falling often upon unaccented inflectional
terminations such as *eth*, *ed*, and *ing*, thus—

> " I fare as one escaped that fleeth,
> Glad he is gone, and yet still feareth
> Spied to be caught, and so dreadeth
> That he for nought his pain loseth."

He makes *other* rhyme with *higher* and *her ; maister* with *nature ;
accited* with *tryed* and *presented.*  In some of his pieces nearly
one-fourth of the rhymes are of this nature.    His metre, also, is
questionable.    He employs words with their foreign accents, and,
generally, seems to study only to have the proper number of
accents.    This is the most charitable supposition : it might be
contended that he simply counts syllables and arbitrarily puts an
accent upon every second syllable without regard to its acknow-

ledged accent.  And with all these licences he has some difficulty
in filling up the measure of his stanzas.  It is, however, only in
his sonnets, and his compositions in *terza rima* and *ottava rima*,
that these defects appear.  His songs are no less flowing than
Surrey's, and to the full as musical.  In them he moves like a
runner escaped from a thicket into the open plain.  He "sends
his complaints and tears to sue for grace" with genuine lyric
rapture—

> " Pass forth my wonted cries
>     Those cruel ears to pierce,
> Which in most hateful wise
>     Do still my plaints reverse.
> Do you, my tears, also
>     So wet her barren heart,
> That pity there may grow
>     And cruelty depart."

## II.—Henry Howard, Earl of Surrey (1516-1547).

The editor of Tottel's Miscellany speaks of "the honourable
style of the noble Earl of Surrey, and the weightiness of the
deep-witted Sir Thomas Wyat the elder's verse."  There is some
discrimination in the epithets.  Surrey has not the deep and subtle
feelings of Wyat; but he has a captivating sweetness, a direct
eloquence, a generous impetuosity, that make him a much more
universal favourite.

Warton dwells at some length on Surrey's life as throwing light
upon the character and subjects of his poetry.  The prevailing
errors in Surrey's biography may have had something to do with
the misconception of his position in literature.  If he had, as was at
one time the accepted belief, been engaged in the battle of Flodden
(three years before he was born), he might well have taken prece-
dence of Wyatt.  Warton does not fall into this mistake: but he
affirms that Surrey was educated at Windsor with Henry's natural
son, the Duke of Richmond; and repeats the fiction of Thomas
Nash that Surrey made the tour of Europe as a knight-errant,
upholding against all comers the superiority of his mistress
Geraldine.  The facts are these.  From his birth till 1524, Henry
Howard lived in his father's house—in the summer time at
Tendring Hall, Suffolk, in the winter time at Hunsdon, in Hertfordshire : he is not known to have been the companion of the
youthful Duke of Richmond till their education (in the limited
meaning of the word) was completed.  Surrey's boyhood was
probably passed·at Kenninghall, under the care of a tutor : the
pleasures that he recounts as passed in Windsor with a king's
son in his childish years were probably not enjoyed till 1534, by
which time both had been at Cambridge, had taken part in royal

pageants, and had been married, or at least affianced, to noble
ladies.   His itinerant championship of Geraldine is purely fabulous.   The lady is conjectured to have been Elizabeth Fitzgerald,
daughter of the Earl of Kildare : but seeing that she was only
four years old when Surrey married in 1532, and was herself
married to Sir Anthony Brown at the age of fifteen in 1543, we
may believe with Dr Nott that the passion was altogether ideal,
and perhaps the effect rather than the cause of Surrey's turn for
sonnet-writing.   Belonging to the most powerful family in England, Surrey was a most prominent figure at Court : in the festiv-
ities at Henry's marriage with Anne of Cleves in 1540, he was
the leader of one of the sides in the tournament.   His imperious
spirit more than once committed him to durance vile : once for
challenging to a duel, and again for breaking the windows of the
citizens of London under the pretence (serious or comical) of
alarming their guilty minds with fear of approaching Divine
vengeance.   He held commands in the unimportant wars with
Scotland and France that occupied the later years of the reign of
Henry, and distinguished himself by his personal courage.   In
December 1546, at the instance of certain enemies, he was lodged
in the Tower ; and in the January following was brought to trial
for high treason, condemned, and executed.   He was charged with
having "falsely, maliciously, and traitorously set up and bore the
arms of Edward the Confessor."

Surrey is described as a somewhat small man, strongly knit,
with a dark piercing eye and a composed thoughtful countenance.
He was much more impetuous and gushing than Wyat : proud,
confident, indiscreet in word and action : profuse in his expenses,
sumptuous in apparel and mode of living : courteous and affable
to inferiors, haughty to equals, and willing to acknowledge no
superior.

Surrey's originality was not of the fastidious kind that rejects
thoughts and images simply because they have occurred to a predecessor.   His imagery is not strikingly new.   In his irresistible
energetic way he made free use of whatever suggested itself in
the moment of composition, no matter where it might have come
from.   He borrowed many phrases, many images, and many hints
of phrases and images, from his friend Wyat.[1]   What he bor-

---

[1] It will at once be asked—How do we know that Wyat was the lender and
not the borrower?  Apart from the probabilities of dates, we know from such
small facts as the following: Surrey assigns to Wyat the significant figure
that the scar of a severe wound is never effaced ; and in the poem containing
that figure we find several other expressions that are used by Surrey.  Such a
fact, of course, is not conclusive ; it might plausibly be turned the other way.
That it points in the way here indicated appears farther from the form of Surrey's
reference ; he quotes Wyat as a master :—

> " Yet Solomon said, the wronged shall recure :
> But Wyat said true, the scar doth aye endure."

rowed, however, he passed through his own mint. He vividly realised in his own experience the feelings that other poets professed, and the imagery they employed to give expression to their feelings. At times, indeed, he seems like a spasmodic poet to be agitating himself for the sake of the experience. All his poetry thus displays a modified originality. He probably would not have observed what he delineates, nor would he have thought of the means of delineation, without an obtrusive stimulus, a broad hint; but once his eyes were turned to the proper quarter, and he was told, as it were, what to look for, he used his own eyesight independently, and cast about him for the means of giving expression to what he saw and felt. He had an energetic, versatile mind, singularly open to impressions and impulses : versifying the moods and circumstances of love in songs and sonnets was merely one of the channels that his energy was guided into; and once set agoing he versified in his own way, just as in war he aspired to direct operations in his own way.

Compared with Wyat, Surrey strikes one as having much greater affluence of words—the language is more plastic in his hands. When his mind is full of an idea, he pours it forth with soft voluble eloquence; he commands such abundance of words that he preserves with ease a uniform measure. Uniformity, indeed, is almost indispensable to such abundance : we read him with the feeling that in a "tumbling metre" his fluency would run away with him. Such impetuous affluent natures as his need to be held in with the bit and bridle of uniformity. A calm, composed man like Wyat, with a fine ear for varied melodies, may be trusted to elaborate tranquilly irregular and subtle rhythms; to men like Surrey there is a danger in any medium between "correctness" and Skeltonian licence.

Surrey goes beyond Wyat in the enthusiasm of nature, in the worship of bud and bloom. In the depths of his amorous despair, the beauty of the tender green, and the careless happiness of the brute creation, arrest his eye, and detain him for certain moments from his own sorrow. His most frequently quoted sonnet is a picture of the general happiness of nature in spring, artfully prolonged to the last line, when his own misery bursts in, refusing any longer to be comforted or held at a distance with other interests. There is great freshness in his enjoyment of spring; he describes what he has seen and felt :—

> " When Summer took in hand the Winter to assail,
> With force of might, and virtue great, his stormy blasts to quail ;
>   And when he clothed fair the earth about with green,
> And every tree new garmented that pleasure was to seen :
>   Mine heart gan new revive, and changed blood did stur
> Me to withdraw my winter woe, that kept within the durre.

> Abroad, quod my desire, assay to set thy foot,
> Where thou shalt find the summer sweet, for sprung is every root :
> And to thy health, if thou wert sick in any case,
> Nothing more good than in the spring the air to feel a space.
> There thou shalt hear and see all kinds of birds y-wrought,
> Well tune their voice with warble small, as Nature hath them taught.
> Thus pricked me my lust the sluggish house to leave,
> And for my health I thought it best, such counsel to receive.
> So on a morrow forth, unwist of any wight,
> I went to prove how well it would my heavy burden light.
> And when I felt the air so pleasant round about,
> Lord ! to myself how glad I was that I had gotten out.
> There might I see how Ver had every blossom bent ;
> And eke the new betrothed birds y-coupled how they went.
> And in their songs methought, they thanked Nature much,
> That by her licence all that year to love their hap was such."

Nature, however, was not always a soothing balm to his restlessness : her sweet dews fell unheeded on the tumult of his veins ; his hurrying thoughts would not obey the admonition of her stately movements. In the repose of midnight his complaint rose with unabated anguish :—

> "Alas ! so all things now do hold their peace !
>     Heaven and earth disturbed in nothing :
> The beasts, the air, the birds their song do cease ;
>     The nightes chair the stars about doth bring :
> Calm is the sea ; the waves work less and less.
>     So am not I, whom love alas doth wring,
> Bringing before my face the great increase
>     Of my desires, whereat I weep and sing,
> In joy and wo as in a doubtful ease.
>     For my sweet thoughts sometime do pleasure bring,
> But by-and-by the cause of my disease
>     Gives me a pang that inwardly doth sting,
> When that I think what grief it is again
> To live and lack the thing should rid my pain."

What a contrast to the repose of Greek sculpture ! how fine a subject for Mr Matthew Arnold's lesson of "Self-Dependence" !

It is exceedingly difficult to trace differences of character in the love-poems of Surrey and Wyat. We find in Surrey a greater richness of circumstance and epithet, a more glowing colour ; but we cannot lay our finger upon any one mood in either poet, and say with confidence that we should be surprised to find it in the other. For one thing Surrey wrote comparatively few poems, so that we have no assurance of having boxed the compass of his moods ; and for another thing, it was part of his energetic versatility to be able to throw himself into an imaginary situation upon any accidental hint, and compose a song or sonnet to correspond.

Surrey, upon the whole, strikes us as more light-hearted and ebullient; less deeply penetrated by the earnestness of passion. None of Wyat's songs open with the ringing strength and joyous brightness of Surrey's "praise of his love, wherein he reproveth them that compare their ladies with his:"—

> "Give place, ye lovers, here before
>     That spent your boasts and brags in vain:
> My lady's beauty passeth more
>     The best of yours, I dare well sain,
> Than doth the sun the candle light,
> Or brightest day the darkest night.
>
> And thereto hath a truth as just,
>     As had Penelope the fair;
> For what she saith, ye may it trust,
>     As it by writing sealed were.
> And virtues hath she many mo
> Than I with pen have skill to show.
>
> I could rehearse, if that I would,
>     The whole effect of Nature's plaint,
> When she had lost the perfect mould,
>     The like to whom she could not paint:
> With wringing hands how she did cry,
> And what she said, I know it, I."[1]

Compliments that flow with such a current, and sparkle with such bubbles, do not come from the depths. Again, Wyat is too intensely in earnest to love on without hope of success: he seeks after a definite sign, and when the signs seem unfavourable, bitterly takes refuge in self-sufficing pride. Surrey, on the other hand, with light-hearted generosity, is content only to be hers "although his chance be nought;" and with a hopefulness that shows how slender a hold the passion has upon him, finds consolation in thinking of the long toils and ultimate triumph of the Greeks before Troy. Once more, when Wyat suspects his

[1] The sonnet by Fiorenzuola, from which this is imitated, was a favourite with the translators and imitators of the sixteenth century. There are other two versions of it in Tottel's Miscellany, one of them attributed to Heywood, which opens with the following rather pretty staves:—

> "Give place you ladies, and begone!
>     Boast not yourselves at all:
> For here at hand approacheth one
>     Whose face will stain you all.
>
> The virtue of her lovely looks
>     Excels the precious stone:
> I wish to have none other books
>     To read or look upon.
>
> In each of her two crystal eyes
>     Smileth a naked boy;
> It would you all in heart suffice
>     To see that lamp of joy."

lady of playing false, he mocks his own stupidity, and gravely resolves to be wiser in future; beneath his assumed indifference of tone, we see that the lesson has been bitter. In a similar situation, Surrey prides himself upon his acuteness in seeing through the practices of faithless women :—

> "Too dearly had I bought my green and youthful years,
> If in mine age I could not find when craft for love appears.
> And seldom though I come in court among the rest,
> Yet can I judge in colours dim as deep as can the best."

In another poem he is represented by the editor of 'Tottel' as "a careless man, scorning and describing the subtle usage of women toward their lovers." Still, all these signs may be deceptive, and one would not care to dogmatise on the difference between the two lovers.

None of Wyat's poems are dramatic : he speaks for himself; he does not put himself in the place of others and express their emotions for them. Two or three of Surrey's poems, on the other hand, have this dramatic turn. He sets himself to express, in two different metres, the complaint of a lady whose lover is absent upon the sea—an early Mariana. The following are three staves of the first complaint :—

> "When other lovers in arms across,
>     Rejoice their chief delight ;
> Drowned in tears to mourn my loss,
>     I stand the bitter night,
> In my window where I may see,
> Before the winds how the clouds flee.
> Lo, what a mariner Love hath made me !
>
> And in green waves when the salt flood
>     Doth rise by rage of wind :
> A thousand fancies in that mood
>     Assail my restless mind.
> Alas ! now drencheth my sweet foe,
> That with the spoil of my heart did go,
> And left me, but alas ! why did he so ?
>
> And when the seas wax calm again,
>     To chase fro me annoy ;
> My doubtful hope doth cause me plain,
>     So dread cuts off my joy.
> Thus is my wealth mingled with wo,
> And of each thought a doubt doth grow,
> Now he comes ! will he come ? alas ! no, no.

The forms of sonnet used by Wyat and Surrey are various; they were experimenting, and neither of them seems to have been fascinated by any one form. They several times attempted constructing the fourteen lines throughout upon two rhymes, as in Surrey's—"Alas! so all things now do hold their peace" (p. 126); a form of no particular beauty, and attractive to verse-writers chiefly as an exercise of skill in rhyming. The two most important types are seen in their rival versions of the same sonnet, quoted at p. 118. Wyat follows the arrangement observed by Petrarch, and thus loosely spoken of as the Italian form; Surrey, the arrangement adopted by Shakespeare, and thus loosely spoken of as the English form. The fourteen lines of Wyat's version are divided into two parts: first a stanza of eight lines, consisting of two quatrains banded together by common rhymes; then a stanza of six lines, consisting of two *tercettes*, also banded together by common rhymes. In this type of sonnet, a certain variety was permitted in the disposition of the rhymes within these limits: in the banded quatrains, they might either be alternate, or successive as in Wyat's sonnet; and in the tercettes there might be two rhymes or three connected in any order that the sonneteer could devise. The form of Surrey's version, the English form, is an easier arrangement, which came into use in Italy in the beginning of the sixteenth century. In it the division into two stanzas is broken up, and the fourteen lines arranged in three independent quatrains closed in by a couplet. As we shall see, the form was adopted and regularly used by Daniel for his "Sonnets to Delia"; and from him was adopted by Shakespeare. Before the "Sonnets to Delia," the Italian form was rather the favourite with English sonneteers: it was employed constantly by Sidney.

Surrey's poem composed during his imprisonment in Windsor, is claimed by Dr Nott, who edits Surrey with more than a biographer's enthusiasm, as the first specimen of our elegiac stave— four heroic lines rhyming alternately. This poem contains twelve such staves. Curiously enough, however, the whole is shut in with a final couplet, so that the poem is really a sonnet with twelve quatrains instead of three. It is a confirmation of Mr Guest's intrinsically probable conjecture that the elegiac stave arose from the breaking up of the sonnet into easier forms. Mr Guest, however, is wrong in saying that the final stage of dropping the couplet did not come on till after Milton. Elegiacs without any such appendage are found in the poems of Robert Greene.

The chief feather in Surrey's plume as a verse-writer is his introduction of blank verse. He employed it in his translation of the Second and Fourth Books of the Æneid, which is memorable also as an indication of the growing study of the ancient classics in England. Although Gawain Douglas is a prior claimant to the honour of producing the first English translation of an ancient classic (if Douglas's language is entitled to be called English), Surrey has sufficient honour in his choice of the unrhymed form.

I

About the same time the Italians were beginning to experiment in
dispensing with rhyme ; and Surrey had the good fortune, or the
good sense, to apply to the translation of the great Roman epic
the form that has since been established as English heroic verse.
His blank verse is described by Conington as a good beginning,
but "not entitled to any very high positive praise," being "languid
and monotonous, and sometimes unmetrical and inharmonious."
Surrey's direct knowledge of the classics preserved him as it preserved Wyat and others of the time from the gross mediæval
blunders : yet it is significant of his being only among the pioneers
that in his praise of Wyat he speaks of "*Dan* Homer's rhymes,"
"who feigned gests of heathen princes sung."

We should not omit to notice, among other evidences of Surrey's
searching versatility and eager activity seeking vent in many forms,
that he made an attempt also at pastoral poetry.  His "Complaint of a dying Lover refused upon his Lady's unjust mistaking
of his writing," is put into the mouth of a shepherd.  In this he
followed the example of the Italian imitators of Virgil.  His
metre seems to be a modification of the old ballad form of long
rhyming couplets : he shortens the first line of the couplet by an
accent, or two syllables, thus—

> " In Winter's just return, when Borcas gan his reign,
> And every tree unclothed fast as Nature taught them plain ;
> In misty morning dark, as sheep are then in hold,
> I hied me fast, it set me on, my sheep for to unfold.
> And as it is a thing that lovers have by fits,
> Under a palm I heard one cry as he had lost his wits."

### III.—*Writers of Mysteries, Moralities, " Moral Interludes":*
#### JOHN BALE.

The writers that fall under this section lay wholly out of the
current of Italian influences.  The common stage did not feel
these influences till later.  The primitive English drama was as
little affected by the causes that furthered the poetry of Wyat
and Surrey as it had been a century and a half before, by the
movement of which the main English outcome was Chaucer.  With
its firm hold of popular sympathies, through its ministration to
simple inartificial wants, it continued to flourish when the spirit
of Chaucer decayed, and maintained a certain struggle for existence even after the full maturity of the Elizabethan drama, of
which it had, as we shall see, some claim to be considered the
parent.  Throughout its lease of life it was a direct response to
a popular demand : it knew its audience, and gave them what
they desired.

In one view, indeed, this rude religious drama cannot be held to have remained unaffected by surrounding influences. The Moral-plays, in which the characters were personified virtues and vices —Reason, Repentance, Avarice, Sensuality, Folly, &c.—may be regarded as a modification produced, not by a development from within, but by the action of neighbouring forces. As the materials of one section of Chaucer's poetry were the offspring of a union between Abstraction and Sense, so the moral plays may be looked upon as a cross between Abstraction and the Miracle-plays. It really is immaterial to this view what conclusion we adopt as to the precise transition from miracle-play to moral-play, whether we suppose the transition to have taken place by the gradual introduction of abstract personifications among Scriptural and legendary individuals, or suppose it to have taken place at a leap by the use of moral tales of personifications instead of Scripture and legend as subjects for dramatic representation. In either view, we are at liberty to regard the transition as an encroach-ment made by the abstracting tendency of the Middle Ages upon a simple popular entertainment.

Moral-plays, in whatever way they were suggested, were com-mon throughout the fifteenth century, and had not quite died out at the end of the sixteenth. They, as well as Mysteries, were largely used by the advocates and the opponents of the Reforma-tion to promote their respective views. To give some idea of their nature, we may look at "The World and the Child," *Mundus et Infans*, which is called "a proper new interlude," showing the estate of childhood and manhood.[1] It has no regard for the unity of time : it conducts a child from the cradle to the grave without change of scene. It has no plot : it is really a descrip-tive or panoramic dialogue, in which the Prince of this World holds conversations with a human creature at various stages of its existence, giving his commands to it, and receiving at the end of every seven years an account of its proceedings. The outline is something like this. Mundus enters boasting of his palace, his stalled horses, his riches, his command of mirth and game. He is prince of power and of plenty; and he smites with poverty all that come not when he calls. Infans next tells us that he is a child like other children, "gotten in game and in great sin," and complains of his nakedness and poverty. He beseeches Mun-dus to clothe him and feed him—

> "Sir, of some comfort I you crave
> Meat and cloth my life to save,
> And I your true servant shall be."

---

[1] Mr Collier gives a particular account of "Nature," a morality by Henry Medwall, chaplain to Cardinal Morton.—Hist. of Dram. Poet. ii. 298. See Mr Collier's work for a complete account of our primitive drama.

Mundus hearkens to his prayer, gives him gay garments, names him Wanton, and bids him return for further consideration when fourteen years are come and gone. Wanton is delighted, and repeats with great zest the various amusements and tricks of sportive boydom—top-spinning, biting and kicking, making mouths at his seniors and skipping off, telling lies, dancing, playing at cherry-pit, whistling, plundering orchards, harrying nests. It is considered quite enough for Wanton simply to recapitulate those recreations to give the audience to understand that, he has lived through them ; and after the recapitulation he says—

> " But, sirs, when I was seven year of age
> I was sent to the World to take wage,
> And this seven year I've been his page
> And kept his commandement.
> Now I will wend to the World and worthy emperor.
> Hail, Lord of great honour !
> This seven year I have served you in hall and in bower
> With all my true intent."

Mundus has not left the stage all this time, and he returns a gracious answer, calling Wanton his darling dear. He christens him anew Lust and Liking, and bids him enjoy all game and glee and gladness, and come again at the end of seven years. After another speech, enumerating the doings of lusty youth, Lust and Liking returns aged twenty-one, ready for further orders. Mundus christens him Manhood, and bids him worship seven kings, which are no other than the seven deadly sins—Pride, Envy, Wrath, Covetousness, Sloth, Gluttony, Lechery. Manhood promises to honour them all, and presently announces himself a stalwart and stout lord, of wide dominion and wide fame. While he is boasting of his might and main, Conscience passes by, and they have a dialogue, Conscience discoursing good counsel, meeting at first with much insolence, but ultimately succeeding in making Manhood very uncomfortable. Manhood is glad when Conscience says farewell, although he admits the truth of what he has said. Folly next enters, brimful of audacious impertinence, and after some disputation, persuades Manhood that he is a better leader than Conscience. Just as Manhood is about to follow Folly, Conscience returns, and finding it impossible to restrain Manhood, calls in the aid of Perseverance. Before Perseverance has well explained his functions, Manhood returns in the guise of Age, lamenting his bowed body and his former service of the seven deadly sins. In this mood he is converted, receives the name of Repentance, and so the play ends.

Another piece of this class, with more pretence to plot and vivacity, is " Hick-Scorner," also written during the reign of Henry VIII. The personages are Freewill and Imagination (two dissolute characters, companions of Hick-Scorner); Pity (who tries to mediate between these two worthies when they quarrel, and is seized upon, after the usual fate of peace-makers, by both the wranglers and put in the stocks); and Perseverance and Contemplation (who succeed in reclaiming Freewill and Imagination to a virtuous life). This play gives a really lively picture of manners; Hick-Scorner representing the travelled gallant; Freewill and Imagination, the "rufflers," profligate swaggering fellows, not very particular in their ways of making money; Pity, the good man who laments the degeneracy of the age, and thinks that wickedness was never so prevalent as in his own time; and Perseverance and Contemplation, ideals of virtuous conduct and humane desire for the good of mankind.

The influence of this popular drama in forming public opinion was deeply respected by Henry and his successors, who framed acts and issued proclamations lamenting the inquietation of their people by diversity of opinion, and interdicting all plays that had not received the royal sanction. Both Mysteries and Moralities were used to leaven the popular mind with sound doctrine.

JOHN BALE (1495-1563), a zealous reformer, favoured by Cromwell, forced to flee the country after his death in 1540, recalled by Edward VI. and made Bishop of Ossory, exiled under Mary, restored once more at the accession of Elizabeth, wrote no less than nineteen plays to promote the Reformation. "God's Promises," reprinted in Dodsley's Old Plays, was written in 1538, and entitled "A Tragedy or Interlude, manifesting the chief promises of God unto man by all ages in the old law, from the fall of Adam to the incarnation of the Lord Jesus Christ." The composition is much more solid than that of the "World and the Child," but the plan of the work is very much the same. It is divided into seven Acts, in each of which God sustains a dialogue with a Scriptural patriarch or a prophet: Adam, Noah, Abraham, Moses, David, Isaiah, John the Baptist. Each of the Acts begins with a declaration of God's anger against man, proceeds with deprecating entreaties from the representative of man, and ends with a promise of mercy. The pious author thus embraces within his play the chief promises of a Saviour, as made to Adam, Abraham, David, and Isaiah. Three other mysteries by Bale are extant—"The Three Laws, of Nature, Moses, and Christ;" "John the Baptist's Preaching in the Wilderness;" and "The Temptation of Christ." This last is called by the author a comedy.[1]

---

[1] Bale, says Mr Collier, was the first to apply, or rather to misapply, the words "tragedy" and "comedy" to dramatic representations in English. Mr Collier attributes to him also the curious play *King Johan*, a "morality" with a political intention, and historical characters mixed with such abstractions as "Civil Order," "Treason," and "Verity."—*Camden Society*, 1838.

Bishop Bale used Scripture-plays seriously for the purpose of disseminating his own views of Biblical truth. It is to his plays that we must go if we wish to keep up the idea that the object and function of mysteries was to diffuse among the people a knowledge of Holy Writ. Moral-plays were also utilised by the champions of the Reformation. In the battle against the old faith, mysteries and moralities may be said to have served two separate functions —mysteries being employed in the constructive work of spreading the light of the Bible, and moralities in the destructive work of ridiculing the priests and tenets of Roman Catholicism. In the moral-play of "Lusty Juventus," written during the reign of Edward VI., the ministers and the ritual of Roman Catholicism are represented as being the offspring of hypocrisy, the daughter of the devil, and he is represented as complaining that the Reformation is taking away his choicest instruments. It was natural that when Mary ascended the throne, her party should employ the same organ to play a very different tune. Under Mary it was the new faith and its professors that had to be discredited and made odious. In the "Interlude of Youth," Youth is seduced by the ordinary means of Riot and Pride, and reclaimed by Charity with sound Catholic doctrine. And in a "merry interlude, entitled *Respublica*," Reformation figures as an *alias* of Oppression, with Insolence and Adulation as his comrades; and the three behave so badly, that Nemesis comes down from heaven with her four fair ladies to chastise them, and redress their perversion of "all right and all order of true justice." The three iniquities pay court to Avarice, a touchy old gentleman. Reformation says—

> "And to you have we borne hearty favours alway."

To which Avarice replies shortly and sharply—

> "And I warrant you hanged for your labours one day."

Whereupon Reformation and Adulation chime in together, but get little encouragement from their irascible patron—

*R. & A.*    Even as our God we have alway honoured you.
*Avar.*    And e'en as your God I have aye succoured you.
*R. & A.*    We call you our founder by all holy hallows.
*Avar.*    Founder me no foundering, but beware the gallows.

This employment of a rude drama for political and religious purposes is heavy reading, now that the freshness of its applications is gone. It has little interest as literature side by side with the poetry of Wyat and Surrey. Occasionally, however, the dreary waste is relieved by a sparkling interval. There are two songs in "Lusty Juventus" which step out of their lifeless surroundings, and challenge comparison with the new poetry of the period.   They appeal to us as things of native growth against the imports of the Italian school.   They are genuinely English, and have something of the quality of the snatches of song interspersed through the mature Elizabethan drama.   The first of them is the opening of the play, and is sung by Lusty Juventus himself upon his entrance :—

> " In a herbere green asleep whereas I lay,
>     The birds sang sweet in the midst of the day ;
>     I dreamed fast of mirth and play.
>         In youth is pleasure—in youth is pleasure.
>
> Methought I walked still to and fro,
>     And from her company I could not go ;
>     But when I waked, it was not so.
>         In youth is pleasure—in youth is pleasure.
>
> Therefore my heart is surely pight,
>     Of her alone to have a sight,
>     Which is my joy and heart's delight.
>         In youth is pleasure—in youth is pleasure."

The other is in a similar strain :—

> " Why should not youth fulfil his own mind,
>     As the course of nature doth him bind ?
>     Is not everything ordained to do his kind ?
>         Report me to you—report me to you.
>
> Do not the flowers spring fresh and gay,
>     Pleasant and sweet in the month of May ?
>     And when their time cometh they fade away.
>         Report me to you—report me to you.
>
> Be not the trees in winter bare ?
>     Like unto their kind, such they are.
>     And when they spring their fruits declare.
>         Report me to you—report me to you.
>
> What should youth do with the fruits of age
>     But live in pleasure in his passage ?
>     For when age cometh his lusts will 'suage.
>         Report me to you—report me to you.
>
> Why should not youth fulfil his own mind,
>     As the course of nature doth him bind ?"

IV.—John Heywood : *"Merry Interludes"—The Four P's— Thersites.*

The "merry interludes" of John Heywood, an epigrammatist and noted jester or wit, in great favour with Mary, but driven

abroad, on the accession of Elizabeth, by his adherence to the
Roman Catholic faith, lie between moralities, otherwise called
"moral interludes," and the regular comedy.   They have not
the plot of regular comedy, and they are superior to moralities
in the exhibition of character, because they bring on the stage
not personified abstractions but representatives of professions.   In
spirit they have much in common with the modern farce, being
designed for the same purpose of keeping an audience in broad
enjoyment for a short time.   Heywood's "merry interludes" are
fine examples of broad, boisterous, healthy English humour.   He
took a pride in his own "mad merry wit."

> " Art thou Heywood, with thy mad merry wit?
>     Yea! forsooth, Master, that name is even hit.
>   Art thou Heywood, that appliest mirth more than thrift?
>     Yes, sir, I take merry mirth a golden gift.
>   Art thou Heywood, that hast made many mad plays?
>     Yea, many plays, few good works in my days."

It seems a strange thing that this madcap should have suffered
persecution for his religious faith : it is a parallel to the contemporary paradox of the facetious but fundamentally serious Sir
Thomas More.   From his interludes one might suppose Heywood's leanings to have been the other way—towards the Reformers rather than the Papists : in his extant plays, priests,
palmers, and pardoners are the chief butts of his ridicule.   One
of them—"The Pardoner, the Friar, the Curate, and neighbour
Pratt"—exhibits a struggle between a Pardoner and a Friar for
the temporary use of the Curate's church, and the vain efforts of
the Curate and neighbour Pratt to keep the peace.   Another, entitled "A merry play between John the husband, Tib the wife,
and Sir Jhan the priest," has for its subjects a henpecked husband and a clerical paramour.   The main fun of a third—"The
Four P's, or the Palmer, the Pardoner, the Potecary, and the Pedlar"—turns upon engaging three notorious liars in a competition
to prove which can tell the biggest lie, the fourth standing by as
judge.

The "Four P's," which is reprinted in Dodsley's Old Plays, is
brimful of bright broad humour.   The Palmer enters and tells
what he is, where he has travelled, and why he goes on pilgrimage.   So far all is serious : we have a pious man before us, enumerating his pilgrimages, and crossing himself as he repeats his
devout motives :—

> " To these, with many other one,
>   Devoutly have I prayed and gone,
>   Praying to them to pray for me
>   Unto the blessed Trinity.

> By whose prayers and my daily pain
> I trust the sooner to obtain
> For my salvation, grace, and mercy.
> For be ye sure I think assuredly
> Who seeketh saints for Christës sake
> And namely such as pain do take
> On foot to punish their frail body,
> Shall thereby merit more highly
> Than by anything done by man."

But the Pardoner enters, and dissipates the devout atmosphere with mad spirit. "For all your labour and ghostly intent," he says to the Palmer, "you return as wise as you went." The pilgrim should have come to him.

> " Now mark in this what wit ye have,
> To seek so far and help so nigh ;
> Even here at home is remedy :
> For at your door myself doth dwell
> Who could have saved your soul as well
> As all your wide wand'ring shall do,
> Though ye went thrice to Jericho.
>
> .     .     .     .     .     .
>
> Give me but a penny or twopence,
> And as soon as the soul departeth hence,
> In half-an-hour or three-quarters at the most,
> The soul is in heaven with the Holy Ghost."

The Apothecary now enters with an irreverent inquiry, and proceeds to boast with coarse strong humour that he is of more service to the health of souls than either Pardoner or Palmer.

> " No soul, ye know, entreth heaven gate
> Till from the body he be separate :
> And whom have ye known die honestly
> Without help of the Potecary ?
>
> .     .     .     .     .     .
>
> Since of our souls the multitude
> I send to heaven when all viewed,
> Who should but I then all together
> Have thank of all their coming thither ? "

And the Pardoner and the Potecary assert their rival claims as follows :—

> " *Par.* If ye killed a thousand in an hour space,
>      When come they to heaven dying out of grace ?
>   *Pot.* But if a thousand pardons about their necks were tied,
>      When come they to heaven if they never died ? "

Thus the two knaves jest about serious things. Then the Pedlar enters and sets forth his wares ; and after much humorous sparring, chiefly between the Pardoner and the Potecary, who make very rough fun of one another's pretensions, they settle down into the serious competition in lying. The comparatively quiet Palmer outwits his more boisterous companions, and tricks them into a confession of his superiority. Gravely taking up the Pardoner's tale of a visit to hell, and of the devil's desire to get his kingdom kept clear of women, the Palmer wonders how women can be such shrews in the nether world, for in all his travels, in the course of which he has seen three hundred thousand women, he has never seen one woman out of patience. All cry out that this is a great lie.

This kind of "merry interlude" was in high favour; its heroes must have been felt to be an advance in point of comical interest upon the "vice" of the moralities. The fun, indeed, was of the same boisterous breadth in the moralities, and grew out of similar conceptions and situations; but in the interludes the comical element was extracted and the heavy prosy element left behind. This process of extraction is seen in the interlude of "Thersites,"[1] a revel of gross exaggerated boasting and violent contrast between pretension and performance. Thersites is very much the same character as the Herod of the Mysteries and the Magnificence of the Moralities, only he is exhibited without any admixture of more serious elements; he is a pure extravagance from beginning to end. The hero enters with a club on his neck, shouting—

> " Have in a ruffler, forth of the Greek land,
>     Called Thersites, if ye will me know ;
> Aback, give me room, in my way do not stand,
>     For if ye do, I will soon lay you low."

He speaks with contempt of the Greek chiefs, vowing that if he meets them he will make the dastards "run into a bag to hide them fro me, as from the devil of hell." After some comical misunderstanding, he obtains from Mulciber various pieces of armour, boasting louder and louder after each successive piece, adjuring all the great heroes of antiquity — Hercules, Samson, Cacus, Arthur, Launcelot, &c., &c.—to come and fight with him, declaring them to be puny things. "O good Lord," he cries, "how broad is my breast !"

> " Behold you my hands, my legs, and my feet,
>     Every part is strong, proportionable, and meet :
> Think you that I am not feared in field and street."

Getting more and more intoxicated with the idea of his own might, he avows his intention of making a voyage to hell, to beat the

---

[1] Written apparently in 1537; not printed till 1561; reprinted for the Roxburghe Club in 1820.

devil and his dame and bring away the souls. Then he will go to
old purgatory, and will supersede the need of pardons to let out
the sufferers. Finally, he will climb to heaven, fetch away Peter's
keys, keep them himself, and let in a great rout, for " why should
such a fisher keep good fellows out?" By-and-by his mother
enters, and he expresses a vehement desire to fight with some lion
or other wild beast, resisting his mother's tearful and kneeling
entreaties that he will stay at home. Not Jupiter himself could
restrain him. Presently a snail comes in, at which Thersites falls
into a cold perspiration, in his alarm mistaking it for a sow or a
cow; he fights against it with his club, then casts away his club
and takes to his sword, whereupon the snail draws his horns in,
and he professes himself satisfied. Miles has entered while the
combat was going on, and at the termination, when Thersites
renews his bragging, offers to fight him. Thersites takes refuge
at his mother's back, crying out that he is pursued by a thousand
horsemen. This is the end of the plot; what follows is an incoherent appendage—a visit from Telemachus with a flattering introduction from Ulysses, asking Thersites to make his old mother
charm the boy for a juvenile complaint of a not particularly
delicate nature.


V.—NICHOLAS UDALL (1505-1556): *Ralph Roister Doister—
Gammer Gurton's Needle.*

Udall, sometime head-master at Eton, and celebrated for the
severity of his discipline, is the founder of English comedy.
Evidences remain of his liking for Terence and for Erasmus: in
1533 he compiled and published certain translations from Terence
under the title of ' Flowers from Latin speaking;' and he translated Erasmus's Apophthegms in 1542, and his Paraphrase of the
New Testament between 1542 and 1545. He early acquired, and
maintained to the close of his life, a reputation for the writing of
plays and pageants. He was employed along with Leland in
1533 in composing verses for the city pageant exhibited before
Anne Boleyn, when she rode through London to her coronation.
And he was mentioned by Mary in a document of 1554 as one
that had " heretofore showed and mindeth hereafter to show his
diligence in setting forth of dialogues and interludes before us for
our regal disport and recreation."
The date of the composition of his comedy ' Ralph Roister
Doister,' is not ascertained:[1] Mr Collier suggests that it was

[1] The only extant copy wants the title-page. We know that a printer had a
licence to print the play in 1566. It is reprinted by the Shakespeare Society,
and is included by Mr Arber in his series of English Reprints.

written in Udall's youth.   It is a great step in advance of moralities and interludes.   The author names Plautus and Terence as
his models, and terms the work an interlude *or comedy*, as if wishing to claim kindred with a higher order of composition.   He had
sufficient genius to borrow from the Romans a superior construction of play without sacrificing any of his native humour to foreign
affectations.   Roister Doister rises above preceding dramatic representations in English in the formal excellence of being divided
into Acts and Scenes, and, still more, in having a plot based upon
lively misunderstandings—the proper and peculiar plot of comedy.
Its leading characters, too, are deliberate studies. . The action of
the play consists in the wooing of a widow, Dame Constance, by
a boastful half-witted rich fellow, Ralph Roister Doister, who is
set on and befooled by Matthew Merrygreek, an imitation of
Terence's clever rogue and parasite.   The play opens with the
entrance of Merrygreek singing and cheerfully recounting his
various shifts to gain an idle livelihood.   Ralph, he says, is his
chief banker and sheet-anchor, and one of the greatest louts in
the kingdom.   Presently Ralph enters, and from that moment till
the end of the play is the victim of Merrygreek's tricks and extortions.   The rogue discovers that he is in love, and ready to run
mad ; and after hearing of the lady's wealth, and moralising that
marriage money usually shrinks, he works in the most amusing
way on the hero's vanity.

Ralph is a fine subject for ludicrous misadventures, and Merrygreek fools him to the top of his bent.   His loutish character is
kept up with many delightful touches of consistent humour.
Acting always with the malicious Merrygreek at his elbow, he tries
to follow Ovid's precept of gaining over the lady's servants : but
not having the courage to approach Tibet Talkapace, a saucy
coquettish handmaid, he makes up to old Madge Mumblecrust,
the nurse, and while he is whispering into her ear, Merrygreek
comes up with a following, pretends to take old Madge for the
object of Ralph's devotion, and salutes her with absurd courtesy,
much to Ralph's fury.   Next Merrygreek acts as ambassador,
brings back an insulting reply, and on Ralph's declaring himself
unable to survive the shock, has a funeral service performed over
him.   Then Ralph employs a scrivener to write a moving letter,
and Merrygreek in reading it to the lady, punctuates it, as Quince
does the prologue in " Midsummer Night's Dream," in such a
way as to reverse the meaning, send her away in a passion, and
make Ralph vow to have the scrivener's life.   Finally Merrygreek
eggs him on to take the lady by force : she arms her maid-servants
for the defence, and a comical battle ensues in which Ralph is
ignominiously beaten.

The play is saved from being a mere extravagance by the danger of serious consequences to Dame Constance from the suit of her foolish admirer. She is affianced to an honest merchant, Gawin Goodluck; and he, on hearing mistaken reports which cause him to doubt her fidelity, is disposed to break off the engagement. However, all comes right in the end : the faithful Constance is married to honest Gawin, and Ralph is pardoned his troublesome advances.

It is impossible to say what may have been the single influence of 'Roister Doister' on English comedy : the probability is that its influence was inconsiderable. It was not printed till 1566, and by that time the more powerful influences of early Italian comedy were beginning to operate. Besides, with all its cleverness and delicate humour, the spirit of 'Roister Doister' is essentially boyish : it was written to be acted by boys, and its extravagant incidents are of a kind to draw shouts of delight from boys. There are shrewd touches of worldly wisdom in it; but, as a whole, it has not the robustness of comedy framed for the enjoyment of full-grown men and women. Our early comedy was largely coloured by the circumstance that much of it was written for boys. The interlude of 'Jack Juggler'[1] is another example. This interlude was produced under the inspiration of Plautus, and it is superior in point of construction to earlier interludes, being, indeed, a farce with a plot perfectly rounded off. But it is too extravagant and unreal for our national comedy. It is entitled "a new interlude for children to play; both witty and very pleasant." The personages are Master Boungrace, a gallant; Dame Coy, a gentlewoman; Jack Juggler, "the vice"; Jenkin Careaway, a lackey; and Alice Trip and Go, a maid. Poor Careaway, the lackey, has need for all his powers of banishing melancholy. His mistress is a pretty gingerly piece, as dainty and as nice as a halfpennyworth of silver spoons, but, like all other women, "a very cursed shrew by the blessed Trinity, and a very devil," and she takes special delight in getting him now and then by the pate as an afternoon exercise for her bodily health. His master is worse even than his mistress, once he is thoroughly angered. The maid Alison is a mincing, bridling, simpering, pranking young lady, quavering and warbling with every joint in her body when she goes out, chatting like a pye, speaking like a "parrot popinjay," "as fine as a small silken thread;" and, what is of more consequence to the unfortunate lackey, a spiteful lying girl, never so happy as when she has a tale against him, and enjoying unbounded credit with her mistress. To crown all, he has a cunning and revengeful enemy in Jack Juggler. When he has

<hr>

[1] Entered in the Stationers' Book, 1562-3 : reprinted for the Roxburghe Club in 1820.

been sent out on a message, and has loitered, as he usually does, playing at bucklers, overturning the fruiterer's wife's basket and stealing her apples, losing his money at dice, and so forth, Jack Juggler puts on a suit of the same livery, takes possession of the house gate, and swears to the delinquent idler, that he is Jenkin Careaway, and boldly calls the real Jenkin a drunken knave for pretending to that name. Juggler beats the puzzled Jenkin till he denies his own identity, and bewilders him by telling him all that he has done that day, till the boy is disposed to think as well as to say that he is not himself. When left alone, he cries—

> "Good Lord of heaven, where did I myself leave?
> Or who did me of my name by the way bereave?
> For I am sure of this in my mind
> That I did in no place leave myself behind.
> If I had my name played away at dice,
> Or had sold myself to any man at a price,
> Or had made a fray and had lost it in fighting,
> Or it had been stolen from me sleeping,
> It had been a matter and I would have kept patience,
> But it spiteth my heart to have lost it by such open negligence."

In his anxiety about his personality, he forgets all the lies he has invented to excuse his delays to his mistress and his master, and tells them what he has done; so that Juggler has the satisfaction of seeing "the calf" soundly thrashed, Dame Coy shouting to her enraged husband—

> "Lay on and spare not for the love of Christ,
> Joll his head to a post, and favour your fist:
> Now, for my sake, sweetheart, spare and favour your hand,
> And lay him about the ribs with this wand."

The interlude concludes with moralisings by Jenkin on the wrongs inflicted on innocent simplicity by strength and subtlety.

The well-known play of 'Gammer Gurton's Needle' (which is entitled a right pithy, pleasant, and merry comedy, and is divided into Acts and Scenes), is supposed to have been written about 1560, and, before the discovery of 'Roister Doister,' enjoyed the distinction of being considered our first regular comedy. It is said to have been written by "Mr S., Master of Arts"; and its humour, which is certainly more robust than the humour of 'Roister Doister,' may have been considered suitable to the expanded tastes of Eton boys after they became undergraduates. It has, however, less of the character of a comedy than 'Roister Doister;' it is essentially a farce, designed throughout for the free play of lungs and diaphragm, and the broadening and empurpling of long and pale countenances. An irascible old gammer, such as Noah's wife, has always been a favourite character on the farcical stage : we see at the present day in Christmas Pantomimes how much can be got out of such a personage when enacted by a man, and in those days when greater freedom was allowed, we may imagine how laughter was made to hold both his sides. Gammer Gurton's temper is sorely tried. One day when she is mending her husband's breeches, Gib, the cat, seizes the opportunity of indulging herself with a little milk. Gammer starts up and flings the breeches at the thief. On taking them up again, she cannot find the needle, and turns the house topsy-turvy in the search for it, interfering sadly with the comfort of goodman Hodge, who makes desperate suggestions as to possible places of concealment. A mischievous neighbour Diccon is tickled by the loss, and devises sundry practical jokes out of it. He tells the Gammer that Dame Chat has stolen it, and then goes to Dame Chat and tells her that Gammer Gurton accuses her of stealing her cock : in consequence of which malicious misinformation the two dames proceed to words, and from words to blows. Again, Diccon informs Dr Rat the curate that, if he goes to Dame Chat's, he will find her sewing with the very needle ; and then informs Dame Chat that that evening Hodge intends to make a return visit to her roost : the result of which plot is that the curate's skull is nearly fractured by the enraged dame with a door-bar. Ultimately the needle is discovered by accident embedded in the part of Hodge's apparel on which he usually sits.

### VI.—THOMAS SACKVILLE (1536-7—1608): *The Mirror for Magistrates.*

In 1559, two years after the publication of Tottel's Miscellany, was published a collection of poems more sombre in their hues than the gay songs and sonnets of Surrey and Wyat. Instead of Love, their burden was the mutability of Fortune as shown in the rise and fall of kings, rebels, and noble ministers of state ; and the gloomy record of ambition and disaster was called 'The Mirror for Magistrates'—a glass wherein rulers might see the dangers that wait on greatness.

The work was projected in 1555, about the middle of the reign of Mary : and critics have not failed to remark how naturally the time called for such a mirror. It should, however, be borne in mind, that in the same year, 1555, appeared an edition of Chaucer ; and that Tottel's Songs and Sonnets first saw the light in print during the same "bloody" reign. I have already (p. 70) made some remarks on the dubiety of the connection between literature and politics. The origin of the 'Mirror for Magistrates' is one

of the facts that most strikingly illustrate how quietly literary
operations proceed in the midst of political disquietude.  In 1554
or 1555, Wayland the printer was producing an edition of Lydgate's translation of Boccaccio's 'Fall of Princes' (in rivalry to an
edition by Tottel), and was advised by several of his patrons,
"both honourable and worshipful," "to have the story continued
from whereas Bochas left unto this present time, chiefly of such as
Fortune had dallied with here in this island, which might be a
mirror to all men as well nobles as others."  Wayland applied to
one William Baldwin—a graduate of Oxford, who in 1549 described
himself as "servant with Edward Whitchurch" the printer,[1] and
who was prepared to write plays and philosophical treatises as
well as poems ; but Baldwin would not undertake the task without assistance.  Accordingly, learned men, to the number of seven,
were invited to a consultation, to which Baldwin resorted with
Lydgate's translation under his arm ; and there and then they
agreed to supplement Boccaccio (who had left off with the capture
of the King of France at Poictiers) by calling up the shades of
unfortunate English kings and ministers, from the time of Richard
II., and making them bewail "their grievous chances, heavy
destinies, and woful misfortunes."  It was agreed that Baldwin
should "usurp Bochas' room," the ghostly figures being supposed
to address themselves to him, and that each of the company
should take upon him some unfortunate's lament.  George Ferrers—a lawyer who maintained himself in Court favour under
Henry, Edward, Mary, and Elizabeth, and who was noted as a
director of dramatic pageants—undertook the first of the tragic
series, the fall of Chief-Justice Tresilian, remarking òn the abundant material in our earlier history, but deferring to the printer's
wish to have merely a continuation of Boccaccio as an experi-
mental speculation.  This was the origin of the 'Mirror for
Magistrates.'  An enterprising printer was eager for trade, ready
to print anything, whether grave or gay, that was ready to sell ;
and when he had in hand an edition of Lydgate's translation of
the 'Fall of Princes,' one of his customers suggested a continuation of the work to modern times.  This is what it comes to when
we scrutinise the phantom of a gloomy book rising out of a gloomy
reign.  It rises side by side with another bookseller's speculation
of gayer aspect, both fitted to gratify interests that never die out
among the reading portion of any community.  The imagination
can never live upon comedy alone ; some of us are more mirthful
than others, and more mirthful at sometimes than at other times,
but nearly all of us desire to alternate the gay with the grave.
As the 'Mirror' itself was designed to show, no period in our

---

[1] Printers now began to be, to some extent, the patrons of literary men ; who
still, however, depended more upon the munificence of noble patrons.

annals had been exempt from the caprices of Fortune; had such a reign as Mary's been enough to extinguish love and mirth among her subjects, all our poetry anterior to her reign would have been overhung by the gloom of Erebus.

The first edition of the 'Mirror,' published as we have said in 1559,[1] contained nineteen legends from the reigns of Richard II., Henry IV., Henry V., Henry VI., and Edward IV. Twelve of these are attributed to Baldwin, three to Ferrers: Baldwin was also general editor, and wove the stories together by a prose narrative of the remarks made when they were first read in the conclave of authors. In 1563 appeared a second edition, with eight more legends of later date. In 1574, John Higgins went back to the fabulous beginnings of our history, and wrote sixteen legends of unfortunate British princes between "the coming of Brute and the incarnation of our Saviour." In 1578, Thomas Blennerhasset wrote twelve legends of the times between Cæsar and the Conquest. Various scattered additions were made during the reign of Elizabeth; but the next great event in the bibliography of the work was the collection of the whole by Richard Niccols in 1610. Niccols took great liberties with the text, and omitted all the intermediate *l'envoys* of Higgins and conversations of Baldwin and Blennerhasset. The standard modern edition is Haslewood's, 1815.

Thomas Sackville, created Baron Buckhurst in 1567 and Earl of Dorset in 1603, has no right to be called the "primary inventor" of the 'Mirror for Magistrates,' seeing that his Induction and his Legend of the Duke of Buckingham were not printed till the second edition in 1563; but his name may still be associated with the work as its most distinguished contributor. He infused into it a new and higher spirit. His coadjutors would have been content to drone on with scattered legends on the old plan,\ but Sackville aspired to emulate Dante with a connected epic.\ His language, also, as well as his conception, is fresh and powerful: his singing-robes are new and rich, and throw a double dinginess on the verses of his associates, which are covered with mean and incongruous patches.

Sackville's plan is this. He walks out at nightfall towards the close of autumn, when the declining light and the approaching winter remind him sharply of the changes of fortune. In the midst of his gloomy meditations, there suddenly appears before him a hideous figure in the extremity of grief and despair. This figure is sorrow, who discourses to him of the frailty of human greatness, and conveys him through a gloomy entrance to the abode of departed spirits, proposing to show him the ghosts of unfortunate peers and princes, and to make . them relate their

---

[1] The publication was delayed by Mary's Chancellor.

history.　The first of these unfortunates is the Duke of Buckingham, who was decapitated by Richard III.　Sackville's purpose was to continue the list of ill-starred British warriors and statesmen backwards to the Conquest, working into his plan the legends already versified by Ferrers and Baldwin.　Very naturally and properly he deposed Baldwin from the place of Boccaccio, and made the ghost of Buckingham address himself :—

> "And, Sackville, sith in purpose now thou hast
>   The woful fall of princes to descrive,
> Whom Fortune hath uplift, and 'gain down cast,
>   To show thereby the unsurety in this life," &c.

Sackville never went beyond his one legend, and the other contributors do not seem to have been prepared to merge themselves in his plan, so that his complaint of Buckingham, with the Induction prefixed, was simply printed among the rest in the original chronological order.[1]

Sackville's position in literature is unique.　He projected and began our first grand epic, and wrote our first tragic drama,[2] at once taking a permanent rank in the history of our poetry, and placing himself at the head of contemporary English poets, before he had completed his twenty-seventh year: then, so far as is known, he abandoned the Muses for good.　After a short period of dissipation and reckless profusion, he reformed, entered public life, was employed on diplomatic service by Elizabeth, succeeded Burleigh as Lord High Treasurer, and continued to be the greatest subject of the realm during the first five years of the reign of James; but though he lived to the age of seventy-one, he is not known to have written one line after his contribution to the ' Mirror for Magistrates.'

The ' Mirror for Magistrates,' being designed as a continuation of Lydgate's translation, was written chiefly in the same seven-line stanza.　It is probably in consequence of his study of Lydgate that Sackville, while writing in this stanza, uses a greater number of archaic words than in ' Gorboduc,' which is written in blank verse.　His turns of expression generally afford abundant traces of

---

[1] When Higgins subsequently went back to Brute the Trojan, he aspired to be the leading figure, and copied Sackville's Induction.　He failed, however, to digest the unmanageable mass of legends, so that the ' Mirror for Magistrates ' remained to the last a crude abortion of the grand epic.　The authors were certainly not a "mirror for magistrates" in their unsubordinated action and craving for personal pre-eminence.

[2] ' The Tragedy of Ferrex and Porrex,' first acted in the Christmas Revels of the Inner Temple, afterwards before Elizabeth at Whitehall, Jan. 18, 1561. It was published by the authors in 1570, having previously appeared in a surreptitious edition.　In the edition of 1590 the title was altered to ' Gorboduc.' . Thomas Norton was conjoined in the authorship, but his share cannot be traced, and is believed to be small.

the influence of Wyat and Surrey: echoes of Wyat's Penitential Psalms are especially frequent. As he wrote in youth, and probably also in haste, his debts to predecessors are particularly easy to follow; and it is obvious that he was a careful student of Dante and Virgil, as well as of our native poets. From Dante, undoubtedly, he received his main inspiration.

The personified abstractions that Sackville met in the abode of fallen princes are drawn with great power and harmony of attributes. In the opening of his Induction, as we have said, he describes himself as meeting the hideous figure of Sorrow at nightfall in a dreary evening, when the bare trees and blustering winds reminded him of Fortune's changes; and he observes the same propriety in describing the tenants of the infernal gulf with their behaviour and various circumstances. Sackville's personifications of Sorrow, Remorse, Dread, Revenge, Misery, Care, Sleep, Old Age, Malady, Famine, Death, War, were conceived with a sustained energy and pregnant significance then unparalleled in our literature. They were not eclipsed by the efforts of Spenser in the same vein;[1] and they held their ground till the freshness of such creations had faded. The following is his picture of Misery :—

> " His face was lean and somedeal pined away,
> And eke his hands consumed to the bone ;
> But what his body was I cannot say,
> For on his carcase raiment had he none,
> Save clouts and patches pieced one by one ;
> With staff in hand and scrip on shoulders cast,
> His chief defence against the winter's blast.
>
> His food for most was wild fruits of the tree,
> Unless sometimes some crumbs fell to his share ;
> Which in his wallet long, God wot, kept he,
> As on the which full daintily would he fare :
> His drink the running stream, his cup the bare
> Of the palm closed ; his bed the hard cold ground.
> To this poor life was Misery ybound."

This picture is all the more remarkable when we consider the rank of the poet. And when we consider his youth, we are also surprised at his vivid picture of hoary, trembling Old Age, bemoaning with broken and hollow plaint his forepast youth, but still clinging to life, and praying that he be not yet sent down to the grave, to lie for ever in darkness :—

> " Crook-backed he was, tooth-shaken, and blear-eyed,
> Went on three feet, and sometimes crept on four,
> With old lame bones that rattled by his side,

---

[1] They are all quoted in England's Parnassus, 1600.

> His scalp all pill'd, and he with old forlore:
> His wither'd fist still knocking at death's door;
> Fumbling and drivelling as he draws his breath
> For brief, the shape and messenger of death."

The grisly shape of Famine is described as tearing her own flesh for hunger, clutching at everything that comes near her, and gnashing on her own bones.  Her destruction by Death is a fearful picture of fiendish triumph :—

> " On her while we thus firmly fixed our eyes,
> That bled for ruth of such a dreary sight,
> Lo! suddenly she shrieked in so huge wise,
> As made hell-gates to shiver with the might :
> Wherewith a dart we saw how it did light
> Right on her breast, and therewithal pale Death
> Enthrilling it to reave her of her breath."

Campbell has compared the Induction to "a landscape on which the sun never shines."  The gloom is farther intensified by some exquisite hints of what the landscape was before "hawthorn had lost his motley livery," and before "the naked twigs were shivering all for cold."  We pass through the horrors of the nether world with a feeling that it is winter also in the upper world : and we shudder still more when we think on the sweet season that winter has supplanted.  In the middle of the "Complaint of Buckingham" there is another powerful effect of contrast.  Buckingham swoons at the recollection of a dependant's treachery ; and while he lies between death and life, the poet relieves the horrors of the scene by a description of midnight peace :—

> " Midnight was come, and every vital thing
> With sweet sound sleep their weary limbs did rest;
> The beasts were still, the little birds that sing
> Now sweetly slept beside their mothers' breast :
> The old and all were shrouded in their nest.
> The waters calm, the cruel seas did cense,
> The woods, the fields, and all things hold their peace.
>
> The golden stars were whirl'd amid their race,
> And on the earth did laugh with twinkling light,
> When each thing, nestled in his resting-place,
> Forgat day's pain with pleasure of the night :
> The hare had not the greedy hounds in sight,
> The fearful deer of death stood not in doubt,
> The partridge dreamt not of the falcon's foot.
>
> The ugly bear now minded not the stake,
> Nor how the cruel mastives do him tear ;
> The stag lay still unroused from the brake,
> The foamy boar feared not the hunter's spear.
> All thing was still in desert, bush, and brear.
> With quiet heart now from their travails cease,
> Soundly they slept in midst of all their rest."

The tragedy of "Gorboduc" was written by one profoundly interested in grave problems of state, and was designed for an audience whose interests were also deeply political. Gorboduc, a fabulous King of Britain, B.C. 500, takes counsel about dividing his realm in his lifetime between his two sons, Ferrex and Porrex, and makes the division against the advice of his wisest counsellors. Ferrex and Porrex are jealous of each other: this jealousy is fanned by mischievous flatterers: Porrex, the younger, suddenly issues from his own dominions with an invading army and puts his brother to death: in revenge, he is assassinated by their mother Videna: finally, Videna and Gorboduc are murdered by the populace to avenge the assassination of Porrex, and the race of Brutus being thus extinguished, the kingdom is left a prey to contending factions. The story gives ample scope for the display of political wisdom; and the various opportunities are used with a fulness that no doubt sustained the interest of Elizabeth and her courtiers, though it would be dull enough to the play-goers of our time. But the story contains also tragic materials of universal interest. The unnatural jealousy of Ferrex and Porrex, inflamed by devilish suggestions to the horror of fratricide; the love of Videna for her eldest son, begetting the fierce thirst for a revenge so monstrous; the blind fury of the populace lighting upon innocent old Gorboduc, whose only crime was infatuated parental fondness; and the final reduction of a well-ordered prosperous kingdom to a confused and embroiled anarchy, form no ordinary complication of human passions and human weakness leading to tragic consequences.

Although, however, Sackville is the author of the first extant tragedy in the English language, and though it deserves all Pope's encomium for its propriety of sentiments, unaffected perspicuity, easy flow of numbers, "chastity, correctness, and gravity," he is not to be called the "founder of English tragedy." That title is reserved for Marlowe. The reason for the seeming inconsistency is, that Sackville adhered to classic models, and did not adapt himself to the changed mode of representation. There is a radical difference between "Gorboduc" and the form of tragedy that established itself on the English stage. The actors of Greek and Roman tragedy, to suit their large public theatres, were raised on thick-soled buskins, and stuffed out to more than human bulk. Thus stiffened, they could not represent animated action, and were forced to suppose such action to take place behind the scenes, and to communicate the state of affairs to the audience, in narrative, soliloquy, and dialogue. English actors, on the other hand, were hampered by no bodily encumbrance, and were free to engage in battle, murder, and violent struggle: and thus it was possible for English dramatists to bring the action on the stage. Apart, therefore, from the debated question of good or bad taste in filling the stage with violent action, it is clear that this was not possible for the classical dramatist, whereas it was possible for the English dramatist. Now Sackville, in our first English tragedy, did not fully avail himself of the possibilities of the modern stage. The war between Porrex and Ferrex, the murder of Porrex by Videna, the storming of the palace and the massacre of old Gorboduc by the rabble, were narrated, not represented, as they would have been by the later Elizabethan actors. It is, however, worthy of notice, that he did to some extent avail himself of the modern possibilities in 'the "dumb show" before the Acts. "The order and signification of the dumb show before the Fifth Act," is set down as follows: "First the drums and flutes began to sound, during which there came forth upon the stage a company of harque-bushers and of armed men, all in order of battle. These after their pieces discharged, and that the armed men had three times marched about the stage, departed, and then the drums and flutes did cease. Hereby was signified tumults, rebellions, arms, and civil wars to follow, &c." There we have a certain anticipation of the "excursions" and hand-to-hand fighting afterwards incorporated with the play. Although, therefore, we may not call Sackville the "founder," we may very well call him the "pioneer," of English tragedy, as well as of our grand epic.

## VII.—RICHARD EDWARDS (1523-1566): *Damon and Pythias—Paradise of Dainty Devices.*

About the time of the first representation of "Gorboduc," was presented also for the entertainment of her Majesty the comedy of "Damon and Pythias," which is in some respects of a higher order than the imitations of Plautus and Terence, composed for the boys of Eton or the undergraduates of the Universities. The author was Richard Edwards, Master of the Children of the Chapel Royal, a poet and a musician, formerly a student of Christ Church, Oxford : and he would seem to have kept in mind in whose presence his play was to be acted. It is to be presumed, from bloodthirsty Mary's preference for Heywood and Udall, that she enjoyed a hearty laugh for its own sake; but her successor, if we may judge from her warm commendations of "Damon and Pythias," though not averse to comic scenes of a broad character, desired to encourage a more decorous order of play with some pretence to gravity, wisdom, and refined sentiment—an easy, pleasant, witty play, enforcing a lofty sentiment and a lesson of state, such as she and her statesmen might listen to with pleasure, and without incurring the charge of frivolity. At any rate this was the kind of

play that Edwards furnished and that her Majesty commended.
It is a praise of true friendship and an exposure of false friendship,
ending with the moral that—

> "The strongest guard that kings can have
> Are constant friends their state to save"—

and a prayer that God grant such friends to Queen Elizabeth.
Edwards goes to classical story for a pair of noble friends, Damon
and Pythias, and exhibits them at the Court of the tyrant Dionysius
the younger in glaring contrast to two false friends, two men who
pretend friendship from interested motives—Aristippus, the world-
ly-wise philosopher, a type of an urbane courtier, and Carisophus,
a vile type of spy and informer. The devotion of the two faithful friends is fiercely tried and nobly maintained, while the other
partnership is dissolved the moment it ceases to be useful to one of
the parties. A good deal of amusing action and witty dialogue is
got out of the relations of Aristippus and Carisophus to the Court
and to each other : and a passage of more boisterous entertainment
is rather forcibly provided by introducing Grim, a collier of Croy-
don, as purveyor of coals to Dionysius.

Edwards starts in his prologue with very sound principles for
the composition of comedy :—

> "In Comedies the greatest skill is this, rightly to touch
> All things to the quick, and eke to frame each person so,
> That by his common talk you may his nature rightly know :
> A Roister ought not to preach, that were too strange to hear,
> But as from virtue he doth swerve, so ought his words appear :
> The old man is sober, the young man rash, the Lover triumphing in joys,
> The Matron grave, the Harlot wild and full of wanton toys.
> Which as in one course all they no wise do agree :
> So correspondent to their kind their speeches ought to be."

And it must be owned that he fulfils these conditions with no
small success. He is not particular to realise the political or
religious talk that may be supposed to have taken place at the
Court of Syracuse, but he makes the most of the common hints of
the character of Dionysius, and develops Aristippus with considerable spirit from the famous line of Horace—

> "Omnis Aristippum decuit color et status et res."

One very striking passage in the play is that where Damon
quotes the description of Ulysses in Horace's version of the
opening lines of the Odyssey as the description of "a perfect
wise man"—*qui mores hominum multorum vidit et urbes*—one
who had seen cities and the manners of many different men.
This ideal is significant of the coming excellence of English

drama; and there are not wanting other evidences that observation of character was then quite a mania among literary men.

Edwards was the author also of a play on "Palamon and Arcite," which has not been preserved. We have, however, another monument of his poetical taste and talent in the 'Paradise of Dainty Devices,' a miscellany of amatory and moral pieces, similar to Tottel's Miscellany. It was not published till 1576, ten years after the death of its editor. It ran through several editions before the end of the century. This paradise was described by a critic of the period as "a packet of bald rhymes"; and the description could not easily be improved. It is lugubrious and barren of genius to a degree. All the contributors write in the same doleful strain. As a whole, it gives an impression of dismal monotony; and when we put together the productions of the several writers, we find them one and all in doleful dumps. Edwards laments the prevalence of flattery, the subtle sleights practised at Court, the slow fulfilment of promises, the general want of truth, the rapid decay of worldly beauties, the delay of his desires, the cruel power of Fortune. He denounces the frauds that beguile simple honesty :—

> "I see the serpent vile, that lurks under the green,
> How subtilly he shrouds himself that he may not be seen :
> And yet his foster'd bane his leering looks bewray.
> Wo worth the wily heads that seeks the simple man's decay !
>
> Wo worth the feigning looks on favour that do wait !
> Wo worth the feigned friendly heart that harbours deep deceit !
> Wo worth the viper's brood ! O thrice wo worth I say
> All worldly wily heads that seeks the simple man's decay !"

His coadjutors are equally miserable and indignant against wrong-doing. W. Hunnis is eloquent in lover's melancholy : he repents the folly of misplaced affection and misspent youth : he compares himself to a dove on a leafless branch weeping and wailing and tearing its breast : finding no joy in life he desires death. He is no less unhappy in his notions of friendship. Thomas, Lord Vaux, several of whose pieces had appeared in Tottel's Miscellany, is also a sorrowful singer : and Jasper Heywood, Francis Kinwelmarsh, Sands, F. M., and Richard Hill, are all laid under contribution for poems of a grave or lugubrious cast. The liveliest of the company is Edward, Earl of Oxford. He also, indeed, bewails the loss of his good name, and cries for help to gods, saints, sprites, powers, and howling hounds of hell ; writes of rejected loves and unattained desires, of trickling tears and irremediable pensiveness. But his wounds are obviously shallow. The sprightly verses on a reply given by Desire have more of his heart in them :—

"The lively lark did stretch her wing
The messenger of morning bright :
And with her cheerful voice did sing
The day's approach, discharging night,
When that Aurora blushing red
Descried the guilt of Thetis' bed.
    Laradon tan tan, Tedriton teight.

I went abroad to take the air,
And in the meads I met a knight,
Clad in carnation colour fair.
I did salute the youthful wight ;
Of him his name I did inquire ;
He sighed and said, I am Desire.
    Laradon tan tan, Tedriton teight.

Desire I did desire to stay,
Awhile with him I craved talk :
The courteous wight said me no nay,
But hand in hand with me did walk.
Then in desire I asked again
What thing did please and what did pain.
    Laradon tan tan.

He smiled and thus he answered me :
Desire can have no greater pain,
Than for to see another man
The thing desired to obtain.
No joy no greater too than this
Than to enjoy what others miss.
    Laradon tan tan."

## VIII.—GEORGE GASCOIGNE (1525-1577).

Within the first ten years of Elizabeth's reign another novelty
was added to the drama. In 1566, George Gascoigne translated
from Ariosto, for representation at Gray's Inn, the prose comedy
*Gli-Suppositi.* This, acted under the title of "The Supposes," is
the first comedy written in English prose, and in plot, situation,
and character, it approaches nearer than "Damon and Pythias"
to the established type of English comedy. One great tribute
to its excellence is the use made of its plot and its situations by
Shakespeare : the underplot in the "Taming of the Shrew" is
an adaptation of the plot of "The Supposes," and a great many
of the situations or relations between the various characters might
be paralleled from Shakespeare's comedies.

George Gascoigne, "soldier and poet" as he loved to describe
himself, was the most versatile writer belonging to the first half
of Elizabeth's reign ; and contrived to anticipate more than one
of the forms of composition in which the later Elizabethans
achieved their fame. Few writers can claim a more varied list of

literary exploits. Besides his prose comedy, he translated from the Italian of Bandello the prose tale of "Jeronimi," perhaps the first novel printed in English : wrote the mock-heroic poem of "Dan Bartholomew," our first attempt to rival the mock-heroic poetry of the Italians : wrote three acts of "Jocasta," the first adaptation of a Greek tragedy performed on the English stage : prepared masques for Queen Elizabeth : composed in prose a dull "tragical comedy" "The Glass of Government": and wrote the "Steel Glass," the first extensive English satire.

His personal history is not without interest. It affords a touching example of middle - age rendered miserable by thoughtless youth. When he went up from Cambridge to the Inns of Court, a vigorous, enthusiastic young fellow, "well-born, tenderly fostered, and delicately accompanied," he was ready to join friends and companions in any excitement, animal or intellectual. One of his earliest adventures in London was a temporary imprisonment during the year 1548, on a charge of dicing and other disreputable practices. Entering into the fashion of the time, he wrote love-verses whose coarse boisterous humour was warmly resented by the graver sort when first they appeared in print. Aspiring to political distinction, he sat as a burgess for Bedford during the reign of Mary. When play-writing became the rage, he at once figured in the front of play-wrights. Before this, having impaired his estate by his extravagance, and being disinherited as a prodigal son, he had sought to retrieve his fortunes by marrying a rich widow ; but either the money was tied up from him for behoof of the lady's children by her former husband, or he got it into his hands and ran through it before 1572, for at that date he endeavoured to gain admission into Parliament as burgess for Midhurst, and was defeated by formal objections, which represented him as being a slanderous rhymer, a notorious ruffian, an atheist, a manslaughterer, and an extensive debtor lurking about in fear of apprehension, and seeking admission to Parliament that he might be able to defy his creditors. It may have been this last ignoble motive, if not the motive of retrieving his name by brave achievements, that induced him to cross over to Holland and seek a commission under the Prince of Orange. After his return from Holland in 1573, he made shift to live by his pen. He was now well on to fifty, harassed by debt, met on all sides with cold looks, bitterly regretful of the mad follies of his youth. During his absence, some of his questionable poesies had been printed, and were read with indignation by the guardians of public morality. Soon after his return, in 1575, he issued an edition of his works under the title of 'Flowers, Herbs, and Weeds.' In a prefatory epistle to "reverend divines," he apologises humbly but with some bitterness for the faults of his youth ;

and out of deference to them reprints his youthful effusions in a purified form, and with the self-accusing title of "weeds." There is a bitterness in all his later compositions. He often writes as if experience had taught him that he must not speak evil of dignitaries, while he chafed against the enforced restraint; in the tone of his protestations of respect, he betrayed a somewhat savage sense of the injustice done him by merciless remembrance of his misspent youth. Poor man: he might have written well if the world had gone pleasantly with him, but he was disconcerted and embittered by coldness and suspicion. Yet he was not wholly without countenance and patronage. Arthur Lord Grey of Wilton was a steady friend to him, and might have secured him preferment had he not himself fallen into disgrace. He was asked by the Earl of Leicester to help in the pageants for the entertainment of Elizabeth in the famous reception at Kenilworth. Still his poems have a consistent tinge of gloom. In the epistle dedicatory to his "Steel Glass" (1576), he records how he was "derided, suspected, accused, and condemned; yea, more than that, vigorously rejected when he proffered amends for his harm." "The Drum of Doomsday," "The View of Worldly Vanities," "The Shame of Sin," "The Needle's Eye," "Remedies against the Bitterness of Death," "A Delicate Diet for Daintymouthed Drunkards," "The Grief of Joy," "The Griefs or Discommodities of Lusty Youth," "The Vanities of Beauty," "The Faults of Force and Strength," "The Vanities of Activities," are the significantly cheerless titles and sub-titles of his last productions. He died at Stamford towards the end of 1577.

Not that Gascoigne was a man of first-rate genius. He never would have been anything higher than a versatile master of verse. But his energy was prodigious; and the career of such energy is always an interesting spectacle.

Some of the precepts in his "Notes of Instruction"[1] in verse-making may be put in evidence regarding his qualifications as a poet. The most suggestive is his advice to young poets in search of rhyme—"When you have set down your first verse, take the last word thereof, and count over all the words of the self-same sound by order of the alphabet." Another sound practical advice is to use as few polysyllables as possible; first, because the most ancient English words are of one syllable, but also because "words of one syllable will more easily fall to be short or long as occasion requireth." Characteristic of his own clearness and vigour is his advice to study perspicuity, to abstain from Latin inversions, to be sparing of poetical licences, and to avoid commonplaces. It is remarkable, also, that he enunciates a prin-

---

[1] Reprinted by Mr Arber along with the "Steel Glass" and the "Complaint of Philomene."

ciple which is sometimes spoken of as being of later growth—
" Remember to place every word in his natural emphasis or sound
—that is to say, in such wise, and with such length or shortness,
elevation or depression of syllables, as it is commonly pronounced
and used." He also lays down a strict rule of cæsura.

The "Jocasta," an adaptation from the "Phœnissæ" of Euripides, contains some powerful situations, but they are lost in the
mass of tedious narrative dialogue. The blank verse has every
appearance of having been patched up hurriedly. One of the best
passages is the interchange of defiance between Etiocles and Poly-
nices in the presence of their mother : it would have been difficult
to destroy the tragic force of such a situation.

The tale of Ferdinando Jeronimi and Leonora de Valasco is a
voluptuous story of warm but fickle love, won easily and lost
through exacting causeless jealousy. It was probably one item
in the education of that generation of poets in the arts and ways
of love : its main lesson, apart from its exquisite little windings
and turnings, being that where a woman yields her whole heart
she is implacably offended when she discovers that she is not
trusted. In style the tale is the parent of the tales of Lyly and
Greene. Its " euphuism " is not so methodical as euphuism
strictly so called—the developed mannerism of Lyly : but one
might quote from Gascoigne passages that contain all the elements
of that mannerism. Gascoigne, however, was too robust a nature
to develop this sort of figurative language into a system. After
a euphuistic passage, he begins a new paragraph by saying—" to
speak English."

His love-verses are not the verses of a sentimental inamorato,
or impassioned lover. He woos more like Diomede than like
Troilus, praising his lady's beauty with humorous ardour, and
bidding her "farewell with a mischief" when she proves incon-
stant. Grave and reverend divines had some reason to complain
of a poet who published three sonnets written upon the occasion
of presenting his mistress with a copy of the "Golden Ass" of
Apuleius. His more serious lyrics have an impetuous movement
and rough fire in them that make us think of poor George as an
imperfect Byron,—resembling Byron as he did not a little in his
life, and complaining of the same identification of himself with
his heroes.

There is abundance of comic vigour and mad rollicking humour
in "Dan Bartholomew of Bath." It may be made another point
of comparison with Byron ; but its general strain bears more resemblance to Lockhart's "Mad Banker of Amsterdam." The
hero's courtship and deceptive triumph, his discomfiture and dolo-
rous laments, his Last Will and Testament, his Subscription and
Seal, his Farewell, and " The Reporter's " conclusion in the style

of the 'Mirror for Magistrates,' are executed with great spirit.
The account of his falling in love will give an idea of the
style :—

> " For though he had in all his learned lore
> Both read good rules to bridle fantasy,
> And all good authors taught him evermore
> To love the mean and leave extremity ;
> Yet Kind hath left him such a quality,
> That at the last he quite forgot his books,
> And fastened fancy with the fairest looks.
>
> For proof : when green youth leapt out of his eye,
> And left him now a man of middle age,
> His hap was yet with wandering looks to spy
> A fair young imp of proper personage,
> Eke born (as he) of honest parentage :
> And truth to tell, my skill it cannot serve
> To praise her beauty as it did deserve.
>
> First for her head : the hairs were not of gold,     .
> But of some other metal far more fine,
> Whereof each crinet seemed, to behold,
> Like glistering wires against the sun that shine ;
> And therewithal the blazing of her eyne
> Was like the beams of Titan, truth to tell,
> Which glads us all that in this world do dwell.
>
> Upon her cheeks the lily and the rose
> Did intermeet with equal change of hue,
> And in her gifts no lack I can suppose
> But that at last (alas) she was untrue :
> Which flinging fault, because it is not new
> Nor seldom seen in kits of Cressid's kind,
> I marvel not, nor bear it much in mind.
>
> .     .     .     .     .     .     .
>
> That mouth of hers which seemed to flow with mell
> In speech, in voice, in tender touch, in taste :
> That dimpled chin wherein delight did dwell,
> That ruddy lip wherein was pleasure placed ;
> Those well-shaped hands, fine arms, and slender waist,
> With all the gifts which gave her any grace,
> Were smiling baits which caught fond fools apace."

"The Glass of Government" belongs to the broken-down and
disheartened period of his life. It was published in 1575. He
calls it a tragical comedy to illustrate the rewards and punish-
ments of virtues and vices, consecrates the title-page with a quotation from Scripture, and fills a preliminary fly-leaf with pious,
loyal, patriotic, and moral saws. The prologue forbids all expectations of merry jest and vain delight, referring wanton play-
goers to interludes and Italian toys, and announcing that the
comedy is not a comedy in Terence's sense, but a mirror to lords

and citizens, and a beacon to rash youth.   The argument is the
history of four young men, two of quick capacity, who become
dissipated, and end their careers in shame—two of dull understanding, but steady industry, who are preferred to honourable
positions.   The play is saturated with good advice, the education
of the young men affording opportunities for commonplace counsel
and the exposition of learned precepts by exemplary parents and
teachers, possessing the profoundest sense of their responsibilities.
Copious citations are made from Scripture, and from Greek and
Roman moralists and poets.   It is virtually a moral-play, with individual names given to the abstractions, and the parasite of Latin
comedy in place of the Vice of the Moralities.

"The Steel Glass" shows poor Gascoigne sunk deep in the
slough of despondency and bitterness.   And in one of his smaller
poems it is sad to find him thus looking back to the strength of
his youth, and reflecting that strength is after all a dangerous
thing, which may in the end prove to be a less bountiful gift of
nature than weakness :—

> " I have been strong (I thank my God therefore)
> And did therein rejoice as most men did:
> I leapt, I ran, I toiled and travailed sore,
> My might and main did covet to be kid.[1]
> But lo : behold : my merry days amid,
> One heady deed my haughty heart did break,
> And since (full oft) I wished I had been weak.
> The weakling he sits buzzing at his book,
> Or keeps full close, and loves to live in quiet :
> For lack of force he warily doth look
> In every dish which may disturb his diet.
> He neither fights nor runneth after riot.
> But stays his steps by mean and measure too,
> And longer lives than many strong men do."

## IX.—Thomas Churchyard (1520-1604).

Much tamer in every way than Gascoigne was this other soldier
and poet, yet he is an interesting man, if for no other reason than
that he saw the wonderful growth of the Elizabethan literature
from its beginnings to its maturity.   He lived for some two years
in the service of the Earl of Surrey, contributed to Tottel's Miscellany and to the 'Mirror for Magistrates,' and survived to issue
several books contemporaneously with the plays of Shakespeare.
He began life as a gay gallant or "royster" at the Court of
Henry VIII., and he saw the accession of James I.   Though
his poetry is of small account, his life was eventful and interest-

[1] Known.

ing. In the war with Scotland under Edward VI. he was taken prisoner; being ransomed, he returned to Court, found himself forgotten and neglected, and turned his face, swearing, "as long as he his five wits had, to come in Court no more." He courted a widow, who shamelessly told him he had too little money for her: whereupon, in the rage of his disappointment, he broke his lute, burnt his books and MSS., and went abroad to the Emperor as a soldier of fortune.

He served in Mary's wars with France in the last year of her reign; was taken prisoner; became very popular among the cultivated French, and rewarded their courtesy by cleverly escaping to England. He lived through the whole of the reign of Elizabeth, engaging in various warlike adventures, for which he seems to have received very poor recompense, and making some effort to live by his pen. His chief writings,[1] besides the stories of Lord Mowbray and Shore's Wife in the 'Mirror for Magistrates,' were extracts from his own experience;—Churchyard's Chips, 1565; Churchyard's Choice, 1579; Churchyard's Charge, "a light bundle of lively discourses," 1580; Churchyard's Challenge, 1593; and Churchyard's Charity, "a musical consort of heavenly harmony," 1595. In these works he appears as a garrulous, gossiping old fellow, fond of reciting his own exploits, and overflowing with good advice and general goodwill—on easy confidential terms with the public. So far as his works afford indications, he was tolerably happy in his old age. There would seem to have been a change in his circumstances between 1565 and 1580. In 1565 he narrated his own life in most lugubrious Mirror for Magistrates strain, under the title of "A tragical discourse of the unhappy man's life." In 1578 he translated Ovid *De Tristibus.* But in 1580 he gave another version of his life in dancing ballad couplets as "a story translated out of French," dwelling with particular gusto on his powers of amusing and gaining the friendship of his enemies during his periods of captivity in Scotland and France. He kept on writing with great activity till the very last, publishing no less than thirty-five works during the last twenty-five years of his long life. Such was the Nestor of the Elizabethan heroes.


### X.—TRANSLATORS OF SENECA AND OVID.

Our translators were drawn to Seneca by the same feelings that led to the production of the 'Mirror for Magistrates.' They found in him a similar vein of declamation on the downfall

[1] For reprints see 'Bibliographical Miscellanies,' Oxford, 1813; *Frondes Caducæ*, Auchinleck Press, 1816-17; and (specially) 'Chips concerning Scotland,' edited, with Life, by George Chalmers, 1817.

of greatness, the evanescent character of prosperity, the slipperi-
ness of the heights of pride. Thomas Newton, who collected the
translations of the several tragedies in 1581, enlarged expressly
on their moral tone. He affected to believe that Seneca might
be charged with encouraging ambition, cruelty, incontinence, &c.;
and affirmed in denial of any such charge that "in the whole
catalogue of heathen writers there is none that does so much
with gravity of philosophical sentences, weightiness of sappy
words, and authority of sound matter, to beat down sin, loose
life, dissolute dealing, and unbridled sensuality."

It is not worth while, if it were possible, to recall the personalities of the several translators. The first of them was Jasper
Heywood, then an Oxford undergraduate, who set to work to
translate the 'Troas,' immediately after the publication of the
'Mirror for Magistrates' in 1559. He was followed by Alexander
Nevile, John Studley, and Thomas Nuce: and the separate translations were collected into one volume by Thomas Newton in
1581. The translations are avowedly free. In his preface to the
'Troas,' Heywood says that he has endeavoured to keep touch
with the Latin, not word for word or verse for verse, but in such
a way as to expound the sense; and Nevile, who was but sixteen
when he wrote, and whose preface is an amusing study of inflated
precocity and stilted moralising, boldly affirmed his intention of
wandering from his author, roving where he listed, adding and
subtracting at pleasure. Of course none of the translators make
the remotest approach to the style of Seneca: they simply transmute him into the poetical commonplaces of Lydgate and the
'Mirror.' Look, for instance, at Studley's rendering of the invocation of Medea in the Fourth Act :—

<blockquote>
" O flittering flocks of grisly ghosts<br>
    that sit in silent seat,<br>
O ugsome Bugs, O Goblins grim<br>
    of hell, I you entreat !<br>
O lowering Chaos, dungeon blind<br>
    And dreadful darken'd pit<br>
Where Ditis muffled up in clouds<br>
    of blackest shades doth sit!<br>
O wretched woful wawling souls<br>
    your aid I do implore,<br>
That linked lie with jingling chains<br>
    on wailing Limbo shore !<br>
O mossy den where death doth couch<br>
    his ghastly carrion face :<br>
Release your pangs, O sprites, and to<br>
    this wedding hie apace.<br>
Cause ye the snaggy wheel to pause<br>
    that rents the carcase bound ;<br>
Permit Ixion's racked limbs<br>
    to rest upon the ground ;
</blockquote>

> Let hunger-bitten Tantalus
>   with gaunt and pined paunch,
> Sup by Pirene's gulphed stream,
>   his swelling thirst to staunch."

A collector of "sound and fury" would find many amusing passages in these translations. At the same time, the raw material, very raw though it was, may have been useful to Shakespeare or any dramatist that knew how to refine it. It is not impossible that Shakespeare derived from these rude translations some hints for his incomparable studies of oppressed and desperate women.

What drew Arthur Golding to translate Ovid's Metamorphoses, is hard to conjecture. If it had been Ovid's 'Art of Love,' one might have pointed to the translation as part of the amatory movement in literature, standing to the translation of Seneca as Tottel's Miscellany to the 'Mirror for Magistrates.' But Golding was not the sort of man from whom one would expect a translation of an amatory work. He was an indefatigable translator from Latin, but his subjects generally were of a different cast. He began in 1562 by translating with fervent Protestant zeal a brief treatise on the burning of Bucer and Phagius in the time of Queen Mary, setting forth "the fantastical and tyrannous dealings of the Romish Church, together with the godly and modest regiment of the true Christian Church." The tract is picturesque and forcible. His next performance was a translation of Aretine's history of the wars between "the Imperials and the Goths for the possession of Italy," published in 1563. He translated from Justin in 1564; Cæsar's Commentaries in 1565; and numerous ecclesiastical and other works. His translation of Ovid's Metamorphoses was completed in 1567. It is not very exact, nor calculated to convey an idea of the poet's exquisite delicacy of expression; but it was quite good enough to reveal to non-classical readers a new world of graceful fancies. Shakespeare must have revelled in it, denuding the exquisite fancies of what was rough in the manner of their presentation, and letting them lie in his mind, and stimulate his imagination to beget many others of the same kind. The following is a specimen which may have been in Shakespeare's mind when he imagined the station of Mercury new lighted on a heaven-kissing hill :—

> " And thereupon he call'd his son that Maia had him born,
> Commanding Argus should be killed. He made no long abode,
> But tied his feathers to his feet, and took his charmed rod
> (With which he bringeth things asleep, and fetcheth souls from hell,)
> And put his hat upon his head ; and when that all was well,

> He leaped from his father's towers and down to earth he flew,
> And there both hat and wings also he lightly from him threw,
> Retaining nothing but his staff, the which he closely held
> Between his elbow and his side, and through the common field
> Went plodding like some good plain soul that had some flock to feed."

Prefixed to the work is an epistle also in Alexandrines, moralising the various fables, asking the pious reader to understand *good men* by "gods," and to see in Fate and Fortune aspects of the eternal Providence; and arguing that, though the Scriptures are the only true fountains of knowledge, yet much may be learnt from these pagan writers when rightly interpreted.   The following is part of the moral of Phaeton :—

> " This fable also doth advise all parents and all such
> As bring up youth to take good heed of cockering them too much."

# CHAPTER IV.

## EDMUND SPENSER.

### (1552-1598.)

### I.—His Life and Character.

ALTHOUGH, in Dryden's phrase, "Spenser more than once insinuates that the soul of Chaucer was transfused into his body," there can be no doubt that Spenser's chief impulse in the composition of his principal poem was derived from Ariosto and Tasso. It is, indeed, not difficult to adduce passages from the 'Faery Queen,' founded on Chaucer or Sir Thomas Malory. Spenser was a most learned poet, more so probably than any great English poet, except Mr Swinburne; and he assimilated and incorporated material from many predecessors—English, French, Italian, Latin, and Greek. "E. K.," the inspired commentator on his 'Shepherd's Calendar,' after enumerating as writers of pastoral poetry Theocritus, Virgil, Mantuanus, Petrarca, and Boccaccio, comes finally to Marot, Sanazarro, "and also divers other excellent both Italian and French poets," and adds, "whose footing this author everywhere followeth, yet so as few, but they be well scented, can trace him out." Our poet laid all under contribution, not stealing clumsily and mechanically, but using · the products of other imaginations as food for his own. The Italian masters, undoubtedly, were his chief models and exemplars, although he never followed them to the oppression, still less to the suppression, of his own spirit. The 'Faery Queen' is of the same kindred with the 'Orlando Furioso' and the 'Gerusalemme Liberata.' In Spenser's poem, perhaps, the allegory had greater generative force: but all three agree in the essential respect of having the elements of chivalrous romance used by great artists for purely artistic purposes.

The translations of Ariosto and Tasso executed about the time of the appearance of the 'Faery Queen,' are a proof of the interest

then prevailing in these poems of chivalry.  A translation of
Ariosto's 'Orlando Furioso,' by Sir John Harrington, was published in 1591 : one translation of Tasso's 'Godfrey of Bulloigne,'
or 'Jerusalem Delivered,' by Richard Carew, in 1594, and another,
more celebrated, by Sir Edward Fairfax, in 1600.  Both Harrington's and Fairfax's are smooth and copious, and supplied 'England's Parnassus' with many choice extracts.  They are in *ottava
rima*, and are far from having Spenser's inimitable music; yet, if
an unobservant reader were set down to some of those extracts,
the general resemblance of strain, of matter and imagery, is such
that he would probably refer them at once to Spenser.[1]

Spenser's lineage and life have been made subjects for laborious
inquiry and nice speculation.  He was born in London, and is
supposed to have belonged to a Lancashire branch of the ennobled
family of Spencer.  The date of his birth is generally fixed about
1552.  He entered Pembroke Hall, Cambridge, as a sizar, in 1569 ;
became B.A. in 1573, M.A. in 1576.  After his residence at Cambridge, he is believed to have gone to the north of England; to
have returned south in 1578 by the advice of his college friend
Gabriel Harvey; and to have been introduced by Harvey to Sir
Philip Sidney.  Sidney and the Earl of Leicester took him by the
hand and advanced his fortunes.

In 1579 he dedicated to Sidney his first poetical effort, 'The
Shepherd's Calendar,' containing twelve pastorals, one for each
month, classified as moral, plaintive, and recreative.  About this
time, in his correspondence with Harvey, mention is made of
various works now lost, but probably, with the exception of his
'Nine Comedies,' partially embodied in what he afterwards published.  By that time, also, he had begun the 'Faery Queen.'

In 1580, at the age of twenty-seven, he entered upon official
life : in that year he went to Ireland as secretary to the viceroy,
Lord Grey.  He is usually said to have returned to England in
1582, when Lord Grey was recalled : and his business employment
for the rest of his life is ignored.  Only three facts are known,
but they are significant.  In 1581 he was appointed clerk to the

---

[1] Sir John Harrington might be taken as a typical Elizabethan courtier—a
handsome young fellow, possessed of a keen eye for fun as well as for beauty,
and a very ready command of language.  Besides translating 'Orlando Furioso,'
which the Queen is said to have imposed upon him as a punishment for translating the episode of 'Alcina and Ruggiero,' he wrote epigrams, composed 'Polindor
and Flostella,' a mock-heroic poem in couplets, full of fresh feeling and cleverness, and expounded the merits of one of the most valuable sanitary contriv-
ances of civilised life in a prose treatise—'Ajax Metamorphosed'—boiling over
with gross Rabelaisian humour.  Fairfax was a quieter man, of secluded studious
habits.  Dryden, in the preface to his fables, is loud in praise of the beauty of
Fairfax's numbers, which, he says, Waller himself owned to have been his model.
"Milton was the poetical son of Spenser, and Mr Waller of Fairfax."

Irish Court of Chancery. In 1588 he resigned that appointment for the office of Clerk to the Council of Munster. In 1598 he was recommended by the Queen as a suitable person to be Sheriff of Cork; but had to flee the country in less than a month afterwards. For eighteen years, therefore, with the exception of two brief ascertained visits to England, the author of the 'Faery Queen' remained in Ireland, nominally at least, as an official clerk; and the last appointment would seem to show that his duties were more than nominal, and were efficiently discharged.

In 1586 his friends obtained for him a grant of three thousand acres of forfeited land at Kilcolman, near Cork. It being a condition of the grant that the holder should cultivate the soil, our poet probably at once went into residence. There, on the borders of a lake, amid beautiful scenery, with easy official duties, and with occasional visits from his friends—Sir Walter Raleigh among the number—he placidly elaborated his 'Faery Queen.' In 1590 he crossed St George's Channel in Raleigh's company, with three books ready for the printer; saw to the publication of them; was introduced to Elizabeth; and recrossed to Kilcolman, probably in the spring of 1591, with a substantial proof of her Majesty's favour in the shape of a grant for a yearly pension of fifty pounds, and the consequent honorary title of Poet-Laureate. In 1591, some minor poems of his were published, with or without his superintendence: "The Ruins of Time," "The Tears of the Muses," "Virgil's Gnat," "Prosopopœia, or Mother Hubbard's Tale," "Muiopotmos, or the Fate of the Butterfly," and "Visions of the World's Vanity." About the same time[1] he wrote his "Daphnaida," an elegy on the death of a noble lady. His next publications were in 1595: when Ponsonby issued in separate volumes, and at different times, 'Colin Clout's Come Home Again' (a poem interesting from its allusions to his contemporaries), along with a lament for Sir Philip Sidney, and his "Amoretti" and "Epithalamion," love-sonnets and a marriage-song, occasioned by his wooing and its successful termination in 1594. In 1596 he went over to England and superintended the publication of three more Books of the 'Faery Queen,' along with a second edition of the first three. In the same year appeared in one volume his "Prothalamion" (spousal verses), the elegiac "Daphnaida" already mentioned, and four Hymns. In 1598 he was driven from Kilcolman by the outbreak of Tyrone's rebellion. His wife and himself escaped, but in the hurry and panic they left a little child behind them, and never saw it again. Their house was sacked and burned. He died soon after in London, January

---

[1] Probably before. It is dated Jan. 1, 1591; and we know (Preface to 'Shepherd's Calendar') that Spenser made the year begin with January, and not, as was then usual, with March.

1599. His 'View of the State of Ireland,' a prose dialogue, completed in 1596, was not published till 1633.

"Short curling hair, a full moustache, cut after the pattern of Lord Leicester's, close-clipped beard, heavy eyebrows, and under them thoughtful brown eyes, whose upper eyelids weigh them dreamily down; a long and straight nose, strongly developed, answering to a long and somewhat spare face, with a well-formed sensible-looking forehead; a mouth almost obscured by the moustache, but still showing rather full lips, denoting feeling, well set together, so that the warmth of feeling shall not run riot, with a touch of sadness in them;—such is the look of Spenser, as his portrait hands it down to us."[1]

What may have been the extent of his official duties we do not know; but, to judge from internal evidence, no man ever lived more exclusively in and for poetry than Spenser. We try in vain for any image to express the voluptuous completeness of his immersion in the colours and music of poetry. He was a man of reserved and gentle disposition, and he turned luxuriously from the rough world of facts to the ampler ether, the diviner air, the softer and more resplendent forms of Arcadia, and the delightful land of Faery. While the dramatists were labouring to make the past present, his imagination worked in an opposite line: his effort was to remove hard, clear, visible, and tangible actualities to dreamy regions, and there to reproduce them in a glorified state with softer and warmer forms and colours, or, as the case might be, in a degraded state, with attributes exaggerated in hideousness. His own Pastoral land and Faery land he had furnished with a geography, a population, and a history of their own, and there chiefly his imagination loved to dwell and pursue its creative work. But his spirit, restless and insatiate in its search for deliverance from the cold and definite world, never disdained to enter the abodes prepared by other poets. He expatiated freely through the realms of ancient mythology, and often soared up and poised his wing in mystical contemplation of love and beauty.

More than one of Spenser's contemporaries expressed admiration of his "deep conceit." The luxuriance of leaf and blossom in his poems is deeply rooted in meditation. The profound allegory of the ' Faery Queen ' has been supposed to be alarming to the easy general reader; and several critics, out of a laudable desire to extend Spenser's popularity, have assured us that we may give over all anxiety about the hidden meaning and yet lose none of the enjoyment of the plain story. If, indeed, we desire

---

[1] Rev. G. W. Kitchin, in Clarendon Press edition of ' Faery Queen.'

to understand fully the rich activity and subtlety of the poet's imagination, we do well to get possession of the allegorical groundwork, and study from that point the luxuriant growth of enfolding images. But that effort is necessary only if we desire to feel stems growing and leaves and flowers bursting about us with unceasing energy and boundless profusion.

Many have asserted, and Christopher North indignantly denied, that Spenser's imagination overpowered his judgment. The meaning of the assertors seems to be, that Spenser's fertile mind conceived many images that offend against good taste or that twine themselves together with bewildering intricacy, and his judgment was not strong enough to keep them back. In all such cases the critic can speak only for himself. Warton, and many soberminded people who read poetry with a certain amount of pleasure, would doubtless often be bewildered and occasionally disgusted in journeying through the intricate paths and encountering some of the monstrous personages of the land of Faery. Wilson was too enraptured with the poem to be conscious of any such faults: he was not, perhaps, so easily bewildered nor so easily disgusted by strongly painted "lumps of foul deformity."

Spenser was not without a full share of the poet's alleged peculiar failings, vanity and irritability. Like Sir Walter Scott, our other great poet of chivalrous heroism, he loved to dwell on his ancestry : he somewhat ostentatiously claimed kindred with the noble house of Spencer. Over his natural pride in the exercise of his great gift, he spread but a thin disguise : his transparent compliments to himself are almost unique. He wrote, or procured or allowed a mysterious friend to write, under the initials E. K., an introduction and explanatory notes to his 'Shepherd's Calendar,' comparing this trial of his wings with similar essays by Theocritus and Virgil, and announcing him as "one that in time shall be able to keep wing with the best." Among the shepherds he represents himself under the names of Colin Clout and young Cuddy, and makes other shepherds speak of these sweet players on the oaten pipe with boundless admiration as the joy of their fellows and the rivals of Calliope herself.[1] As for the poet's irritability, that appears in the covert bitterness of his attacks on Roman Catholics and other subjects of his dislike, but most unmistakably in his 'View of the State of Ireland.' His temper was too thin for the asperities of public life. These, however, are the unfavourable aspects of the poet's amiable nature. More favourable aspects of the same reserved meditative disposition appear in his warm gratitude to benefactors, his passion for temperance and purity, and his deep religious earnestness.

[1] See also Appendix.

## II.—His Words, Metres, and General Form.

Consistently with his shrinking from the cold realities of the present, Spenser gave a softer tinge to his diction by here and there introducing a word of the Chaucerian time. Even his diction was to be slightly mellowed with antiquity; he loved now and then to have upon his tongue a word with this soft unction round it. It is strange that the archaic character of his diction should ever have been doubted. The fact was recognised at the time. F. Beaumont, in an epistle prefixed to Speght's Chaucer, says that "Maister Spenser, following the counsel of Tully in *De Oratore* for reviving of ancient words, hath adorned his own style with that beauty and gravity which Tully speaks of, and his much frequenting of Chaucer's ancient speeches causeth many to allow far better of him than otherwise they would." And a still better and earlier authority, the shadowy E. K., anticipated the objections to disused words, saying that the poet, "having the sound of ancient poets still ringing in his ears, mought needs in singing, hit out some of their tunes." "But whether he useth them by such casualty and custom, or of set purpose and choice, as thinking them fittest for such rustical rudeness of shepherds, either for that their rough sounds would make his rhymes more ragged and rustical, or else because such old and obsolete words are most used of country folk, sure I think, and I think not amiss, that they bring great grace, and as one would say authority to the verse." "Ancient solemn words are a great ornament." "Tully saith that ofttimes an ancient word maketh the style seem grave, and as it were reverend, no otherwise than we honour and reverence grey hairs for a certain religious regard which we have of old age." Yet what Spenser prided himself upon was denied of him by some modern admirers, who thought it a detraction.

Our poet had, however, in the rich music of his verse, a fuller protection to interpose between himself and the harsh discords of real life. He was a great metrician. With his friend Gabriel Harvey at Cambridge, with Sidney at Penshurst, with Raleigh at Kilcolman, his talk ran often on the subject of metres. He interested himself in Harvey's enthusiasm for unrhymed dactylic hexameters; but though he approved of them in theory, and produced a specimen with which he was himself highly pleased, he was not so unwise as to waste upon the experiment a poem of any length. Some of the stanzas in his 'Shepherd's Calendar' are exceedingly pretty, particularly the light, airy, childlike jig of the contest between Perigot and Willy. But his greatest achievement was the stanza that bears his name, which he formed by adding an Alexandrine to the stave used in Chaucer's Monk's Tale. In the last great revival of poetry this stanza was warmly adopted. "All poets," says Wilson, "have, since Warton's time, agreed in thinking the Spenserian stanza the finest ever conceived by the soul of man—and what various delightful specimens of it have we now in our language! Thomson's 'Castle of Indolence,' Shenstone's 'Schoolmistress,' Beattie's 'Minstrel,' Burns's 'Cotter's Saturday Night,' Campbell's 'Gertrude of Wyoming,' Scott's 'Don Roderick,' Wordsworth's 'Female Vagrant,' Shelley's 'Revolt of Islam,' Keats's 'Eve of St Agnes,' Croly's 'Angel of the World,' Byron's 'Childe Harold'!" It lends itself with peculiar harmony to impassioned meditation and luxurious description.

Spenser's sonnets, entitled "Amoretti," composed to commemorate his love for the lady whom he afterwards married, are very intricate in form. They consist of three quatrains closed in by a couplet, the first quatrain being interwoven with the second and the second with the third. They obey the rule that confines each sonnet to a distinct idea. Their beauties, however, are wholly technical; their thin pale sentiment and frigid conceits are fatal to anything like profound human interest.

Very different from the involved and timid sonnets is the triumphant "Epithalamion," which celebrates the completion of the same courtship. I know no poem that realises so directly and vividly the idea of winged words: no poem whose verses soar and precipitate themselves with such a vehemence of impetuous ardour and exultation.

Spenser followed the example of Virgil in trying his skill first upon pastoral poetry. This poetical exercise of his has been criticised by various standards, and pronounced wanting. The 'Shepherd's Calendar' was unhappily praised by Dryden as showing mastery of the northern dialect, and as being an exact imitation of Theocritus: this was subsequently seen to be a mistake, and, the standard of comparison being retained, Spenser was blamed because he did not imitate Theocritus. Amid the mass of confused criticism of these pastorals, where each critic pronounces from some vague ideal of what pastoral poetry ought to be, the fundamental objection has always been that they do not represent the actual life of shepherds. Shepherds in real life do not sit in the shade playing on pan-pipes, improvising songs for wagers of lambs and curiously carved bowls, and discoursing in rhymed verse about morality, religion, and politics. But it was not Spenser's design to paint real shepherds, or to copy the features of real pastoral life. His shepherds are allegorical representatives of his friends and his enemies, and exponents of his artistic, moral, and other theories, the whole drifted into a land of the imagination. If we are asked why he chose such a disguise, we must go back to his character, and point to his turn for the picturesque, and his delight in withdrawing from direct contact with the actual world. He loved to wrap hard facts in soft and picturesque allegory. Sir Philip Sidney killed at Zutphen becomes the shepherd Astrophel of Arcadia torn to death by a savage beast, and transformed along with his love Stella into a red and blue flower like a star. Such an Arcadia is purely fanciful, and must be criticised as such not from an unsympathetic distance but out of the mood in which it was conceived. If, indeed, it is said that in the strictly pastoral parts of the poem, Spenser is far inferior to Theocritus, that he neglects the minuter daily and hourly changes of aspect in field and sky, and that there is too little sunshine in his Arcadia, one can understand this criticism as indicating positive defects: the poet might have brought more of this into his Arcadia with the effect of enriching it, and without doing harm to his design. But we miss the whole intention and effect of the poetry if we exact from the poet an adherence to the conditions of the actual life of shepherds. The picturesque environment of hill, wood, dale, silly sheep and ravenous wild beasts, is all that the poet cares for: if he helps us to remember that we are amongst such scenery, he has fulfilled his design. We are not to look for North of England dialect or North of England scenery: if we would enjoy Spenser's Arcadia, we must simply let ourselves float into a dreamland of unsubstantial form and colour. The pastoral surroundings are of value only in so far as they colour and transfigure the sentiments of the poetry.

It was again in professed imitation of Virgil that our poet raised his pipe "from rustic tunes to chant heroic deeds." His knights are as shadowy as his shepherds. Spenser's design was not, like Sir Walter Scott's, to revive in imagination the manners, customs, and adventures of chivalry. In the 'Faery Queen,' as in the 'Shepherd's Calendar,' his design was to translate bare realities into poetical form and colour. Stating the general scope of the work, and passing over his adumbrations of living characters, we may say that his knights and fair ladies are virtues impersonated; his monsters and feigned fair ladies, vices impersonated. So far there is a resemblance between the 'Shepherd's Calendar' and the 'Faery Queen:' both lead us into allegorical worlds. But the two worlds are very different; they rose up in the poet's imagination at the bidding of very different emotions. In the 'Shepherd's Calendar' all is pan-piping and peace, composed sadness and grave moral reflection. In the 'Faery Queen,' on the other hand, we are brought into a land of storms and sunshine, fierce encounter and rapturous love-making; we are hurried in rapid change through lively emotions of mystery, terror, voluptuous security, heartrending pity, and admiration of superhuman prowess—through various scenes, from the "Den of Error" to the "House of Holiness," from the "Bower of Bliss" to the "Gardens of Adonis": now hideousness triumphs, and beauty is in distress; and anon the gates are burst open by a blast of Arthur's horn, or Britomart charges with her charmed spear. The pastoral allegory is insipid if we ignore the hidden meaning; but Faery land is a land of wonder and beauty, where we need remember the hidden meaning only if we desire to pay just homage to the genius of the poet.

Dryden and many others have complained of occasional intricacy and incoherence in the 'Faery Queen.' The admirers of the poet should not meet this complaint by denying the fact: for a fact it is that Spenser does often violate the plain laws of space and time.[1] To maintain coherence, prolonged actions must sometimes be supposed to happen in no time: and personages are sometimes present or absent as it suits the poet's convenience, coming or going without remark. The proper excuse is to say that the scene is laid "in the delightful land of Faery," where perplexity and confusion are as natural as in a dream. The real explanation probably is, that the poet wrote with great facility, and that in "winging his flight rapidly through the prescribed labyrinth of sweet sounds," he sometimes sang himself to sleep, and forgot exactly where he was.

### III.—THE CHIEF QUALITIES OF HIS POETRY.

In Thomas Campbell's criticism of the 'Faery Queen,' it is said that, "on a comprehensive view of the whole work, we certainly miss the charm of strength, symmetry, and rapid or interesting progress." The criticism, like all others from the same pen, is carefully studied and just; but it is somewhat startling without farther explanation of the terms. By rapid or interesting progress we must not understand rapid or interesting succession of events; we must lay emphasis on the word *progress*. Incidents succeed one another quickly and suddenly as in a dream: but they do not progress with the interest of increasing suspense towards their professed end, the accomplishment of the commands of Gloriana, "that greatest glorious Queen of Faery land." Nor, had the poem been completed, is it easy to see how the additional cantos could have corrected what we have, and made part answer to part with even balance: the poet makes no apparent effort to proportion with nice care the weight and space assigned to each personage, situation, and adventure. This will be readily allowed. But the critic's meaning in saying that we miss the charm of strength, is more liable to be misunderstood.

---

[1] See, for very decided cases, Book IV., Cantos 8, 9, 10.

If by "strength" is meant the sentiment inspired by the ideal presence of superior might, then, so far from missing that charm in the 'Faery Queen,' we are kept under its fascination from beginning to end of the poem : imposing situations and mighty beings surround us on every hand. We are carried through waste wildernesses and interminable forests, the haunts of monsters and powerful magicians : forests darkened by frightful shadows, and filled with sad trembling sounds. Hideous giants and dragons, puissant knights, enchanted weapons, grim caves, stately palaces, gloomy dungeons—these and suchlike conceptions in the 'Faery Queen' occupy our imaginations with a perpetual stir of wonder, admiration, and awe. "We do not often," says I. Disraeli, "pause at elevations which raise the feeling of the sublime." If that is so, which I very much doubt, it must be because, in that land of wonders, one thing is not felt to be more wonderful than another. We are sustained at a sublime elevation throughout : we move among the primeval elements of sublimity : even on the Idle Lake, or in the Bower of Bliss, or in the Gardens of Adonis, where the senses ache with beauty, our voluptuous delight is permeated and elevated by the presence of supernatural agency. It may perhaps be pleaded by the nice discriminators of language that there is too much grotesqueness and excitement in Spenser's Faery land to warrant the application of the term "sublime" : many, doubtless, would restrict the name to Miltonic sublimity, the steady planetary sublimity that overawes into calmness. Spenser, it is true, sustains us at a different pitch from Milton. To come fully under the spell of the 'Faery Queen,' we must make ourselves as little children listening to the wondrous tales of a nurse : the very diction has in it something of the affected strange words, feigned excitement, and mouthed tones of softness and wonder put on by a skilful story-teller to such an audience : and when we yield ourselves to the poet in such a spirit, he makes our hearts throb with the same absorbing emotions. Of these emotions perhaps the most fitting names are wonder and dread ; but they are also fitly termed modes of sublimity, when they rise to a certain pitch. We should call both Milton and Spenser sublime, but sublime in different ways.

What then did Campbell mean by saying that in the 'Faery Queen' we miss the charm of strength ? He meant, probably, the strength arising from clearness and brevity of expression : in description, he says, Spenser "exhibits nothing of the brief strokes and robust power which characterise the very greatest poets." It would perhaps be more accurate to say that the brief strokes are supplemented and their abrupt concentrated effect weakened or at least softened by subsequent diffusion. Compare, for example, with Lucrece's frantic exclamations against Night, the following

by impatient Arthur when darkness comes between him and his
pursuit of Florimel (iii. 4) :—

> "Night ! thou foul mother of annoyance sad,
>   Sister of heavy Death, and nurse of Woe,
>   Which wast begot in Heaven, but for thy bad
>   And brutish shape thrust down to Hell below,
>   Where by the grim flood of Cocytus slow,
>   Thy dwelling is in Erebus' black house,
>   (Black Erebus, thy husband, is the foe
>   Of all the gods) where thou ungracious
> Half of thy days dost lead in horror hideous.
>
>   What had the Eternal Maker need of thee,
>   The world in his continual course to keep,
>   That dost all things deface, ne lettest see
>   The beauty of his work ?   Indeed in sleep
>   The slothful body that doth love to steep
>   His lustless limbs, and drown his baser mind,
>   Doth praise thee oft, and oft from Stygian deep,
>   Calls thee his goddess, in his error blind,
> And great dame Nature's handmaid cheering every kind.
>
>   But well I wot that to an heavy heart,
>   Thou art the root and nurse of bitter cares,
>   Breeder of new, renewer of old smarts ;
>   Instead of sleep thou lendest railing tears,
>   Instead of sleep thou sendest troublous fears
>   And dreadful visions, in the which alive
>   The dreary image of sad Death appears :
>   So from the weary spirit thou dost drive
> Desired rest, and men of happiness deprive.
>
>   Under thy mantle black there hidden lie
>   Light-shunning Theft, and traitorous Intent,
>   Abhorred Bloodshed, and vile Felony,
>   Shameful Deceit, and Danger imminent,
>   Foul Horror, and eke hellish Dreariment :
>   All these I wot in thy protection be,
>   And light do shun for fear of being shent :
>   For light y-like is loathed of them and thee ;
> And all that lewdness love do hate the light to see."

Here we have no lack of brief strokes, but they are not final and
solitary : the poet does not leave his conceptions pent up and
struggling with repressed force, but expands them into sublime
images.  Another way of understanding how Spenser's wide ex-
pansive manner is opposed to abrupt strength, would be to
compare any of his pitched duels with similar performances by
Mr Tennyson, in which brevity and symmetry are carried almost
to the pitch of burlesque.  Compare, for example, the encounter
of Guyon and Britomart (iii. 1), with the fight between Gareth
and the Evening Star.

The visit of Duessa to Dame Night, and the journey of the
weird pair to bring the wounded Sansjoy to Æsculapius, who had
been thrust down to hell by the jealousy of Jove, is a passage of
magnificent power; the terrible figure of the ancient but still
mighty mother out of whose womb came earth and the ruler of
heaven and earth, at whose presence dogs bay, owls shriek, and
wolves howl, and whose arrival causes such excitement amidst the
ghastly population of hell, is quite a typical conception of wild
Gothic grandeur (I. 5) :—

> "So wept Duessa until eventide
> That shining lamps in Jove's high house were light.
> Then forth she rose, ne longer would abide,
> But comes unto the place where the heathen knight
> In slumbering swound, nigh void of vital sprite,
> Lay covered with enchanted cloud all day :
> Whom when she found, as she him left in flight,
> To wail his woful case she would not stay,
> But to the eastern coast of Heaven makes speedy way.
>
> Where grisly Night, with visage deadly sad,
> That Phœbus' cheerful face durst never view,
> And in a foul black pitchy mantle clad,
> She finds forth coming from her darksome mew,
> Where she all day did hide her hated hue.
> Before the door her iron chariot stood,
> Already harnessed for journey new,
> And coal-black steeds yborn of hellish brood
> That on their rusty bits did champ as they were wood.
>
> Who when she saw Duessa, sunny bright,
> Adorned with gold and jewels shining clear,
> She greatly grew amazed at the sight,
> And the unacquainted light began to fear,
> (For never did such brightness there appear) ;
> And would have back retired to her cave,
> Until the witch's speech she gan to hear,
> Saying—'Yet, O thou dreaded dame, I crave
> Abide, till I have told the message which I have.'
>
> She stayed ; and forth Duessa gan proceed :
> 'O thou, most ancient grandmother of all,
> More old than Jove, whom thou at first didst breed,
> Or that great house of gods celestial :
> Which was begot in Demogorgon's hall,
> And sawest the secrets of the world unmade !
> Why sufferest thou thy nephews dear to fall
> With elfin sword, most shamefully betrayed ?
> Lo, where the stout Sansjoy doth sleep in deadly shade !
>
> 'And, him before, I saw with bitter eyes
> The bold Sansfoy shrink underneath his spear :
> And now the prey of fowls in field he lies,
> Nor wailed of friends nor laid on groaning bier,
> That whilom was to me too dearly dear.

Oh ! what of gods them boots it to be born
If old Aveugle's sons so evil hear ?
Or who shall not great Nightës children scorn,
When two of three her nephews are so foul forlorn !

'Up, then ; up, dreary dame, of darkness queen !
Go, gather up the relics of thy race !
Or else go them avenge ; and let be seen
That dreadest Night in brightest day hath place,
And can the children of fair Light deface !'
Her feeling speeches some compassion moved
In heart, and change in that great mother's face ;
Yet pity in her heart was never proved
Till then, for evermore she hated, never loved.

.         .         .         .         .         .         .

Then to her iron wagon she betakes,
And with her bears the foul well-favoured witch ;
Through mirksome air her ready way she makes.
Her twofold team (of which two black as pitch,
And two were brown, yet each to each unlitch)
Did softly swim away, ne ever stamp
Unless she chanced their stubborn mouths to twitch ;
Then, foaming tar, their bridles they would champ,
And trampling the fire element would fiercely ramp.

So well they sped that they be come at length
Unto the place whereas the Paynim lay
Devoid of outward sense and native strength,
Covered with charmed cloud from view of day
And sight of men since his late luckless fray.
His cruel wounds with cruddy blood congealed
They binden up so wisely as they may,
And handle softly till they can be healed ;
So lay him in her chariot close in night concealed.

And all the while she stood upon the ground,
The wakeful dogs did never cease to bay ;
As giving warning of the unwonted sound,
With which her iron wheels did them affray,
And her dark grisly look them much dismay.
The messenger of death, the ghastly owl,
With dreary shrieks did also her bewray ;
And hungry wolves continually did howl
At her abhorred face, so filthy and so foul.

Thence turning back in silence soft they stole,
And brought the heavy corse with easy pace
To yawning gulf of deep Avernus hole ;
By that same hole an entrance, dark and base,
With smoke and sulphur hiding all the place,
Descends to Hell ; there creature never past,
That back returned without heavenly grace ;
But dreadful furies, which their chains have brast,
And damned sprites sent forth to make ill men aghast.

> By that same way the direful dames do drive
> Their mournful chariot, filled with rusty blood,
> And down to Pluto's house are come belive :
> Which passing through on every side there stood
> The trembling ghosts with sad amazed mood,
> Chattering their iron teeth, and staring wide
> With stony eyes ; and all the hellish brood
> Of fiends infernal flocked on every side
> To gaze on earthly wight that with the night durst ride."

Other celebrated passages of powerful composition in the 'Faery Queen' are—the Cave of Despair (i. 9); the fight between St George and the Dragon, where the partition between the sublime and the ridiculous is specially thin (i. 11); the Cave of Mammon (ii. 7); the despair of Malbecco (end of iii. 10): the house of Ate (iv. 1); the protracted tournaments in iv. 3 and iv. 4; the exploits of Arthegal and Talus (v. 2). The situation of Britomart in the forest when her companions suddenly disappear in chase of the sudden apparition of Florimel and the foster (iii. 1); and her situation in the enchanter's palace when the house is shaken and the doors clapped by the sudden whirlwind that preludes the Mask of Cupid (iii. 12), may be mentioned as specially effective movements. The action of Britomart's enchanted spear through- out Books iii. and iv. would satisfy Campbell's desideratum of a "brief stroke": there is, however, a touch of the ludicrous in the amazement of the unhorsed champions.

Spenser's Arcadia is not a region of absolutely unruffled peace, seeing that some of the poet's shepherds are sufficiently miserable and irate to have recourse to satire. Satire, however, in the mouths of creatures so simple and shadowy, cannot sound harsh and biting: it rather amuses us gently than fills us with sym- pathetic bitterness. Most of the poems in the 'Shepherd's Calendar' fall under the heads "recreative" and "plaintive." The pictures of pastoral recreation are very sweet and pretty. In the eclogue for May, old Palinode thus exquisitely describes a merry-making of the young folks, and sighs that his old limbs are now too stiff for the furious glee of their innocent sports :—

> " Sicker this morrow, no longer ago,
> I saw a shoal of shepherds outgo
> With singing, and shouting, and jolly cheer:
> Before them yode a lusty tabrere,
> That to the menyie a horn-pipe played,
> Whereto they dancen each one with his maid.
> To see those folks make such jovisance,
> Made my heart after the pipe to dance.
> Tho to the greenwood they speeden hem all,
> To fetchen home May with their musical ;

> And home they bringen in a royal throne,
> Crowned as king ; and his queen attone
> Was lady Flora, on whom did attend
> A fair flock of fairies, and a fresh bend
> Of lovely nymphs.   O that I were there,
> To helpen the ladies their May bush to bear !

But his pastoral lays and ditties, with their cold atmosphere and simple staves, become intolerably tame and insipid after the wondrous beauties and full rich music of the 'Faery Queen.' With all its lofty character as a chronicle of martial deeds, and though the stately Muse is here presented "with quaint Bellona in her equipage," the softer passages will always be read as the most incomparable fruits of the poet's genius.   The Idle Lake (ii. 6), the Bower of Bliss (ii. 12), and the Gardens of Adonis (iii. 6), are unrivalled as pictures of voluptuous dreamy delight. Una among the worshipping Satyrs, with the fair Hamadryades and light-foot Naiades running to see her lovely face (i. 6); the huntress Belphœbe with her broad forehead stepping forth from the thicket (ii. 3); the courting of Florimel by the witch's son (iii. 7); Pastorella among the shepherds (vi. 9),—are pictures that touch our fancies with a livelier, less languid, but not less exquisite, sense of beauty.   Again in the fourth canto of the Third Book, which describes the Rich Strand or Pretious Shore of Marinell, and the journey of sad Cymoent with her team of dolphins over the broad round back of Neptune, the voluptuous elements of the description are interpenetrated by the impassioned grief of the goddess for her beloved son, and the hushed anxiety and tender handling of the sympathising nymphs ; in that passage we taste the last extreme of tender ecstasy :—

> " Eftsoons both flowers and garlands far away
>     She flung, and her fair dewy locks yrent ;
> To sorrow huge she turned her former play,
>     And gamesome mirth to grievous dreariment :   .
> She threw herself down on the continent,
>     No word did speak but lay as in a swown,
> Whiles all her sisters did for her lament
>     With yelling outcries, and with shrieking sown ;
> And every one did tear her garland from her crown.

> Soon as she up out of her deadly fit
>     Arose, she bade her chariot to be brought ;
> And all her sisters that with her did sit,
>     Bade eke at once their chariots to be sought :
> Tho full of bitter grief and pensive thought
>     She to her wagon clomb : clomb all the rest
> And forth together went with sorrow fraught :
>     The waves obedient to their behest
> Them yielded ready passage and their rage surceast.

M

Great Neptune stood amazed at their sight,
Whiles on his broad round back they softly slid,
And eke himself mourned at their mournful plight,
Yet wist not what their wailing meant, yet did
For great compassion of their sorrow, bid
His mighty waters to them buxom be :
Eftsoons the roaring billows still abid,
And all the grisly monsters of the sea
Stood gaping at their gait, and wondered them to see.

A team of dolphins ranged in array
Drew the smooth chariot of sad Cymoent ;
They were all taught by Triton to obey
To the long reins at her commandëment :
As swift as swallows on the waves they went,
That their broad flaggy fins no foam did rear,
No bubbling roundel they behind them sent ;
The rest of other fishes drawen were
Which with their finny oars the swelling sea did shear.

Soon as they been arrived on the brim
Of the rich strond, their chariots they forbore,
And let their timid fishes softly swim
Along the margent of the foamy shore,
Lest they their fins should bruise, and surbate sore
Their tender feet upon the stony ground :
And coming to the place where all in gore
And cruddy blood enwallowed they found
The luckless Marinell lying in deadly swound.

His mother swooned thrice, and the third time
Could scarce recovered be out of her pain ;
Had she not been devoid of mortal slime,
She should not then have been relieved again :
But soon as life recovered had the rein,
She made so piteous moan and dear waiment,
That the hard rocks could scarce from tears refrain ;   .
And all her sister nymphs with one consent   ,
Supplied her sobbing breaches with sad complement.

　　·　　　·　　　·　　　·　　　·　　　·　　　·

Thus when they all had sorrowed their fill,
They softly gan to search his grisly wound :
And that they might him handle more at will,
They him disarmed ; and spreading on the ground
Their watchet mantles fringed with silver round,
They softly wiped away the jelly blood
From the orifice ; which having well upbound,
They poured in sovereign balm and nectar good,
Good both for earthly medicine and for heavenly food.

Tho, when the lily-handed Liagore
(This Liagore whilom had learned skill
In leech's craft, by great Apollo's lore,
Sith her whilom upon high Pindus hill
He loved, and at last her womb did fill

With heavenly seed, whereof wise Paeon sprung)
Did feel his pulse, she knew there stayed still
Some little life his feeble sprites among ;
Which to his mother told, despair she from her flung.

Tho, up him taking in their tender hands
They easily unto her chariot bear ;
Her team at her commandment quiet stands,
Whiles they the corse into her wagon rear,
And strow with flowers the lamentable bier ;
Then all the rest into their coaches climb,
And through the brackish waves their passage shear ;
Upon great Neptune's neck they softly swim,
And to her watery chamber swiftly carry him.

Deep in the bottom of the sea her bower
Is built of hollow billows heaped high,
Like to thick clouds that threat a stormy shower,
And vaulted all within like to the sky,
In which the gods do dwell eternally ;
There they him laid in easy couch well dight,
And sent in haste for Tryphon, to apply
Salves to his wounds, and medicines of might :
For Tryphon of sea-gods the sovereign leech is hight."

. To get a full notion of Spenser's power of "ravishing human sense" with word-music, one must read at least a canto, if not a whole book of the 'Faery Queen.' The dreamy melodious softness of his numbers and his ideas has something of the luxurious charm that the song of the mermaids had for the ear of Guyon (Book ii. Canto 12) :—

"And now they nigh approachèd to the stead
Whereas those mermaids dwelt ; it was a still
And calmy bay, on th' one side shelterèd
With the broad shadow of an hoary hill.

 .  .  .  .  .  .

So now to Guyon as he passed by,
Their pleasant tunes they sweetly thus applied ;
'O thou fair son of gentle Faëry,
Thou art in mighty arms most magnified
Above all knights that ever battle tried :
O turn thy rudder hitherward a while !
Here may thy storm-beat vessel safely ride;
This is the port of rest from troublous toil,
The world's sweet inn from pain and wearisome turmoil.'

With that the rolling sea, resounding soft,
In his big base them fitly answerèd ;
And on the rock the waves breaking aloft
A solemn mean unto them measurèd ;
Tho whiles sweet Zephyrus loud whistlelèd
His treble—a strange kind of harmony,
Which Guyon's senses softly tickelèd,
That he the boatman bade row easily
And let him hear some part of their rare melody."

It is usually said that Spenser has no humour.  His humour, indeed, is of the most quiet and lurking order, and may easily pass unobserved among so many objects of wonder and beauty. But though unobtrusive it is nevertheless there.  The drowsy irritability of Morpheus (i. 1), and the idiotic "He could not tell" of the grave and reverend Ignaro (i. 8), are in the most delicate vein of humour.  Archimago's disguise as a hermit, and his affectation of childish senility and unworldly simplicity, are also very delicately touched off: the enemy of mankind appears as—

> "An aged sire, in long black weeds y-clad,
>   His feet all bare, his beard all hoary grey,
>   And by his belt his book he hanging had ;
>   Sober he seem'd and very sagely sad ;
>   And to the ground his eyes were lowly bent,
>   Simple in shew, and void of malice bad ;
>   And all the way he prayed as he went,
> And often knocked his breast, as one that did repent.
>
>   He fair the knight saluted, louting low,
>   Who fair him quited, as that courteous was ;
>   And after asked him, if he did know
>   Of strange adventures, which abroad did pass,
>   'Ah ! my dear son,' quoth he, 'how should, alas !
>   Silly old man that lives in hidden cell,
>   Bidding his beads all day for his trespass,
>   Tidings of war and worldly trouble tell ?
> With holy father sits not with such things to mell.'"

We may be certain, from Spenser's antipathy to the Roman Catholics, that this was a character in one of the lost nine Comedies : the sudden casting off of the disguise, and the flaming out in his true colours as—

> "A bold bad man ! that dared to call by name
>   Great Gorgon, prince of darkness and dead night—"

would have been a startling effect.

The most openly humorous character in the 'Faery Queen' is Braggadocio, whose behaviour is often farcical.  See his bold pretences to Archimago, and his abject terror and ignominious skulking, in Book ii. 3.

Spenser has been accused of bad taste in mixing up heathen mythology with the narratives of the Bible.  In Book ii. Canto 7, he represents Tantalus and Pontius Pilate as suffering in the same place of punishment.  The answer that wicked men of all ages and creeds may reasonably be supposed to suffer together, is complete.

He has also been accused of interfering with ancient mythology, marrying Clio to Apollo, making Cupid the sister of the Graces, bringing Neptune to the marriage of the Thames and the Medway, and adding without authority to Neptune's retinue. On this great liberty I do not venture to pronounce.

He has been accused of extravagant violations of probability. To this it may be answered that, when we consent to be introduced to Faery land, we sign a dispensation from the ordinary conditions of life.

These charges are frivolous: much more plausibility attaches to his alleged transgressions of the boundary between pleasure and disgust. The picture of Error is said to be intolerably loathsome—

> "Therewith she spew'd out of her filthy maw
> A flood of poison horrible and black,
> Full of great lumps of flesh and gobbets raw,
> Which stunk so vilely that it forc'd him slack
> His grasping hold, and from her turn aback ;
> Her vomit full of books and papers was,
> With loathly frogs and toads, which eyes did lack,
> And creeping sought way in the weedy grass ;
> Her filthy parbreak all the place defiled has."

The picture of Duessa unmasked is still more disgusting. And yet Burke is said to have been fond of quoting the description of Error. To persons of sober refinement, for whom the energy of indignant disgust has no fascination but is merely repulsive, such passages can be justified only as being occasional discords, heightening by contrast the surrounding harmonies, or at the worst, disagreeable episodes tided over by the general sublimity and beauty. Yet the critic should not ignore the fact that great poets of our race have created such passages, and that many readers are drawn to them by irresistible fascination. It is a paradox that descriptions of things so foul and odious should possess any spell : but it is not to be denied that they do possess a strong spell, and that for minds of the most poetical constitution. Spenser's design may have been entirely moral in drawing repulsive pictures of Error and Popery; but there is, whatever may have been his design, a certain intrinsic charm of sublime exaltation in the supreme energy of loathing.

# CHAPTER V.

## ELIZABETHAN SONNETEERS.

THE last ten or fifteen years of the sixteenth century was a period of amazing poetic activity: there is nothing like it in the history of our literature. Never in any equal period of our history did so much intellect go to the making of verses. They had not then the same number of distracting claims: literary ambition had fewer outlets. Carlyle, Grote, Mill, Gladstone, Disraeli, had they lived in the age of Elizabeth, would all have had to make their literary reputation in verse, and all might have earned a respectable place among our poets—might, at least, like Francis Bacon, have composed some single piece of sufficient excellence to be thought worthy of the 'Golden Treasury of Songs and Lyrics.' Amidst a general excitement and ambition of fame the gift of song may be brought to light where in less favourable circumstances it might have been extinguished by other interests. And the rivalry of men endowed with eager and powerful intellects must always act as a stimulus to the genuine poet, although all their efforts come short of the creations of genius.

Three fashions of love-poetry may be particularised as flourishing with especial vigour during those ten or fifteen years—pastoral songs and lyrics, sonnets, and tales of the same type as Venus and Adonis. Spenser did much to confirm if not to set the pastoral fashion; but perhaps still more was done by Sir Philip Sidney with his 'Arcadia' and his sonnets of Astrophel to Stella. These two poets leading the way to the sweet pastoral country of craggy mountain, hill and valley, dale and field, the greater portion of the tuneful host crowded after them, transforming themselves into Damons, Dorons, and Coridons, and piping to cruel Phillises, Phillidas, and Carmelas.[1] Out of this masquerading grew many

---

[1] The land of ideal shepherds was only one of the ideal countries frequented by the artistic courtiers of Elizabeth. They were as eager to descry new worlds of imagination as her navigators were to discover new regions in the terraqueous globe. In the masques presented at Court we find inhabitants of four great worlds or continents—the country of Shepherds, the country of Faeries, the Mythological world, and the world of Personified Abstractions.

beautiful lyrics. 'England's Helicon,' which was published in 1600, and which gathered the harvest of this pastoral poetry, is by many degrees the finest of the numerous miscellanies of the Elizabethan age. It contained selections from Spenser, Sidney, Greene, Lodge, J. Wootton, Bolton, Barnefield, "Shepherd Tonie," Drayton, Shakespeare, and others of less note.

Many of these pastorals took the form of sonnets, but I single out sonnet-writing as a fashion by itself, in order to draw attention to the numerous bodies of sonnets published in the last decade of the century as lasting monuments of sustained passion, real or ideal. The list is very remarkable. It opens with the publication of Sidney's sonnets to Stella in 1591, and includes— Daniel's sonnets to Delia, published in 1592 ; Constable's sonnets to Diana, 1592 ; Lodge's sonnets to Phillis, 1593 ; Watson's Tears of Fancy, or Love Disdained, 1593 ; Drayton's Idea's Mirror, "amours in quatorzains," in 1594 ; and Spenser's Amoretti or Sonnets in 1596.[1]

Hardly less notable is the fancy for short mythological or historical love-tales. The way in this form of composition was led by Thomas Lodge, who published in 1589 the poem of 'Glaucus and Scylla,' narrating with many pretty circumstances the cruelty of Scylla to Glaucus, in punishment whereof she was transformed into a dangerous rock on the coasts of Sicily. Marlowe began and Chapman finished the tale of Hero and Leander ; Shakespeare sang the love of Venus and Adonis : Drayton the love of Endymion and Phœbe ; Chapman (in ' Ovid's Banquet of Sense ') the love of Ovid and Julia. The voluptuous descriptions of these tales could not have been expected to go on without sooner or later exciting the spirit of derisive parody : and accordingly, in 1598, Shakespeare's "Venus and Adonis" was rudely burlesqued by the satirical Marston in a comical version of the tale of "Pygmalion and Galatea." To prevent any undue indignation at the liberty thus taken with our great dramatist, I may here intimate a suspicion, for which I shall afterwards produce some grounds, that certain of Shakespeare's sonnets — those, namely, from the 127th to the 152d inclusive—were designed to ridicule the effusions of some of his seriously or feignedly love-sick predecessors. Marston's profane parody may thus assume the aspect of a Nemesis.

The enthusiasm of beauty was strong in the Elizabethan poets. With many of them it was a fierce and earnest thirst. Their lives were hot, turbulent, precarious : they turned often to the bloom of fair checks and the lustre of bright hair as a passionate relief from desperate fortunes. Beauty was pursued by Greene

---

[1] In this chapter I have used the order of the publication of these sonnets as a basis of arrangement for the predecessors of Shakespeare in that form of composition.

and Marlowe not as a luxury but as a fierce necessity—as the
only thing that could make life tolerable.  Such visions as Hero
and fair Samela filled them with mad ecstasy in the height of
their intemperate orgies, and were called back for soothing
worship in their after-fits of exhaustion and savage despondency.
In many others of calmer and more temperate lives, beauty
excited less ardent transports, and yet was a powerful influence.
Beauty was a very prevailing religion ; the perfections of woman,
excellence of eye, of lip, of brow, were meditated on and adored
with devout rapture ;  and though the votary's enthusiasm in
some cases travelled into licentious delirium, in gentler natures it
bred soft and delicate fancies, of the most exquisite tenderness.
Beauty was part of all their lives, and shaped itself in each mind
according to the soil.  A very surprising number of different soils
it found to grow in, and very remarkable were the products.  One
meets the same flowers again and again, but always with some individual grace.  Even third-rate and fourth-rate poets do not seem
to be weaving garlands of flowers plucked from the verses of the
masters : they develop the common seeds in their own way.  Consider, for example, the following madrigal by John Wootton,
a name now uttterly forgotten by the generality, and a poet of
whose personality nothing survives but his name and his contributions to ' England's Helicon : '—

> " Her eyes like shining lamps in midst of night,
>     Night dark and dead :
> Or as the stars that give the seamen light,
>     Light for to lead
>     Their wandering ships.
>
> Amidst her cheeks the rose and lily strive,
>     Lily snow-white :
> When their contend doth make their colour thrive,
>     Colour too bright
>     For shepherd's eyes.
>
> Her lips like scarlet of the finest dye,
>     Scarlet blood-red :
> Teeth white as snow, which on the hills doth lie,
>     Hills overspread
>     By Winter's force.
>
> Her skin as soft as is the finest silk,
>     Silk soft and fine :
> Of colour like unto the whitest milk,
>     Milk of the kine
>     Of Daphnis' herd.
>
> As swift of foot as is the pretty roe,
>     Roe swift of pace :
> When yelping hounds pursue her to and fro,
>     Hounds fierce in chase
>     To reave her life."

## I.—SIR PHILIP SIDNEY [1] (1554-1586).

In 1591 a volume of sonnets was issued under the editorship of Thomas Nash, containing Sidney's "Astrophel and Stella," twenty-eight sonnets by Samuel Daniel, and other poems by "Divers Noblemen and Gentlemen." The publication was most probably surreptitious: Daniel, who published his "Sonnets to Delia" in the following year, complained that "a greedy printer had published some of his sonnets along with those of Sir Philip Sidney;" and a corrected and authentic edition of Sidney's sonnets was issued before the close of 1591.

The main attraction of Nash's volume was the "Astrophel and Stella" series of sonnets; this was the title of the work, the other poems being merely appended. The editor extolled Sidney with characteristic eloquence and extravagance. He apologises for commending a poet "the least syllable of whose name, sounded in the ears of judgment, is able to give the meanest line he writes a dowry of immortality." He deplores the long absence of England's Sun, and ridicules the gross fatty flames that have wandered abroad like hobgoblins with a wisp of paper at their tails in the middest eclipse of his shining perfections. "Put out your rush candles, you poets and rhymers," he cries; "and bequeath your crazed quatorzains to the chandlers; for lo! here he cometh that hath broken your legs."

The story of the romantic passion between Sidney and Penelope Devereux, Astrophel and Stella, is well known to readers of literary history. Lady Penelope, sister of the unfortunate Earl of Essex, was some nine years younger than her distinguished lover. Her father had formed a high opinion of Sir Philip's promise, and on his deathbed expressed a wish for their union: but her guardians were in favour of a wealthier match, and two or three years after the old Earl's death, she was married at the age of seventeen, much against her own wishes, to an unattractive young nobleman, Lord Rich. This event may have been hastened by Sidney's attitude before the marriage. If his self-reproaches in the sonnets were well founded, he would seem to have been undecided and vacillating in his addresses, his natural impulses being obstructed by a pedantic fancy that love was unworthy of a great thinker like himself—perhaps a temporary result of his correspondence with Languet: but when the lady was married out of his reach, his love became most ardent, and he courted her favours in a long series of passionate sonnets. Seeing that he very soon after married another lady—a daughter of Sir Francis Walsingham—it

---

[1] I have given some account of Sidney's life and character in my Manual of English Prose Literature, and shall here confine myself to his sonnets.

might with some reason be inferred that there was in Sidney's as in other sonnets not a little make-believe passion, and that his delight as an ambitious young poet at finding such an amount of literary capital was quite as strong as the pain of the disappointment. Certainly, however, Lady Rich, whose rare charms of beauty and wit were the theme of many celebrated Elizabethan pens, was likely enough to be the object of a genuine passion. As the wife of a man whom she disliked and kept in thorough fear and subjection, and as the sister of an ambitious nobleman nearly related to the throne, she led as she advanced in years a brilliant and a troubled life, and was in the Court of England the most conspicuous and fascinating woman of her generation. When Sidney wrote his sonnets she was in the prime of her beauty, and he may well have been sincere in deploring the loss of such a prize, and praying in wailful sonnets that he might continue to have a place in her affections.

In the choice of ideas for his sonnets Sidney prided himself on being original.[1] This was a natural reaction from the long line of imitators between Surrey and himself. In Watson's ' Hecatompathia, or Passionate Century of Love,' published in 1582, about the time when Sidney was composing his sonnets, the imitative and artificial character of the fashionable English love-poetry was specially illustrated by the candid acknowledgments of the accompanying notes. The poet makes no pretence to spontaneous effusion. Prefixed to the many ingenious praises of his lady's beauty, and allegations of her cruelty, and his own varied professions of unalterable love and consuming pangs of despair, are full references to the literary sources of his inspiration. Before depicting the pangs of Cupid's deadly dart and praying for its withdrawal, the commentary informs us that " the author hath wrought this passion out of Stephanus Forcatulus." Before a dire lament that Neptune's waves might be renewed from the poet's weeping eyes, Vulcan's forge from the flames within his breast, and the windbags of Æolus from his sobbing sighs, we are candidly informed that " the invention of this Passion is borrowed for the most part from Seraphine, Son. 125." A praise of his lady is imitated from Petrarch : a sweet fancy about the capture of Love by the Muses, from Ronsard : a vision of his lady in sleep from Hercules Strozza. Another commendation of the most rare excellencies of his mistress is imitated from a famous sonnet by Fiorenzuola the Florentine, which was imitated also by Surrey and by two other writers in Tottel's Miscellany. So with the majority of Watson's " passions," as he called his poems ; very few of them professed to be wholly

---

[1] He carried his disdain of commonplace into other walks of love. The ladies of the Court thought him a dry-as-dust because he wore no particular colours " nor nourished special locks of vowed hair."—Son. 54.

original, and the adaptation was generally very slight. Now Sidney revolted from this habit of adopting the praises, vows, and "deploring dumps" of other amorous singers. He swore "by blackest brook of hell," that he was "no pick-purse of another's wit." His eloquence came from a different source : "his lips were sweet, inspired with Stella's kiss." He had tried the old plan—

> "I sought fit words to paint the blackest face of woe
> Studying inventions fine, her wits to entertain ;
> Oft turning others' leaves to see if thence would flow
> Some fresh and fruitful showers upon my sunburned brain."

But Invention, the child of Nature, fled from the blows of Study. He sat biting his pen, and beating himself for spite, till at last—

> "Fool ! said my Muse to me, look in thy heart and write."

His success was such that he could not refrain from boastful tirades against the old imitators—

> "You that do Dictionary's method bring
> Into your rhymes, running in rattling rows ;
> You that poor Petrarch's long deceased woes
> With new-born sighs and denizened wit do sing,
> You take wrong ways, those far-fetched helps be such
> As do betray a want of inward touch."

This and many other passages in Sidney illustrate the almost Homeric complacency of self-estimate among the Elizabethans.

Most of the conceptions and conceits in Sidney's sonnets are really his own; and they display very exquisite subtlety and tenderness of fancy. In these respects they deserve all the admiration they received from his contemporaries. What, for example, could be finer than the ruling conceit of his 38th sonnet ?

> "This night while Sleep begins with heavy wings,
> To hatch mine eyes, and that unbitted thought
> Doth fall to stray, and my chief powers are brought
>   To leave the sceptre of all subject things :
>   The first that straight my fancy's error brings
> Unto my mind, is Stella's image, wrought
> By Love's own self, but, with so curious draught
>   That she, methinks, not only shines but sings.
> I start, look, hark : but what in closed-up sense
>   Was held, in open sense it flies away,
> Leaving me nought but wailing eloquence :
>   I, seeing better sights in Sight's decay
> Called it anew, and wooed sleep again :
> But him, her host, that unkind guest had slain."

The first fifty or sixty sonnets exhibit Astrophel's love in what may be called in fashionable mathematical language the statical stage : the subsequent dynamical stage being composed of sonnets descriptive of moods and conceits occasioned by a sequence of incidents between the lovers—supposed encouragement, venturous liberties, discouragement, despair, and so forth. During the statical or brooding stage, the poet-lover's mind is occupied with similitudes and all sorts of fanciful inventions to set forth the imcomparable charms of his mistress and the unexampled force of his passion. During that period his love is subject to no fluctuations, no dynamic change ; it suffers neither increase nor abatement. It is chiefly in this stage that the soft gracefulness and ethereal reach of Sidney's fancy are displayed. Instead of the sighing lover's commonplace raw assertion that his mistress is fairer than Helen, or Semele, or Ariadne, or Chloris, or any other mythological beauty, or that she would have borne away the apple from Juno, Pallas, and Venus, Astrophel presents Stella with the following ingenious and delicately wrought conceit, enlivened by a sportive breath of tender humour :—

> "Phœbus was judge between Jove, Mars, and Love,
> Of those three gods whose arms the fairest were :
> Jove's golden shield did eagles sable bear,
>   Whose talons held young Ganymede above :
> But in vert field Mars bore a golden spear,
>   Which through a bleeding heart his point did shove.
>   Each had his crest ; Mars carried Venus' glove,
> Jove on his helm the thunder-bolt did rear.
>   Cupid then smiles : see ! on his crest there lies
> Stella's fair hair ; her face he makes his shield,
> Whose roses gules are borne in silver field.
>   Phœbus drew wide the curtains of the skies
> To blaze these last, and sware devoutly then
> The first thus match'd, were scantly gentlemen."

He is brimful of fancies equally delicate. Venus falls out on Cupid because under terror of the threats of Mars he would not wound that god deep enough. The angry mother breaks her son's bow and shafts, and the poor boy is disconsolate—

> "Till that his grandame Nature, pitying it,
> Of Stella's brows made him two better bows,
> And in her eyes of arrows infinite :
> O how for joy he leaps ! O how he crows !
> And straight therewith, like wags new got to play,
> Falls to shrewd turns,—and I was in his way."

The commonplace that his mistress's eyes are like stars he builds up into a profession of faith in Astrology. He takes

Plato's saying, that if Virtue could come directly in contact with our eyes, it would raise flames of love in our souls, and maintains the truth of the doctrine, for Virtue has taken Stella's shape, and he is conscious of the effect in his own person. He exults over Reason, who at first intermeddled and decried, but when Stella appeared, knelt down and offered to produce good reasons for loving her. He is puzzled to make out why his plaints move her so faintly. He will not admit that she is hard-hearted; but at last he hits upon the true explanation :—

> " I much do guess, yet find no truth, save this,
> That when the breath of my complaints doth touch
> Those dainty doors unto the court of bliss,
> The heavenly nature of that place is such
> That once come there the sobs of mine annoys
> Are metamorphosed straight to tunes of joys."

These sweet fancies rise in the head when the heart is comparatively tranquil. When storms began to agitate, the lover's strains became more impassioned. The following is the 48th sonnet :—

> " Soul's joy, bend not those morning stars from me,
> Where virtue is made strong by beauty's might;
> Where Love is chasteness, pain doth learn delight,
> And humbleness grows on with majesty.
> Whatever may ensue, O let me be
> Copartner of the riches of that sight :
> Let not mine eyes be hell-driven from that light :
> O look ! O shine ! O let me die, and see !
> For though I oft myself of them bemoan,
> That through my heart their beamy darts be gone,
> Whose cureless wounds, e'en now, most freshly bleed ;
> Yet since my death-wound is already got,
> Dear killer, spare not thy sweet cruel shot:
> A kind of grace it is to slay with speed."

Farther on in the series, having so far conquered the lady's indifference, he prays for and receives a kiss, "poor hope's first wealth, hostage of promised weal, breakfast of Love," and expresses his rapture in several most impassioned sonnets. The following is the 81st :—

> " O kiss, which dost those ruddy gems impart,
> Or gems, or fruits, of new-found Paradise :
> Breathing all bliss and sweet'ning to the heart ;
> Teaching dumb lips a nobler exercise !
> O kiss, which souls, even souls, together ties
> By links of Love, and only Nature's art :
> How fain would I paint thee to all men's eyes,
> Or of thy gifts, at least, shade out some part !

> But she forbids ; with blushing words she says,
> She builds her fame on higher-seated praise :
> But my heart burns, I cannot silent be.
> Then since, dear life, you fain would have me peace,
> And I, mad with delight, want wit to cease,
> Stop you my mouth with still, still kissing me. "

Sidney observes the Petrarchian form of the sonnet in so far as
regards the division of the stanza into two staves, the first of eight
lines with two rhymes, the second of six lines with three rhymes.
Whether for ease or for variety, he is not particular about the
arrangement of the rhymes within these limits.   In the first stave
he employs sometimes the alternate, sometimes the successive
arrangement ; and when the rhymes are alternate, he sometimes
reverses but oftener repeats in the second quatrain the order of the
first.   In the second stave, he sometimes interweaves the lines so
as to make a stave proper ; but oftener he subdivides it into a
quatrain followed by a couplet.   Sometimes, as in two of the
sonnets above quoted, he begins with the couplet and ends with
the quatrain ; and the arrangement is seemingly dictated not by
ease or accident, but by a just sense of metrical effect.

Interspersed with the sonnets are several songs, and in these our
poet is happier than in the more confined measures.   The last of
these songs, which is in the form adopted by Shakespeare for the
serenade to Silvia (Two Gent. of Ver., iv. 2), contains some very
sweet staves.   The two first lines go to the lady ; the three following to the lover :—

> " Who is it that this dark night
>     Underneath my window plaineth ?
> It is one, who from thy sight
>     Being (ah !) exiled, disdaineth
> Every other vulgar light.
>
> Why, alas ! and are you he ?
>     Be not yet those fancies changed ?
> Dear, when you find change in me
>     Tho' from me you be estranged
> Let my change to ruin be.
>
> .     .     .     .     .     .     .
>
> But Time will these thoughts remove :
>     Time doth work what no man knoweth.
> Time doth as the subject prove,
>     With time still affection groweth
> In the faithful turtle-dove.
>
> What if ye new beauties see
>     Will not they stir new affection ?
> I will think they pictures be
>     Image-like of saint-perfection,
> Poorly counterfeiting thee. "

Two such songs as this and the one to Silvia make the stave seem the only true form for a lover's lyric: the lines run into music of their own accord, and scatter sweet perfumes with their light motion. There is nothing more ravishing in the language.

## II.—Samuel Daniel (1562-1619).

Daniel, born near Taunton in Somersetshire, was the son of a music-master, but somehow obtained a university education at Oxford. He published a translation of Paulus Jovius's 'Discourse of Rare Inventions' in 1585 at the age of twenty-three, and soon afterwards became tutor to Lady Anne Clifford. A man of taste and refined feeling, very unlike some of the sturdy contemporary plants who lived by acting and play-writing, Daniel grew up under the shelter of noble patronage, conciliating favour by the amiability of his disposition as well as by the gracefulness of his literary compliments. He enjoyed the patronage of the Earl of Southampton and of the Pembroke family. Through the influence of his noble friends, he had obtained in 1593, the Mastership of the Revels, for which poor John Lyly had waited so long and begged so earnestly; and after the accession of James, he was made Gentleman-Extraordinary, and subsequently one of the Grooms of the Privy Chamber to the Queen Consort. His chief poetical works were—Sonnets to "Delia," 1592; "Delia" augmented, along with the "Complaint of Rosamond" and the "Tragedy of Cleopatra," 1594; metrical history of the "Civil Wars," 1604; "Tragedy of Philotas," 1611; "Hymen's Triumph, a pastoral tragi-comedy," not published till 1623. He wrote several other pieces of less importance. His plays were produced for the entertainment of the Court; and it may have been this connection that dictated his choice of the Wars of the Roses as a subject. He also wrote in prose a History of England.

Had Daniel lived in the present day, his destiny probably would have been to write scholarly and elegant articles in the magazines, ripe fruits of leisurely study, cultivated taste, and easy command of polite English. His was not one of the stormy irregular natures that laid the foundation and raised the structure of the English drama: the elements of his being were softly blended, and wrought together mildly and harmoniously. In the prologue to "Hymen's Triumph," he declares that he has no rude antique sport to offer—

> " But tender passions, motions soft and grave
> The still spectators must expect to have."

He wrote for Cynthia, and therefore his play—

> " Must be gentle like to her
> Whose sweet affections mildly move and stir."

He might have said the same about all his poetry. He was no master of strong passions : he never felt them, and he could not paint them. Between his Cleopatra and Shakespeare's there is a wide gulf. But he is most exquisite and delicate in pencilling " tender passions, motions soft and grave."

Without being strikingly original, Daniel has a way and a vein of his own. He fills his mind with ideas and forms from extraneous sources, and with quietly operating plasticity reshapes them in accordance with the bent of his own modes of thought and feeling. He had not the Shakespearian lightning quickness in adaptation and extension ; the process in him was more peaceable and easy. The diction of his poems is choice ; the versification easy and flowing. He often puts things with felicitous terseness and vigour, and his words almost invariably come together happily and harmoniously.

The publication of Daniel's sonnets in 1592 is an epoch in the history of the English Sonnet. This was the first body of sonnets written in what is sometimes called by pre-eminence the English form—three independent quatrains closed in by a couplet. Daniel also set an example to Shakespeare in treating the sonnet as a stanza, connecting several of them together as consecutive parts of a larger expression. Apart from their form, there is not very much interest in the sonnets to Delia. They have all Daniel's smoothness and felicity of phrase, and are pervaded by exceedingly sweet and soft sentiment. Though they rouse no strong feelings, they may be dwelt upon by a sympathetic reader with lively enjoyment. One of them, with somewhat greater depth of feeling than most of the others, the sonnet beginning—"Care-charmer Sleep, son of the sable Night," is ranked among the best sonnets in the language. But their most general interest is found in their relation to Shakespeare's sonnets, several of which seem to have been built up from ideas suggested by the study of those to Delia.[1] In the following sonnets, for example, readers familiar

---

[1] The Sonnets to Delia on their first issue were preceded by a prose dedication to the Countess of Pembroke, "Sidney's sister, Pembroke's mother" : the poet desiring "to be graced by the countenance of your protection ; whom the fortune of our time hath made the happy and judicial patroness of the Muses (a glory hereditary to your house)." To the second issue was prefixed a dedicatory sonnet to the same lady, entitling her as the " wonder of these, glory of other times " ; affirming that his sonnets were " her own, begotten by her hand " ; and that though the travail was his, the glory must be hers. These facts, and some of the expressions, are interesting to those who believe that the friend of Shakespeare's sonnets was this lady's son.

with Shakespeare's will not fail to remark a certain similarity of
idea, although the two series of sonnets differ as widely as the
genius of the two poets.

### SONNET 37.

" But love whilst that thou mayst be loved again,
    Now whilst thy May hath filled thy lap with flowers ;
Now whilst thy beauty bears without a stain :
    Now use the summer smiles, ere winter lowers :
And whilst thou spreadst unto the rising Sun
    The fairest flower that ever saw the light,
Now joy thy time before thy sweet be done ;
    And, Delia, think thy morning must have night,
And that thy brightness sets at length to west,
    When thou wilt close up that which now thou show'st,
And think the same becomes thy fading best,
    Which then shall most inveil and shadow most.
Men do not weigh the stalk for that it was,
When once they find her flower, her glory pass."

### SONNET 39.

" When winter snows upon thy sable hairs,
    And frost of age hath nipt thy beauties near;
When dark shall seem thy day that never clears,
    And all lies withered that was held so dear :
Then take this picture which I here present thee,
    Limned with a pencil that's not all unworthy :
Here see the gifts that God and Nature lent thee ;
    Here read thyself, and what I suffer'd for thee.
This may remain thy lasting monument,
    Which happily posterity may cherish ;
These colours with thy fading are not spent,
    These may remain, when thou and I shall perish.
If they remain, then thou shalt live thereby :
They will remain, and so thou canst not die."

### SONNET 41.

" Be not displeased that these my papers should
    Bewray unto the world how fair thou art ;
Or that my wits have showed the best they could
    The chastest flame that ever warmed heart !
Think not, sweet Delia, this shall be thy shame,
    My Muse should sound thy praise with mournful warble ;
How many live, the glory of whose name
    Shall rest in ice, when thine is graved in marble !
Thou mayst in after-ages live esteemed
    Unburied in these lines, reserved in pureness ;
These shall entomb those eyes, that have redeemed
    Me from the vulgar, thee from all obscureness.
Although my careful accents never moved thee,
Yet count it no disgrace that I have loved thee."

N

SONNET 52.

" Let others sing of knights and paladins,
  In aged accents and untimely words ;
Paint shadows in imaginary lines
  Which well the reach of their high wits records ;
But I must sing of thee, and those fair eyes
  Authentic shall my verse in time to come
When yet th' unborn shall say, ' Lo where she lies
  Whose beauty made him speak, that else was dumb.'
These are the arks, the trophies I erect,
  That fortify thy name against old age ;
And these thy sacred virtues must protect,
  Against the dark and Time's consuming rage.
Though th' error of my youth in them appear
  Suffice they show I lived and loved thee dear."

Daniel's genius is best shown in the expression of bereaved love in the "Complaint of Rosamond," and in "Hymen's Triumph"—as Spenser said, "in tragic plaints and passionate mischance." In the expression of courtship love, his imagination is cold and acts artificially and mechanically : but when the beloved object is taken away, he is moved to the depths, and pours forth his strains with genuine warmth. The passion has still a certain softness in it : his lovers have not the inconsolable fierce distraction of Shakespeare's forsaken lover, "tearing of papers, breaking rings atwain :" they do not shriek undistinguished woe : but they sigh deeply, and their voices are richly laden with impassioned remembrance. The plaintive sorrow of Thyrsis is sweet and profound. But nothing that Daniel has written flows with surer instinct and more natural impulse than the agonised endearments of Harry over the body of Rosamond. Wholly different in character from the frantic doting of Venus over her lost Adon, these verses are hardly less perfect as the utterance of a milder and less fiercely fond passion. The deep heart's sorrow of the bereaved lover makes itself felt in every line—

" Then as these passions do him overwhelm
He draws him near my body to behold it ;
And as the vine married unto the elm
With strict embraces, so doth he enfold it :
And as he in his careful arms doth hold it
Viewing the face that even death commends
On senseless lips millions of kisses spends.

' Pitiful mouth,' said he, ' that living gavest
The sweetest comfort that my soul could wish :
O be it lawful now, that dead thou havest,
This sorrowing farewell of a dying kiss.
And you, fair eyes, containers of my bliss,
Motives of love, born to be matched never,
Entomb'd in your sweet circles, sleep for ever.

'Ah, how methinks I see Death dallying seeks
To entertain itself in Love's sweet place !
Decayed roses of discoloured cheeks,
Do yet retain dear notes of former grace,
And ugly Death sits fair within her face ;
Sweet remnants resting of vermilion red,
That Death itself doubts whether she be dead.

'Wonder of beauty, O receive these plaints,
These obsequies, the last that I shall make thee :
For lo, my soul that now already faints,
(That loved the living, dead will not forsake thee)
Hastens her speedy course to overtake thee.
I'll meet my death, and free myself thereby,
For ah, what can he do that cannot die?

'Yet, ere I die, thus much my soul doth vow,
Revenge shall sweeten death with ease of mind :
And I will cause posterity shall know,
How fair thou wert above all womankind.
And after-ages monuments shall find
Showing thy beauty's title, not thy name,
Rose of the world that sweetened so the same.' "

### III.—Henry Constable (1555 ?–1610 ?).

Constable was of Roman Catholic family, and was educated at
St John's, Cambridge, where he took the degree of B.A. in 1579.
He was obliged to leave England in 1595, from suspicion of trea-
sonable practices.  Venturing back in 1601 or 1602, he was committed to the Tower, from which he was not released till towards
the close of 1604.  He is mentioned as if he were still alive in the
'Return from Parnassus' (1606), and in Bolton's 'Hypercritica'
(1616) as if he were then dead.  The first edition of his sonnets
to "Diana" appeared in 1592, and contained 23 ; a second was
issued in 1594, containing 27.  Sixty-three sonnets by Constable,
methodically arranged in sevens, are printed in the Harleian Miscellany from a MS. known as Todd's MS. : this collection comprises
all that appear in the printed collections.  Constable wrote also
certain 'Spiritual Sonnets,' and a version of the tale of Venus
and Adonis, which was not published till 1600, but is believed to
have been written earlier.

Like Daniel, Constable does not attempt the delineation of
stormy passions, yet his deepest vein is quite different from
Daniel's.  He has a more ardent soul than Daniel : his imagination is more warmly and richly coloured : he has more of flame
and less of moisture in him.  Daniel's words flow most abundantly
and with happiest impulse when his eye is dim with tears ; Constable's when his whole being is aglow with the rapture of beauty.
Tears fall from the poet's eyes in the following sonnet, but they

fall like rain in sunshine. The occasion is his lady's walking in a garden :—

> " My lady's presence makes the roses red
>   Because to see her lips they blush for shame :
>   The lily's leaves for envy pale became,
> And her white hands in them this envy bred.
> The marigold abroad its leaves did spread
>   Because the sun's and her power is the same ;
>   The violet of purple colour came,
> Dyed with the blood she made my heart to shed.
>   In brief, all flowers from her their virtue take ;
> From her sweet breath their sweet smells do proceed ;
>   The living heat which her eyebeams do make
> Warmeth the ground, and quickeneth the seed.
>   The rain wherewith she watereth these flowers
>   Falls from mine eyes which she dissolves in showers."

The following is more characteristic of his soaring ardour—"rapture all air and fire;" though the structure is somewhat artificial :—

> " Blame not my heart for flying up so high,
>   Sith thou art cause that it this flight begun,
>   For earthly vapours, drawn up by the sun,
> Comets become, and night-suns in the sky.
> My humble heart so with thy heavenly eye
>   Drawn up aloft, all low desires doth shun :
>   Raise thou me up, as thou my heart has done,
> So during night, in heaven remain may I.
>   Blame not, I say again, my high desire,
> Sith of us both the cause thereof depends :
>   In thee doth shine, in me doth burn a fire ;
> Fire draweth up others, and itself ascends,
>   Thine eye a fire, and so draws up my love ;
>   My love a fire, and so ascends above."

The most exquisite of his sonnets for sweet colour and winning fancy is that where he compares his love to a beggar at the door of beauty—

> " Pity refusing my poor Love to feed,
>   A beggar starved for want of help he lies,
>   And at your mouth, the door of beauty, cries
> That thence some alms of sweet grants may proceed.
> But as he waiteth for some almës-deed,
>   A cherry tree before the door he spies—
>   O dear, quoth he, two cherries may suffice,
> Two only life may save in this my need.
>   But beggars can they nought but cherries eat ?
> Pardon my Love, he is a goddess' son,
>   And never feedeth but of dainty meat,
> Else need he not to pine as he hath done.
>   For only the sweet fruit of this sweet tree
>   Can give food to my love, and life to me."

In one of his sonnets he makes the same glorious claim for his lady that Shakespeare makes for the fair youth of his adoration—

> "Miracle of the world ! I never will deny
> That former poets praise the beauty of their days ;
> But all those beauties were but figures of thy praise,
> And all those poets did of thee but prophesy."

His amorous sonnets and other light poems were the effusions of his youth, and like Spenser he turned in his older years to the contemplation of heavenly beauty.  He concludes his love-sonnets by saying—

> "For if none ever loved like me, then why
> Still blameth he the things he doth not know ?
> And he that hath so loved will favour show,
> For he hath been a fool as well as I."

And adds in prose—"When I had ended this last sonnet, and found that such vain poems as I had by idle hours writ, did amount just to the climacterical number 63 ; methought it was high time for my folly to die, and to employ the remnant of wit to other calmer thoughts less sweet and less bitter." There can be little doubt that the beautiful "spiritual sonnets" ascribed to him by Mr Park, and printed in vol. ii. of the 'Heliconia,' are his composition.  Those addressed to "our Blessed Lady" are particularly fine.

## IV.—THOMAS LODGE (1556–1625).

Lodge, the next in order of our sonneteers, led rather a varied life.  His father was a grocer in London, who in 1563 attained to the dignity of Lord Mayor.  He entered Trinity College, Oxford, in 1573, and Lincoln's Inn in 1578 ; but literature seems to have had more attraction for him than the bar.  In 1586, and again in 1591-3, we find him engaged in privateering expeditions to the West Indies, in search of excitement and adventure.  He belonged to the wild society of Greene, Marlowe, and Nash ; but if he took much part in their dissipations, he had strength enough to survive it, and when the leaders of the set died off, he became sober and respectable, studied medicine, gave up poetry, and spent the leisure of his professional life in translating Josephus, and the "works, both natural and moral," of Seneca.  His chief productions were—A 'Defence of Poetry, Music, and Stage-plays,' in reply to Stephen Gosson's 'School of Abuse,' 1580 ; 'Alarm against Usurers,' along with the novelette of 'Forbonius and Prisceria,' 1584 ; 'Scylla's Metamorphosis,' with "sundry most absolute Poems and Sonnets," 1589 ; 'Euphues Golden Legacy,' (reprinted in Mr Collier's 'Shakespeare's Library,' as being the basis of "As You Like It," 1590; 'Phyllis honoured with Pastoral Sonnets,' 1593; 'The Wounds of Civil War,' a tragedy on the history of Marius and Sylla, 1594; 'A Fig for Momus,' a body of satires, 1595; 'Wit's Misery and the World's Madness,' a prose satire, 1596; 'A Marguerite of America,' a very tragical novel, 1596.

Lodge's love-poems have an exquisite delicacy and grace: they breathe a tenderer and truer passion than we find in any of his contemporaries. His sonnets are more loose and straggling, slighter and less compactly built, than Constable's or Daniel's; but they have a wonderful charm of sweet fancy and unaffected tenderness. His themes are the usual praises of beauty and complaints of unkindness; but he contrives to impart to them a most unusual air of sincere devotion and graceful fervour. None of his rivals can equal the direct and earnest simplicity and grace of his adoration of Phyllis, and avowal of faith in her constancy.

> "Fair art thou, Phyllis; ay, so fair, sweet maid,
>     As nor the sun nor I have seen more fair;
> For in thy cheeks sweet roses are embayed
>     And gold more pure than gold doth gild thy hair.
> Sweet bees have hived their honey on thy tongue,
>     And Hebe spiced her nectar with thy breath:
> About thy neck do all the graces throng
>     And lay such baits as might entangle Death.
> In such a breast what heart would not be thrall?
>     From such sweet arms who would not wish embraces?
> At thy fair hands who wonders not at all,
>     Wonder itself through ignorance embases.
> Yet nathöless tho' wondrous gifts you call these,
> My faith is far more wonderful than all these."

There is a seeming artlessness in Lodge's sonnets, a winning directness, that constitutes a great part of their charm. They seem to be uttered through a clear and pure medium straight from the heart: their tender fragrance and music come from the heart itself. If the poet's design was to assume a pastoral innocence and simplicity, he has eminently succeeded. There are many conceits in his sonnets, but they are expressed so simply and naturally that they take on the semblance of half-earnest beliefs. A simple silly Arcadian may be allowed the sweet fancy of supposing a storm to be the result of Aurora's envy and despair at seeing his lovely mistress.

> "The dewy roseate Morn had with her hairs
>     In sundry sorts the Indian clime adorned;
> And now her eyes apparelled in tears
>     The loss of lovely Memnon long had mourned:

> Whenas she spied the nymph whom I admire,
>     Kembing her locks, of which the yellow gold
> Made blush the beauties of her curled wire,
>     Which heaven itself with wonder might behold:
> Then red with shame, her reverend locks she rent,
>     And weeping hid the beauty of her face—
> The flower of fancy wrought such discontent:
>     The sighs which 'midst the air she breathed a space
> A three days' stormy tempest did maintain,
> Her shame a fire, her eyes a swelling rain."

And when despair seizes him, with what earnestness he makes his appeal to the last relief !—

> " Burst, burst, poor heart, thou hast no longer hope :
>     Captive mine eyes unto eternal sleep ;
> Let all my senses have no further scope ;
>     Let death be lord of me and all my sheep.
> For Phyllis hath betrothed fierce disdain,
>     That makes his mortal mansion in her heart ;
> And tho' my tongue have long time taken pain,
>     To sue divorce and wed her to desart,
> She will not yield ; my words can have no power ;
>     She scorns my faith ; she laughs at my sad lays ;
> She fills my soul with never-ceasing sour,
>     Who filled the world with volumes of her praise.
> In such extremes what wretch can cease to crave
> His peace from Death who can no mercy have ? "

It may, however, be acknowledged that Lodge's nature was not specially fitted for the sonnet form of composition ; he was not sufficiently patient and meditative to elaborate intricate stanzas. His lines have on them the dewy freshness of an impulsive gush, —a freshness off which the dew has not been brushed by the travail of thought ; and the opening of his sonnets in many cases leads us to expect better things than we find as we proceed when the leading idea has been hammered out into a quatorzain.   In the sonnet that opens with the lines—

> " Ah, pale and dying infant of the spring,
>     How rightly now do I resemble thee !
> That self-same hand that thee from stalk did wring,
>     Hath rent my breast and robbed my heart from me "—

the conclusion is laboured and disappointing.   And still more disappointing is the sonnet to his lady on her sickness, which opens with the exquisitely tender verses—

> " How languisheth the primrose of love's garden ?
> How trill her tears the elixir of my senses ? "

Although it contains two other beautiful lines of adjuration—

> " Ah, roses, love's fair roses, do not languish :
> Blush through the milk-white veil that holds you covered."

Mixed with his sonnets to Phyllis, and scattered through his prose tales, are many lyrics of less intricate measure, which show Lodge's charm at the height of its power.   Take, for example, the two following in honour of Phyllis :—

"Love guards the roses of thy lips,
    And flies about them like a bee ;
If I approach, he forward skips,
    And if I kiss, he stingeth me.
Love in thine eyes doth build his bower,
    And sleeps within their pretty shine ;
And if I look the boy will lower,
    And from their orbs shoot shafts divine.
Love works thy heart within his fire
    And in my tears doth firm the same ;
And if I tempt, it will retire,
    And of my plaints doth make a game.
Love, let me cull her choicest flowers,
    And pity me, and calm her eye;
Make soft her heart, dissolve her lowers,
    Then will I praise thy deity.
But if thou do not, Love, I'll truly serve her,
In spite of thee, and by firm faith deserve her.

"My Phyllis hath the morning sun,
    At first to look upon her,
And Phyllis hath morn-waking birds
    Her risings for to honour.
My Phyllis hath prime feathered flowers
    That smile when she treads on them,
And Phyllis hath a gallant flock
    That leaps since she doth own them.
But Phyllis hath so hard a heart,
    Alas that she should have it !
As yields no mercy to desart
    Nor grace to those that crave it.
Sweet sun, when thou lookest on,
    Pray her regard my moan.
Sweet birds, when you sing to her,
    To yield some pity woo her.
Sweet flowers, whenas she treads on,
    Tell her her beauty deads one.
And if in life her love she nill agree me,
Pray her before I die she'll come and see me. '

Not less exquisite is Rosalind's Madrigal :—

"Love in my bosom like a bee
    Doth suck his sweet :
    Now with his wings he plays with me,
        Now with his feet.
    Within mine eyes he makes his nest,
    His bed amid my tender breast,
    My kisses are his daily feast,
    And yet he robs me of my rest.
        Ah, wanton, will ye ?

And if I sleep then percheth he
  With pretty flight,
And makes his pillow of my knee
  The livelong night.
Strike I my lute, he tunes the string,  ˙
He music plays if so I sing,
He lends me every lovely thing :
Yet cruel he my heart doth sting.
  Whist, wanton, still ye,

Else I with roses every day
  Will whip you hence ;
And bind you when you long to play
  For your offence.
I'll shut mine eyes to keep you in,
I'll make you fast it for your sin,
I'll count your power not worth a pin,
Alas ! what hereby shall I win,
  If he gainsay me !

What if I beat the wanton boy
  With many a rod ?
He will repay me with annoy,
  Because a god.
Then sit thou safely on my knee
And let thy bower my bosom be :
Lurk in mine eyes, I like of thee :
O Cupid, so thou pity me,
  Spare not but play thee."

˙ "Scylla's Metamorphosis," the tale of Glaucus and Scylla, is interesting on its own account, and further, as the probable model of Shakespeare's "Venus and Adonis," whose unhappy loves it introduces as an episode. It is at least the first published of the apocryphal classical tales which at that time became a transient fashion—the English anticipator, if not the model, of Marlowe's "Hero and Leander," Drayton's "Endymion and Phœbe," and Chapman's "Ovid's Banquet of Sense." I need not follow the windings of the tale. The gist is that Scylla was metamorphosed as a punishment for her cruelty to Glaucus, a sea-god : and the interest of the poem lies in its voluptuous descriptions. I may quote his picture of the anguish of Venus for comparison with Daniel's Henry and Shakespeare's Venus : it is more a pretty grief than a deep passion : its sweetness reminds us of a child's endearments to a dead pet bird.

" He that hath seen the sweet Arcadian boy
    Wiping the purple from his forced wound,
  His pretty tears betokening his annoy ;
    His sighs, his cries, his falling on the ground ;
  The echoes ringing from the rocks his fall,
  The trees with tears reporting of his thrall.

> And Venus starting at her love-mate's cry
>   Forcing her birds to haste her chariot on ;
> And, full of grief, at last, with piteous eye,
>   Seen where all pale with death he lay alone
> Whose beauty quail'd as wont the lilies droop
> When wasteful winter winds do make them stoop.
>
> Her dainty hand addressed to claw her dear,
>   Her roseal lip allied to his pale cheek,
> Her sighs, and then her looks and heavy cheer,
>   Her bitter threats, and then her passions meek ;
> How on his senseless corpse she lay a-crying,
> As if the boy were then but new a-dying."

Lodge's "Fig for Momus" is often amusing, but the satire is
not very pungent.   He was much too good-natured a man to be a
satirist : he was not capable even of smiling spite, much less of
bitter derision.   His "Epistles" are entitled to the claim that he,
makes for them, of being the first productions of the kind in
English, and their date disposes at once of Joseph Hall's conceited
boast—

> "I first adventure, follow me who list
> And be the second English satirist."

But priority is their chief merit : they are colourless imitations of
Horace.   Marston is the first real English satirist.

Nor can Lodge be said to have been successful as a dramatist.
The "Wounds of Civil War" is a heavy drama.   Sylla is drawn
with considerable power as a bold rough man with a certain sense
of humour in him : ambitious, boastful, treating his enemies with
scoffing contempt, making a jest of death and cruelty, rudely
repelling compliments, provoking public censure for the pleasure
of defying it.   He may have supplied some raw material for
Shakespeare's "Coriolanus."   Sylla talks very much in the vein
of Tamburlaine ; and it is probable from this that Lodge may
fairly get the credit or discredit of the extravagant ramps of
Rasni in the "Looking-glass for London," which he wrote in
conjunction with Greene.   It is a curious thing that men like
Lodge and Peele should quite equal, if not surpass, even Marlowe
in outrageous heroics.   One wonders that the Herod of the
Mysteries should be out-Heroded by one who dwells with such
fresh enthusiasm on tender beauties.   How different are Sylla's
rants from this strain !—

> "O shady vale, O fair enriched meads,
>   O sacred woods, sweet fields, and rising mountains ;
> O painted flowers, green herbs where Flora treads,
>   Refreshed by wanton winds and watery fountains."

Perhaps, however, it is not more surprising than that the author
of "Tamburlaine" should be the author of "Hero and Leander."

## V.—THOMAS WATSON (1557?–1592?).

We have mentioned incidently the ʿΕκατομπαθία, or Passionate Century of Love,' by Thomas Watson. Watson first appeared as an author in 1581, with a translation into Latin of the 'Antigone' of Sophocles. The "Passionate Century" (that is, *Hundred*) was published in 1582. Three years after, he executed a Latin elegiac poem, entitled "Amyntas." He continued the practice of Latin verse alongside of English: in 1590 he published an "Eglogue upon the Death of Sir Francis Walsingham" in Latin and English, adopting in this case the title of "Meliboeus." In 1593, in which year he was mentioned as if then dead,[1] his last work was published—a collection of sixty sonnets, entitled "The Tears of Fancy, or Love Disdained."

Neither the "Century of Love" nor the "Tears of Fancy" belongs to a high order of poetry. The "Century" was avowedly an exercise of skill: the love-passion, he tells us in the Preface, was "but supposed." With this the critic has no quarrel: so far Watson differs from many of his poetical brethren, only in the perhaps superfluous candour of the avowal. The misfortune is that the supposition, the imaginative passion, is weak. There is no constructive vitality in his lines; the words and images seem brought together by a process of mechanical accumulation. The "Tears of Fancy" are decidedly superior to the "Love-passions," but here also there is a fatal lack of spontaneity and freshness: the superiority has every appearance of being due to the author's study of Spenser.

The "Passionate Century" is worth reading as a repertory of commonplace lover's hyperboles. There never was so sweet a lady, never so fond nor so distraught a lover. Hand, foot, lip, eye, brow, and golden locks are all incomparable. The ages never have produced, and never will produce, such another; Apelles could not have painted her, Praxiteles could not have sculptured her, Virgil and Homer could not have expressed her, and Tully would not have ventured to repeat the number of her gifts. She is superior to all the mythological paramours of Jove. The various goddesses have contributed their best endowments, mental and physical, to make her perfect. Her voice excels Arion's harp, Philomela's song, Apollo's lute; yea—

> "Music herself and all the Muses nine
> For skill or voice their titles may resign."

The despair produced in the lover's heart by the disdain of such a paragon is in a corresponding ratio. Vesuvius is nothing to

---

[1] See the introduction to Mr Arber's reprint.

the fire that consumes his heart.   The pains of hell would be a
comparative relief.   He suffers the combined tortures of Tantalus,
Ixion, Tityus, and Sisyphus :—

> " If Tityus, wretched wight, beheld my pains,
>     He would confess his wounds to be but small :
> A vulture worse than his tears all my veins,
>     Yet never lets me die, nor live at all,
> Would God a while I might possess his place,
>     To judge of both which were in better case."

The "Tears of Fancy," which, as we have said, are chiefly imitation gems, observe the same form as Daniel's.   The two following quatrains, with their pretty *anadiplosis*, or doubling in one
line upon the last words of the preceding, are an extreme example
of the poet's imitation of Spenser.   Cupid is the eager fugitive,
bent on mischief :—

> " Then on the sudden fast away he fled,
>     He fled apace as from pursuing foe :
> Ne ever looked he back, ne turned his head,
>     Until he came whereas he wrought my woe.
> Tho' casting from his back his bended bow,
>     He quickly clad himself in strange disguise :
> In strange disguise that no man might him know,
>     So coucht himself within my Lady's eyes."

The two following conceits are in his best manner, and derive
a certain interest from their having apparently been imitated in
Shakespeare's sonnets 46 and 47 :—

> " My heart imposed this penance on mine eyes,
>     Eyes the first causers of my heart's lamenting :
> That they should weep till love and fancy dies,
>     Fond love the last cause of my heart's repenting.
> Mine eyes upon my heart inflict this pain,
>     Bold heart that dared to harbour thoughts of love !
> That it should love and purchase fell disdain,
>     A grievous penance, which my heart doth prove.
> Mine eyes did weep as heart had then imposed,
>     My heart did pine as eyes had it constrained :
> Eyes in their tears my paled face disclosed,
>     Heart in his sighs did show it was disdained.
> So th' one did weep, th' other sigh'd, both grieved,
> For both must live and love, both unrelieved."

> " My heart accused mine eyes and was offended,
>     Vowing the cause was in mine eyes' aspiring :
> Mine eyes affirmed my heart might well amend it,
>     If he at first had banished love's desiring.
> Heart said that love did enter at the eyes,
>     And from the eyes descended to the heart :
> Eyes said that in the heart did sparks arise,
>     Which kindled flame that wrought the inward smart.

> Heart said eyes' tears might soon have quench'd that flame,
> Eyes said heart's sighs at first might love excite.
> So heart the eyes, and eyes the heart did blame,
> Whilst both did pine, for both the pain did feel.
> Heart sighed and bled, eyes wept and gazed too much :
> Yet must I gaze because I see none such."

These sonnets, with or without the following beginning of Watson's 22d Love-passion—

> "When wert thou born, sweet Love ? who was thy sire ?
> When Flora first adorn'd Dame Tellus' lap,
> Then sprung I forth with wanton Hot Desire.
> Who was thy nurse, to feed thee first with pap ?
> Youth first with tender hand bound up my head,
> Then said, with looks alone I should be fed ——"

may have suggested the song in the 'Merchant of Venice,' Act iii. 2, "Tell me, where is Fancy bred."[1]

## VI.—MICHAEL DRAYTON (1563–1631).

In Spenser's "Colin Clout's Come Home Again," published in 1595, occur four lines that are commonly supposed to refer to Shakespeare—

> "And there though last not least is Action ;
> A gentler shepherd may nowhere be found :
> Whose muse, full of high thought's invention,
> Doth like himself heroically sound."

A much stronger probability may be made out for Drayton. Drayton made his *début* as a pastoral poet in 1593, with his "Idea : Shepherd's Garland, fashioned in Nine Eclogues ;" and followed this up in 1594 with a body of sonnets—"Idea's Mirror, Amours in Quatorzains"—and the mythological tale of "Endymion and Phœbe." It has been considered conclusive against the probability of his being referred to by Spenser that "he had published nothing in an heroical strain even in 1595 ;" and that "it would be difficult to assign any meaning to the assertion that his name did, *like himself,* heroically sound." But Drayton's first publication, 'Harmony of the Church,' 1591, versified the highest poetry of the Old Testament, and loftily disclaimed all intention of "feeding any vain humour"; while the poetical name that he assumed was Rowland or Roland, the most heroic name in

---

[1] A writer in the 'Quarterly Review,' No. 267, ascribes the suggestion of this song to a sonnet by Jacopo da Lentino. The sonnet is not known to have been printed before 1661, but the writer supposes Shakespeare to have seen it in MS., and considers it a proof that Shakespeare could read Italian, if not that he had been in Italy ! The coincidence is certainly striking, but the birthplace of Love or Fancy in the eyes was a commonplace. I have remarked several English poems of the time quite capable of having given the suggestion.

chivalry.  Spenser, full as he was of Ariosto, was much more
likely to be struck with the heroic sound of Roland than of
Shakespeare.  Further, the aspiring character of Drayton's muse
would seem to have struck other minds than Spenser's.  Prefixed
to "Endymion and Phœbe" is a commendatory poem containing
the following lines :—

> "Rowland, when first I read thy stately rhymes
> In shepherd's weeds when yet thou livedst unknown,
>
> I then beheld thy chaste Idea's fame
> Put on the wings of thy immortal style.
>
> Thy fiery spirit mounts up to the sky,
> And what thou writest lives to Eternity."

Drayton did more afterwards to show the loftiness or heroism
of his thoughts.  His chief productions were—"Mortimeriados"
(a poem on the civil wars in the reign of Edward II., recast and
published in 1603 under the title of the "Barons' Wars"), 1596;
"England's Heroical Epistles" (imaginary letters after the manner
of Ovid between lovers celebrated in English history), 1598;
"Polyolbion" (a metrical description of England, county by
county), eighteen books in 1612, thirty complete in 1622; "The
Battle of Agincourt," 1627.

Not much is known of his personal history.  He was born at
Hartshill, Atherston, Warwickshire, near the river Anker.  In
one of his poems he speaks of himself as having been a "proper
goodly page."  His relations with patrons and patronesses are
known only from his dedications, which are addressed to various
honourable and noble personages.  In the course of his numerous publications, he fell out lamentably with the booksellers:
in a letter to Drummond, he calls them "a company of base
knaves, whom I both scorn and kick at."  In person, he was a
swart little man, full of energy and an enthusiastic sense of his
own powers; erudite, laborious, versatile; noted for the respectability of his life, and distinguished by the ardour of his orthodox
and patriotic sentiments.  I doubt whether he had any special
call to poetry beyond the contagion of circumstances; ambition
made his verses.  No person with literary gifts could have lived
in such an atmosphere without catching something of the poetic
frenzy: one could hardly have helped learning how to express the
fiery touch of love, and the sweet influences of nature.  Drayton
has a suspicious pride in the exercise of his gift: originality and
versatility are the two qualities that he boasts of, as if he had
overmastered the muse by intellectual force rather than won her
by natural affinity.  Yet he has written some interesting poetry:
his "Nymphidia" is a pretty burlesque of love, jealousy, combat,

and reconciliation at the Court of Faeryland; his "Polyolbion,"
a miracle of industry and sustained enthusiasm, contains some
fine descriptions; one, at least, of his sonnets (that quoted in
Mr Palgrave's 'Golden Treasury') is exceedingly happy and ingenious; and his poem on the Battle of Agincourt is vivid,
stirring, and filled throughout with the most glowing patriotism.
His ode on the Battle of Agincourt is, perhaps, his masterpiece:
Mr Swinburne ranks it with Campbell's "Battle of the Baltic,"
of which it seems to have been the model.

> " Fair stood the wind for France,
> When we our sails advance,
> Nor now to prove our chance
>   Longer not tarry,
> But put into the main :
> At Kaux the mouth of Seine
> With all his warlike train
>   Landed King Harry.
>
> And taking many a fort
> Furnish'd in warlike sort
> Coming toward Agincourt
>   In happy hour ;
> Skirmishing day by day
> With those oppose his way
> Whereas the general lay
>   With all his power.
>
> And ready to be gone,
> Armour on armour shone,
> Drum unto drum did groan,
>   To hear was wonder ;
> That with the cries they make
> The very earth did shake ;
> Trumpet to trumpet spake,
>   Thunder to thunder.
>
> Well it thine age became,
> O noble Erpingham !
> That didst the signal frame
>   Unto the forces ;
> When from a meadow by,
> Like a storm suddenly,
> The English archery
>   Stuck the French horses.
>
> When down their bows they threw,
> And forth their bilboes drew,
> And on the French they flew,
>   No man was tardy.
> Arms from the shoulder sent ;
> Scalps to the teeth were rent ;
> Down the French peasants went :
>   These were men hardy.

> On happy Crispin day
> Fought was the noble fray,
> Which Fame did not delay
>     To England to carry.
> O when shall Englishmen
> With such acts fill a pen,
> Or England breed again
>     Such a King Harry ! "

There is something of the same fire in his poem on the same
glorious battle, though it is weighted and obscured by the laborious
circumstantiality, the industrious particularisation, which is so
conspicuous also in his "Polyolbion."  He names the various
ships, and describes the colours and ensigns of the various companies, with Homeric minuteness and more than Homeric ardour :
and realises such scenes as the two camps on the night before the
battle with great variety of vivid details.  His circumstantiality
sometimes has the powerful effect so often remarked in the
descriptions of Defoe : for example, the following incidents in
the siege of Harfleur :—

> "Now upon one side you should hear a cry
>     And all that quarter clouded with a smother ;
> The like from that against it by and by,
>     As though the one were echo to the other,
> The king and Clarence so their turns can ply ;
>     And valiant Glo'ster shows himself their brother,
> Whose mines to the besieged more mischief do,
> Than with the assaults above, the other two.
>
> An old man sitting by the fireside
>     Decrepit with extremity of age,
> Stilling his little grandchild when it cried,
>     Almost distracted with the batteries' rage ;
> Sometimes doth speak it fair, sometimes doth chide :
>     As thus he seeks its mourning to assuage,
> By chance a bullet doth the chimney hit,
> Which falling in doth kill both him and it.
>
> Whilst the sad weeping mother sits her down,
>     To give her little new-born babe the·pap,
> A luckless quarry, levelled at the town,
>     Kills the sweet baby sleeping in her lap,
> That with the fright she falls into a swoon ;
>     From which awaked, and mad with the mishap,
> As up a rampier shrieking she doth climb,
> Comes a great shot, and strikes her limb from limb.
>
> Whilst a sort run confusedly to quench
>     Some palace burning, or some fired street,
> Called from where they were fighting in the trench,
>     They in their way with balls of wildfire meet,

So plagued are the miserable French,
    Not above head but also under feet ;
For the fierce English vow the town to take,
Or of it soon a heap of stones to make.

Hot is the siege, the English coming on
    As men so long to be kept out that scorn,
Careless of wounds, as they were made of stone,
    As with their teeth the walls they would have torn :
Into a breach who quickly is not gone,
    Is by the next behind him overborne ;
So that they found a place that gave them way,
They never cared what danger therein lay."

If his sonnets have no great intrinsic interest, they derive a certain adventitious interest from their illustrative bearing on the sonnets of Shakespeare. The following, with its curious points of resemblance to Shakespeare's 144th sonnet—"Two loves I have of comfort and despair"—raises a doubt whether that perplexing sonnet is not more figurative than is commonly supposed. If I am right in my recollection that it did not appear before the edition of 1602, it may have been imitated from Shakespeare's, which appeared in 1599; and at any rate, taken in connection with the last lines of Shakespeare's sonnet, it raises the question whether Shakespeare's worser spirit was so serious an evil as the first part of the sonnet represents.

" An evil spirit your beauty haunts me still,
    Wherewith, alas ! I have been long possesst,
Which ceaseth not to tempt me to each ill,
    Nor gives me once but one poor minute's rest :
In me it speaks whether I sleep or wake,
    And when by means to drive it out I try,
With greater torments then it me doth take,
    And tortures me in most extremity :
Before my face it lays down my despairs
    And hastes me on unto a sudden death ;
Now tempting me to drown myself in tears
    And then in sighing to give up my breath :
Thus am I still provoked to every evil
By this good wicked spirit, sweet angel devil. "

In Drayton's sonnets we find several of the conceits that appear in Shakespeare's, such as the warfare between heart and eyes and the play upon the identity of the lover and his beloved ; but it may perhaps be more serviceable to quote his version of another commonplace, the promise of immortality to his mistress, to help to correct a vulgar notion that Shakespeare stood alone in the lofty confidence of eternal memory.  ·

" How many paltry, foolish, painted things,
    That now in coaches trouble every street,
Shall be forgotten, whom no poet sings,
    Ere they be well wrapped in their winding-sheet !

> Where I to thee eternity shall give,
>   When nothing else remaineth of these days,
> And queens hereafter shall be glad to live
>   Upon the alms of thy superfluous praise ;
> Virgins and matrons reading these my rhymes,
>   Shall be so much delighted with thy story,
> That they shall grieve they lived not in these times
>   To have seen thee, their sex's only glory :
> So shalt thou fly above the vulgar throng
> Still to survive in my immortal song."

> " Stay, speedy Time, behold before thou pass,
>   From age to age, what thou hast sought to see,
>   One in whom all the excellencies be ;
> In whom Heaven looks itself as in a glass :
> Time, look thou too in this tralucent glass
>   And thy youth past in this pure mirror see,
>   As the world's beauty in his infancy,
> What it was then, and thou before it was ;
> Pass on, and to posterity tell this ;
>   Yet see thou tell but truly what hath been :
>   Say to our nephews, that thou once hast seen
> In perfect human shape, all heavenly bliss :
> And bid them mourn, nay more, despair with thee
> When she is gone, her like again to see."


## VII.—WILLIAM SHAKESPEARE—*Sonnets.*

After a survey of the huge issue of sonnets between 1591 and
1594, the characteristics of the sonnets of Shakespeare seem to
stand out with greater distinctness. They divide themselves into
three classes. First come the sonnets of the ' Passionate Pilgrim,'
some of which rise out of the relations between Venus and Adonis,
and most of which are in the same strain, treating the theme of
love with a certain lightness. Next come the twenty-six sonnets placed among his Sonnets so - called, between the 127th
and the 152d inclusive : sonnets sufficiently alarming at first sight,
but not so very terrible when we examine them boldly. Finally
comes the main body of his sonnets, addressed to his friend.
These are in every way more powerful and mature. The second
and third classes are, as we shall see, strongly contrasted in
sentiment with the effusions of preceding sonneteers.

In 1598, one Francis Meres, in a work entitled ' *Palladis Tamia,
Wit's Treasury,*' eulogised the various English poets, finding par-
allels for them among the Greek and Latin poets. Among others,
he remarked on Shakespeare, and said : " As the soul of Euphor-
bus was thought to live in Pythagoras, so the sweet, witty soul
of Ovid lives in mellifluous and honey-tongued Shakespeare ;
witness his *Venus and Adonis*, his *Lucrece*, his sugared *Sonnets*
among his private friends," &c. The sonnets published in the

following year in the 'Passionate Pilgrim,' which bore Shakespeare's name on the title-page, fully answer this description:[1] they may with sufficient propriety be said to be animated by the sweet witty soul of Ovid. The rest of Shakespeare's sonnets were not published till 1609, when they were issued as 'Shakespeare's Sonnets,' "never before imprinted"; and some critics have asseverated with unaccountable confidence that the second issue *must* be the sonnets spoken of by Meres, although the publication of them had been delayed. There is not the slightest ground for this assertion: "among his private friends" cannot be taken to mean "to his private friend." In the sonnets of the 'Passionate Pilgrim' there is quite enough to justify the words of Meres. Besides, Meres seems to have made his comparison with some notion of its meaning, seeing that "Venus" and "Lucrece" at once carry us to the *Amores* and the *Heroides;* and in the case of the sonnets addressed to a friend the comparison would be wholly inapplicable. Further, the 107th sonnet, containing the line—

: "The mortal moon hath her eclipse endured,"

*must* have been written after the death of Elizabeth, to whose name of "Cynthia" the line is an undoubted reference.

Sonnets cxxvii.-clii. are, as I have said, startling at first sight. They are unmistakably addressed to a woman of loose character, and they seem to represent the poet as involved in a disreputable passion. But when we look more closely into them, we begin to suspect that, if those sonnets are to be treated as bearing all on one subject, we do wrong to take too serious a view of them. One must not treat published sonnets addressed to a courtesan as earnest private correspondence, or as grave confessions whispered in the ear of a ghostly counsellor. I believe that the proper view is to regard them as exercises of skill, undertaken in a spirit of wanton defiance and derision of commonplace. When young Hal was told of his father's triumphs, the humorous youth indulged in a curious eccentricity, which, if I am not in error, represents exactly the spirit of these sonnets—

> " His answer was, he would unto the stews,
> And from the commonest creature pluck a glove,
> And wear it as a favour; and with that
> He would unhorse the lustiest challenger."

Now those who have gone through the overwhelming mass of

[1] Part, at least, of the 'Passionate Pilgrim' was composed by Shakespeare. See Mr Collier's remarks on the subject. I should be disposed to assent to nearly all, if not all, that Messrs Clark and Wright have published as Shakespeare's under that title. (See under "Marlowe.") The name "sonnet" was not confined to quatorzains; several of the Passionate Pilgrim's sonnets are in the six-line staves used in Watson's "Passionate Century of Love."

sonnets poured out about the time when Shakespeare began to
write—sonnets in admiring praise and mournful blame of Stella,
Delia, Diana, Phyllis, and Idea—will not be slow to understand,
if not to sympathise with, the wanton outburst of impatient genius.
The new sonneteer lays down a humorous challenge—Give place,
ye lovers, who boast of beauty and virtue : my mistress is neither
fair nor faithful, yet I can praise her with as much zeal and fury
as the best of you—

> " My mistress' eyes are nothing like the sun ;
>     Coral is far more red than her lips' red :
> If snow be white, why then her breasts are dun ;
>     If hairs be wires, black wires grow on her head.
> I have seen roses damasked, red and white,
>     But no such roses see I in her cheeks ;
> And in some perfumes is there more delight,
>     Than in the breath that from my mistress reeks.
> I love to hear her speak, yet well I know
>     That music hath a far more pleasing sound ;
> I grant I never saw a goddess go:
>     My mistress, when she walks, treads on the ground :
> And yet, by Heaven, I think my love as rare
> As any she, belied by false compare."

He is no tame admirer and adorer, seeing nothing in his mistress
but perfection : he woos with a bolder cheer.   He tells her plainly
that he does not love her with his eyes, for they see in her a thousand errors : yet his heart loves her in spite of them (cxli.)   He
speculates on the cause of the lover's blindness : concludes that it
comes from watching and tears : and apostrophises the cunning of
Love in thus hiding his mistress's imperfections (cxlviii.)   When
she swears that she is made of truth, he believes her—although he
knows that she lies (cxxxviii.)   He must surely be frantic mad to
swear her fair and think her bright when she is black as hell and
dark as night (cxlvii.)   His complaints of unkindness and allegations of cruelty might easily pass as serious, did not the other sonnets reveal the humorous mockery : yet they are not without the
jocular touch.   He complains of unkindness with a leniency hardly
consistent with serious passion—

> " Tell me thou lovest elsewhere ; but in my sight,
>     Dear heart, forbear to glance thine eye aside."

That is to say, do whatever you please behind my back, but do not
ogle other men before my eyes (cxxxix.)   He accuses her of pride
and cruelty, but warns her not to carry it too far—lest he do—
what ? commit suicide ? no, but—

> " Lest sorrow lend me words, and words express
>     The *manner* of my pity-wanting pain."

Two or three of the series, and particularly cxxviii., praise the lady without obvious mockery, yet with a certain gay familiarity. The only sonnet of the series radically inconsistent with this theory is the 146th. Down to the 143d the gay defiant tone is unmistakable : two or three after that are uncertain and equivocal, and the 146th seems unmistakably serious. Must we then give up the theory? I think not. There is an obvious explanation which one may produce without being liable to a charge of sophistry; and that is, that Shakespeare, having taken up the relation between a lover and a courtesan originally in wanton humorous defiance of somewhat lackadaisical effusions, his dramatic instinct could not be restrained from pursuing the relationship farther into more serious aspects.

The sonnets addressed to a friend—a young nobleman, apparently, whose bounty the poet has experienced, and whose personal gifts and graces he admires with impassioned fondness—depart very strikingly from the sonnets of Shakespeare's predecessors. He ceases to reiterate Petrarch's woes, and opens up a new vein of feeling. Love is still the argument—love's fears and confidences, crosses and triumphs—but it is love for a different object under different conditions. We find in Shakespeare's sonnets most of the commonplaces of the course of true love, coldness and reconciliation, independence and devoted submission, but they are transferred to the course of impassioned friendship, and thereby transfigured. Are, then, these moods of impassioned friendship real or feigned, utterances from the heart, or artificial creations to break the monotony of the language and imagery of passionate admiration between the sexes? Some modern critics would have us believe that the theme is not friendship in any shape, real or feigned: the sentiment of the sonnets, they say, is too warm to be inspired except by the charms of woman : Shakespeare could not have admired beauty so fondly in any youth however beautiful. These critics maintain that the sonnets must have been addressed to a woman : and Coleridge went the length of saying that one sonnet where the sex is indisputable must have been introduced as a blind.[1] All this is the mere insanity of critical dogmatism, maintained in defiance of the most obtrusive facts. Mr Gerald Massey, not being able to get over masculine pronouns and other indications of gender, but still unwilling to admit that some of the sonnets could have been addressed to a man, professes to distinguish between sonnets of friendship and sonnets of sexual love, and redistributes them accordingly. In sonnets addressed unequivocally to his youthful friend, it is, says Mr Massey, manly

---

[1] This is hardly less curious than the amiable Opium-eater's notion that Hamlet's character was exceedingly like his own.

beauty that the poet extols.  What, then, are we to make of
Sonnet iii., where the young man is told—

> "Thou art thy mother's glass, and she in thee
> Calls back the lovely April of her prime"?

Mr Massey draws the line between manly beauty and womanly
beauty at whiteness of hand and fragrance of breath : when
Shakespeare praises these points of beauty, he must be addressing a woman.[1]   Yet in Sonnet cvi. Shakespeare ascribes "sweet
beauty's best" without distinction to ladies and lovely knights—

> "When in the chronicle of wasted time
>     I see descriptions of the fairest wights,
> And beauty making beautiful old rhyme
>     In praise of ladies dead and *lovely knights;*
> Then in the blazon of sweet beauty's best,
>     Of hand, of foot, of lip, of eye, of brow,
> I see their antique pen would have express'd
>     Ev'n such a beauty as you master now."

Further, Mr Massey, if I mistake not, ascribes to the friend
Sonnet liii. containing these lines—

> "Describe Adonis, and the counterfeit
>     Is poorly imitated after you ;
> On Helen's cheek all art of beauty set,
>     And you in Grecian tires are painted new."

And when we look to the description of Adonis we find such
lines as—

> "Once more the ruby-coloured portal opened
> That to his mouth did honey passage yield."

And—

> "Who when he lived his breath and beauty set
> Gloss on the rose, smell to the violet."

It is bad enough to defy all indications of gender and declare
that none of these sonnets were addressed to a young man : it is
perhaps worse to say that some are and some are not, and to
make an arbitrary selection, taking one's own feelings as the
exact measure of the poet's.   Admiration of the personal beauty
of his friend is too closely woven into the sonnets to be detached
in this way.   They are interpenetrated with it : it is expressed
as warmly in sonnets when the sex happens to be unequivocal,
as in others where the rashness of dogmatic ingenuity is restrained
by no such accident.

[1] Gilderoy, in the ballad, is said to have a breath as sweet as rose, and a
hand fairer than any lady's, and yet he was a manly youth whom none dared
meet single-handed, and who "bauldly bare away the gear of many a Lawland
loon."

The friendship expressed in Shakespeare's sonnets was probably no less real than the love professed for their mistresses by other sonneteers. Friendship is not quite dead even in these degenerate days. There are still people alive to whom the warmth of the warmest of Shakespeare's sonnets would not appear an exaggeration. But there would seem to have been a peculiar exaltation of the sentiment of friendship among the Elizabethan poets. The titles of Edward's plays are "Damon and Pythias" and "Palamon and Arcite"; and in the one that has been preserved friendship is extolled above all other blessings. The 'Paradise of Dainty Devices' is full of "praises of friendship." The dramatists did not hesitate to bring it into collision with love, and to represent it as rising in some cases higher than love itself. Marlowe makes Edward II. desert his queen for the sake of Gaveston, and declare that he will rather lose his kingdom than renounce his favourite. In Lyly's "Endymion," Eumenides affirms that "such is his unspotted faith to Endymion, that whatsoever seemeth a needle to prick his finger is a dagger to wound his heart;" and when it is in his power to obtain whatever he asks, he hesitates between the recovery of his friend Endymion and the possession of his mistress Semele, and is finally decided by an old man in favour of the friend. Shakespeare himself has treated the problem in his "Two Gentlemen of Verona." In Proteus, the weaker-willed nature, new love is an irresistible passion stronger than friendship, and stronger also than old love; but in the manlier Valentine friendship is the nobler sentiment of the two, and even when his friend is convicted of the grossest treachery he comes generously forward and says, "All that is mine in Silvia I give thee." Commentators unable to understand this supreme and perhaps fantastic generosity of friendship, as Mr Gerald Massey is unable to understand the impassioned friendship of the sonnets, think there must be something wrong with the conclusion of the play: they wholly miss the design of the dramatist, and cry out that he has had recourse to a forced and unnatural expedient to extricate himself from a difficult complication. All these that I have mentioned, with the exception of Edward and Gaveston, were cases of friendship between equals. Bacon laid down that friendship could not exist between equals; and the Elizabethans were familiar with the often quoted friendships between Alexander and Hephæstion, Hercules and Hylas, Achilles and Patrocles, Socrates and Alcibiades, in which the sentiment was enhanced by the charms of strength on the one hand, and youth and beauty on the other. It is not impossible that the influence of the maiden queen had something to do with the laudation of friendship in the Elizabethan age; and the representation of women's parts on the stage by boys may have fostered to an unusual degree the sentimental admiration of beautiful youths. This last influence could hardly but have affected Shakespeare, seeing that he acted up to boys in that character, and that they must occasionally have crossed his mind with their "small pipes" and "smooth and rubious" lips when he was composing praises of the beauty that they represented. And it is difficult to see what can have been meant by the expression "Socratem ingenio"—a Socrates in disposition—in Shakespeare's epitaph, if it does not point to his sentiment for beautiful young men.

The sonnets, with the exception perhaps of the first seventeen advising his beautiful friend to marry, which may have been the poet's first offering of verses, or may have been composed at any time and placed first as a suitable preface, seem to follow the history of the friendship. I do not quite agree with Mr Armitage Brown's division of the 'Sonnets' into separate poems, in each of which the sonnet form is merely used as a stanza; but it seems to me unmistakable that there is a sequence in them, not only to this extent that several consecutive sonnets are occupied with the same theme, but to this further extent that the themes are consecutive, arising naturally as if in the course of the poet's varying relations with his friend, relations real or imagined. Certainly there is no justification for the course that Mr Massey has adopted of treating the sonnets as if they had been written on separate slips to different persons for different purposes, and shuffled together by the publisher.

The great question in connection with the sonnets is, who was Shakespeare's friend and the object of his praises? The poet's lofty promise of immortal memory has been fulfilled more liberally and less exactly than he intended: he, or his publisher for him, may be said to have immortalised everybody in that generation whose initials are known to have been W. and H., read either way; and the actual friend comes in for nothing more than a share of the disputed honour, if, indeed, he has as yet been recognised at all.

By the testimony of the sonnets themselves, Shakespeare's friend was young and beautiful, of rank superior to the poet, a bountiful patron, and very much courted by rival poets. Now two young noblemen are known to have extended their patronage to Shakespeare—Henry Wriothesley, Earl of Southampton, and William Herbert, Earl of Pembroke. It was to Southampton that Shakespeare dedicated 'Venus and Adonis'—the first heir of his invention—in 1593, and 'Lucrece' in the following year. The first dedication was couched in terms of distant respect: the second, which was as follows, bears in its warmth of expression a striking similarity to the language of the sonnets, particularly sonnet 26,—"The love I dedicate to your lordship is without end;

whereof this pamphlet, without beginning, is but a superfluous
moiety. The warrant I have of your honourable disposition, not
the worth of my untutored lines, makes it assured of acceptance.
What I have done is yours; what I have to do is yours; being
part in all I have, devoted yours. Were my worth greater, my
duty would show greater; meantime, as it is, it is bound to your
lordship, to whom I wish long life, still lengthened with all happiness." There is also a tradition that Southampton at one time
made the poet a present of a thousand pounds. The evidence for
the patronage of Shakespeare by Pembroke is not so pointed, but
is quite trustworthy. Shakespeare's fellow-players, Heming and
Condell, dedicated the folio of 1623 to the "incomparable pair
of brethren," the Earl of Pembroke and the Earl of Montgomery,
calling the poet "your servant Shakespeare," and mentioning that
they had "prosecuted both the plays and their author living with
much favour." Both Southampton and Pembroke were younger
men than the poet, Southampton by nine years (being born in
1573), Pembroke by sixteen years (being born in 1580). There is
no record of personal beauty in Southampton, while there is in the
case of Pembroke: but the known partiality of affection forbids
us to lay much stress on that. Both were bountiful patrons of
literature, and had sonnets addressed to them by Daniel, Chapman, Withers, and many others.

When we cast about for presumptions to turn the balance of
probability one way or the other, we naturally look first to the
inscription prefixed to the sonnets by the publisher. It runs as
follows: "To THE ONLIE BEGETTER OF THESE INSUING SONNETS
Mr W. H. ALL HAPPINESS AND THAT ETERNITIE PROMISED BY
OUR EVER - LIVING POET WISHETH THE WELL-WISHING ADVEN-
TURER IN SETTING FORTH T.T." Now the phrase "only begetter"
sounds strange in nineteenth-century ears; *we* should call the poet
the only begetter.[1] But the humility of dedication was carried
much farther by the Elizabethans. Shakespeare himself, in
dedicating his "Lucrece" to Southampton, used the expression—
"what I have done is yours; what I have to do is yours." It
is in allusion to this practice of poets that the Duke in "Twelfth
Night," apostrophising greatness cries—

> "Thousand escapes of wit
> Make thee the *father* of their idle dreams."

And in the dedication of Daniel's sonnets to "Delia," to the
Countess of Pembroke, the mother of the young Earl of Pembroke

---

[1] Too much stress should not be given to the "only." It need mean nothing
more than "matchless," "incomparable"; a strong superlative, as in the phrases
"*only* rare poet," "*only* expected imp of a noble house," or Shakespeare's
own expression in the first sonnet—"*only* herald of the gaudy spring."

just mentioned, we seem to have the very original of "T. T.'s"
expression.[1]   "Vouchsafe," the poet says—

> "Vouchsafe now to accept them as thine own,
>   *Begotten* by thy hand and my desire,
>   Wherein my zeal and thy great might is shown."

And this although Lady Mary was not Delia, but only lent her
name to countenance the young poet's first effusion.   Had, then,
Mr W. H. no nearer relation than this to Shakespeare's Sonnets:
was he not the noble young friend, but only some person whose
favour T. T. was anxious to conciliate?   One does not like to say
dogmatically what a bookseller might or might not have done
in those days, but I am inclined to think that "Mr W. H." must
stand for Shakespeare's friend and patron—for this reason, that
I cannot bring myself to believe that any bookseller would have
dared to divert the poet's promise of immortality from a person
of rank such as Shakespeare's friend and patron undoubtedly was.
I do not think the "Mr" need stand in our way.   Sidney is
called *Master* Philip Sidney in Webbe's 'Discourse of English
Poetry,' and Lord Buckhurst is entered as *M.* Sackville in 'England's Parnassus.'   Certainly, although so great an authority as
Mr Collier considers "Mr" a serious difficulty, it is much easier
to find probable reasons for the title than to find any tolerable
reason for the bookseller's appropriating the poet's promise for
the benefit of a friend of his own so obscure that history has
preserved no memorial of his name.   This would have been so
idiotic that it is incredible.   I see no reason for refusing to believe
that W. H. are the initials of the name of Shakespeare's friend.
Now, curiously enough, W. H. are the initials of William Herbert, Earl of Pembroke, and H. W. are the initials of Henry
Wriothesley, Earl of Southampton.   Dr Nathan Drake contended
that the Earl of Southampton was meant, and that the inversion
of the initials was intended as a blind.   But if any blind was
thought necessary, why have a dedication at all?   And why use
a blind that must at once draw suspicion on the Earl of Pembroke?   If the "Mr" was blind enough, the inversion of the
initials was unnecessary—and if it was not, then the Earl of Pembroke was pointed to; and if the sonnets were such that the
Earl of Southampton was ashamed of them, it is not likely that
T. T. would have fathered them on the Earl of Pembroke.   But
though the initials have proved a sufficient blind to the eyes of
posterity, I doubt very much whether any blind was intended
or effected by them when they first appeared.   In all probability,

---

[1] But the truth is, that the original might have been found in any dedication
from Geoffrey of Monmouth's downwards.   It is a commonplace compliment
from poet to patron.—1885.

tho object of Shakespeare's sonnets was perfectly well known to the first readers of them: and W. H. pointed to William Herbert as surely as T. T. pointed to Thomas Thorpe the bookseller.[1]

There is one circumstance which at first glance appears insignificant, but which, when considered, appears an almost conclusive presumption in favour of the Earl of Pembroke, and that is the parent that Shakespeare's friend is said to take after. In tho 3d sonnet the friend is told—

> " Thou art thy *mother's* glass, and she in thee
> Calls back tho lovely April of her prime."

Now it is open to say that this means no more than that Shakespeare's friend bore a resemblance to his mother more than to his father. But it is difficult to be satisfied with this interpretation when we remember who was " Pembroke's mother," and recall Ben Jonson's famous epitaph—

> " Underneath this sable hearse
> Lies the subject of all verse,
> Sidney's sister, Pembroke's mother ;
> Death ! ere thou hast slain another
> Learned and fair and good as she,
> Time shall throw a dart at thee."

No illustrious family ever won the hearts of the poets so completely as the Sidneys, and not of the poets only but of all men : they were universal favourites. As Sidney was considered the jewel of Elizabeth's Court, and his sister the paragon of her sex, so Pembroke was said to be "the most universally beloved and esteemed of any man" of his age. This lends additional point to Shakespeare's urgency for the marriage of his friend : he might well be anxious for the preservation of so noble a stock.

Any inference to be drawn from dates is also on the whole favourable to the claims of Pembroke as against Southampton. One thing, indeed, at first seems to be in favour of Southampton —namely, the number of coincidences in expression between the sonnets and comedies composed before the end of the century. But two facts combine to deprive this argument from coincidences

---

[1] Seeing that Shakespeare lays so much stress on their difference of rank in the sonnets, and agrees that he cannot always be acknowledged in public, it would have been inconsistent for him to have dedicated them openly in his own name to his patron at full length. This may account for the publisher's taking the dedication in hand, and as it were endorsing the compliments of the poet. It might even have been necessary that the sonnets should appear to be published without consent of either poet or patron, and that the publisher should use the timid but transparent veil of " Mr W. H." as if he had made the dedication of his own accord and without permission. But this, of course, is pure speculation.

of any value.   One is that it was in those plays that Shakespeare made his first studies of the non-tragical relations between lovers, and formed his ways of looking at and expressing those relations : it was inevitable, therefore, that when he took up the parallel relations of friendship, the treatment should exhibit coincidences. And the other is that the comedies were frequently repeated, so that the poet was not allowed to forget his earlier studies : he might have gone home any evening before 1609 with his head full of "Love's Labour Lost" or the "Comedy of Errors."   We cannot, therefore, argue from coincidences in idea and expression that a sonnet and a play were composed at the same date.   The only sonnet of really indisputable date is the 107th, containing the reference to the death of Elizabeth or "Cynthia" as the eclipse of "the mortal moon" : this must have been composed after it had been seen that Elizabeth's death was to be followed by no dangerous consequences.   This sonnet must have been composed some time after March 1603.   Now, in the 104th sonnet, the poet tells his friend that three winters and three summers have passed since first they met.   If, then, there is any chronological sequence in the sonnets, if there is not a gap of several years between the 104th and the 107th—and in the absence of evidence to the contrary the presumption is that there is not—this would seem to show that Shakespeare made the acquaintance of his friend not long before the beginning of the century.   Which conclusion exactly suits the claims of Pembroke, who came to London in 1598, a youth of 18—and is radically adverse to the claims of Southampton, whom Shakespeare knew at least as early as 1594. The argument is not entitled to much weight, inasmuch as it presumes a chronological sequence, but it deserves to be mentioned as a slight corroboration.

Again, in the first sonnet, where the poet opens his recommendations of marriage, the friend is called "only herald to the gaudy spring."   What gaudy spring ?   Is this another reference to the time described in the 107th sonnet—

> "Incertainties now crown themselves assured,
> And peace proclaims olives of endless age.
> Now *with the drops of this most balmy time*
> My love looks fresh, and Death to me subscribes" ?

The minds of men seem to have been agitated by the fear of a disputed succession after the death of Elizabeth, and there was a disposition, partly from relief at the passing of the crisis without disturbance, and partly from a desire to flatter the new king, to hail the accession of James hopefully and joyfully as a spring. Thus Daniel in his Panegyric to the King's Most Excellent Majesty, exclaimed—

" What a return of comfort dost thou bring,
  Now at this fresh returning of our blood !
This meeting with the opening of the spring,
  To make our spirits likewise to embud !
What a new season of encouraging
Begins to enlength the days disposed to good !
What apprehension of recovery
Of greater strength, of more ability !

The pulse of England never yet did beat
  So strong as now : nor ever were our hearts
Let out to hopes so spacious and so great
  As now they are : nor ever in all parts
Did we thus feel so comfortable heat
  As now the glory of thy worth imparts :
The whole complexion of the commonwealth
  So weak before, hoped never for more health."

It is not at all improbable that Shakespeare's " gaudy spring " was
this same exultant season ; and if so, Southampton cannot have
been the friend addressed with such glowing flattery and urgent
fervour, seeing that he had then been married for several years.
Pembroke was then twenty-three years of age, and, as the representative of the Sidneys, might well be hailed as " the world's fresh
ornament," and " only herald of the gaudy spring."   The fact is,
that the more one looks into this vexed question, the more does
one find little particulars emerging, singly inconclusive, but all increasing the weight of the probability that Pembroke was the man.[1]

Let us turn now for a moment to a question hardly less interesting, namely—Who was the rival poet alluded to in the sonnets ?
So complete is the parallel of this course of true friendship to
the course of true love that even the passion of jealousy finds a
place.   Nine sonnets (lxxviii. - lxxxvi.) are occupied with the
pretensions of other poets, and one poet in particular, to the
gracious countenance of his patron.   In the 80th sonnet he
cries :—

" O how I faint when I of you do write,
  Knowing a better spirit doth use your name,
And in the praise thereof spends all his might,
  To make me tongue-tied, speaking of your fame !
But since your worth, wide as the ocean is,
  The humble as the proudest sail doth bear,
My saucy bark inferior far to his
  On your broad main doth wilfully appear."

Who was this " better spirit " ?   I hope I shall not be held
guilty of hunting after paradox if I say that every possible poet

<hr>

[1] Mr Thomas Tyler and Rev. W. A. Harrison have recently adduced new arguments in favour of Pembroke.  See *Academy*, March 8 and 22, April 19, June 7
and 21, July 5, 1884.

has been named but the right one, nor of presumption if I say that he is so obvious that his escape from notice is something little short of miraculous.   The 86th sonnet supplies ample means of identification :—

> " Was it the proud full sail of his great verse,
>     Bound for the prize of all too precious you,
>   That did my ripe thoughts in my brain inhearse,
>     Making their tomb the womb wherein they grew ?
>   Was it his spirit, by spirits taught to write
>     Above a mortal pitch, that struck me dead ?
>   No, neither he, nor his compeers by night
>     Giving him aid, my verse astonished.
>   He, nor that affable familiar ghost
>     Which nightly gulls him with intelligence,
>   As victors of my silence cannot boast :
>     I was not sick of any fear from thence :
>   But when your countenance filled up his line,
>   Then lacked I matter ; that enfeebled mine. "

The allusions to supernatural assistance are here very pointed, and upon the strength of them Marlowe has been suggested as having been a man of dark and mysterious reputation, who was suspected of dealings with evil spirits.   The insuperable objection to Marlowe is that he died in 1593 ; and even supposing Southampton to have been Shakespeare's patron, we have no evidence of their acquaintance prior to 1593, and there is no evidence that Marlowe was acquainted with Southampton at all.   Mr Massey, however, argues confidently for Marlowe, on the ground that there was nobody else to whom the pointed charge of supernatural dealing could apply.   But there was another to whom the allusions apply more pointedly than to Marlowe, and that was George Chapman, a man less honoured now, but numbered in his own generation among the greatest of its poets.   Chapman was a man of overpowering enthusiasm, ever eager in magnifying poetry, and advancing fervent claims to supernatural inspiration.   In 1594 he published a poem called the "Shadow of Night," which goes far to establish his identity with Shakespeare's rival.   In the Dedication, after animadverting severely on vulgar searchers after knowledge, he exclaims—"Now what a supererogation in wit this is, to think Skill so mightily pierced with their loves that she should prostitutely show them her secrets, when she will scarcely be looked upon by others *but with invocation, fasting, watching ; yea, not without having drops of their souls like a heavenly familiar.*" Here we have something like a profession of the familiar ghost that Shakespeare saucily laughs at.   But Shakespeare's rival gets his intelligence by night : special stress is laid in the sonnet upon the aid of his compeers by night, and his nightly familiar.   Well, Chapman's poem is called the "Shadow of Night," and its purpose is to extol the wonderful powers of Night in imparting knowledge to her votaries. He addresses her with fervent devotion :—

> "Rich tapered sanctuary of the blest,
> Palace of ruth, made all of tears and rest,
> To thy black shades and desolation
> I consecrate my life."

And he cries :—

> "All you possessed with indepressed spirits,
> Endued with nimble and aspiring wits,
> Come consecrate with me to sacred Night
> Your whole endeavours and detest the light.
>
> No pen can anything eternal write
> That is not steeped in humour of the Night."

It is not simply that night is the best season for study : the enthusiastic poet finds more active assistance than silence and freedom from interruption. When the avenues of sense are closed by sleep, his soul rises to the court of Skill (the mother of knowledge, who must be propitiated by drops of the soul like an heavenly familiar), and if he could only remember what he learns there, no secret would be hid from him.

> "Let soft sleep,
> Binding my senses lose my working soul,
> That in her highest pitch she may control
> The court of Skill, compact of mystery,
> Wanting but franchisement and memory
> To reach all secrets."

As regards the other feature in the rival poet, "the proud full sail of his great verse," that applies with almost too literal exactness to the Alexandrines of Chapman's Homer, part of which appeared in 1596; and as for its being bound for the prize of Shakespeare's patron, both Pembroke and Southampton were included in the list of those honoured with dedicatory sonnets in a subsequent edition. Chapman's chief patron was Sir Francis Walsingham, whose daughter Sir Philip Sidney had married, and nothing could have been more natural than that the old man should introduce his favourite to the Countess of Pembroke or her son. But apart from Alexandrines and proved or probable connection with Southampton and Pembroke, I contend that the other reference to Chapman is too pointed to be mistaken ; and though Chapman's name has not received due prominence in the manuals of our literature, no one who has read any of his poetry, and who knows his own lofty pretensions and the rank accorded him in his own generation, will think that his "proud sail" has been unduly honoured by the affected jealousy and good-humoured banter of the "saucy bark" of Shakespeare.

# CHAPTER VI.

### DRAMATISTS BEFORE SHAKESPEARE.

A VERY natural question to ask, in beginning the study of the Elizabethan drama, is, What were the causes of that extraordinary outburst of creative genius?  No satisfactory answer has yet been given to that question : perhaps none can be given.  There the literature stands full grown ; but when we are asked how it came there, we can do little more than point to the names of its creators, and say that their genius was equal to the task of producing it.

Time, with its slow development of new theatrical customs out of new social needs, brought them their opportunity.  The stimulating novelty of the form must stand first in the list of " causes " of the greatness of the Elizabethan drama.  The significance of this simple fact, as generally happens with obvious facts, has been overlooked by ætiological speculators.  Two great types of drama —using the word as equivalent to tragic drama—have been born into the world ; both attained their supreme height within a generation of their birth, and all subsequent attempts to revive their early magnificence have been little better than mechanical attempts to make a living body.  If we wish to know what the Greek type of drama is capable of, we must go to the Athenian dramatists of the fifth century B.C. ; and if we wish to know what the English type of drama is capable of, we must go to Shakespeare and his immediate contemporaries and successors.  The fascination of these organs of expression for the human spirit was greatest while they were new.  To put it somewhat mathematically, in the first generation of their existence they drew towards them irresistibly a larger proportion of free intellect than they were ever able to attract in subsequent generations.  This is the law of all subjects of disinterested intellectual effort, whether artistic or scientific.  The most ambitious intellects rush after the newest subjects with which they have affinity : if the subjects are great, and succeed in fascinating congenial minds, then the results are great.

Such was the happy fortune of the Elizabethan drama — a fortune that comes to the human race at rare intervals. While Sackville, Gascoigne, and Daniel were composing scholarly imitations of the Greek drama to produce a feeble agitation of pity and terror in the minds of Cynthia and her courtiers, lifeless shadows of a once glorious form, Fortune beckoned to Marlowe and showed him the way to a new dramatic world. Marlowe was really the Columbus of the English drama. It is not very easy to say now what it was that induced him, a university man, to give his pen to the service of the common stage, and try to redeem it from " the jigging veins of rhyming mother-wits ; " it is not impossible that he had heard of the success of the popular drama in Spain. But whatever moved him to write "Tamburlaine" for a vulgar audience, he was the first to enter in and take possession of a region which offered infinite new possibilities to the dramatist.

The representation of passionate conflict was insuperably hampered by the conditions of the Greek stage. The large Greek theatres necessitated masks and padded and stiffened figures : and thus lively conflict, whether of mind or of body, was rendered impossible. English dramatists, writing for actors who came on the stage in their natural faces and figures, were throwing away their opportunities for giving a more vivid representation of life when they accommodated themselves to Greek models. By good luck or sagacious insight, Marlowe initiated a drama that took full advantage of the changed manner of stage representation. Men could now be brought face to face in passionate antagonism, and all the vicissitudes of the struggle put before the spectator with lifelike force. What a revelation it was ! what a fascination it must have had upon all dramatic minds ! The Elizabethans were called upon to re-write the history of human passion in all its phases and stages : and there were men among them who took delight in the task that Fate or Fortune had imposed. They fulfilled their mission with keen emulation : they reaped the harvest with such thoroughness as to leave little behind for the gleaners of after-times.

Many circumstances favoured them : many things must contribute to the success of such an enterprise. England had very recently passed through the crisis of the Reformation, and was still excited and exalted to an unusual pitch of energy by apprehensions of intestine plots and foreign invasion : the pulse of the country beat high with success and thirst for new enterprise. When men are unfortunate and despondent, they have no heart to go and look at the mimicry of action and passion : it is only when their enterprises succeed that they can go with free hearts and applaud the heroics of Tamburlaine or weep over the sorrows of Desdemona. The Elizabethans were prosperous in war and

P

in commerce : they repelled the Spaniard, and brought home richly laden argosies from east and west : they were strong, thriving, hopeful men, with nerves that could bear a good thrill of tragic horror, and sides that the most boisterous laughter was unable to shake too rudely. But one must have no small confidence in the power of general conditions over specific effects who would venture to say that our dramatists would never have come into existence, or would have sought some other line of activity, had Mary remained upon the throne instead of Elizabeth, and had England continued at peace with Spain. Doubtless a material basis of prosperity was indispensable to the support of dramatic entertainments : it was absolutely necessary that there should be enough free wealth to fill the theatres. But one fails to see what the stir of the Reformation had to do with the dramatic tendencies of Marlowe, or how the defeat of the Armada was concerned in the migration of Shakespeare from Stratford to the London stage.

A more vital condition of the great dramatic outburst was the abundance of material lying ready to the shaping and inspiring genius of the dramatist. There were numberless tales and chronicles of love and war to furnish him with plots or suggestions of plots : even if he knew no language but his own, the enterprise of printers had furnished him not only with the works of native poets and chroniclers, but with hosts of translations from Italian, French, and Latin. Observation of men was a prevailing passion, and literature was crowded with sententious maxims of character and politics. The passion of love had been expressed in many different moods and phases, and attempts had been made to treat with becoming gravity the tragic themes of disaster and death. Literature was undoubtedly ripe for dramatic embodiment.

In studying the development of the drama under Elizabeth, a broad distinction must be drawn between the Court stage and the popular stage. The Court stage was ruled by classical traditions and Italian precedents ; it was in the popular stage that the new drama was rooted, and it is there that we must look for the first sprouts of its vigorous life. It was an age of widespread interest in play-acting ; but there were two very different kinds of theatrical audience, and the plays that pleased the one would have been far from satisfactory to the other. The difference was as great as the difference now is between east-end theatres and west-end, probably greater and more clearly marked. The audiences had different tastes, and plays were written and acted to correspond. Amateur companies were formed at the public schools, at the universities, at the Inns of Court, and their performances were graced occasionally with the presence of royalty. Between 1568 and 1580, Mr Collier tells us, some fifty dramas were presented at Court. To judge from such specimens as remain, the authors of these fashionable plays followed literary usages in their compositions. Their comedies were modelled on the new Italian comedy; their tragedies abstained from the actual exhibition of violent passion, and dreadful deeds were told but not enacted. Lyly and Daniel, rivals for the Mastership of the Revels, furnish a clue to the Queen's taste, by which the fashion was determined. Her predecessor, "Bloody" Mary, had apparently a liking for broad and boisterous farce. But Queen Elizabeth was a person of much more culture and refinement. The light sparkling word-play of Lyly, and the gentle decorous passion of Daniel, were more after her standard than farcical buffoonery or violent tragedy. How high the quarrel ran at the end of her reign between the fashionable critics and the caterers for the common stage, we may gather from the conversation between Hamlet and Rosencrantz on the subject: "There was, for a while, no money bid for argument, unless the poet and the player went to cuffs in the question."

This rough distinction between the Court stage and the common stage is of importance, because it is true in the main to say that the great work effected by the genius of Shakespeare and his contemporaries was the reconciliation of the two stages by the union of what was best in both. Doubtless, in all that they had to say against coarseness, rant, bombast, absurd and revolting incident, the literary critics were in the right. So far, their contemptuous laughter at the common stage was well founded. But they failed to see that the common stage, in throwing off the restrictions of Horace and Aristotle upon violent incident—restrictions due to the accidents of Greek theatrical representation—had set dramatists free for a new kind of work. The preposterous half-serious tyrants of Mysteries, Moralities, and Chronicle Histories, the Pilate, the Herod, the Magnificence, the King Cambyses, when they committed and superintended deeds of blood before the eyes of a half-shuddering, half-laughing audience, were making possible the full presentation on the stage of such characters as Othello and Macbeth. But for the infusion of new life from the common stage, Daniel's "Cleopatra" might have remained the high-water mark of the poetic drama; and but for the ingrafting of the culture of centuries on its wild stock, the common stage might never have risen above the vein of King Cambyses.

· Marlowe was not exactly the first to represent on the stage actions that the Greek dramatist supposed to take place behind the scenes and communicated to the audience in a subsequent narrative by an eyewitness. Among Mr Collier's reprints is an example of a mixed morality and history, containing the revenge of Orestes upon his mother and her paramour, and mixing up personified abstractions, Vice, Nature, Truth, Fame, Duty, with Orestes, Clytemnestra, Ægisthus, Menelaus, and other actual personages.   In this drama there is a lively battle upon the stage, with a direction, "let it be long ere you can win the city;" and though Clytemnestra is dismissed under custody, Ægisthus is seized, dragged violently, and hanged before the audience in spite of his entreaties for mercy.   The date of this drama is 1567, and from it we may conclude that as early as that date the popular instinct had broken through the restrictions of Horace, founded as they were upon the natural limitations of a stage wholly different in structure and appointments from our own.   While, at Court, frigid and artificial restrictions were maintained when the necessity for them no longer existed, they were cast aside in performances for the entertainment of the rude vulgar.   Marlowe's position, therefore, is this: he did not originate the idea of bringing tragic action on the stage, but he was the first writer of plays whose genius was adequate to the powerful situations introduced by the popular instinct for dramatic effect.

## I.—John Lyly (1554–1606).

John Lyly, the Euphuist,[1] "the witty, comical, facetiously quick and unparalleled John Lyly," was our first extensive writer of comedies.   He produced no fewer than nine pieces—one in blank verse, seven in prose, and one in rhyme.   "The Woman in the Moon" (which is in blank verse, and which he calls "his first dream in Phœbus' holy bower," though not printed till 1597); "Alexander and Campaspe" (printed in 1584); "Sappho and Phao" (1584); "Endymion" (1591); "Galathea" (1592); "Midas" (1592); "Mother Bombie" (1594); "The Maid's Metamorphosis" (in rhyme and only probably his, 1600); "Love's Metamorphosis" (1601).   Lyly's plays are the sort of gay, fantastic, insubstantial things that may catch widely as a transient fashion, but are too extravagant to receive sympathy from more than one generation: critics in general set their heels on his delicate constructions.   His plays were acted by the children of the Revels, and he would seem to have indulged in airy and childish caprices of fancy to match.   Perhaps he wrote with an abiding consciousness that ladies were to make the chief part of his audience, and thought only of bringing smiles on their faces with pretty quibbles and mildly sentimental or childishly jocular situations.   In "Endymion," Tellus expresses surprise that Corsites, being a captain, "who should sound nothing but terror, and suck nothing but blood," talks so softly and politely.   "It agreeth not with your

[1] I have given some account of his Euphuism in my 'Manual of English Prose Literature.'  Lyly was a great tobacco-taker; one wonders that no devoted champion of the weed has ever remarked the coincidence between its introduction and the beginning of the greatness of the English drama.

calling," she says, "to use words so soft as that of love." And Corsites replies with the utmost urbanity—"Lady, it were unfit of wars to discourse with women, into whose minds nothing can sink but smoothness." In accordance with this idea, Lyly's subjects, except in "Alexander and Campaspe" and "Mother Bombie," are mythological and pastoral: and in none of them is any deep feeling excited. He is careful not to alarm his courtly audience with the prospect of terrible consequences : the stream of incidents moves with very slight interruptions to a happy conclusion, enlivened with fantastic love-talk, fantastic moralisings on ambition, war, peace, avarice, illicit love, and other commonplaces, and the pranks and puns of mischievous vivacious boys. The fabric is so slight and artificial that we are in danger of undervaluing the powers of the workman, who was a most ingenious and original man, and deserved all the adjectives of his publisher. His plays are vessels filled to the brim with sparkling liquor, which stands to Shakespeare's comedy in the relation of lemonade to champagne. The whole thing is a sort of ginger-pop intoxication ; with airy bubbles of fanciful conceits winking all over.

If there is no extravagance of passion in Lyly, there is the utmost extravagance of ingenious fancy. Wit being defined as an ingenious and unexpected play upon words, Lyly's comedies are full of it. There is hardly a sentence in the whole of them that does not contain some pun, or clever antithesis, or far-fetched image. He is so uninterruptedly witty that he destroys his own wit : the play on words and images ceases to be unexpected, and so falls out of the definition. Yet a little of it is very pretty even now ; and if we could call up the Children of the Chapel Royal to fire off his crackers, and poise his glittering conceits, and imagine ourselves listening with the much-flattered Cynthia, we might conceive the possibility of sitting out a whole comedy with pleased faces.

Lyly carries his love of contrast and delicate symmetrical arrangement into the structure of his plays, scene being balanced against scene, and character against character. In "Alexander and Campaspe," his first published play, he attempted, after the model of Edwards's "Damon and Pythias," more substantial characters than he afterwards produced in his mythological and pastoral conceptions. One of his most elaborate and characteristic personages is Sir Tophas, in "Endymion," a fat, vainglorious, foolish squire, who struts about armed with weapons of sport, and breathing out bloodthirsty sentiments against wrens, blackbirds, sheep, and other such harmless enemies. Sir Tophas is the Falstaff of children, reminding us of the story that Shakespeare when a boy used to kill a calf with an air : he has also points of resemblance with Pistol, Holofernes, and Don Armado. He has a little follower Epiton, like Armado's Moth, with whom he holds discourses, and he falls in love with Dipsas, as Armado with Jaquenetta.

"*Tophas.* Epi.

*Epiton.* Here, sir.

*Top.* I brook not this idle humour of love; it tickles not my liver, from whence lovemongers in former ages seemed to infer it should proceed.

*Epi.* Love, sir, may lie in your lungs, and I think it doth, and that is the cause you blow and are so pursy.

*Top.* Tush, boy; I think it is but some device of the poet to get money.

*Epi.* A poet; what's that?

*Top.* Dost thou not know what a poet is?

*Epi.* No.

*Top.* Why, fool, a poet is as much as one should say—a poet. But soft! yonder be two wrens; shall I shoot at them?

*Epi.* They are two lads.

*Top.* Larks or wrens, I will kill them.

*Epi.* Larks? are you blind? they are two little boys.

*Top.* Birds or boys, they are but a pittance for my breakfast; therefore have at them, for their brains must as it were embroider my bolts."

The finest things in Lyly's plays are the occasional songs. "Cupid and my Campaspe played" is often quoted, and Sappho's song is hardly less pretty.

> "O cruel Love! on thee I lay
> My curse, which shall strike blind the day;
> Never may sleep with velvet hand
> Charm thine eyes with sacred wand;
> Thy jailors shall be hopes and fears;
> Thy prison-mates groans, sighs, and tears;
> Thy play to wear out weary times
> Fantastic passions, vows, and rhymes;
> Thy bread be frowns; thy drink be gall;
> Such as when you Phao call
> The bed thou liest on by despair;
> Thy sleep, fond dreams: thy dreams, long care;
> Hope (like thy fool), at thy bed's head,
> Mock thee, till madness strike thee dead.
> As Phao, thou dost me, with thy proud eyes;
> In thee poor Sappho lives, for thee she dies."

## II.—CHRISTOPHER MARLOWE (1564–1593).

When we pass from Lyly to Marlowe we find ourselves in a wholly different atmosphere. They wrote for a different audience, a different stage, different actors; and the plays are not more unlike than were the lives and characters of the authors. The plays written by Lyly for the Court, and represented by the children of the Chapel Royal, do not come up to M. Taine's description of the ferocity of English manners in that age: their mythological and pastoral worlds are the opposite of a violent and complete expansion of nature. In Marlowe's plays, on the other hand, written for the public theatre, there is ferocity enough, and a good many of the restraints of nature as well as of probability are violently broken through. Passing from Lyly to Marlowe is like passing from sentimental modern comedy to the blood and convulsion, powder and poison drama that still keeps its hold in many of our theatres. M. Taine should not have been so anxious to make out that the Elizabethan drama was a faithful reflection of the manners of the Court: one might as soon take Mr Boucicault's Irish dramas as an index to the character of the modern English gentleman. It is the pit and not the boxes that theatrical managers must chiefly keep in view, if they wish their theatres to pay: we are not entitled to infer, from the thrilling agonies, fierce passions, and bloodthirsty heroics of the Elizabethan drama, anything except that they pleased the body of the house. Modern critics have endorsed the judgment of the Elizabethan pit; Lyly and Daniel, with their gentle plays adapted to gentle ears, now require an education to appreciate them, while we are never weary of admiring the gigantic powers that dared to express the tempest and whirlwind of unrestrained passion. But it is not by any means certain that this was the view taken by the gallants of the day, who lounged on the stage or in the boxes ("rooms," as they were then called), and exchanged chaff with the groundlings: it is not impossible that the violent passions of the drama, so far from being an attraction for them by natural affinity, were the subjects of their derision, torn to tatters as the passions most usually have been by robustious actors. The passion for heroics and horrors was by no means universal in the Elizabethan age any more than in our own. Thomas Nash ridiculed vainglorious tragedians with their swelling bombast of bragging blank verse. Lodge even ventured to deride the cries for revenge uttered by the Ghost in "Hamlet," a part represented, according to tradition, by the divine dramatist himself. Tragedy was one of the themes of the weak and conceited satires of Joseph Hall. The eulogists of Shakespeare lay stress not upon his power of expressing tragic passions, but upon his sweet witty soul, his mellifluous and honeyed tongue, his silver tongue, his honey-flowing vein, and the sugared tongues and attractive beauty of his personages. Entries remain in the 'Accounts of the Revels,' of dramas by Shakespeare presented at the Court of James: the list comprises one tragedy, one historical play, and eight comedies. Everything goes to show that in the Elizabethan age persons of fashion and refinement, if they did not actually consider tragedy vulgar, at least had a preference for comedy. The spirit then prevailing on that point at Court was not so very different from what prevailed when Chaucer wrote, and made his representative of "the gentles" put a stop to the tragic recitals of the Monk.

The tragic drama emanated from the people. It had its beginnings in the public theatre, and its first and greatest authors were men of the people. Men do not learn passion and the expression of passion, so far as these can be learnt, from national movements, but from the experience of their own individual struggle for existence or fame. Men of easy unvaried lives, who have never had to fight with poverty or slander, the malice of fortune or the malice of men, cannot be dramatists.

Marlowe was only two months older than Shakespeare, having been born in February 1564. His father was a shoemaker in Canterbury, with a somewhat numerous family. His first education was probably got at the endowed king's school, and he went to Cambridge (Benet College, Corpus Christi) in 1581. He is not recorded to have held a scholarship, and he may have owed his maintenance at college to a wealthy relative or other patron. He received the degree of M.A. in 1587, but before that he would seem to have renounced the sure prospects of the staid professions for the precarious career of actor and playwright. "Tamburlaine the Great" is inferred by Collier and Dyce to have been his first play, and to have been acted anterior to 1587, though not printed till 1590. None of his other plays were printed till after his death; but Mr Dyce supposes them to have been produced in the following order—"Faustus," "Jew of Malta," "Edward II.," "Massacre at Paris." He lost his life in 1593 in a miserable brawl. Among the papers left behind him were part of the tragedy of "Dido," afterwards completed by Nash; a metrical paraphrase of part of Musæus's "Hero and Leander," afterwards continued by Chapman; a translation of some of Ovid's Elegies; and a translation into blank verse of the First Book of Lucan.[1]

Marlowe's life was brief and probably dissolute. We have no right to identify a dramatist with his characters, but it is impossible to disregard the combined evidences of his dramatic conceptions and the accusations brought against him by more respectable contemporaries. His chief characters, Tamburlaine, Faustus, and the Jew of Malta, are not the creations of a calm mind: their

---

[1] For the discussion of other works attributed to him see the 'Account of Marlowe and his writings' in Mr Dyce's edition, pp. lviii-lxvii. (1850); and Bell's Greene and Marlowe, p. 150 (1856). I adhere to Bell's remarks on the authorship of "Lust's Dominion" and "The First Part of the Contention." If isolated coincidences of expression are taken as proof of authorship, almost any given play in the Elizabethan age might be assigned to any given author: the dramatists made so communistically free with the productions of their fellows. In spite of its dealing with events subsequent to Marlowe's death, "Lust's Dominion" is, on the whole, much more like his work than "The First Part of the Contention."

volcanic passions and daring scepticism are the offspring of a turbulent, vehement, irregular nature, bold and defiant of public opinion. Marlowe's alleged writings against the Trinity have never been seen ; in all probability, like some alleged infidel works of the Middle Ages, they never existed : but there seems no reason to doubt that he was, as his accusers stated, a man that neither feared God nor regarded man. Beauty, which he worshipped with passionate devotion, was the only sunshine of his life, and it shone with a burning fierceness proportioned to the violence of his tempestuous moods. The vision of Hero and Leander is a rapt surrender of the whole soul to impassioned meditation on luxurious beauty. In his life as in his plays, such intervals of delight were probably rare. Tamburlaine is a most impassioned adorer of divine Zenocrate ; Faustus hangs in ecstatic worship on the lips of Helen ; but these are only brief transports in lives where energy and ambition are devouringly predominant. Marlowe's genius was little adapted to sonneteering and pastoral poetry : he stigmatised the fashionable love-lyrics as "egregious foppery," and derided them with rough ridicule. He wrote no sonnets ; only one pastoral song has been ascribed to him,[1] and it is direct, and fresh, a movement of impatient captivating sweetness, an impulsive tone of invitation that will take no denial. Marlowe was a clear and powerful genius, and we often seem to catch in his poetry an undertone of almost angry contempt for commonplace.

The most generally impressive of Marlowe's works is his fragment on the tale of Hero and Leander, and if we founded solely upon this, we should form most erroneous notions of his genius. We should suppose his worship of beauty, which was but a rare and transient passion, to have been the presiding force of his imagination. It is in his plays that we find the world of storm and strife wherein he delighted to expatiate, and a most Titanic world it is, immeasurably transcending nature in breadth and height of thought, feeling, and destructive energy ; a region where everything is on a gigantic scale, peopled with creatures that are monstrous in the largeness of their composition and the fierceness of their passions. "Tamburlaine the Great" was his first play, and serves as well as any other to give a notion of his grand manner. Tamburlaine (better known as Timour the Tartar) is represented as a Scythian shepherd, whose ambition, fed by

---

[1] The song of the "Passionate Shepherd to his Love" is ascribed to Marlowe in 'England's Helicon,' but this is not conclusive, as pieces were not always given to their true authors in these miscellanies. The curious thing is, that in the "Passionate Pilgrim," where it is given as Shakespeare's, all the staves would pass for his : but in E. H. two more staves are given that seem to be in Marlowe's distinctive vein.

heavenly portents and oracles, soars to the height of subduing the
three continents : he aspires to spread his name

> " As far as Boreas claps his brazen wings,
>   Or fair Bootes sends his cheerful light."[1]

Theridamas, a Persian general, is sent to take the mad shepherd
prisoner, but when he sets eyes on him he is seduced from his
allegiance by miraculous fascination.  He stands rooted to the
earth, and exclaims :—

> " Tamburlaine ! a Scythian shepherd so embellished
>   With Nature's pride and richest furniture !
>   His looks do menace Heaven and dare the gods ;
>   His fiery eyes are fixed upon the earth,
>   As if he now devised some stratagem,
>   Or meant to pierce Avernus' darksome vaults
>   To pull the triple-headed dog from hell."

When this tremendous being breaks silence, his speech is pregnant
with sublime energy :—

> " Forsake thy king, and do but join with me,
>   And we will triumph over all the world :
>   I hold the Fates bound fast in iron chains,
>   And with my hand turn Fortune's wheel about ;
>   And sooner shall the sun fall from his sphere
>   Than Tamburlaine be slain or overcome.
>   Draw forth thy sword thou mighty man at arms,
>   Intending but to raze my charmed skin,
>   And Jove himself will stretch his hand from heaven
>   To ward the blow, and shield me safe from harm."

Tamburlaine's vaunts are justified by events : he soon gains the
crown of Persia : then turns his arms against the countless legions
of the Turks, subdues their emperor Bajazeth (whom he carries
about in a cage and uses upon occasion as a footstool), and
bestows kingdoms upon his most eminent followers.  Towards
the end of the First Part of his eventful drama, he thus sums
up his achievements :—

> " The god of war resigns his seat to me,
>   Meaning to make me general of the world :
>   Jove, viewing me in arms, looks pale and wan,
>   Fearing my power should pull him from his throne :
>   Where'er I come the Fatal Sisters sweat,

---

[1] This passage seems to be referred to in Nash's celebrated Epistle prefixed to
Greene's " Menaphon," where he speaks of vainglorious tragedians who think
themselves all right " if they once but get Boreas by the beard and the heavenly
Bull by the dewlap."  If so, this would confirm Mr Collier's opinion that Marlowe is the " idiot art-master " assailed in that connection, and cast some doubt
on the propriety of M. Taine's taking Marlowe's plays as the standard of English
taste in that age.

And grisly Death, by running to and fro,
To do their ceaseless homage to my sword :
And here in Afric, where it seldom rains,
Since I arrived with my triumphant host,
Have swelling clouds, drawn from wide-gaping wounds,
Been oft resolved in bloody purple showers,
A meteor that might terrify the earth,
And make it quake at every drop it drinks :
Millions of souls sit on the banks of Styx,
Waiting the back-return of Charon's boat ;
Hell and Elysium swarm with ghosts of men,
That I have sent from sundry foughten fields,
To spread my fame through hell and up to heaven."

In the Second Part the poet's imagination expatiates in a still ampler range of extravagance. Two of the conqueror's sons display their father's spirit. "Wading through blood to a throne" would be but a tame image to them. When their father talks of what must be the character of his successor, one of them says that, were the throne placed in a sea of blood, he would prepare a ship and sail to it ; and the other, with still greater hardihood, cries :—

" And I would strive to swim through pools of blood,
Or make a bridge of murdered carcases,
Whose arches should be framed with bones of Turks,
Ere I would lose the title of a king."

His wife Zenocrate falling sick, he consoles himself with sublime fancies of the reception preparing for her in heaven :—

" Now walk the angels on the walls of heaven
As sentinels to warn th' immortal souls
To entertain divine Zenocrate.

.    .    .    .    .    .

The cherubins and holy seraphins
That sing and play before the King of kings,
Use all their voices and their instruments
To entertain divine Zenocrate :
And in this sweet and curious harmony,
The god that tunes this music to our souls,
Holds out his hand in highest majesty
To entertain divine Zenocrate."

His raving over her death is hardly less extravagant :—

" What, is she dead ?  Techelles, draw thy sword,
And wound the earth that it may cleave in twain,
And we descend into the infernal vaults,
To hale the Fatal Sisters by the hair,
And throw them in the triple moat of hell,
For taking hence my fair Zenocrate.
Cassane and Theridamas, to arms !
Raise cavalieros higher than the clouds,

> And with the cannon break the frame of heaven :
> Batter the shining palace of the sun
> And shiver all the starry firmament,
> For amorous Jove hath snatched my love from hence,
> Meaning to make her stately queen of heaven."

Tamburlaine is, if possible, increased in fierceness by the death of his queen.  He lays waste the town where she died with fire and sword : and proceeding in his irresistible career of conquest, harnesses kings to his chariot, and stabs one of his own sons for effeminate shirking of war.  His last exploit is the capture of Babylon.  He binds the Babylonians hand and foot, and drowns man, woman, and child ; then burns the sacred books of Mahomet, daring the prophet, if he have any power, to come down and take vengeance.  Immediately thereafter he is seized by a sudden and mysterious distemper.  He maintains his sublime spirit to the last. He represents death as afraid to confront him eye to eye :—

> " See where my slave, the ugly monster Death,
> Shaking and quivering, pale and wan for fear,
> Stands aiming at me with his murdering dart,
> Who flies away at every glance I give,
> And, when I look away, comes stealing on ! "

Yet once more, in spite of Death, he takes the field, and scatters his enemies "like summer's vapours vanished by the sun : " then calls for a map that he may trace the extent of his conquests, and see how much of the world remains to subdue ; commends the completion of the triumph to his son ; and bids his friends farewell—

> " For Tamburlaine, the scourge of God, must die."

It is not alone the inflated ambition and miraculous success of the hero, that raise and swell the effect of this play to dimensions so astounding.  His chief followers and his chief enemies express themselves with hardly inferior energy ; and our minds are filled with amazement at the hundreds of thousands under various kings and emperors arrayed for and against the magnificent conqueror.[1]

"Tamburlaine" was Marlowe's first play, but the impetuous swell of his conceptions cannot be said to have been much moderated as he went on.  His "raptures all air and fire" were not, I believe, the extravagance of youth ; still less could they have been,

---

[1] The resources of the scene-painter and the stage machinist were not then developed.  A board with a name upon it indicated the place of the action ; and supernatural personages descended and reascended only when the carpenter "could conveniently."  But it seems probable that part of the success of 'Tamburlaine' was due to its spectacular effect, introducing as it did potentates in the costumes of their several regions.  Greene and Peele seem to have taken the hint.  Belinus and Abdelmelec may have invoked the aid of the Turkish emperor to afford an opportunity of exhibiting the gorgeous costumes of himself and his retinue of kings.

as Mr Collier seems to think, the result of inexperience in blank
verse, and mistaken effort to make up by bombastic terms for the
absence of rhyme; they were part of the constitution of this individual man. It is impossible to say what he might have done
had his life been longer: he might have exhausted this high astounding vein, and proved himself capable of opening up another.
But as long as he lived he found fuel for his lofty raptures. He
could not repeat another conqueror of the world, but his heroes are
all expanded to the utmost possible limit of their circumstances.
The Jew of Malta is an incarnation of the devil himself: he is no
less universal in his war against all mankind that are within reach
of his power: he fights single-handed with monstrous instruments of
death against a whole city, and does not scruple to poison even his
own daughter. Faustus is not a malevolent being, but his ambition is even greater than Tamburlaine's; he soars beyond the petty
possibilities of humanity, leagues himself with superhuman powers,
and rides through space in a fiery chariot exploring the secrets of
the universe. Even in his historical play of Edward II., where
he is bound by the shackles of recent history more or less known
to his audience, the conflict of explosive passions is superhuman
in its energies; the king's court is a hell of extravagant affection
and fiendish spite, wanton tyranny and mutinous unapproachable
fierceness—a den of wild beasts.[1]

It is sometimes said by way of superlative eulogy that the
tragedy of Edward II. is worthy of Shakespeare. Such a notion
could not be held for a moment by any one accustomed to draw
distinctions among the objects of his admiration. The manner of
Marlowe is as different as possible from the manner of Shakespeare.
Not to enter into minute comparisons of expression, which, though
somewhat tedious, is perhaps the most distinct way of conveying
how radically they differ, it is sufficient to mention two great
points of contrast, significant of the deepest differences of constitution. Marlowe has very little humour, and very little sense of
varied aspects of character. Shakespeare is said to have borrowed
the idea of Richard II. from Marlowe's Edward II., and his Hotspur from Marlowe's young Mortimer. Now, compare the conceptions of the two dramatists. Edward and Richard agree only in
being weak and wasteful kings, Mortimer and Hotspur in being
irrepressible noblemen, with a natural delight in war. On the
throne and in the dungeon Edward is more contemptible than
Richard. Edward, indeed, is a spoiled child of Titanic breed: he
has the infatuated loves and spites of a spoiled child; and the
cruel indignities put upon him after his dethronement seem aimed

---

[1] This would almost seem to be the original of M. Taine's conception of six-
teenth-century England.

in contempt at his effeminacy.   He clings to Gaveston as to a forbidden toy.   When his nobles stalk defiantly from his presence and leave him to storm in monologue, he takes revenge by bullying his wife.   In the true spirit of a wayward child, he loads Gaveston with honours to spite the fractious noblemen : he affirms that he cares for the throne only as a means of indulging his favourite. Shakespeare's Richard II. is a very different being.   He is said to be wasteful and given to favouritism : but in all his appearances upon the stage he comports himself with royal dignity.   The faults that work his overthrow are impetuous indiscretion and a greater love for Fine Art than the duties of government.   His reverses turn upon a much finer pivot than Edward's gross abuse of power : he might have kept his throne had he not on a random impulse stopped the combat between Bolingbroke and Mowbray, and sent them both into banishment :—

> "O when the king did throw his warder down,
>   His own life hung upon the staff he threw."

Richard's death is heroic ; and his reflections in the dungeon may be contrasted with Gaveston's schemes for the amusement of Edward, as showing the higher reach of his philosophic and artistic culture.   A close comparison of Mortimer and Hotspur reveals still more striking dissimilarities.   Mortimer is outspoken and delights in war like Hotspur, but he shows no trace of the amiable qualities of Harry Percy.   He is actuated by a coarse ambition to marry the queen and seize the throne, and is the author of the gross cruelty wreaked upon the helpless king. Harry Percy is presented in more varied as well as more amiable lights.   He chafes and "chaffs" Glendower with impudence privileged by its happy audacity.   He is wrapt up in warlike schemes : he gives playful evasive answers to his wife's questions ; sometimes he is so preoccupied that he does not answer till an hour afterwards.   He is fondly beloved by his Kate : while he is alive, he is her "mad ape," her "paraquito," a dear provoking fellow ; and when he dies, her noble eulogy of his chivalrous nature shows how deep was his hold of her affections.   To his rival Hal, his overpowering devotion to war sometimes appears a little comical ; but his courage and prowess receive all deference and honour.   Of all those traits that give Harry Percy individual life, there is not the faintest prefiguration in Marlowe's young Mortimer.   Character - painting, indeed, was not in Marlowe's way : his personages do not show many-sided character in their different relations.   All his creations relax under the charms of love, and express themselves with glowing affection ; but they all relax and warm into raptures very much after the same fashion. There is no such discrimination in Marlowe as the distinction between the wooing of Troilus and the wooing of Diomede, not to speak of finer distinctions. Even Edward's love for Gaveston and the Jew's love for his daughter flow into the same current of language as Tamburlaine's love for Zenocrate, and Faustus's admiration of Helen.

The fragment of "Hero and Leander" is incomparably the finest product of Marlowe's genius: it is one of the chief treasures of the language. The poet is fairly intoxicated with the beauty of his subject: he has thought about the two lovers, and dreamed about them, and filled his imagination with their charms; he writes with ecstasy as if obeying an impulse that he can resist no longer, and in every other line expressions escape him that have all the warmth of involuntary bursts of admiration. He dashes into the subject with passionate eagerness, outlining the situation with a few impatient strokes, and at once proceeding to descant on the beauty of Hero :—

> " On Hellespont, guilty of true lovers' blood,
> In view and opposite two cities stood,
> Sea-borderers, disjoined by Neptune's might;
> The one Abydos, the other Sestos hight.
> At Sestos Hero dwelt; Hero the fair,
> Whom young Apollo courted for her hair,
> And offered as a dower his burning throne
> Where she should sit for men to gaze upon.
>
> .    .    .    .    .    .
>
> Some say for her the fairest Cupid pined,
> And looking in her face was strooken blind.
> But this is true; so like was one the other,
> As he imagined Hero was his mother;
> And oftentimes into her bosom flew,
> About her naked neck his bare arms threw,
> And laid his childish head upon her breast,
> And with still panting rock, there took his rest.
> So lovely fair was Hero, Venus' nun,
> As Nature wept thinking she was undone,
> Because she took more from her than she left,
> And of such wondrous beauty her bereft :
> Therefore in sign her treasure suffered wrack,
> Since Hero's time hath half the world been black."

From Hero he passes to Leander—

> " Amorous Leander, beautiful and young,
>  Whose tragedy divine Musæus sung,
> Dwelt at Abydos; since him dwelt there none
> For whom succeeding times make greater moan."

Leander's beauty is painted in even more glowing colours than Hero's. In his picture of the infatuated doting of Edward II. on Piers Gaveston, Marlowe had already shown that he understood the passion that may be felt for the beauty of young men, and here we have a stronger evidence. He describes Leander with something like a Greek feeling for his beauties, his arms, his smooth breast, his white shoulder, his orient cheeks and lips: some of the particulars would seem to have been adopted by Shakespeare and applied to the praise of his beautiful friend. The poem as a whole is more voluptuous and earnestly impassioned in sentiment than Shakespeare's corresponding poem of "Venus and Adonis": the poet did not live to carry the tale into its tragic stage.

### III.—ROBERT GREENE (1560–1592).

To class Greene among the dramatists is rather a harsh measure for his reputation, although the arrangement is justified by his relations with the stage. When Shakespeare began to write, Marlowe and Greene were the most firmly established playwrights, and both himself and his friends testify to the eagerness of rival managers to obtain the hastiest of Greene's performances. Yet Greene's plays are by no means the best fruits of his pen. He began his literary career as an author of love-tales or novels in prose interspersed with songs and lyrics: and as he had a most rich and vivid feeling for colour, and a fine ear for the music of verse, these occasional pieces are by far his best productions. If, therefore, we were to estimate him by quality rather than by quantity, we should place him rather among the love-poets than among the dramatists. As a dramatist he was a follower of Lyly and Marlowe: as a writer of pastoral lyrics he was Marlowe's predecessor and superior.

The earliest production of Greene's hitherto discovered is "Mamillia," an imitation to a certain extent of Lyly's "Euphues," published in 1583, while the author was in residence at Clare Hall, Cambridge, just before taking the degree of M.A. He had come up from Norwich to St John's, and had graduated B.A. in 1578: after that, though his father would not seem to have been a rich man, he found means to travel in Spain, Italy, and other parts of the Continent. According to his own account, written in deathbed repentance, he had learnt in Italy luxurious, profligate, and abominable habits, and on his return soon exhausted both his money and his credit, and was at his wits' end for a suitable profession. After vacillating for a little between the Church and Physic, he finally gravitated to the last resort of such unsteady spirits—"became an author of plays and a penner of love-pamphlets." "Mamillia" was rapidly followed by a host of other love-pamphlets: "Morando," "Menaphon," "Perimedes the Blacksmith," "Pandosto, the Triumph of Time" (reprinted by Mr Collier as the foundation of the "Winter's Tale"), "Philomela, the Lady Fitzwater's Nightingale" (reprinted along with "Mena-phon" in Brydges' "Archaica"), and many others. These euphuistically embellished tales were the fashionable reading of ladies on their first appearance, and afterwards went through many editions, to the delight of sentimental maids in humbler life. Greene's fertility is all the more amazing when we consider the debauched life that he led: we need not wonder at his early death when we see how he burnt the candle at both ends—hard work and immoderate dissipation. Five of his plays have come down to us: "Orlando Furioso" (published 1594); "Looking-Glass for London and England" (1594, written in conjunction with Lodge); "Friar Bacon and Friar Bungay" (1594); "James the Fourth" (1598); "Alphonsus, King of Arragon" (1599). "George-a-Green, the Pinner of Wakefield" (1599), is also attributed to him.

Greene saw a great deal of villanous company during his brief career in London. His own excuse for his choice of depraved associates was that he wished to paint their manners. It is not impossible that this was part of his motive for consorting with rogues and sharpers: it may even have been the apology that he offered to his own conscience. Yet with all allowances for his thus stooping to gain professional ends, we shall probably not be far wrong if we accept Mr Dyce's conclusion, that of all "the Muse's sons whose vices have conducted them to shame and sorrow, none, perhaps, have sunk to deeper degradation and misery." We must not be prejudiced against Greene because he assailed the youthful Shakespeare so bitterly, nor must we take Gabriel Harvey's picture as accurate in every particular. But it seems indisputable that Greene reduced himself to extreme distress by extravagant profligacy; that he spent recklessly, and was not over-scrupulous in replenishing his coffers; and that in his struggle for the means of debauchery he was bitterly jealous and envious of all literary competitors. Marlowe as well as Shakespeare had been an object of attack when he began his career of playwright: he was seemingly attacked in Nash's preface to Greene's "Menaphon," and afterwards his "Tamburlaine" and its blank verse were directly sneered at by Greene himself. Indeed, Greene confessed in his repentant fit that he could not keep a friend: he behaved to his friends in such a way as to turn them into utter enemies.

It seems possible to trace the reaction from this intemperate life of debauchery, hard work, and bitterness, in the passionate beauty of Greene's lyrics: one can understand with what a trans-port of relief he would throw himself out of his base surroundings into the dreams of a happy pastoral country and the music of sweet verse. There is nothing in his dramas to suggest the prof-ligacy of the author. They are of the nature of comedies: they terminate happily, and in accordance with the strictest principles

of morality.   His heroines—Angelica, the fair maid of Fressingfield, Dorothea, Isabel—are models of moral no less than of physical beauty.

On the whole, Greene seems to have been a clever ready-witted
fellow, with a gift of sweet song, and unbounded facility in the
use of words : bold, shameless, somewhat cynical and bitter : prepared to write to the utmost of his ability in any vein that would
sell : a boisterous reveller, incapable of foregoing a rough joke
even at the expense of his dearest friend.   This was the man as he
appeared to his fellows.   But he would seem to have had an inner
life of remorseful fits, abject in proportion to the intemperate
height of his orgies.   If indeed we had no authority beyond his
" Repentance" and his "Groat's Worth of Wit" we might easily
believe these to have been written for the sole purpose of replenishing his purse.   But there are trustworthy accounts of his deathbed behaviour, when his "jolly long red peak" and "well-propor-
tioned body" were finally prostrated ; and these accounts lead us
to believe that his repentance was unfeigned.   And, indeed, the
tone of his plays, and his delight in the imagination of beauty,
innocence, and country joys, are indications of a better nature that
lay hid under poor Robert's outer profligacy.

Greene has no claim to high rank as a dramatist, and yet he
deserves considerable study as a precursor of Shakespeare.   Although his blank verse is somewhat monotonous, yet there is
incisive and vivid energy in his language : and he had probably
more influence than Marlowe in forming or enriching Shakespeare's
diction.   Take at random, as an illustration, the induction to Act
ii. of "Alphonsus" :—

> " Thus from the pit of pilgrim's poverty
> Alphonsus 'gins by step and step to climb
> Unto the top of friendly Fortune's wheel.
> From banished state, as you have plainly seen,
> He is transform'd into a soldier's life,
> And marcheth in the ensign of the King
> Of worthy Naples, which Belinus hight ;
> Not for because that he doth love him so,
> But that he may revenge him on his foe.
> Now on the top of lusty barbèd steed
> He mounted is, in glittering armour clad,
> Seeking about the troops of Arragon,
> For to encounter with his traitorous niece.
> How he doth speed and what doth him befall,
> Mark this our act, for it doth show it all."

The versification of this is exceedingly flat, but here and there are
touches of vivid expression.   The opening of this Act is energetic,
reminding us of Gloucester's "Down, down to hell, and say I sent
thee thither."   Alphonsus kills Flaminius, and exclaims—

> " Go, pack thee hence unto the Stygian lake,
> And make report unto thy traitorous sire
> How well thou hast enjoyed the diadem
> Which he by treason set upon thy head;
> And if he ask thee who did send thee down,
> Alphonsus say, who now must wear thy crown."

Greene is sometimes accused of ranting. The chief basis for this accusation is the character of Rasni, King of Nineveh, in the "Looking-Glass for London and England." This "Imperial swaggerer," as Campbell calls him, is puffed up with immeasurable pride till the prophet Jonah lets the wind out of him; and glories in a strain somewhat like Tamburlaine, but more like the conventional Herod of the Mysteries:—

> " Great Jewry's God, that foiled stout Benhadad,
> Could not rebate the strength that Rasni brought;
> For be he God in heaven, yet, viceroys, know,
> Rasni is god on earth and none but he."

It should be remarked, however, that this play was written by Greene in conjunction with Lodge, and that Greene's portion of the work was probably the delineation of the extortion, roguery, and debauchery of Nineveh, which was to say, of London. The particulars of the sumptuous wedding, indeed, are quite in Greene's style; he was at home in the exercise of accumulating gorgeous particulars. But there is nothing to approach the extravagant inflation of Rasni in any play of Greene's sole workmanship. He essayed a counterpart to Tamburlaine in his Alphonsus, and there had ample opportunity for unbounded rant; but Alphonsus bears his exploits lightly, and indulges but sparingly in the swelling utterance of aspiration and triumph. Greene was too cynical to have command of language for a character of sustained pride; he could pump up expression for a good many emotions, but his nature was dry in that region. He is, indeed, a standing refutation of the plausible idea that rant belongs to the infancy of the drama. Rant goes rather with the nature of the individual; and Greene, with all his roughness and recklessness, was fitted to be the pupil of Lyly more than of Marlowe.

Like most of his predecessors, from Chaucer downwards, Greene makes frequent use of the goddesses and celebrated beauties of Grecian mythology for purposes of comparison. But he does more than merely repeat the names, saying that a heroine is as fair as Helen or as faithful as Penelope: he evidently exerted his imagination to conceive them in a certain visual semblance of beauty. We are not, of course, to suppose that he had any notion of conceiving classical beauty as different from English beauty: when he spoke of the port of Juno and the foot of Thetis, he probably had in his mind's eye a gait and an instep that had charmed him in the neighbourhood of St Paul's. Still, he had the notion of giving life to dead names. He had also the notion of conceiving these antique paragons at supreme moments in their history when their charms were at full height. Semele, Chloris, Daphne, Thetis, and others, are taken at the moment when their beauty proved irresistible even to the gods: Venus at the moment of her highest triumph. Amurack exclaims of his wife Fausta—

> " Behold the gem and jewel of mine age !
> See where she comes, whose heavenly majesty
> Doth far surpass the brave and gorgeous pace
> Which Cytherea, daughter unto Jove,
> Did put in ure whenas she had obtained
> The golden apple at the shepherd's hands."

This vein of classical allusion is one of the outcomes of Greene's passion for beautiful forms and colours. It is carried out to a weakness in his dramas, rendering him peculiarly open to the charge made at the time against University poets generally—he "smacks too much of Ovid." He sadly violates dramatic propriety by ascribing an acquaintance with the Roman poet to all his characters indiscriminately. Even lovely Peggy, the keeper's daughter at Fressingfield, can discourse of Phœbus courting lovely Semele, of the matchless hue of Helen, of the scrolls that Jove sent to Danae; she puts up an appeal to "fond Ate, doomer of bad-boding fates;" and says with enthusiasm that Lacy is

> " Proportioned as was Paris when, in gray,
> He courted Œnon in the vale of Troy."

If, however, we wish to see Greene at his best, we must go to the occasional songs in his prose tales.[1] We might, indeed, compile from his plays a florilegium of pretty lines, such as—

> " Thou gladsome lamp that wait'st on Phœbus' train,
> Spreading thy kindness through the jarring orbs,
> That in their union praise thy lasting powers;
> Fair pride of morn, sweet beauty of the even ! "

Or—

> " Sleep like the smiling purity of heaven,
> When mildest wind is loath to blend the peace."

But a collection of his lyrics—songs, roundelays, jigs, sonettos, madrigals, ditties, and odes—is really like his own Cuba, a region enriched

> " With favours sparkling from the smiling heavens."

---

[1] These are reprinted in Bell's Poets, along with "Hero and Leander"—a charming volume."

Very often he rounds off in a few lines a perfect subject for the painter,[1] as in the burden of Sephestia's song to her child—

> " Weep not, my wanton, smile upon my knee;
>   When thou art old there's grief enough for thee."

Or the opening lines of Menaphon's roundelay—

> " When tender ewes, brought home with evening sun,
>     Wend to their folds,
>     And to their holds
>   The shepherds trudge when light of day is done."

In the tales these verses come in as if the author's thoughts were tired of their prose vehicle, and spontaneously and irresistibly blossomed into song. His excellence in short verses, or in a capricious mixture of short verses with long, is a curious contrast to the baldness and monotony of his blank verse: it surprises us as when an indifferent walker proves a light and graceful runner. There is nothing in any of his plays to suggest a possibility of such as the following :—

> " Ah, what is love ?  It is a pretty thing,
>   As sweet unto a shepherd as a king ;
>     And sweeter too,
>   For kings have cares that wait upon a crown,
>   And cares can make the sweetest love to frown:
>     Ah then, ah then,
>   If country loves such sweet desires do gain,
>   What lady would not love a shepherd swain ?
>
>   His flocks are folded, he comes home at night,
>   As merry as a king in his delight ;
>     And merrier too,
>   For kings bethink them what the state require,
>   Where shepherds careless carol by the fire :
>     Ah then, ah then,
>   If country loves such sweet desires do gain,
>   What lady would not love a shepherd swain ? "

In more regular and even measures, Greene is comparatively stiff and restrained. One of his longest poems, which contains passages equal to his best, is printed in the 'Phœnix Nest,' with the title "A most Rare and Excellent Dream, learnedly set down by a worthy gentleman, a brave scholar, and M. of Arts in both universities." It has not been identified as Greene's by Mr Dyce or Mr Bell ; but the title, taken in conjunction with the style, may be considered conclusive evidence. The measure is the seven-line stave of Troilus verse.

---

[1] Since this was written, Mr Gosse has suggested that Greene's sense of colour was probably cultivated by the study of Italian paintings, which he might have seen during his travels.

## IV.—GEORGE PEELE (1558–1598).

Peele was a few years older than either Marlowe or Greene, and had published a rhymed play before Marlowe began to write, but we place him after these two, because he probably followed them as a writer for the public stage.   He was a gentleman by birth, took the degree of M.A. at Oxford (Broadgates Hall, now Pembroke College) in 1579, and possessed some land in right of his wife : but, eschewing the steady professions, he went up to London in 1581, and soon became known as one of the authors whose living was gained by their wits.   He was a conspicuous figure in the same dissipated circle as Marlowe and Greene : and acquired such notoriety as a profligate wit that a body of 'Merry Conceited Jests'[1] was fathered upon him—apparently without much mistake of paternity.

The plays attributed to Peele in Mr Dyce's edition are " The Arraignment of Paris " (1584, a rhymed play, written for private representation before the Queen by the children of the Chapel); " The Chronicle History of Edward I." (1593); " The Battle of Alcazar " (1594); " The Old Wives' Tales " (1595, supposed to be the basis of Milton's " Comus "); " David and Bethsabe " (1599, the best of Peele's Plays); " Sir Clyomon and Sir Clamydes " (1599).   He was frequently employed to devise pageants, and several of these have been preserved.   He wrote also a poem in heroic couplets, " The Tale of Troy," and various miscellaneous poems.   His extant works are not so numerous as Greene's ; and he would seem to have been a much less productive writer.   His literary career was twice as long as Greene's.   In the 'Jests' we are told that " George was of the poetical disposition, never to write so long as his money lasted :" and if we may trust that authority, he had many madcap and unscrupulous ways of " raising the wind," from nominal borrowing to downright cozenage.

Peele was a man of softer and subtler make than Greene : a handsome person with a thin womanish voice ; of light and nimble fancy, and smooth ingenious execution : without the faintest desire to use honest means in procuring a livelihood.   Poor Greene was not very scrupulous, but he thought it necessary to justify his keeping company with blackguards ; he worked hard, advocated high morality, and suffered occasional visitations of conscience. Peele's choice of subjects does not betray any stifled morality in him.   The most marked hint of the writer's personality appears in the ingenuity of his compliments direct and indirect to his audience.   The *dénouement* of " The Arraignment of Paris " is an audacious compliment to Elizabeth.   The idea is that the judg-

---

[1] " Jest " meaning *practical joke.*

ment of Paris is called in question, as being unjust and partial; Paris is arraigned before a council of the gods; the matter is referred to the arbitration of Diana; and she, to keep the peace of Olympus, awards the apple to Elizabeth, a peerless nymph, a paragon, as stately as Juno, as wise as Minerva, as lovely as Venus, and as chaste as Diana herself.[1] His two chronicle histories had a large adventitious interest for the time, as gratifying the prevailing English hatred of Spain and Popery. Elinor, the Spanish queen of Edward I., is represented as a monster of cruelty and pride: and Stukely, the hero of the " Battle of Alcazar," is a renegade Englishman, commissioned by the Pope to raise a rebellion in Ireland. Most Elizabethan dramatists paid incidental compliments to Elizabeth, and to their country: Peele seems to have deliberately aimed at securing patronage by making whole plays a bolus of flattery. Spenser's ' Faery Queen ' and Lyly's " Midas " as well as his " Endymion," were also designed to flatter Elizabeth ; but Spenser and Lyly used a decorous veil of allegory. It pleased the erratic Nash to commend Peele in 1587 "as the chief supporter of pleasance now living, the Atlas of poetry, and *primus verborum artifex*,"—"chief engineer of phrases." This was in opposition to Marlowe. Posterity has certainly reversed this haphazard judgment as regards the general power of the rival poets: it is universally allowed that "Marlowe had a far more powerful intellect than Peele, and a far deeper insight into the human heart"—was, in short, a poet of immeasurably higher order. On the matter of skill in blank verse, Campbell and Mr Payne Collier are at variance. Campbell spoke strongly in favour of Peele : "There is no such sweetness of versification and imagery to be found in our blank verse anterior to Shakespeare." Mr Collier ascribes this honour to Marlowe, pointing out the fact that Peele did not write a complete play in blank verse till Marlowe had set the example, and declaring his best blank verse to be for the most part monotonous. Mr Collier is too truculent on this point of versification. The general strain of the two poets is so very different, that one cannot decide the question by counting their pauses and their trochaic and monosyllabic endings. The versification of "David and Bethsabe" is undoubtedly sweet. Blank verse would not have been suitable for " The Arraignment of Paris," a piece moving with almost pantomimic gaiety. Peele acted with judgment in reserving blank verse for the formal orations of Paris and Diana.

The occasional ranting in "Edward I.," and the prevailing

---

[1] Udall paid a similar compliment to Anne Boleyn in 1532, representing that the golden apple was not worthy of her ; and a Mr Pownd repeated it for the gratification of Elizabeth in 1566 ; but these did not carry it to the extent of making it the aim of an entire play.

extravagance of the "Battle of Alcazar," are remarkable as coming from the same pen as "The Arraignment of Paris" and "David and Bethsabe." I can hardly believe that the bombast of Muly Mahamet—whom even more than Tamburlaine Shakespeare had in his eye in the burlesque of Pistol—was a serious expression according to the author's notions of art : we reconcile it with Peele's character only by supposing it to have been an audacious experiment in rivalry of the heroics of Tamburlaine. It seems to have succeeded. The incident burlesqued in "Feed and grow fat, my fair Calipolis," was specially famous. The Moor, Muly Mahamet, with his wife Calipolis and his son, are fleeing before the army of Abdelmelec, when Calipolis grows faint from hunger. Muly rushes off the stage shouting—"Famine shall pine to death, and thou shalt live ;" and re-enters with a piece of flesh upon his sword—

> " Hold thee, Calipolis, feed, and faint no more ;
> This flesh I forced from a lioness,
> Meat of a princess, for a princess meet :
>
> .        .        .        .        .        .
>
> Feed, then, and faint not, fair Calipolis ;
> For rather than fierce famine shall prevail
> To gnaw thy entrails with her thorny teeth,
> The conquering lioness shall attend on thee.
>
> .        .        .        .        .        .
>
> Jove's stately bird with wide-commanding wings
> Shall hover still about thy princely head,
> And beat down fowl by shoals into thy lap ;
> Feed, then, and faint not, fair Calipolis."

This incident struck the popular fancy very much like Tamburlaine's entrance in a car of gold drawn by two kings with bits in their mouths; and offered a bright mark for Shakespeare's ridicule. Pistol's strong language about the Furies, Pluto's damned lake, Erebus, and tortures vile also, seems to be founded on passages in the same play. In the explanation of the dumb-show before Act I. we find the following :—

> " Till Nemesis, high mistress of revenge,
> That with her scourge keeps all the world in awe,
> With thundering drum awakes the God of War,
> And calls the Furies from Avernus' crags,
> To range, and rage, and vengeance to inflict,
> Vengeance on this accursed Moor for sin."

In the dumb-show before Act II. Nemesis again uses her drum, and—

> " 'Larums aloud into Alecto's ears,
> And with her thundering wakes whereas they lie
> In cave as dark as hell and beds of steel,
> The Furies, just imps of dire revenge."

In Act I. Muly Mahamet Seth exclaims—

> " Sheath not your swords, soldiers of Amurath,
> Sheath not your swords, you Moors of Barbary,
> That fight in right of your anointed king,
> But follow to the gates of death and hell,
> Pale death and hell, to entertain his soul;
> Follow, I say, to burning Phlegethon,
> This traitor-tyrant and his companies."

Muly Mahamet himself ends off Act IV. with an apostrophe to the Furies, and a mad frenzy of imprecation :—

> " You bastards of the Night and Erebus,
> Fiends, Furies, hags that fight in beds of steel,
> Range through this army with your iron whips.
>
> .    .    .    .    .    .
>
> And lastly for revenge, for deep revenge,
> Whereof thou goddess and deviser art,
> Damned let him be, damned, and condemned to bear
> All torments, tortures, plagues, and pains of hell. "

We see in these passages where Pistol may have caught his trick of repeating emphatic words. The facetious Peele in all likelihood piled up these agonies for popular effect with hardly less sense of their ludicrous extravagance than Shakespeare himself.

In strange contrast to these mad explosions are the rich fancy and tender feeling of "David and Bethsabe" and the delicate airy wit of "The Arraignment of Paris." Campbell has quoted the finest passage in "David and Bethsabe," but the following is not much inferior. It is David's exclamation at the sight of Bethsabe approaching in obedience to his summons :—

> " Now comes my lover tripping like the roe,
> And brings my longings tangled in her hair.
> To joy her love I'll build a kingly bower,
> Seated in hearing of a hundred streams,
> That for their homage to her sovereign looks,
> Shall, as the serpents fold into their nests
> In oblique turnings, wind their nimble waves
> About the circles of her curious walks ;
> And with their murmur summon easeful sleep
> To lay his golden sceptre on her brows."

The following is also a sweet picture, although, perhaps, the sweetness is too surfeiting :—

> " The time of year is pleasant for your grace,
> And gladsome summer in her shady robes
> Crowned with roses and with painted flowers,
> With all her nymphs shall entertain my lord,
> That, from the thicket of my verdant groves,
> Will sprinkle honey-dews about his breast,
> And cast sweet balm upon his kingly head."

The sprightly art of the "Arraignment" would seem but stale in a quotation.   The most elaborate joke in it seems intended to ridicule the amorous pining of Spenser's 'Shepherd's Calendar.' Colin is introduced bewailing the cruelty of Love, and commiserated by his friends Hobinol, Diggon, and Thenot: shortly afterwards his hearse is brought in, and shepherds sing welladay over his untimely death.   His sweetheart Thestylis woos and is rejected by a "foul crooked churl."   Our knowledge of the personal jealousies and friendships of the period is imperfect and perplexing; but it is probable that the "Palin" whom Spenser mentions in Colin Clout as "envying at his rustic quill" was George Peele, and that this was the expression of the envy.


### V.—Thomas Nash (1558–1600 ?).

Marlowe's unfinished tragedy of "Dido" was completed by Thomas Nash; and though this clever writer is memorable chiefly as a prose satirist, yet his name will always be remembered most naturally in connection with his poetical associates, Greene, Marlowe, Lodge, and Peele.   Nash was educated at Cambridge, which he seems to have left in some disgrace, and his first essay in print was the dashing critical preface to Greene's "Menaphon" in 1587. A clever harum-scarum fellow, with a quick sense of the ludicrous, and an unsparing tongue, he found admirable scope for his powers in replying to the Martin Marprelate tracts, which he did in some four or five different pamphlets in and about the year 1589.   In the same year he opened up a vein of general prose satire in his 'Anatomy of Absurdity,' a general attack on whatever struck him as ridiculous in contemporary literature and manners—ranging consequently within a wide circle.   In 1592 he continued his exercitations in this vein with 'Pierce Penniless, his Supplication to the Devil.'   But meantime he had become involved in a quarrel with Gabriel Harvey, the friend of Spenser, and his brothers, of which a full account is given in D'Israeli's 'Quarrels of Authors.'   The original cause of Nash's ire seems to have been the offensive conceit of Richard Harvey, who in the Marprelate controversy had tried "to play Jack of both sides," sneering at all parties to the dispute, and had repeated the offence in a subsequent publication, in which he went the length of terming all poets and writers about London "piperly make-plays and make-baits."   Nash was thoroughly in his element in taking up such a taunt.   Throughout the various pamphlets of the celebrated logomachy, he seems never to lose for a moment his feeling of complete and easy mastery over his opponent, writing always with good-humoured assurance of victory, and with the unsparing

derision of one who fears no retort. In the opening of his
'Strange News,' a reply to Harvey's attack on the deceased
Greene, he bids the Lord have mercy on poor Gabriel, for he
is fallen into hands that will plague him. Harvey's poetical pretensions, and, above all, his hexameters, are ridiculed in this
pamphlet with wonderful spirit and direct freshness and copiousness of language. It confirms Nash's protestations that the
quarrel was none of his seeking, to find him in his 'Christ's
Tears over Jerusalem,' a religious and moral performance strangely
different from the writer's previous effusions, making certain overtures towards reconciliation. These overtures being rejected, he
returned with redoubled incisiveness to his former ways of warfare,
which continued till the mouths of the antagonists were shut by
the intervention of the scandalised Government.

Nash was imprisoned in 1597 for his share in a play called the
"Isle of Dogs," which has not been preserved. "Summer's Last
Will and Testament" is the only play of his that has come down
to us. It is of the nature of a Masque, in which the seasons are
the prominent figures; was written for representation on the
private stage of some nobleman, whose name is unknown, and
was acted in 1592, though not published till 1600. On the whole
it is a somewhat dull production, as the author himself seems to
have felt. Frantic efforts are made to say witty and pretty things
about the seasons, and to deliver striking saws about miscellaneous
objects, dogs and drunkards, bookish theorists, and misanthropists.
The best part of it is the song quoted in Palgrave's Treasury.
Nash has no marked dramatic talent. His forte lay in what Mr
Collier calls "humorous objurgation": he throws himself into
that vein with a sad want of continence, but with unflagging
vivacity, and unfailing copiousness both of words and of conceptions.
He tried also a tale—"Jack Wilton"—but did not succeed: he
never is anything except when in the full swing of harum-scarum
raillery.


VI.—THOMAS KYD. (?)


The author of "Jeronimo" (produced in 1588) and its continuation "The Spanish Tragedy, or Hieronimo is mad again,"
belongs to the "robustious" school of rampant heroism. Ben
Jonson's calling him the "sportive Kyd" is a joke. Kyd, however, possesses merits and a character of his own. In direct and
vivid energy of language, in powerful antithesis of character, and
in skilful and effective construction of plot, in the chief qualities
that make a good acting play, "The Spanish Tragedy" will bear
comparison with the best work of any of Shakespeare's predecessors. That it passed through more editions than perhaps any play

of the Elizabethan age is not at all surprising; it offered many points for ridicule to the wits of the time, but its unflagging interest and strong emotions of pity and suspense went straight to the popular heart.

The prominence of " Hieronimo " in the public mind is shown by the mention made of it in Jonson's " Cynthia's Revels," the " Return from Parnassus," Thomas May's " Heir," and other writings of the time. A less obtrusive evidence—but more complimentary to Kyd if it arose from choice and not from necessity—is the fact of Shakespeare's familiarity with the play, as proved by numerous echoes and adaptations of its phraseology and its situations.

One remarkable point in the plot of this double play is the breadth and scope of the action. Lorenzo, an antitype of Iago, plans the murder of his brother-in-law Andrea, and the dishonour of his sister Belimperia. Jeronimo and his son Horatio, the friend of Andrea, become aware of the plot, and write to Andrea warning him of his danger. Were the villain at this point to be exposed and the intended victim preserved for a happy life, or were all the principal personages to perish tragically, the action of the play would still be of ordinary breadth. But this is only half of the action of the First Part of Jeronimo. Jeronimo's letter never reaches Andrea, and Lorenzo's plot miscarries by an ingeniously conceived accident; yet, after all, the man whose assassination was arranged is dishonourably killed in battle by the myrmidons of Balthazar, the young prince of Portugal, and the First Part ends with Andrea's ghost bequeathing to Horatio the duty of revenge. In the Second Part, a marriage is contrived between Balthazar, who has been taken prisoner, and Belimperia the widow of Andrea. She loathes him and falls in love with Horatio. Horatio, the appointed revenger of Andrea's death, is hanged in his father's garden by Lorenzo and Balthazar. This takes place in the first two Acts. The remaining three are occupied with Hieronimo's madness at the loss of his only son, partly real, partly feigned. Like Hamlet, he is not at first certain of the murderers, and even when he discovers them indubitably, he bides his time. At last he hits upon the scheme of representing a play before the Court, and procuring that the actors be Lorenzo, Balthazar, Belimperia, and himself. They kill in earnest where they should kill but in jest: Belimperia stabs Balthazar, whose servants had killed her husband, and then stabs herself; Hieronimo stabs Lorenzo, the murderer of his son, then makes a speech disclosing to the horrified Court the " realism " of the play, and hangs himself.

## VII.—ANTHONY MUNDAY (1553–162–?).

Munday is known to have been employed in fourteen plays between 1597 and 1603, and he was probably a constant writer for the stage for many years before that date. When quite a youth he seems to have been seized with a passion for travel, and to have run away from his father's with as much money as he could scrape together, and crossed the Channel strange countries for to see. He and his companion were robbed on their way through France, and after some adventures were persuaded to join the English Seminary in Rome. After a time he made his way back to England, and published an account of his experiences under the title 'The English Roman Life,' "discoursing the lives of such Englishmen as by secret escape leave their own country to live in Rome under the servile yoke of the Pope's government." This was in 1582, and he would seem to have now made his living by translating from French and Italian, and composing rhymed plays. A rhymed play of his—"Fidele and Fortunatus," was entered on the Stationers' Books in 1584. The "Downfal of Robert Earl of Huntingdon," which was published in 1601, is supposed to have been originally and chiefly the work of Munday, modified by Chettle. Later in life, he seems to have abandoned the stage for the counter : he devised and wrote the Lord Mayor's pageant in 1605, entitling it—"The Triumphs of Reunited Britannia," and is described on the title-page as "citizen and draper." He was several times employed after this to write these pageants, and was driven to complain of the difficulty of finding new subjects. The Golden Fleece being the drapers' coat of arms, he twice made use of the voyage of the Argo : and when the Mayor happened to be a fishmonger, he treated the citizens to "Chrysanaleia, or the Golden Fishing," to signify the close alliance between the Fishmongers and the Goldsmiths.
·There is nothing in Munday's compositions above the tamest mediocrity, and he is worth mentioning only as a specimen of the literary journey man of the time.

## VIII.—HENRY CHETTLE (1563–160–?).

Chettle, the editor of Greene's posthumous "Groatsworth of Wit," which contained the memorable attack on Shakespeare, was very much superior to Munday. He seems to have been originally a printer or stationer (he subscribes himself "stationer" in a note of acknowledgment to Henslowe in 1598), and probably took to writing plays about the same time as Marlowe. Between 1597 and 1603, during which time he was often in distress from want of money, his name is connected with the production of forty-seven plays, of sixteen of which he was sole author. Of his sixteen original plays, only one survives, "Hoffman, or a Revenge for a Father," a tragedy, written probably about 1602, to compete with Shakespeare's "Hamlet," then in course of successful performance at the Globe Theatre. Of the thirty-one plays that he had a share in, all but three are lost—"Patient Grissell" (Chettle, Dekker, and Haughton), "Robin Hood" (Chettle and Munday), "Blind Beggar of Bethnal Green" (Chettle and Day). In 1607, Dekker speaks of Chettle as being in the Elysian fields, and gives the only record we have of his personal appearance—namely, that he was a fat man.

"Hoffman" is a horrid inflated thing, absurd and bloody. The hero in revenging his father certainly does not suffer from the weakness of irresolution. Fortune throws an opportunity in his way, and he seizes it pitilessly, and makes it beget other opportunities, till a long list of enemies, their relatives, and the stranger within their gates, perish by poison or steel. His mission of slaughter is very nearly fulfilled when he has the weakness to fall in love with the Duchess of Luneberg, one of his intended victims, who pretends to listen to his addresses, and betrays him to his father's death by a red-hot crown of iron. It is remarkable that Chettle, like so many other of the Elizabethan poets, no matter how inflated he is in expressing vehement passions of rage, hatred, and revenge, displays considerable felicity in the expression of the tender feelings. One might apply to the poets of that age two lines used by old Janicolo in "Patient Grissell"—

> "Indeed, my child, men's eyes do nowadays
> Quickly take fire at the least spark of beauty."

The beginning of the Third Act of "Hoffman" is very beautiful. It is a moonlight scene between the runaways Lodowick and Lucibella, imitated apparently from the "Merchant of Venice." They have walked till they are weary, the moon strewing silver on their path, and weeping a gentle dew on the flower-spotted earth. The flowers are beguiled by the light of Lucibella's eyes to open their petals "as when they entertain the lord of May." They rest on a bank of violets, and talk themselves asleep.

> "*Lod.* O Love's sweet touch ! with what a heavenly charm
> Do your soft fingers my war-thoughts disarm !
> Prussia had reason to attempt my life,
> Enchanted by the magic of thy looks
> That cast a lustre on the blushing stars.
> Pardon, chaste Queen of Beauty ! make me proud,
> To rest my toiled head on your tender knee !

> My chin with sleep is to my bosom bowed ;
> Fair, if you please, a little rest with me !
> > [*He reclines his head upon her lap.*
>
> *Luci.* No, I'll be sentinel ; I'll watch for fear
> Of venomous worms or wolves, or wolvish thieves.
> My hand shall fan your eyes, like the filmed wing
> Of drowsy Morpheus : and my voice shall sing
> In a low compass for a lullaby.
>
> *Lod.* I thank you ! I am drowsy ; sing, I pray,
> Or sleep ; do what you please : I'm heavy, I !
> Good night to all our care !  Oh ! I am blest
> By this soft pillow, where my head doth rest !
> > [LODOWICK *sleeps.*
>
> *Luci.* In sooth, I'm sleepy too ; I cannot sing :
> My heart is troubled with some heavy thing.
> Rest on these violets, whilst I prepare
> In thy soft slumber to receive a share !
> Blush not, chaste moon, to see a virgin lie
> So near a prince ! 'tis no immodesty ;
> For when the thoughts are pure, no time nor place
> Have power to work fair chastity's disgrace.
> Lod'wick, I clasp thee thus ! so, arm clip arm ;
> Let sorrow fold them that wish true love's harm !
> > [*She sleeps, embracing* LODOWICK."

The finest lines in the play are the exclamation of Matthias when he believes that he has killed Lucibella unjustly, and finds that she still breathes—

> " There's life in Lucibella, for I feel
> A breath more odoriferous than balm
> Thrill through the coral portals of her lips."

The beautiful song in " Patient Grissell," quoted in Palgrave's Treasury under the title of " The Happy Heart," is in all probability the work of Dekker.   But Chettle also had a certain gift of song.   He appended to his " Mourning Garment, in memory of the death of Elizabeth," a " Shepherd's Spring Song," in celebration of the accession of James.   Such raptures can hardly be other than feigned ; still, there are touches of beauty in the song.

> " Thenot and Chloris, red-lipped Driope,
> Shepherds, nymphs, swains, all that delight in field,
> Living by harmless thrift, your fat herds yield,
> Why slack ye now your loved company ?
> Up sluggards, learn, the lark doth mounted sing
> His cheerful carols, to salute our king.
>
> The mavis, blackbird, and the little wren,
> The nightingale upon the hawthorn brier,
> And all the wing'd musicians in a quire
> Do with their notes rebuke dull lazy men.
> Up, shepherds, up, your sloth breeds all your shames ;
> You sleep like beasts, while birds salute K. James.

The gray-eyed morning with a blustering cheek,
  Like England's royal rose mixt red and white,
  Summons all eyes to pleasure and delight :
Behold the evening's dews do upward reek,
  Drawn by the sun, which now doth gild the sky
  With its light-giving and world-cheering eye.

Oh, that's well done ! I see your cause of stay
  Was to adorn your temples with fresh flowers ;
  And gather beauty to bedeck your bowers
That they may seem the cabinets of May.
  Honour this time, sweetest of all sweet springs,
  That so much good, so many pleasures brings."

# CHAPTER VII.

## WILLIAM SHAKESPEARE.

### I.—His Life and Character.

STEEVENS, Hallam, and Dyce are unreasonably sceptical and depressing in their summary of "all that is known with any degree of certainty concerning Shakespeare." It is our own fault if we are disappointed and perplexed by what antiquaries have discovered, and if we refuse to interpret facts, because they do not illustrate Shakespeare's character in the precise way that we desire. A good deal more is known concerning Shakespeare than that "he was born at Stratford-upon-Avon—married and had children there—went to London, where he commenced actor, and wrote poems and plays—returned to Stratford, made his will, died, and was buried." The industry of antiquaries has brought to light many significant facts concerning the poet's family; concerning the public institutions and customs at Stratford during his boyhood; and concerning the life of a player in London when Shakespeare belonged to the profession. To the same industry we are indebted for some suggestive particulars more directly personal: we know some facts about his marriage, his wife, and his children; we have memorials of the effect that his poems and plays produced upon his contemporaries; we know whether he returned to Stratford poor or rich, from necessity or from choice, a broken-down Bohemian or a prosperous and respected townsman; and we know that after his death and burial, a bust was erected to his memory in the church of his native town, and that this bust still exists to show what sort of man he was in outward appearance.

Shakespeare died on the 23d of April 1616, and the tradition is that he died on his birthday.[1] The register of his baptism is

---

[1] Mr Bolton Corney contests this on the ground that Shakespeare is said by the monument to have died in his 53d year. But if he had completed his 52d year, he might have been said to be in his 53d.

consistent with this: he was baptised on the 26th of April 1564. But the exact day of Shakespeare's birth is not worth discussing: much more important is it to know what were the surroundings of his childhood, what was his father's business, and the probable condition of his father's household. When the future "myriad-minded" dramatist came into the world, his father's household seems to have been radiant with the good-humour of prosperous industry and enterprise. The son of a substantial farmer at Snitterfield, three or four miles from Stratford, John Shakespeare had some thirteen years before opened a shop in Henley Street, Stratford. What he sold in this shop has been much disputed: he certainly sold gloves, and he probably sold also meat, wool, and barley. It is not uncommon now for farmers' sons in the neighbourhood of towns to set up as corn-merchants or butchers; and there is nothing improbable in supposing that in those days, when there was less trade and less division of labour, John Shakespeare may have retailed farm produce to the townspeople of Stratford, selling them barley, mutton, wool, and sheepskin gloves. But whatever he sold, the important fact is that he had prospered. Three years after he had settled in Stratford he had been able to buy two small copyhold properties. Soon after (probably in 1557) he had married Mary Arden of Wilmecote, daughter of a substantial yeoman or proprietor-farmer in the neighbourhood, and heiress to a small farm called Ashbies. He had mixed with credit in the public affairs of the town: he had been appointed an ale-taster and elected a burgess; and before 1564 had filled in succession the offices of constable, affeeror (assessor of fines), and chamberlain.

Such were the circumstances that Shakespeare was born into. Two little sisters, born before him, had died in infancy; another brother, named Gilbert, was baptised on October 13, 1566; a sister, named Joan, on April 15, 1569; another sister, named Anna (who died in infancy), on September 28, 1571. During this time John Shakespeare continued to prosper and rise in the esteem of the corporation. When little William was seven years old, his father attained the summit of municipal dignity,—being on September 5, 1571, elected chief alderman for the ensuing year.

Our next question is—What were the provisions for school education in Stratford?[1] A free school had been restored to the town in the reign of Edward VI., and to this in all probability Shakespeare was sent at an early age, six or seven, and taught the rudiments of Latin. He learned at least enough to enter into the humour of Sir Hugh Evans's lesson to Master William Page; to smell Costard's false Latin; and to put jocularly into the mouth

---

[1] This subject has been thoroughly discussed by Professor Spencer Baynes in a series of papers in 'Fraser's Magazine,' 1879-80. Mr Baynes supplies most ingenious and conclusive proof that Shakespeare read Ovid in the original.

of Holofernes the first line of the eclogues of Mantuanus the Car-
melite—lines then as familiar to schoolboys as the first lines of
Virgil's eclogues are now.  Such, so far as his plays afford any
warrant, was the extent of Shakespeare's Latin knowledge.  Ben
Jonson's saying that he knew small Latin and less Greek, is
obviously an epigrammatic way of saying that he knew no Greek
at all.

Take Shakespeare next at a point where his schoolboy days are
over.  How long did he continue at school?  There is a tradition
that he was withdrawn from school earlier than he might otherwise have been by the narrow circumstances of his father.  So far
this is substantiated by the ascertained fact that in 1578, when
Shakespeare was fourteen years old, his father mortgaged the
estate at Ashbies: from that date onwards there are unmistakable
evidences of poverty gaining upon John Shakespeare's resources.
Under such stress of circumstances nothing could be more natural
than to withdraw the eldest boy from school to assist in the miscellaneous business of butchering, wool-selling, glove-making, and
farming.  There is nothing more unlikely, more incongruous, or
more derogatory in Shakespeare's helping to kill a sheep, or make
a glove, or herd cows in his boyhood, than in Burns's casting peats,
pulling turnips, or gauging beer-barrels in his manhood.  Such
occupations gave strength to their minds as well as to their bodies:
it brought home to them the earnestness of the struggle for existence, and widened and deepened their sympathies with the mass of
their fellowmen.

To account for Shakespeare's knowledge of legal terms, Malone
conjectured that after leaving school he was articled to an attorney in Stratford.  But Shakespeare needed no experience of an
attorney's office to awaken his interest in legal terms.  He had
motive enough without going beyond his father's household.
There are no family secrets from the children of the poor.  Shakespeare doubtless heard the painful deliberations of his once prosperous parents, knew all their difficulties, and perused the mortgage
bond with a boy's grave curiosity and awe.  Then, and more than
once again, before he established himself and his parents in assured
comfort, he received the sharpest of stimulants to make out the
exact meaning of legal terms.

This, however, is the serious side of our poet's youth.  It
doubtless had a brighter side.  Poverty could not repress such
energy, ebullient spirits, and fresh open senses.  We may imagine
the boy often running cheerfully between the shop in the town
and the farm in the country: sticking a cowslip in his breast, and
looking down at its cinque spots; whistling after the birds; rolling in the sun upon a bank of wild thyme; reading and spouting
Sir Bevis of Southampton or Sir Guy of Warwick, and building,

perhaps, many a boyish castle in the air.  He was doubtless
popular among his father's and his grandfather's ploughmen and
shepherds: a leading spirit in the antics on Plough-Monday and at
the Feast of Sheep-shearing.  We may imagine him a favourite
with some garrulous old repository of "merry tales of errant
knights, queens, lovers, lords, ladies, giants, dwarfs, thieves,
cheaters, witches, fairies, goblins, friars, &c.," which Burton says
were among the ordinary recreations of winter: we may imagine
the boy listening gratefully to such tales while the old gossip is—

> " Sitting in a corner turning crabs,
> Or coughing o'er a warmed pot of ale."

If we imagine him thus employed in his boyhood, we can understand with what delight he reverted to such scenes amidst the excitement and nerve-shattering racket of an actor's life in  London :
we can enter with more vivid sympathy into his songs about spring
freshness and simple winter comforts when they take us back with
him from the hot exhaustion of the playhouse to the brightness of
his youth in Stratford.

But while we imagine Shakespeare engaging with high spirits in
every sort of game and glee, one form of recreation in particular
demands our attention as having probably exercised a powerful influence on his future career.  This was the representation of plays
in Stratford.  We know from the records of the corporation of
Stratford that it was visited by various companies of players, the
Queen's Company, the servants of Lord Worcester, of Lord Leicester, of Lord Warwick, and of other noblemen.  There was a
performance by such a company in the Guildhall when John
Shakespeare was bailiff: and some of the actors were probably
entertained in his house, and gazed at with wonder by his little
son, then a child of five years.  From his sixth year onwards,
Shakespeare had thus frequent opportunities of witnessing plays.
By the time he was two-and-twenty, he may have seen, as Mr
Dyce says, "the best dramatic productions, such as they were, represented by the best actors then alive."  Further, our knowledge
of the customs of the country enables us to conjecture with reasonable probability that Shakespeare was more than a spectator of
play-acting.  Apart from the well-known tendency of schoolboys
in a country town to imitate the latest sensation in their play-
ground, we know that throughout England in Shakespeare's youth
dramatic pageants of various kinds, from "storial shows" to
morris-dancing, were regular features in the amusements of the
established festivals—Twelfth-Night, Shrove-Tuesday, Hock-Tues-
day, May-day, Whitsuntide, &c.  In Stratford, Whitsuntide seems
to have been the favourite season for these exhibitions: as Hock-

Tuesday was the usual time for the annual plays of the men of Coventry.   In the " Winter's Tale," Perdita is made to say—

> " Methinks I play as I have seen them do
> In *Whitsun' Pastorals.*"

And in the " Two Gentlemen of Verona," Julia, disguised as a page, feigns that—

> "*At Pentecost,*
> *When all our pageants of delight were played,*
> Our youth got me to play the woman's part."

The exhibition of the Nine Worthies in " Love's Labour Lost" and the " tedious brief scene of young Pyramus and his love Thisbe" in "Midsummer Night's Dream," were in all likelihood caricatures of the sort of thing that young Shakespeare actually saw in Stratford, and actually took part in.   In these annual midsummer pageants of delight doubtless were included many varieties of performance—from the more ambitious efforts of the schoolmaster to the humble endeavours of hard-handed men that had never laboured in their minds before, and toiled their unbreathed memories for the first time.   We may imagine Shakespeare, while still a schoolboy, with his small features and elegant shape, chosen to " play the woman's part," and instructed in such undertakings as—

> " Ariadne passioning
> For Theseus' perjury and unjust flight."

We may imagine him at a somewhat later stage writing a play for a party of his boon companions, and organising of an evening in the woods about Stratford some such rude rehearsals as Peter Quince superintended " in the palace wood, a mile without the town, by moonlight."   Holofernes, who plays three " worthies " himself, and Bottom, who covets every effective part, who can " speak in a monstrous little voice," who can roar either terribly or " as gently as any sucking dove," and whom the politic Quince propitiates by assigning him Pyramus—" a sweet-faced man ; a proper man, as one shall see in a summer's day ; a most lovely gentleman-like man "—were doubtless caricatures from nature.   Another reminiscence of these extravagantly amusing rehearsals—the most enjoyable part of all amateur representations—may be traced in " Love's Labour Lost " in Boyet's account of the preparations for the Russian masquerade (Act v. 2, 107).

If, then, we take any part of Shakespeare's life between boyhood and manhood, we find nature making great preparations for the future many-sided dramatist.   We find the boy's life placed at times under deep shadows, and we find the shadows left at home and forgotten, returning, perhaps, with momentary pang to mingle sadness with mirth. When he went out thinking gloomily of his father's accumulating distress and of the cheerless prospect for his little brothers and little sister, the darkness would often be chased from his susceptible spirit by spring freshness, sunshine, and bird-singing, or by the company of light-hearted friends; and he thus had early experience of all varieties of mood between despair and immoderate mirth. Had Shakespeare's life been all light and no shadow during that plastic period of youth when the man's chief tendencies are formed, he could never have searched so thoroughly the depths and the heights of the human heart.

Further, when we know the dramatic tendency of Stratford, we lessen the miracle of his sudden rise as an actor and a dramatist. That a raw youth from the country, unused to the stage and the pen, should in the course of five or six years have risen to the highest rank as a writer of plays, is simply incredible. The boy is always father to the man : supreme achievements demand a prolonged conspiracy of circumstances. It need not lessen our reverence for the mighty genius of Shakespeare to find reason for believing that he was to the manner born; that reckoning Time with her millioned accidents gave him a special education for the stage. Not only had he in his youth witnessed plays and taken part in plays, but in all likelihood he had even as a boy read tales and romances with a special eye to plots and incidents suitable for dramatic representation. This much, in the failure of assured knowledge, we may reasonably conjecture as quite within the probabilities, or at least the possibilities, of the case.

The first documentary memorial of Shakespeare, next to the record of his baptism, is his marriage bond. This is dated November 28, 1582 : he being then under nineteen years of age. His bride was Anne Hathaway, daughter of Richard Hathaway, a substantial yeoman, living at Shottery, a hamlet about a mile from Stratford. Anne was about eight years older than her boy-husband. From the signatures to the document Mr Halliwell-Phillipps argues that the parents of both parties approved of the match. One thing at least is clear, that there was in some quarter a certain eagerness for the ceremony : they were married " with once asking of the banns of matrimony between them," and there is a clause in the bond throwing all the responsibility upon "the said William" himself, and "saving harmless" the Lord Bishop and his officers. The most probable reason for this expedition appears in the date of the baptism of their first child, Susanna, May 26, 1583.

The next great event in his life is traditionary : he is said to have been prosecuted for stealing Sir Thomas Lucy's deer. Malone, De Quincey, and many others reject this incident, founding triumphantly on the fact that Sir Thomas Lucy had no park. It is alleged, on the other hand, that though Sir Thomas had no park, "he may have had deer; for his son and successor sent a buck as a present to Lord Ellesmere in 1602." There is nothing improbable in the incident; and it is no whit more derogatory to the dignity of Shakespeare than the mere fact of his humble birth. To call the offence deer-*stealing* is to name it from the point of view of a game-preserver or a gamekeeper. We know that Lucy and the townsmen of Stratford were not on good terms: Mr Halliwell-Phillipps has discovered a "riot" made "upon" him; and the excitable son of a popular burgess would· doubtless consider it a good joke to carry off the unpopular gentleman's deer, more particularly if he had few of them. But it is unnecessary to suppose that Shakespeare was actuated by anything beyond a natural liking "to hunt the wild deer, and to follow the roe."

The tradition is that his trespass against Sir Thomas compelled Shakespeare to leave Stratford. Another reason may have co-operated in persuading him to seek fortune elsewhere—namely, his father's accumulating embarrassments. He may also have been somewhat frightened at the prospect of a large family: twin-children of his, Hamnet and Judith, were baptised on Feb. 2, 1585. From whatever reason, he left Stratford and became a player in the Queen's company, performing at Blackfriars Theatre. The supposed date of this step is 1586. The probability is that he joined the Queen's or some other company as it passed through Stratford. The story given in Greene's 'Groatsworth of Wit' of the beginning of his connection with the stage shows by what inducements the profession was recruited. The player that persuaded Greene to join him had been a "country author, passing at a Moral," had seen the time when he carried his playing fardle or bundle on his back, and had risen to have a share in playing apparel alone worth more than two hundred pounds. Such an example of success might well have induced Shakespeare to leave his dull and cramped life at home: and he may have been employed from the first, upon a reputation as a "country author," to remodel and adapt plays.

The notion that Spenser referred to Shakespeare as "our pleasant Willy" in the 'Tears of the Muses' in 1591 is a most mistaken and almost ludicrous attempt to snatch a compliment for the great dramatist. It would indeed have been more of a compliment to Spenser to make out that he discerned the coming man: but the possibility vanishes before the slightest attention to the real circumstances. The Tears of the Muses were supposed to be shed over the decay of learning. Thalia, the Muse of Comedy, was particularly sad over the absence of "learning's treasure" from the theatres, and the presumption of illiterate upstarts. Learned men, men of university education, no longer wrote comedy for the stage: it was abandoned to the base-born and illiterate. The lament was very characteristic of the aristocratic and refined Spenser, who had himself written comedies that were never represented. With what reason, then, is it supposed that Spenser included Shakespeare among the learned men whose absence Thalia deplored? Is there any evidence for supposing that Shakespeare at the age of twenty-seven could be spoken of as a writer of comedies who had of late ceased writing in disgust at the prevailing scurrility and ribaldry? Could he, while struggling as an actor and playwright to maintain himself and his family, be said to be holding haughtily aloof from the stage, because it had been taken possession of by base-born men with no university education? Supposing that Shakespeare had written any comedies before that time, and supposing that Spenser, who lived for the most part in Ireland, had ever heard of his name, there would have been some ground for construing the lines—

> " Each idle wit at will presumes to make,
> And doth the learned's task upon him take,"

into an ill-natured sneer at the extra-academical poet. I do not believe that these lines were pointed at Shakespeare, but I have no doubt that he smarted under their arrogance, and resented Spenser's academic pride in his sarcastic parody of the title of the work in " Midsummer Night's Dream "—

> " The thrice three Muses mourning for the death
> Of learning, late deceased in beggary."

It is no doubt pleasing to suppose that when the gracious light of Shakespeare appeared in the orient, all other poets at once did homage to his sacred majesty. But the academic poets, even such of them as had condescended or been driven to write for the public stage, Marlowe, Greene, Nash, and Lodge, would have had to swallow very strong prejudices before they admitted Shakespeare to their fellowship, and recognised his claims to equal criticism. Marlowe opened his " Tamburlaine " with a contemptuous go-by to the " jigging veins of rhyming mother-wits." Nash, in his epistle to Greene's " Menaphon," sneers at the efforts of "those that never were gowned in the university," laughs at the idea of men "busying themselves with the endeavours of art that could scarcely Latinise their neck-verse if they should have need : " they live by crumbs from the translator's trencher, and obtain from English Seneca " whole *Hamlets*—I should say, handfuls of tragical speeches." [1] These were general denunciations of extra-academical presumption. But Greene, in his dying ' Groatsworth of

---

[1] This was in 1587. There are certain slight traces of Seneca in Shakespeare's "Hamlet," but this was probably an earlier version of the play on which Shakespeare founded.

Wit,' made a direct attack on Shakespeare. He recommended his friends to give up play-writing as no longer a fit occupation for gentlemen; censured the ingratitude and presumption of players, and assailed in particular one "upstart crow beautified with our feathers, that with his *Tiger's heart wrapt in a player's hide*, supposes he is as well able to bombast out a blank verse as the best of you; and being an absolute *Johannes Fac-totum*, is, in his own conceit, the only Shakescene in a country." It is unnecessary to suppose that this bitter outburst, the best of all testimonies to Shakespeare's power, was caused by his having been employed to remodel any of Greene's plays. The phrase "beautified with our feathers" may be, as we are entitled to infer from the tone of Nash's epistle, nothing more than an expression of academical arrogance, looking down with supreme contempt upon the ungowned playwright as one that could not possibly have anything except what he stole from more learned authors.[1]

In Lodge's prose satire, 'Wit's Misery or the World's Madness,' of date 1596, there is a passage that may or may not be another insult to our dramatist from the same set of university pens. He is describing a personification of Envy, and goes on to say among other things that "he walks in black under colour of gravity, and looks as pale as the visard of the ghost which cried so miserably at the theatre like an oysterwise,[2] *Hamlet, revenge.*"[3] Now, if there is anything in the tradition that Shakespeare played the part of the ghost in "Hamlet," we have here a slight touch of ridicule at Shakespeare's acting, and a partisan support by Lodge of his old friend Greene. That, however, depends entirely upon the worth of the tradition, which certainly has a good many plausible considerations in its favour. Be that as it may, there is another passage in this same work of Lodge's a few pages farther on which has an undoubted interest. Lodge enumerates the "divine wits" of the time, and the following is his list: "Lyly, the famous for facility in discourse; Spenser, best read in ancient poetry; Daniel, choice in word and invention; Drayton, diligent and formal; Th. Nash, true English Aretine." Shakespeare is not mentioned.

Lodge's mention of Drayton confirms my opinion (p. 205) that he and not Shakespeare is the Aetion of Spenser's "Colin Clout."

---

[1] There is a remarkable passage in "Hamlet" (ii. 2, 353-370), where the habit of attacking "the common stages" is sharply ridiculed. The poet is advised not to be so severe on the common player, because he may be obliged to take to the trade himself.

[2] *Oysterwise*, whether misprint or not, is the reading, not *oysterwife*, as always quoted. Oysters do gape very much, as actors often do in mouthing this cry.

[3] This passage at least establishes one of two things: either that Shakespeare's "Hamlet" was upon the stage in 1596, or that the preceding play on the same subject also contained the ghost. Shakespeare was as likely to have played the ghost in the one version as in the other.

True, "diligent and formal" are epithets very different from Spenser's high eulogium; but the expression "choice in word and invention," applied to Daniel, is not more unlike Spenser's praises of that poet. The fact is that Lodge's epithets apply, and apply with much discrimination, chiefly to the sonnets of the two poets. And apart from this mention of Drayton by Lodge, I doubt very much whether "Venus and Adonis" would have suited the taste of Spenser. The man who considered it necessary to apologise for the sensuous freedom of his own descriptions of earthly beauty, may well be supposed to have looked coldly on the rampant paganism of the first heir of Shakespeare's invention. No; I believe that Shakespeare struggled into fame in the teeth of strong prejudices, and that the established potentate of the literary world, the refined and haughty Spenser, did nothing to help his ascent. Shakespeare was an enthusiastic admirer of Spenser, but the elder poet was much less catholic, infinitely more narrow and exclusive. In the very passage where he praised Aetion, Spenser declared that no living poet was to be compared to Sir Philip Sidney—always, of course, excepting himself. The first recognitions of Shakespeare came from humbler pens. Henry Chettle, the stationer and playwright, who edited Greene's 'Groatsworth of Wit,' apologised a few months afterwards for the attack on Shakespeare, and mentioned his civil demeanour, his excellence as a player, his honesty, and his facetious grace in writing, the two last particulars being "reported by divers of worship." This is the first complimentary notice of Shakespeare, and it comes from one who was himself an ungowned playwright. The compliments paid by Barnfield, Meres, Weever, and others to Shakespeare's honey-flowing vein, and suchlike, were not only the homage of very inferior men, but followed upon a wide public recognition of the poet's power. The general public were really the first to recognise Shakespeare : no literary potentate bailed him out of obscurity. His "Venus and Adonis," published in 1593, ran rapidly through several editions, reaching a fifth in 1602. His "Lucrece," published in the following year, though not so popular as its forerunner, still was widely sold. His plays became the talk of the town. In the 11th satire of his "Scourge of Villainy," 1598, Marston asks what is doing in the theatres, and finds that the rage is all for "Romeo and Juliet."

> " Luscus, what's played to-day !  Faith now I know ;
> I set thy lips abroach, from whence doth flow
> Nought but poor Juliet and Romeo."

The Queen heard of Shakespeare's fame, had his plays represented at Court, and was " taken " with them : seeing Falstaff in " Henry IV.," she is said to have desired to see the fat knight in love, and thus to have suggested the "Merry Wives of Windsor." There was a demand for his plays in print. In 1597 he published three tragedies, "Richard II.," "Richard III.," and "Romeo and Juliet." In 1598 he published "Love's Labour Lost" and "Henry IV.," besides second editions of "Richard II." and "Richard III.": in 1599, second editions of "Romeo" and "Henry IV.": in 1600, two editions of a "Midsummer Night's Dream," two editions of the "Merchant of Venice," "2 Henry IV.," "Henry V.," "Much Ado about Nothing," and a second edition of "Titus Andronicus." After 1600 he seems to have felt his fame to be assured, and to have found it more profitable to let his plays be seen only in stage representation. He probably made an agreement with the management of Blackfriars Theatre to refrain from publication that he might not damage the attendance at the playhouse. Even before 1600 he did not publish every play that he wrote : Meres enumerates six comedies and six tragedies of his put upon the stage before 1598 : namely, "Two Gentlemen of Verona," "Comedy of Errors," "Love's Labour Lost," "Love's Labour Won" (supposed to be the play now known by the title "All's Well that Ends Well"), "Midsummer Night's Dream," "Merchant of Venice," "Richard II.," "Richard III.," "Henry IV.," "John," "Titus Andronicus," and "Romeo and Juliet." Four of these were not published till after his death.

Shakespeare was thus in high repute before the close of the century. His popularity did not decrease after the accession of James. Such was the demand for his works that in 1603 a piratical bookseller issued an unauthorised and imperfect edition of "Hamlet," based, probably, upon notes of the play taken during the representation : this provoked him to break through his rule, and he published a correct edition in the following year. In 1608, for some reason unknown, he made another exception to his rule, and published the tragedy of "King Lear": it was so popular that three editions were printed in the same year. In that year, also, a third and a fourth edition of "Richard II." were called for; besides a third edition of "Henry V." and a fourth edition of "Henry IV." He frequently received the honour of having his plays represented at Court : he was the king's favourite dramatist, and there is a tradition that he received a complimentary letter from the king's own hand. There are evidences, also, that he was prospering in worldly affairs as well as in the good opinion of those around him. Early in 1597 he bought for £60 (equivalent to ten times as much of our money) one of the best houses in Stratford, called New Place. Fortunately, also, there have been preserved letters written in that and the following year by natives of Stratford : in which correspondence the poet is spoken of as a man likely to invest money in Stratford, is asked for the loan of £30, and is recommended as a person likely to procure a loan for a friend and countryman. In 1602 he made a more extensive investment near his native town—buying for £320 a hundred and seven acres of arable land in the parish of Old Stratford. In the same year he purchased some property in the town of Stratford. In 1605 he made his largest purchase: paying £440 for the remainder of a lease—granted in 1544 for ninety-two years—of the tithes great and small of Stratford, Old Stratford, Bishopton, and Welcombe.

At what time he retired from the stage is not known with certainty, any more than the date of his entrance upon it. A tradition is recorded in Ward's Diary, extending from 1648 to 1679, that Shakespeare "frequented the plays all his younger time, but in his elder days lived at Stratford, and supplied the stage with two plays every year, and for it had an allowance so large that he spent at the rate of £1000 a-year, as I have heard." Ward was vicar of Stratford-on-Avon, and as he may have had his information from persons that had been acquainted with Shakespeare, there is no reason to discredit the main fact. We may lawfully suppose that Shakespeare spent his latter years at Stratford in comfortable ease, looking after his farm and his tithes, and enjoying the conversation of his friends. His father had died in 1601, and his mother died in 1608; but his wife was still alive, and his daughter was well married to a doctor in Stratford, and presented him with a little grand-daughter to be the old man's darling. Some traditions are preserved of his witty repartees in genial Stratford society; but none of them bear any internal evidence of genuineness.

Shakespeare died at New Place, on the 23d of April 1616. The only record of the cause of his death is the following entry in the Diary just mentioned: "Shakespeare, Drayton, and Ben Jonson had a merry meeting, and it seems drank too hard, for Shakespeare died of a fever there contracted." On this Mr Dyce remarks: "That such a symposium was held is likely enough. Drayton, a native of Warwickshire, and frequently in the neighbourhood of Stratford, may fairly be presumed to have partaken at times of Shakespeare's hospitality; and Jonson, who, about two years after, wandered on foot into Scotland and back again, would think little of a journey to Stratford for the sake of visiting so dear a friend; nevertheless, we should hardly be justified in determining the cause of Shakespeare's death on the authority of a tradition which was not written down till nearly half a century after the event."

Three elaborate works have been written on the portraits of

Shakespeare: Boaden's, 1824; Wivell's, 1827; and Friswell's, 1864. Friswell's, entitled 'Life Portraits of Shakespeare,' is recommended by its containing photographs of the principal portraits—the Stratford bust, the Droeshout engraving, the Chandos painting (the original of the most common Shakespeare face), the Jansen painting, and the Felton head. Only the first two of these portraits are known for certain to be portraits of Shakespeare. The bust, probably put up very soon after the poet's death, was seen and praised as a faithful likeness in 1623. The Droeshout engraving appeared on the title-page of the first edition of Shakespeare's plays in the same year, and received a high compliment in Ben Jonson's famous commendatory verses: it is a bad engraving, but may have been a fair likeness. The bust, however, which is believed to have been copied from a cast taken after death—a practice then sufficiently common—may be accepted upon all considerations as the most trustworthy memorial of the poet's face; the top and back part of the head seem to be rounded off in a regular oval without any pretension to phrenological fidelity. The forehead is not so high as in the ideal Shakespeare's head, but is broad, full, and smoothly arched; it is well balanced by the substantial English yeoman jaw and double chin. In proportion to the full forehead and full underface, the intermediate features are small and delicate, and they are set with the same easy symmetry. From the shortness of the nose and the length of the upper lip, it has been conjectured that the sculptor had an accident with the nose; but we should remember that Scott's upper lip was also irregularly long, and that Shakespeare's admirers were not likely to accept a maimed sculpture. Originally the bust was coloured: the hands and face of a flesh colour, the eyes of a light hazel, the hair and beard auburn. Towards the end of last century, it was coated over with white paint by one of those respectable mediocrities whose sense of propriety is sometimes more destructive than the most outrageous Vandalism. It has since been restored to its original colours.

It is a favourite way with some eulogists of Shakespeare to deny him all individuality whatsoever. He was not one man, they say, but an epitome of all men. His mind, says Hazlitt, "had no one peculiar bias or exclusive excellence more than another. He was just like any other man, but that he was like all other men. He was the least of an egotist that it was possible to be. He was nothing in himself; but he was all that others were or that they could become." Against such a degradation of Shakespeare's character, or of any man's character, it is our duty to protest. In trying to make Shakespeare more than human, the reckless panegyrist makes him considerably less than human: instead of the man whose prudence made him rich, whose affectionate nature made him loved almost to idolatry, and whose genius has been the wonder of the world, we are presented with plasticity in the abstract, an object not more interesting than a quarry of potter's clay.

One of the most curious traits in Shakespeare's character is his worldly wisdom. I do not allude to what is called the wisdom of Shakespeare, as displayed in his maxims of morality and politics. I mean the commonplace virtue, rarely exhibited by men of genius, of prudently expending the material rewards of their toil. We are indebted to the antiquaries for the illustration of this. Not only have they shown us how he invested large savings in his native town, but by ransacking corporation records and other public archives they have discovered for us how firmly he looked after his property. We find him in 1604 prosecuting one Rogers who had bought malt from him and failed to pay. We find him in 1608 bringing an action against John Addenbroke for recovery of a small debt, and thereafter, on the flight of the debtor, proceeding against the security. In 1612 we find him conjoined in a petition to the Court of Chancery to compel certain sharers in the farming of the tithes to pay their just proportions of a common burden. In 1614 he took measures to resist the proposed enclosure of certain common lands which would have affected the value of his property. These little items are not without an interest: they are small in themselves, but they suggest a good deal. The hardships of Shakespeare's early days, the misfortunes of his father, had taught him prudence: he was evidently a firm man of business, not to be imposed upon or cheated with impunity.

This combination of sure and firm-set prudence with heaven-climbing genius is the fundamental wonder in Shakespeare, the permanent marvel of his constitution. From whatever point we look at him, this wonder emerges. With all his capricious streamers of fancy, he does not gyrate off into aimless oddity and eccentricity. The torrent, tempest, and whirlwind of impassioned imagination is, in him, controlled by a temperance that pulls it back from the raving frenzy of incontinent riot. He is copiously inventive and original, but he does not vex, strain, and dislocate his faculty by striving after plots, characters, maxims, words, and images that had never before been seen in print, or heard upon the stage. Large, steadfast, clear-eyed sagacity and sanity are everywhere conspicuous in Shakespeare.

Readers of Shakespeare not familiar with the antecedent literature are naturally enough betrayed into thinking that he drew all his wise sentences about character, morality, and politics from his own experience and observation. Now this is the very thing that his sagacity kept him from attempting. He knew how poor a

show one man's experience can make, and he opened his mind
freely to the accumulated experience of ages.  There were abundant stores within his reach.  The moral-plays were store-houses of
proverbial philosophy : the common wisdom of many generations
was harvested and preserved there as in granaries.  The works of
all our poets from Chaucer downwards were full of similar gen-
eralisations : they were studiously affected in the tales and plays
of his immediate predecessors.  To have neglected these accumulations, if it had been possible, would have been the reverse of
wise : Shakespeare used them liberally.  It is not to be supposed
that he deliberately and in cold blood searched in these reposi-
tories for matter to fill up a dialogue ; but his mind was full of
them, and he took what came to him in the act of composition
and what best suited his purposes, without troubling himself as
to whether it was original or commonplace.  And in like manner
with his imagery.  Before he began to write, nature had been
ransacked and even a fabulous natural history invented in the
craze for imagery.  This, doubtless, gave an immense stimulus to
the poet's original faculty, as the passion for moral and political
saws gave to his powers of observation.  But had Shakespeare
resolved to use no weighty sentence and no figure of speech that
had ever been used before, he would have been forfeiting all hope
of success as a dramatist ; deliberately taking up with the glean-
ings, the husks, and the crumbs.  A play furnished only with
recondite maxims and [far-fetched imagery would have been intolerably thin and meagre.  One thing, however, was and is to be
expected from dramatists having recourse to the great accumulated
wealth of literature : we expect them to give a new application,
and, above all, a new expression, to what they borrow.  We give
them liberty to take the seeds, but not to take the plant.  This
was what Shakespeare did.  Now and then, perhaps, he carried off a whole plant, when he was in a hurry ; but in nearly
every case he took only the seed, the suggestion, and from it
reared a plant far excelling the original stock.  So incomparable
was his genius for expression, that very rarely did he fail to im-
prove what he appropriated.  And therein lay his power and excellence : not in that he added more than any other man to the immense stock of old-world wisdom, but in that he gave to what he
adopted an expression so superlative that generalised observations
centuries older than him have passed into common speech in his
forms.  His wisdom was the wisdom of sagacious choice and happy
application : but his genius was his own.

If we wish to have a vivid impression of the superiority of
Shakespeare's judgment, we cannot do better than compare his
plays with tales on which they have been founded.  He did not
exhaust himself in trying to discover new situations ; but going in

with victorious opulence of matter, took the best situations that occurred to him, from his own mind or from novels, poems, histories, or even from plays then upon the stage, and filled them out in a way that transcended all competition. When our dramatic antiquaries meet in Shakespeare with a story that they have not hitherto discovered in any previous writer, they pursue their inquiries with full confidence that they will some day stumble upon the original. And these discoveries, so far from hurting Shakespeare's reputation, are the most astonishing disclosures of his power. Not only does he enrich the story, and give an incomparable embodiment and expression to the characters, but he recasts the plot and the relations of the *dramatis personæ* with large and clear judgment, so as to produce a more harmonious whole.

"Myriad-minded" has become a favourite epithet for Shakespeare: "myriad-mooded," if it did not sound so odd, might be more precisely descriptive of the dramatist's most essential endowment. One man becomes able to understand the mental habits of many other men if he passes through many changes of mood: if the world presents itself to him in many different lights according to his varying states of mind. A stolid, immobile man—or a man, however mobile, whose life was easy, unvaried, unexcited— could not be a dramatist of any considerable range: no power of imaginative genius can go far in constructing states of mind that have never fallen within the lines of its experience. But, indeed, active imaginative genius, combined with keen interest in human beings, must inevitably produce incessant variableness of mood: a man with these qualities in him must be constantly and incontinently changing his imaginary relations with the world: his imagination will not allow him to be tranquil: moodiness, variableness, is the imperious law of his being. Shakespeare, in imagining the general mental attitude of crafty Bolingbroke, cynical Timon, melancholy Jacques, mad-headed Hotspur, or even dare-devil Richard, and unconscionable Falstaff, fell back upon more or less temporary attitudes of his own variable mind. There could not be a more monstrous mistake than to suppose the great dramatist to have been a calm man, who was never melancholy, and who sat comfortably in a study turning the world round for his amusement, and meditating quietly on the strange fellows that nature had formed in her time. He could not have understood so many of those strange fellows unless he had for however brief an interval passed through the experience of their moods. We know that Shakespeare lived a life of changeful circumstances. In his boyhood, his father's position underwent a gradual change in the eyes of the townspeople of Stratford; and in his youth he took an unusual step that also exposed him to various comments. In London he experienced the feelings of gradually making his way in the world through various obstructions, and at all times he occupied a doubtful position, exposing him to great variety of treatment between the extremes of insult and admiration. He was brought into direct contact with men of all classes, and received with all the diversity of manner experienced by men whose position is not fixed by rigid convention. Now a man of active imagination and quick susceptibilities could not but have approached these changing circumstances in different moods; now melancholy, now defiant, sometimes eager, sometimes cool and indifferent, disposed sometimes to laugh at everything, and sometimes to cry at nothing. In the course of his varied life, he had, doubtless, a touch of the dissolute and reckless spirit of his favourite "Hal"—"of all humours that have showed themselves humours since the old days of goodman Adam;" as well as of the grave, politic, and resolute spirit of Hal's father, Bolingbroke, or Hal himself when he became the heroic Harry the Fifth.

The amazing thing is to find all this variableness, without which dramatic insight is impossible, in combination with the fundamental steadiness, without which dramatic execution is impossible. All this variableness had, as it were, a centre—was an incessant movement above, below, and around a fixed centre of gravity. For all his presumable moodiness, Shakespeare would seem to have never composed but in one mood—the mood of dramatic impartiality. Nobody has been able to detect in his character any strong bias of opinions held dogmatically by himself. He would seem to have composed with intense concentration, setting himself with all the strength of his imagination to express the particular concerns, passions, follies, vices, virtues, actions, and motives that emerged from his story of love or revenge, and allowing himself to be swayed by no considerations except dramatic effect. Preachers sometimes essay to prove his religion and morality by choice excerpts, but they only prove that he put such sentiments into the mouths of his characters : he holds the mirror up to the irreligion and immorality of Edmund and Iago, and displays them with equal clearness and force. One of his characters explains away prophecy, another rationalises presentiments, a third declares that miracles are ceased, and that we can admit only natural means: yet ghosts walk in his dramas, men are haunted by evil forebodings, and calamities are heralded by monstrous portents. It is vain to look for consistent opinions where the dramatist's principle is to embody men of all shades with strict impartiality in their exact form and pressure.

The most amiable and one of the best attested features of Shakespeare's character, is the constancy of certain attachments. We may well suppose that, with an imagination ever ready to invest objects with attributes not their own, and sufficiently subtle to find for Titania points of attraction in the head of an ass, Shakespeare had many passing loves and friendships. But he was capable also of constant attachment. The strongest evidence of this is found in his continued visits to his native place, and his final settlement there in the evening of his life. True, had we no other evidence of his intense affections, the fact of his retirement to Stratford might be otherwise interpreted : it might be said that he left London and its pleasant society because there his profession as an actor exposed him to indignities that his pride would not brook, and went to Stratford because there he was treated as a person of consequence. In support of this might be alleged the significant fact that in 1596 his father, probably at his instigation, applied for a grant of arms at the Heralds' College. We know from Shakespeare's sonnets that he felt keenly the inferiority and disgrace attaching to his profession ; and it is not unlikely that he went back to the scenes of his boyhood with a certain feeling of relief from the scene of his humiliation. It is not perhaps to be denied that Shakespeare was glad to leave London, with all the attractions of wit-combats with Ben Jonson at the Mermaid, because he had not Big Ben's rough indifference to public opinion, and could not bear to be patronised for his genius by men that felt themselves above his profession. But while we acknowledge all this, we have still to account for the fact that his native town of Stratford was the chosen place of his retirement : he might have invested his gains in some quarter where he was utterly unknown, but for the desire to be near the friends and the scenes of his youth. And we are entitled to put upon the fact its most natural construction, when we find that supported by the warmth of attachment expressed in his sonnets, and the recorded testimonies of the gentleness of his nature. "I loved the man," said Ben Jonson, "and do honour his memory, on this side idolatry, as much as any. He was, indeed, honest, and of an open and free nature."


## II.—His Words and Imagery.

The art of putting things cleverly and playing upon words was never carried to a greater height than in the age of Elizabeth. The Elizabethans were conscious word-artists — "engineers of phrases," as Thomas Nash said. "To see this age !" cries the clown in "Twelfth Night," "a sentence is but a cheveril glove to a good wit ; how quickly the wrong side may be turned outward !" And this same clown was acting in delicious caricature of the age, when he fastidiously rejected the word "element"— "Who you are and what you would are out of my welkin, I might say 'element,' but the word is overdone."

The delight in similitudes went naturally with this extravagant craze for uncommon expression : the fancy was solicited, and when solicitation failed, was tortured to satisfy the reigning fashion. They ransacked for comparisons the heavens above, the earth beneath, the waters under the earth, and the historical and mythical generations of earth's inhabitants. The wit of those days viewed the whole world as so much figurative material; he knew it as a painter knows his box of colours, or an enthusiastic botanist the flora of his own parish.

That was the sort of fermentation likely to produce great masters of words. To call a spade a spade is a most benumbing and stifling maxim to literary genius : an Elizabethan would not have called a spade a spade if he could possibly have found anything else to call it. The Elizabethan literature would not have been the rich field that it is had a wretched host of Dean Alfords been in the ascendant, with their miserable notions about idiomatic purity and Queen's English.

The number of words used by Shakespeare is said to be 15,000; and the prodigious magnitude of this number is usually brought out by comparing it with Milton's number, which is 8000.[1]  We might say to him as Katherine said to Wolsey :—

> " Your words,
> Domestics to you, serve your will as't please
> Yourself pronounce their office ; "

and add that his verbal establishment was upon an unparalleled scale.  To some extent, indeed, it would seem that those hosts of

---

[1] Shakespeare's use of technical terms and phrases deserves special notice, as having created quite a department of literature.  Several volumes have been written, dwelling upon all phraseology that belongs, whether exclusively or not, to special trades, occupations, or professions ; each contending for some one occupation that Shakespeare must have engaged in before he could have been able to use its technicalities with such abundance and discrimination. The phraseology of law, medicine, surgery, chemistry, war, navigation, music, field-sports, black-art—the phraseology of each of these was used by Shakespeare, it is argued, with the intelligence of an experienced proficient.  We have also special treatises on his acquaintance with botany, entomology, and ornithology. When each of several volumes contends for a different occupation as the occupation of Shakespeare's youth or early manhood, and each argues on the same fundamental principle with equal conclusiveness, they refute each other and discredit their common principle.  The principle underlying all these arguments is, that a man cannot use the phraseology of an occupation without having practised that occupation.  It is reduced to an absurdity by the latest work in the department, Mr Blades's 'Shakspere and Typography,' in which it is cleverly argued from Shakespeare's use of printing technicalities that he must have been a printer.  The fact is that Shakespeare's contemporaries as well as himself ransacked all trades and professions for striking phrases.  Legal terms were in particular request, and it was not necessary for Shakespeare to study, much less to practise law, in order to acquire them : they abounded in the general literature of the period.

servants were too officious; obtruding their services in such jost-
ling numbers as to embarrass operations. It would appear as if,
when Shakespeare sat in the heat of composition, every word in
the sentence just penned overwhelmed him with its associations;
so perfectly were his intellectual forces mobilised, and so fresh
and eager were they for employment. And besides these officious
troops of words, he had in his service troops of images no less
officious, no less ready to appear upon the slightest hint. Upon
the slightest hint that they were wanted, they came flashing in
with lightning excitement from all quarters; from pages of
poems, histories, and even compendiums, from echoes of the
stage, from all regions of earth and sky that he had seen or
realised in thought.

M. Taine lays most stress upon the copiousness of Shakespeare's
imagery. "It is a series of paintings which is unfolded in his
mind. He does not seek them, they come of themselves; they
crowd within him, covering his arguments; they dim with their
brightness the pure light of logic. He does not labour to explain
or prove; picture on picture, image on image, he is for ever copy-
ing the strange and splendid visions which are engendered one
within another, and are heaped up within him."

Now I am not prepared to admit that Shakespeare's argumentative faculty was thus overwhelmed by the enthusiasm of imagery.
If the dramatist's mind had been thus overpoweringly pictorial, he
would have been too much carried away by the imagination of the
splendid portents, the blazing meteors, and feverish earthquakes,
that prefigured Glendower's birth, to be capable of meeting it with
Hotspur's rejoinder, conceived on the soundest principles of induc-
tive philosophy; the fascination of the fiery heaven and shaking
earth would have prevented him from seeing that the same things
might have happened if Glendower's mother's cat had but kittened
though himself had never been born. That is a typical instance
of logical faculty rising superior to the engrossing force of imagination. Apart, however, from that, I am of opinion that M.
Taine exaggerates the pictorial side of Shakespeare's genius. It
doubtless affords a very plausible explanation of Shakespeare's
mixed metaphors to say that they were produced by the press and
crush of thronging images; as his liberties with grammatical usage
arose from over-abundance and strong pressure of words. But
there is reason to believe that Shakespeare, like every other great
verbal artist, took more delight in words than in forms and colours,
as a painter takes more delight in forms and colours than in words:
and that he was tempted both to mixed metaphors and to violations of grammatical usage by a desire for fresh and startling
combinations of words. This thirst of his ear for new conjunc-
tions overpowered every other consideration. When he was

importuned by several images at once, he knocked two or three of them forcibly together; but I believe that the temptation to do so came chiefly from his delight in the new marriage of words thus consummated.

Indeed, we spread a radical misconception of the poet's art, of the means whereby he gains his hold upon our sensibilities, when we lay M. Taine's stress upon the genesis of his imagery. It is not the pictures of form and colour that are the principal ingredients in the poet's charm: they complete the spell, but are not the essence of it. What takes us captive is the gathering up of ideas in new groups under new bands of words; our senses are ravished by new combinations of words in a poem as by fresh harmonies in an oratorio. In a new combination of words, of course, we are affected by much beyond the mere sound, though that, doubtless, is a large element to many minds. The words appeal to us by multitudinous associations, awake slumbering echoes in many different chambers of our being: the charm of the new encounter is that it rouses and locks together many memories never before united. Several people in the Elizabethan age, or indeed in any other age, could have led us through "a wood, crowded with interwoven trees and luxuriant bushes, which conceal you and close your path, which delight and dazzle your eyes by the magnificence of their verdure and the wealth of their bloom." Spenser comes very much nearer this description than Shakespeare, to my mind: to me it conveys not the remotest approach to the peculiar effect of Shakespeare. Simple and easy as the operation seems, the power of fresh and effective word-combination is one of the rarest of gifts: it is indispensable to a great poet; and part of Shakespeare's main distinction among great poets is the possession of this power in an incomparable degree. Something in the effect of his combinations upon us is due, no doubt, to change in the usage of words: many words whose conjunction raised no surprise in an Elizabethan, have since wandered away from each other and gathered other associations about them, so that their reunion in our minds is like the reunion of youthful friends in old age. The words lay near each other then, and had little variety of idea to bring into collision: now, in this later stage of their existence, they have lived long apart, they surprise us by their mutual recognition, and they bring many memories into shifting indefinite comparison, indefinably charming collision.

In reading Shakespeare's predecessors, we often meet with what appear to have been the suggestions or seeds of passages in his plays; and the comparison of the suggestion with its development gives a most vivid notion of the amplitude and rapidity of growth in Shakespeare's mind. So abundant and mobile were words and

images in that soil, so warm its generating force, that a seed fallen
there at once germinated and shot up with the utmost facility
of assimilation into a complete organism.    Take a simple case.
When Gaveston, in Marlowe's "Edward II.," returns from banishment, and is recognised as the king's favourite, he is besieged
by a host of hunters for patronage.    Among the rest is a traveller,
at whom Gaveston looks for a moment, and then says—"Let me
see : thou wouldst do well to wait at my trencher and tell me lies
at dinner-time ; and as I like your discoursing, I'll have you."
Shakespeare seems to have been tickled with this deliberate utilisa-
tion of the traveller, for he makes the Bastard in "King John,"
when he has obtained royal favour, take delight in the prospect of
the same entertainment.    But in Shakespeare's mind the idea
ripens into a complete picture of well-fed satisfaction, condescension,
obsequiousness, and rambling after-dinner talk ("King John," i.
1, 190).

### III.—Certain Qualities of his Poetry.

The most general reader is impressed by the width of Shakespeare's range through varied effects of strength, pathos, and
humour : and minute methodical reading brings an increase of
admiration.    It must not, however, be supposed that Shakespeare's
poetry embraces all the qualities to be found in all other poets—
that every effect producible by poetry on the human spirit finds
its most conspicuous exemplification in his plays.    He fills us
with wonder, with submissive awe, with heroic energy ; he runs
us through the gamut of tears and laughter, smiling and sadness :
no mortal man has struck so many different notes ; yet with all
his marvellous versatility, he had his own individual touch, and
he left an inexhaustible variety of notes to be sounded.    Shakespeare was a man of wonderful range ; but his plays are not a
measure of the effects that lie within the compass of poetic
language.
    The might that Shakespeare excels in expressing is not the
might of slow and regular agencies, but the might of swift and
confounding agencies.    His power is figured in the boast of
Prospero—

> " To the dread rattling thunder
> Have I given fire, and rifted Jove's stout oak
> With his own bolt."

The awful energies that he sets in motion move with lightning
swiftness and overpowering suddenness : the sublime influence
does not soar and sail above us ; it comes about our senses, flashing and crackling, dazzling and confounding, like Jove's own bolt.
His words pass over us like the burst and ear-deafening voice of

the oracle over Cleomenes, surprising the hearer into nothingness; or flame before our amazed eyes like the sight-outrunning activity of Ariel on board the king's ship in the tempest. Milton's sublimity has not the same life, the same magic energy: it is statelier and less intimate: the effect is not so sudden and overwhelming. There is an excitement akin to madness in the swiftly concentrated energy of some of Shakespeare's occasional bursts. Lear's curses are quivering with compressed force—

> " All the stored vengeances of heaven fall
> On her ungrateful top !  Strike her young bones,
> Ye taking airs, with lameness ! "

And again—

> " Now all the plagues that in the pendulous air
> Hang fated o'er men's faults light on thy daughters ! "

There is a similar half-maddening excitement compressed, as it were, with strong hand, but trembling on the verge of frantic explosion, in Lucrece's invocation of Night—

> " O comfort-killing Night, image of hell !
> Dim register and notary of shame !
> Black stage for tragedies and murders fell !
> Vast sin-concealing chaos ! nurse of blame !
> Blind muffled bawd ! dark harbour for defame !
> Grim cave of death ! whispering conspirator
> With close-tongued treason and the ravisher."

Claudio's anticipation of the horrors of death ("Measure for Measure," iii. 1, 118), Lady Macbeth's invocation (i. 5, 40), Calphurnia's description of the portents ("Julius Cæsar," ii. 2, 13), Othello's imprecation on himself (v. 2, 277), are pregnant with a similar energy. Such passages are few and far between, as in a volcanic country you find many grandeurs with supreme accumulations here and there. In Macbeth's dark hints to his wife about the plot to murder Banquo, the sublime passion is calmer and less thrilling, but there is a lurking devil of swift excitability even in that lofty passage :—

> " *Macb.* There's comfort yet ; they are assailable :
> Then be thou jocund ; ere the bat hath flown
> His cloister'd flight, ere to black Hecat's summons
> The shard-borne beetle with his drowsy hums
> Hath rung night's yawning peal, there shall be done
> A deed of dreadful note.
> 　*Lady Macb.*　　　　　What's to be done ?
> 　*Macb.* Be innocent of the knowledge, dearest chuck,
> Till thou applaud the deed.  Come, seeling night,
> Scarf up the tender eye of pitiful day ;
> And with thy bloody and invisible hand
> Cancel and tear to pieces that great bond

> Which keeps me pale !   Light thickens; and the crow
> Makes wing to the rooky wood :
> Good things of day begin to droop and drowse ;
> While night's black agents to their preys do rouse."

I am not aware that any passage can be quoted from Shakespeare with the composed, stately, sustained grandeur of Milton's description of Satan : Shakespeare's sublime agencies do not move with the same massive dignity—they are instinct with quick life and motion, and their change of attitude is like lightning. The planetary Miltonic grandeur was not, indeed, suited to his purposes as a dramatist.   A Satan of Miltonic dignity put upon the stage must have appeared more or less of a bombast Tamburlaine.   Cæsar, "the foremost man of all this world," who, as Casca mockingly said, " bestrode the narrow world like a Colossus," and who, as he said himself, was "constant as the northern star," is Shakespeare's nearest approach to Miltonic grandeur of conception ; but the grandeur is not sustained as in Milton, it is made up by momentary glances of the poet's swift-ranging imagination. Othello is grand with a volcanic grandeur : he is easily moved ; he blazes out suddenly with such commands as—

> " Hold, for your lives !
>
> He that stirs next to carve for his own rage
> Holds his soul light; he dies upon his motion."

Henry V. was a favourite with the poet, and the prologue to the play where he appears, after shaking off the base contagious clouds that smothered up his beauty from the world, is conceived in a spirit of swelling sublimity ; but mark the nature and attitude of the powers held in reserve by the mighty monarch—

> " O for a Muse of fire, that would ascend
> The brightest heaven of invention !
> A kingdom for a stage, princes to act
> And monarchs to behold the swelling scene !
> Then should the warlike Harry, like himself
> Assume the port of Mars ; *and at his heels*
> *Leash'd in like hounds, should famine, sword, and fire*
> *Crouch for employment.*"

In accordance with this characteristic, Shakespeare's descriptions of storms and tempests, or the dread witching hour with devilry in the mysterious background ; of hurly-burly, riot, and confusion, or vague impending terrors ; of hell let loose or hell pent up and stealthily preparing to spring out,—are far and away incomparable.   Description is more in the way of the epic poet than of the dramatist ; but the dramatist also, even in the modern drama, often has occasion to describe what his personages saw before

they made their appearance on the stage.  Shakespeare loses no
opportunity for description.  Sometimes, as in the beginning of
the Second Act of "Othello," he makes personages on the stage
describe with vivid effect what they see taking place behind the
scenes—the struggle of vessel after vessel on a fiercely tempestuous
sea.  In "Pericles," he brings a storm as it were on the stage,
asking the audience to imagine the stage to be the deck of the
sea-tost mariners, and making his personages speak and act as if
on shipboard.  The scene ("Pericles," iii. 1) is one of Shakespeare's
most magnificent passages.

Storms in the social world, "the grappling vigour and rough
frown of war," were large elements in the Elizabethan drama, and
Shakespeare entered into them with delighted energy.  The
various circumstances of war are described in his historical plays
with a spirit and vividness that one might expect from a
professional man of blood, possessed with the habitual fierceness
of M. Taine's typical Elizabethan.  His imagination revelled in
the scenic glories and horrors of invasion and conflict.  The
picture of the invading army in "Richard II." ii. 3, 95—

> " Frighting the pale-faced villages with war
> And ostentation of despised arms "—

carries his peculiar thrill in its compressed force : and there is a
still more unhinging panic-striking energy in the announcement
made to King John (v. 1, 35)—

> " And wild amazement hurries up and down
> The little number of your doubtful friends."

He describes the night watch before the battle with the dreadful
note of preparation ("Henry V." iv., Prologue), and the bloody
field after the battle ("Henry V." iv. 7, 74).  The actual horrors
of extended conflict he would not seem to have realised minutely,
or to have considered fitted for narration, except in such special
episodes as the death of York and Suffolk ("Henry V." iv. 6).
Conflict on the large scale he expressed in vague powerful figures,
such as the following in a speech of the Bastard's (" King John,"
ii. 1, 350)—

> " Ha, majesty ! how high thy glory towers,
> When the rich blood of kings is set on fire !
> O, now doth Death line his dead chaps with steel :
> The swords of soldiers are his teeth, his fangs :
> And now he feasts, mousing the flesh of men
> In undetermined differences of kings.
> Why stand these royal fronts amazed thus ?
> Cry ' havoc ! ' kings ; back to the stained field
> You equal potents, fiery kindled spirits !
> Then let confusion of one part confirm
> The other's peace ; till then, blows, blood, and death !"

So much for scenic grandeurs, which are but accidents in the drama; let us look now at spiritual grandeurs, which are the dramatic pith and essence. One main function of the drama is to conceive and express the storms of the individual heart under all the variety of passions that stir it to the depths—love, jealousy, despair, revenge, ambition. These storms may arise under endless variety of conditions, and we require of the dramatist not only adequate energy of expression but a certain truth to nature in the origin and fluctuation of passion: the passion must neither arise nor change without just motive. As the passion transcends nature, so may—indeed, so must—the motive: but the relation between the two must not outrage nature. In this correspondence between the motive and the passion consists dramatic truth: dramatic subtlety is shown chiefly in the fluctuations of passion. It is Shakespeare's supreme pre-eminence to combine this truth and subtlety with incomparable energy of expression.

Many people believe that there is hardly a situation in life that cannot be paralleled from Shakespeare; and, curiously enough, this contrast between physical and spiritual commotions is definitely expressed by one of his dramatic creatures, and the spiritual declared to be the more impressive. In "King John" (v. 2, 40), Lewis replies as follows to Salisbury's agitation and conflict of spirit at following the banners of his country's invader :—

> " A noble temper dost thou show in this:
> And great affections, wrestling in thy bosom,
> Doth make an earthquake of nobility.
>
> .    .    .    .    .    .
>
> My heart hath melted at a lady's tears,
> Being an ordinary inundation;
> But this effusion of such manly drops,
> This shower, blown up by tempest of the soul,
> Startles mine eyes, and makes me more amazed
> Than had I seen the vaulty top of heaven
> Figured quite o'er with burning meteors."

Bacon wondered why a woman's eye should be so gazed at when the beauties of the heavens were so little regarded. That wonder spoke the philosopher no less unmistakably than the above passage speaks the dramatist. Human passion affected him more than the grandest phenomena of inanimate nature.

No poet has approached Shakespeare in imagining and expressing the tempest raised in the soul by supernatural apparitions. This is another aspect of his power over the expression of wild, swift-thrilling excitement. Macbeth's agitation after his first interview with the witches, his quivering horror and hoarse cries before the ghost of Banquo, the suppressed delirium of Hamlet's first address to the ghost of his father, exhibit the poet's power in its maturity, when art moves with the freedom of instinct, and imagination and expression go together with hand loosely in hand. Clarence's dream ("Richard III.," i. 4, 43) is an earlier effort, and more commonplace in conception; but the apparition of Edward, a swift interlacing of heaven and hell, has the inexpressible Shakespearian thrill.

The fierce passions of the fight, the fiery exhortations of excited leaders, ferocious teeth-grinding challenge and indignant defiance, infuriated pursuit and savage standing at bay, are prominent in several of Shakespeare's plays. We must not, however, suppose that his imagination worked to gratify a blood-sucking disposition, a savage thirst for wounds and falls, and agonised contortions, the delight of strong nerves in drums, trumpets, the clash of swords and shields, the discharge of small-arms and cannon, the hurried movements of charge and retreat. Mere warlike enthusiasm, the thirst for fighting and glory, is never more than a subordinate passion in his dramas. Its various moods—its hardy aspiration "to pluck bright honour from the pale-faced moon" ("1 Henry IV.," i. 3, 201); its eager revelling in the anticipated combat ("1 Henry IV.," iv. 1, 111); its delight in the most deafening sounds of war ("King John," ii. 1, 372); its contemptuous braving of the enemy ("King John," v. 2, 130)—are rendered with the greatest spirit in the speeches of the hot-headed, "wasp-stung and impatient," Hotspur, and the strong humorous soldier of fortune, Faulconbridge. When the warlike fit is on him, Hotspur is the very incarnation of the demon of war, the unmistakable son of Bellona: he speaks plain cannon-fire and breathes cannon-smoke: in his dreams he mutters words of encouragement to his horse, and his face is strained with phantom effort. But both Hotspur and the Bastard are exhibited to the audience rather as characters, or, as they were then called, "humours," than heroes. Hotspur's uncontrollable ardour is snubbed sarcastically by his uncle and his father, and his fire-eating propensities generally are ridiculed by the more versatile Prince Harry. And similarly, when the Bastard, a more robust warrior than Percy, gives his bragging message to the King of France, he is called a scold, and contemptuously interrupted by the rattle of drums. Achilles and Ajax, the champions of the Greeks, are mere fighting machines, senseless blocks, coarse and insolent as buffaloes. Coriolanus and Antony, who go to battle like the war-horse of the Bible, are moved by nobler passions than the savage instinct for bringing their strength to the trial of mortal combat. Shakespeare, while he recognised the nobility of the soldier's aspiration—

> "To win renown
> Even in the jaws of danger and of death "—

had a most civilised contempt for the causeless exercise of brute
force.

A spirit of deeper and more bitter fierceness is shown by men
that fight not for the mere love of fighting, but in defence of in-
sulted honour, or in support of incensed hatred.   The cross accusations and challenges of Bolingbroke and Mowbray in the First
Act of " Richard II." are an example.   The two enemies assail
each other with indignant words before the King, such terms passing between them as "traitor and miscreant," "pale trembling
coward," "a slanderous coward and a villain."   Gages are thrown
and taken up, when the King and Gaunt interfere to keep the
peace.   "Cousin," says the King to Bolingbroke, "throw up your
gage ; do you begin."   Bolingbroke refuses—

> " O God defend my soul from such deep sin !
>   Shall I seem crest-fallen in my father's sight ?
>   Or with pale beggar fear impeach my height
>   Before this out-dared bastard ?   Ere my tongue
>   Shall wound my honour with such feeble wrong,
>   Or sound so base a parle, my teeth shall tear
>   The slavish motive of recanting fear
>   And spit it bleeding in his high disgrace
>   Where shame doth harbour, ev'n in Mowbray's face.'

This indomitable ferocity is from the politic and normally
self-restrained Bolingbroke : no wonder that M. Taine found it
difficult to see the soft moods of such a character.   In the lists,
however, when their hatred is settling into their arms and their
tongues are correspondingly relieved, their mutual defiance is
perceptibly milder : they take their stations no less gaily than two
duellists from the Court of Louis XIV.   The ferocity of speech is
left for the impatient onlooker, old Gaunt : the combatants go to
mortal battle—

> " As gentle and as jocund as to gest."
> —*Richard II.*, i. 3, 60-90.

Warlike fury becomes most impressive, and demands the utmost
strain of imagination to give it deep and full body, when it
rises out of the decay of hope, when the soldier's arm is his last
refuge against the falling off of friends and the thickening troops
of enemies.   It is when the warrior is baited like Macbeth, or
hunted like Richard, or caught in the toils like Antony, that the
war passion concentrates for a burst of supreme energy, quickening
the most peaceful pulses and thrilling the least combustible nerves
with sympathetic fire.   In the case of Richard, indeed, there is
less propriety in the word concentration ;—

> " Let's to 't pell-mell,
> If not to heaven, then hand in hand to hell "—

is a resolution that mounts very little above his uniform level of dare-devilry.  We are conscious of hardly any rise of temperature in Richard till we reach the peremptory savage fury of his last moments, and he can hardly be said to concentrate, to bend up, his energies for this culmination of rage — it is only that the exasperation of circumstances has blown his normal fiendishness to a white heat.  His energies are maintained throughout at a fiendish pitch : he was created when the young dramatist had not ventured on deep fluctuations.  With Macbeth the supreme moment comes when the promise is explained away that had before steeled him with a trust in invulnerable destiny.  For a moment the stripping off of that supernatural protection cows his better part of man, but it is only a momentary crouch : there is a depth beneath undrawn : and what condensed firmness and ferocity there is in his bearing when he towers up and fronts Macduff with his last defiance—

> " I will not yield,
> To kiss the ground before young Malcolm's feet,
> And to be baited with the rabble's curse,
> Though Birnam wood be come to Dunsinane,
> And thou opposed, being of no woman born,
> Yet I will try the last.  Before my body
> I throw my warlike shield," &c.

In the "old ruffian," the magnanimous "sworder," Antony, when hemmed in like a lion by overpowering numbers, the spirit mounts above the dark fierceness of despair.  He goes to battle with savage laughter : his bloodthirsty ferocity is strangely tempered with sweetness, if not with light.  Bewitched by his passion for Cleopatra, he has let slip opportunity after opportunity till the final struggle can be delayed no longer : he rouses himself perforce and puts forth his strength to show the world that—

> " 'Tis better playing with a lion's whelp,
> Than with an old one dying."

His talk with Cleopatra at the banquet on the evening before his last effort, is a fine illustration of Shakespeare's bold and sure treatment of the stormiest passions.  The dramatist takes on the situation as it were instinctively : the words seem to come by spontaneous impulse.  Antony's last " gaudy night " is no carousal to drown care : no effort to forget the coming morrow.  War is not excluded from the banquet : on the contrary, he is the guest of the evening : he sits on Antony's right, while Love is on the left.

Akin to martial rage is fiery invective, the warfare of the tongue, the last resource of women and misanthropes, of oppressed Margarets and soured Timons. Amidst the circle of tearful afflicted women bereaved by the multiplied villanies of Richard III., Margaret stands out with irrepressible fierceness flashing through and burning up her tears, husbandless, childless, friendless, utterly impotent, but indomitable. In her young and beautiful days, when Suffolk brought her from France as "nature's miracle," to be the wife of King Henry, she gave ample proof that she was a woman of spirit. She came among Henry's mutinous nobles and haughty ladies with an imperial resolution to be no nominal queen. She bitterly resented the king's unmanliness. She boxed the ears of the proud wife of Gloucester. When Henry weakly made over the succession to the Duke of York, she took the field in behalf of her defrauded son; defeated York and took him prisoner; dipped a handkerchief in the blood of the boy Rutland, and offered it to the captive father to wipe his eyes with. She stabbed York with her own hand. Such was the beautiful "she-wolf of France," the "tiger's heart wrapped in a woman's hide," in the prime of her youth. In "Richard III.," she reappears withered and wrinkled, bereft of husband, son, and every vestige of power; but neither age nor misfortune can quench her fiery energy. She is turned all to envenomed bitterness, hungry for revenge, "well skilled in curses," never opening her mouth save to give passage to "the breath of bitter words." No hope but the hope of revenge survives to detain her longer in England. Herself impotent, she hangs about the Court to ease her heart with curses, and pray that her eyes may see revenge; she lies in wait for opportunities of chilling the prosperous with prophecies of pain and ruin, and adding with her bitter tongue to the miseries of the wretched. When poor Elizabeth, the wife of dying Edward, exclaims—"Small joy have I in being England's queen," Margaret enters behind with the bitter addition—

> "And lessened be that small, God, I beseech thee !
> Thy honour, state, and seat is due to me."

Richard alone is a match for her. He treats her curses with humorous indifference. She assails him with a torrent of incomparably savage epithets—"elvish-marked, abortive, rooting hog," "slander of thy mother's heavy womb," &c.,—and he takes even her breath away for a moment by coolly completing the curse with her own name. But her hard bitter spirit encounters no such check, and moves on with triumphant volubility in the incomparable scene ("Richard III." iv. 4), where she intrudes upon the prostrate mourners Elizabeth and the Duchess of York. This was one of Shakespeare's earlier efforts; but he never again equalled the concentrated bitter fierceness of this she-wolf's hunger for

revenge, fiendish laughter over its partial accomplishment, and
savage prayer for its completion.   Words could not hiss and sting
with more envenomed intensity than in the speech that she concludes with the prayer for Richard's death—

> " Cancel his bond of life, dear God, I pray,
> That I may live to say, The dog is dead."

The general misanthropy of Timon is a more massive feeling
than Margaret's sharp and piercing special hatred and keen hunger
for revenge, the rage of a tigress robbed of her whelps.   There
is the difference between them that there is between piercing personal invective and large denunciations of universal depravity.
There is a grandeur in Timon's misanthropy, as there was in the
imperial munificence of his better days : his feelings at no time
are in the common roll : there is a largeness of heart about him,
an impassioned superiority to ordinary prudence and ordinary
sobriety of judgment.   His affections move not in petty rivulets
within severely restraining bounds of intellect : their motion is
oceanic.   When he was rich he gave about him without a thought
of consequences, and without the faintest suspicion of human
honesty and gratitude ; and when the scales are plucked rudely
from his eyes, and friend after friend in quick succession proves
ungrateful, his impetuous tide of disgust is too powerful to receive
the slightest check from the arguments of temperate judgment.
From first to last he is a creature of unreasoning impulse and
passion.

The surest evidence that a dramatist has taken hold of the
complete body of a strong passion is seen in his representation of
its transfiguring power.   The power of strong feeling to transfigure and distort, to make foul things seem fair to the impassioned vision and fair things foul, is a very familiar fact, understood to a certain depth by the most ordinary novelist.   Almost
anybody could have conceived the perversion of the brave o'erhang-
ing firmament by the force of melancholy into a foul and pestilent
congregation of vapours.   But there are much more startling and
sweeping transfigurations wrought by the fire of passion among
Shakespeare's characters.   One of the most striking is the revelation of his mother's guilt by Hamlet in the closet scene (" Hamlet,"
iii. 4, 40).   In the rising frenzy of his moral indignation, all
nature seems to join with the avenger in flaming horror and
hideous disgust at the monstrosity of the crime :—

> " Heaven's face doth glow ;
> Yea, this solidity and compound mass,
> With tristful visage as against the doom
> Is thought-sick at the act."

But for a sudden marvellous leap of passion even this shudder-
ing frenzy is inferior in power to Isabella's fierce rejection of the
unworthy proposals of Angelo ("Measure for Measure," ii. 4, 100).

But if Shakespeare is supreme in angry invective, he is equally
supreme in the expression of the impassioned transports of love.
The whole soul agitated by love was no less at his command :
the tumults and steady raptures, the sudden bursts and overwhelming tides of absorbing passion, whether of hatred or of
love, found in him an understanding heart and a copious tongue.
His two great love tragedies, "Romeo and Juliet," and "Antony
and Cleopatra," certainly not inferior to the greatest of his works,
were a sufficient peace-offering to Venus for his disparagement
of her power in his sonnets and his "Two Gentlemen of Verona :"
they recanted his trifling with friendship as a master-passion, and
laid the strongest ties of kindred and ambition at the feet of the
all-powerful goddess.  Juliet may for a moment be angry with
Romeo for the death of her kinsman Tybalt, but her whole soul is
up in arms when she hears the words, "Shame come to Romeo!"—

> " Blistered be thy tongue
> For such a wish !  He was not born to shame :
> Upon his brow shame is ashamed to sit ;
> For 'tis a throne where honour may be crowned
> Sole monarch of the universal earth ! "

There is a fine contrast throughout between the two pairs of lovers,
Romeo and Juliet and Antony and Cleopatra.  Juliet's fiery brevity
and flashing sublime splendour is no less in keeping with her
virgin youth, than is the magnificent torrent of hyperboles with
which the passionate Queen of Egypt deifies her paramour characteristic of her meretricious maturity and experience.  In vain
poor Dolabella makes polite efforts to be heard : there is no resisting the tide of Cleopatra's eloquence—

> "*Cleo.* I dreamed there was an Emperor Antony :
> O, such another sleep, that I might see
> But such another man !
>    *Dol.*                    If it might please ye——
>    *Cleo.* His face was as the heavens : and therein stuck
> A sun and moon, which kept their course and lighted
> The little O, the earth.
>    *Dol.*                    Most sovereign creature——
>    *Cleo.* His legs bestrid the ocean : his rear'd arm
> Crested the world : his voice was propertied,
> As all the tuned spheres : and that to friends ;
> But when he meant to quail and shake the orb,
> He was as rattling thunder.  For his bounty
> There was no winter in't ; an autumn 'twas
> That grew the more by reaping : his delights

> Were dolphin-like; they show'd his back above
> The element they lived in : in his livery
> Walk'd crowns and crownets ; realms and islands were
> As plates dropp'd from his pocket."

Shakespeare was just such a servant as Venus loves; not too tamely obedient and reverential, often breaking loose in fits of capricious mockery and flat contradiction, yet every now and again giving unequivocal tokens of respect. So perfect was his mastery over the language of genuine passion, that he was never afraid to bring it into contrast with mock hyperbole or unsentimental worldliness. His sympathies with Biron, Benedick, Mercutio, and Diomede, did not prevent him from giving earnest expression to the soaring raptures of the youthful lovers, Romeo and Troilus. Even the mocking Biron himself is touched with the sacred flame, and renders homage to the power of his divinity in verses of dazzling magnificence ("Love's Labour Lost," iv. 3, 231). But though Biron raises his divinity to a dazzling height, and draws a fine scenic picture of her majesty, his transports are formal compared with the agonised soul's hunger of Troilus, stalking about Cressid's door—

> "Like a strange soul upon the Stygian banks
> Staying for waftage."

And all other lovers' raptures must yield to the world-absorbing passion of Romeo in the Sixth Scene of the Second Act, where the violent delights of the lovers are approaching their culmination—

> " *Friar.* So smile the heavens upon this holy act,
> That after hours with sorrow chide us not !
> *Rom.* Amen, amen ! but come what sorrow can,
> It cannot countervail the exchange of joy
> That one short minute gives me in her sight :
> Do thou but close our hands with holy words,
> Then love-devouring death do what he dare ;
> It is enough I may but call her mine."

The dazzling and confounding power of the sudden apparition of beauty is described with inspired zeal in the unexpected outburst of the merry lord, Biron. But Biron's description of the majesty of his mistress is surpassed in idolatrous elevation and enraptured homage by Cassio's welcome to Desdemona ("Othello," ii. 1, 83).

> "O, behold,
> The riches of the ship is come on shore !
> Ye men of Cyprus, let her have your knees.
> Hail to thee, lady ! and the grace of heaven,
> Before, behind thee, and on every hand,
> Enwheel thee round !"

T

Such a reception is worthy of the lady "that paragons description, and wild fame." When, however, the poet has to describe the power of more than mortal charms, he surpasses his wildest tributes to mortal beauty. Oberon's account of the effects of the mermaid's song ("Midsummer Night's Dream," ii. 1, 148) dwindles all other hyperboles into meanness—

> " My gentle Puck, come hither. Thou rememberest
> Since once I sat upon a promontory,
> And heard a mermaid on a dolphin's back
> Uttering such dulcet and harmonious breath,
> That the rude sea grew civil at her song,
> And certain stars shot madly from their spheres
> To hear the sea-maid's music."

In all these passages the energy is swift and darting, with here and there a momentary poise or slowing of speed, as it dwells on some revelation of spiritual or scenic grandeur. There is no end to the variety of movement, no bounds to its range : it ascends to the most passionate heaven of love, and enters with equal zest the gloomiest hell of hatred and desperate fury, of bitter curses and set teeth. But wherever the energy goes, it goes swiftly. It does not wait calmly to gather body and proceed with quietly overbearing stateliness : when checked, it rages impatiently, and pierces irresistibly through all impediments.

This is the general character of the strength of Shakespeare's genius. We must not, however, allow this dazzling movement of lightnings in the atmosphere of his tragedies to blind us to the vast firmament that overhangs the whole, and displays itself in quiet grandeur when the hurly-burly of conflicting passions has stormed itself to rest. The poet recognises an overruling Destiny above all the tumult. It is not a cold remote power of marble majesty : it is represented (Sonnet 115) as being in intimate connection with human affairs—

> " Reckoning Time, whose million'd accidents
> Creep in 'twixt vows and change decrees of kings,
> Tan sacred beauty, blunt the sharp'st intents,
> Divert strong minds to the course of altering things."

Nothing is more remarkable in Shakespeare's plays, and nothing contributes more to make them a faithful image of life, than the prominence given to the influence of chance, of undesigned accidents. The most tragic events turn on the most trifling circumstances. The fate of Richard II. is traced to a momentary impulse. When Bolingbroke and Mowbray are mounted for the encounter, and waiting for the signal to charge, the king on a sudden thought throws down his warder, stops the fight, and sends the combatants into exile. That impulse cost him kingdom and life ("2 Henry IV.," iv. 1, 125)—

> "O when the king did throw his warder down,
> His own life hung upon the staff he threw."

Poor Desdemona's fate hangs on the accidental dropping of a handkerchief. The unhappy deaths of Romeo and Juliet are the result of the miscarriage of a letter. "The most noble blood of all this world" might not have been spilt untimely had Cæsar not postponed reading the schedule of Artemidorus. Wolsey fell from the full meridian of his glory through a single slight inadvertence : one fatal slip which not all his deep sagacity could redeem. But the predominance of chance over human designs is most powerfully brought home in the tragedy of "Hamlet," whose fate turns on accident after accident. The passage just quoted from the sonnets reads as a commentary on the fortunes of Hamlet, and should be printed in the beginning of all copies of the play, to induce the lofty vein of reflection designed by the poet as the main effect of the whole, and to undo the wretched criticism that would degrade it to the level of a sermon against procrastination. The poet leaves us in no doubt as to his intention, although one might easily have apprehended it from his treatment of slight turning-points and weak beginnings of things in other plays. In the Second Scene of the last Act, Hamlet tells Horatio how accidentally and how rashly he discovered the treachery of Rosencranz and Guildenstern. He lay sleepless in his cabin, when an impulse took him to rise and rob them of their packet—

> "Sir, in my heart there was a kind of fighting,
> That would not let me sleep ; methought I lay
> Worse than the mutines in the bilboes. Rashly,
> And praised be rashness for it, let us know,
> *Our indiscretion sometimes serves us well*
> *When our deep plots do pall;* and that should teach us
> There's a divinity that shapes our ends,
> Rough-hew them how we will."

That is Shakespeare's poetical religion : a power variously denominated Destiny, Fate, Chance, Providence — supreme over mortal affairs. The varied energies of the world, which no man has ever embodied with such force and subtlety of conception and expression, are governed and shut in by great sublimities of time and space. Read his sonnets and mark how frequently his meditations fall into this vein—

> "When I consider everything that grows
> Holds in perfection but a little moment,
> That this huge stage presenteth nought but shows
> Whereon the stars in secret influence comment."

It is the stars that guide our moving, that govern our conditions.
But nothing can preserve us against "confounding age's cruel
knife"—

> "Like as the waves make toward the pebbled shore,
> So do our minutes hasten to their end."

Sometimes his spirit revolts against the tyranny of Time and Fate.
He imparts fresh vigour to the commonplace boast that the record
of his love shall outlive ruin and decay.   At other moments, the
relentless march of time is evidently disquieting to him, and he
seems ready to cry with his own Henry IV. (iii. 1, 45)—

> "O God ! that one might read the Book of Fate
> And see the revolution of the times
> Make mountains level, and *the continent*
> *Weary of solid firmness*, melt itself
> Into the sea ! and, other times, to see
> The beachy girdle of the ocean
> Too wide for Neptune's hips ; *how chances mock,*
> *And changes fill the cup of alteration*
> *With divers liquors !*   Oh, if this were seen,
> The happiest youth, viewing his progress through,
> What perils past, what crosses to ensue,
> Would shut the book, and sit him down and die."

The thought of Destiny expands the sadness of tragic conclusions to more voluminous dimensions and invests them with a softer complexion : conducting the living river of tears to the ocean,
carrying the visible smoke of sighs into the vague all-embracing
air.   But apart from this thought, the tendency of all tragic
agitation is to subside into the calm of sadness.   The fiercest
storms of passion wear a sad look when viewed from the repose of
the conclusion.   Even the arrogance of Coriolanus and the heady
impetuosity of Hotspur make us shake the head when we see the
curtain fall on their dead bodies, and go back in imagination to
the powerful manner of their life.   Think of the warm rhapsodies
of Romeo and Juliet, intoxicated by "the strong new wine of
love," when you see them lying before the tomb of the Capulets,
and you cannot keep your heart from filling.
    The pathos of sad conclusions is the proper pathos of tragedy.
Not till all is over are we suffered to lapse into the attitude of
sadness.   If an agent of prime importance gives way under the
blows of outrageous fortune, is utterly bereft of hope, whether in
his own powers or in external aid, as happens in "Henry VIII."
to Wolsey,—we are not permitted to linger over his downfall—we
must on with the march of events till the play is played out.   The
dramatist must not induce us to yield to the fascination of passing
calamities : we may follow him with tears in our eyes as we

glance backward on fallen idols, but to persevere in a worship of sorrow before the play is ended, would be a course of undramatic stubbornness.

If we detach individual lives from the rich interdependent complexity of a play, the pathetic moment, the moment seized upon by the mind under the fascination of pity, is analogous to the close of the Fifth Act—is the end of some great hope, or of all hope, the moment of special or general despair. So long as the spirit is militant against calamity, it appeals to the sympathies of the energetic; not until it succumbs does it claim the sympathy of the sad. Dido with the willow in her hand, the pale forsaken maid "shrieking undistinguished woe"—

> "Tearing of papers, breaking rings atwain,
> Storming her world with sorrow's wind and rain "—

are pathetic objects, on which we dwell with sorrow undisturbed by forward-looking excitement: their drama is ended, they are beyond the reach of aid; there is no prospect of deliverance to hold us in suspense. Ariadne passioning for the perjury and cruel flight of Theseus is an object of pathetic meditation only when we look beyond her bitter hours of desertion to her final deliverance: if we vividly realise the moment when she first discovers her lover's perjury, and cries desperately for help, we are too much disturbed by anger and anxiety to wrap ourselves up in heavy folds of sadness.

Individual lives may be dwelt upon with least abnegation of rich general effects, in the historical plays, which are more loosely woven together; and the case of Constance in "King John" is one of the finest of our dramatist's studies of heart-broken women. When the message is brought to her that the King of France has abandoned her quarrel and compounded peace with England, she is fitful and capricious in her sorrow, but her spirit does not fail: her sorrows are proud: and when the kings enter, she rises up and assails them with acrimonious accusations of oppression and perjury. Margaret herself is not more skilled in curses, more instinct with the breath of bitter words. When, however, Arthur is taken prisoner, her defiance breaks down; and she walks about invoking Death, with dishevelled hair—

> " Look, who comes here! a grave unto a soul;
> Holding the eternal spirit against her will
> In the vile prison of afflicted breath."

"Patience, good lady!" says Philip, tenderly; "comfort, gentle Constance!" But there is no comfort for her.

> " No, I defy all counsel, all redress,
> But that which ends all counsel, true redress,

> Death, death ; O amiable, lovely Death !
> Thou odoriferous stench ! sound rottenness !
> Arise forth from the couch of lasting night
> Thou hate and terror to posterity,
> And I will kiss thy detestable bones
> And put my eyeballs in thy vaulty brows,
> And stop this gap of breath with fulsome dust,
> And be a carrion monster like thyself :
> Come grin on me, and I will think thou smilest,
> And bless thee as thy wife.   Misery's love,
> O, come to me !"

Grief has full possession of her; all thoughts of redress and revenge have died out; bitterness is transfigured into ecstatic sweetness.   Deeply touched by her passion, Philip pleads—

> " O fair affliction, peace !"

But this only gives a new motive to her outcries, supplies new fuel to the chemistry that converts every thought, word, and sight into images of despair.

> " No, no, I will not, having breath to cry ;
> O that my tongue were in the thunder's mouth !
> Then with a passion would I shake the world ;
> And rouse from sleep that fell anatomy
> Which cannot hear a lady's feeble voice,
> Which scorns a modern invocation."

Philip tells her that this is madness ; whereupon she wishes that she were mad if thereby she might "madly think a babe of clouts were he."   Then he also gives way to piteous fancies, unable longer to comfort her with formal words of compassion and consolation :—

> " Bind up those tresses.   O, what love I note
> In the fair multitude of those her hairs !
> Where but by chance a silver drop hath fallen,
> Even to that drop ten thousand wiry friends
> Do glue themselves in sociable grief,
> Like true, inseparable, faithful loves
> Sticking together in calamity."

She hears him as if she heard him not, and says mechanically and incoherently—"To England, if you will."   He repeats, "Bind up your hairs," recalling her to his meaning.   She rouses herself, and instantly turns this also into a mournful symbol :—

> " Yes, that I will ; and wherefore will I do it ?
> I tore them from their bonds and cried aloud
> ' O that these hands could so redeem my son
> As they have given these hairs their liberty !'
> But now I envy at their liberty,
> And will again commit them to their bonds
> Because my poor child is a prisoner."

To my mind Shakespeare's mastery over keys of sadness is the most memorable side of his mighty genius. His intimate knowledge of the sorrows of women is hardly more remarkable than the varieties of pathos in his representations of unfortunate kings and ministers. Richard II., Henry VI., Gloucester, and Wolsey bear the crush of misfortune each in different spirit, characteristic of their several frames of mind. There is a certain mournful gaiety in Richard's demeanour in accordance with his magnanimous dignity and indifference to life: he says farewell to his queen with exquisite tenderness, yet with epithets that look like an ostentation of light-heartedness :—

> " Join not with grief, fair woman, do not so,
> To make my end too sudden : learn, good soul,
> To think our former state a happy dream ;
> From which awaked, the truth of what we are
> Shows us but this : I am sworn brother, sweet,
> To grim Necessity, and he and I
> Will keep a league till death. Hie thee to France,
> And cloister thee in some religious house :
> Our holy lives must win a new world's crown,
> Which our profane hours here have stricken down."

Of his queen he says :—

> " She came adorned hither like sweet May.
> Sent back like Hallowmas or short'st of day."

The weak Henry VI. pines for rest as rest : he would gladly lay aside the cares of state if only he could get in exchange the crown of a peaceful life :—

> " O God ! methinks it were a happy life,
> To be no better than a homely swain ;
> To sit upon a hill as I do now,
> To carve out dials quaintly, point by point,
> Thereby to see the minutes how they run,
> How many make the hour full complete ;
> How many hours bring about the day ;
> How many days will finish up the year ;
> How many years a mortal man may live."

Compare, again, Gloucester and Wolsey, in their decline and fall. The good Duke Humphrey is moved deeply by the degradation of his "sweet Nell"; but his own fall he takes with the matter-of-fact callousness of an unromantic man of the world, prepared for reverses as the natural course of things. (" 2 Henry VI.," ii. 4, 1)—:

> " Thus sometimes hath the brightest day a cloud ;
> And after summer evermore succeeds
> Barren winter, with his wrathful nipping cold :
> So cares and joys abound, as seasons fleet."

Poor Wolsey, aspiring and demonstrative, the man of grand and studied manners, whose every public act is impressive, cannot creep into his narrow bed so quietly: his last words touch our deepest feelings with the skill of a profound theatrical artist.   His end is thus described ("Henry VIII.," iv. 2, 18):—

> " At last, with easy roads, he came to Leicester,
>     Lodged in the abbey ; where the reverend abbot,
>     With all his convent, honorably received him ;  ·
>     To whom he gave these words—' *O, father abbot,*
>     *An old man, broken with the storms of state,*
>     *Is come to lay his weary bones among ye ;*
>     *Give him a little earth for charity !* '
>     So went to bed ; where eagerly his sickness
>     Pursued him still ; and, three nights after this,
>     About the hour of eight, which he himself
>     Foretold should be his last, full of repentance,
>     Continual meditations, tears and sorrows,
>     He gave his honours to the world again,
>     His blessed part to heaven, and slept in peace."

All these wrecks of fortune are touching, inexpressibly touching, but each in a way consistent with the character of the individual.

Our poet's sympathies with humanity were wide-reaching, but they did not exhaust the fine energy of his imagination.   The lower creation claimed a share of his interest ; importuned him, as it were, to devote some passing moments to the realisation of their joys and agonies.   The observations of the melancholy Jacques on the wounded deer have always been held among the most prized "gems of Shakespeare ;" and none of his descriptions are more touching and tender than the picture of the protracted anxieties of the hunted hare in "Venus and Adonis," (*l.* 678).

The close alliance in Shakespeare's mind between sadness and love is shown in the moonlight scene between Lorenzo and Jessica ("Merchant of Venice," v. 1).   The lovers walk in an avenue under bright moonlight in perfect stillness—

> " When the sweet wind did gently kiss the trees,
>     And they did make no noise,"—

and conjure up pictures in harmony with the scene.   One of the pictures that the moonlight pours in upon their happy hearts is the sorceress Medea gathering her enchanted herbs—a conception in the finest harmony with the soft mysterious light of the moon. But the other three are pictures of sighing, ill-starred, forlorn lovers, Troilus, Thisbe, and Dido.   The moonlight hours are peculiarly sacred to lovers, and their placid influence tends to tranquillity and sadness.   Happy successful love is akin to sad- ness ; it is unsatisfied sighing that raises tempests in the soul, and confident hope or reckless despair that inspires to heroic deeds. In the moment of assured success the lover may be seated on the highest pinnacle of triumph, in rapture at having won the world's dearest possession ; but triumph soon gives place to more tranquil joy, falls naturally into the common pathetic key of love and soft diffused sadness.

Shakespeare shows in many passages his deep feeling for the pathos and witchery of moonlight.   In the "Two Gentlemen of Verona" (iii. 2), Proteus thus advises Thurio—

> " Visit by night your lady's chamber-window
> With some sweet concert; to their instruments,
> Tune a deploring dump : the night's dead silence
> Will well become such sweet complaining grievance."

'Who is Silvia' sung in the still moonlight, is certainly fitted to ravish human sense.   One can never cease to be astonished at the commentary of Gervinus on this most exquisite of songs; he refuses to accept it as a specimen of the genuine Shakespearian love-lyric, and supposes it to be accommodated to the cloddy and stupid character of Thurio !   These exquisite strains should always be conceived in their original connection sounding through the still silvery-lighted air.   Shakespeare's delight in music under such circumstances appears to have been ecstatic.   His famous commendation of music is put into the mouth of Lorenzo in the scene already referred to : the musicians are introduced with the thrilling line—

> " Come, ho! and wake Diana with a hymn "—

and when the ears of the lovers are surfeited with sweet sounds, the music dies away at the softly breathed command—

> " Peace, ho! the moon sleeps with Endymion,
> And would not be awaked."

There are some exquisite moonlight scenes in "Midsummer Night's Dream."   Oberon's vision of the wonderful sea-maid is granted him by the light of the moon ; and all the fun and pathos of that delightful night is transacted under the same bewitching luminary.

It is a familiar law of our nature that we never admire things so profoundly as when we are in danger of losing them : love is always increased by the near prospect of separation.   In the garden scene between Romeo and Juliet, the danger of interruption and death to the daring youth gives a keener passion to the mutual confessions' and protestations of the lovers, and helps to make this scene the finest love-passage in the whole range of our drama.   One does not wonder that this play took London by storm, and that play-goers could not open their mouths without talking of Juliet and Romeo. Othello's endearments to Desdemona before committing the fatal act, which have an inexpressible power over our deepest feelings, are a more extreme case of the same principle. Perhaps the most touching lines in Shakespeare are those beginning—" When I have plucked the rose" (" Othello," v. 2, 13).

Of all Shakespeare's Comedies, perhaps "Twelfth Night" is the most richly woven with various hues of love, serious and mock-heroic. The amorous threads take warmer shifting colours from their neighbourhood to the unmitigated remorseless merry-making of the harum-scarum old wag Sir Toby and his sparkling captain in mischief, the "most excellent devil of wit," Maria. Beside their loud conviviality and pitiless fun the languishing sentiment of the cultivated love-lorn Duke stands out seven times refined, and goes with exquisite touch to the innermost sensibilities.

The two comedies most rich in scenic beauty, in dazzling play of fancy, are the "Tempest" and "Midsummer Night's Dream." The beauties of the ".Tempest" are comparatively stately : dainty Ariel is a gentle obedient spirit, affectionately and minutely attentive to his master's behests, and these behests have a certain colour of Prospero's own dignity and lofty tenderness. The masque of Iris, Ceres, and Juno, unfolded to the wondering eyes of the young couple as an indulgent display of the magician's art, is a majestic vision, a richly-coloured representation of stately beneficence. The character of the "Tempest" is seen in Caliban's summation of the wonders of the island. This is one of those prodigal efflorescences that dazzle even the mind accustomed to the luxuriance of Shakespeare : it is as if the poet had exerted himself to gather together all the celestial effects of that astonishing play and overwhelm the senses by a sudden revelation of accumulated beauties ("Tempest," iii. 2, 143) :—

> " Be not afeard ; the isle is full of noises,
> Sounds and sweet airs, that give delight and hurt not.
> Sometimes a thousand twangling instruments
> Will hum about mine ears, and sometimes voices
> That, if I then had waked after long sleep,
> Will make me sleep again : and then, in dreaming,
> The clouds methought would open and show riches
> Ready to drop upon me, that, when I waked,
> I cried to dream again."

The "Midsummer Night's Dream" has none of this stateliness : it is a wild revel of fancy, "a debauch of the senses and the imagination." Puck, the presiding spirit, has a very different master from Ariel, and very different notions of duty. He is, indeed, "the pert and nimble spirit of mirth;" a mistake of

Oberon's orders does not lic heavy on his conscience—the more mistakes the merrier—

> " And those things do best please me,
> That befal preposterously."

In this play, also, there is the happiest use of contrasts. The airy debauch of fancy is mixed up with a debauch of farcical invention. The graceful delicate little shapes of the fairies, with their swift motions, their pretty spites and shudders, their nomad life among Nature's choicest treasures of form and colour, are a fine contrast to the hard-handed, thick-headed, honest workmen. The beauty as well as the fun of the piece is heightened by the earnestness of everybody except Puck, the chuckling contriver of so much confusion. It was not without propriety that Shakespeare put into this play his famous account of the seething brains and shaping fantasies of " the lunatic, the lover, and the poet ;" at the close of the story of that wonderful night, he might well reflect upon the nature of the poet's imagination.

Two qualities that deeply affect Shakespeare's sense of the ludicrous are conspicuous in the " Midsummer Night's Dream "— the essential sympathetic kindliness of his nature, and the astonishing swiftness of his transitions from the serious to the ridiculous point of view. The fine taste of Sir Philip Sidney objected to making sport of the mispronunciations of foreigners, as being an offensive assumption of superiority, and Shakespeare seems to have felt compunctions about laughing at the honest efforts of poor fellows that had never laboured in their minds before. Accordingly, the gentle-hearted Hippolyta is made to protest against this source of amusement, saying—

> " I love not to see wretchedness o'ercharged
> And duty in his service perishing."

And Theseus is saved from the vulgar littleness of seeking amusement in the blunders of men anxious to do him service, by being made to express a greater pleasure in the modesty of fearful duty than in the rattling tongue of saucy and audacious eloquence. Our conscience is thus set at rest, and we are enabled to laugh at the absurdities of Pyramus, Thisbe, Wall, Moonshine, and Lion with genial good-nature, and without any odious contempt for the honest amateurs.

The lightning swiftness of Shakespeare's intellect is in nothing more conspicuous than in the rapidity of his transitions from the serious to the ludicrous, such as we have in the love-making of Titania to Bottom, and the translated weaver's grovelling asinine replies. The essence of the ludicrous is the sudden degradation

of things or the turning of them upside down, and in the rapidity
and completeness of this operation Shakespeare is incomparable—
even "the merry Greek, tart Aristophanes" must yield the palm.
Shakespeare has such variety that he never exhausts you with one
thing : when you have laughed your fill he changes the scene, and
does not bring you back to ludicrous conceptions till your lungs
have been refreshed by an interval of rest.  And when he is in
the ludicrous vein, he throws his heart into it : the mischievous
spirit of comical degradation coming upon him after a fit of
serious creation finds him ready and willing for the wildest
pranks.  With what profane glee he upsets all the grave emotions
proper to the piteous tale of Pyramus and Thisbe, which Chaucer
handles with such tender sympathy among his " Legends of Good
Women." [1]   Shakespeare also could take a pathetic conception of
Thisbe fearfully o'ertripping the dew ; but when the tale came in
his way as a subject for comic treatment, he carried out the work
of ludicrous subversion with pitiless completeness.  He thoroughly
enjoyed putting off the buskin and playing riotous capers in the
sock.  He might well have applied to himself part of Falstaff's
self-complacent reflection, and said—"The brain of this foolish
compounded clay, man, is not able to invent anything that tends
to laughter more than I invent."  The marvel is that his own
serious conceptions were safe in his hands ; that one with so quick
an eye for the ludicrous and so thorough an execution could allow
his imagination to persist in a serious vein at all.  This is, indeed,
another aspect of the fundamental wonder in Shakespeare—self-
command : command over forces that have proved absolute and
ungovernable in every other case where they have existed in equal
degree.

One of the best examples of Shakespeare's extraordinary swiftness in changing his point of view is found in the Second Scene
of the Fifth Act of "Troilus and Cressida," where Troilus and
Ulysses are eavesdropping and commenting on the behaviour of
Cressida with Diomede, while Thersites stands behind and remarks
on the whole situation.  The comment of the impish mocker upon
the passionate apostrophe of the indignant betrayed lover is incomparably fine : it takes us by surprise, and the more we dwell upon
it, the more exquisite its edge seems to be :—

> " *Tro.* Ay, Greek ; and that shall be divulged well
> In character as red as Mars his heart
> Inflamed with Venus : ne'er did young man fancy
> With so eternal and so fixed a soul.

---

[1] There is a full version of the story in the 'Gorgeous Gallery of Gallant
Inventions,' not nearly so delicate as Chaucer's, and this may have been Shakespeare's basis.

> Hark, Greek: as much as I do Cressid love,
> So much by weight hate I her Diomed:
> That sleeve is mine that he'll bear on his helm;
> Were it a casque composed by Vulcan's skill,
> My sword should bite it: not the dreadful spout
> Which shipmen do the hurricano call,
> Constringed in mass by the almighty sun,
> Shall dizzy with more clamour Neptune's car
> In his descent than shall my prompted sword
> Falling on Diomed.
>     *Ther.* He'll tickle it for his concupy."

Two of Shakespeare's comedies, the "Taming of the Shrew" and the "Comedy of Errors," belong mainly to the province of farce: they are longer, and contain more fully delineated characters than modern farces, but their chief incidents are of the extravagant sort generally understood as farcical. The "Taming of the Shrew," indeed, is now usually acted in a curtailed form, in which only the more extravagant incidents are retained: and in this form it has all the broad effect of a boisterous afterpiece. It should be remarked, however, that the most farcial incidents in both stories—the behaviour of Petruchio in church, and the wild revenge taken by Antipholus on the lean-faced anatomy of the conjuror Pinch—are narrated and not represented on the stage.

I have more than once spoken of Shakespeare's self-restraint as a most marvellous thing, considering the sort of self that he had to restrain. In all cases where he is alleged to have been hurried beyond his own control into bewildered excitement, the ground of the allegation lies in the critic's inability to rise to the heights of tragic emotion: the poet's imagination is sure and unfaltering at the most dizzy elevations, though the critic, hampered, probably robbed of his natural strength and palsied by artificial notions of what is becoming, cannot follow him with the same certainty of step. Most persons of the same race with Shakespeare should be able to feel his firm mastery over the most perturbing passions, if only they could give themselves up to the guidance of his imagination without constraint.

A standing count against Shakespeare, among those who looked upon him as a wild irregular genius, was the unbecoming intrusion of low comedy into tragic situations. His worst offences in this respect were considered to be the Clown in the last Scene of "Cleopatra," the Porter in Act ii. Scene 3 of "Macbeth," and the Fool in Act iii. Scene 2 of "Lear." An easy and satisfactory explanation of the Gravedigger in "Hamlet" might be found in the general distemperment of that play; but those others were coarse violations of propriety, to be dismissed simply as examples of the gross taste of the age that could tolerate them. Now, doubtless, those passages are too gross for modern ears: and yet, we cannot condemn them except when we come upon them without having entered into the stormy passions in the midst of which they occur. The Fool in "Lear" comes in when the poor, infirm, weak, and despised old man has been, scene after scene, gradually wrought up to almost inarticulate frenzy, and is wandering shelterless amidst unheard-of bursts of thunder, sheets of fire, and groans of roaring wind and rain; to fix one's thoughts continuously on the maddening situation of the poor old man would be insupportable—some relief is imperatively demanded. And a very touching relief it is to pass from the monstrous unkindness of the daughters and the growing madness of the old man to the devotedness of the hired boy Fool, following his master through such a tempest, and trying to divert him with his professional sallies, as if neither daughters nor elements were unkind. Nor is the matter of the Fool's wit so incongruous: laughter is a natural outlet for absorbing agitation—poor old Lear is too far gone to laugh, his brain is beginning to turn, but he smiles at the boy's efforts, and is soothed by them. The case of the Fool in "Lear" is thus exceedingly complicated: his presence affects us powerfully in many and shifting ways, which cannot be clearly stated. The other two cases are very much simpler: in them the art of the dramatist is less subtle and more unmistakable. Nobody capable of being absorbed and fascinated by the horrors of the scene in the court of Macbeth's castle can fail to acknowledge the gratefulness of the transition to the unconcern and coarse humour of the Porter. De Quincey wrote in delighted admiration of the perfection of dramatic skill that recalls us from the demoniac world of the murderers by the knocking at the gate. The many-sided significance of that startling knock, the rush of reflection that it sets free, makes it indeed an incomparable stroke of dramatic genius: but it does not necessarily recall us from the murder; for a moment it aggravates the strain of our suspense; we do not breathe freely till the sleepy, unconcerned, and deliberate porter appears with his utter relaxation of the preceding tragic intensity. The change is complete in several aspects, and we return with all the greater force to the evolution of the tragedy after this brief interval of free breath. The case of the Clown in "Antony and Cleopatra" is somewhat more subtle and difficult for cool reason to comprehend. His stupid lumpish answers about the worm are also of the nature of a relief to tragic intensity of strain in the audience; but they are more: like the sayings of the Fool in "Lear," they enter into the main current of the play— they are a relief to the high-strung excitement of the queen. Cleopatra is working herself up to the pitch of self-destruction, and the insensate dull stupidity of the Clown comes in oppor-

tunely to keep her from passing out of her resolution into deliri-
ous hysterics. Neither she nor Charmian could die with calm
bravery: they keep down their fears of death with forced laughter and forced attention to trifles: they trifle with death, and put
off the fatal moment as long as they can, and you feel that any
untoward turn might make them shriek with horror and fall down
in trembling impotence to despatch themselves.

To many minds Isabella's protestation to Angelo and Constance's
invocation of Death must appear extravagant and unnatural. To
understand them one must be able to recognise the transfiguring
force of intense passion ; one must understand the alchemical brain
that our dramatist ascribes to lunatics, lovers, and poets. Other
passions than love are a momentary madness, and change whatever the eye falls upon into accórdance with their imperious needs :
and whoever has not a living knowledge of this transfiguring
power, cannot but think it an extravagance to speak of wearing
the impression of keen whips as rubies, or to hail the hideous
skeleton of death as an object to be embraced and kissed as
a longed-for husband. There is strict dramatic truth in Macbeth's
fancy that the blood on his hands would incarnadine the multitudinous seas, making the green, one red. The same law of the
human mind is the justification of little Arthur's agonised plead-
ings for his life to Hubert in "King John" (iv. 1, 100), which
might otherwise appear to be cold, artificial, and incongruous
conceits. The poor child's frenzy of terror and eager clinging to
life transforms the murderer's implements into active advocates
for his safety—

> "*Arthur.* . . . . O spare mine eyes,
> Though to no use but still to look on you !
> Lo, by my troth, the instrument is cold
> And would not harm me.
>     *Hubert.*      I can heat it, boy.
>     *Arth.* No, in good sooth : the fire is dead with grief,
> Being create for comfort, to be used
> In undeserved extremes; see else yourself ;
> There is no malice in this burning coal ;
> The breath of heaven has blown his spirit out
> And strewed repentant ashes on his head.
>     *Hub.* But with my breath I can revive it, boy.
>     *Arth.* An if you do, you will but make it blush
> And glow with shame of your proceedings, Hubert :
> Nay, it perchance will sparkle in your eyes ;
> And like a dog that is compelled to fight,
> Snatch at his master that doth tarre him on.
> All things that you should use to do me wrong
> Deny their office : only you do lack
> That mercy which fierce fire and iron extends,
> Creatures of note for mercy-lacking uses.
>     *Hub.* Well, see to live ; I will not touch thine eye

> For all the treasure that thine uncle owes :
> Yet am I sworn and I did purpose, boy,
> With this same very iron to burn them out."

Finally, let us see what can be said for and against the extravagant ramps of some of Shakespeare's heroes.   There are passages in "Julius Cæsar" and "Coriolanus" almost as bombastic as anything to be found in Shakespeare's dramatic predecessors. Cæsar's bearing in the interview with the conspirators, when they beg the repeal of Publius Cimber's banishment, is not less lofty than Tamburlaine's inflation, though more calm and dignified—

> "Know Cæsar doth not wrong, nor without cause
> Will he be satisfied."

And the speech beginning—

> "I could be well moved, if I were as you"—

may not be an offence against the modesty of nature, but taken by itself, is an offence against the modesty of art.   The boasts and brags of Coriolanus out-Herod the Herod of the Mysteries.   For example (i. 1, 200)—

> "Would the nobility lay aside their ruth,
> And let me use my sword, I'd make a quarry
> With thousands of these quarter'd slaves, as high
> As I could pick my lance."

And (iv. 5, 112)—

> "Let me twine
> Mine arms about that body, where against
> My grained ash an hundred times hath broke
> And scarr'd the moon with splinters."

It is a noticeable circumstance that these inflated speeches—as well as one or two in "Antony and Cleopatra"—are put in the mouths of Roman heroes.   I am not quite sure that this is not one explanation and justification of them : they may have been Shakespeare's ideal of what appertained to the Roman character. But apart from their being true to the Roman manner, they may be justified also on the principle of variety.   It must have been a relief to Shakespeare's mind, ever hungry for fresh types of character, to expatiate in the well-marked high-astounding ideal ; and it is equally a relief to the student or spectator who may have followed his career and dwelt with appreciative insight on his varied representation of humanity.   This is the broadest justification : if we consider more curiously, other justifications make themselves palpable.   The inflation of Coriolanus and Cæsar is not like Tamburlaine's presented to us as a thing unquestioned and admired by those around them, as being, for aught said upon the stage to the contrary, the becoming language of heroic manhood. The violent language of Coriolanus is deprecated by his friends, and raises a furious antagonism in his enemies. Side by side with Cæsar's high conception of himself, we have the humorous expression of his greatness by blunt Casca and the sneering of cynical Cassius. In the case of Cæsar, too, there is a profound contrast between his lofty declaration of immovable constancy and the immediate dethronement of the god to lifeless clay. We must not take the rant of Cæsar, Coriolanus, or Antony by itself simply as rant, and wish with Ben Jonson that it had been blotted out. We must consider whether it does not become the Roman character: we must remember that a varied artist like Shakespeare may be allowed an occasional rant as a stretch to powers weary of the ordinary level; and above all, we must observe how it is regarded by other personages in the drama—in what light it is presented to the audience.

## IV.—His Delineation of Character.

One large deduction must always be made from our assertion of Shakespeare's truth to nature. All his personages, except intended Malaprops, are supposed to have the gift of perfect expression. The poet is the common interpreter. Gervinus, indeed, professes to find in some cases a correspondence between characters and their mode of expression; but we may rest assured that all such discoveries are reached by twisting accident into the semblance of design. We might as soon try to argue that it was natural for Shakespeare's personages to speak in blank verse. It is expected of a dramatist that he shall give as perfect expression as he can to the emotions and thoughts that occur: the conditions of his art impose no limits upon him in this direction except that his personages must not illustrate their meaning by allusions flagrantly beyond the possibilities of their knowledge. If the emotions of the *dramatis personæ* are in keeping with their characters and their situations, and are at the same time theatrically effective, the dramatist has fulfilled the weightier part of dramatic law.

Shakespeare's personages have all their author's vividness, energy, and delicacy of language, and all the abstractness of phrase and profusion of imagery characteristic of the Elizabethans. Shakespeare could never have been what he is had he been fettered by considerations of exact truth to nature or to history. We are not to believe that when he put into Macbeth's mouth the famous adjuration of the witches, he paused to consider whether a man in such a situation would naturally have so much to say: he took a firm grasp of the heroic exaltation proper to such a moment, and gave his imagination full swing to body it forth to the audience. Nor must we take exception to the abstruse, antithetical, and metaphysical statement of the conflict of motives in Macbeth's soliloquies, and say that such coherence and figurative force of expression would have been impossible in a rude thane so violently agitated; enough that such an internal conflict was natural to a man of Macbeth's character—the poet must be left free to express the fluctuating passion with all the force of his genius.

Nor did Shakespeare impede the free movement of his genius by vexatious attention to little details of costume and surroundings: he makes Romans toss caps in the air, and wave hats in scorn, makes Hector quote Aristotle, makes Mantuan outlaws swear by the bare scalp of Robin Hood's fat friar. Yet such was the vivid and searching force of his intellect, the quickness of his constructive energy, that in a brief effort of intense concentration, he was able to realise a scene in its essential circumstances and feelings with a propriety that the mere scholar would not have attained after years spent in the laborious accumulation of accurate particulars. He could hardly have seized the leading features with such freshness had he stood hesitating and consulting authorities about details: he went in boldly, and his clearness of insight kept him right in the main. Hazlitt quotes his picture of Caliban as a special example of his truth to nature. Now the realisation of Caliban is not faultless. It does not seem to have been observed that though Caliban tastes intoxicating liquor for the first time from the flask of Stephano, yet, at the end of the play, he expresses a civilised contempt for a drunkard. Still we should not be disposed for a slight inadvertence like this—which doubtless might be plausibly argued to be no inadvertence at all, but a stroke of profound wisdom—to moderate very much what Hazlitt says, that " the character of Caliban not only stands before us with a language and manners of its own, but the scenery and situation of the enchanted island he inhabits, the traditions of the place, its strange noises, its hidden recesses, his frequent haunts and ancient neighbourhood, are given with a miraculous truth of nature, and with all the familiarity of an old recollection." This is very far from being literally true; yet when we compare Shakespeare's characters with what other dramatists have accomplished, we must admit that some such superhuman exaggeration is needed to give the ordinary reader a just idea of his marvellous pre-eminence.

Shakespeare's historical plays afford the most unambiguous and indisputable evidence of his close study of character, and his inexhaustible fertility in giving it expression. He could not merely sum up a character in such general language as he puts into the mouth of the Duchess of York concerning her son Richard :—

> " Tetchy and wayward was thy infancy ;
> Thy school-days frightful, desperate, wild, and furious,
> Thy prime of manhood daring, bold, and venturous,
> Thy age confirmed, proud, subtle, bloody, treacherous."

But he had a living and manageable knowledge of the subjective moods and objective manifestations of the character thus summed up; he could imagine the feelings, actions, and artifices of such a man under a great variety of circumstances. Many people have knowledge of character enough to draw the general outlines of Richard, but who has shown sufficient knowledge of character to embody such a conception? This power is shown in all his plays, but is most conspicuous and easily recognised in his historical plays, because there he had more definite materials for his imagination to lay hold of and work into consistent characterisations. What chiefly makes his characters so life-like is their many-sidedness. The poet's just sense of clear broad dramatic effect is shown in making his leading characters approach to well-marked types; but the various characters are much more than narrow abstractions —each has traits that individualise him, and strongly colour his behaviour. Take his soldiers, his mighty men of war, the bastard Faulconbridge in " King John," Hotspur in " Henry IV.," Coriolanus, and Antony. All have a powerful theatrical effect as men of heroic strength and courage, but each is a distinct character: the Bastard is individualised by his robust hearty humour and unpretentious loyalty; Hotspur, by his wasp-stung impatience, absorbed manner, and irresistible ebullience of animal spirits; Coriolanus, by his patrician pride; Antony, by his oratorical skill, his fondness for the theatre, and his sensuality. The various qualities of each are consistent with their warlike reputation, and studiously consistent with one another. So his kings, John, Richard II., Henry IV., Henry V., Henry VI., Henry VIII., all have a certain kingly dignity, and yet they are distinct individuals: the weak kings, Richard, John, and Henry VI., are weak in different and characteristic ways—Richard from impulsive generosity, John from moral obliquity, Henry from constitutional imbecility. Look again at the extraordinary circle of sorrowing women round Richard III, how skilfully they are distinguished: the she-wolf Margaret, the motherly old Duchess, the weak and yielding Anne, the high-spirited and clever Elizabeth, bear their sorrows in widely different attitudes. Or we might make a small gallery of portraits of high ecclesiastics—the worldly smooth papal legate Pandulph in " King John," the fiery unscrupulous Beaufort in " Henry VI.," the ambitious noble-minded Wolsey, the meek but firm Cranmer—all exhibited with unmistakable individuality.

Of his historical plays, the First " Henry IV." is one of the finest in study of character. The classical histories also abound in fine discrimination. "Troilus and Cressida" is strongly coloured by the mediæval prejudice in favour of the Trojans, which has led the dramatist to present the fighting heroes of the Greeks as stupid blocks, mere draught-oxen yoked by superior intellect to plough up the wars; but the various conceptions are worked out with very skilful touches. "Julius Cæsar" also contains very clearly marked delineations,—Brutus, Cassius, Casca, Antony, Portia: the dramatist worked from translated authorities, but no one has ventured to dispute the essentials of his interpretations. None of the Roman plays, however, contain finer characterisation than the two parts of "Henry IV.," which between them exhibit the characters of the King himself, the Prince, Hotspur, Glendower, Lady Percy, Falstaff and his companions. The great magician, Glendower, is drawn with remarkable delicacy; his indulgence towards the whims of Hotspur is a very happy stroke, in fine keeping with the qualities found in union with his deep knowledge and lofty pretensions ("1 Henry IV.," iii. 1) :—

> " In faith he is a worthy gentleman,
> Exceedingly well read, and profited
> In strange concealments, valiant as a lion
> And wondrous affable, and as bountiful
> As mines of India."

There are a good many points of resemblance between Prince Henry and Hamlet, although they seem to stand contrasted as examples of princely gaiety and princely melancholy. Harry might pass for Ophelia's picture of Hamlet before his noble mind was overthrown: he has "the courtier's, soldier's, scholar's eye, tongue, sword." True, these qualities in Harry are smothered up from the world when first he is introduced to us; but when he has mounted the throne his friends reckon up his virtues and argue that he must have used wildness as a veil to contemplation. They say ("Henry V.," i. 1, 38) :—

> " Hear him but reason in divinity,
> And all-admiring with an inward wish
> You would desire the king were made a prelate ;
> Hear him debate of commonwealth affairs
> You'ld say it hath been all in all his study ;
> List his discourse of war, and you shall hear
> A fearful battle rendered you in music ;
> Turn him to any course of policy
> The Gordian knot of it he will unloose
> Familiar as his garter : that, when he speaks,
> The air, a chartered libertine, is still,
> And the mute wonder lurketh in men's ears
> To steal his sweet and honeyed sentences."

Further, as Harry is opposed to impatient and warlike Hotspur, and is anxious to try skill in arms with him, so Hamlet is opposed to Laertes. And the resemblance goes deeper. Harry is eminently a conscientious man : he assumes the crown with a deep sense of his responsibilities, and will not undertake the war with France and involve the two nations in bloodshed until he is fully assured by his counsellors of the perfect justice of his cause ("Henry V.," i. 2, 10–30). In like manner Hamlet abstains from the bloody business of revenge till he obtains unequivocal proofs of his uncle's guilt and utter badness of heart. Nor is Harry's companionship with Falstaff inconsistent with Hamlet's character. The prince goes with that wild set for the purpose of studying them and seeing life ("2 Henry IV.," iv. 4, 68), as Hamlet frequented the players. And he is not without gloomy fits : he is not always in the vein for doffing the world aside and bidding it pass. His father's description of him would apply exactly to Hamlet :—

> " For he is gracious, if he be observed ;
> He hath a tear for pity and a hand
> Open as day for melting charity :
> Yet notwithstanding, being incensed, he's flint,
> As humorous as winter and as sudden
> As flaws congealed in the spring of day,
> His temper, therefore, must be well observed :
> Chide him for faults, and do it reverently,
> When you perceive his blood inclined to mirth ;
> But being moody, give him line and scope."

Such a prince might very easily fall into melancholy, if an uncle married his mother within two months of his father's death and "popped in between the election and his hopes."

Hamlet, however, is younger than the companion of Falstaff. There is no ground whatsoever for the prevailing notion that Hamlet's age must be set down as thirty. It proceeds upon two quite unfounded assumptions : that the married life of the player King and Queen corresponds exactly in its duration of thirty years to the married life of Hamlet's father and mother, and that the Gravedigger is our only explicit authority. Several circumstances show that Hamlet's age is at the utmost seventeen or eighteen. He has just returned from the University of Wittenberg, and wishes to go back ; the boy that played the woman's part when he was there is not yet too old for the office ; his friend Horatio is still there, Laertes is just setting out on his travels. The usual age for youths at that stage of their education in Shakespeare's England was between sixteen and eighteen. And if our philosophical German friends should insist that Shakespeare had his own idea of the proper age for leaving the University, and that that age was thirty, what are we to

make of the passage where Polonius and Laertes warn Ophelia
against entertaining the youth's professions of love, alleging
among other things, that his love is but "a violet in the youth
of primy nature," and will change when he grows older ?   Laertes
actually speaks of him as not yet full grown (i. 3, 11)—

> " For nature, crescent, does not grow alone
>   In thews and bulk, but as this temple waxes,
>   The inward service of the mind and soul
>   Grows wide withal.   Perhaps he loves you now," &c.

The chief difficulty in the play of Hamlet is the prince's delay
in the execution of his revenge.   When his father's ghost makes
the first revelation of foul play, he cries—

> " Haste me to know't, that I with wings as swift
>   As meditation or the thoughts of love
>   May sweep to my revenge."

Yet when he is told that the murderer is his uncle, he is so amazed
and staggered that he does not at once proceed to execute vengeance, but adds delay to delay, and at last kills the murderer
upon an unpremeditated impulse.   Goethe's well-known theory
is that this delay proceeds from irresolution and weakuess.   The
key to Hamlet's character is found in the words—

> " The time is out of joint : O cursed spite
>   That ever I was born to set it right."

Hamlet is a soft, calm-tempered, cultivated prince : he has not
the strength of nerve to be a hero.   "Shakespeare meant in the
present case to represent the effects of a great action laid upon a
soul unfit for the performance of it."   Now to ascribe Hamlet's
delay to weakness of character, and not to the overwhelming
shock of the ghost's monstrous revelations, is to miss the just
effect of the tragedy.   This I take to be compassion for the struggles of a noble youth, confronted as he steps across the threshold
of life in all the generous ardour and sweetness of "primy nature"
by the discovery of an unnatural crime, perpetrated by those
whom he most loves and trusts; confounded, distempered, un-
hinged, jangled by this horrible discovery ; summoned to revenge,
but reluctant to believe facts so foul; distrustful, his faith in
humankind blasted, seeking bitterly for a revenge that shall be
adequate, and guided to it at last by the "Divinity that shapes
our ends when our deep plots do pall."

Goethe tried to form an idea of what Hamlet might have been
had his father's life been prolonged.   Now the value of this as
a critical method will appear if we apply it to the life of Prince
Henry.   But at any rate, we are bound to take into account what

happened when Hamlet's father's life was cut short; we cannot be allowed to substitute our own conception of what a young prince delicately reared ought to be, for the real Hamlet as revealed by the play. What evidence, then, is there for saying that Hamlet was weak, irresolute, cowardly? When he hears that his father's spirit is in arms he resolves to watch for it: he crosses its path and addresses it at the risk of being blasted: not setting his life at a pin's fee, he disregards the warnings of his companions, throws them off when they seek to restrain him, and puts himself in the power of the dread figure without knowing whether it comes from heaven or from hell. When the monstrous revelation is made, his heart and strength threaten to fail him: he cries:—

> " Hold, hold, my heart;
> And you, my sinews, grow not instant old,
> But bear me stiffly up."

And we are asked to believe that this was the effect of fear: the man who has just displayed superhuman daring and reckless indifference to life, and who afterwards leads the way in boarding a pirate, quakes at the prospect of putting his life in danger! Nothing but theory-blunderers could fail to see the real meaning of Hamlet's agitation: he is for a moment astounded and staggered at the monstrosity of the crime. But why does he not recover himself, rush off, and despatch his uncle at once, or at least rouse the people as Laertes afterwards did when his father was killed, and besiege the palace? Was not this consideration paralysing action? Most undoubtedly, consideration here interposed beween impulse and action; but we do not call that weakness, irresolution, or cowardice. We call it a proof of strength to refrain from rushing intemperately into action. Mark the contrast between Hamlet and Laertes: it is the same contrast that Shakespeare draws between Henry and Hotspur. Laertes impetuously raises the people, and threatens to punish—the wrong man: he is, like Hotspur, a " wasp-stung and impatient fool." And that is what we should have called Hamlet if he had run upon the instant at the bidding of the ghost, and thrust his sword into his uncle: and if he had gone to the people shouting what his father's ghost had revealed, they would very properly have thought him mad or cunningly ambitious. But Hamlet, like Henry, is a man of larger intelligence looking before and after: he is no more a coward than Henry was when he summoned his counsellors before rushing into war; but he desires to be assured of the justice of his cause. He at once resolves upon a plan: he will put an antic disposition on, and watch for confirmation. But is not his outcry against the cursed spite of fortune a proof that he was unwilling to undertake the task of revenge? It proves, at least, that he did not like the situation that the spite of fortune had thrust upon him. But was it weak, irresolute, or cowardly, to be agonished by the thought that his father had been killed and his mother strumpeted by his uncle, and under the anguish of this thought to express a passing wish that he had never been born into a world where such crimes were possible?

For some time Hamlet's cloak of madness helps him to discover nothing: he only finds spies set upon him to discover the secret of his derangement. With characteristic recklessness he does not carry the pretence far: he merely goes about in disordered dress, and in rapt study, and makes himself disagreeable to the astonished court by the causticity of his remarks: in fact, he uses the pretence of madness as a privilege. The King and Queen suspect the cause of his melancholy, and employ Rosencranz and Guildenstern to sound him; but at the same time they allow the obtrusive wiseacre, old Polonius, who knows all about everything and is never wrong, to use means for testing his confident theory of the Prince's madness. The employment of Ophelia as a decoy increases Hamlet's sense of the foulness of the world, and throws him with increased force on his friendship with Horatio; but he can discover nothing. At last chance throws the players in his way, and he at once concocts a scheme for turning them to account. In the meantime, however, the emotion shown by one of the actors in reciting a passionate speech makes him accuse himself of cowardice in thus delaying the execution of the Ghost's commands; and if Goethe had been present at his deliberations, he would have seconded the young Prince's morbid self-accusings. But reason prevails: he reflects justly that the Ghost may have been sent by the devil to tempt him to damnation, and resolves to have proof of his uncle's guilt more relative than the word of an ambiguous apparition.

But why does Hamlet still delay when he has received strong confirmation from the play? He gets an opportunity: he comes upon his uncle kneeling in prayer: why does he withhold? Not from fear: not from irresolution: but from cold iron determination sure of its victim and resolved not to strike till the most favourable moment. He is tempted to the weakness of yielding to impulse; but he holds back with inflexible strength. His words are instinct with the most iron energy of will (iii. 3, 73). In the interview with his mother, hearing somebody stir behind the arras, he either conceives that now he has caught the villain in an unsanctified moment, or he cannot resist the excitement of the unexpected opportunity: he makes a pass through the arras, and kills Polonius. When he is harrowing his mother's soul with reproaches, the Ghost reappears avowedly to whet his almost blunted purpose, but with the effect of diverting the rising frenzy of his invective : the departed spirit retains it tenderness for the weak woman, and is pained to see her thus tormented by exposure and remorse. And Hamlet still bides his time. Was this cowardice ? In his sharp self-questionings, he calls it so himself. On his way to England another incident occurs that makes him reflect on his own conduct, and he says :—

> " Now whether it be
> Bestial oblivion, or some craven scruple
> Of thinking too precisely on the event,
> A thought which quartered, hath but one part wisdom
> And ever three parts coward, *I do not know*
> *Why yet I live to say ' This thing's to do ;'*
> *Sith I have cause and will and strength and means*
> *To do 't.*"

His delay was inexplicable to Hamlet himself, though we are all so confident in explaining it for him. One might have pointed out to him, without seconding his own morbid and unjustifiable accusation of cowardice, that he had still no means of satisfying the people that he was a pious avenger and not merely a mad or an ambitious murderer, more particularly after he had incurred the accidental taint of the murder of Polonius, whom he was not to know that the King would inter in hugger-mugger. And the desire to be above suspicion, to have an unblemished reputation, was a strong motive with Hamlet, as we see from his dying injunction to Horatio to tell his story to the world and clear his wounded name from unjust aspersion. But I do not think that it was the dramatist's intention to represent this as the chief motive for Hamlet's delay, otherwise he would have brought it out more strongly. No; the above passage, taken in conjunction with Hamlet's communications to Horatio in the beginning of the last Scene, supplies the real clue to the dramatist's intention in the concluding Acts. Hamlet does not know why he delays : he is not afraid—there is not the slightest trace of such a motive in his behaviour from first to last—but he restrains himself in a blind inexplicable vague trust that some supremely favourable moment will occur. Meantime Destiny is ripening the harvest for him : a Divinity is shaping his ends : his indiscretions serve him when his deep plots do pall. The measure of his uncle's guilt, already full, is now heaped over ; crime begets crime ; Hamlet returns from England with documentary evidence of the villain's designs upon his own life. He has no time to lose : the news will soon be brought from England of the result of his stratagem : he resolves to make swift use of the interim. But the supreme moment comes after all without his contrivance, and is more comprehensive in its provisions for justice than any scheme that could have been devised

by single wisdom, and executed by single power.   Claudius is at
last caught by vengeance in an act that has no relish of salvation
in it, is surprised in an infamous plot, and sent to hell with a
heavier load of guilt upon his back : and others brought within
the widening vortex of the original crime, are involved in the final
ruin.   Horatio is left to sum up the story :—

"Of carnal, bloody, and unnatural acts,<br>
Of accidental judgments, casual slaughters,<br>
Of deaths put on by cunning and forced cause,<br>
And in this upshot purposes mistook<br>
Fallen on the inventors' heads."

Volumes might be written, and indeed have been written, on
Shakespeare's characters.   Their sayings and doings are not an
exact transcript of life ; but they produce the dramatic illusion of
life more perfectly than if they were actual copies.   The varied
concerns of life do not divert and distract his personages in exactly
the same way as in the course of an actual ruling passion ; and
yet the diversion of circumstances in real life is represented in his
plays and gives his personages the appearance of actual beings.
Although Hamlet vows to wipe everything from his memory save
'the Ghost's commandment, Nature is too strong for him : he is
interested in the news from Wittenberg, he cannot resist the old
desire to see his play acted in a becoming and workmanlike manner, and even when the crisis is at hand, he is sufficiently disen-
gaged to bandy words with the Gravedigger and with Osric.   Such
is life, a mixture of great concerns and small : a man possessed
with one great unintermitted object is a madman ; and plays that
represent the reciprocal action and reaction of such characters, are
not a representation of life.
   The greatest of Shakespeare's comic characters is Falstaff, and
he also, curiously enough, has suffered somewhat at the hands of a
friendly German commentator.   Gervinus alleges "sensual pleasure
and brutishness as the starting-point and aim of Falstaff's whole
being."   Now this is taking too serious and unsympathetic a view
of " that huge bombard of sack, that grey iniquity, that father
ruffian, that vanity in years ; " and if the ghost of Sir John could
address a word to this defamer, he would doubtless ask—" I would
your commentatorship would take me with you ; whom means
your commentatorship ? "   There is not a little in common between Falstaff and Autolycus.   Their moral (or rather immoral)
principles are the same, and they have the same witty resourceful-
ness.   Both have come down in the world from being pages to
being " squires of the night's body," "Diana's foresters, gentlemen of the shade, minions of the moon."   If the fat knight had
had " but a belly of any indifferency," he says, " he would simply

have been the most active fellow in Europe :" and in that case, had he only not lost his voice by halloing and singing of anthems, the resemblance between him and Autolycus would have been tolerably complete. The starting-point and aim of Sir John as a subject to invent laughter and an object for laughter to be invented on, is his fat unabashed self-satisfaction, and good-humoured volubility in the conscious absence of nearly all the virtues. He is an absolute negation of the cardinal virtues of temperance and piety, and of the hardly less important virtues of honesty, veracity, active courage, and chastity : but when any breach of these virtues is brought home to him, when he is caught telling incomprehensible lies or abusing his friends behind their back or "misusing the king's press most damnably," he is not ashamed, but is ever ready with some quick-witted excuse. Virtue contends with the fat rogue and is worsted : he is impervious to the arrows of remorse : no amount of plain tales can put him down, disturb the serenity of his chuckle, or abate his hunger and thirst for sugar and sack. It is this complete rout of Virtue by the old rascal that is so ludicrous. If his delinquencies were more serious than they are, if he were a man scattering firebrands, arrows, and death, our moral sentiments would be too much outraged to laugh over his victory. But he is comparatively harmless : he is too fat "with drinking of old sack and unbuttoning after supper, and sleeping on benches after noon," to be a dangerous character : and we cannot help extending a laughing sympathy to his presence of mind, readiness of wit, volubility of tongue, and good-humoured surrender of his person to be the occasion of wit in others. Gervinus, if I mistake not, accuses him of wanting courage. This depends upon what meaning is attached to courage. Sir John, as we know him, is not much of a fighting man ; he does not fight longer than he sees reason : but he is too self-complacent and self-confident to be called a coward. In the Gadshill encounter, he heads the attack on the travellers : afterwards he makes a few passes before he runs away, while his comrades take to their heels at once : and he leads his ragamuffin company where they are peppered, although he does despise honour and fall down pretending to be dead before the infuriated Douglas. But granting his physical courage to be but small, his moral courage is dauntless. When the sheriff comes to the door of the tavern with his formidable train, Sir John is not in the least disconcerted, but is eager to have the play played out, and he falls asleep behind the arras in a situation where a cowardly breaker of the laws would have been perspiring with fear. Even the excitement of battle does not unhinge his fat composure :—

" *Prince.* . . . . I prithee, lend me thy sword.
*Fal.* O Hal, I prithee, give me leave to breathe awhile. Turk Gregory

never did such deeds in arms as I have done this day.   I have paid Percy,
I have made him sure.
 *Prince.* He is, indeed ; and living to kill thee.  ·I prithee lend me thy
sword.
 *Fal.* Nay, before God, Hal, if Percy be alive, thou get'st not my sword ;
but take my pistol, if thou wilt.
 *Prince.* Give it me : what, is it in this case ?
 *Fal.* Ay, Hal ; 'tis hot, 'tis hot ; there's that will sack a city.
   [*The Prince draws it out, and finds it to be a bottle of sack.*]"

He pursues his intrigues with the " Merry Wives of Windsor "
with a boldness equally imperturbable : he is not deterred by one
mishap after another from again running into danger.   No : if we
overlook Sir John's courage, we miss the essence of his humour.
Sir John is no sneaking sinner : he meets all charges of iniquity
with a full unabashed eye glistening out of his fat countenance,
with voluble assertions of his own virtue and loud denunciations
of the degeneracy of the times.   After his flight from Gadshill he
does not hide his face for shame, but enters the " Boar's Head "
shouting for sack and exclaiming against cowardice :—

 " You rogue, here's lime in this sack too : there is nothing but roguery
to be found in villanous man : yet a coward is worse than a cup of sack
with lime in it.  A villanous coward !  Go thy ways, old Jack ; die when
thou wilt ; if manhood, good manhood, be not forgot upon the face of the
earth, then am I a shotten herring.   There live not three good men un-
hanged in England ; and one of them is fat and grows old : God help the
while a bad world, I say.   I would I were a weaver ; I could sing psalms
or anything.   A plague of all cowards, I say still."

In his exquisite interview with the Lord Chief-Justice, he abuses
these costermonger times, says he has lost his voice with halloing and singing of anthems, wishes to God his name were not so
terrible to the enemy, and crowns his impudence by asking the
loan of a thousand pounds.   There is a good deal more than " sensual pleasure and brutishness " in the character of Sir John : it is
not his sensual pleasure and brutishness that we laugh at, but the
ingenuity and brazen presence of mind with which he glosses over
his vices.   Humour involves a surprise of mood as wit involves a
surprise of words : and Falstaff's way of taking things is certainly
very different from what the ordinary way of the world leads us
to expect.   Sir John, too, is a wit as well as a besotted volup-
tuary and a willing butt for the wit of others.   His ridicule of
Bardolph's nose is incomparable.   Down in Gloucestershire we
see him watching Shallow and Slender with observant eye, and
contemptuously noting their peculiarities with a view to future
capital.   " I will devise matter enough out of this Shallow to
keep Prince Harry in continual laughter the wearing out of six
fashions, which is four terms, or two actions, and a' shall laugh
without intervallums."

## V.—THE INTER-ACTION OF HIS CHARACTERS.

A writer may have the power of expressing many varieties of passion, may have a profound sense of beauty, a quick sense of the ludicrous, and a perfect knowledge of character, and yet fail in the dramatist's most essential faculty—the power of representing one character in active influence upon another. The dramatist has to deal not with still life or with tranquil exposition: he must bring impassioned men and women face to face, and show how their words operate upon one another to comfort, to cajole, to convince, to soothe, and to inflame. The problem ever before the mind of the dramatist is, in mathematical language, to estimate the effect of a given expression on a given character in a given state of feeling. Then this effect reacts, and the reaction reacts, and other influences come in and join in the complicated process of action and reaction, so that the ability to hold your shifting data unconfused, to solve problem after problem with unerring judgment, and to keep all your results within the just limits of dramatic effect, is one of the rarest of human gifts. This is dramatic genius.

Shakespeare's swiftness of intellect, fine emotional discrimination, and unfailing self-command, were tasked to the utmost in the representation of this reciprocal action. In his three greatest triumphs in the exhibition of what Bacon calls "working" a man—the instigation of Othello's jealousy by Iago ("Othello," iii. 3), the puffing up of Ajax's pride by Ulysses ("Troilus and Cressida," ii. 3), and the wooing of Anne by Richard III. ("Richard III.," i. 2)—the influence can hardly be said to be reciprocal: the agent stands with immovable self-possession, only keeping himself on the alert to follow up with all his dexterity the effect produced by each stroke. A similar remark may be made concerning the half-wilful torture of Juliet by her Nurse ("Romeo and Juliet," iii. 2), or the gradual agitation of Posthumus by the lies of the villain Iachimo ("Cymbeline," ii. 4), or the annoyance and final discomfiture of the Chief-Justice by the imperturbable Falstaff ("2 Henry IV.," i. 2). So, too, in the swaying of the passions of the "mutable rank-scented" Roman mob in "Coriolanus" and "Julius Cæsar," there is not much reaction: the dramatist has set himself to represent the fluctuations of an excitable crowd under the power of adroit oratory, the orator himself in each case persevering steadily in his objects. But Shakespeare did not shrink from the infinitely more difficult task of making both parties to a dialogue exert a powerful influence on each other. Of this there are memorable examples in the opening acts of "Macbeth," and in several scenes of "Coriolanus" and "Julius Cæsar." The quarrel between Brutus and Cassius ("Julius

Cæsar," iv. 3), and the interview of Coriolanus with his mother, his wife, and his son ("Coriolanus," v. 3), are managed with consummate knowledge of the heart, and unerring grasp of imagination upon its slightest and most shifting fluctuations. One would not venture to say that Shakespeare's power of identifying himself with his characters, and wonderful swiftness in passing from one personality to another, increased after the time when he composed "Richard III.," and delineated the scenes between Margaret and the objects of her hatred : but certainly he increased in the masterly ease of his transitions. The greatest monument of his dramatic subtlety is the tragedy of "Antony and Cleopatra." With all its noble bursts of passion and occasional splendour of description, this play has not perhaps the massive breadth of feeling and overpowering interest of the four great tragedies, "Macbeth," "Hamlet," "Lear," and "Othello"; but it is greater even than "Macbeth" and "Othello" in the range of its mastery over the fluctuations of profound passion : it is the greatest of Shakespeare's plays in the dramatist's greatest faculty. The conflict of motives in "Hamlet" is an achievement of genius· that must always be regarded with wonder and reverence ; but, to my mind, "Antony and Cleopatra" is the dramatist's masterpiece. One may have less interest in the final end of the subtle changes wrought in the hero and heroine : but in the pursuit and certain grasp of those changes, Shakespeare's dramatic genius appears at its supreme height.

Schlegel quotes with approbation a saying of Lessing's regarding Shakespeare's exhibition of the gradual progress of passion from its first origin. "He gives," says Lessing, "a living picture of all the slight and secret artifices by which a feeling steals into our souls, of all the imperceptible advantages which it there gains, of all the stratagems by which it makes every other passion subservient to itself, till it becomes the sole tyrant of our desires and our aversions." This incautious hyperbole tends to confuse the boundaries between the drama and the novel or epic of manners. The remark is more applicable to the novels of George Eliot, or to the "Troilus and Cressida" of Chaucer, than to the plays of Shakespeare. The slight and stealthy growth of passion is wholly unsuited for the stage. In the drama, life is condensed and concentrated ; the pulses of life and the energies of growth are quickened. Passions spring up with more than tropical rapidity. The mutual love of Romeo and Juliet, the misanthropy of Timon, the ambition of Macbeth, Hamlet's thirst for revenge, Lear's fatal hatred of Cordelia, Othello's jealousy—are all passions of sudden growth. Iago's artifices are subtle but swift and instantaneously effectual : Othello's pang at his first stab (iii. 3, 35) is not less sharp than the heart's wound of young Romeo by the first shaft from Juliet's eyes.  The dramatist is very well aware that the first suggestion commonly works more slowly : he makes Iago say—

> "Dangerous conceits are, in their natures, poisons,
> Which at the first are scarce found to distaste,
> But with a little act upon the blood—
> Burn like the mines of sulphur."

But his poison must work swiftly; inflammatory insinuations must be accumulated and compressed so as to force the passion at once into a blaze : before an hour is over, Iago exclaims in agony—

> "Not poppy, nor mandragora,
> Nor all the drowsy syrups of the world,
> Shall ever medicine thee to that sweet sleep
> Which thou owedst yesterday."

Hamlet's action is tempered by subsequent reflections, but his desire for revenge attains its utmost vehemence at the first supernatural solicitation : he at once passionately vows to wipe from his memory every record but the ghost's commandment. Macbeth does not proceed instantly to murder Duncan ; but the confirmation of part of the promise of the witches immediately raises the terrible suggestion—

> "Whose horrid image doth unfix his hair
> And make his seated heart knock at his ribs,
> Against the use of nature."

The great stages of the growth of passion are indicated in Shakespeare's dramas with all the power of his genius, but the development proceeds with fiery vehemence.  Slight and stealthy development belongs to the domain of the novelist.


## VI.—The Tranquillising Close of his Tragedies.

I have already drawn attention (p. 290) to the presence of Destiny or Fortune as an impelling or thwarting influence in Shakespeare's dramas.  In all his tragedies the influence of this mighty World-power on the concerns of men is more or less suggested.  Romeo takes refuge in death from its persecutions : "O, here," he cries at the tomb of Juliet—

> "O, here
> Will I set up my everlasting rest,
> And shake the yoke of inauspicious stars
> From this world-wearied flesh."

Before the battle of Philippi, when even Cassius begins partly to credit things that do presage, Brutus, who in the end prefers leaping into the pit to tarrying till he is pushed, is resolute to hold out while any hope remains :—

> " Arming himself with patience
> To stay the providence of some high powers
> That govern us below."

Macbeth at first is disposed to commit himself to the control of Chance :—

> " If Chance will have me king, why Chance may crown me,
> Without my stir."

And his wife sees the hand of Fate in the half-fulfilled predictions of the witches and the entrance of Duncan under her battlements.  The bastard Edmund ridicules the excellent foppery of the world in making guilty of our disasters the sun, moon, and stars ; but later in the play old Kent can find no other satisfactory way of accounting for the cruelty of Goneril and Regan, and the kindness of Cordelia :—

> " It is the stars,
> The stars above us, govern our conditions."

Othello exclaims of the supposed treachery of Desdemona :—

> " 'Tis destiny unshunnable as death."

And when he calls to mind his prowess in happier days, cries :—

> " O vain boast !
> Who can control his fate ?"

The magnanimous Antony rises superior to the enmity of Fate : when his soldiers are lamenting round him, he says to them :—

> " Nay, good my fellows, do not please sharp Fate
> To grace it with your sorrows : bid that welcome
> Which comes to punish us, and we punish it
> Seeming to bear it lightly."

The thought of inevitable Destiny, iron Fate, is a great tranquilliser, and rolls over tragic catastrophes like the calm grandeur of stars after a storm.  When our minds are fatigued by the spectacle of horrors, or poignant griefs, or violent struggles of fatal issue, this thought unfolds itself to soothe the tumult.  We subdue the keen agitation of particular calamities by fixing our eyes on the calm majesty of the irresistible forces of the universe : we take some part of the disturbing culpability of individual agents off their shoulders, and lay it on the Stars, dread agents equally above our love and our hatred. Before the awful magnificence of their doings, our fierce detestation of individual malice is subdued, and the sorrows of the individual lose their sharpness merged in the sorrows of mankind.

The power that overhangs Shakespeare's tragedies appears also in the aspect of an inexorable and relentless Justice, blindly dealing out the punishment of death to all who are wilfully or accidentally brought within the sweep of her sword. Not the slightest culpability is left unavenged. None remain alive at the end who have been so intimately mixed up with the chief victims that their survival would chafe our sense of justice and vex our meditations on the impartial rigour of the Destinies. Not one false step within the tragic circle can be withdrawn. Conscious or unconscious, intentional or unintentional, all complicity is fearfully punished. We ask what poor Cordelia had done that she should perish untimely; and Justice points to her wayward refusal to humour the exacting irritability of her doting old father. Ophelia? She was thrust for a moment by the wretched rash intruding Polonius between Hamlet and his revenge: for one moment she was the innocent tool of the guilty, and though her sad fate was avenged on Hamlet, she could not escape. Consider how you should have felt had Cordelia survived Lear or Ophelia survived her father, her brother, and her lover, and you will recognise the dramatic justice of involving them in the general ruin of their friends and enemies. The fate of Desdemona is too harrowing if we miss the completeness of the dramatist's design in the outlines of her character. In the first frenzy of our grief and anger, our thoughts run fiercely towards revenge. We do not regret the death of Emilia, remembering that she had been guilty of stealing the fatal handkerchief. We behold with savage satisfaction the remorse of Othello, and his desperate retribution on himself. We exercise our ingenuity in devising tortures for Iago, the fiendish contriver of all the mischief. Then when justice has been surfeited, and the awful question—Who can control his fate? rolls its starry grandeurs over the fatigued spirit, we revert to the life of the victim, and in that mood we recognise a sinister influence even in the stars of poor Desdemona. She was not a pale creature of colourless blood, framed for a long unruffled life. Her nature was capable of the intemperate passion that leads too surely to tragic consequences. That passionate love of hers for the warlike Moor, which seemed so monstrous and unnatural to her father, and which was construed so craftily by Iago, was too immoderate to be innocuous: "such violent delights have violent ends." The powers that gave her the heart to slight men of her own complexion and degree and fix her affections on a

X

Moor, had destined her to unhappiness. Remove this vicious mole of nature from Desdemona, leave her a cold pattern of propriety reserved to her lover and obedient to her parents, and you find it much more difficult to quell your uneasiness at the crushing of such a flower under the wheel of Destiny. The vicious mole is small in proportion to the retribution : but the fact that she was in a measure, however faint, accessory to her own ruin, blends with other mitigations of the final horror.

# CHAPTER VIII.

## SHAKESPEARE'S CONTEMPORARIES AND SUCCESSORS.

THE more we read of Elizabethan literature, the more we become convinced of the vast superiority of Shakespeare. If one begins the study of the Elizabethan dramatists with a stern resolution to throw aside all prepossessions, and judge every man as if one had heard nothing whatever about him before, the first conclusion reached from dipping here and dipping there into choice passages may well be, that they all wrote with very much the same kind of power. But when we have lived in their company for some time, and studied their works in various lights, we become aware of immeasurable differences. Gradually we come to see that each man applies a different kind of power to the expression of every thought, the conception of every character, the construction of every scene; and the sum of these individualities is enormous.

But though no other Elizabethan dramatist could make the shadow of a claim to be the equal of Shakespeare, there were other men among them justly entitled to be called great. Why, it is often asked, was there such a cluster of great dramatists in that age? Why, we may reply, should there not have been? The drama at that time offered a new and exciting field to the English imagination; and the English imagination, finding the field congenial, rushed into it, and worked at the exalted pitch of energy which new things inspire. Marlowe was really the Columbus of a new literary world. He emancipated the English mind from classical notions of stiff decorum—the necessary accompaniments of the large theatre and the cothurnus and the mask—and by so doing, opened up infinite possibilities to the dramatist. Now, indeed, the drama could be a representation of passionate life. Men struggling passionately after antagonistic aims could now be brought face to face; and the ups and downs, the hopes and fears, the shrinkings and the darings of the struggle and the characters of the combatants, could be placed in swift and dazzling and heart-shaking succession visibly before the eyes of the spectators. The stage even dared to show how men and women bore themselves in the presence of incensed Death—how their spirits quailed or remained constant in fierce defiance with the knife at their throat. Never was there an emancipation so calculated to excite the human intellect to the very utmost of its powers. No wonder that the age should have produced the largest cluster of great names in our literature.

Further, I believe it may be said that it is indispensable to the production of a very great man that a number of great men should work side by side. They not only stimulate one another to extreme effort, but they also, consciously and unconsciously, get from one another invaluable helps and suggestions. In literature, in art, in commerce, all through life, I believe this rule holds. In all things it is an infallible source of degeneration to keep company with inferior minds. You cannot even have a good whist-player, or billiard-player, or cricketer, without others to spur him on; remove the stimulus of competition, and inevitably he is demoralised. Distinguished criminals do not occur singly. What great orator ever rose up from a low general level? When one man makes a tremendous fortune, you are certain to find others following hard in his wake. Greatness in the humblest walks as well as in the highest is so difficult an achievement, and demands such a persistence in heroic effort, that men cannot persevere unto the end, but fall away from the straight course unless they are kept to it by the most powerful of human motives—the ambition of making or keeping a reputation.

The dramatists of greatest general repute next to Shakespeare are Ben Jonson and John Fletcher.[1] There are good grounds for their pre-eminence. Among their contemporaries and competitors were men of higher and rarer qualities; men of more interesting character; but no others, excepting always Marlowe and Shakespeare, gave so much original impulse to the drama, established themselves so firmly and unmistakably as leaders of literature. We shall see that it is a mistake to regard Jonson as an imitator of classical models; and that he himself took a juster view of his position when he disclaimed adherence to Plautus and Terence, and declared himself the inventor of a new comedy. Jonson was the first English dramatist who found the whole materials of his comedy in contemporary life. He may have taken this idea from the Latin comedians. But his method as well as his spirit was essentially different from theirs. Chapman was an older man than Jonson, and Dekker excelled him in the fidelity and delicacy of his delineation of life; but both were his disciples. As regards

---

[1] I shall show reason for believing that injustice is done to Fletcher by writing his name with Beaumont's.

Fletcher, who threw into the drama not only the high spirits and daring manner of aristocratic youth, but also a sweet odour of poetry brought from the vales of Arcadia and the gardens of the Faëry Queen, he is the real progenitor of the drama of the Restoration. Charles Lamb was not strictly correct in saying that "quite a new turn of tragic and comic interest came in with the Restoration." It was not strictly new: it had at least been foreshadowed by Fletcher. Dryden was Fletcher's pupil in tragedy as Wycherley was in comedy. Their work was the natural development of his when relieved from the restraining influences of his age—in tragedy, the competition of men who wrote with a high sense of artistic responsibility, and in comedy, the regard to decency, imposed by a decorous female sovereign and her successor, a royal old woman. The young barbarians who enjoyed the obscenities of Fletcher would not have been shocked by the indecent wit of Wycherley or Congreve, and probably looked upon Shakespeare as old-fashioned and stilted.

I have said nothing about the influence of the Spanish drama on Elizabethan dramatists, because I do not believe that it could have exercised, or did exercise, any appreciable influence. It may have been that Marlowe was induced to write for the public stage by hearing of a great popular drama in Spain—news which he might have had from his friend Greene if he did not know it otherwise; but once the Elizabethan drama was in full career, it was no more possible to turn it into the channels of the Spanish drama, than to turn the Rhine at Frankfort into the Rhone, or to sensibly change the waters of the Ganges by bucketfuls from the Volga. Much of the material of the English drama was taken from Southern Europe, where intrigue and passion have freer play than with us; but the mode of representation was wholly indigenous.


## I.—George Chapman (1559–1634).

George Chapman is conspicuous among the mob of easy and precocious writers in his generation for his late entrance into the service of the Muses, and his loudly proclaimed enthusiasm and strenuous labours in that service. He made no secret of the effort that it cost him to climb Parnassus, or of his fiery resolution to reach the top; he rather exaggerated his struggles and the vehemence of his ambition. He refrained from publication till he was thirty-five years old, and then burst upon the world like a repressed and accumulated volcano. The swelling arrogance[1] and lofty

---

[1] A profession of contempt for critics was quite a commonplace in those days; but Chapman is peculiarly earnest. His fury at some exceptions taken to his Homer was boundless: he fairly gnashed his teeth at the frontless detractions

expectations with which he had restrained his secret labours display themselves without reserve in the 'Shadow of Night'—his first contribution to print.  The dedication of that poem and the poem itself strike the key-note of his literary character.  "It is," he bursts out, " an exceeding rapture of delight in the deep search of knowledge . . . that maketh man manfully endure the extremes incident to that Herculean labour : from flints must the Gorgonian fount be smitten." . . . " Men must be shod by Mercury, girt with Saturn's adamantine sword, take the shield from Pallas, the helm from Pluto, and have the eyes of Graia (as Hesiodus arms Perseus against Medusa), before they can cut off the viperous head of benumbing ignorance, or subdue their monstrous affections to a most beautiful judgment."  If Night, " sorrow's dread sovereign," will only give his " working soul " skill to declare the griefs that he has suffered, she will be able to sing all the tortures of Earth,—

> "And force to tremble in her trumpeting
>   Heaven's crystal spheres."

He adjures Night, the mother of all knowledge, to give force to his words :—

> "Then let fierce bolts, well ramm'd with heat and cold,
>   In Jove's artillery my words unfold
>   To break the labyrinth of every ear,
>   And make each frighted soul come forth and hear.
>   Let them break hearts, as well as yielding airs,
>   That all men's bosoms (pierced with no affairs
>   But gain of riches) may be lanced wide,
>   And with the threats of virtue terrified."

One cannot wonder that this fiery aspirant to fame, so lofty in his pretensions, so novel in his strain, drew all men's eyes upon him, and found many admirers eager to support his claim to stand among the greatest poets.  Englishmen have never been deficient in the worship of force : and the vehement enthusiasm of George Chapman exerted a strong fascination.[1]

Very little is known concerning Chapman prior to 1594, the date of the publication of his 'Shadow of Night.'  He is believed to have been born at Hitchin, and to have studied at Oxford, and perhaps also at Cambridge.  The probability is that he had matured several works before he began to publish, because he issued three or four different productions in rapid succession, and then remained silent for six or seven years, presumably till he was ready for another attack upon the public.  He followed up his

of some stupid ignorants that, " no more knowing me than their own beastly ends, and I ever (to my knowledge) blest from their sight, whisper behind me, vilifying of my translation."

[1] See above, p. 223.

'Shadow of Night' in 1595 with a luxurious study in sensuous description—'Ovid's Banquet of Sense;' and his "Blind Beggar of Alexandria" was played by the Lord Admiral's men in the same year, though not published till 1598.

The chronology of the instalments of his translation of Homer has been greatly obscured by the rash assertions of Warton; but the facts seem to be that he published seven books in Alexandrines in 1598: the 'Shield of Achilles' in heroic couplets in the same year; and twelve books complete in 1606. "A Humorous Day's Mirth," a comedy, was published in 1599, having been sundry times acted before. He offered no other play to the public till 1605, when he printed the comedy of "All Fools." Thereafter he seems to have divided his energies between writing comedies and tragedies and translating from the Classics. His COMEDIES, in addition to those already mentioned, were,—"Monsieur D'Olive," 1606; "The Gentleman Usher," 1606; "May-Day," 1611; "The Widow's Tears," 1612. His TRAGEDIES,— "Bussy d'Ambois," 1607; "Revenge of Bussy d'Ambois," 1613; "The Conspiracy and Tragedy of Charles, Duke of Byron," in two plays, 1608; "Cæsar and Pompey," not published till 1631; "Alphonsus," 1654; "Revenge for Honour," 1654. As regards translations, he was able to boast towards the close of his career that he had translated all the works attributed to Homer. He published a continuation of Marlowe's "Hero and Leander" in 1606.

The circumstantial richness of description in Chapman's two earliest pieces is very remarkable. That was evidently his first study, and he pursued it with untiring enthusiasm till he obtained complete mastery. In the 'Shadow of Night' there are some studiously elaborate descriptions, such as the following :—

> "And as, when Chloris paints th' enamelled meads,
> A flock of shepherds to the bagpipe treads
> Rude rural dances with their country loves :
> Some afar off observing their removes—
> Turns and returns, quick footing, sudden stands,
> Reelings aside, odd motions with their hands,
> Now back, now forwards, now locked arm in arm—
> Not hearing music, think it is a charm,
> That like loose fools at bacchanalian feasts
> Make them seem frantic in their barren jests." .

But ' Ovid's Banquet of Sense ' is his most fervent and indefatigable effort in the way of rich description. As if he had resolved to acquire once for all a complete command of sensuous expression, he there narrates a happy adventure that procured the gratification of all the senses, and tasks the whole power of his fancy in a protracted endeavour to depict the sweet tumult raised in the soul by their various objects. The argument of the poem is, that Ovid having fallen in love with Julia, daughter of Augustus, whom he celebrated under the name of Corinna, found means to enter the imperial gardens and see Corinna playing on her lute and singing, and afterwards entering her bath, which had been filled with the richest perfumes. In this adventure all Ovid's senses were feasted; his hearing with her voice and lute, his sense of smell with the dispersed odours, his eye with her disrobed figure, his mouth with a kiss. He is permitted also to touch her side—the gratification of Feeling, which Chapman calls the senses' groundwork, the emperor of the senses, whom it is no immodesty to serve. 'Ovid's Banquet of Sense' is really a banquet of most exquisite poetry—a most determined effort by the indomitable poet to eclipse by fervid elaboration all the raptures of previous pairs of mythological lovers—Lodge's Glaucus and Scylla, Marlowe's Hero and Leander, Shakespeare's Venus and Adonis, Drayton's Endymion and Phœbe. How elaborately, for example, and with what glowing colours, he describes Ovid's feelings when Corinna stooped down to kiss him!—

> " Her moving towards him made Ovid's eye
>     Believe the firmament was coming down
> To take him quick to immortality,
>     And that the ambrosian kiss set on the crown:
> She spake in kissing, and her breath infused
>     Restoring syrup to his taste in swoon;
> And he imagined Hebe's hands had bruised
> A banquet of the gods into his sense,
> Which filled him with this furious influence.
>
> The motion of the heavens that did beget
>     The golden age, and by whose harmony
> Heaven is preserved, in me on work is set.
>     All instruments of deepest melody,
> Set sweet in my desire, to my love's liking,
>     With this sweet kiss in me their tunes apply,
> As if the best musician's hands were striking:
> This kiss in me hath endless music closed,
> Like Phœbus' lute, on Nisus' towers imposed.
>
> And as a pebble cast into a spring,
>     We see a sort of trembling circles rise,
> One forming other in their issuing,
>     Till over all the fount they circulise;
> So this perpetual motion-making-kiss
>     Is propagate through all my faculties,
> And makes my breast an endless fount of bliss;
> Of which if gods would drink, their matchless fare
> Would make them much more blessed than they are.
>
> But as when sounds do hollow bodies beat,
>     Air gathered there, compressed and thickened,

> The self-same way she came doth make retreat,
>   And so affects the sounds re-echoed
> Only in part, because she weaker is
>   In that redition than when first she fled.
> So I, alas ! faint echo of this kiss,
> Only reiterate a slender part
> Of that high joy it worketh in my heart."

This fervid vividness and laboured-minuteness of realisation is characteristic of all Chapman's descriptions. All his pictures, whether of beauty or of grandeur, whether voluptuous or horrible, strike us as if they had been executed under a fiery determination to make them thorough. In translating Homer, he was rarely content to dismiss a simile with the simple handling of the original : he usually conceived the image for himself, and wrestled with it vehemently to make it yield up greater plenitude of detail.

What chiefly strikes us when we survey Chapman's career through his successive publications, is his steady improvement in every vein that he set himself to master. We should naturally infer from his late appearance in print, which is altogether without a parallel in that age, that his intellect was somewhat stiff and stubborn, not easily set in motion or put upon a track ; and this inference is confirmed by an examination of his beginnings and gradual progress in different veins. Sensuous description would seem to have been his first ambition, and to this he held his intellect by sheer force of ardent enthusiasm till he succeeded up to his ideal. In translating Homer, he had reached the thirteenth book before he fairly entered into the heart of his subject : "when driving through his thirteenth and last books, I drew the main depth, and saw the round coming of this silver bow of our Phœbus ; the clear scope and contexture of his work ; the full and most beautiful figures of his persons." Once warmed to his subject and fairly got under way, his motion was rapid enough ; bodies that are difficult to move are also difficult to stop. He boasted that he drove through the last twelve books in fifteen weeks.[1] When we look to his comedies and his tragedies, we find in like manner poor beginnings and determined improvement. "All Fools" is a great advance on the "Blind Beggar of Alexandria," and "May-Day," with all its coarseness, is in many respects a more masterly composition than "All Fools." The "Revenge for Honour" is incomparably the best of his tragedies.

One great aim in his comedies is to exhibit the gulling of one personage by another. If one were to take Chapman's comedies

---

[1] It is somewhat curious that want of competent time is one of his excuses for making so little of the first twelve books. One often finds very stiff laborious men anxious to have credit for rapid composition.

as mirrors of the time, one would suppose that the chief recreation
of the young courtiers of Elizabeth and James was to find butts
for their wit and subjects for practical jokes.  Chapman was probably put on this track by Jonson's "Every Man in his Humour,"
and he hammered at the idea with characteristic pertinacity.
There is much clever deception—clever, indeed, to extreme im-
probability—in the "Blind Beggar," which was produced before
Ben Jonson's first play ; but Chapman's first effort in the representation of deliberate gulling appears in his "Humorous Day's
Mirth," where the old husband Labernel, the old father Foyes,
and the young pretentious simpleton Bestia (the same character
as Jonson's 'Stephen'), are notoriously deceived by a pack of
waggish gallants.  The gulling in "All Fools," as the title
indicates, is universal :[1]  every one of the *dramatis personæ* is
more or less victimised.  Again, Monsieur D'Olive is gulled by
two young courtiers ; and the Gentleman Usher, Bassiolo, by the
two lovers Vincentio and Margaret, who make him their medium
of communication, and flatter him into the belief that they are a
pair of foolish bashful lovers, very much indebted to his kindly
offices for helping them to declare their mutual passion.  The
"Gentleman Usher" is, taken all in all, the best of Chapman's
comedies ; it contains a certain admixture of serious plot (which
would have been better if he could have refrained from introducing the supernatural), and the gulling of Bassiolo is his masterpiece in that way.  The most riotous and laughable gulling,
however, occurs in the coarsest of his comedies, "May-Day,"
which contains more spirited dialogue, more piquant characters,
and more ludicrous incidents, than any of its predecessors.

Another of his comic aims, persisted in with no less resolution,
is to exhibit the hypocrisy, inconsistency, and general frailty of
women.  This, indeed, may be said to be one of his aims in all
his plays : he has not drawn a single fine female character of any
mark in any play from the "Blind Beggar" to the "Revenge for
Honour": all from Ægiale to Caropia have some taint upon them.
Chapman would almost seem to have been like his own Rinaldo
in "All Fools," who had vowed eternal war against the whole
sex.  And in displaying their frailties, as in other aims that he
took in hand, he improved very much with practice.  The behaviour of Samathis and Elimine in the "Blind Beggar," though
a sufficiently malicious conception, is too violently improbable to
have much point as a satire : Irus, who figures as four different
personages in the play, marries Samathis as Leon, and Elimine
as Hermes, and afterwards as Hermes, seduces Samathis, and as
Leon, Elimine.  Florila, the fair Puritan, in the "Humorous

___________
[1] It is difficult to see why Mr Hallam speaks of this play as a tragi-comedy.

Day's Mirth," is more of a satire on female weakness. But Chapman's greatest achievement in this vein is the "Widow's Tears," in which he makes young Tharsalio conquer a youthful widow, who had sworn eternal constancy, within a few months of her husband's death, and that, too, by representations of the least reputable sort; and, as a secondary plot, elaborates Petronius Arbiter's story of the widow of Ephesus,[1] who went to starve herself to death in her husband's tomb, and was there wooed and won by a soldier stationed near on guard of some crucified bodies.

In his first tragedies, Chapman's main endeavour was to build up a majestic dialogue with weighty moral sentences. In the dedication of his " Revenge of Bussy d'Ambois " he falls out upon certain critics who seem to have found fault with the want of probability both in the characters and in the action of his plays. " And for the authentical truth," says he in defence, " of either person or action, who (worth the respecting) will expect it in a poem, whose subject is not truth, but things like truth? Poor envious fools they are that cavil at truth's want in these natural fictions : material instruction, elegant and sententious excitation to virtue, and deflection from her contrary being the soul, limbs, and limits of an authentical tragedy." His sententious excitations to virtue are powerfully expressed. He would seem to have studied to fulfil his early prayer to Night, concentrating explosive forces, and firing off each word of his maxims like a cannon-ball. But the thunder of this moral artillery is too continuous and deafening; the interchange of elaborate sentences between his personages, especially in the two Byron plays, becomes intolerably tedious. In his latest tragedies, however, Chapman observes a much better proportion of weighty saws. In the " Revenge for Honour " the dialogue is much more full of life than in any of his previous tragedies.

Chapman's designs were always ambitious; but he was guided more like a pedant by authoritative models than like a genuine artist by a clear judgment and sure instinct of his own. He had, undoubtedly, immense power; but his sail was a great deal prouder and fuller than his ship. Both in his comedies and in his tragedies he burdened himself with an unavailing effort to imitate the Latin and Greek classics : he probably flattered himself in so doing with a feeling of superiority to less learned playwrights; but he might have been more successful if he had imitated the published works of Shakespeare. But ambitious and resolute George would have scorned to imitate consciously any of his contemporaries : he aspired to stand out among them as a heaven-sent genius, in rapt communion with the great empress

<hr>

[1] Repeated in Jeremy Taylor's ' Holy Dying.'

of all secrets.   He might, indeed, hold intercourse with the mighty minds of old, and submit to their teaching; he might also take up the conceptions of contemporary writers, and show the proper way to carry them out; but imitate—never.   How, then, is this reconciled with what I have just said, that Chapman imitated like a pedant?   The explanation is, that Chapman, like many other men, was self-deluded in his conviction of originality and inspiration.   His originality was of the nature of oddity, eccentricity, quaintness — a forcible wrench given to commonplace or borrowed ideas, characters, images, and turns of expression.   He was really very much influenced by contemporaries, and commonly for good.   The influence of Shakespeare, to all appearance, operated strongly on the composition of his "Revenge for Honour"; and it is, as I have already said, by far the best of his tragedies.   His earliest tragedies contain splendid passages of description, and a plethora of pithy and noble sentences; but his "Revenge for Honour" is, in respect of lively dialogue, powerfully drawn character, clearly conceived interaction, absorbing plot, and terrible catastrophe, entitled to a high place among the works of the best tragedians.   The chief drawback to Chapman's comedies is the universal ignobility of the characters—the title "All Fools" might almost be extended to his comedies generally.   And one fatal drawback to all his plays is his low conception of female character.   No plays can have a durable popularity that have none of the softer gifts and graces to mingle with their comic humours or tragic horrors.


## II.—JOHN MARSTON (157 ?–1634).

John Marston is the Skelton or Swift of the Elizabethan period. Like them, he wrote in denunciation and derision of what seemed to him vicious or weakly sentimental; and like them, he impatiently carried a passion for directness of speech to the extremes of coarseness.   He was for no half‑veiled exposure of vices. "Know," he cried, in the preface to 'The Scourge of Villany,' his first furious lash at the age, "I hate to affect too much obscurity and harshness, because they profit no sense.   To note vices so that no man can understand them is as fond as the French execution in picture."   And a contemporary (in the anonymous "Return from Parnassus") confirmed this self-estimate of his purposes :—

> "Tut, what cares he for modest close-couched terms
>   Cleanly to gird our looser libertines ?
> Give him plain naked words, stript from their shirts,
>   That might beseem plain-dealing Aretine ! "

Marston's satires are not elegant, self-complacent exercitations in imitation of Horace, such as Hall was so vain of writing; he wrote in a more savage and less affected vein :—

> "Unless the Destin's adamantine band
> Should tie my teeth, I cannot choose but bite."

One of his mottoes is taken from Juvenal, with whom he had more in common than with Horace—*Difficile est satiram non scribere*—"It is difficult *not* to write satire." There would be an almost Timonic grandeur in the swelling energy of his defiance of public opinion were it not for the satirist's half-humorous enjoyment of his own position. "I dare defend my plainness against the verjuice face of the crabbedest Satirist that ever stuttered. He that thinks worse of my rhymes than myself, I scorn him, for he cannot; he that thinks better is a fool. . . . If thou perusest me with an impartial eye, read on; if otherwise, know I neither value thee nor thy censure." Whatever other people are afraid to do has a great charm for Marston. He dedicates his "Scourge of Villany" to Detraction, and bids her snarl, bark, and bite,— for his spirit scorns her spite :—

> "My spirit is not puft up with fat fume
> Of slimy ale, or Bacchus' heating grape;
> My mind disdains the dungy muddy scum
> Of abject thoughts and Envy's raging hate."

With somewhat less coarse bravery he consigns himself to everlasting oblivion—"mighty gulf, insatiate cormorant"—in opposition to the usual aspirations for eternal memory :—

> "Let others pray
> For ever their fair poems flourish may;
> But as for me, hungry Oblivion,
> Devour me quick."

He beseeches the wits to malign him; nothing could give him greater pleasure :—

> "Proface, read on; for your extremest dislikes
> Will add a pinion to my praise's flights.
> Oh! how I bristle up my plumes of pride!
> Oh! how I think my satires dignified!
> When I once hear some quaint Castilio,
> Some supple-mouthed slave, some lewd Tubrio,
> Some spruce pedant, or some span-new-come fry
> Of Inns-o'-Court, striving to vilify
> My dark reproofs! Then do but rail at me—
> No greater honour craves my poesy."

Almost nothing is known concerning Marston's private life. He is believed to be the John Marston who was admitted B.A. at Oxford in 1593, as being the eldest son of an Esquire, his father belonging to the city of Coventry. He began his literary career in 1598, publishing in that year "Pygmalion's Image, and certain Satires," and "The Scourge of Villany, Three Books of Satires." He is supposed to be the Maxton or Mastone, "the new poet," mentioned in Henslowe's Diary in 1599; and the play there referred to is supposed to be his "Malcontent," published in 1604 in two editions—one with, and the other without, an Induction by Webster. His other plays published were—"Antonio and Mellida," 1602; "Antonio's Revenge," 1602; "The Dutch Courtesan," 1605; "Parasitaster," 1606; "Sophonisba," 1606; "What you Will," 1607; "The Insatiate Countess," 1613. He was also conjoined with Chapman and Jonson in the composition of "Eastward Ho!" certain passages of which, written by Chapman and Marston between them, gave such offence to the Scotch predilections of the king that it brought the trio to prison, and very nearly to the pillory. Marston and Jonson were less friendly in after life, as they had been at enmity before.[1] Jonson told Drummond that he once "beat Marston and took his pistol from him." Marston's total abstinence from literature during the last twenty years of his life is not explained.

One of Marston's favourite butts, both in his Satires and in his plays, was the puling sentimentality of enamoured sonneteers. He goes beyond himself in the invention of mad indignities, coarse and subtle, overt and sly, for these forlorn creatures; parodies them and scoffs at them; buffets them, as it were, tweaks their noses, stealthily pulls out hairs and puts in pins, kicks them out of his presence.

> "Sweet-faced Corinna, deign the riband tie
> Of thy cork-shoe, or else thy slave will die:
> Some puling sonnet tolls his passing bell;
> Some sighing elegy must ring his knell.
> Unless bright sunshine of thy grace revive
> His wambling stomach, certes he will dive
> Into the whirlpool of devouring death,
> And to some mermaid sacrifice his breath."

I have endeavoured to show that Shakespeare co-operated with this derision of forced love-sighs, writing certain of his sonnets in ridicule of their windy suspiration. But Shakespeare himself was not always above the contempt of the predestined cynic. 'Venus and Adonis' was singled out by Marston as the type of dangerously voluptuous poetry, and unmercifully parodied in his "Pygmalion's Image," the arts of the goddess to win over the cold

---

[1] Jonson made Marston the subject of a play in 1601—"The Poetaster." He, and not (as D'Israeli states) Dekker, is Crispinus: the parody of Marston's style in the Fifth Act is unmistakable. The reconciliation must have been only temporary. Marston dedicated his "Malcontent" to Jonson in 1604.

youth being coarsely paralleled in mad mockery by the arts of
Pygmalion to bring his beloved statue to life.  The risk in all
such parodies is that they be taken as serious productions.  This
has been the fate of Shakespeare's sonnet parodies; and Marston
either feared or had actually incurred a similar calamity.

> " Curio, know'st my sprite,
> Yet deem'st that in sad seriousness I write
> Such nasty stuff as is Pygmalion?
> .    .    .    O barbarous dropsy noll!
> Think'st thou that genius that attends my soul,
> And guides my fist to scourge magnificoes,
> Will deign my mind be rank'd in Paphian shows?"

Marston seems to have had rather a fancy for parodying Shakespeare: he more than once has a fling at "A horse, a horse! my
kingdom for a horse!" and in "The Malcontent" he has several
hits at passages in Hamlet, including " Illo, ho, ho, ho, art there,
old Truepenny?" and a parody on Hamlet's reflection, "What a
piece of work is man!"   But he also paid the great dramatist the
compliment of imitating from him.  In "The Malcontent," the
conception of the villain Mendozo is indebted in several particulars
to Richard III.   And the hinge of the plot is borrowed indirectly
from "Hamlet."   A banished Duke of Genoa returns to court in
the disguise of Malevolo, an ill-conditioned cynic, who deliberately
uses his reputation for craziness as a licence to tell people of their
vices in very surly terms face to face.  This origin of the idea of
Malevolo might not have occurred to us but for the parodies of
Hamlet in the play: and it has a certain value as showing
Marston's notion of the feigned madness of Hamlet.

Marston's plays are very remarkable and distinctive productions.  They are written with amazing energy—energy audacious,
defiant, shameless, yet, when viewed in the totality of its manifestations, not unworthy to be called Titanic.  They make no pretence
to dramatic impartiality; they are written throughout in the spirit
of his satires; his puppets walk the stage as embodiments of
various ramifications of deadly sins and contemptible fopperies,
side by side with virtuous opposites and indignant commenting
censors.  His characters, indeed, speak and act with vigorous life:
they are much more forcible and distinct personalities than Chapman's characters.  But though Marston brings out his characters
sharply and clearly, and puts them in lifelike motion, they are too
manifestly objects of their creator's liking and disliking: some are
caricatured, some are unduly black, and some unduly stainless.
From one great fault Marston's personages are exceedingly free:
they may be overdrawn, and they may be coarse, but they are
seldom dull—their life is a rough coarse life, but life it is.  And
all his serious creations have here and there put into their mouths

passages of tremendous energy. Charles Lamb has gathered from Marston, for his 'Specimens of English Dramatic Poets,' extracts of passionate declamation and powerful description hardly surpassed in all that rich collection.

As we read Marston's plays, too, the conviction gains ground upon us that, after all, he was not the ill-conditioned, snarling, and biting cur that he would have us believe himself to be, but a fairly honest fellow of very powerful intellect, only rude and rugged enough to have a mad delight in the use of coarse paradox and strong language. He was not a self-satisfied snarler, girding freely at the world, but tender of his own precious personality. His plays convince us that there was a touch of sincere modesty in his prayer to Oblivion :—

> " Accept my orison,
> My earnest prayers, which do importune thee
> With gloomy shade of thy still empery
> To veil both me and my rude poesy.
> Far worthier lines, in silence of thy state,
> Do sleep securely, free from love or hate."

In the Induction to "What you Will," he makes Doricus turn round on Philomene, who is railing against the stupidity of the public in the vein of the "Scourge of Villany," and call the strain rank, odious, and leprous—"as your friend the author . . . seems so fair in his own glass . . . that he talks once of squinting critics, drunken censure, splay-footed opinion, juiceless husks, I ha' done with him, I ha' done with him." And in the body of the same play he is hardy enough to make Quadratus fall out upon Kinsayder, his own *nom de plume* in his early satires :—

> " Why, you Don Kinsayder,
> Thou canker-eaten, rusty cur, thou snaffle
> To freer spirits."

We cannot complain of ill-treatment from a cynic so unmerciful to himself, so uncompromising in his gross ebullient humour. We are inclined to concede to him that, like his own Feliche, he "hates not man, but man's lewd qualities." There are more amiable and admirable characters in his plays than in Chapman's. He has good characters to set off the bad : the treacherous, unscrupulous Mendozo is balanced by the faithful Celso ; the shamelessly frail Aurelia by the constant Maria ; the cruel, boastful Piero by the noble Andrugio ; the impulsive, unceremonious, warm-hearted, pert, forward, inquisitive, chattering Rossaline, by the true and gentle Mellida.

## III.—BEN JONSON (1573-1637).

Ben Jonson had a mind of immense force and pertinacious grasp; but nothing could be wider of the truth than the notion maintained with such ferocity by Gifford, that he was the father of regular comedy, the pioneer of severe and correct taste. Jonson's domineering scholarship must not be taken for more than it was worth: it was a large and gratifying possession in itself, but he would probably have written better plays and more poetry without it. It is a sad application of the mathematical method to the history of our literature to argue that the most learned playwright of his time superseded the rude efforts of such untaught mother-wits as Shakespeare with compositions based on classical models. What Jonson really did was to work out his own ideas of comedy and tragedy, and he expressly claimed the right to do so. The most scrupulous adherence to the unity of time, and the most rigid exclusion of tragic elements from comedy, do not make a play classical. Ben Jonson conformed to these externals; but there was not a more violently unclassical spirit than his among all the writers for the stage in that generation.[1] His laborious accumulation of learned details, his fantastic extravagance of comic and satirical imagination, the heavy force of his expression, his study of "humours," had their origin in his own nature, and not in the models of Greece and Rome.

Jonson, according to his own account, was of Scotch extraction, his grandfather being a Johnstone of Annandale, who settled in Carlisle, and was taken into the service of Henry VIII. His father, who suffered persecution under Mary, and afterwards became "a grave minister of the gospel," died before our poet's birth. Whether or not his mother married a bricklayer as her second husband, it would seem that in his youth he was apprenticed to that trade, but not before he had received at least the rudiments of a good education at Westminster School under Camden, a patron to whom he was never backward in acknowledging his obligations. From bricklaying he went in disgust to soldiering, and served a brief campaign in the Low Countries, distinguishing himself in a single combat with a champion of the enemy, whom he killed and stripped in the sight of both camps. How he began his connection with the stage is not known. He is called "bricklayer"[2] in 1598 in a letter of Henslowe's giving an account of a

---

[1] His picture of the Court of Augustus, which Lamb praises so highly, was founded probably on what he saw or what he desiderated at the Court of England. Jonson seems always to have had friends among the courtiers.

[2] Collier's 'Memoirs of Edward Alleyn,' p. 50. It would not have been at all unlike the man to work as a bricklayer while writing for the stage. He might have enjoyed the defiance of public opinion in honest labour. This would give

duel that he fought in that year with a player; but before that time he had begun to write plays. A version of his " Every Man in his Humour " would seem to have been put on the stage in 1596, and the play was published in 1598. The dates of the production of his subsequent plays, as given by Gifford, are as follows: " The Case is Altered," published 1598; " Every Man out of his Humour," 1599; " Cynthia's Revels," 1600; " Poetaster," 1601; " Sejanus," 1603; " Eastward Ho!" (written in conjunction with Chapman and Marston), 1605; " Volpone, or The Fox," 1605; " Epicœne, or The Silent Woman," 1609; " The Alchemist," 1610; " Catiline," 1611; " Bartholomew Fair," 1614; " The Devil is an Ass," 1616; " The Staple of News," 1625; " The New Inn," 1630; " The Magnetic Lady," 1632; " The Tale of a Tub," 1633. These plays were not the author's chief means of living: they were not as a rule popular. He told Drummond in 1618 that all his plays together had not brought him £200. A more lucrative employment was the preparation of Masques for the Court: he seems to have furnished the Court with a masque or other entertainment almost every year from the accession of James till 1627, when his quarrel with Inigo Jones lost him this pleasant source of income. In 1613 he went abroad in charge of the eldest son of Sir Walter Raleigh. In 1616 he obtained from the Crown a pension of 100 marks. This was confirmed to him by Charles; yet from his loss of the Court entertainments, and the failure of the last plays that he wrote, his closing years were embittered by distressful poverty. In his celebrated conversations with Drummond during his visit to Scotland in 1618-19, he complained that poetry had " beggared him when he might have been a rich lawyer, physician, or merchant;" and his circumstances at that time were affluent compared with what they were in his later years.

Jonson's person was not built on the classical type of graceful or dignified symmetry: he had the large and rugged dimensions of a strong Borderland reiver, swollen by a sedentary life into huge corpulence. Although in his later days he jested at his own " mountain belly and his rocky face," he probably bore his unwieldy figure with a more athletic carriage than his namesake the lexicographer. Bodily as well as mentally he belonged to the race of Anak. His position among his contemporaries was very much what Samuel Johnson's might have been had he been contradicted and fought against by independent rivals, jealous and resentful of his dictatorial manner. Ben Jonson's large and irascible personality could not have failed to command respect; but

a literality to Dekker's taunt of " the lime-and-mortar poet." But Jonson is entered as " player" in 1596. He can hardly be supposed to have returned to bricklaying.

his rivals had too much respect for themselves to give way absolutely to his authority. They refused to be as grasshoppers in his sight. We should do wrong, however, to suppose that this disturbed the giant's peace of mind. Gifford, who makes a good many mistakes in the course of his rabidly one-sided memoir of Jonson, is certainly right in saying that he was not an envious man. His arrogance was the arrogance of irascible and magnanimous strength—good-natured when not thwarted, and placable when well opposed. If his rivals refused to be as grasshoppers, he accepted them contentedly at their own valuation, with, perhaps, passing fits of occasional ill-temper. There is no evidence to support his alleged jealousy of Shakespeare : it is quite possible that he may have made occasional sharp remarks about his great contemporary ; but when he sat down to remember the worth of the mighty dead, his words breathed nothing but sincere and generous admiration and warm friendship. His relations with Marston and Inigo Jones are typical of the man. He quarrelled with them and showed them up, was reconciled, and quarrelled again. He took offence at Marston, and ridiculed him unmercifully as Crispinus "The Poetaster"; became friends with him again ; received the dedication of his "Malcontent"; and wrote with him and Chapman in "Eastward Ho!" yet told Drummond that he had many quarrels with Marston. He scoffed at Inigo Jones in "Bartholomew Fair" as Lanthorn Leatherhead, a puppet-seller and contriver of masques ;[1] co-operated with him afterwards in the preparation of Court entertainments ; and finally broke with him utterly, and tried to extinguish him with lofty contempt. There seems to be no denying that Ben was irascible and difficult to get on with. Yet there was a fundamental large-hearted good-humour in him too. We must not judge of him altogether by his conversations with Drummond, as Drummond himself did : he was the sort of man that falls into fits of incontinent railing and depreciation, and so conveys an erroneous impression of his normal inner nature. In his better moods he was not unwilling to laugh at his own failings. He had many friends among the great patrons of poetry.

When we examine into the alleged correctness of Jonson's plays, we find curious evidence of how his known acquaintance with the classics has imposed upon his critics. "Generally speaking," says Gifford, "his characters have but one predominating quality : his merit (whatever it be) consists in the felicity with which he combines a certain number of such personages, distinct from one

---

[1] Gifford denied this without authority. It is supported by the Drummond conversations, in which Jonson said (in 1618) that he had told Prince Charles that "when he wanted words to set forth a knave, he would name him an Inigo;" and also by the language of his final "Expostulation with Inigo Jones."

another, into a well-ordered and regular plot, dexterously preserving the unities of time and place, and exhibiting all the probabilities which the most rigid admirer of the ancient models could
possibly demand." The regularity of the plot and the observation
of the probabilities are parts of Gifford's preconceived ideal, formed
without the slightest attention to the facts. As regards regularity,
Jonson is so far regular that in most of his plays four acts are
occupied in exhibiting every man in his humour,[1] while the fifth
act exhibits every man out of his humour; and the "humours"
overmaster every other consideration. In the running criticisms
of Mitis and Cordatus, the author's friends, in "Every Man out of
his Humour," he is careful to point out that "herein his art
appears most full of lustre, and approacheth nearest the life:" it
is like the course of things in reality that his actors should for
some time "strongly pursue and continue their humours," and
thereafter, in the flame and height of them, be suddenly laid flat.
Macilente, Carlo Buffone, and others, in "Every Man out of his
Humour"; Amorphus in "Cynthia's Revels"; Crispinus in "The
Poetaster"; Volpone and his dupes in "The Fox"; Face and
Subtle and their dupes in "The Alchemist"; Overdo and his
friends in "Bartholomew Fair"; Fitzdottrel in "The Devil is an
Ass";—all come to grief in the last act, after a triumphant career
in their several humours. So far, Ben Jonson's comedies are well-
ordered and regular—so far they have a rigorous and unbending
unity; but the connection between the various victims of tyran-
nical humours is of the loosest kind, and there is no attempt at
subtlety of construction or artful excitation of suspense in preparing the way for the final collapse: the whole interest lies in the
representation of the characters and the incidents.[2] Probability,
either of character or of incident, is about the last thing one would
think of alleging. Ben Jonson's "humours," by his own definition of them, are caricatures. It is ridiculous to suppose that they

[1] The word "humour" was much in use in Jonson's time. He complained
that it was abused to signify any capricious fancy or affectation: a man wore a
pied feather, or a cable hat-band, or a three-piled ruff, or a yard of shoe-tie, and
called it his humour. Nym, in Henry IV., uses it in a still looser sense. Jonson is careful to explain the signification of the term in his plays (" Every Man
in his Humour," Induction). I need not quote his etymology at length—he
often shows a scholarly hankering after etymological fancies—but his conclusion
is, that the term may, by metaphor, apply itself—

> " Unto the general disposition ;
> As when some one peculiar quality
> Doth so possess a man that it doth draw
> All his effects, his spirits, and his powers,
> In their confluctions all to run one way,
> This may be truly said to be a humour."

[2] The celebrated band of amateurs—including Charles Dickens and Mr G. H.
Lewes—who acted "Every Man in his Humour" with such success, chose the
play, I believe, chiefly on account of the number of good characters in it.

were taken from life: there never was any such drawing of the thoughts and feelings one way outside the walls of Bedlam. The "humour" of legacy-hunting was never so omnipotent over all effects, spirits, and powers, in real life, as it is made out to be in "The Fox." And the incidents—such as the swooning of Fungoso at sight of Brisk's new suit, the sealing up of Buffone's mouth, the inexpressibly ludicrous tournament in court-compliment between Azotus and Mercury, the vomiting of Crispinus, &c., &c.—are conceived in the spirit of the wildest farce or the most bitterly exaggerated satire. There is, indeed, a parallel to Jonson's mad upsetting of things among the classics: Aristophanes is a devil of mirth no less fantastic and much more unconstrained than Jonson; but we do not look to Aristophanes for good order, regularity, or "all the probabilities which the most rigid admirer of the ancient models could possibly demand."

Jonson, indeed, explicitly professed his independence of correct classical models, and proclaimed his affinity with the older and more licentious forms. In the Induction to "Every Man out of his Humour," Cordatus, the man "inly acquainted with the scope and drift of the plot," explains that the play is "strange, and of a particular kind by itself, somewhat like 'Vetus Comœdia.'" "Does the author," asks Mitis, "observe all the laws of comedy in it, according to the Terentian manner?" "O no," replies Cordatus, "these are too nice observations." He can discern no necessity for adhering to the Terentian model. The laws of comedy were not a revelation or a sudden inspiration of genius: each playwright reserved the fullest liberty to innovate upon his predecessors "according to the elegancy and disposition of those times wherein he wrote." "I see not then but we should enjoy the same licence, or free power to illustrate and heighten our invention, as they did; and not be tied to those strict and regular forms which the niceness of a few, who are nothing but form, would thrust upon us." It is a curious illustration of the blindness of preconception that Gifford should have read this and yet persisted in magnifying Jonson as the apostle of regularity—the very thing that he contemptuously disclaimed. True, Jonson might not have understood himself. We know that, although he professed to cleanse the stage of ribaldry, foul and unwashed brothelry, and suchlike, he nevertheless, like many another professed and earnest moralist, drew in the interests of morality foul and disgusting pictures, quite as demoralising as anything that the most licentious dramatist ever ventured to portray. None of the Elizabethan dramatists exceed in unwashed filth some of the passages in "The Silent Woman" and "Bartholomew Fair." We should not have suspected that Jonson was an apostle of decency, if he had not told us. But in the matter of correctness and regularity, it needed no

Cordatus, inly acquainted with the author's drift, to inform us that Jonson's study of "humours" is "strange, and of a particular kind by itself, somewhat like 'Vetus Comœdia,' "—a very remarkable outcome of a powerful and original mind, which was not very popular at the time, but which strongly affected the practice of contemporary dramatists, and has been fully honoured by posterity.

The only sense in which correctness can be applied to Jonson is careful elaboration—laborious filling in of details. Whether in the exhibition of character, or in the description of places or things, he is never content with a bold sketch and a few significant particulars. The characteristic of plodding dogged thoroughness runs through all his work, but is most conspicuous and obtrusive in passages where he has an opportunity of displaying technical knowledge,—as when he expounds the stock-in-trade and the business cares of a draper, or the various vessels and other implements of an alchemist's laboratory, or the ingredients of a fine lady's cosmetic or a witch's charm, or the precise language of the acknowledged processes for raising the devil, or transmuting the baser metals into gold. It is in studying this peculiarity that we get a just idea of the vastness of Jonson's scholarship, his prodigious patience of research, and strength of memory. His scholarship was not so much an athletic scholarship, like Spenser's, as a vast knowledge of all sorts of dry details from all sorts of sources ; and when we consider the extent of it, we cannot sufficiently admire the power and the patience that have compelled it into dramatic existence, and endowed it with a certain dramatic life.

We need not dwell on Ben Jonson's tragedies, "Sejanus" and "Catiline." His warmest admirers have not much to say in favour of them. "Catiline" is better than "Sejanus," but even "Catiline" wants the elements of an effective drama. Looking at these tragedies, I am wholly at a loss to understand M. Taine's opinion that Jonson possesses in an eminent degree the art of development, of drawing up ideas in connected rank. The primary rule of development is to present your audience first with the broad outlines, and then to fill in the details clearly. This is the rule of development observed by Shakespeare and by all conscious or unconscious masters of the art of presentation. But this rule is not observed by Johnson : in spite of his Herculean efforts to marshal his vast scholarship, he was too much overwhelmed by it to put his readers in clear possession of character and situation by bold decisive strokes and well-judged and opportune sequence. Compare the opening of his "Sejanus" with the opening of "Titus Andronicus." In "Titus Andronicus" the dramatist had to deal with numerous characters and complicated relations, yet we take them all in at our first reading of the first act : the leading parties are brought boldly and clearly on the stage at once in such

a way as to command our interest, and minor relations appear as
we proceed with perfectly-judged sequence. The same may be
seen in Shakespeare's more mature Roman dramas, " Julius Cæsar"
and " Coriolanus." In " Sejanus," on the other hand, laborious
attention and several readings of the opening passages are needed
before we comprehend the situation. Two unimportant personages
come in with long-winded talk about the arts of worldly advance-
ment, and describe some half-dozen characters in a string in such
a way that the sharpest hearer must get bewildered as to their
relative positions and claims upon his interest. It seems to me
that M. Taine must have formed his opinion of Jonson's skill in
development from observing his persistent iteration throughout
each play of the main characteristics of his personages, and his
habit of expounding the intention of important passages, as if he
could not trust to the unaided understanding of the audience.
Thus Ben hammers into us the daring, forward, impetuous character of Cethegus; and before the scene in which Catiline practises
to win over allies, makes the arch-conspirator unfold to his wife
how he means to work upon their various weaknesses. But this is
not so much skilful development as superfluous care and weak dis-
trust of the intelligence of his hearers.

In Jonson's comedies there are occasional passages that may
justly be called tragic, but they belong to low, coarse, revolting
tragedy. The misanthropy of Macilente in " Every Man out of
his Humour" is tragic; it is the Timonism of a thoroughly ill-
conditioned foul-mouthed churl. The scene between Volpone,
Corvino, and Celia (" The Fox," iii. 5)—the foul abuse of his wife
by Corvino, and the struggle between Volpone and Celia—is mon-
strously tragic: if the moralist desired to heal spiritual diseases
by such an exhibition, he has not scrupled to administer a very
strong medicine. The opening scene of " The Alchemist," between the sharpers Subtle and Face and their confederate and
common mistress Dol, might pass in a modern sensational drama
from the south side of the Thames but for the coarseness and the
power of the language: it is a unique revelation of hellish discord
and odious patching up of a villanous alliance; and its initiatory
fascination was doubtless a chief cause in making " The Alchemist"
Jonson's most successful play.

The most generally pleasing remains of Jonson's genius are his
occasional songs, his Masques, and his "Sad Shepherd." The
"Sad Shepherd" is not quite complete; but, though not without
a few blots and stains, it contains some of Jonson's finest poetry.
The shepherdess Amie is such a sweet creation that one is indignant at the dramatist for the vulgar and wholly superfluous
immodesty of one of her expressions in her first confession of
unrest: to the pure all things are pure, but it exposes the simple

shepherdess to unnecessary ridicule from the ordinary reader.
One is surprised to find such sympathy with simple innocence in
rare but rough Ben—all the more that the "Sad Shepherd" was
written in his later years, when he was exacerbated by failure and
poverty.

> " I do remember, Marian, I have oft
>     With pleasure kist my lambs and puppies soft ;
>     And once a dainty fine roe-fawn I had,
>     Of whose out-skipping bounds I was as glad
>     As of my health ; and him I oft would kiss ;
>     Yet had his no such sting or pain as this :
>     They never prick'd or hurt my heart ; and for
>     They were so blunt and dull, I wish no more.
>     But this that hurts and pricks doth please ; this sweet
>     Mingled with sour, I wish again to meet :
>     And that delay, methinks, most tedious is
>     That keeps or hinders me of Karol's kiss."

## IV.—THOMAS DEKKER (1577–1638).

The skirmish between Marston, Jonson, and Dekker, is one of
the most famous "quarrels of authors."   Who gave the first offence is a matter of dispute : Jonson said it was Marston and Dekker, and Dekker said it was Jonson.   When Jonson caricatured
Marston as Crispinus the Poetaster, with a very slight passing
thrust at Dekker under the name of Demetrius, he professed that
he had received information of their intention to attack him ; and
when Dekker replied with "Satiromastrix, or The Untrussing of
the Humorous Poet," he read Jonson a dignified lecture on his
jealous disposition, and represented himself and Marston as acting
reluctantly in self-defence.   On which side the truth lies, it is impossible to say ; the facts are against Jonson, inasmuch as he
struck the first blow ; and his alleged acquaintance with the evil
intentions of Marston and Dekker is such as might easily have
been inserted between the first acting of "The Poetaster," and the
publication of it.[1]   At any rate, Dekker had very much the best
of the contest.   From Gifford's saying that "Dekker writes in
downright passion, and foams through every page," we should infer that he had never read "Satiromastrix," were it not the case
that he makes mistakes equally gross concerning plays that he
must have read.   Dekker writes with the greatest possible lightness of heart, easy mockery, and free abuse.   It is absurd to say
that he "makes no pretensions to invention, but takes up the
characters of his predecessor, and turns them the seamy side

---

[1] All the part of Demetrius looks as if it had been inserted after Jonson was
informed of Dekker's intention to "untruss him " in revenge of Marston.

without." Tucca is the only character that he borrows, and a very ingenious idea it is—one of the best parts of the joke—to set Jonson's own free-spoken swaggerer to abuse himself.  Dekker's Tucca is much more ably wrought out than Jonson's; he has a much finer command of what Widow Minever calls "horrible ungodly names"; and his devices to obtain money are equally shameless and amusing.  All the other characters, and what plot there is, are Dekker's own; he, of course, uses the names Horace, Crispinus, and Demetrius, otherwise there would have been no point in his reply—but he gives them very different characters.  William Rufus, whom Gifford supposed to be the "rude and ignorant soldier" of that name, is conjectured to have been no other than Shakespeare—"learning's true Mæcenas, poesy's King"; and perhaps to a playwright like Dekker, Shakespeare might appear a true Mæcenas, although at first sight one would naturally think rather of the Earl of Pembroke or some other noble patron of letters.  I am surprised that so able a critic as Mr Symonds should say that "Satiromastrix" is not to be named in the] same breath with the "Poetaster," and that its success must have been due to the acting.  To be sure it does not reproduce the Court of Augustus with the same verisimilitude—its flight is much too light-winged and madding for any such scholarly achievement. The Court of Augustus would have broken the continuity of the play with yawning intervals; the frail, fallible, and romantic Court of William Rufus is more in keeping with its ebullient and victorious humour.  "Satiromastrix," the castigation of the satirist, is not in itself a satire so much as a genial confident mockery: it accomplished the main end of such productions — the applause of the playgoers; and I must confess that I for one should have been inclined to give the clever rogue a hand, however badly his counterblast had been put on the stage.

Of Dekker's personal history few particulars are known.  The dates both of his birth and of his death are only approximate conjectures.  He seems to have made his living by plays, pageants, and prose pamphlets, and to have been almost as prolific and versatile as Defoe, although his labours did not always suffice to keep him out of "the Counter in the Poultry," and the King's Bench Prison.  He is first named in 'Henslowe's Diary' in 1597, and he would seem to have been conjoined with Chettle, Haughton, Day, and Jonson on several plays before the close of the century.  The first play published as his was "The Shoemaker's Holiday," in 1600: and the subsequent list is—"The Pleasant Comedy of Old Fortunatus," 1600; "Satiromastrix," 1602; "Patient Grissel" (in conjunction with Chettle and Haughton), 1603; "The Honest Whore" (Part I.), 1604; "The Whore of Babylon," 1607; "Westward Ho!" "Northward Ho!" and "Sir Thomas Wyatt" (in conjunction with Webster), 1607; "The Roaring Girl" (in conjunction with Middleton), 1611; "If it be not Good, the Devil is in it," 1612; "The Virgin Martyr" (in conjunction with Massinger), 1622; "Match me in London," 1631; "The Wonder of a Kingdom" 1636; "The Sun's Darling" (not published till 1656); and "The Witch of Edmonton," 1658 (written in conjunction with Ford).

Dekker was a man of less determined painstaking than Chapman or Jonson, but of greater natural quickness and fineness of vision, more genial warmth of sympathy, and more copious spontaneity of expression. The fertility of his conception and the sweetness of his verse were not surpassed by any of his great contemporaries: his melting tenderness of sympathy and light play of humour are peculiarly his own. He had more in common with Shakespeare than with any of the three sturdy writers whom we have been discussing. Hazlitt complains of Shakespeare's comic Muse, as such, that it is "too good-natured and magnanimous," that it "does not take the highest pleasure in making human nature look as mean, as ridiculous, and as contemptible as possible." This is plainly a characteristic of Shakespeare's comedy as distinguished from the Terentian manner; but I should not call it a fault. I know no reason why this should be placed outside the limits of what is strictly called comedy. I should be inclined to call this the crowning excellence of English comedy—that it is able to present such a web of the admirable and the ridiculous as life itself appears when viewed in a pleasant mood. This is the kind of comedy that Dekker naturally pursued. He had a very strong propensity towards fun, darted into every opening that promised laughter with the gleefulness of a boy; but he had also a strong love for the virtues, and a genial belief in human goodness, and delighted to picture an honest citizen, a repentant sinner, a relenting father, a merciful prince. Neither his humour nor his love for gentleness of heart was diminished by his poverty and frequent distress. If Dekker, as Jonson said, "was a rogue and not to be trusted," he always took a kinder and more lenient view of humanity than appears in the plays of his enemy,—the stern scourge of vice and folly. Dekker's genius had many points of resemblance with Chaucer's.

If, with Hamlet, we take the purpose of playing to be "to show virtue her own feature, scorn her own image, and the very age and body of the time his form and pressure," Dekker must receive a high place among the dramatists. There is none of them that has preserved so many lifelike intimations of the state of the various classes of society in that age. His plots are loosely constructed; but occasional scenes are wrought out with the utmost vividness, and the most complete and subtle exhibition of character and habits.   Dekker's being born in London, and his exceptional acquaintance with strange bedfellows in the course of his miserable life, gave him an advantage as the abstract and brief chronicle of the time over Shakespeare, who was bred in the country, and passed a comparatively prosperous and respectable life in London — apart altogether from the fact that Shakespeare's imagination would not let him rest content with so close a transcript of nature.

## V.—Thomas Middleton (1570–1627).

Middleton has not Dekker's lightness of touch and etherial purity of tenderness, but there are qualities in which he comes nearer than any contemporary dramatist to the master mind of the time.   There is a certain imperial confidence in his use of words and imagery, a daring originality and impatient force of expression, an easy freedom of humour, wide of range yet thoroughly well in hand, such as we find in the same degree even in that age of giants in no Elizabethan saving only Shakespeare. It was as a comedian that Middleton first made his reputation, about the year 1607, comparatively late in life ; and it would seem that he despaired of obtaining recognition for his powers in tragedy, for two of his most striking performances in that kind are interwoven with comic stories and the whole plays named after leading characters in the comic under-plot.   Nobody would expect from the title of the "Mayor of Queenborough," the intensity and force that Middleton shows in the tragic scenes of that play.   The title seems to require our attention for the humorous antics of the Mayor, Simon the tanner, an imitation of Dekker's Simon Eyre the shoemaker, Mayor of London.   And similarly in "The Changeling," which Middleton wrote in conjunction with Rowley, the dramatists seem to modestly intimate that they set store chiefly on the comic portions.   Yet there are tragic passages in "The Changeling" unsurpassed for intensity of passion and appalling surprises in the whole range of Elizabethan literature.   That these scenes were devised and written by Middleton will hardly be doubted by anybody acquainted with "The Mayor of Queenborough," and his later pure tragedy, "Women Beware Women."   This last play is literally open to Jonson's sarcastic note on "Hamlet"—"Here the play of necessity ends, all the actors being killed."   The slaughter in "Women Beware Women" extends to every character honoured with a name. Regarded as wholes, Middleton's tragedies fall very far short of the dignity of Shakespeare's.   His heroes and heroines are not made of the same noble stuff, and their calamities have not the same grandeur. The characters are all so vile that the pity and terror produced by their death is almost wholly physical. But in the expression of incidental moments of passion, Middleton often rises to a sublime pitch of energy.

It may have been that Middleton, though only six years younger than Shakespeare, was born too late for tragedy. A complaint is made in "The Roaring Girl," in the composition of which he was conjoined with Dekker, that tragedies had gone out of fashion. "In the time of the great crop doublet," it is said, "your huge bombasted plays quilted with mighty words to lean purpose, were only then in the fashion; and as the doublet fell, neater inventions began to be set up." Under King James the taste was all for "light colour summer stuff, mingled with divers colours." Thus by the time that Middleton came into favour as a playwright, the atmosphere of the theatre was not encouraging to tragic composition. How far this influenced him in the devotion of his versatile powers to comedy, and how much was due to his individual character, it is of course impossible now to determine, for we have nothing but his plays to judge by. He began his literary life, like Marston, as a satirist, writing in the style popular at the end of the sixteenth century; but he achieved no great success in this artificial line of composition. His first triumph as a writer of comedy would seem to have been "A Trick to Catch the Old One."[1] This, along with four others, was licensed in 1607. Chapman's "All Fools," the great exemplar and prototype of the English comedy of "gulling," had taken the town two years before, and Middleton threw himself into the fashion. In this type of comedy he is exceedingly happy, and surpasses his masters in ingenuity of construction, and easy accumulation of mirthful circumstances. The fun begins early, and goes on to the end with accelerating speed. Middleton excels peculiarly in the dramatic irony of making his gulls accessory to their own deception, and putting into their mouths statements that have, to those in the secret, a meaning very much beyond what they intend. "A Mad World, my Masters," licensed in 1608, is one of his happiest efforts in this vein. As bearing on Jonson's description of him as "a base fellow," it may be remarked that he professes to be more decent than some of his predecessors, and has a gird apparently at Marston or Jonson, as some obscene fellow, who cares not what he writes against others, yet rips up the most nasty vice in his own plays, and presents it to a

---

[1] This play furnished the plot of Massinger's "New Way to Pay Old Debts." The titles of the plays, in fact, are interchangeable: both the scapegrace heroes extract by the same device rather more than their rights from usurious and grasping uncles. The character of Sir Giles has more force than any creation of Middleton's; but the germ of the character was probably taken from Middleton's "Pecunious Lucre," or Sir Alexander Wargrave in "The Roaring Girl."

modest assembly. It is the excellency of a writer, says Middleton, to leave things better than he finds them. According to this principle, in the "Trick to Catch the Old One," and the "Mad World," the courtesans are married and made honest women—the rakes are reclaimed; and though no lesson is weightily inculcated, there is less indecency than in the works of more pretentious moralists.

Middleton's name has of late been revived in connection with the authorship of "Macbeth." It has been conjectured, on the ground of certain slight coincidences between Middleton's play and the witch scenes, that Middleton had a hand in the composition of "Macbeth."[1] The supposition is about as groundless as any ever made in connection with Shakespeare, which is saying a good deal. Even if either author borrowed the words of the song from the other, that is no evidence of further co-operation. The plays are wholly different in spirit. "The Witch" is by no means one of Middleton's best plays. The plot is both intricate and feeble; and the witches, in spite of Charles Lamb's exquisite comparison of them with Shakespeare's, are, as stage creations, essentially comic and spectacular. With their ribald revelry, their cauldrons, their hideous spells and weird incantations, they are much more calculated to excite laughter than fear as exhibited on the stage, however much fitted to touch the chords of superstitious dread when transported by the imagination to their native wilds. The characters of the play do not treat them with sufficient respect to command the sympathy of the audience for them. Familiarity breeds contempt: if they had been consulted only by the Duchess with a view to the murder of her husband, they might have kept up an appearance of dignity and terror; but when the drunk Almachildes staggers in among them, upsets some of the beldams, and is received by Hecate as a favoured lover, we cease to have much respect for them, even though they do profess to exercise the terrible power of raising jars, jealousies, strifes, and heart-burning disagreements like a thick scarf o'er life. The visit of the fantastical gentleman whom Hecate has thrice enjoyed in incubus, is a very happy inspiration in the same vein as Tam o' Shanter's admiration of the heroine of Alloway Kirk: the scene is a fine opportunity for a comic actor; but it is damaging to the respectability of the dread Hecate.

[1] The chief resemblances are, that both poets introduce Hecate as the queen of the witches, and that the songs "Come away" and "Black Spirits," of which only the first words are given in "Macbeth," are set down in full in "The Witch." "The Witch" was not printed till 1778, when it was discovered in MS. by Mr Isaac Reed. If the songs were popular witch-songs, whether written before or after Shakespeare wrote "Macbeth," they may have been adopted in the stage copy of the play.

## VI.—JOHN FLETCHER (1579-1625).

It is not without compunction that one ventures to dissolve the long-established union between the names of Beaumont and Fletcher, and to characterise the second and principal member by himself. The rigour of my plan demands it. There are ample materials for forming an estimate of Fletcher, because he wrote plays unassisted probably before, and certainly after, his partnership with Beaumont; while in groping after the character of Beaumont we must trust chiefly to imperfect materials—a masque, a few poems, vague traditions, and arbitrary recognition of portions of his joint work with Fletcher. If there had been marked differences between the plays written by Fletcher alone, and those written by him in conjunction with Beaumont, one might have proceeded with some confidence to allocate their respective shares in the joint compositions. But I must confess for myself that there is no passage in any of the joint plays that I could affirm with any confidence not to be Fletcher's—not to contain traces of his hand. Of the three plays in which it is known for certain that Beaumont took part — the "Maid's Tragedy," "Philaster," and "A King and No King"—all have the same complexion as Fletcher's single compositions, similar characters, similar sentiments, and similar impelling forces. One would expect the metre to be a good criterion of separate identity. The abundance of feminine endings in Fletcher's undoubted verse, and his habit of running one line into another, have been suggested as tests; but the application of these tests, is rendered uncertain by the fact that they do not apply to Fletcher's "Faithful Shepherdess." We cannot pick out certain passages as being Beaumont's, simply on the ground that they contain a smaller proportion of feminine endings than certain other passages which may be supposed to be Fletcher's. On the whole, I see no reason to doubt the opinion currrent during the reign of Charles I., and communicated by Bishop Earle to Aubrey, that Beaumont's chief share in the plays lay in correcting the exuberance of Fletcher. Almost all the commendatory poems prefixed to the edition of 1647—poems by Denham, Waller, Lovelace, Herrick, Lowell, Cartwright, Richard Brome, &c.—are addressed to Fletcher alone. Richard Brome, Jonson's servant and pupil, who knew Fletcher intimately, and was as likely as any man to be aware of the exact relationship between the two dramatists, gives all the glory to Fletcher. The truth probably is, that Beaumont applied his superior judgment to the task of amending Fletcher's first drafts, seeing that his prolific partner was strongly averse to the labour of correction. I cannot say that there is any one scene in the plays of Beaumont and Fletcher which I should feel warranted in assigning to Beaumont alone, although it is quite possible that he contributed whole Scenes, if not whole Acts.

All the dramatists hitherto considered in our survey agree in being men of humble extraction, who had to fight their way in the world through manifold difficulties. Fletcher is only partly an exception to this agreement. He was the son of a Kentish clergyman, who rose to the rank of bishop; but his father died in 1596, when he was seventeen years old, and left a widow and a large family in distressed circumstances. Five years before his father's death, Fletcher had entered Bennet College, Cambridge, and he was resident there in 1593. No other particulars of his private life have been ascertained. He seems to have begun to write for the stage about 1606, the supposed date of his "Woman-Hater"; and before he was cut off by the plague in 1625, he had written or co-operated in writing no less than sixty plays.

Fletcher entered the dramatic field when the rivalry of wit was at its hottest. He belonged to the lighter build of combatants—the saucy bark, rather than the imperious, proud, full sail. It is significant of his personal appearance that his portraits were considered failures: there was no catching the quick play of his vivacious features. His first dramatic effort—if the "Woman-Hater" is so—was in the mock-heroic vein, and gave proof of a comic genius second only to Shakespeare's. There are two comic heroes in the play—Gondarino, a ridiculously ill-conditioned and techy hater of women; and Lazarillo, a fanatic and insatiable gourmand. Gondarino's sourness takes the fancy of a mischief-loving young lady, Oriana, who amuses herself and gives rise to some most ludicrous scenes by making violent love to the old porcupine, very much to his disgust. In the pursuit of her whim, however, she compromises herself by equivocal behaviour, and narrowly escapes falling a victim to the cynic's ludicrously diabolical project of revenge. Alongside this series of incidents, and partly interwoven with them, runs the mock-heroic passion of Lazarillo, whose sole aim in life is to get possession of dainty food without paying for it. His goddess is Plenty, and his daily prayer to her is, "Fill me this day with some rare delicates." A sumptuous feast is the sacrifice that he vows to perform. Bills of fare are his holy scriptures, which he never fails to take up with reverence. Lazarillo's page, whose office it is to haunt the kitchens of the great, and bring instant word of forthcoming dishes, in order that his master may devise stratagems and ambuscades to procure a taste of them, one day reports that the Duke's table is to be graced by—the head of an Umbrana. "Is it possible?" cries Lazarillo; "can heaven be so propitious to the Duke?" And forthwith he vows to pursue this Umbrana's head with all his

strength, mind, and heart.  He procures an introduction to the
Duke, only to find that the Duke has sent the object of his
idolatry to Gondarino : when good fortune has thrown Gondarino
in his way, and he is beginning to rejoice, he finds that it has
gone to Gondarino's mercer : when he has skilfully engineered an
invitation to dine with the mercer, he finds that the mercer has
sent it to a woman of doubtful fame.  After these and other
checks at moments when the Umbrana's head was almost between
his teeth, he at last attains it by marrying the mercer's mistress.
The intensity of Lazarillo's passion for the rare morsel, his ecstasies
when he is on the point of attaining it, his profound dejection and
distraction after each temporary repulse to his hopes, are in the
maddest vein of mock-heroism.

The " Woman-Hater " is a good introduction to Fletcher's gay
and daring humour.  He indulged it without much regard for
decency : he had less veneration than Shakespeare to check him :
he is more coolly contemptuous in laying serious respectabilities
by the heels.  The " Faithful Shepherdess " gives us a more
beautiful side of his character, developed with the same freedom and abandonment of himself to the full swing of a ruling
sentiment.  This masque, though naturally enough condemned
when put on the public stage as a drama, furnished Milton
with a model for his " Comus," and is in itself one of the finest
monuments of our moralising pastoral poetry.  Fletcher throws
himself unreservedly into the loves and crosses of Amoret and
Perigot, and the pious austerity of the bereaved Clorin, and lets
his imagination revel in picturing the scene of their adventures.
The wood where the mistakes of a night are enacted is very
fitting for a romantic drama :—

> " For in that holy wood is consecrate
>     A virtuous well, about whose flowery banks
>     The nimble-footed fairies dance their rounds
>     By the pale moonshine, dipping often-times
>     Their stolen children, so to make them free
>     From dying flesh and dull mortality.
>     By this fair fount hath many a shepherd sworn
>     And given away his freedom ; many a troth
>     Been plighted, which nor Envy nor old Time
>     Could ever break, with many a chaste kiss given,
>     In hope of coming happiness."

The mad irrepressible humour of the poet, however, broke
through the sweet surface of his romantic conception : he spoiled
his paradise by introducing, as evil principles, the wantons Cloe
and Alexis, and the malignant Sullen Shepherd, and investing
them with characters so disgusting, that their gross humour,
instead of operating as an elevating contrast, tends rather to
throw a taint of ridicule on the whole composition.

From Dryden down to Coleridge, all Fletcher's critics have remarked his success in representing the easy and animated conversation of young gentlemen. Don John in the "Chances," Mirabel in the "Wild Goose Chase," Cleremont in the "Little French Lawyer," Don Jamie and Leandro in the "Spanish Curate," Monsieur Thomas, and many others, use much less abstruse language than Shakespeare's Biron, Gratiano, Benedick, and suchlike, and language consequently better suited to the mouths of young men of blood and fashion. The truth is, that Fletcher's easy, rapid, copious style, preserved by his good taste and sense of humour from conceits, and by his superficial nature from any kind of depth or intricacy, approaches nearer the language of polite conversation than the style of any of his contemporaries: the ease and sprightliness is not specially put on for young men of spirit, but is a pervading characteristic of his style. There is a similar dash and abandonment in the language of all his personages: he throws himself heartily and impetuously, but not deeply, into a situation, and expresses the sentiment of the moment with unfailing' abundance of clear, bright-coloured, gracious, and noble words.

Apart from his fertile humour, which is no less varied than unscrupulous, the main charm of Fletcher lies in the plentiful stream of simple ideas and readily understood feelings, expressed in felicitous and animated language. When we try to grasp the consistency of his characters, and regard his plays as wholes, we discover many evidences of weak characterisation and hasty construction. It is remarkable how few of his personages are throughout admirable, beautiful, or venerable; and this arises not from cynical purpose, as in Jonson, but from sketchiness and shallowness of conception. He is fond of delineating exemplarily virtuous women; but chastity is too often and too prominently their sole claim upon our interest, and many of them pollute their lips with language the reverse of lovely. His magnanimous heroes, also, harp too much on one string: he could not have ventured to show a hero in his domestic and playful side, as Shakespeare does with Hotspur. And many of his personages, both male and female—Sorano, Protaldye, Brunhalt, &c. &c.—are abominably vile,—vile almost beyond parallel. One cannot say that in the plays pruned by the revision or enlarged by the co-operation of Beaumont, there is much difference in these respects. There are exquisite passages in the sad stories of Aspatia and Euphrasia, as there are in the stories of Amoret or Evanthe, showing them to be children of the same delicate fancy; but there is a want of body in the appeal that they make to our sympathies: they are, besides, brought into too close contact with the pitch that defiles. And both the "Maid's Tragedy" and "Philaster" are seriously disfigured by the ignoble and repulsive character of the impelling forces : the shameless intrigue of Evadne and the king is too violent an outrage on decency, too base and animal, to permit any dignity to envelop its tragic consequences ; and the easy credence given to the filthy accusations of Megra, so base, unsupported, and obviously malicious, makes us look upon the hero as a fool, and seriously affects his claims to our interest and admiration.

## VII.—John Webster (?).

Dekker's partner in " Westward Ho ! " " Northward Ho ! " and " Sir Thomas Wyatt," was to all appearance as different from himself as one man of genius could be from another—a man who sank deep shafts into the mines of tragedy; and built up his plays with profound design and deliberate care. Dekker is not more remarkable for his genial reproduction of city life in loosely contrived scenes, and for his easy unstudied sympathy with deep heart's-sorrowing and keen heart's-bitterness, than Webster is for his penetrating grasp of character, meditated construction of intricate scenes, and elaborate, just, and powerful treatment of terrible situations. One would expect from the joint work of two such men results of the most supreme kind—plays that might compete with the unrivalled Shakespeare. But the excellent qualities of two men cannot be fused into one work of art : two minds cannot work as one with the united strength of the strong faculties of both. Of the three joint plays of Dekker and Webster, two of them, " Westward Ho ! " and " Northward Ho ! " are not distinguishable from the unaided productions of Dekker ; while the third, " Sir Thomas Wyatt," in the mutilated and imperfect shape that has been handed down to us, contains strong marks of Webster, and may be regarded as being, in great part, the first effort of his powerful genius.

Concerning Webster's life one can only repeat the same tale of ignorance that must be told concerning so many of our dramatists. He was born free of the Merchant Tailors' Company ; began to write for the stage as early as 1601 ; and we may conjecture, from his predilection for scenes in courts of law and his elaborate treatment of them, that he had been bred to the profession. His quotations show that he had at least been taught Latin, and so far had received a learned education. His fame rests on three tragedies and a tragic comedy,—" Vittoria Corombona, the White Devil," published in 1612 ; " The Duchess of Malfi," 1623 ; " The Devil's Law-Case," a tragi-comedy, 1623 ; and " Appius and Virginia," not published till 1654.[1]

[1] Mr E. Gosse argues that the main plot in " A Cure for a Cuckold " is Webster's. But the share of each of two joint authors must always be doubtful. See article on Middleton, 'Academy,' August 22, 1885.

In the preface to "Vittoria Corombona," Webster defends himself against the charge of being a slow composer. We find this charge also in a contemporary satirist ('Notes from Blackfriars,' 1620), who draws a very lively picture of "crabbed Websterio" :—

> "See how he draws his mouth awry of late,
> How he scrubs, wrings his wrists, scratches his pate ;
> A midwife, help !   .   .   .   .
> Here's not a word cursively I have writ
> But he'll industriously examine it ;
> And in some twelve months thence, or thereabout,
> Set in a shameful sheet my errors out."

Webster does not deny the charge ; but he answers his critics with a bold tradition : "Alcestides objecting that Euripides had only in three days composed three verses, whereas himself had written three hundred ; 'Thou tellest truth,' quoth he, 'but here's the difference : thine shall only be read for three days, whereas mine shall continue three ages.'" Webster's characters could not have been drawn nor his scenes constructed in a hurry. Appius and Romelio are unsurpassed as broad and elaborate studies, filled in with indefatigable detail and accommodated with subtle art to a profound conception. In following these masterpieces the student of character is kept in an ecstasy of delight by stroke after stroke of the most unerring art. In every other scene their replies and ways of taking things surprise us, yet every such paradox on reflection is seen to accord with the central conception of their character, and increases our admiration of the dramatist's deep insight and steady grasp. And these plays are not merely closet-plays, whose excellences can be picked out and admired only at leisure. The characters have not the simplicity and popular intelligibility of Shakespeare's Richard or Iago. The plots, too, except in "Appius and Virginia," where all the incidents lie in the direct line of the catastrophe, are involved with obscure windings and turnings. Yet all the scenes are carefully constructed for dramatic effect. Mark how studious Webster has been that his actors shall never go lamely off the stage : they make their exit at happily chosen moments, and with some remark calculated to leave a buzz of interest behind them. When we look closely into Webster's plays we become aware that no dramatist loses more in closet perusal : all his dialogues were written with a careful eye to the stage. Everywhere throughout his plays we meet with marks of deep meditation and just design. It is not with his plays as with Fletcher's. The more we study Webster, the more we find to admire. His characters approach nearer to the many-sidedness of real men and women than those of any dramatist except Shakespeare ; and his exhibition of the changes of feeling wrought in them by the changing progress of events, though characterised by less of revealing instinct and more of penetrating effort than appear in Shakespeare, is hardly less powerful and true.

Webster did not attempt comedy, unless in conjunction with Dekker, and before he had felt where his strength lay. The moral saws wrought into his dialogues show that his meditations held chiefly to the dark side of the world. In forming our impression of the man, we are perhaps unduly dominated by the concluding scenes of "Vittoria Corombona" and "The Duchess of Malfi": it is from these scenes that he has received the name of "the terrible Webster." It showed a strange ignorance of his own power that in the preface to "Vittoria" he regretted that the nature of the English stage would not permit him to write sententious tragedy after the model of the ancients, "observing all the critical laws, as height of style and gravity of person, enriching it with the sententious chorus, and, as it were, *enlivening death in the passionate and weighty* NUNTIUS." He does undoubtedly observe height of style, and his persons are exempt from meanness and ignobility. Uncontrollable passionate love, and a temporary insanity of avarice pursued with subtle policy and bitterly repented of, are the chief impelling forces of his four great plays; and even inferior instruments of villany, such as Ludowick, Flamineo, and Bosola, are invested with a certain dignity. But that Webster should have desired to relate those terrific death-scenes instead of exhibiting them as he has done, showed a strange obliviousness of the basis of his own fame and the excellence of modern tragedy. Not to mention his grander scenes, how tame and unimpressive would have been the fate of the poisoned Brachiano in the narrative of a messenger to his beloved mistress Vittoria, compared with what it is when we are brought face to face with the fearfully punished sinner and the passionately interested witnesses of his agony.

> "*Brach.* Oh! I am gone already. The infection
> Flies to the brain and heart. O thou strong heart!
> There's such a covenant 'tween the world and it,
> They're loath to break.
>     *Giovanni.* O my most loved father!
>     *Brach.* Remove the boy away:
> Where's this good woman? had I infinite worlds,
> They are too little for thee. Must I leave thee?
> What say you, screech-owls? is the venom mortal?
>     *Physician.* Most deadly.
>     *Brach.* Most corrupted, politic hangman!
> You kill without book; but your art to save
> Fails you as oft as great men's needy friends.
> I that have given life to offending slaves
> And wretched murderers, have I not power
> To lengthen mine own a twelvemonth?

Do not kiss me, for I shall poison thee ;
This unction is sent from the Great Duke of Florence.
   *Fran. de Medici [his enemy the Great Duke in disguise].* Sir, be of
      comfort.
   *Brach.* O thou soft natural death, that art joint-twin
To sweetest slumber ! no rough-bearded comet
Stares on thy mild departure ; the dull owl
Beats not against thy casement ; the hoarse wolf
Scents not thy carrion. Pity winds thy corse
Whilst horror waits on princes.
   *Vittoria Corombona.* I am lost for ever !
   *Brach.* How miserable a thing it is to die
'Mongst women howling ! what are these !
   *Flamineo. Franciscan.*
They have brought the extreme unction.
   *Brach.* On pain of death let no man name death to me :
It is a word most infinitely terrible.
Withdraw into our cabinet."

Brachiano's bidding Vittoria not kiss him or she will be
poisoned, is characteristic of Webster's subtle art. The wretched
man had been moved by his passion for Vittoria, the "white
devil," to poison his wife, and the deed had been heartlessly done
by anointing with a deadly unction the lips of a picture of her
husband which the poor lady was in the habit of kissing every
night before she went to bed ; and this line at once shows the
direction of Brachiano's franticly shifting thoughts, and brings the
crime by a sudden flash side by side with the punishment and the
impassioned motive.

## VIII.—CYRIL TOURNEUR (?).

Tourneur's name will always be associated with Webster's,
because his nature led him within the same circle of terrible
subjects. Only two of his plays survive, the . "Revenger's
Tragedy" and the "Atheist's Tragedy"—the one first published
in 1607, the other in 1611. Nothing more is known about him,
except that he wrote also a play called the "Nobleman," which
was utilised by Warburton's cook.

Tourneur was far from having the breadth and the weight of
Webster's genius : he does not take so deep a hold of the being of
his personages. Yet he is entitled to a high and unique place
among the Elizabethan dramatists. There is a piercing intelligence
in his grasp of character, a daring vigour and fire in his expression.
His two plays show no elaborate study of variety of character ;
but he burns the chief moods of his principal characters deep into
the mind.

Vindici, in the "Revenger's Tragedy," forms an interesting
comparison with Hamlet. His character, one need hardly say, is

not so versatile and complete as Hamlet's; but "Hamlet," also, is a revenger's tragedy: and it is worth while to look at the two side by side.   Vindici is sustained throughout in one mood: from the first he knows who it is that has robbed him of his mistress, and he pursues the murderer with unwavering hatred.   At no time is his spirit filled with weariness of the whole course of the world: he lives throughout at a demoniac pitch, turned all to gall and wormwood by the bitter wrong done to him, and expatiating on the world with daring wit, fierce biting mockery.   The critics of last generation, in their remarks on the unseasonable levity of Hamlet, seemed to have lost sight of the fact that the deepest and most wringing sorrow, when it is not too strong for the frame of the sufferer, finds vent more in laughter than in tears.   Vindici's laughter is still more terrible than Hamlet's, because his angry bitterness is so unrelaxed and unvaried by gentle moods.   Even his anger does not pass through many phases.   There is no sustained weight of indignation in it: the intense scoffing vein is paramount, and the earnestness of his passion only flashes through at fiery intervals.   In the scene in which he explains to his brother the plan of revenge that he has formed, his fantastic demoniac mirth, his bitter buffoonery is at its height; and the passage is one of the many that show how much higher those dramatists rose into the extravagances of human passion than sober-footed critics have since been able to follow them.   Vindici's bride, Gloriana, had been ravished and poisoned by the Duke, and Vindici, the better to effect his revenge, had fiercely forced himself to assume the disguise of a pander.   In this disguise he had been employed by the Duke to procure a mistress, and he explains (Act iii.) to his brother with bitter delight who the mistress is that he has provided.   He keeps the skull of his dead bride in his study, and he has resolved to bring this veiled to the old "luxur" at the appointed spot, and when the deception is discovered, to consummate his revenge.

> "*Enter* VINDICI *with* HIPPOLYTO *his brother.*
>
> *Vind.* O sweet, delectable, rare, happy, ravishing!
> *Hipp.* Why, what's the matter, brother!
> *Vind.* O, 'tis able to make a man spring up and knock his forehead against
>         yon silver ceiling.
> *Hipp.* Pr'ythee tell me  .     .     .     .
>
> *Vind.*               The old Duke .     .     .
> Hires me by price to greet him with a lady
> In some fit place, veiled from the eyes of the court.
>     .     .     .     .     I have took care
> For a delicious lip, a sparkling eye!
> You shall be witness, brother.
> Be ready; stand with your hat off.

*Hipp.* Troth I wonder what lady it should be;
Yet 'tis no wonder, now I think again,
To have a lady stoop to a Duke.

*Enter* VINDICI *with the skull of his love dressed up in tires.*

*Vind.* Madam, his grace will not be absent long.
Secret ?   Ne'er doubt us, Madam.   'Twill be worth
Three velvet gowns to your ladyship.   Known ?
Few ladies respect that disgrace ; a poor thin shell !
'Tis the best grace you have to do it well.
I'll save your hand that labour.   I'll unmask you.
   *Hipp.* Why, brother, brother ?
   *Vind.* Art thou beguiled now ?
Have I not fitted the old surfeiter
With a quaint piece of beauty ?  .     .     .
  .     .     .     .     Here's an eye,
Able to tempt a great man—to serve God.
A pretty hanging lip, that has forgot now to dissemble.
Methinks this mouth should make a swearer tremble,
A drunkard clasp his teeth, and not undo them
To suffer wet damnation to run through them.
Here's a cheek keeps her colour, let the wind go whistle.
Spout, rain, we fear thee not : be hot or cold,
All's one with us.   And is not he absurd
Whose fortunes are upon their faces set,
That fear no other God but wind and wet.
   *Hipp.* Brother, you've spoke that right.
Is this the form that living shone so bright ?
   *Vind.* The very same.
And now methinks I could e'en chide myself
For doating on her beauty, though her death
Shall be avenged after no common action."

There are many striking passages in Tourneur of splendid declamation and masterly description.   Perhaps none is more remarkable than that quoted by Lamb under the title of "The Drowned Soldier."   With all one's reverence for Lamb as a critic, one cannot help saying that this title and his slightly disparaging remark about the weaving of parenthesis within parenthesis shows that he did not feel the peculiar and wonderful power of the description.   It is not the drowned soldier that we are interested in : it is the movements of his terrible murderer.   I know nothing comparable to this passage as a description of the fearfulness of the sea : it makes one shudder to read it—as if the gigantic sea-serpent himself were hissing and wallowing before us in his uncouth and horrible pity.

    " Walking upon the fatal shore,
Among the slaughtered bodies of their men,
Which the full-stomached sea had cast upon
The sands, it was my unhappy chance to light
Upon a face, whose favour when it lived

> My astonished mind informed me I had seen.
> He lay in his armour, as if that had been
> His coffin ; and the weeping sea (like one
> Whose milder temper doth lament the death
> Of him whom in his rage he slew) runs up
> The shore, embraces him, kisses his cheek ;
> Goes back again, and forces up the sands
> To bury him ; and every time it parts,
> Sheds tears upon him ; till at last (as if
> It could no longer endure to see the man
> Whom it had slain, yet loath to leave him) with
> A kind of unresolved unwilling pace,
> Winding her waves one in another (like
> A man that folds his arms, or wrings his hands
> For grief), ebbed from the body, and descends
> As if it would sink down into the earth,
> And hide itself for shame of such a deed."

## IX.—JOHN FORD (1586–1640 ?).

Whoever wishes to fully understand Ford's genius should read Mr Swinburne's paper in the 'Fortnightly Review' of July 1871. All other criticisms must appear faint and colourless after that masterpiece of searching criticism and noble language.   It is still, however, open to consider Ford more especially as a dramatist. In what follows, my endeavour has been to trace the influence of Ford's character on the structure of his plays.

Little is known of Ford's life.   Two doggerel lines that have come down in a contemporary satire on the poets of the time are rather expressive of what seems to have been the character of the man :—

> " Deep in a dump John Ford alone was got,
> With folded arms and melancholy hat."

He seems to have been a proud, reserved, austere kind of man, of few and warm attachments, with but slender gifts in the way of ebullient spirits or social flow.   He was a barrister, with a respectable ancestry to look back to ; and though he wrote several plays, and did not disdain to work in conjunction with such a professional playwright as Dekker, he was nervously anxious lest it should be supposed that he made his living by play-writing.   In his first Prologue he spoke contemptuously of such as made poetry a trade, and he took more than one opportunity of protesting that his plays were the fruits of leisure, the issue of less serious hours. Some of his plays he dedicated to noblemen, but he was careful to assure them that it was not his habit to court greatness, and that his dedication was a simple offering of respect without mercenary motive.   His first play, "The Lover's Melancholy," he dedicated to his friends in Gray's Inn, avowing that he desired not to please the many, but to obtain the free opinion of his equals in condition.

Ford had good reason for making this independent stand. Although Shakespeare had made his living chiefly by poetry, and had been not very scrupulous in using the fancies and inventions of others, there were many traders in play-writing with whom it was not so reputable to be classed. The servility of begging dedications, too, had become quite loathsome. At the same time, the haughty reserved disposition out of which this independence came was not favourable to dramatic excellence. A play written to please the few is not likely to be a good play. The dramatist must be above the narrowness of sympathy that this implies. And this ungeniality produces failure where, on first consideration, a nineteenth-century reader would least expect it. Such a reader, on hearing of an Elizabethan playwright anxious to please the few, would expect to find him abstaining from the indecency that makes so many of these plays unfit for family reading. But it is quite the other way. Ford's low-comedy scenes are very coarse and very dull. To be sure, the gentlemen of Gray's Inn, the few for whom Ford wrote, were not particular on this point. But this was not the main cause of the offensiveness of Ford's attempts at humour. The main cause was his want of sympathy with his low-comedy puppets. He makes them express themselves as if he disliked them and wished to make them odious and contemptible: their coarseness is unprovoked, gratuitous, with very little of wit or humour to redeem it. Fletcher's Megra and other creations of that type are quite as gross as Ford's Putana; but the dramatist enters into their obscene humour, and in some degree takes away the attention from its obscenity by the cleverness of its intrusions, the comical irrepressibility of its chuckle. Now Ford had not sufficient freedom of high spirits to enter into the humour of his Putanas and Berghettos, and there is a cynicism, a harshness, an offensive exaggeration, in his representation of the frankness of their language.

But the haughty reserve and want of heartiness in Ford's nature told against his plays in a much more serious respect. He would not seem to have looked at his plays from the point of view of his audience, or to have exerted himself to stir their interest or to keep it from flagging. There is a certain haughtiness of touch even in his language; sometimes a repudiation of emphasis, as if he did not care to be impressive on a slight occasion; sometimes a wilful abstruseness, as if it mattered nothing though his words were misunderstood. This alone is often the cause of considerable reaches of dull dialogue—dull, that is to say, for the purposes of the stage. In his first play, also, "The Lover's Melancholy," three acts pass before any very strong interest is excited in the personages or the action. The main issues presented to us are—what is the cause of the Prince of Cyprus's melancholy, and whether he will recover from it. It is hinted that this melancholy may have dangerous consequences—that discontent is muttering at home, and that enemies are gathering on the borders of the kingdom, presuming on the inactivity of the prince; but these consequences, instead of being powerfully represented, so as to throw the interest of a mixed audience keenly on the prince's dejection and indifference to affairs of state, are only dimly and faintly mentioned, in such a way that no ordinary hearer would perceive their importance. In the underplot we are never agitated by any fear of an untoward issue. We never have any serious apprehension that the haughty Thaumasta will eventually reject Menaphon, or that the noble and prosperous Amethus will falter in his love to Cleophila. And the story of the Prince Palador and his mistress Eroclea, with its picture of the forlorn Eroclea, and its finely wrought presentation of their reunion, is not by itself, without further development, enough for a drama: it is better suited for a descriptive epic.

It is only in his two great tragedies, the "Broken Heart" and "'Tis Pity she's a Whore," that Ford's power is unmistakably shown. In them he has to deal, from the first scene, with men under the full sway of intelligible passion; and in the presence of passion his haughtiness, his reserve, his indifference, vanishes, and he enters earnestly into the work of interpretation. The second of these two plays, in spite of the harsh, affected, and offensive levity of the title, is Ford's masterpiece,—the play that justifies Mr Swinburne's eloquent panegyric, and will always be most in the critic's mind in all attempts to fix Ford's place among the dramatists. In the "Broken Heart," notwithstanding its many powerful and touching passages, there is somewhat too much of learned delineation of character: the noble heroism of strength and impetuosity in Ithocles and Calantha is too obtrusively balanced against the tamer heroism of determined endurance in the other pair of lovers, Orgilus and Penthea. All the persons of the drama have names expressive of their leading qualities; and at the close, our wonder at the strangeness of the lunatic jealousy of Bassanes, the pitiless, dogged, irreconcilable revengefulness of Orgilus, the bitter constancy of Penthea in starving herself to death, seriously obstructs the nobler emotions of horror and pity. Even the closing scene, in which the heroic Calantha hears of the death of her father and her lover, and gives no sign of sorrow till the duties of her high state have been performed, when her over-strained heart-strings break, and she falls dead on the body of her slain lover, is more likely to stun and amaze all but the select few, than to come home powerfully to their sympathies. But there are no such scholarly obstructions to the terrible tragedy of fate-driven love between Brother and Sister. In it passion is supreme from the first scene to the last.

A man can never wholly hide a ruling tendency in his nature; and even Ford's great tragedies are not without traces of his harshness and severity. There is something very unsatisfactory in the characters of Bassanes and Vasques: it frets and vexes us at the end to see such base deformities stand by and triumph at the fall of nobler natures. We may think them unworthy of the sword of poetic justice—we may reason them out of the sphere of guilt in the tragedy; but their triumph disconcerts us.

### X.—Philip Massinger (1584–1640).

Massinger had less original force than any of the other great dramatists. He was eminently a cultivated dramatist, a man of broad, liberal, adaptive mind, fluent and versatile, with just conceptions of dramatic effect, and the power of giving copious expression to his conceptions without straining or dislocating effort. Yet he was much too strong and vigorous to be a mere imitator. His nature was not such as to fight against the influence of his great predecessors: his mind opened itself genially to their work, and absorbed their materials and their methods; but he did not simply reproduce them—they decomposed, so to speak, in his mind, and lay there ready to be laid hold of and embodied in new organisms. So far he resembled Shakespeare, in that he had good sense enough not to harass himself in straining after little novelties: his judgment was broad and manly. But he was far from resembling Shakespeare in swiftness and originality of imagination: his muse was comparatively tame and even-paced. The common remark that his diction is singularly free from archaisms shows us one aspect of the soundness of his taste, and bears testimony, at the same time, to his want of eccentricity and original force. He was the Gray of his generation—greater than Gray, inasmuch as his generation was greater than Gray's—a man of large, open, fertile, and versatile mind.

His personal career is obscure. His father was "a servant" in the family of the Herberts of Pembroke, as we know from the dedication of his "Bondman," and "spent many years in the service of that honourable house;" but whether the service was menial, or such as might be rendered by a gentleman, there is no means of ascertaining. At any rate, Massinger's position was not such as to prevent him from going to Oxford in 1602, or from being in a debtor's prison about 1614, and under the necessity of joining with two others in begging an advance of £5 from Henslowe to procure his release. From the almost desperate mendicancy of his dedications, which are the extreme opposites of Ford's, one would judge him to have lived in wretched poverty: and the entry of his death in the register of St Saviour's —"buried Philip Massinger, a stranger"—gives us no ground for hoping against the most natural inference.

The probability is that Massinger began to write for the stage about 1606, if not a year or two earlier, going up from the university as Marlowe and Thomas Nash had done some twenty years before, in search of literary fame and the mysteries of London life. He did not, however, begin to publish till much later, his first printed play being "The Virgin Martyr," which appeared in 1622, and in which he had the assistance of Dekker. Only twelve of his plays were published during his lifetime, out of the thirty-seven which he is known to have written. Perhaps we have the less reason to regret this, because the plays published in his lifetime are decidedly superior to those published after his death. He himself saw in print, besides "The Virgin Martyr,"— "The Duke of Milan," 1623; "The Bondman," 1624; "The Roman Actor," 1629; "The Picture," 1630; "The Fatal Dowry," 1632; "The Maid of Honour," 1632; "A New Way to Pay Old Debts," 1633; and "The Great Duke of Florence," 1636. After all, it may be that Mr Warburton's cook, who is said to have covered his pies and lighted his fires with some twelve of Massinger's plays, may have done both the world and the poet a service.

Gifford entertained the notion that Massinger must have turned Roman Catholic when he was at Oxford. The notion is based upon the use that Massinger makes of a Roman Catholic legend in "The Virgin Martyr," and the fair character that he gives to a Jesuit priest in "The Renegado." One wants proof more relative: this only proves that Massinger was able to treat Roman Catholics with dramatic impartiality.[1] Coleridge's notion about Massinger's democratic leanings is equally questionable. Massinger, indeed, makes one of his characters sigh for the happy times when lords were styled fathers of families. He makes another say that princes do well to cherish goodness where they find it, for—

> " They being men and not gods, Contarino,
> They can give wealth and titles, but not virtues."

He makes Timoleon administer a sharp rebuke to the men of Syracuse for corruption prevailing in high places, and rate them soundly for preferring golden dross to liberty.

In the same play ("The Bondman"), he takes an evident pleasure in representing the indignities put upon high-fed madams by their insurgent slaves: and in "The City Madam" he ridicules

---

[1] But see article on Massinger in 'Encyclopædia Britannica.'

with much zest the pretensions of upstart wealth. But all these
things are as consistent with a benevolent paternal Toryism as with
Whiggery, and are to be looked upon as indications simply of the
dramatist's range of sympathies, and not of any discontent on his
part with the established framework of government or society.

Hartley Coleridge, in his rambling and racy introduction to
Massinger and Ford, commits himself to the extraordinary statement that Massinger had no humour. "Massinger would have
been the dullest of jokers, if Ford had not contrived to be still
duller." I have already remarked on the severity and ungeniality
of Ford's character; but there is nothing connected with Massinger to imply that he bore the least resemblance to Ford in this
point. On the contrary, all Massinger's characteristics are those
of a widely sympathetic man, with a genial propensity to laughter.
He has written several very obscene passages, such as the courtship of Asotus by Corisca in "The Bondman," but they are all
pervaded by genuine humour; and a countless number of his
scenes, such as that between Wellborn and Marrall in "A New
Way to Pay Old Debts," are irresistibly laughable. It may perhaps be said with justice that there is often a certain serious
motive underlying Massinger's humour, which connects itself with
the earnestness of his distressed life; but humour he undoubtedly had, and that of the most ebullient and irrepressible sort.

One fancies indeed, but it may be the result of our knowledge
of his painful life, that there is a certain sad didactic running
through all Massinger's work. The "Duke of Milan," by far his
greatest drama, has not the satisfying close of Shakespeare's
tragedies. It preaches directly the moral deducible from "Romeo
and Juliet," that violent delights have violent ends; but whereas
we do not vex ourselves with vain wishes that Romeo and Juliet
had been united in happy marriage, we are at the death of Sforza
and Marcelia disconcerted by the feeling that their fate ought to
have been, and easily might have been, different. And in his
other tragedies we are haunted at the close by a similar uneasiness: the purgation of the mind by pity and terror is not effected
—the tumult that they raise is not tranquillised. All tragedies,
of course, are susceptible of a didactic interpretation; but those
in which the didactic has a sharp edge, affect us in quite a different
way from those in which it is vaguely present as part of a grand
and overwhelming impression; and Massinger's conclusions have
a sharp edge. Again, his romantic tragi-comedies, and even his
comedies, have also a serious tinge, apart from the natural interest
of the development of the story. They do not directly preach at
us, but the colour of the subject-matter suggests that the dramatist
was not wholly free-minded and studious only of dramatic and
scenic impressions.

## XI.—JAMES SHIRLEY (1596–1667).

More is known about Shirley than about some of his more distinguished, or at least abler contemporaries. He was born in London, and educated at Merchant Tailors' School, St John's College, Oxford, and Catherine Hall, Cambridge. He took orders, and was presented to a living in Hertfordshire; but in a short time he became Roman Catholic, left his living, turned schoolmaster for a while; and at last, finding this employment also "uneasy to him, he retired to the metropolis, lived in Gray's Inn, and set up for a playmaker." He was twenty-eight or twenty-nine when he went up to London (probably in 1624 or 1625), and in the course of a few years he got into the full swing of dramatic composition, and produced plays at the rate of two or three or four a-year. The chief were—"Love's Tricks," a comedy, 1625; "The Maid's Revenge," a tragedy, 1626; "The Brothers," a comedy, 1626; "The Witty Fair One," a comedy, 1628; "The Wedding," a comedy, 1628; "The Grateful Servant," a tragi-comedy, 1629; "The Changes, or Love in a Maze," 1632; "The Ball" (written in conjunction with Chapman, but almost wholly Shirley's), 1632; "The Gamester," a comedy, 1633; "The Example" (containing an imitation of Ben Jonson's *humours*), 1634; "The Opportunity," 1634; "The Traitor," a tragedy (perhaps Shirley's best), 1635; "The Lady of Pleasure" (perhaps the best of his comedies), 1635; "The Cardinal," a tragedy (an attempt to compete with Webster's "Duchess of Malfi"), 1641. Under the Commonwealth, Shirley, after some vicissitudes during the civil war, was obliged to return to his old trade of teaching; and at the Restoration, though several of his plays were revived, he made no attempt to resume his connection with the stage.

Shirley's first essay in print was a poem entitled "Echo" (afterwards printed under the more suggestive title of "Narcissus"). A man's youthful work is always a good index of his tendencies and powers, and in this poem the nature of Shirley's gifts shines unmistakably through the lines. He goes boldly to work with jaunty self-assured ease: there is pith and "go" in his style; he is borne on with pride in his triumphs of expression, but he is victorious with weapons which other men have provided. He has no originality of idea, or situation, or diction.

The same thing strikes us in his plays. Lamb says of him that "he was the last of a great race, all of whom spoke nearly the same language, and had a set of moral feelings and notions in common." But the really great men of the race, not merely Shakespeare, Jonson, and Fletcher, but Chapman, Dekker, Webster, Ford, and Massinger, spoke the same language with a difference; and each had moral feelings and notions of his own. In Shirley the distinctive individual difference was small, both in amount and in kind: he was not a great man in himself, but an essentially small man inspired by the creations of great men. Fletcher was his master and exemplar, as Shakespeare was Massinger's; but he imitated much more closely, was much more completely carried away by this model than Massinger was. And although his language and moral feelings and notions (even as regards female types and kings) are Fletcher's, and he had most ambition to emulate Fletcher's dashing and brilliant manner, yet Shirley's plays contain frequent echoes of other dramatists. One great interest in reading him is that he reminds us so often of the situations and characters of his predecessors. It is good for the critic, if for nobody else, to read Shirley, because there he finds emphasised all that told most effectively on the playgoers of the period. We read Greene and Marlowe to know what the Elizabethan drama was in its powerful but awkward youth; Shirley to know what it was in its declining but facile and still powerful old age.

------

There were many other able playmakers in the great dramatic period, and notably four Thomases, Thomas Heywood, Thomas Rowley, Thomas Randolph, and Thomas May, but no other that can be called great, either by originality or by imitation. True, Charles Lamb has called Thomas Heywood "a prose Shakespeare," and that prolific author of 250 plays doubtless has a certain sweet vein of grandmotherly tenderness in him; but if Elia had lived till now, he would, perhaps, have described good old Heywood more accurately by calling him a garrulous Longfellow.

One may hope to be excused for feeling no desire to go farther down the scale than Middleton and Shirley. In studying the literature that led to the supreme efflorescence of the Elizabethan drama, one thinks no relic too humble to be worth discussing; but when so many large and powerful minds invite our companionship, and continue always to lay before us fresh points of interest and fresh matter for thought, it is intolerably dull to turn from them to the crowd of mediocrities who hang about their doors and follow their footsteps.

# APPENDIX  A.

## OUR PLEASANT WILLY.

THREE stanzas are often quoted from Thalia's complaint regarding the decay of the theatres in Spenser's "Tears of the Muses," and it has been elaborately argued that they refer to Shakespeare.   The date of their publication is 1591.

> " And he, the man whom Nature's self had made
>     To mock herself, and truth to imitate,
> With kindly counter under mimic shade,
>     Our pleasant Willy, ah ! is dead of late; '
> With whom all joy and jolly merriment
> Is also deaded, and in dolour drent.
>
> Instead thereof scoffing Scurrility,
>     And scornful Folly with Contempt is crept,
> Rolling in rhymes of shameless ribaldry
>     Without regard or due decorum kept ;
> Each idle wit at will presumes to make,
> And doth the learned's task upon him take.
>
> But that same gentle spirit from whose pen
>     Large streams of honey and sweet nectar flow,
> Scorning the boldness of such base-born men,
>     Which dare their follies forth so rashly throw ;
> Doth rather choose to sit in idle cell,
> Than so himself to mockery to sell."

I have stated some reasons (p. 263) for refusing to believe that these stanzas, however appropriate to Shakespeare we may think them, can possibly have been applied to him in 1591.   I believe that death is, in the first stanza, real and not metaphorical, and that Willy is Spenser's friend Sidney.   Sidney's death is lamented under that name in an eclogue in Davidson's Poetical Rhapsody—"an eclogue made long since upon the death of Sir Philip Sidney."

> " Ye shepherds' boys that lead your flocks,
>     The whilst your sheep feed safely round about,
>     Break me your pipes that pleasant sound did yield,
>     Sing now no more the songs of Colin Clout :

> Lament the end of all our joy,
>   Lament the source of all annoy ;
>       Willy is dead
>       That wont to lead
> Our flocks and us in mirth and shepherds' glee :
>       Well could he sing,
>       Well dance and spring ;
> Of all the shepherds was none such as he.
>
> How often hath his skill in pleasant song
> Drawn all the water-nymphs from out their bowers !
> How have they lain the tender grass along,
> And made him garlands gay of smelling flowers !
>       Phoebus himself that conquer'd Pan,
>       Striving with Willy nothing wan ;
>           Methinks I see
>           The time when he
> Pluckt from his golden locks the laurel crown ;
>           And so to raise
>           Our Willy's praise,
> Bedeckt his head and softly set him down.
>
> The learned Muses flockt to hear his skill,
> And quite forgot their water, wood, and mount ;
> They thought his songs were done too quickly still,
> Of none but Willy's pipe they made account.
>       He sung ; they seem'd in joy to flow :
>       He ceast : they seem'd to weep for woe ;
>           The rural rout
>           All round about
> Like bees came swarming thick to hear him sing ;
>           Ne could they think
>           On meat or drink
> While Willy's music in their ears did ring.
>
> But now, alas ! such pleasant mirth is past ;
> Apollo weeps, the Muses rend their hair.
> No joy on earth that any time can last.
> See where his breathless corpse lies on the bier.
>       That self-same hand that reft his life
>       Hath turned shepherd's peace to strife.
>           Our joy is fled,
>           Our life is dead,
> Our hope, our help, our glory, all is gone :
>           Our poet's praise,
>           Our happy days,
> And nothing left but grief to think thereon."

The only difficulty in the way of supposing our pleasant Willy to be Sir Philip Sidney is purely factitious.[1] It is taken for granted that all the three of Spenser's stanzas refer to the same person as the first ; and then it is argued that the death of our pleasant Willy must be only metaphorical in the first, meaning really his cessation from the composition of comedies, because in the third he is said to be producing large streams of tragedies. But any person who looks at

---

[1] The fact that Sidney did not write comedies, if we exclude his "Lady of the May" from that title, is immaterial. The poet only says that Nature had made him to write comedies—"to mock herself with kindly counter under mimic shade."

the whole lament will see that two different persons must be intended. The sequence of thought is this: The first of the three stanzas laments that Willy is dead ; the second, that scoffing scurrility and scornful folly have occupied the stage in his stead ; the third approves the conduct of a living and producing writer in abstaining from co-operation with base-born play-wrights. If we suppose "that same gentle spirit" to refer back to our pleasant Willy, and not forward to the next line, we land ourselves in a contradiction whether we regard Willy's death as literal or metaphorical, because this gentle spirit is both really and poetically alive—large streams of honey and nectar are flowing from him. I believe that in the third stanza Thalia refers to Spenser himself, and that here we have his justification of himself for complaining of the withdrawal of learning from the stage, and yet sending no compositions of his own to prop it up. Some such justification was certainly required : Spenser could hardly have asked why learning had forsaken the stage, without giving a reason for withholding contributions from his own copious pen. The vanity of the excuse will not surprise any one who knows what he makes Hobinol and others say concerning Colin Clout.

# APPENDIX B.

---

### AN UNRECOGNISED SONNET BY SHAKESPEARE !

In the Elizabethan age of our literature, when there were neither dailies, weeklies, monthlies, nor quarterlies in which it might be possible to express a friendly partiality for a new book, it was a common mark of friendship to send to an author a set of eulogistic verses, to be printed at the beginning of his book as a guarantee of its worth. In those days very few books were published without one or more such introductory poems of commendation. It was, perhaps, inevitable that this peculiar form of literature should, even in the rich Elizabethan age, be remarkable chiefly for poverty of invention ; the circle of ideas for these commendations is almost necessarily limited. We find in great plenty such verses as the following :—

> He that shall read thy characters, Nic. Breton,
> And weigh them well, must say they are well written ;

or—

> Who reads this book with a judicious eye,
> Will in true judgment true discretion try ;

or—

> Read with regard what here with due regard
> Our second Ciceronian Southwell sent.

Such is the commonplace commendatory poem ; and the friendly eulogiums of the greatest masters, Ben Jonson, Beaumont, Fletcher, Chapman, or Ford, rise very little, if at all, above the level. Most of them are of the three-piled hyperbolical order—containing loud assertions of merit with loud defiance of contradiction, and playing if possible upon the name of the piece or of the author. Even Chapman's ingenuity could devise nothing better than the following lines in a eulogium on Ben Jonson's "Volpone, or The Fox :"—

> Come yet more forth, Volpone, and thy chase
> Perform to all length, for thy breath will serve thee ;
> The usurer shall never wear thy case,
> Men do not hunt to kill but to preserve thee.

A very fair impression of the general character of commendatory verses may be got from the following set composed by Henry Upcher for Greene's "Menaphon": in cleverness and prettiness this is distinctly above the average :—

> Delicious words, the life of wanton wit,
>   That doth inspire our souls with sweet content,
> Why hath your father Hermes thought it fit,
>   Mine eyes should surfeit by my heart's consent?
> Full twenty summers have I fading seen,
>   And twenty Floras in their golden guise ;
> Yet never viewed I such a pleasant *Greene*,
>   As this whose garnish'd gleads, compar'd, devise.
> Of all the flowers a *Lilly* once I loved,
>   Whose labouring beauty branch'd itself abroad ;
> But now old age his glory hath remov'd,
>   And greener objects are mine eyes abroad.
> No country to the downs of *Arcadie*,
>   Where Aganippe's ever-springing wells
> Do moist the meads with bubbling melody,
>   And makes me muse what more in Delos dwells.
> There feeds our *Menaphon's* celestial Muse,
>   There makes his pipe his pastoral report ;
> Which strained now a note above his use,
>   Foretells he'll ne'er come chaunt of Thoae's sport.
> Read all that list, and read till you mislike,
>   Condemn who can, so envy be not judge ;
> No, read who can, swell higher, lest it shriek,
>   *Robin*, thou hast done well, care not who grudge.

It has been remarked that Shakespeare is not known to have contributed any such expression of goodwill to the works of any of his friends, and the reason has been supposed to be that he shrank from the suspicion of hollowness and insincerity to which the practice had become liable. But I am half inclined to believe that I have fallen upon an exception to this rule, made, in fact, before the rule was formed, a few years after Shakespeare's arrival in London. There is a sonnet prefixed to John Florio's 'Second Fruits,' published in the spring of 1591, which is not without certain marks of Shakespearian parentage. 'Second Fruits' is not, perhaps, *primâ facie*, a book where one would naturally expect to find a recommendation by Shakespeare ; being nothing but a book of dialogues and aphorisms, printed in parallel columns of English and Italian, to help those speaking the one language to acquire a knowledge of the other. But those who remember the interest then taken in the Italian language, the probability that Shakespeare shared that interest, and the fact that both Shakespeare and Florio, who was a famed teacher of Italian, were *protégés* of the young Earl of Southampton, will not be inclined to deny the authorship on external probabilities, if the sonnet seems otherwise worthy of so distinguished an origin. It runs as follows, the compliment turning upon the title "Fruits," the name Florio, and the season of publication :—

PHAETON TO HIS FRIEND FLORIO.

Sweet friend, whose name agrees with thy increase,
How fit a rival art thou of the Spring !
For when each branch hath left his flourishing,
And green-lock'd Summer's shady pleasures cease,
She makes the Winter's storms repose in peace
And spends her franchise on each living thing :
The daisies sprout, the little birds do sing ;
Herbs, gums, and plants do vaunt of their release.
So when that all our English wits lay dead
(Except the Laurel that is ever green),
Thou with thy fruits our barrenness o'erspread
And set thy flowery pleasance to be seen.
Such fruits, such flow'rets of morality,
Were ne'er before brought out of Italy.

The concluding couplet is bald, apparently from the necessity that the author was under of returning from his description of the seasons to the dry reality in hand ; but otherwise, those familiar with the commendatory verses of the period will recognise at once its superiority to commonplace. Excepting always the splendid sonnet signed " W. R.," prefixed to the second issue of Spenser's ‘Faery Queen,’ which is so good that it is hard to resist a conviction that it is Spenser's own, one might safely challenge all detractors to produce half-a-dozen better commendatory poems from the works of that generation. Whereas most others strike us as making desperate efforts to find something to say, Phaeton seems to hit easily upon a fresh and fruitful idea. He is hyperbolical, of course, in his praise, but his hyperbole is not three-piled ; on the contrary, there is a peculiar earnestness and simplicity in his tone. This is all the more noticeable because the main idea would seem to have been suggested by one of the sonnets of Petrarch, which professes to have been sent with a present of flowers in the spring. There is no imitation beyond the borrowing of the main thought : Phaeton follows it out in his own way. It is no exaggeration to say that almost any other panegyrist in that age would have played upon the words " Florio " and " Fruits " from beginning to end of the sonnet.

Nothing is more distinctive of Shakespeare than the intense earnestness of his descriptions of the coming on of Winter and of Night, corresponding naturally to the genuine ecstasy of his descriptions of Spring and of Morning. This is no idolatrous fancy about Shakespeare, but a conclusion that is irresistible when we place his descriptions side by side with the descriptions of his contemporaries. It is not easy to analyse the peculiarities of expression that produce this effect in terms impervious to cavil ; but one may venture to say that in their descriptions of Winter and Spring, or of the allied seasons, Night and Morning, his contemporaries are quainter, or more diffuse, or more frivolous, or more conventional, than he is. Shakespeare does use the conventional classical personifications in his less serious moods ; but much more habitually than his contemporaries he personifies the powers of Nature directly for himself. Thus where Spenser has—

>     At last fair Hesperus in highest sky
>     Had spent his lamp and brought forth dawning light,—

Shakespeare has—

>     Night's candles are burnt out, and jocund Day
>     Stands tiptoe on the misty mountain tops.

Where Spenser has—

>     The joyous day 'gan early to appear,
>     And fair Aurora, fro the dewy bed
>     Of aged Tithon 'gan herself to rear
>     With rosy cheeks, for shame as blushing red,—

Shakespeare has the incomparable lines—

>     And sullen Night with slow sad steps descended
>     To ugly hell ; when lo ! the blushing Morrow
>     Lends light to all fair eyes that light will borrow.

Take, again, Drayton's description of the morning twilight—

>     Now ere the purple dawning yet did spring,
>     The joyful lark began to stretch her wing ;
>     And now the cock, the morning's trumpeter,
>     Play'd " Hunt's-up " for the day star to appear:
>     Down slideth Phoebe from her crystal chair,
>     'Sdaining to lend her light unto the air.

This is very sweet and pretty, but it wants the glowing earnestness
of Shakespeare's description of a somewhat later moment—

>     Lo ! now the gentle lark, weary of rest,
>     From his moist cabinet mounts up on high,
>     And wakes the Morning, from whose silver breast
>     The Sun ariseth in his Majesty :
>     Who doth the world so gloriously behold
>     That cedar-tops and hills seem burnish'd gold.

In all Shakespeare's descriptions we are conscious of a deep and
vivid sense of the pains of darkness and barrenness, and the pleasures
of relief from them.  And in the sonnet of Phaeton's, though the
occasion did not call for the deepest feeling, and though the expression
is not so uniformly mature, we are conscious of the same genuine
earnestness.  Phaeton also personifies directly, and gives to his personification of Spring a fuller and less conventional life than we have
seen in any other Elizabethan poet.  The reader will best understand
our argument by comparing Phaeton's treatment of the Seasons with
the following passages from Drayton :—

>     As when fair Ver, dight in her flowery rail,
>     In her new-colour'd livery decks the earth :
>     And glorious Titan spreads his sunshine veil,
>     To bring to pass her tender infants' birth :
>     Such was her beauty which I then possest,
>     With whose embracings all my youth was blest.

> As in September, when our year resigns
> The glorious sun unto the watery signs,
> Which through the clouds looks on the earth in scorn,
> The little bird yet to salute the morn
> Upon the naked branches sets her foot
> (The leaves now lying on the mossy root),
> And there a silly chirruping doth keep,
> As though she fain would sing, yet fain would weep:
> Praising fair Summer, that too soon is gone,
> Or mourning Winter too fast coming on ;
> In this sad plight I mourn for thy return.

When we compare more minutely the diction of Phaeton's sonnet with the language used by Shakespeare in his plays and his sonnets regarding the Seasons, some very curious coincidences are brought to light. The word "franchise," which occurs in Phaeton's sonnet, has a curious history in Shakespeare's early plays. This fine-sounding word and its compounds, which Dryden thought worthy of his "majestic march and energy divine," was not by any means common among the Elizabethan writers : Spenser does not use it in the first three books of his 'Faery Queen,' though he has plenty of opportunities. But it was a very favourite word with Shakespeare in his early days. He uses "enfranchise" in the sense of setting at liberty in "Titus Andronicus," in the "Two Gentlemen of Verona," in "Richard III.," twice in "Richard II.," and in "Venus and Adonis"—all written, according to Malone, before 1593. He seems then to have felt that he had rather overdone the figure ; for, in "Love's Labour's Lost" (supposed to be his next play), he puts it into the mouth of Don Adriano de Armado—"Sirrah Costard, I will enfranchise thee ; " and after having thus, with characteristic self-irony, laughed at his own fine-sounding term, he thenceforth uses it more in a political and technical sense, as in "Coriolanus" and in "Antony and Cleopatra."

But it would be idle to found any identification upon single words. What any person ought to do who is disposed to discuss, if not to believe in, the identity of Phaeton and Shakespeare, is to examine minutely Shakespeare's conceptions of the Seasons, together with the words and images he uses in expressing them. If one finds in Shakespeare the peculiar circle of ideas and diction which appear in Phaeton's sonnet, and the same circle cannot be shown to exist in any other Elizabethan poet, then one is entitled to claim a presumption, though far from a certainty, in favour of the identity of Phaeton with Shakespeare. This circle of expressions, and not any single expression, must be made the basis of the argument.

Let us look, then, at Shakespeare's sonnets, where, as in his earlier plays, the Seasons frequently occur. In the opening sonnets, as our readers remember, Shakespeare urges his friend to preserve his beauty to another generation, warning him of the rapid and inevitable progress of decay. In the fifth sonnet he says :—

> For never-resting Time leads Summer on
> To hideous Winter, and confounds him there ;
> Sap check'd with frost and lusty leaves quite gone
> Beauty o'ersnow'd and bareness everywhere :

> Then, were not summer's distillation left,
>     A liquid prisoner pent in walls of glass,
> Beauty's effect with beauty were bereft,
>     Nor it nor no remembrance what it was.
> But flowers distill'd, though they with Winter meet,
> Leese but their show; their substance still lives sweet.

Here the idea of the vital principles, the germs, of natural things kept alive throughout the Winter as "liquid *prisoners*," corresponds exactly with Phaeton's idea of Spring spending her *franchise* on each living thing, and with the idea of natural things vaunting of their *release*. The ideas are, as it were, segments of the same circle. And looking at the words used to express them, it may be noticed that "imprisonment" and "enfranchisement" occur as obverse expressions of the same idea in one of Shakespeare's earliest plays—"Titus Andronicus," iv. 2, 124—

> And from that womb where you *imprison'd* were
> He is *enfranchised* and come to light.

They occur also in the same connection in one of his latest plays—the "Winter's Tale," ii. 2, 60—

> This child was *prisoner* to the womb, and is
> By law and process of great Nature thence
> Freed and *enfranchised*.

The idea of Summer's distillation as a liquid prisoner during Winter is a carrying out and completing of the less recondite idea of Spring as an enfranchising power. Simple as the conception may seem, the present writer has met neither the one expression nor the other among all the numerous descriptions of Spring by other Elizabethan writers; and it seems to him to have the peculiar vividness and depth that are characteristic of Shakespeare's conception of the seasons of Winter and Spring. Can any more patient and learned student of Elizabethan poetry produce the same conception from any of Shakespeare's contemporaries?

In Sonnet XII. we find the following picture of the mournful time of the year:—

> When lofty trees I see barren of leaves,
> Which erst from heat did canopy the herd,
> And Summer's green all girded up in sheaves,
> Borne on the bier with white and bristly beard.

The aspects here presented correspond very closely with the aspects in Phaeton's sonnet, the succinct "shady pleasures" being represented by a whole line; but there is nothing very distinctive in the expression, and one would not build upon that. What one does to some extent build upon, is the association of death ("borne on the *bier*") and bareness, as in Phaeton's sonnet, with the approach of the season of Winter. The same association appears in Sonnet XIII. (where also there is a condensation of impressions similar to the condensation in "green-lock'd Summer's shady pleasures," and peculiarly Shakespearian):—

> Which husbandry in honour might uphold
> Against the stormy gusts of Winter's day,
> And barren rage of death's eternal cold.

Again, in Shakespeare's 98th Sonnet, we find the following description of the reviving influence of Spring :—

> From you have I been absent in the spring,
> When proud-pied April, dress'd in all his trim,
> *Hath put a spirit of youth in every thing,*
> That heavy Saturn laugh'd and leap'd with him.

The mood here is lighter, more ebullient, than in Phaeton, as becomes the occasion, and harmonises with the playful treatment of the grim classical personage : but the italicised line has a certain correspondence in form with Phaeton's—"*And spends her franchise on each living thing;*" and the epithet "proud-pied" corresponds both in form and in position with "green-lock'd." Apart, however, from this, let the reader note from the two passages Shakespeare's association of a *vaunting youthful spirit* with Spring, and then turn to the play of "Richard II.," act i. scene 3. Young Bolingbroke and Mowbray have quarrelled mortally, and the lists have been set up at Coventry before the King and his nobles that they may fight their quarrel to the death. In the course of the preliminary formalities Bolingbroke expresses his confidence in the issue, and vaunts in his youthful sap, saying that he is—

> Not sick, although I have to do with death,
> But *lusty, young,* and *cheerly* drawing breath.

He invokes the blessing of his father upon his arms—

> O thou, the earthly author of my blood,
> Whose *youthful spirit,* in me regenerate,
> Doth with a twofold vigour lift me up
> To reach a victory above my head,
> Add proof unto mine armour with thy prayers.

Gaunt, in answer to this, bids him "rouse up his youthful blood." Shakespeare has now to find for Mowbray a suitable balance to this vaunting. He wishes to make Mowbray express in turn how delighted *he* is at the prospect of the encounter. When Marlowe in "Edward II." had to make Gaveston express intense delight at his return from banishment, he used the following image :—

> The shepherd nipt with biting Winter's rage
> Frolics not more to see the painted Spring
> Than I do to behold your Majesty.

Now the form used by Shakespeare in the following lines to express Mowbray's exultation is so similar to this passage in Marlowe, with which Shakespeare must have been familiar, that it almost looks as if this had been in his mind when he wrote them ; and if so, the association between Spring and enfranchisement had occurred to him directly, as it had to Phaeton :—

> However God or fortune cast my lot,
> There lives or dies, true to King Richard's throne,
> A loyal, just, and upright gentleman.
> *Never did captive with a freer heart*
> *Cast off his chains of bondage and embrace*
> *His golden uncontroll'd enfranchisement,*
> More than my dancing soul doth celebrate
> This feast of battle with mine adversary.

The pride of the youthful spirit, the "gleeful boast" of everything in the Spring, and the sense of newly acquired freedom as expressed by the word enfranchisement, would seem to have been in Shakespeare's mind parts of one circle of ideas and expressions. The same association of youthful spirit and enfranchisement appears in his description of Adonis's horse—

> But when he saw his love, his *youth's* fair fee,
> *He held such petty bondage in disdain ;*
> Throwing the base thong from his bending crest,
> *Enfranchising* his mouth, his back, his breast.

Can this same definite circle of words and ideas be pointed out in any other Elizabethan writer? If not, is there not some probability that Shakespeare and Phaeton are the same? While Shakespeare makes the Spring "put a spirit of youth in everything," Phaeton makes the Spring "spend her franchise on each living thing"; but Shakespeare twice uses youthful spirit and enfranchisement as allied words and ideas, and twice describes birth as an enfranchisement. Moreover, Shakespeare speaks of the child as being imprisoned before its birth, and of natural things as being imprisoned before their birth in the Spring-time. The word "vaunt" is so common that we should not care to lay any stress upon its being used both by Shakespeare and by Phaeton to express the personified feelings of the Spring. One thing, however, we may remark as characteristic of Shakespeare. Phaeton does not use the word in the same conventional meaningless way as "Summer's *pride*," or "Spring's *proud* livery" : he carries the figure a little deeper, gives it a meaning and a new life by suggesting *why* things vaunt in the Spring-time—they "*vaunt of their release*" from the tyranny of Winter.

Such an identification, of course, does not admit of demonstrative proof : all that we can possibly provide in the absence of authentic contemporary testimony that Shakespeare and Phaeton were the same, is a concurrence of presumptions, separately feeble, severally open to banter, but together affording as firm a ground for belief as can be had in such matters. I fear the attempt to trace the movements of Shakespeare's mind may be regarded as supersubtle ; but I cannot refrain from noting another small coincidence. In the "Two Gentlemen of Verona," written, according to Malone, in the same year as the sonnet, the word "enfranchise" occurs in curious proximity to "Phaethon." When the Duke (iii. 1) detects Valentine in a design to carry away Silvia, and takes a sonnet from the lover's person, he cries—

> What's here!
>   'Silvia, this night I will *enfranchise* thee.'
> 'Tis so : and here's the ladder for the purpose.
> Why, *Phaethon*,—for thou art Merops' son,—
> Wilt thou aspire to guide the heavenly car,
> And with thy daring folly burn the world.

Now there is not a very strong similarity between the situation of Phaethon and the situation of a young man about to elope with his mistress—at least not enough for the one directly to suggest the other. The elopement of the Duke's daughter with Valentine was not likely to set the world on fire. If, however, Shakespeare wrote Phaeton's sonnet, the marked word "enfranchise," which was evidently a sweet morsel to his mouth, would naturally suggest the sonnet ; and the faint resemblance between Valentine and Phaethon would flash upon his mind when the idea of Phaethon's ambition had been suggested by this accidental reminder ! I need hardly say that the coincidence may be purely accidental, and that the ambition of Valentine in "reaching at stars because they shone over him," may have been quite enough to suggest the ambition of Phaethon.

So much for the correspondence of the words and substance of Phaeton's imagery with the Shakespearian circle. The rest of the sonnet offers less field for telling correspondence : every poet in those days played upon names, every poet admired Spenser, and every poet was interested in what came out of Italy. Shakespeare indulged in all sorts of puns upon names, serious and sportive ; he admired Spenser, as appears from traces of Spenser's influence, even if we reject the open compliment in the disputed "Passionate Pilgrim"; and the beginning of act i. of the "Taming of the Shrew" shows that his thoughts had turned to Italy as the nursery of arts (although a passage in "Richard II." shows that he had no liking for the slavish imitation of Italian manners). But in these respects he stood by no means alone. In Phaeton's manner, however, of playing upon the name there is something Shakespearian, if not peculiarly and distinctively so. The reader will have noticed that both in Harry Upcher's verses and in Chapman's, the puns upon the names are introduced indirectly : we are not expressly informed that the names are susceptible of such and such an interpretation, but the pun is made, and we are left to see it for ourselves. I have looked over a good number of these sonnets and verses, and find the same thing in them all. But in Phaeton's sonnet it is different. Here there is no pun at all in the strict sense of the word, there is merely a serious abstract statement—"whose name agrees with thy increase." Now this form occurs several times in Shakespeare. In "Richard II.," when the king asks, "How is't with aged Gaunt ?" the sick old man answers—

> O, how that name befits my composition !

In "Cymbeline," when Imogen tells Lucius that her name is Fidele, he answers—

> Thou dost approve thyself the very same ;
> Thy name fits well thy faith, thy faith thy name.

In both these cases the form of the expression corresponds as closely as possible with Phaeton's; and simple as the form may appear, and though it might in the present day be paralleled from Bret Harte, I have not found the same form in any Elizabethan except Shakespeare.

If it proved anything, one might go through Phaeton's sonnet word by word, as well as line by line, and point out that the cardinal verbs occur in Shakespeare in similar situations. "Agrees with," "left" (for *left off*), "spends," "set," and words cognate to them, are to be found in exactly parallel situations. But, although I have a general impression that these four constructions are not so common in other Elizabethans as in Shakespeare, one does not pretend to the super-human reading that would entitle one to affirm that proposition absolutely and dogmatically. I therefore only suggest, with all willingness to accept demonstrated correction, whether it is not the case.

An obvious objection might be raised on the form of Phaeton's sonnet. It is not composed like Shakespeare's in the form of three quatrains and a couplet, but consists of an eight-line stave and a six-line stave. This objection is met by pointing to the date, 1591. The form ultimately adopted by Shakespeare was established in England by Daniel and Drayton in 1592 and 1594. Sidney, who set the fashion of sonnet-writing at the time, followed the Italian model, as Phaeton does.

Finally—I put this argument last, though it was the first to strike me—attentive readers of poetry must have remarked that the effort of fully realising what they read differs for different poets. In all poets we may encounter passages of special difficulty; but, on the whole, each poet keeps us at a particular intellectual strain. This is determined chiefly by the degree of abstractness or abstruseness in the language, and by the degree of clearness and power in the ideas. Shakespeare's language is peculiarly abstract, but his ideas are clear and definite: as we read, we are baffled by the abstractness, but stimulated by the clearness and power: once excited and braced up to the requisite intellectual pitch, we read him with greater ease than a less abstract but more intangible and feeble writer. Phaeton's sonnet is not a large field to experiment upon; but, as nearly as I can judge, it requires very much the same intellectual strain as one of Shakespeare's sonnets. Let the reader compare it for himself with the sonnets of Sidney, Daniel, Drayton, and Shakespeare; he will be struck both with special expressions and with a certain clear firmness and boldness in the general method. Phaeton's sonnet, in fact, first struck me as being Shakespeare's some thirteen years ago, when I had been spending some weeks over the sonnet literature of the Eliza-bethan period. I had met with the sonnet before and been suffi-ciently impressed by it to copy it out simply as a very superior specimen of the commendatory sonnet; but it did not strike me as Shakespeare's till I happened to take it up when my mind was full of the styles of the various sonneteers of the time. I afterwards made the detailed comparisons which are here set forth.

On the whole I venture to think that I have altogether produced a sufficient number of presumptions in favour of the identification of

Shakespeare and Phaeton to warrant me in submitting the sonnet to the consideration of those who take an interest in such matters. *If* this sonnet is Shakespeare's, it was the first known composition of his that saw the light of print. When we remember how the player was jeered at by University men for trying to write plays and thus attempting the task of the learned, we see a characteristic meaning in his use of the name 'Phaethon.'

Of course, seeing that Phaeton's sonnet appeared in 1591, it is open to anybody to argue that Shakespeare may have read the sonnet, and been so impressed by it that it formed his whole habit in dealing with the Seasons for the rest of his life. For any critic who is base enough to upset my elaborate arguments in this way, I have no answer but astonished silence.

A few particulars may be added about John Florio, to whom the sonnet was addressed. He was the most eminent teacher of Italian in London at the end of the sixteenth and the beginning of the seventeenth century, and ultimately numbered Prince Henry and the Queen among his pupils. Naturally also at a time when the literature of Italy was exercising so powerful an influence on our own, he was a favourite with poets. Ben Jonson presented a copy of 'The Fox' to him with the inscription, "To his loving father and worthy friend, master John Florio, Ben Jonson seals this testimony of his friendship and love."

Florio was born in London in 1545, his parents being Italian refugees, belonging to the persecuted sect of the Waldenses. During the reign of Mary, they had to seek an asylum on the Continent, but Florio reappeared in 1576 as tutor to a son of the Bishop of Durham, at Magdalen College, Oxford. His first publication was in 1578, an extraordinary collection of wise sayings on all subjects from Italian authors. It bore the alliterative and punning title—'Florio, his First Fruits.' Shakespeare was evidently familiar with this storehouse of gnomic wisdom, which deserves the attention of the New Shakspere Society. It was dedicated to the Earl of Leicester. Thereafter Florio, who loved to subscribe himself "Resolute John Florio," and was evidently a man of great energy and industry as well as learning and wit, matriculated at Oxford, his college being Magdalen, and apparently remained there for some time teaching Italian and French to certain scholars of the University. His 'Second Fruits' appeared in 1591. This is the work to which Phaeton's sonnet is prefixed. It would appear from the preface that by this time he was established in London, and was already engaged on his most laborious work, an Italian dictionary, which was published in 1598, under the title 'A World of Words.' In the preface to this last book, he speaks of himself as having been for some years in "the pay and patronage" of the Earl of Southampton, Shakespeare's first patron. There is a curious passage in the address to the reader, which seems to refer to Phaeton's sonnet: "There is another sort of leering curs, that rather

snarl than bite, whereof I could instance in one, who lighting upon a
good sonnet of a gentleman's, a friend of mine, that loved better to be
a poet than to be counted so, called the author a rymer, notwithstanding he had more skill in good poetry than my sly gentleman
seemed to have in good manners or humanity." That this refers to
Phaeton's sonnet is probable from the fact that the whole address is a
boisterously vituperative retort in the manner of the period to some
'H. S.,' who had spoken disrespectfully of Florio's 'Second Fruits.'
Florio's last publication was a translation of Montaigne's essays,
undertaken on the advice of Sir Edward Wotton, and prosecuted
under the encouragement of six noble ladies, his pupils. This
appeared in 1603. Thereafter Florio was fortunate enough to obtain
royal patronage, and lived to the good old age of eighty, dying in
1625. To Warburton we owe the supremely absurd suggestion that
this versatile Italian was the original of Holofernes in ' Love's Labour's
Lost.' Shakespeare was conjectured to have thus caricatured him
because he criticised the Chronicle Histories in vogue on the English
stage when Shakespeare began to write.

PRINTED BY WILLIAM BLACKWOOD AND SONS.

## Opinions of the British and American Press—*Continued.*

**Civil Service Gazette.**—"We have had occasion to notice the peculiar features and merits of 'Stormonth's Dictionary,' and we need not repeat our commendations both of the judicious plan and the admirable execution. . . . This is a pre-eminently good, comprehensive, and authentic English lexicon, embracing not only all the words to be found in previous dictionaries, but all the modern words—scientific, new coined, and adopted from foreign languages, and now naturalised and legitimised."

**Notes and Queries.**—"The whole constitutes a work of high utility."

**Dublin Irish Times.**—"The book has the singular merit of being a dictionary of the highest order in every department and in every arrangement, without being cumbersome; whilst for ease of reference there is no dictionary we know of that equals it. . . . For the library table it is also, we must repeat, precisely the sort of volume required, and indispensable to every large reader or literary worker."

**Liverpool Mercury.**—"Every page bears the evidence of extensive scholarship and laborious research, nothing necessary to the elucidation of present-day language being omitted. . . . As a book of reference for terms in every department of English speech, this work must be accorded a high place—in fact, it is quite a library in itself. . . . It is a marvel of accuracy."

**New York Tribune.**—"The work exhibits all the freshness and best results of modern lexicographic scholarship, and is arranged with great care, so as to facilitate reference."

**New York Mail and Express.**—"It is certainly a monumental work."

**Philadelphia Times.**—"Its merits will be discovered and commended until the book takes its place among our standard and best English dictionaries."

**Christian Intelligencer, New York.**—"A trustworthy, truly scholarly dictionary of our English language."

**Boston Gazette.**—"There can be but little doubt that, when completed, the work will be one of the most serviceable and most accurate that English lexicography has yet produced for general use."

**Boston Post.**—"The work will be a most valuable addition to the library of the scholar and of the general reader. It can have for the present no possible rival in its own field."

**Toronto Globe.**—"In every respect this is one of the best works of the kind in the language."

WILLIAM BLACKWOOD & SONS, Edinburgh and London.

# LIST OF

# Educational Works

Published by

## William Blackwood & Sons

45 GEORGE STREET, EDINBURGH

AND

37 PATERNOSTER ROW, LONDON

# English Composition.

## A Manual of English Prose Literature, Biographical and Critical : designed mainly to show characteristics of style. By WILLIAM MINTO, M.A., Prof. of Logic and English Literature in the University of Aberdeen. Second Edition, crown 8vo, 7s. 6d.

"A masterly manual of English prose literature." —*Standard.*

"Will be welcomed by those who are capable of appreciating excellent workmanship. It is not rash to say that this work is the first scientific treatment of the subject by an English writer. . . . About the ability as well as the originality of the work there cannot be two opinions. The views pronounced are expressed in terse, weighty, incisive *dicta*—sentences to be carried away as a geologist carries away a sample. . . . It is the best English book on the subject."—*Observer.*

"As a history of English literature, the present work is characterised by several features that are novel. . . . He has conceived a methodical plan for exhaustive criticism, founded on the newest analysis of the devices and the qualities of style. . . . It is most elaborate and thorough in the conception, and is expounded with perfect clearness."—*Examiner.*

"Mr Minto's is no common book, but a very careful and well-considered survey of the wide field he traverses—a survey undertaken not without considerable critical competency and large equipment of knowledge."—*Scotsman.*

"It is not often that it is our good fortune to come across so excellent a book as that before us. . . . He has approached his theme from a new point, and treated it in a new manner."—*Educational Times.*

## English Prose Composition; a Practical Manual FOR USE IN SCHOOLS. By JAMES CURRIE, LL.D., Principal of the Church of Scotland Training College, Edinburgh. Thirty-Eighth Thousand. 1s. 6d.

"We do not remember having seen a work so completely to our minds as this, which combines sound theory with judicious practice. Proceeding step by step, it advances from the formation of the shortest sentences to the composition of complete essays, the pupil being everywhere furnished with all needful assistance in the way of models and hints. Nobody can work through such a book as this without thoroughly understanding the structure of sentences, and acquiring facility in arranging and expressing his thoughts appropriately. It ought to be extensively used."—*Athenæum.*

# Mathematics.

## Primer of Geometry. An Easy Introduction to the Propositions of Euclid. By FRANCIS CUTHBERTSON, M.A., LL.D., late Fellow of Corpus Christi College, Cambridge ; Head Mathematical Master of the City of London School. 5th Edition. 1s. 6d.

"The selection is most judicious, and we believe the plan will be successful."—*Spectator.*

## The Theory of Arithmetic. By DAVID MUNN, F.R.S.E., Mathematical Master, Royal High School of Edinburgh. Crown 8vo, pp. 294. 5s.

## Treatise on Arithmetic, with numerous Exercises for Teaching in Classes. By JAMES WATSON, one of the Master of Heriot's Hospital. Fcap. 1s.

# Latin and Greek.

**Aditus Faciliores:** an Easy Latin Construing Book, with Complete Vocabulary. By A. W. POTTS, M.A., LL.D., Head-Master of the Fettes College, Edinburgh, and sometime Fellow of St John's College, Cambridge; and the Rev. C. DARNELL, M.A., Head-Master of Cargilfield Preparatory School, Edinburgh, and late Scholar of Pembroke and Downing Colleges, Cambridge. Eighth Edition. Fcap. 8vo. 3s. 6d.

**Aditus Faciliores Graeci:** an Easy Greek Construing Book, with Complete Vocabulary. By the SAME AUTHORS. Fourth Edition. Fcap. 8vo. 3s.

**A Parallel Syntax.** Greek and Latin for Beginners, with Exercises and a Greek Vocabulary. By the Rev. HERBERT W. SNEYD-KYNNERSLEY, LL.M., Trin. Coll., Cambridge; Head-Master of Sunninghill House, Ascot; Author of 'Greek Verbs for Beginners,' &c. Crown 8vo. 3s.

**Practical Rudiments of the Latin Language;** or, LATIN FORMS AND ENGLISH ROOTS. Comprising Accidence, Vocabularies, and Latin - English, English - Latin, and English Derivative Exercises, forming a complete First Latin Course, both for English and Latin Classes. By JOHN ROSS, M.A., Rector of the High School of Arbroath. Second Edition. Crown 8vo, pp. 164. 1s. 6d.

**Introduction to the Writing of Greek.** For the Use of Junior Classes. By Sir D. K. SANDFORD, A.M., D.C.L. New Edition. Crown Svo. 3s. 6d.

**Rules and Exercises in Homeric and Attic Greek,** to which is added a short System of Greek Prosody. By the SAME. New Edition. Crown 8vo. 6s. 6d.

**Greek Extracts, with Notes and Lexicon.** For the use of Junior Classes. By the SAME. New Edition. Crown 8vo. 6s.

---

*In the Press.*

**Greek Testament Lessons for Colleges, Schools,** AND PRIVATE STUDENTS. Consisting chiefly of the Sermon on the Mount, and Parables of our Lord. With Notes and Essays. By the Rev. J. HUNTER SMITH, M.A., First Assistant-Master at King Edward's School, Birmingham. One Volume, crown 8vo, with Maps.

# Mr Stormonth's
## English Dictionaries.

### I.

AN ETYMOLOGICAL AND PRONOUNCING

**Dictionary of the English Language.** Including a very Copious Selection of Scientific, Technical, and other Terms and Phrases. Designed for Use in Schools and Colleges, and as a Handy Book for General Reference. By the Rev. JAMES STORMONTH. The Pronunciation carefully revised by the Rev. P. H. PHELP, M.A. Eighth Edition, revised, with a new and enlarged Supplement. Crown 8vo, pp. 795, 7s. 6d.

"This Dictionary is admirable. The etymological part especially is good and sound. . . . The work deserves a place in every English school, whether boys' or girls'."—*Westminster Review.*

"A good Dictionary to people who do much writing is like a life-belt to people who make ocean voyages: it may, perhaps, never be needed, but it is always safest to have one at hand. This use of a dictionary, though one of the humblest, is one of the most general. For ordinary purposes a very ordinary dictionary will serve; but when one has a dictionary, it is as well to have a good one. . . . Special care seems to have been bestowed on the pronunciation and etymological derivation, and the 'root-words' which are given are most valuable in helping to a knowledge of primary significations. All through the book are evidences of elaborate and conscientious work, and any one who masters the varied contents of this dictionary will not be far off the attainment of the complete art of 'writing the English language with propriety,' in the matter of orthography at any rate."—*Belfast Northern Whig.*

"A full and complete etymological and explanatory dictionary of the English language. . . . We have not space to describe all its excellences, or to point out in detail how it differs from other lexicons; but we cannot with justice omit mentioning some of its more striking peculiarities. In the first place, it is comprehensive, including not only all the words recognised by the best authorities as sterling old English, but all the new coinages which have passed into general circulation, with a great many scientific terms, and those which come under the designation of slang. . . . The pronunciation is carefully and clearly marked in accordance with the most approved modern usage, and in this respect the Dictionary is most valuable and thoroughly reliable. As to the etymology of words, it is exhibited in a form that fixes itself upon the memory, the root-words showing the probable origin of the English words, their primary meaning, and their equivalents in other languages. Much useful information and instruction relative to prefixes, postfixes, abbreviations, and phrases from the Latin, French, and other languages, &c., appropriately follow the Dictionary, which is throughout beautifully and most correctly printed."—*Civil Service Gazette.*

"A really good and valuable dictionary."—*Journal of Education.*

"I am happy to be able to express—and that in the strongest terms of commendation—my opinion of the merits of this Dictionary. Considering the extensive field which it covers, it seems to me a marvel of painstaking labour and general accuracy. With regard to the scientific and technical words so extensively introduced into it, I must say, that in this respect I know no Dictionary that so satisfactorily meets a real and widely felt want in our literature of reference. I have compared it with the large and costly works of Latham, Wedgwood, and others, and find that in the fulness of its details, and the clearness of its definitions, it holds its own even against them. The etymology has been treated throughout with much intelligence, the most distinguished authorities, and the most recent discoveries in philological science, having been laid under careful contribution."—*Richard D. Graham, Esq., English Master, College for Daughters of Ministers of the Church of Scotland and of Professors in the Scottish Universities.*

II.

## The School Etymological Dictionary and Word-

BOOK. Combining the advantages of an ordinary Pronouncing School Dictionary and an Etymological Spelling-Book. Containing: The Dictionary—List of Prefixes—List of Postfixes—Vocabulary of Root-words, followed by English Derivations. By the SAME. Fcap. 8vo, pp. 260. 2s.

"This Dictionary, which contains every word in ordinary use, is followed up by a carefully prepared list of prefixes and postfixes, with illustrative examples, and a vocabulary of Latin, Greek, and other root-words, followed by derived English words. It will be obvious to every experienced teacher that these lists may be made available in many ways for imparting a sound knowledge of the English language, and for helping unfortunate pupils over the terrible difficulties of our unsystematic and stubborn orthography. We think this volume will be a valuable addition to the pupil's store of books, and, if rightly used, will prove a safe and suggestive guide to a sound and thorough knowledge of his native tongue."—*The Schoolmaster.*

"Mr Stormonth, in this admirable word-book, has provided the means of carrying out our principle in the higher classes, and of correcting all the inexactness and want of completeness to which the English student of English is liable. His book is an etymological dictionary curtailed and condensed. . . . The pronunciation is indicated by a neat system of symbols, easily mastered at the outset, and indeed pretty nearly speaking for themselves."—*School Board Chronicle.*

III.

## The Handy School Dictionary. For Use in Ele-

mentary Schools, and as a Pocket Reference Dictionary. By the SAME. Pp. 268. 9d.

# History.

## Epitome of Alison's History of Europe, for the

USE OF SCHOOLS. 29th Thousand. Post 8vo, pp. 604. 7s. 6d., bound in leather. Atlas to ditto, 7s.

## The Eighteen Christian Centuries. By the Rev.

JAMES WHITE, Author of 'The History of France.' Seventh Edition, post 8vo, with index. 6s.

"He goes to work upon the only true principle, and produces a picture that at once satisfies truth, arrests the memory, and fills the imagination. It will be difficult to lay hands on any book of the kind more useful and more entertaining."—*Times.*

## History of France, from the Earliest Times. By

the SAME. 6th Thousand, post 8vo, with Index. 6s.

## History of India: from the Earliest Period to the

CLOSE OF THE INDIA COMPANY'S GOVERNMENT, WITH AN EPITOME OF SUBSEQUENT EVENTS. Abridged from the Author's larger Work. By JOHN CLARK MARSHMAN, C.S.I. Crown 8vo, pp. 568. 6s. 6d. Second Edition, with Map.

"'There is only one History of India, and that is Marshman's,' exclaimed a critic when the original three-volume edition of this book appeared some years ago. He had read them all, and a whole library of books referring to periods of the history, and this was his conclusion. It is a wise and a just verdict."—*Daily Review.*

# Geography.

*Tenth Thousand.*

## Manual of Modern Geography : Mathematical,
PHYSICAL, AND POLITICAL; on a new plan, embracing a complete development of the River Systems of the Globe. By the Rev. ALEXANDER MACKAY, LL.D., F.R.G.S. Revised to date of publication. Crown 8vo, pp. 688. 7s. 6d.

This volume—the result of many years' unremitting application—is specially adapted for the use of Teachers, Advanced Classes, Candidates for the Civil Service, and proficients in geography generally.

*Forty-Ninth Thousand.*

## Elements of Modern Geography. By the SAME.
Revised to the present time. Crown 8vo, pp. 300. 3s.

The 'Elements' form a careful condensation of the 'Manual,' the order of arrangement being the same, the river-systems of the globe playing the same conspicuous part, the pronunciation being given, and the results of the latest census being uniformly exhibited. This volume is now extensively introduced into many of the best schools in the kingdom.

*One Hundred and Sixtieth Thousand.*

## Outlines of Modern Geography. By the SAME.
Revised to the present time. 18mo, pp. 112. 1s.

These 'Outlines'—in many respects an epitome of the 'Elements'—are carefully prepared to meet the wants of beginners. The arrangement is the same as in the Author's larger works. Minute details are avoided, the broad outlines are graphically presented, the accentuation marked, and the most recent changes in political geography exhibited.

*Ninth Edition, Revised.*

## The Intermediate Geography. Intended as an
Intermediate Book between the Author's 'Outlines of Geography' and 'Elements of Geography.' By the SAME. Revised to the present time. Crown 8vo, pp. 224. 2s.

*Eighty-Second Thousand.*

## First Steps in Geography. By the SAME. Re-
vised to the present time. 18mo, pp. 56. Sewed, 4d. In cloth, 6d.

## Geography of the British Empire. By the SAME.
3d.

## Elements of Physiography. By the SAME. 25th
Thousand. *See page 8.*

## OPINIONS OF DR MACKAY'S GEOGRAPHICAL SERIES.

**Annual Address of the President of the Royal Geographical Society.—** We must admire the ability and persevering research with which he has succeeded in imparting to his 'Manual' so much freshness and originality. In no respect is this character more apparent than in the plan of arrangement, by which the author commences his description of the physical geography of each tract by a sketch of its true basis or geological structure. It is, indeed, a most useful school-book in opening out geographical knowledge.

**Saturday Review.—**It contains a prodigious array of geographical facts, and will be found useful for reference.

**English Journal of Education.—** Of all the Manuals on Geography that have come under our notice, we place the one whose title is given above in the first rank. For fulness of information, for knowledge of method in arrangement, for the manner in which the details are handled, we know of no work that can, in these respects, compete with Mr Mackay's Manual.

**A. KEITH JOHNSTON, LL.D., F.R.S.E., F.R.G.S., H.M. Geographer for Scotland, Author of the 'Royal Atlas,' &c., &c.—**There is no work of the kind in this or any other language, known to me, which comes so near my *ideal* of perfection in a school-book, on the important subject of which it treats. In arrangement, style, selection of matter, clearness, and thorough accuracy of statement, it is without a rival; and knowing, as I do, the vast amount of labour and research you bestowed on its production, I trust it will be so appreciated as to insure, by an extensive sale, a well-merited reward.

**G. BICKERTON, Esq., Edinburgh Institution.—**I have been led to form a very high opinion of Mackay's 'Manual of Geography' and 'Elements of Geography,' partly from a careful examination of them, and partly from my experience of the latter as a text-book in the EDINBURGH INSTITUTION. One of their most valuable features is the elaborate Table of River-Basins and Towns which is given in addition to the ordinary Province or County List, so that a good idea may be obtained by the pupil of the natural as well as the political relationship of the towns in each country. On all matters connected with Physical Geography, Ethnography, Government, &c., the information is full, accurate, and well digested. They are books that can be strongly recommended to the student of geography.

**RICHARD D. GRAHAM, English Master, College for Daughters of Ministers of the Church of Scotland and of Professors in the Scottish Universities.—**No work with which I am acquainted so amply fulfils the conditions of a perfect text-book on the important subject of which it treats, as Dr Mackay's 'Elements of Modern Geography.' In fulness and accuracy of details, in the scientific grouping of facts, combined with clearness and simplicity of statement, it stands alone, and leaves almost nothing to be desired in the way of improvement. Eminently fitted, by reason of this exceptional variety and thoroughness, to meet all the requirements of higher education, it is never without a living interest, which adapts it to the intelligence of ordinary pupils. It is not the least of its merits that its information is abreast of all the latest developments in geographical science, accurately exhibiting both the recent political and territorial changes in Europe, and the many important results of modern travel and research.

**Spectator.—**The best Geography we have ever met with.

# Physical Geography.

## Introductory Text-Book of Physical Geography.

With Sketch-Maps and Illustrations. By DAVID PAGE, LL.D., &c., Author of Text-Books of Geology; and Professor CHARLES LAPWORTH. Eleventh Edition. 2s. 6d.

"The divisions of the subject are so clearly defined, the explanations are so lucid, the relations of one portion of the subject to another are so satisfactorily shown, and, above all, the bearings of the allied sciences to Physical Geography are brought out with so much precision, that every reader will feel that difficulties have been removed, and the path of study smoothed before him."—*Athenæum.*

"Whether as a school-book or a manual for the private student, this work has no equal in our Educational literature."—*Iron.*

## Advanced Text-Book of Physical Geography.

With Engravings. By the SAME. Third Edition. 5s.

"A thoroughly good Text-Book of Physical Geography."—*Saturday Review.*

## Examinations on Physical Geography. A Progressive Series of Questions, adapted to the Introductory and Advanced Text-Books of Physical Geography. By the SAME. Sixth Edition. 9d.

## Elements of Physiography and Physical Geography. With express reference to the Instructions recently issued by the Science and Art Department. By the Rev. ALEX. MACKAY, LL.D., F.R.G.S., Author of 'A Manual of Modern Geography, Mathematical, Physical, and Political,' &c. With numerous Illustrations. 25th Thousand, pp. 150. 1s. 6d.

## Comparative Geography. By Carl Ritter. Translated by W. L. GAGE. Fcap. 3s. 6d.

---

## Introductory Text-Book of Meteorology. By ALEXANDER BUCHAN, M.A., F.R.S.E., Secretary of the Scottish Meteorological Society, Author of 'Handy Book of Meteorology,' &c. Crown 8vo, with 8 Coloured Charts and other Engravings. Pp. 218. 4s. 6d.

"A handy compendium of Meteorology by one of the most competent authorities on this branch of science."—*Petermann's Geographische Mittheilungen.*

"We can recommend it as a handy, clear, and scientific introduction to the theory of Meteorology, written by a man who has evidently mastered his subject."—*Lancet.*

"An exceedingly useful volume."—*Athenæum.*

# Botany.

## A Manual of Botany, Anatomical and Physiological. For the Use of Students. By ROBERT BROWN, M.A., PH.D., F.R.G.S. Crown 8vo, with numerous Illustrations. 12s. 6d.

# Geology.

*Eleventh Edition.*

## Introductory Text-Book of Geology. By DAVID
PAGE, LL.D., &c., Professor of Geology in the Durham University College of Physical Science, Newcastle. With Engravings on Wood, and Glossarial Index. 2s. 6d.

"It has not been our good fortune to examine a text-book on science of which we could express an opinion so entirely favourable as we are enabled to do of Mr Page's little work."—*Athenæum.*

*Sixth Edition.*

## Advanced Text-Book of Geology, Descriptive and
INDUSTRIAL. With Engravings, and Glossary of Scientific Terms. By the SAME. Revised and enlarged. 7s. 6d.

"We have carefully read this truly satisfactory book, and do not hesitate to say that it is an excellent compendium of the great facts of Geology, and written in a truthful and philosophic spirit."—*Edinburgh Philosophical Journal.*

"As a school-book nothing can match the Advanced Text-Book of Geology by Professor Page of Newcastle."—*Mechanics' Magazine.*

"We know of no introduction containing a larger amount of information in the same space, and which we could more cordially recommend to the geological student."—*Athenæum.*

*Tenth Edition.*

## The Geological Examinator. A Progressive Series
of Questions, adapted to the Introductory and Advanced Text-Books of Geology. Prepared to assist Teachers in framing their Examinations, and Students in testing their own Progress and Proficiency. By the SAME. 9d.

---

"Few of our handbooks of popular science can be said to have greater or more decisive merit than those of Mr Page on Geology and Palæontology. They are clear and vigorous in style, they never oppress the reader with a pedantic display of learning, nor overwhelm him with a pompous and superfluous terminology; and they have the happy art of taking him straightway to the face of nature herself, instead of leading him by the tortuous and bewildering paths of technical system and artificial classification."—*Saturday Review.*

# German.

## A Handy Manual of German Literature. For
Schools, Civil Service Competitions, and University Local Examinations. By M. F. REID. Fcap. cloth. 3s.

## A Treasury of the English and German Lan-
GUAGES. Compiled from the best Authors and Lexicographers in both Languages. Adapted to the Use of Schools, Students, Travellers, and Men of Business; and forming a Companion to all German-English Dictionaries. By JOSEPH CAUVIN, LL.D. & PH.D., of the University of Göttingen, &c. Crown 8vo, 7s. 6d., bound in cloth.

# Zoology.

## A Manual of Zoology, for the Use of Students.

With a General Introduction on the Principles of Zoology. By HENRY ALLEYNE NICHOLSON, M.D., D.Sc., F.L.S., F.G.S., Regius Professor of Natural History in the University of Aberdeen. Sixth Edition, revised and greatly enlarged. Crown 8vo, pp. 816, with 394 Engravings on Wood. 14s.

"It is the best manual of zoology yet published, not merely in England, but in Europe."—*Pall Mall Gazette.*
"The best treatise on zoology in moderate compass that we possess."—*Lancet.*

## Text - Book of Zoology, for the Use of Schools.

By the SAME. Third Edition, enlarged. Crown 8vo, with 188 Engravings on Wood. 6s.

"This capital introduction to natural history is illustrated and well got up in every way. We should be glad to see it generally used in schools."—*Medical Press and Circular.*

## Introductory Text-Book of Zoology, for the Use

OF JUNIOR CLASSES. By the SAME. Fifth Edition, revised and enlarged, with 156 Engravings. 3s.

"Very suitable for junior classes in schools. There is no reason why any one should not become acquainted with the principles of the science, and the facts on which they are based, as set forth in this volume."—*Lancet.*
"Nothing can be better adapted to its object than this cheap and well-written Introduction."—*London Quarterly Review.*

## Outlines of Natural History, for Beginners ; being

Descriptions of a Progressive Series of Zoological Types. By the SAME. Third Edition. With 52 Engravings. 1s. 6d.

"There has been no book since Patterson's well-known ' Zoology for Schools ' that has so completely provided for the class to which it is addressed as the capital little volume by Dr Nicholson."—*Popular Science Review.*

## Examinations in Natural History ; being a Pro-

gressive Series of Questions adapted to the Author's Introductory and Advanced Text-Books and the Student's Manual of Zoology. By the SAME. 1s.

## Introduction to the Study of Biology. By the

SAME. Crown 8vo, with numerous Engravings. 6s.

## Palæontology.

**A Manual of Palæontology,** for the Use of Students.
With a General Introduction on the Principles of Palæontology.
By Professor H. ALLEYNE NICHOLSON, Aberdeen. Second Edition. 2 vols. 8vo, with 722 Engravings. 42s.

"The most complete and systematic treatise on the subject in the English language. It has not only been thoroughly revised and to a great extent re-written, but so much enlarged by the addition of new matter, that it may claim to be considered to all intents and purposes a new book."—*Saturday Review.*

**The Ancient Life - History of the Earth.** An
Outline of the Principles and Leading Facts of Palæontological Science. By the SAME. With a Glossary and Index. In crown 8vo, with 270 Engravings. 10s. 6d.

## Agriculture.

**Catechism of Practical Agriculture.** By HENRY
STEPHENS, F.R.S.E., Author of the 'Book of the Farm.' 19th Thousand. With Engravings. 1s.

"Teachers will find in this little volume an admirable course of instruction in practical agriculture—that is, the outlines which they may easily fill up; and by following the hints given in Mr Stephens' preface, the course would scarcely fail to be quite interesting, as well as of great practical benefit. Landed proprietors and farmers might with propriety encourage the introduction of this work into schools."—*Aberdeen Journal.*

**Professor Johnston's Catechism of Agricultural**
CHEMISTRY. A New Edition, being the 81st Thousand, revised and extended by CHARLES A. CAMERON, M.D., F.R.G.S.I., &c. With Engravings. 1s.

**Professor Johnston's Elements of Agricultural**
CHEMISTRY AND GEOLOGY. Thirteenth Edition, revised and brought down to the present time, by CHARLES A. CAMERON, M.D., F.R.G.S.I., &c. Foolscap. 6s. 6d.

## Popular Chemistry.

**Professor Johnston's Chemistry of Common Life.**
New Edition, revised and brought down to the present time. By ARTHUR HERBERT CHURCH, M.A. Oxon., Author of 'Food, its Sources, Constituents, and Uses;' 'The Laboratory Guide for Agricultural Students,' &c. Illustrated with Maps and 102 Engravings on Wood. Crown 8vo, pp. 618. 7s. 6d.

"No popular scientific work that has ever been published has been more generally and deservedly appreciated than the late Professor Johnston's 'Chemistry of Common Life.' . . . It remains unrivalled as a clear, interesting, comprehensive, and exact treatise upon the important subjects with which it deals. . . . The book is one which not only every student but every educated person who lives should read, and keep to refer to."—*Mark Lane Express.*

"The established reputation of this volume is not merely maintained, but its value is considerably increased by the care with which every subject has been posted up to the date of publication."—*Athenæum.*

## Mental Philosophy.

*Sixth Edition.*

**Lectures on Metaphysics.** By Sir WILLIAM HAMILTON, Bart., Professor of Logic and Metaphysics in the University of Edinburgh. Edited by the Very Rev. H. L. MANSELL, LL.D., Dean of St Paul's, and JOHN VEITCH, M.A., Professor of Logic and Rhetoric, Glasgow. 2 vols. 8vo. 24s.

*Third Edition.*

**Lectures on Logic.** By Sir WILLIAM HAMILTON, Bart. Edited by the same. 2 vols. 8vo. 24s.

*Third Edition.*

**Discussions on Philosophy and Literature,** EDUCATION AND UNIVERSITY REFORM. By Sir WILLIAM HAMILTON, Bart. 8vo. 21s.

*New Edition.*

**Philosophical Works of the late James** FREDERICK FERRIER, B.A. Oxon., LL.D., Professor of Moral Philosophy and Political Economy in the University of St Andrews. 3 vols. crown 8vo. 34s. 6d.

The following are sold Separately:—

INSTITUTES OF METAPHYSIC. Third Edition. 10s. 6d.

LECTURES ON THE EARLY GREEK PHILOSOPHY. Second Edition. 10s. 6d.

PHILOSOPHICAL REMAINS, INCLUDING THE LECTURES ON EARLY GREEK PHILOSOPHY. Edited by Sir ALEX. GRANT, Bart., D.C.L., and Professor LUSHINGTON. 2 vols. 24s.

*Eighth Edition.*

**Port Royal Logic.** Translated from the French: with Introduction, Notes, and Appendix. By THOMAS SPENCER BAYNES, LL.D., Professor of Logic and English Literature in the University of St Andrews. 12mo. 4s.

*Eighth Edition.*

**Method, Meditations, and Principles of Philo-** SOPHY OF DESCARTES. Translated from the original French and Latin. With a New Introductory Essay, Historical and Critical, on the Cartesian Philosophy. By JOHN VEITCH, LL.D., Professor of Logic and Rhetoric in the University of Glasgow. 12mo. 6s. 6d.

**The Philosophy of History in Europe.** Vol. I., containing the History of that Philosophy in FRANCE and GERMANY. By ROBERT FLINT, D.D., LL.D., Professor of Divinity in the University of Edinburgh. 8vo. 15s.

A SCIENCE PRIMER

**On the Nature of Things.** By JOHN G. MACVICAR, LL.D., D.D. Crown 8vo, with illustrations. 3s. 6d.

NOW BEING ISSUED.

# Philosophical Classics for English Readers.

Edited by WILLIAM KNIGHT, LL.D., Professor of Moral Philosophy, University of St Andrews. In crown 8vo, cloth boards, with Portraits, price 3s. 6d. each.

The aim of this Third Series will be to tell the general reader—who cannot possibly peruse the entire works of the Philosophers—who the founders of the chief systems were, and how they dealt with the great questions of the universe; to give an outline of their lives and characters; to show how the systems were connected with the individualities of the writers, how they received the problem of Philosophy from their predecessors, with what additions they handed it on to their successors, and what they thus contributed to the increasing purpose of the world's thought and its organic development.

The Series will thus unfold the History of Modern Philosophy under the light cast upon it by the labours of the chief system-builders. In each work it will be the aim of the writers to translate the discussion out of the dialect of the Schools, which is often too technical, and which presupposes the knowledge of a special vocabulary, into the language of ordinary life. If the philosophical achievements of such writers as Descartes, Spinoza, Bacon, Hobbes, Locke, Leibniz, Butler, Berkeley, Hume, Stewart, Kant, Fichte, Hegel, Cousin, Comte, and Hamilton (not to refer to other names), were thus recorded,—and the discussion popularised without being diluted, — it is believed that the Series would form a useful assistance to the student of Philosophy, and be of much value to the general reader.

*The Volumes published of this Series contain—*

| | |
|---|---|
| I. DESCARTES, | By Professor MAHAFFY, Dublin. |
| II. BUTLER, | By the Rev. W. LUCAS COLLINS, M.A. |
| III. BERKELEY, | By Professor FRASER, Edinburgh. |
| IV. FICHTE, | By Professor ADAMSON, Owens College, Manchester. |
| V. KANT, | By Professor WALLACE, Oxford. |
| VI. HAMILTON, | By Professor VEITCH, Glasgow. |
| VII. HEGEL, | By Professor EDWARD CAIRD, Glasgow. |
| VIII. LEIBNIZ, | By JOHN THEODORE MERZ. |
| IX. VICO, | By Professor FLINT, Edinburgh. |

*In preparation—*

| | |
|---|---|
| HOBBES, | By Professor CROOM ROBERTSON, London. |
| HUME, | By the EDITOR. |
| BACON, | By Professor NICHOL, Glasgow. |
| SPINOZA, | By the Very Rev. Principal CAIRD, Glasgow. |

## Ancient Classics for English Readers. Edited
by the Rev. W. LUCAS COLLINS, M.A. Complete in 28 vols., price 2s. 6d. each, in cloth (sold separately); or bound in 14 vols., with calf or vellum back, for £3, 10s.

"In the advertising catalogues we sometimes see a book labelled as one 'without which no gentleman's library can be looked upon as complete.' It may be said with truth that no popular library or mechanic's institute will be properly furnished without this series. . . . These handy books to ancient classical literature are at the same time as attractive to the scholar as they ought to be to the English reader. We think, then, that they are destined to attain a wide and enduring circulation, and we are quite sure that they deserve it."— *Westminster Review*.

"It is difficult to estimate too highly the value of such a series as this in giving 'English readers' an insight, exact as far as it goes, into those olden times which are so remote and yet to many of us so close."—*Saturday Review*.

"We gladly avail ourselves of this opportunity to recommend the other volumes of this useful series, most of which are executed with discrimination and ability."—*Quarterly Review*.

CONTENTS.—Homer: The Iliad, by the Editor. Homer: The Odyssey, by the Editor. Herodotus, by G. C. Swayne, M.A. Xenophon, by Sir Alexander Grant, Bart. Euripides, by W. B. Donne. Aristophanes, by the Editor. Plato, by Clifton W. Collins, M.A. Lucian, by the Editor. Æschylus, by Reginald S. Copleston, D.D. (now Bishop of Colombo). Sophocles, by Clifton W. Collins, M.A. Hesiod and Theognis, by the Rev. J. Davies, M.A. Greek Anthology, by Lord Neaves. Virgil, by the Editor. Horace, by Theodore Martin. Juvenal, by Edward Walford, M.A. Plautus and Terence, by the Editor. The Commentaries of Cæsar, by Anthony Trollope. Tacitus, by W. B. Donne. Cicero, by the Editor. Pliny's Letters, by the Rev. Alfred Church, M.A., and the Rev. W. J. Brodribb, M.A. Livy, by the Editor. Ovid, by the Rev. A. Church, M.A. Catullus, Tibullus, and Propertius, by the Rev. James Davies, M.A. Demosthenes, by the Rev. W. J. Brodribb, M.A. Aristotle, by Sir Alexander Grant, Bart., LL.D. Thucydides, by the Editor. Lucretius, by W. H. Mallock. Pindar, by the Rev. F. D. Morice, M.A.

## Foreign Classics for English Readers. Edited
by MRS OLIPHANT. In course of publication, price 2s. 6d. each.

"The wonderful and well-deserved success of the 'Ancient Classics' naturally led to the extension of the design; and the kindred series of 'Foreign Classics' bids fair to rival its predecessor in educational value."—*London Quarterly Review*.

CONTENTS.—Dante, by the Editor. Voltaire, by Major-General Sir E. B. Hamley. Pascal, by Principal Tulloch. Petrarch, by Henry Reeve. Goethe, by A. Hayward, Q.C. Molière, by the Editor and F. Tarver, M.A. Montaigne, by the Rev. W. Lucas Collins, M.A. Rabelais, by Walter Besant, M.A. Calderon, by E. J. Hasell. Saint Simon, by Clifton W. Collins, M.A. Cervantes, by the Editor. Corneille and Racine, by Henry M. Trollope. Schiller, by James Sime, Author of 'Life of Lessing.' Rousseau, by Henry Graham. La Fontaine, and other French Fabulists, by Rev. W. Lucas Collins, M.A. Madame de Sévigné, by Miss Thackeray.